NATCHEZ
BURNING

Greg Iles spent most of his youth in Natchez, Mississippi, and graduated from Ole Miss in 1983. His thirteen *New York Times* bestselling novels have been made into films, translated into more than twenty languages, and published in more than thirty-five countries worldwide. He lives in Natchez with his two teenage children.

www.gregiles.com
www.facebook.com/GregIlesAuthor
@GregIles

BOOKS BY GREG ILES

THE PENN CAGE SERIES

Natchez Burning

The Devil's Punchbowl

Turning Angel

The Quiet Game

OTHER WORKS

Third Degree

True Evil

Blood Memory

Dark Matter (US TITLE: *The Footprints of God*)

Sleep No More

Dead Sleep

24 Hours

Mortal Fear

Black Cross

Spandau Phoenix

NATCHEZ
BURNING

GREG ILES

HarperCollins*Publishers*

HarperCollins*Publishers*
77–85 Fulham Palace Road,
Hammersmith, London W6 8JB

www.harpercollins.co.uk

Published by HarperCollins*Publishers* 2014
1

A catalogue record for this book
is available from the British Library

ISBN: 978-0-00-730485-1

Designed by Lisa Stokes

Printed and bound in Great Britain by
Clays Ltd, St Ives plc

To
Stanley Nelson, of the *Concordia Sentinel*.
A humble hero.

And
all the victims of the Civil Rights movement
Mississippi and Louisiana
1960–1969

For nothing is lost, nothing is ever lost. There is always the clue, the canceled check, the smear of lipstick, the footprint in the canna bed, the condom on the park path, the twitch in the old wound, the baby shoes dipped in bronze, the taint in the blood stream. And all times are one time, and all those dead in the past never lived before our definition gives them life, and out of the shadow their eyes implore us.

—Robert Penn Warren, *All the King's Men*

PROLOGUE

"IF A MAN is forced to choose between the truth and his father, only a fool chooses the truth." A great writer said that, and for a long time I agreed with him. But put into practice, this adage could cloak almost any sin. My mother would agree with it, but I doubt my older sister would, and my fiancée would scoff at the idea. Perhaps we expect too much of our fathers. Nothing frightens me more than the faith in my daughter's eyes. How many men deserve that kind of trust? One by one, the mentors I've most admired eventually revealed chinks in their armor, cracks in their façades, and tired feet of clay—or worse.

But not my father.

A child of the Great Depression, Tom Cage knew hunger. At eighteen, he was drafted and served as a combat medic during the worst fighting in Korea. After surviving that war, he went to medical school, then paid off his loans by serving in the army in West Germany. When he returned home to Mississippi, he practiced family medicine for more than forty years, treating some of the most underprivileged in our community with little thought of financial reward. The *Natchez Examiner* has named him an "Unsung Hero" more times than I can remember. If small towns still have saints, then he is surely one of them.

And yet . . .

As the cynical governor created by my distant relation, Robert Penn Warren, once said: *"Man is conceived in sin and born in corruption and he passeth from the stink of the didie to the stench of the shroud. There is always something."* My younger self sometimes wondered whether this might be true about my father, but time slowly reassured me that he was the exception to Willie Stark's cynical rule. Like poor Jack Burden, my hopeful heart answered: *"Maybe not on the Judge."* But Robert Penn Warren had the kind of courage I've only begun to discover: the will to dig to the bottom of the mine, to shine his pitiless light downward, and to stare unflinchingly at what he found there. And what I found by following his example was proof of Willie Stark's eternal rule: *There is always something.*

It's tempting to think that I might never have learned any of this— that my mother, my sister, and I might mercifully have escaped the consequences of acts committed deep in the haze of history (a time before cell phones and digital cameras and reporters who honor no bounds of propriety, when *N-word* meant nothing to anybody and *nigger* was as common in the vernacular as *tractor*)—but to yearn for ignorance is to embrace the wishful thinking of a child. For once the stone hits the surface of the pond, the ripples never really stop. The waves diminish, and all seems to return to its previous state, but that's an illusion. Disturbed fish change their patterns, a snake slides off the muddy bank into the water, a deer bolts into the open to be shot. And the stone remains on the slimy bottom, out of sight but inarguably there, dense and permanent, sediment settling over it, turtles and catfish prodding it, the sun heating it through all the layers of water until that far-off day when, whether lifted by the fingers of a curious boy diving fifty years after it was cast or uncovered by a bone-dumb farmer draining the pond to plant another half acre of cotton, that stone finds its way back up to the light.

And the man who cast it trembles. Or if he is dead, his sons tremble. They tremble by an unwritten law, one that a fellow Mississippian understood long before I was born and casually revealed to a reporter in a French hotel room in 1956, dispensing eternal truths as effortlessly as a man tossing coins to beggars in the road. He said, *"The past is never dead; it's not even past. If it were, there would be no grief or sorrow."* And ten years before him, my distant relation wrote, *"There is always something."* And six decades after that, I thought: *Please, no, let me remain in my carefully constructed cocoon of Not-Knowing. Let me keep my untarnished idol, my humble war hero, the one healer who has not killed, the one husband who has not lied, the one father who has not betrayed the faith of his children.* But as I know now, and hate the knowing . . . Willie was right: there *is* always something.

So let us begin in 1964, with three murders. Three stones cast into a pond no one had cared about since the siege of Vicksburg, but which was soon to become the center of the world's attention. A place most people in the United States liked to think was somehow different from the rest of the country, but which was in fact the very incarnation of America's tortured soul.

Mississippi.

one true thing by watching musicians pass through his store: the road broke a man down fast—especially a black man.

The white woman screamed in the back. Albert prayed nobody was walking through the alley. Willie was working her hard. Mary Shivers had been married five years and had two kids, but that wasn't enough to keep her at home. Two months ago, she'd struck up a conversation with Willie while he was working on a house next door. Next thing you know, Willie was asking Albert to set up a meeting somewhere. That was the way it went, most times. The black half of the couple would ask Albert to set something up. Might be the man, might be the woman. A few times over the years, a particularly bold white woman had set up a rendezvous in the store, whispering over the sheet music for some hymn or other she was buying. Albert had reluctantly accommodated most of them. That was what a businessman did, after all. Filled a need. Supplied a demand. And Lord knew there was demand for a place where black and white could meet away from prying eyes.

Albert had set up a couple of places where couples could meet discreetly, far away from his shop. But if the white half of the couple had a legitimate interest in music—and enough ready cash—he occasionally allowed a hasty rendezvous in the back of the store. He'd got the idea for using his radio show to set up the meetings from his stint in the navy. He'd only been a cook—that's about all they'd let you be in World War II, if you were black—but a white officer had told him how the Brits had used simple codes during music programs to send messages out to French Resistance agents in the field. They'd play a certain song, or quote a piece of poetry, and different groups would know what the signal meant. Blow up this railroad bridge, or shoot that German officer. Using his Sunday gospel show, Albert had found it easy to send coded messages to the couples waiting to hear their meeting times. And since whites could tune in to his gospel show as easily as blacks, the system was just about perfect. Each person in an illicit couple had a particular song, and each knew the song of his or her partner. As disc jockey of his own show, Albert could say something like "Next Sunday at seven o'clock, I'm gonna be playing a one-two punch with 'Steal Away to Jesus,' by the Mighty Clouds of Joy, followed by 'He Cares for Me,' by the Dixie Hummingbirds. Lord, you can't beat that." And they would know.

Simple.

The rhythm of the sofa springs picked up, then stopped suddenly as Willie cried "Jesus!" with a sinner's fervor. A moment later, the floorboards creaked under Willie's two hundred and thirty pounds. Albert didn't know how that skinny schoolteacher could take what Willie gave her, but that was another thing he'd learned over the years: the size of a woman on the outside didn't mean nothing; it was how much hunger she had on the inside that made her what she was between the sheets. Some of the white women he'd seen come through his store had a desperate hunger that nothing would ever fill.

Albert heard shuffling, then the door opened. Willie Hooks stood there wiping sweat from his forehead with his shirtsleeve. The schoolteacher looked like she'd just run a mile to catch a bus and got run over by it instead. Dazed, she slowly buttoned up her dress with no regard for Albert's presence or what he might see.

"This is the *last* time," Albert said. "For a long time, anyway. And you be damn careful when you go. Big John's cruising around out there, and half the Klan is hunting for Pooky Wilson."

"Big John Law," Hooks said with venom. "What's Pooky done?"

"Don't you worry 'bout that."

"Is that why you sent that little boy to warn me off?" Willie asked, his voice a full octave lower than Albert's. "Why you had that warning light on? 'Cause of Big John?"

"I'll tell you why I sent that boy. Two white men busted up in here today, and one was screaming bloody murder. Screaming 'bout his daughter goin' with a nigger boy."

"What white men?" Willie asked, interested.

"Brody Royal, for one."

Willie blinked in disbelief. "That fine girl he got is doin' Pooky Wilson?"

The schoolteacher elbowed Willie in the ribs.

Hooks didn't flinch. "That skinny little bass player with the crooked back?"

Pooky Wilson had severe scoliosis, but Katy Royal didn't seem to mind. "You forget you ever heard that," Albert said. "You, too," he added, glaring at the white woman, who under any other circumstances could have had him jailed for backtalk.

"I ain't scared of Brody Royal," Willie said. "That rich bastard."

Albert gave Willie a measuring glance. "No? Well, the man with Brody was Frank Knox."

Willie froze.

"You ain't talking so big now, are you?" Albert asked.

"Shit. You let Mr. *Frank's* little girl come up in here to meet somebody?"

Albert stamped his foot in disgust. "I look retarded to you, boy? Frank Knox ain't got no little girl. He was just here to make the point. Now, you get the hell out of my place. You got to find some other place to get your corn ground."

The schoolteacher moaned, sounding more like a feral cat than a human being.

Willie looked at her with frank desire. "Well, if this is the last time for a while . . ."

She opened her mouth and started unbuttoning her dress, but Albert shoved Willie toward the side door. "Get out! And don't come back. Anybody stops you, tell 'em you moved some pianos for me. I'll take care of getting missy out of here."

Hooks laughed and plodded to the side door. "How about a hit of lightnin' for the road, Mr. Albert?"

"I got no whiskey for the likes of you!" He turned back to the woman as Willie cursed and vanished through the door.

The schoolteacher's dress was buttoned now. She looked primly up at him. "You know a lot about a lot of people, don't you?"

"Reckon I would," Albert said, " 'cep' I got a bad memory. Real bad. Forget a face soon as I see it."

"That's good," said Mary Shivers. "We'll all live longer that way."

She started to follow Willie through the side door, but Albert blocked her path and motioned for her to leave by the front. "Pick up some music from the rack on your way out. God help you if you can't lie, but I imagine you're pretty good at it."

After a moment's hesitation, Mary Shivers obeyed.

Albert switched on a box fan to drive her smell from the lesson room. He figured darkness would fall in about fifteen minutes. To pass the time, he walked into his office, knelt beside the desk, and pulled up a pine floorboard. The door of a firebox greeted him. Taking out one of several ledgers he kept inside the box, he sat at his rolltop desk and opened the leather-bound volume, revealing perfect columns of blue-inked names and numbers in his own precise hand.

Albert kept a ledger for everything. He had one for sales of musical instruments, another for rentals. He kept a book for instruments he sold on time, marking in the payments and late charges. He kept a black ledger for whiskey sales, and a red ledger for loans he'd made to people he trusted. He'd loaned out a lot of money over the years, much of it to boys he'd trained in his store, boys sent off to cities like Chicago and Los Angeles with a single marketable skill besides digging ditches or picking cotton—tuning pianos. To a man, they had paid him back their stakes, even if it had taken them years to do it. Those boys were Albert's faith in humanity. It comforted him to know that when Pooky Wilson reached Chicago—*if* he did—he'd probably be able to find work as a piano tuner before the hundred-dollar stake Albert had given him ran out.

In the back of his loan ledger, in red, Albert wrote in the sums he'd loaned to folks in trouble, the kind of trouble where he knew he'd never get the money back. Sometimes you had to do that, even if you were a businessman. That was his mama coming out in him. But the ledger Albert worked in now was special. In this volume he kept a record of every rendezvous he'd ever arranged—the names of the people involved, the times and dates they'd met, the money they'd paid him, their song codes for his radio show. Over eighteen years, quite a few pages had accumulated. There were nearly eighty names in the ledger now. Albert wasn't sure why he kept it. He had no intention of blackmailing anybody, though the ledger would certainly be worth a lot to an unscrupulous man. But a good businessman kept records. It was that simple. You never knew when you might need to refer back to the past.

After writing in the particulars about Willie and the schoolteacher, Albert replaced the ledger in the firebox and covered it with the floorboard. Then he took a quart of corn whiskey from a suitcase, went out to the sales floor, and sat at his favorite piano. He drank in silence until the street went dark outside the display window. Then he got up, switched on the lights, and returned to the piano.

Laying his fingers on the keys, he started with "Blues in the Night," rolling his right hand with a feather-light touch. Then he gently twisted

the melody inside out until it became "Blue Skies," despite not having felt smiled upon in quite a while. It was times like this that Albert
wished his wife had lived. Lilly would always sit at his side while he
played, or on the floor behind him, leaning against his lower back, and
sing over the notes he coaxed from whichever piano they had at the
time. Sometimes she'd sing the way Billie Holiday sang on the radio,
other times she crooned in a language all her own, improvising over
whatever Albert did with the keys. Tonight he'd give all the money he
had in the bank to have recorded the songs his wife had made up on
those nights. But he never did.

And then she died.

Lilly had passed when he was thirty, she twenty-eight. Albert had
never remarried. He'd passed the last twenty years with various girls,
none more special than the last, and he'd stayed away from white
women as much as he could, despite considerable pressure from some
of the housewives whose homes he visited to tune their pianos. He
always tried to make his calls when the husband was home, and he
worked hard to make a good impression. That was how you survived in
cotton country. From one corner of the parish to the other, every white
man of property knew Albert Norris as a "good nigger."

Albert stopped playing in mid-measure, like a walker in mid-stride,
and listened to the suspended chord fade into silence. It took half a
minute, and he knew that a child could probably hear the sound waves
decay for another thirty seconds after that, the way he used to when
he'd sat on the floor by his mother's old Baldwin. Age took those things
from you, though—slow but sure.

In the haunting silence, he heard a muted thump from the workroom. A few seconds later, the sound repeated itself. The trapdoor had
closed. Pooky Wilson was slipping out into hostile night, like a thousand black boys before him.

"Godspeed, son," Albert said softly.

He'd drunk more whiskey than usual tonight, hoping to dull the
memory of the men who'd visited him that afternoon, not to mention
the specter of Big John DeLillo cruising past on the hot asphalt outside.
Sometimes reality crowded in so close on you, not even music could
block it out. He could almost hear Pooky's pounding heart as the boy
tried to cover the two blocks to Widow Nichols's house. Filled with bit-

terness, Albert got up from the piano bench, wobbled, then marched up to the display window and fiddled with some glittery drums to draw the eyes of any watchers outside. After a couple of minutes of this, he staggered to his bedroom at the back of the shop. He could still smell the white woman's sex on the air, and it made him angry.

"Bitch ought to stay with her own," he muttered. "Nothing but trouble."

His last words were mumbled into his bunched pillow.

THE SOUND OF BREAKING glass dredged Albert from a dreamless sleep. Instinctively, he reached for the .32 pistol he kept on his bedside table, but he'd been too drunk to bring it from the office when he went to bed. Somebody fell over a drum set, and a cymbal crashed to the floor. Then a flashlight beam cut through the short dark hallway that led to the sales floor.

"Who's there?" Albert called. "Pooky? That you?"

The noises stopped, then continued, and this time he heard muffled voices. Albert got up, fought a wave of dizziness, then hurried into his office. His pistol was right where he'd left it. He picked up the .32 and padded carefully up the hall. He heard a deep gurgling, like someone emptying herbicide from a fifty-five-gallon drum. Then he smelled gasoline.

Panic and foreknowledge swept through him in a paralyzing wave. He wanted to flee, but the store was all he had. He owned the building—a rare feat for a black man in Ferriday, Louisiana—but he had no insurance. He'd put the premium money into new inventory, those electric guitars all the white boys was wanting since the Beatles hit the TV. Albert flung himself up the hall, then stopped when he saw two black silhouettes in the darkness. The shadow men were emptying gasoline over the piano in the display window, and splashing it high on the guitars hanging on the wall.

"What ya'll doin'?" he cried. "Stop that now! Who is that?"

The men kept emptying the cans.

"I'll call the po-lice! I swear I will!"

The men laughed. Albert squinted, and in the faint light bleeding through the window he saw the paleness of their skin. In the shadows to his right, Albert sensed more than saw a third figure, but it looked larger than a man, almost like a Gemini astronaut with air tanks on his back.

"I got a pistol!" Albert cried, ashamed of the fear in his voice. If he fired now, the muzzle flash or the ricocheting bullet was as likely to set off the fumes as a struck match. "Please!" he begged. "Why ya'll want to ruin my store? What I ever done to you fellas?"

A pickup truck passed on the street outside, and in its reflected headlights Albert recognized the faces of the two men in the window. One was Snake Knox, the brother of Frank, the Klansman who'd visited the store that afternoon. The other was Brody Royal. The third man remained in shadow. *Dear Jesus* . . . These were serious men. They made the regular Ku Klux Klan look like circus clowns. Albert had managed to keep off the wrong side of men like this all his life. He'd bowed and scraped when necessary. He'd ignored the flirtations of their women, greased the right palms, and given gifts of service and merchandise. But now . . . now they wanted the life of a boy who was guilty of nothing but being young and ignorant.

"Mr. Brody, you *knows* me," Albert said with absurd reasonableness. "Please, now . . . I done told you this afternoon, I don't know *nothin'* 'bout your daughter getting up to anything." This lie sounded hollow even to him, but the truth would be worse· *Mr. Royal, your little girl's got a willful streak and she'd hump that black boy right in front of you if he'd let her.* "Please now, Mr. Royal," he pleaded. "Why, I've got your own church organ up in here, fixing it."

"Shut up!" snapped the shadow man. "Tell us where that young buck is right this minute, or you die. Make your choice."

"I don't know!" Albert cried. "I swear! But I do know that boy didn't mean no harm."

Brody Royal dropped his gas can on the floor and walked up to Albert. "Cur dogs don't mean any harm, either, but they'll impregnate your prize bitch if they can get close to her."

"He ain't gonna tell us nothin'," Snake Knox said. "Let's finish the job."

"I thought you were a businessman, Norris," Royal said, his eyes seeming to glow in the pale, angular face. "But I guess in the end, even the best nigra's gonna be a nigger one day a week. Let's go, boys."

Snake picked up the piano bench and tossed it through Albert's plate glass window. The shards tinkled in the street like a shattering dream. Snake leaped through the window after the bench, and Albert saw a man nearly twice his size join him in the street. Brody Royal scrambled out onto the porch, then jumped down to the sidewalk. Instinct told Albert to follow them, but before he could move, the giant figure stepped from the shadows and stared at him with unalloyed hatred. The huge shape was no astronaut; it was Frank Knox, wearing an asbestos suit and some kind of pack on his back.

"You should have talked," he said. "Now you get the Guadalcanal barbecue."

Albert backpedaled in terror, but the roaring jet of flame reached toward him like the finger of Satan, and Knox's eyes flashed with fascination.

The display room exploded into fire.

Facedown in a roaring fog of pain, Albert slowly picked himself up from the floor, then ran blindly from the inferno raging in the front of his store. When he crashed through the back door, arms flailing, he saw that his clothes had already burned away. Like a deer fleeing a forest fire, he bounded toward a bright opening at the end of the alley. There was a service station there—a white-owned station, but he knew the attendant. Maybe somebody would take him to the hospital.

As Albert windmilled down the alley, a big car pulled across the open space, blocking it. The gumball light on its roof came to life, spilling red glare onto the walls of the buildings. A huge shape rose from beside the car. Big John DeLillo.

"Help me, Mr. John!" Albert screamed, running toward the deputy. "Lord, they done burned me out!"

As he ran, Albert saw that his hands were on fire.

CHAPTER 2

Twenty-three days later
Natchez, Mississippi

"IF THEY'D HAVE left them two Jews alone and just shot the nigger," said Frank Knox, "none of this would even be happening. New Yorkers don't give no more of a damn than we do about one less nigger in the world. But you kill a couple of Jewboys, and they're ready to call out the Marines."

"You talking about that Neshoba County business?" asked Glenn Morehouse, a mountain of a man with half the intellectual wattage of his old sergeant.

"What else?" said Frank, flipping a slab of alligator meat on the sizzling grill.

Sonny Thornfield popped the cap on an ice-cold Jax and watched the veins bulge in Frank's neck. The discovery of the three civil rights workers in an earthen dam a few days ago had stirred Frank up in a way Sonny hadn't seen since the Bay of Pigs fiasco. In a way, this whole camping trip had been designed to let off pressure after the FBI's discovery of the bodies up in Philadelphia. After their shift ended Friday, they'd mounted four camper shells on their pickups, then towed Frank's boat and Sonny's homemade grill down to the sandbar south of the Triton Battery plant, where they all worked during the week. The long weekend of sun had pretty much worn everybody out, except the kids. Now the women sat in folding chairs, fanning themselves and swatting mosquitoes in the shade of the cottonwoods. Frank's and Sonny's wives were back there, along with Granny Knox and Wilma Deen, Glenn's divorced sister. The kids who weren't out in the boat were teasing a stray dog down by the riverbank.

The men had spent the weekend practicing their demolition skills on stumps, and on an old Chevy that lay half buried in the sand down by the water. Frank's younger brother Snake was still down there, fiddling with something under the Chevy's dash and flirting with the nineteen-year-old waitress he'd brought with him. All the men on this picnic were old hands with dynamite and Composition B, but Frank had bought some of the new C-4 off a supply sergeant he knew at Fort Polk, and they'd been using it to try to master the art of the shaped charge. Every time they peeled eight inches off a stump top, the kids squealed and hooted and begged for fireworks.

But not even that had calmed Frank down. When they'd driven into town yesterday for cigarettes, he'd used a pay phone to call some buddies and ask about national coverage. He came back to the car saying Cronkite wouldn't shut up about the "national scandal" and all the big-city papers were riding the story hard. All weekend, Sonny had sensed that Frank was coming to some kind of decision. And if he was . . . that meant changes for them all.

Even Morehouse seemed unsettled by the anger that seethed through Frank's pores like sour sweat. Sonny studied the two men with clinical detachment. The gentle giant had done his share of killing during the war, but Morehouse had quickly grown soft in civilian life, putting on eighty pounds of new fat. He stood with his thumbs hooked behind the straps of his overalls and masticated a blade of grass as though it required all his concentration. By contrast, Frank Knox still had a washboard stomach, ropy muscles with pipeline veins running along them, and eyes that Sonny had never seen more relaxed than when behind the sights of a .30-caliber machine gun.

Sonny didn't push Frank for more information; whatever was coming would arrive in its own time. Keeping Morehouse's body between himself and the sinking sun, Sonny sipped the Jax and watched Frank's teenage son spray rooster tails out in the reddish-brown river behind his father's souped-up bass boat.

"There's reporters crawling all over Neshoba County," Frank said, basting the gator meat with his special sauce. "Whole damn country's stirred up, and it's gonna get worse."

Sonny took a bent Camel from his shirt pocket and lit it with a Zippo. "I heard they had navy divers up there, helping search for those corpses. You believe that?"

"Navy pukes," Frank muttered, reaching out to turn up the volume on a GE transistor radio. Marty Robbins was singing "Girl from Spanish Town." Whenever Frank saw a Japanese radio, he'd slam it into the nearest wall, and no one ever protested. "But it wasn't any navy diver found them bodies," he said.

"Who found 'em, then?" asked Morehouse.

"It ain't *who*, Mountain. It's *how*."

Morehouse still looked lost, but Sonny's eyes narrowed. "He's saying they got rats up there just like we do down here."

Frank nodded. "Federal informants, they call 'em. Paid Judases is what they are. Feds never would have found them bodies without help."

"I heard the reward was twenty-five thousand dollars," Morehouse said in an awestruck voice. "That's enough money to buy a house and a truck and a boat besides."

Frank speared him with a glare. "Would you sell out your ancestors for twenty-five grand, Glenn?"

Morehouse's eyes bugged, and his cheeks filled with blood. "Hell, no! You know that, Frank."

"My wife told me something weird this morning," Sonny said thoughtfully. "Her sister lives up in Kemper County, and she heard some Italian bastard was going around Neshoba threatening people. She heard he beat up a Klansman, pulled down his drawers, shoved a pistol up his butt, and asked for the burial location. She said some Klan boys thought he was a mob button man."

"When exactly did she tell you this?" Frank asked.

"This morning, in the camper. She talked to her sister just before we pulled out of town Friday."

While Frank considered this rumor, Jim Reeves began singing "He'll Have to Go." "Gentleman Jim" had died in a plane crash near Nashville only nine days ago, and disc jockeys had been playing his records practically nonstop ever since.

"Bullshit," Frank decided at length. "Not that the FBI hasn't cozied up to the mob some, 'cause I know they did during the Cuba mess. Half the guns coming into our training camps in sixty-one were being supplied by Carlos Marcello's people, and Trafficante's Havana contacts were providing our intel for the invasion. Hoover knew all about that. The CIA ran the South Florida camps, but I met FBI agents down there, too. J. Edgar wouldn't use a wop on something like this, though. If he wants a gun stuck up some Klansman's ass, he's got field agents who'll do it for him. The Bureau's got some hard boys, same as us."

"Yeah," said Morehouse. "They got southern boys in the FBI."

Frank laughed bitterly. "You think there ain't no tough Yankees? Have you forgotten that Irishman, McClaren, on Guadalcanal? He killed more Japs than I ever did, and he was from Boston, just like the Kennedys. Fighting alongside that crazy bastard showed me how we lost at Gettysburg."

Sonny watched Frank like an interrogator waiting for a prisoner to crack. He knew his old sergeant had something to tell them. But hell could freeze over before Frank Knox would show you his hole card. After Sonny's curiosity got the best of him, he said, "Come on, Top. You ain't gonna let this Neshoba County thing pass unanswered, I know."

Frank's eyes shone with menace, like the glow of a tire fire in a dump, which could burn for fifteen years. "That's a fact, Son. Today is a red-letter day. One you boys ain't ever gonna forget."

"How come?" asked Morehouse.

"Because today we're leaving the Klan."

Glenn gasped, and Sonny choked on the smoke in his lungs.

"Don't know why you're surprised," Frank said. "The Klan we got now's about as dangerous as the Garden Club. Every goddamn klavern in the state's eaten up with informants. The whole organization's useless. *Worse* than useless."

Morehouse looked like a Cub Scout whose father had told him they were renouncing American citizenship. "But—but—" he stammered.

"But *nothing*," Frank snapped. "We're splitting off, and that's it."

"We can't quit," Sonny said. "You know that. Once in, never out."

Frank laughed. "We're not *telling* anybody we're quitting. We'll keep going through the motions, wearing the stupid robes and masks, kowtowing to the Dragons and Kleagles and Wizards and all that other Halloween bullshit. But that ain't nothing but cover now. You follow? I'm forming a special unit. An action squad. A wrecking crew."

"Our own wrecking crew," Morehouse echoed, savoring the words on his tongue.

"Sounds good to me," Sonny said. "I never liked hiding my face anyway. When you stand up for what's right, you do it in the open. That's the main reason Daddy never joined the Klan. He said with all the robes and rituals, the KKK looked as silly as the pope and his cardinals. Seems like a pitiful damn joke sometimes."

"It *is* a joke," Frank agreed. "But not for us. The FBI's camped over in the Holiday Inn right now, having a victory party. But we're gonna shut those bastards up. Hoover, too, long as he keeps dancin' to Bobby Kennedy's tune."

"That Harvard pissant," Morehouse muttered. "*Catholic* pissant."

"We're not gonna have to worry about raising money or any of that nonsense, either," Frank said. "Brody Royal's gonna bankroll our whole operation."

Sonny whistled. "How'd you set that up?"

"Brody liked the way we handled the Norris thing, and how we didn't let that Wilson boy get away. Hell, I've known Brody since before I was training the cadres down at Morgan City. He paid for the C-4 we've been blowing all weekend."

"I'll be danged," Morehouse marveled.

"All we have to do in return is a favor here and there," Frank added, "when Brody needs one."

So Royal liked the way we handled the Norris thing, Sonny thought, remembering Albert Norris flaming in the dark, like that guy in the *Fantastic Four* comic books. *And how we didn't let that Wilson boy get away.* Sonny had witnessed horrific brutality on the Pacific Islands during the war—atrocities committed by both sides—but he'd never seen anything like the way Pooky Wilson had died under Snake Knox's hands.

"I can imagine what kind of favors Brody'll be needing," Sonny muttered.

"Nothing we can't handle," Frank said, carefully dipping his basting brush in the pungent sauce bowl. "Now, listen up. We're gonna keep our crew small. Half a dozen good men to start. Only hard-core guys get in. Guys we grew up with."

"Makes sense," Sonny reflected. "But how about Jared Leach? He's from Shreveport, but he's mean as a stepped-on copperhead. He was a marine. How about making an exception for vets, Frank? Vets only, maybe."

"*Combat* vets," Frank said thoughtfully. "Guys who know about killin'."

"Killin' up close," Sonny agreed. "Jared's solid as a rock. He was in the ETO, but he saw some shit, now. The Bulge, for one thing."

"We'll give him a chance to prove it."

Sonny nodded, a bracing excitement building in his chest. "Who else you askin'?"

"I'll let you know. Don't get antsy. We're gonna be methodical about this, like cleaning out machine gun nests. You don't charge in blind like Audie fuckin' Murphy. You flank 'em one at a time, then pour in the lead and grenades. Hold out your hand, Son."

Sonny extended his hand gingerly, half expecting to be cut for a blood oath or branded with some secret insignia. But Frank dropped something heavy and cool into his palm. Sonny saw the flash of gold.

"What the hell?" he asked, recognizing the coin. "Is that a twenty-dollar gold piece?"

"That it is," said Frank. "A Double Eagle."

Sonny whistled with awe. "Haven't seen one of these since my granddaddy showed me one."

"Look at the year it was minted."

He squinted at the coin. "Nineteen twenty-eight?"

"Can you think of anything special about that year?"

"The year of the big flood?" Morehouse guessed, blinking at the gleaming coin.

Frank snorted with contempt. "The flood was in twenty-seven, lug nut."

"I was born in twenty-eight," Sonny said, realizing Frank's intent.

Frank nodded. "That's your dog tag now. Everybody in the unit's gonna carry one. No robes, no masks, no bullshit—just a gold piece. *Your* gold piece." He fished in his pocket, then held out a second Double Eagle to Morehouse.

The giant took the gold coin almost greedily, then held it up in the sun and eyed it like a child examining a rare marble. "Nineteen twenty-seven," he confirmed, grinning. "*Damn*, that's neat."

"They stopped minting these a long time back, didn't they?" asked Sonny.

"Nineteen thirty-three," Frank replied.

"So nobody younger than . . . Bucky Jarrett gets in?"

"That's right. Except for my little brother. Snake wasn't born until thirty-four, but we need that crazy son of a bitch. There's times when crazy is just what the doctor ordered."

Frank's younger brother had volunteered for Korea at seventeen, lying about his age to get early enlistment. Snake had been in the thick of the fighting for most of the war, and he'd learned a lot. Sonny had a feeling that whatever Snake was doing down at the Chevy was designed to prove that to them.

"What are we gonna do first?" Morehouse asked.

"I know what we *ain't* gonna do," Sonny muttered. "We ain't gonna do a lot of gabblin' and then go home drunk like a bunch of broke-dicks."

"That's a stone-cold fact," Frank said, his voice crackling like a live wire.

"We gonna waste somebody?" Sonny asked.

Frank nodded.

"Who?" asked Morehouse. "How 'bout that biggity nigger who works out at Armstrong, that George Metcalfe? Sonny says he's gonna be president of the Natchez NAACP."

Frank shook his head. "We're not going to waste time killing tire builders and handymen. That's for the clowns in the white hoods, if they ever get their nerve up."

"Who, then?" asked Sonny, trying to think like Frank. As soon as he did, a revelation struck him. "Jesus You're thinking about wasting *white guys*. Aren't you?"

"Maybe," Frank conceded, his eyes twinkling.

"What?" Morehouse asked.

"Informants," Sonny explained. "Like Jerry Dugan, out at the plant."

Frank smiled at Sonny's deduction, but once more he shook his head. "It may come to killing Jerry one day, but right now he's off-limits. I want him feeding the FBI a steady stream of bullshit on the regular White Knights. We want Hoover's boys thinking they have their finger on the pulse around here."

"Then *who*?" Sonny asked, genuinely stumped.

Frank grabbed two wooden paddles and shoveled the alligator steak off the grill. One venison tenderloin remained on the hot iron mesh, cut from a doe poached off the International Paper woodlands last night. After fishing a fresh Jax from the cooler, Frank swallowed half the beer in the can, then leveled his gunner's eyes at them.

Snake rolled his eyes, but Sonny and Morehouse held their silence. You never knew when Frank was joking about this kind of thing, and it didn't pay to make assumptions.

"Let's eat that gator," Frank said, turning away and starting up the hill, his big shoulders rolling like a well-oiled machine.

As Snake came alongside him, Sonny said, "He's serious about killing King and Kennedy, isn't he?"

Snake's eyes settled on Sonny with interest. "Why not? Both those guys already lost friends or brothers to bullets. If you step into the gap, you gotta figure you could get the same treatment. That's war, ain't it? We've all been there."

As Sonny walked up the sandbar toward the smoking grill, he had to admit Snake had a point. Only this wasn't the Pacific or Korea—or even Vietnam, wherever the hell that was. This was America. Which meant Snake was talking about a civil war. As soon as this thought flashed through Sonny's mind, everything came clear, and a feeling of peace spread through him. Appomattox hadn't ended anything; it had merely heralded an intermission. The war itself was still raging across the country, right under the shiny plastic surface of the American Dream. Some people pretended not to notice, or made out like the Russians were the real enemy. But anybody who'd read any history knew that great civilizations always crumbled from within. And to prevent that eventuality, Sonny was willing to kill whoever Frank said needed to die.

CHAPTER 3

Four Years Later
March 31, 1968
Near Athens Point, Mississippi

SONNY THORNFIELD STEERED the rusty green johnboat through the darkening swamp with his left hand and held a gun on Jimmy Revels with his right. After three days in Double Eagle captivity, the young Negro wasn't much of a threat. Revels lay in the bottom of the boat, barely conscious, his hands bound behind him. The most he could do now would be to jump out of the boat and drown himself rather than be shot. Sonny had considered simply dumping him among the huge cypress trees, but there was some chance that a fisherman might find his body before the gators did, and Sonny didn't want to take the risk.

Sonny wasn't sure he would survive the night himself. After four years of successful Double Eagle operations, things had finally gone about as wrong as they could go. Three days ago, they'd been on the verge of accomplishing phase one of the mission Frank Knox had outlined on the sandbar that first day back in the summer of '64. But at 4 P.M. on Thursday, Frank had been killed, and five hours later the Eagles had been ordered to stand down. Sonny had no problem with this decision. In his opinion, the Double Eagles without Frank to lead them had no business taking on operations of national scope. But Snake had different ideas. Juiced on white lightning and stoked on speed, Snake Knox had seized upon the notion that if they didn't go through with Frank's original plan, then his older brother had died for nothing.

The black boy in the bottom of the johnboat was the bait Frank had finally settled on, the bait that would lure in the big targets. They couldn't have found a more perfect victim. A former navy cook and noted musician, Jimmy Revels had not only met Martin Luther King in person, but also had worked tirelessly to register black voters in Mississippi. He'd redoubled his efforts in the wake of Robert Kennedy's announcement that he would run for president, which had earned him a personal phone call from Kennedy only a week ago. By an odd coincidence, Revels had also worked for Albert Norris before joining the navy. Stranger still, Revels was the younger brother of Viola Turner, Dr. Cage's nurse, the woman Sonny had secretly lusted after for years. Sonny didn't pretend to understand the mechanics of fate, but he felt that all these connections had somehow brought about Frank's death and stranded them in their current predicament.

Nothing had ever really been the same since Frank's older son was killed in Vietnam. Sonny couldn't remember a single day Frank spent sober after getting that news. *Two years drunk.* Frank functioned well enough, but he'd lost a step. When Frank had outlined his most recent plan, Sonny had worried that grief over his son might be blinding Frank to certain realities. Volunteering to carry out the will of a mob boss like Carlos Marcello was like dealing with the devil. When Sonny pointed out that almost everyone associated with the JFK assassination was now dead, Frank had told him he ought to apply for work in the ladies' underwear section at Coles, the Jew department store downtown. Sonny had shut up after that, but he'd never felt quite right about what they were doing.

Something had changed inside him during the past four years. The early operations back in '64 had felt like war. But what Frank had pushed him to do to get Jimmy Revels out of hiding had left Sonny sick with shame and confusion. Like what the nips had done to the Chinese at Nanking. Sonny had never turned down a free piece of ass, but rape was something else. And raping a woman you cared about . . . that made you want to crawl in a dark hole and never come out again. But what could you do, with Frank Knox giving the order and going first?

As he trolled the boat between the great cypresses, searching for familiar landmarks, Sonny recalled how fired up they'd been after capturing Revels and his big bodyguard, Luther Davis, who was Jimmy's drummer and a former army infantryman. But then death had taken Frank from them, as surely and randomly as it had taken friends in the islands during the war, and Snake had gone batshit crazy. Left to his own devices, he'd have crucified Jimmy Revels on a telephone pole in the center of Natchez, then waited for the big shots to fly in for the protests and the funeral, like ducks to a decoy. But before he could, Brody Royal had sent word that the Eagles were to abort the operation. Royal wanted Jimmy Revels and Luther Davis dropped into a hole so deep that no one would ever find them, and Sonny knew why. The millionaire didn't trust Snake to carry out the operation without landing all of them in prison.

The chaos that followed Royal's decision had resulted in days of brutal torture that shook Sonny to the core. Sleep deprived and high on drugs, Snake had tried to take out his grief on the prisoners in his power. Worse, he'd ordered the kidnapping of Revels's sister Viola, on the pretext that she'd seen their faces when they'd gang-raped her to bring her brother out of hiding. If Sonny could have bailed on that operation, he would have, but by then he was so deep in, there was no way out—only through. That meant forty-eight hours of hell in a machine shop so far out in the woods that no one could hear the screams. When deliverance arrived for Viola like divine intervention, Sonny had said a silent prayer of thanks. But Snake's rage had only escalated, making Sonny fear he would disregard the stand-down order and doom them all.

That was the moment he'd decided to follow Brody Royal's order in spite of Snake's ascension to Frank's post as commander of the Double Eagles. Because an order from Brody Royal might actually be an order from Carlos Marcello, and nobody who disobeyed Carlos survived to tell the tale. When Snake finally crashed—three hours after his brother's funeral—he lay snoring in a chair only feet from his chained and bleeding captives. At that point, Sonny had dragged Glenn Morehouse outside and told him they needed to follow Royal's orders before Snake got them both killed. Morehouse hadn't had the nerve to risk Snake's wrath, but Sonny didn't let that stop him. Since Luther Davis looked likely to die of his wounds anyway, Sonny had cut Jimmy Revels loose, carried him out to his pickup, and driven him to the edge of the Lusahatcha Swamp, where so many other bodies had been dumped over the years.

Revels had stopped talking a couple of hours ago. The only words he'd spoken during the afternoon were to ask about his sister and Luther Davis. Sonny didn't know where Viola was, but he prayed that Luther was at the bottom of the Jericho Hole in Concordia Parish, where Sonny had ordered Morehouse to dump him.

Sonny opened the outboard's throttle a little and nosed the boat through a deeper channel in the cypress trees. They were thirty miles south of Natchez and twenty west of Woodville, deep into Lusahatcha County. This swamp lay mostly on land owned by the Double Eagles' hunting club, but partly on federal land, too—a national forest. Sonny's destination was a stand of virgin cypress that looked like something on the cover of an Edgar Rice Burroughs paperback. At the heart of this swamp, some cypress trunks were fifteen feet in diameter. Sonny and Frank had once tried to stretch a fifty-foot rope around the trunk of the one called the Bone Tree, and they'd come up three feet short. Frank claimed some of those trees were a thousand years old.

"Shit," Sonny muttered, watching the orange sun flare against the purple sky as it sank below the horizon. He was going to have to use a flashlight to get back to civilization. "We shoulda been there by now."

He put down his pistol and picked up a map Snake had drawn for him on a much earlier occasion. As he studied it, Sonny kept glancing over its edge to make sure Jimmy Revels stayed still. The kid's T-shirt was rusty with dried blood and stained black with grease, his left arm wrapped in bloody gauze. In the fading light, Sonny could no longer tell if his eyes were open or closed.

Stinging sweat dripped into Sonny's eyes, and he squinted through it at the map. *I gotta be almost there,* he thought. Then, as though transported by his thought, he realized he was. The normal cypresses had given way to grassy islands, humped mounds of earth crowned by gargantuan trees. The cypress knees alone were larger than the trunks of most trees. Sonny saw paths worn through the grass on some tussocks, probably by hungry deer, exhausted from swimming. Deer were damn good swimmers, though not many people knew it.

Sonny hadn't seen the Bone Tree since 1966, but he remembered it all too well. The colossal cypress reared up out of the swamp like the Tree of Knowledge in the Garden of Eden. But this was no paradise. More than a dozen men Sonny knew of had died under that tree, and Frank claimed the real number was over a hundred. He'd shown Sonny hand-forged chain links embedded in the bark that dated back to slave times. Runaway slaves had supposedly been hanged or hobbled beneath this cypress. High inside the hollow trunk, Sonny had seen carvings Frank swore were Indian sign, from before the French came. Sonny didn't need those facts to make him wary of this place. The things he'd

seen done to men beneath the Bone Tree were seared into his brain. He
was half tempted to carry Jimmy Revels to Baton Rouge and put him
on a northbound bus rather than make the journey out of this snake-
infested swamp alone.

"Glenn don't know how easy he's got it," Sonny muttered. "Compared to this, dumping Luther's car in the Jericho Hole is nothing."

A heavy swish in the water to his right made Sonny's sphincter lock
up. He knew that sound. Sure enough, when he squinted, he saw the
armored back of an alligator swimming alongside the boat. When his
heartbeat finally slowed to normal, Sonny looked forward and saw the
Bone Tree towering a hundred feet above him, its base as broad as a
building blocking his path. The fibrous bark looked like the leathery
skin of some great creature, not dead but only sleeping, and high above,
its branches joined the crowns of other trees to form a thin canopy.
Killing the motor, Sonny let the johnboat glide up onto the edge of the
hummock that surrounded the massive trunk. A narrow, A-shaped
crack of utter darkness offered entrance to the hollow tree, and Sonny
wondered what lay inside that cavelike space on this night. Soon Jimmy
Revels could tell him.

Sonny stood and pointed his pistol down at Revels's bloody form.
"Get out," he said, kicking Revels's foot.

The nigger didn't move.

"Come on, boy!" Sonny's voice sounded higher and thinner than
he'd intended. "I know you're playing possum."

Revels remained still.

"By God, I'll shoot you where you lay." Sonny was lying. The slug
from his .357 Magnum would likely go through Revels and punch a hole
in the bottom of the boat. He didn't plan to spend the night surrounded
by water moccasins and alligators. Hell, there were *bears* in this swamp.

"What difference does it make?" Revels moaned at last.

"Get up, damn you! Or I'll shoot you in the pelvis. That'll make a
difference, I promise you."

"Tell me where my sister is. Then I'll get up."

"I don't know!"

"But ya'll ain't done nothin' else to her?"

"No!" Sonny yelled, blocking out the memory of all they'd done
to Viola Turner. He couldn't bear to think about that. "She got away, I

told you." He squinted at his watch in the dim light. "You saw it happen. She's probably with Dr. Cage right now, all patched up and pretty again."

"That's impossible, after what ya'll did."

"Move, boy!"

Revels struggled to his knees, then crawled out of the rocking boat and collapsed in the grass. He was lying squarely in a deer path.

Sonny picked up his flashlight, climbed out of the boat, and kicked Revels's thigh. "Get your ass up, damn it!"

"Why for? You just gonna shoot me and roll me into the water so the gators get me. Go on and do it."

"That's not what I'm gonna do. I'm just leaving you out here for a couple of days, till things cool down."

"Leave me, then."

"Not here. Inside the tree."

Revels rolled over and looked at the gigantic cypress. *"In* the tree? What you mean?"

"This tree is hollow. I want you to get inside it."

Swollen, bloodshot eyes looked up into Sonny's flashlight beam. "You lyin', man."

"I ain't. The deer get up in there and sleep sometimes, 'cause it's dry. See that crack there? They call this the Bone Tree, 'cause wounded deer crawl up in there to die. You'll get up in there, too, if you want to live. This is gonna be your jail for a couple of days."

Revels stared at the black opening for half a minute, thinking. Then he rolled over and slowly got to his feet. Sonny prodded him in the back, pushing him up the hummock, toward the crack in the fibrous wall of wood. Only eighteen inches wide, it stretched upward for ten feet, gradually narrowing to nothing.

"I ain't going in there," Jimmy said with boyish fear. "Ain't no telling what's up in there."

"Ain't nothing in there now. The animals heard us coming from way off." Sonny stepped forward and rapped the side of the tree with his pistol. "See? If there was a deer in there, he'd have bolted."

"Might be snakes in there."

"You'll just have to take your chances. Go on, now. I got to get out of here."

"I'll just come back out after you leave."

"I'm gonna nail a board up."

Revels stared into the yellow beam and spoke in a voice stripped of all affect. "I know you didn't like what those others did to Viola. Or to me. I saw it in your eyes." He held up his bandaged arm, showing the gauze Sonny had wrapped around the wound made by Snake Knox slicing off the boy's navy tattoo. "You were raised a Christian, just like me, Mr. Thornfield. How can you do this?"

Sonny shook his head and looked away, at the black water to his right. The kid was right about the torture, but he didn't seem to grasp the nature of race war. Having a common faith meant nothing. Niggers weren't true Christians, after all. As slaves, they'd simply latched on to the faith of their masters in desperation, not realizing that the master simply used religion to keep them tame.

"Go on, now," Sonny said, motioning toward the crack with his pistol.

"I ain't going," Jimmy insisted. "I can't."

Sonny gauged his chances of stuffing Revels through the crack if he was dead. The boy was thin enough, but Sonny didn't relish the idea. Moving dead men was hard work. "You go on, Jimmy, or I'll shoot you where you stand. That's the deal."

"Is Luther dead?"

"He is," Sonny said, hoping it was true.

Jimmy's shoulders sank, and whatever resistance he had left went out of him. "At least you told me the truth. So maybe Viola's really all right."

"She is, I swear."

Jimmy intoned something that sounded like a prayer. Then he turned sideways and worked his dark body through the crack in the tree. He might as well have been entering a cave.

Thank God, Sonny thought, as the stained white T-shirt vanished. He shone his flashlight through the crack. Jimmy stood a few feet away, staring at something at the center of the hollow tree. Sonny took the beam off his back and shone it around. The hollow trunk created a round room like some turreted castle tower. The way the walls narrowed as they reached skyward gave him a sort of religious feeling. "What you looking at?" Sonny asked.

Jimmy moved aside and pointed at the floor.

At the center of the round room lay a yellowed skeleton. *Not human,* Sonny realized. "That's just a deer," he said, noticing a carpet of other bones beneath it. "Probably crawled up in here wounded last hunting season."

"You don't have any board to nail up, do you?" Jimmy said in a fatalistic tone.

"No," Sonny said, almost apologetically. "That's a fact."

Jimmy turned slowly and raised a hand against the beam of the flashlight. The whites of his eyes glowed in his black face. Revels was twenty-six years old, but he looked like a teenager.

"You swear my sister's all right?" he insisted.

"I do," Sonny said in a shaky voice. "And if it makes you feel any better, finishing this up out here is going to save your hero's life."

Jimmy blinked in confusion. "Who do you mean?"

"Senator Kennedy."

"What about him?"

"You dying here is going to save his life."

The boy pondered this for several seconds. "It doesn't matter. He'll never be president. If not your bunch, somebody else will get him. The best men never make it. Moses, Jesus . . . Medgar, Malcolm. Even Dr. King. He won't live to see the Promised Land."

Sonny had a feeling the boy was right, but he was glad not to be part of that business anymore.

"Someday," Jimmy said, dropping the hand shielding his eyes, "you tell Viola where to find me, okay? It ain't right to leave a person not knowing about their kin. You were in the service. You know that. Even if you lie about how they died, you tell 'em where the body is. To give the family peace."

Sonny swallowed and raised his pistol. He didn't enjoy killing in cold blood, but neither had he ever hesitated to do his duty. And they'd gone too far to reverse course now. Everything had to be buried. *No body, no crime,* Frank always said. "Maybe someday," Sonny lied, trying to make it easier on the boy.

Revels plainly didn't believe him. Sweat poured off the kid's face, and Sonny had to shake his own head to get the burning sweat out of his eyes.

"You got any last words?" he asked, tilting his head to wipe his face on his shirt.

Revels nodded soberly.

"Get on with it, then."

"Are you listening, Mr. Thornfield?"

Sonny prepared himself for some dreadful curse in the name of God, or perhaps some ancient African demon. "I'm listening."

"I forgive you."

PART TWO

2005

_____

The truth is rarely pure and never simple.

—Oscar Wilde

MONDAY

CHAPTER 4

Natchez, Mississippi

AS A YOUNG LAWYER, I had a recurring dream. My father stood in the dock, accused of some terrible but unknown crime, and I was charged with defending him. There were a dozen versions of this dream, all turned to nightmares by different mistakes on my part. Some were routine, such as realizing I'd failed to file a critical motion or to ask for a continuance, or being physically unable to get into the courtroom. Other variations were more alarming. Sometimes the prosecutor could speak but I was mute; other times everyone could speak but I was deaf, and thus powerless to save my own father. The strangest part of this whole experience was that I was an assistant district attorney—a prosecutor, not a defense lawyer. Stranger still, my father had led an exemplary life. He was a war hero and a beloved physician, without the slightest blemish on his character. Yet in the final episode of this troubling series of dreams, when my father was asked to enter his plea, he stood and opened his mouth, then began coughing uncontrollably. The bailiff handed him a white handkerchief, and when he took it away from his mouth, clotted black blood stained the cotton, like lung tissue coughed up by someone dying of consumption. After a few moments of paralyzed horror, I awakened in my bedroom, my heart thudding against my sternum, and sweating as though I'd run six miles.

That was the last time I had the dream. As the years passed, I occasionally remembered it, but never again did it trouble my sleep. I came to believe that its significance had more to do with my sometimes harrowing experiences in law school and court than anything to do with my father. Other lawyers would occasionally mention similar nightmares, and this convinced me I was right. But then, at the age of forty-five . . . my nightmare came true.

It began with a phone call.

"MR. MAYOR, I HAVE the district attorney for you on line one."

I look up from my BlackBerry, mildly shocked by the identity of the caller. "Did he say what he wanted?"

"What do you think, boss?" A dollop of sarcasm from Rose, my executive secretary. Shadrach Johnson, the district attorney of Adams County, only calls me when he has no way to avoid it.

"Hello, Shad," I say with as much goodwill as I can muster. "What's going on?"

"Strange days, Mayor," he says in a surprisingly diffident voice. "You're not going to believe this. I've got a man in my office demanding that I arrest your father for murder."

I set my BlackBerry on my desk. Surely this is some sort of joke, a prank set up by the DA to pay me back for what he perceives as my many sins against him. "Shad, I don't have time for this. Seriously. What do you need?"

"I wouldn't play games about something like this, Penn. This guy isn't a random citizen. He's an attorney from Chicago. And he means business."

Chicago? "Who's Dad supposed to have killed?"

"A sixty-five-year-old woman named Viola Turner. Do you know that name?"

Viola Turner. "I don't think so."

"Take a minute."

After a disjointed moment of confusion, a Proustian rush of scents and images flashes though my brain. With the tang of rubbing alcohol in my nose, I see a tall, dark-skinned woman who looks very much like Diahann Carroll playing *Julia* on TV in the late 1960s, her white nurse's cap fitted perfectly into diligently straightened black hair, her bright, intelligent eyes set in a café au lait face. *Nurse Viola.* I never saw

Viola Turner after I was eight years old, yet this image remains star-tlingly true. Viola administered my tetanus and penicillin shots when I was a boy, and held my hand while my father stitched up my knees after I ripped them open on the street. During these stressful episodes, I almost never cried, and now I remember why. While Dad hooked that curved needle through my torn skin, Viola would chant or sing softly to me in a language I had never heard. My father later told me this was Creole French, which only confused me. I'd taken French in elementary school, but Nurse Viola's songs resembled nothing I had heard within the walls of St. Stephen's Prep. Only now do I realize that Viola's gift for empathy and her exotic voice must have imprinted her indelibly in my young mind.

"I don't understand," I say softly. "I thought she lived far off some-where. L.A. or—"

"Chicago," Shad finishes. "For the past thirty-seven years."

A rush of dread overpowers my initial skepticism. "Shad, what the hell's going on?"

"As far as I understand it, several months ago, Mrs. Turner was diagnosed with lung cancer. Terminal. Her treatment didn't go well. A few weeks ago, she decided to come home to Natchez to die."

"After thirty-seven years?"

"Happens all the time, brother. Black folk might have run from the South as fast as they could when they were young, but they miss it when they get old. Don't you know that?"

Shad's down-home soul brother voice is an act; a Mississippi-born African-American, he lost his drawl a month after his parents moved him north to Chicago to attend prep school.

"The son," he goes on, "whose name is Lincoln Turner, says his mother worked as a nurse for your papa back in the sixties. Anyway, after Viola came back here, Dr. Cage started treating her at home. Or at her sister's house, rather. The sister never left Natchez. Her name is Revels—Cora Revels. She never got married. So Viola started out a Revels, too. That's a famous black surname, you know? First black man to serve in the U.S. Senate."

"But Dad's not even working right now. He's taking time off to recover from his heart attack."

"Well, he's apparently been making house calls on his old nurse. For the past several weeks, at least. The victim's sister verifies that."

The victim. Christ. "Keep going."

"According to Cora Revels—and to Viola's son—your father and Mrs. Turner had some sort of pact between them."

"What kind of pact?"

"You know what kind," Shad says in his lawyer-to-lawyer voice. "An agreement that before things got too bad, your father would help the old lady pass without too much suffering." Shad's voice carries the certainty of an attorney who has seen most things in his time.

Sixty-five's not that old. "How did this even wind up in your office? She was terminal, you said. The police don't usually get called in these situations."

"I know. It's the son pushing this thing. He seems to feel your father crossed whatever line exists, and Turner's a lawyer. He's sitting outside my office right now."

"Where's my father? He hasn't been arrested, has he?"

"Not yet. But that's what Turner wants."

"How does he think Dad crossed the line?"

"Turner was driving down here from Chicago when it happened. His mother died thirty minutes before he got here, so he didn't get any last visit with her. He believes his mother could easily have lasted another day, or maybe even a few weeks. I'm hoping he'll calm down after the reality sinks in."

A faint buzzing has started in my head, the kind you're not sure belongs to a honeybee or a yellow jacket. "Are you, Shad?"

"You're goddamn right. I haven't forgotten what you've got on me. Pushing this case has no upside whatever for me."

At least Shad hasn't lost his instinct for self-preservation. "What else does the sister say?"

"Not much. I think Cora Revels is sort of simple-minded, to tell you the truth."

"Well, what are you going to do? Did you say the son is talking about a *murder* charge?"

"At first he was, but then he went online and checked the Mississippi statutes. We have an assisted suicide law, in case you didn't know. Now he's asking that your father be charged under that."

"What's the penalty?"

"Ten-year maximum."

"Fuck! That's a life sentence for my father."

"I know, I know. Take it easy, Penn. There's no way it's going to come to that. I made a couple of calls before I phoned you. Cases like this hardly ever make it to trial. When they do, it's usually nonphysicians who are charged, not doctors. Unless you have a nut like Kevorkian, which your father obviously isn't."

It's odd hearing Shad Johnson talk this way, because under normal circumstances, the DA would be thrilled to deliver any news that caused me grief. But eight weeks ago, I gained some unexpected leverage over him, and our relationship skidded far outside the bounds of normalcy.

"Still . . . this doesn't sound good."

"That's why I called. You need to talk to your father fast, find out exactly what happened last night. I want to reassure you, okay? But I have to tell you, the assisted suicide statute is pretty broadly written. Technically your father could be convicted just for providing a lethal dose of narcotics, and from what little I know already, he did more than that."

"A minute ago you were telling me not to worry."

"I'm just saying take it seriously. The chance of this going to trial is small. We just need to find a way to nip it in the bud."

"I hear you."

"As far as an arrest, I honestly don't think there's a cop or a deputy in town who would serve a warrant on your father."

Shad is probably right about this.

"Call me as soon as you talk to your dad. I can't stall Lincoln Turner forever. Call my mobile, not my office. You still have the number?"

"I always know how to find you, Shad."

The DA clicks off.

"*Viola Turner,*" I murmur, setting down my telephone with a shaking hand.

The district attorney has given me a gift, but only out of self-interest. During one of the most harrowing nightmares this town ever experienced, I discovered a digital photograph of Shadrach Johnson in the act of committing a career-ending felony. And though I gave Shad what I told him was the original SD card containing that image (in exchange for his not running for reelection), he can never be sure that I didn't keep a copy, and that I won't use it against him if he pushes me too far.

I glance around my office while my heart tries to find its rhythm again. My gaze wanders over the framed photographs on the wall to my left. Most are family snaps spanning the years from 1960 through the last tumultuous months, which have been filled with work generated by Hurricane Katrina, whose fury reached Natchez two days after it slammed into the Gulf Coast. But centered among the photos of New Orleans refugees and downed trees is a more formal portrait, shot seven years ago by a Houston photographer: the last pristine photograph of my family before my own personal hurricane hit. In this photo I am thirty-eight years old; my wife, Sarah, is thirty-six and vitally, startlingly alive; seated between us is our daughter, Annie, four years old and smiling like a sprite sprung from the dewy grass. My eyes are drawn to Sarah today, for just before this photograph was taken, we'd learned that she had breast cancer, stage IV, already metastasized. Above her smiling lips I see the knowledge of mortality in her eyes, an awareness that only self-deception could suppress, and Sarah was never one for denial. My eyes, too, are freighted with the terrible knowledge that happiness, like life itself, is ineffably fragile. Only Annie's eyes are clear in the picture, but soon even she would sense the soul-crushing weight pressing down on the adults around her.

This portrait always triggers a flood of memories, both good and bad, but what comes clearest today is the night of Sarah's death—an experience I rarely revisit, and one I've never fully recounted to a living soul. In those final weeks I saw something unfamiliar enter my wife's eyes—fear. But on the last night it left her, washed out by peace and acceptance. Only the next day did I understand why, and I've never asked my father to confirm my judgment. But now my mind superimposes Viola Turner's beautiful young face upon that of my wife. Viola probably suffered as terribly as Sarah did as death approached (I watched a strong uncle die of lung cancer, and it left me forever shaken). But what I know in this moment is simple: whatever Viola Turner's son believes my father might have done to his mother last night, he could be right. For where assisted suicide is concerned, one thing is certain:

Dad has done it before.

"MOM, IS DAD HOME?"

"No," says Peggy Cage, her voice instantly taut with concern. "Is something the matter?"

Instinct says not to reveal too much to my mother. "No, I just wanted to ask him something."

"Are you sure?" Definite stress in her voice. "You don't sound like yourself, Penn."

Trying to fool my mother is a challenge akin to flying a 747 beneath NORAD coastal radar. "There's a lot going on in City Hall. Do you know where Dad is?"

"I think he's at his office, working on records. Penn, the last thing you need to do is worry your father over something. His angina hasn't let up for days, and I know he's taken at least one nitro already this morning."

I'd like to ask Mom what time Dad left the house this morning, and also whether he was home last night, but my gut tells me to ask him first. "Seriously, it's nothing major. I just need to ask him something about his retirement plan."

"Well, I keep up with most of that information. You know your father. I'm sure I can help you."

Christ. "No, I need to talk to him."

A long pause. "All right, then. Try the office."

"Thanks, Mom."

Before she can say anything else, I click off. But instead of dialing my father's office, I set the phone on the cradle and leave my hand on it. For the past few weeks, I've assumed that my father, after nearly fifty years of practicing medicine, has been dealing with his traumatic but inevitable decision to retire. Seven weeks ago he suffered a myocardial infarction that he survived only by virtue of luck and heroic medical intervention. Had not my mother, one of the most compulsively prepared humans on the planet, insisted that Dad keep portable defibrillators both in their house and at his clinic, my father would probably be dead now. He always argued that defibrillators only helped in certain types of heart attacks, so keeping them around didn't justify the cost. Thus, no one was more surprised than Dad when, after dropping to the floor in his office, he was brought back to life by his young partner, Drew Elliott, using the defib unit Mom had demanded be always ready to hand.

Despite this brush with death—not his first, by far—my father has been driving to his office occasionally to catch up on charts, and making trips to the nursing homes to check on special patients during his "convalescence." Dad and Mom have been arguing about his driving alone, but you can't tell a doctor anything, so I decided not to intervene. His continued work has surprised no one, since despite several chronic illnesses—plus multiple heart and vascular surgeries—Dad has always soldiered on with a determination so relentless that his patients and colleagues have come to see it as normal. Chalk that up to the work ethic of a man born in 1932. I'd hoped that his desultory dabbling in medicine over these past weeks was part of the weaning process, leading slowly but surely toward full disengagement. But if Shad Johnson is right, Dad has been actively treating at least one patient during his recuperation period, and going to great lengths to do it.

"Miss Viola," I murmur, wondering when I last spoke that name before today. "My God."

According to the district attorney, my perfect vision of a nurse came back to Natchez after thirty-seven years in Chicago not to retire, as so many Natchez natives, both black and white, do—but to die. If Dad has been treating Viola, he has his reasons. And if her death was hastened a little in the name of lessening pain or maintaining dignity, he had reasons for that, too. I'd like nothing better than to leave all this between my father and his former nurse. Unfortunately, I don't have that option today.

Lifting the phone, I dial the private number of my dad's office. Sometimes he answers this line (if he's between patients, for example), but today it's answered by a warm, alto female voice I recognize as that of Melba Price, my father's head nurse. Much like Viola in the 1960s, Melba is my father's right hand in the clinic, and like every other woman who's occupied that position since 1963, she is black. I've never questioned the reason for this, and now that I do, I see one obvious possibility. Since more than half my father's patients are black, perhaps he feels that black nurses make those patients more comfortable in clinical situations. Or maybe he just likes black women.

"Melba, this is Penn."

"Lord, Penn, have you seen your daddy this morning?"

"No, but I need to."

"He's not here, and I haven't seen him. Nobody has."

"He didn't leave word where he'd be?"

"No. But some of the things on his desk have been moved. I've wondered if he came in last night and worked on his records like he does sometimes."

Since Melba occupies the position that Viola herself once did, I wonder if she shares the confidence my father placed in Viola. "Melba, I'm calling about a patient. A special patient. I know about the HIPAA rules and all that, but this has to do with Dad's personal welfare. Do you know if he's been treating a woman named Viola Turner? She has lung cancer."

I hear a short inspiration, then a long sigh. "I wish I could help you, Penn. But that's your daddy's business. I can't get mixed up in that. I'm not sure you should, either."

Oh, boy. "I don't want to, Melba. But I don't have any choice. Viola's dead, and there may be legal repercussions because of it. Problems involving Dad. Do you understand?"

"You need to talk to your father. Have you tried his cell phone?"

"He never answers his cell, you know that."

"Try it anyway. He answers it sometimes."

I thank Melba and hang up, then dial Dad's cell phone, a number I use so rarely I can barely remember it. The phone kicks me straight to voice mail, which hasn't even been set up to accept messages.

Man plans, God laughs, reads a framed cross-stitch on my wall, in both English and Yiddish. My first literary agent sent it to me. Placed around this proverb are framed advertisements from my mayoral campaign against Shadrach Johnson. *If you want a mayor for black people, vote for the other fellow. If you want a mayor for white people, vote for the other fellow. If you want a mayor for all the people, vote Penn Cage.* And this one: *Historic Change for a Historic Town.* Then my personal favorite: *I don't owe anybody in Natchez a favor. I owe everybody.*

I wrote those slogans myself, but two years after being elected mayor of my hometown by a wide margin, I have inescapably failed to deliver the changes I promised. The reasons are legion, but at bottom I blame myself. Two months ago (after two years of beating my head against a wall of indifference), I decided to resign the office and return to writing novels. Then God laughed, and a series of shattering events suggested I might not have the moral right to abdicate the responsibility I'd so blithely taken on. My parents, my daughter, a good friend, and my fiancée reinforced fate's suggestion, and my father's heart attack finally crystallized my resolve to serve out my term.

In the weeks since, I have worked like a man possessed, dividing my time between cleaning up the fallout from the near sinking of a riverboat casino below the Natchez bluff and remaking our local government by forming improbable alliances, calling in favors, and raising money from the unlikeliest of sources. Working at my shoulder throughout this period has been my fiancée, Caitlin Masters, publisher of the *Natchez Examiner.* And pulsing beneath all this activity have been the preparations for our wedding, scheduled to take place twelve days from now, on Christmas Eve. Ever since the district attorney's call, an itch of intuition has told me that whatever my father did last night is ultimately going to require the postponement of my wedding. I shudder to think of how my fiancée and my daughter would react to this eventuality.

"Mr. Mayor," says Rose, "I've got your father on line one."

Relief surges through me. "Thanks." I press the button on the phone base. "Hello?"

"Penn?" In a single syllable, my father's powerful baritone inspires calming confidence. "Peggy told me you were looking for me."

"Dad, where are you?"

"Just running some errands."

Errands! With my father, that could mean anything from shuffling through old bookstores to searching out ammunition for a Civil War–vintage musket. Before I blunder into a conversation about Viola Turner's death, my lawyerly instincts kick in with surprising force. I spent most of my legal career as a prosecutor, but I've always known the first rule of defense lawyers: never ask your client if he did it. Even those who protest their innocence will be putting their lawyer in an untenable position. For if your client gives you one version of the truth, you cannot knowingly put him on the stand later and listen to him tell another. And no defense attorney wants to be bound by something as unforgiving as the truth.

The most alarming thing about this train of thought is that I can't remember a single occasion when my father lied to me. So why am I planning for the possibility now? Paranoia? Or is the knowledge that Shad Johnson is an unscrupulous man with no love for my family forcing me into such pragmatism? "Dad, is anybody with you?"

"No. Why?"

"I got a call a couple of minutes ago from the district attorney. I don't want you to say anything until I finish telling you what he said. All right?"

He hesitates before replying. "All right."

As concisely as possible, I brief him on my conversation with Shad Johnson. "Viola's son is still in Natchez," I conclude. "He's pressing Shad to charge you with assisted suicide. At first he asked for murder, but he's since checked the Mississippi statutes. Now, I'm not asking you to tell me what happened at Cora Revels's house, or even if you were there last night. But will you tell me if you have been treating Viola?"

Dad waits a considerable time before he answers. "I have."

"Does anybody know that?"

"Melba knows. And Cora Revels, of course."

"Mom?"

Another pause. "No. A local pharmacist knows. Maybe some people who lived near the Revels house. I've stopped by there every couple of days, sometimes once a day, for the past six weeks. People out that way know my car. Viola was in bad shape, son."

"Lung cancer?"

"That's right. It metastasized some time ago."

The very word *metastasized* brings back all the horror of my wife's illness. Almost against my will, I ask for details. "Were you at Cora Revels's house last night?"

"I'd prefer not to discuss it, Penn."

"I understand. But with a family member pushing for criminal charges, you're going to have to say something if you want to avert a very public mess."

Dad pauses again, and I can hear him breathing. "I'm not concerned about that. Whatever happened between Viola and me last night occurred between a patient and her physician. I have nothing to say to Shad Johnson about it—or to you or anybody else. I'm sorry if that sounds harsh, but there it is."

This statement leaves me speechless for several seconds. "Dad, the penalty for assisted suicide is ten years. Even without prison, you could lose your medical license."

"I realize that. But I still won't talk about it. If Shad Johnson wants to arrest me, he can do it. I'm not hard to find."

Jesus Christ. "You and I should speak face-to-face."

"There's no point, Penn. I have nothing else to say about the matter."

"Silence isn't an option! Viola's son is an attorney. If he keeps push-ing the DA, and there's corroborating evidence, you could well be tried in criminal court. Believe it or not, Shad Johnson would like to avoid that prospect. But to help him, we're going to have to give him your side of the story."

"I don't *have* to do anything," Dad says, neatly separating his fate from my own in a tone I recognize all too well.

"Refusal to talk about what happened is going to be viewed as an admission of guilt."

"Don't American citizens have the right to remain silent?"

"Yes, but—"

"I don't think the Miranda rules have the word *but* in them, Penn. The Constitution, either, as I recall."

God spare me from amateur lawyers. "Do you know Viola's son?"

"Never laid eyes on him."

"Well, the vibe I'm getting from Shad is that if you handle this right, it could all go away."

"And what would the 'right' way be?"

"I'm not sure. Telling the truth, maybe. Unless . . ."

"What?"

I close my eyes. "Unless you did it."

This time the silence is alarmingly protracted. "I can't say anything else about this. The doctor-patient privilege is sacred to me."

"I'm afraid that privilege ended with Viola's death. Under these cir-cumstances, anyway."

"Not in my book."

His voice carries absolute conviction. I might as well hang up now. "Dad . . . *please* reconsider. You're required by law to assist the coroner in determining the cause of your patient's death. I'm not even the pros-ecutor, and what I'm hearing sounds like a doctor admitting he helped someone to die."

"People hear what they want to hear. I told you, if Shad Johnson wants to arrest me, let him do it. I'm through talking, and I'm sorry you were bothered with this. I'll see you later."

"Dad!"

But he's gone.

Reaching behind me, I take down the Annotated Mississippi Code of 1972 and page through it, searching for the assisted suicide statute, but before I can get my bearings the phone rings again.

"The district attorney again," says Rose. "Line two."

I stab the second button on my phone. "Shad?"

"Tell me you've got a miracle story," he says. "The ultimate alibi."

"I wish I did."

"What do you have?"

"Nothing."

"You couldn't find your father?"

"Oh, I found him. He won't talk to me."

"*What?*"

"He's giving me the Ernest Hemingway treatment. Stoic and silent. He says whatever happened last night is none of my business. Doctor-patient privilege."

"I hope you told him that's not going to fly."

"He doesn't care, Shad. He's as stubborn as they come when he wants to be."

"But he admitted to being there? At the woman's house?"

"He admitted nothing. He told me he'd been treating the lady, that's it."

"Penn, are you being straight with me? Was my call the first you've heard about all this?"

"Absolutely. But I think we'd better stop the questions for now."

"What the hell am I supposed to tell Roy Cohn down here? He wants your father's hide nailed to the courthouse door."

"I don't know. I'm thinking."

"Think faster."

"Maybe I should talk to the son myself."

"Forget it. I don't want Lincoln Turner even knowing I called you. If you can't come up with a medical justification for whatever happened last night—one that will stand up in court—your father is screwed. Turner wants Tom Cage in jail, and the evidence apparently supports his version of things. I'll tell you something else for free: Turner is already playing the race card."

"The race card? How?"

"He told me that if a black doctor had euthanized a white woman, and her son had complained, the doctor would already be in jail."

I try to imagine our black DA reacting to Turner's accusation. "What did you tell him?"

"I told him I'm handling this case just like I would any similar case. But I'm not sure he's wrong."

"Have you ever *had* a similar case?"

"Hell, no. Have you?"

"I prosecuted one once. Not exactly like this one, though. The doctor was a nut job. But what you told me before held true in Houston. Ninety-nine percent of these cases never get to the police, much less the DA's office."

Shad grunts. "I'll tell you something else for free. Lincoln Turner isn't impressed by my melanocytic credentials. He thinks I'm some kind of stooge for the Man."

Despite the gravity of the situation, I can't help but chuckle at Shad's predicament. "How old is this guy?"

"Forty, maybe? He did just lose his mother. I keep thinking he's bound to calm down. But that doesn't help us *today*."

"How long can you stall him?"

"I suppose I can tell him I'm not going to arrest a community physician of spotless reputation without one hundred percent documented evidence. I can take statements from the sister and anyone else who knew what was going on, process the physical evidence. But by tomorrow morning—afternoon at the latest—you'd better have the straight story out of your old man. If you don't, he's going to need a first-rate criminal defense attorney."

As Shad waits for my reply, my eyes lock on to the assisted suicide statute in the 1972 Code. One quick scan starts a chain of muscle spasms up my back. "Shad, what exactly does Turner say happened? Is he saying my father provided the morphine, or that he injected the drug himself?"

"He didn't say. He just kept yelling about morphine and a syringe. Why?"

"The way I read the statute, if Dad provided the drug and Viola injected herself, that's assisted suicide. But if he injected her himself . . . that's murder. Have you checked for precedents?"

"Not yet. But I suggest you get on it. Ten minutes ago I heard that

Sheriff Foti down in Orleans Parish is thinking about prosecuting a respected lady doctor who may have euthanized patients during Katrina. And the charge will be murder."

My heart thumps. "Tell me you're kidding."

"I'm not. And Viola Turner wasn't exactly a nobody, Penn. She had a younger brother who was a civil rights martyr. Jimmy Revels. Revels was kidnapped with a friend in 1968. Bodies never found."

I recall this incident from the newspaper stories by a crusading reporter from across the river. "What does that have to do with anything?"

"Just this. If I get Al Sharpton down here yelling to Greta Van Susteren about racial genocide by euthanasia on Court TV, I'll have no choice but to send your father to Parchman, no matter what kind of leverage you've got on me."

"Don't say that, man."

"Then get your ass in gear. The clock's ticking."

CHAPTER 5

TOM CAGE STARED down at his ringing cell phone, then looked through the bottom of his trifocals to read the name on the caller ID: ROSE MEADOWS. Penn's secretary, cliché name and all. He'd already received two additional calls from City Hall, which he'd ignored. Rose's call from her cell meant that Penn was pushing her hard to reach him again. Tom wished he could have been more forthcoming with his son, but Penn could do nothing to mitigate the situation, while he might easily aggravate it. And by getting involved at all, Penn might be putting himself and his daughter in harm's way. Tom took a deep breath and switched off his phone.

He didn't consider himself a sentimental man. He wasn't the type to wistfully return to the town of his boyhood or attend a high school reunion and get maudlin over his fourth bourbon. A child of the Depression, he had always moved forward, never back. His war experiences in Korea had only reinforced this habit. But there was one building in Natchez that Tom never passed without a tightening in his chest, and the events of the past twelve hours had brought him back to it like an icy comet returning to the star where it began its journey through the cosmos.

The house stood on Monroe Street, a rambling one-story structure in the shadow of the massive water tower that supplied the north side of town. In this residence Tom had first begun practicing medicine as a civilian, after being discharged from the army in 1962. He only passed it now on the rare occasions when he broke his own rule and attended a service at Webb's Funeral Home, or when he made a house call on the north side of town. But today he'd parked his aging BMW beside the wrought-iron fence that bordered the yard of his old office, and stared at the familiar oak door while images of the distant past flowed through his mind.

A surgeon named Wendell Lucas had founded the clinic that once occupied this house. Over the years Lucas had hired a progression of young GPs to handle daily patients and refer him the appendectomies and gallbladder resections that gave him his living. Lucas was a better businessman than a surgeon, and the GPs who had good business sense moved on after three or four years, establishing their own practices in Natchez or other towns. But Tom had cared only about practicing medicine, and having the old surgeon take care of the business side of things freed him up for that, so he'd remained in the arrangement. He had always known the older man was taking advantage, but he was too embarrassed for Lucas to confront him about it. Peggy had ridden Tom about it sometimes, but after enough years even she had given up, and then in 1980 Lucas finally retired to play golf full-time. Tom abandoned the old clinic and moved into a modern new office complex beside St. Catherine's Hospital, the same one he occupied now.

In many ways, this old clinic represented Tom's growth into manhood. Here he had truly come into his own as a physician. He'd experienced great triumphs and made sickening mistakes. The triumphs had been silent for the most part, inspired diagnoses arrived at after deep study and research, and only after following the diagnoses of other doctors to demoralizing dead ends. That was in the days before nuclear imaging and complex lab screening, when all he had to go on was education, experience, and instinct. But the life-and-death intensity of the work Tom had done here was only part of the invisible web that tied him to this building. More than anything else, this was the place where he'd come to know Viola Turner.

As a rule, Dr. Lucas always kept two GPs working under him at the clinic. Most had been decent docs, with only a couple of bad apples over the years. But one of those apples Tom had never forgotten. Gavin Edwards had been at the clinic when Tom arrived in 1963. Viola Turner was Edwards's nurse, but as soon as Tom was hired, Dr. Lucas had transferred Viola to him. Tom figured Lucas had made this change to ease him into the practice (and increase his production numbers), but before long Tom deduced that Viola had requested the transfer. The reason was simple: Gavin Edwards would screw anything in a skirt, and he devoted most of his waking hours to trying. Despite being married, he'd had flings with both receptionists and the lab technician, a full-blown affair with the insurance girl, and he'd possibly even molested some patients.

Viola was the only one of "the girls" Edwards hadn't nailed, and he was clearly itching to do so. He often commented on her physical assets, even after Tom pointedly discouraged him. The irony was that Gavin Edwards was as racist as the average welder at Triton Battery, yet he still wanted to sleep with Viola. Of course, that particular hypocrisy had flourished in America since the seventeenth century. White men loved having sex with black women, so long as they would never have to treat them as equals. And in Mississippi in the early 1960s, there was no risk of that. Truth be told, there wasn't much risk of it in New York, either. In Natchez, Edwards probably could have raped Viola and gotten away with it, but he didn't have the guts to go quite that far. Viola took great pains to avoid being alone with him, but still he persisted. Eventually, Tom began to wonder what he would do if Edwards, who was senior to him, made an overt advance toward Viola. Dr. Lucas would undoubtedly support Edwards in such a circumstance. And if that happened . . . what would Tom do?

Fate soon answered the question for him. It was Viola's duty to unlock the clinic every morning, then set up the examining rooms and the surgery for the day. The other girls came in thirty minutes later, and the docs a half hour after that, after completing morning rounds at the hospital. Dr. Edwards always arrived last, but not because of rounds. He was usually visiting a bored housewife whose husband left early for work. But one morning in 1965, Gavin Edwards was waiting inside the clinic when Viola arrived. He told her he'd come in early to catch up on his records, but within three minutes his hands were all over her. When he tried to pin her in a corner of an examining room, Viola pretended to cooperate just long enough to get a ceramic mug filled with tongue depressors into her hand. Then she cracked him across the face with it.

Tom's first knowledge of the incident came when Dr. Lucas called him into his office. Viola had reported Dr. Edwards's behavior, and the surgeon had already called Edwards in to question him. Edwards told Lucas that he'd been having consensual sex with Viola for a couple of weeks, and she'd only hit him when he admitted that he had no feelings for her and had simply wanted to find out what it was like to "dip his pen in ink." Lucas believed Edwards, mostly because of his track record with the other female employees, yet something had made him ask Tom's opinion. Almost before he knew what he was going to say, Tom blurted out, "Gavin Edwards is a damned liar."

Dr. Lucas's mouth dropped open as though he'd seen a pig start to dance. Then he drew himself up and gave Tom a stern glare. "That's a pretty serious charge against a colleague, Tom. Not to mention the obvious."

"What's the 'obvious'?" Tom asked, wondering if Lucas had the balls to say that Edwards was white and Viola black.

"Are you taking the word of an unregistered nurse over that of a fellow medical man?"

"Viola Turner is the best nurse I've ever worked with," Tom replied, his chin quivering with fury. "Gavin Edwards is a lazy bastard who can't keep his prick in his pants. Worse, he's a lousy diagnostician. I don't think he can even read an EKG."

Dr. Lucas started to say something, but Tom cut him off with an ultimatum. "If you fire Viola, you're firing me as well. Then you and Edwards can do *all* the diagnosing around here." Then he walked out.

After two face-saving days, Dr. Lucas fired Gavin Edwards. Tom had no illusions that this was anything other than a business decision. Edwards might have been a good golfing partner, but it was Tom who kept the practice humming. More than half the patients openly praised him as the best doctor Lucas had ever employed, and Lucas was too greedy to let a frustrated cocksman like Edwards hurt his bottom line.

Viola stayed home from work during those two days, and the clinic suffered mightily because of it. It was like an army company trying to get along without its top sergeant. Her absence quickly revealed just how much work she'd been doing during the course of each day. Patients constantly complained, despite Tom working the substitute nurse off her feet. The day after Edwards cleaned out his desk, Viola reappeared, looking more serene than she ever had. Within hours the clinic was back on keel. But late in the afternoon, as Tom was searching for a chart in the clutter atop his desk, she'd stepped into his private office and closed the door.

"I want to thank you for what you did," she said softly.

Tom felt blood rush to his face. He couldn't look her in the eyes. "It was nothing. Anybody in my place would have done it."

"No," Viola replied. "Nobody else would have done it. No doctor who ever came through here, anyway. I was sure I was going to be fired. Dr. Lucas told me what you said."

Tom stared at Viola's hands, which were folded in front of her white skirt. He couldn't bear to look into her eyes. Perhaps, he thought guiltily, because he shared Edwards's desire. And because of this, he deserved anything but gratitude. As he stared, he realized Viola's hands were clenched so tightly that her skin was bloodless where her thumbs and fingers pressed into it.

"I just told the truth," he said awkwardly, trying to speak around his seemingly swollen larynx. At last he looked up into her big brown eyes. "You're a fine nurse. As good as any I've ever worked with."

"Even in the war?"

"Yes. I wasn't a doctor in Korea, of course. Just a medic. But I saw a good bit of work at the clearing stations, and at a MASH unit after I was wounded."

"You don't know what that means to me." Her hands parted, and Tom saw that they were shaking. "Your next patient is ready in room four."

"Thank you," Tom said, and hesitantly started forward.

Viola stepped aside as if to let him pass, but as she did, she turned into him, buried her face in his chest, and wrapped both arms around him in a fierce hug. Though she was shaking badly, she must have felt his heart pounding. Stunned by the sudden intimacy, he encircled her in his arms and just stood there, holding her. After what seemed a full minute, she drew back, and he saw tears on her face. She wiped them unself-consciously, then smiled.

"Did I say room four or room five?"

"I have no idea."

Viola laughed. "I'll go find out."

And that was that.

They spent the next three years pretending this moment had not passed between them. They were both married, after all. Of course, marriage didn't stop people like Gavin Edwards, and in all truthfulness it might not have stopped them, either. The real barrier to any deeper relationship was simpler and more frightening: Tom was white and Viola black. That gulf could not be bridged in Natchez, Mississippi, in the 1960s, not without casualties. They both knew it, and they lived under the tyranny of that unwritten code.

Playing the role of objective employer with Viola was the hardest thing Tom had ever done. He soon learned the basic human truth that the more you try to put something out of your mind, the more difficult it becomes to think of anything else. Oscar Wilde's dictum that the only way to get rid of a temptation is to yield to it quickly lost any humor it had once had. Five days a week, Tom worked within eight feet of Viola for most of the day, and within two feet for much of it. When they labored over an open wound in the surgery, their heads sometimes touched, and he almost couldn't stand her proximity. He knew the tightly restrained curves of that white uniform more intimately than he knew his wife's naked body. He came to think of Viola's scent like the smell of the caramel candy his grandmother had made when he was a boy—unobtainable in the real world, but vividly, mouthwateringly alive in his mind.

Sometimes he wondered if he should tell Dr. Lucas he wanted to switch nurses. By then there was a new GP working in the clinic, and Lucas wouldn't have hesitated to give Viola to him, knowing that the younger doctor's profitability would improve. But Tom couldn't bring himself to do it. Sometimes he thought he sensed Viola suffering the same torture, trying to reconcile an all consuming attraction with a deeply ingrained moral code. Because not only did Viola Turner love her husband; she was also a devout Catholic. More often than not, when she wasn't in the office, Viola was working at Sacred Heart Church or doing service work in the community. Several times Tom had gone so far as to assist with these projects, doing free physicals for some of the Negro schools' sports teams, or inoculating some of the poorest black children against various diseases. It amazed him that some of his colleagues traveled hundreds of miles to do mission work in Central America when there was dire medical need within two miles of their clinics. Dr. Lucas frowned on these "socialist pro bono crusades," as he dubbed them, but since Tom funded them out of his own pocket, the surgeon didn't make much of a fuss. The end result of all this compensatory effort on Tom's part was that he and Viola spent even more time together and developed an intimacy that spouses waiting at home could not begin to share.

This tense emotional stalemate took a shocking turn in 1967, when Viola's husband was drafted and sent to Vietnam. James Turner was an auto mechanic, but he'd spent a year working on helicopters in the peacetime army in 1960, and that made him valuable in Southeast Asia. In 1967 the army recalled him. Tom vividly remembered a conversation with Viola's anxious husband before he left for New Orleans and his commercial flight to Vietnam. James Turner knew Tom had seen action in Korea, and he wanted to get the best advice he could about staying alive in combat. Tom's cautions were simple and based on experience. "First, don't volunteer for anything. Second, keep your head down and listen to your sergeant. Third, if you're ever ambushed, run toward the fire, not away from it. The first shots are meant to drive you into the waiting machine guns. Your best chance is forward. Fourth, every war's different, so listen to your sergeant. Fifth . . . listen to your sergeant. Are you getting the message?" James had laughed, but Tom could see he was scared to death, and no man in his right mind would have wanted to leave Viola to spend a year in a hostile jungle ten thousand miles away.

For the first month after James's departure, Viola had seemed a different woman. The romantic tension between her and Tom dissipated as though it had never existed, and he felt its absence like a troubling tooth that had finally been pulled, leaving an aching socket. Viola's thoughts were clearly with her husband—yet Tom's jaw still throbbed. She lived with a new tension, one that waxed and waned with Cronkite's daily report on the conflict on the far side of the world. James sent regular letters, and his tone was always upbeat, so after a while Viola settled into a sort of low-grade anxiety. At work she kept up a cheerful front that could have won her an Academy Award. But five months after James Turner left Natchez, two army officers wearing dress uniforms showed up at Viola's home. When they told Viola that her husband was dead, she gave a slight shake of the head—one small gesture of denial—then collapsed to the floor. Dr. Lucas told her to take the week off, and Tom concurred. But the next morning, Viola was back at work, perfectly coiffed and acting with her usual professionalism. The only indication of her loss was a black ribbon worn on the left side of her uniform collar.

From that point forward, Tom had no idea how to behave. Viola's stoicism had moved him beyond words, and from his own war experiences he knew better than to try to lessen her grief. Looking back, Viola's heroic response to young widowhood had probably pushed him further toward love than any physical attraction. But strangely, Viola seemed even more preoccupied over the next months than she had when her husband was in Vietnam. Only after several awkward attempts did Tom finally discover the reason for Viola's worry.

She had a younger brother named Jimmy Revels, and Jimmy was "in trouble." When Tom asked what kind of trouble, Viola shook her head and refused to say. But over the course of a week she finally revealed that Jimmy was involved in the civil rights movement. This worried her on several fronts. Not least was her fear that Dr. Lucas would fire her if he learned she was related to a civil rights activist. Tom assured her that he could protect her job, but Viola thought he was naïve. "Dr. Lucas might have let you desegregate the waiting room," she said, "but that was just good business, since you pull in so many colored patients. Working in the movement is something else."

Viola also worried about the Ku Klux Klan, which had grown rabidly active across the state during the past four years. Jimmy was a musician, but he'd become obsessed with the Reverend Martin Luther King, adopting both his nonviolent philosophy and his habit of putting himself in harm's way. Jimmy's nocturnal activities were making Viola a nervous wreck. Tom tried to reassure her, but the danger could not be denied. As the company doctor for Triton Battery (a deal negotiated by Dr. Lucas), Tom had discovered that a significant fraction of the company's white workers were racists of the first order. They didn't even try to hide their membership in the Klan, or the fact that they were "taking a stand" in the battle for white supremacy. Because Tom was white, they simply assumed that he shared their prejudices.

The tension between Tom and Viola mounted in concert with the racial tension on the streets of Natchez, but whatever barrier remained between their professional and personal lives was shattered not long after a black man was murdered by a white deputy in a barbecue restaurant across the river. On a night when the KKK and the black Deacons for Defense were preparing for armed conflict, a midnight phone call awakened Tom from an uneasy sleep.

"Dr. Cage," he said with a military alertness developed in Korea and West Germany.

"Dr. Cage?" whispered a female voice. "This is Viola. I need help. I'm in trouble."

Tom's heart began hammering, and blood surged through his arteries. "Where are you?"

"At the clinic."

Tom could barely hear her. He looked at his watch. *One twenty-five* A.M. "What's happened?"

"Jimmy's hurt. Bad. I wouldn't have called you, but he can't go to the hospital. I tried to handle it myself, but I can't stop the bleeding."

Tom heard her usually calm voice spiraling into panic. Common sense told him to ask whether the police were involved, but instead he said, "Just try to stabilize him. I'm on my way."

When he arrived at the clinic fifteen minutes later, Tom found Viola in the surgery with her brother and a huge young man named Luther Davis. Both men had been beaten with two-by-fours, but that wasn't the worst of it. Jimmy Revels had been stabbed in the back, and Davis had slashing knife wounds on his arms. The pair had been ambushed by Klansmen outside the Flyway Drive-In between Vidalia and Ferriday, Louisiana. The Flyway was an all-white place, though colored patrons could walk up to the back window and buy a Coke or some french fries if they kept their heads down. Apparently, Jimmy and Luther had pulled into a regular bay and ordered milk shakes like white customers. This created confusion at first, until a pickup truck carrying two Ku Klux Klansmen arrived. The unmasked men got out carrying wooden staves, and everybody had expected a beating, but then Davis had driven his Pontiac convertible over the concrete curb and managed to escape.

The pickup chased Luther's Pontiac for more than a mile, until a second car cut them off near Pelham's lumberyard. With no avenue of escape, Revels had gotten out and tried to reason with their pursuers, but this only earned him a green-stick fracture of his right humerus. Then Luther Davis joined the fray. Luther in a fight was more than most men could handle, even with odds of five against two. He'd done serious damage to their assailants, but eventually superior numbers took their toll. Realizing that he and Jimmy might die beside the road, Luther had fought his way back to the Pontiac and retrieved a .25-caliber pistol from the glove box. He told Tom he'd tried to intimidate the Klansmen into stopping the beating, but one had made him use the gun. Luther shot one man in the leg, then dragged Jimmy's bleeding body back to the car and made their getaway. Only then had Jimmy realized he'd been stabbed in the back.

Tom learned all this while treating the men's injuries, Viola assisting with shaking hands. He'd always made it a point not to learn how to shoot X-rays, so he wouldn't have to feel guilty about referring late-night trauma cases to the ER, but Viola had taught herself to do it by watching the X-ray tech. Within minutes Tom had a beautiful set of films with which to evaluate Jimmy's fracture. Despite his pain, Jimmy thanked Tom profusely for taking the risk of treating them, while Luther bore everything in sullen silence. Viola barely spoke except to tell Jimmy to keep his voice low. Tom knew she was terrified of being fired for bringing trouble to the clinic. He wasn't sure what to do about the situation, but one thing was certain: the actions he was taking now put him far over the line of neutrality in the conflict between the races, and well into the danger zone when it came to the Ku Klux Klan.

He'd stitched a rubber drain into Jimmy's stab wound and was beginning to suture Luther's remaining lacerations when he heard a desperate pounding on the clinic's front door. His first thought was the police, but Jimmy assured him that they'd parked their car far way. Viola had ferried them to the clinic. Tom kept working and hoped the knocking would cease, but it didn't. As he leaned over the sink to wash his hands, he heard a gasp, then turned and saw Viola staring at a pistol in Luther Davis's hand. Tom started to speak, then held his silence. It would be useless to tell the man to put it away.

"You two stay in here," Tom told the men. "Viola, get into Exam Three. And nobody make a peep, no matter how close anybody comes to this room."

Tom switched off the light. As Viola padded across the floor behind him, fresh knocking echoed through the clinic. "I'm going to say I'm alone," he told her, "but if it's the police, and they get pushy, I'll tell them I met one of my nurses up here for a late-night rendezvous. Can you play that role?"

"I'll prance out in my Playtex if it will save Jimmy," Viola whispered.

"It just might."

Leaving her in Exam Three, Tom went to the front of the clinic, checked his shirt for blood, then opened the shuddering front door.

What he saw on the concrete steps was not the police, but three Klansmen he knew all too well. All were employees of Triton Battery. In front stood Frank Knox with his blazing eyes and military crew cut. Behind him stood a giant of a man named Glenn Morehouse, holding up the wiry frame of Sonny Thornfield, whose face was twisted in agony. Thornfield's T-shirt was soaked with blood, and even in the weak light spilling from the doorway, Tom could see his left pant leg plastered to his swollen thigh, a belt fastened tight just above the knee. All three men were shivering in the cold.

"Evenin', Doc," said Frank Knox. "Your wife told us you was out on a house call, but she didn't know where. We couldn't go to the hospital with this, so we was gonna bust in and try to use your equipment. Then we saw your light."

"Why can't you go to the hospital?" Tom asked in the most ingenuous voice he could muster. "Did you rob a bank or something?"

Frank laughed. "Nah. This is nigger trouble. There's too much FBI in town to risk the hospital. We got a doctor over in Brookhaven who helps us out sometimes—a morphine addict—but that's too far for this. I'm worried the bullet nicked his femoral artery."

Tom shook his head. "That leg would be much bigger, or he'd be dead. I'm surprised you didn't call Dr. Lucas. He's a surgeon, which is what it looks like you need."

Knox snorted in contempt. "That son of a bitch don't care about nothin' but his bank balance. You think he'd get out of bed to help a workin' man?"

"Well—"

"Frank can patch this leg," Thornfield said through gritted teeth. "We just need the equipment."

"I saw a lot of gunshot wounds in the Pacific," Knox explained. "Even patched a couple myself. But I'd feel a hell of a lot better with a trained pair of hands on this."

Tom bent and pretended to examine the wound by porch light, but he knew full well he was looking at Luther Davis's handiwork. "How did this happen?"

"You don't want to know, Doc," Thornfield grunted.

"How 'bout we get off this porch?" Frank suggested. "Where you can take a better look?"

Before Tom could protest, all three men were inside the clinic, the door closed behind them. "Where you want us?" Frank asked.

Knox knew where the surgery was. Most of the Triton Battery men had been to the clinic for physicals, if nothing else. Tom was afraid that if they even went close to the surgery, Luther Davis would charge out and finish the work he'd started across the river.

"There's an examining table in the room next to my private office," Tom said, pointing. "Down there, to your right. Room one. Go on in there."

While the men carried their comrade through the waiting room like exhausted soldiers, Tom walked back toward the surgery. "I'll be right there," he assured them. "I need some of Dr. Lucas's instruments."

"Go help him, Glenn," Frank ordered.

"No, I've got it!" Tom called with a pounding heart, looking back to make sure he wasn't being followed.

He hurried back to the surgery, flicked on the light, and held his finger to his lips. Luther was crouched in a fighting stance with his pistol, while Jimmy sat on the examining table, motionless as an ebony Buddha.

"It's your Klan friends," Tom whispered. He looked at Luther. "The one you shot's bleeding like a hog."

"Good," Luther whispered, rising and pacing in the little room. "I'm gon' have to kill them goddamn sons of bitches yet."

"Stop taking the Lord's name in vain," Jimmy said mildly.

"You're not killing anybody," Tom said, blocking the big man's path. "There's three of them, and they've certainly armed themselves by now. You sit here and don't move a muscle. If you make any noise, you'll have klukkers all over you. And nobody wins a gunfight in a twelve-by-twelve room. I can tell you that from experience. Understood?"

After Luther nodded, Tom grabbed some instruments and went back to the room where he'd sent the Klansmen.

The next forty-five minutes were the tensest of his civilian life. All three Klansmen were accustomed to dealing with wounds, but their residual anger was palpable. Most alarming, they knew the identities of "both them niggers" who'd tried to "personally integrate the Flyway" that night. As Tom probed Sonny Thornfield's leg for the .25 slug, Frank said, "What you doing up here at this hour, Doc? Your wife said you was on a house call."

Tom shook his head and kept working. "To tell you the truth, I was banging one of my nurses till you assholes showed up."

After a moment of stunned silence, all three men burst out laughing.

"I thought you guys were my wife come to catch me," Tom added. "That's what took me so long to answer the door. I had to get the girl out with her clothes on."

"We definitely owe you one, then," Frank said. "Any time you need a favor, you let us know."

"Count on it," Tom said, finally extracting the slug to the accompaniment of Thornfield's screams.

"Which nurse you bangin'?" Sonny asked, breathing hard. "You ain't bangin' that colored girl, are you?"

Tom's face heated instantly. "Why?"

"Sonny's jealous," Frank said, laughing. "He's got the hots for that one."

"Bullshit," Sonny growled. "It was her brother who—"

"Quit your bitchin'," Frank snapped. "When the time comes, I'll let you skin the buck who done this. Till then, take it like a man."

"I'll make that nigger squeal, all right," Sonny vowed. Then he went white and vomited over the edge of the table.

"Aw, hell," Frank groaned, backing away. He picked the bloody and deformed slug out of the kidney-shaped metal tray. "Messing up Doc's floor for a little pimp bullet like this. Clean that puke up, Glenn. Doc ain't got no nurse on duty." Frank punched Tom on the arm and laughed. "Least not no more, he don't!"

While Morehouse obediently cleaned up the vomitus, Tom finished working in silence. Twenty minutes was all it took to deal with the superficial injuries, but as he worked, he wondered whether Luther Davis had obeyed his order to remain in the surgery. More than anything, he worried how Viola was holding up in the darkness of Exam Three. He prayed she wouldn't snap and try to check on her brother. Surely she wasn't that crazy—

"Like we said, Doc," Frank said expansively. "Anything you ever need, you let us know."

"Just don't let this happen again. You're cutting into my sex life."

The three men laughed heartily as Tom led them out, Thornfield limping along with Morehouse's support.

"Get home and rest that leg," Tom advised. "You can get your revenge next month. Come to the office tomorrow and let me check it. You all need rest, by the way. Head injuries are nothing to fool with."

Frank laughed. "We'll rest when we're dead, Doc. Take it easy, okay? And sorry 'bout your pussy."

Tom shook his head and shut the door, sweat suffusing his skin in a sudden wave. He'd felt fear like this during the war, but something was different now. In Korea he'd mostly worried about himself. Now he had a wife and two children to protect. And tonight he'd stepped between two warring armies—small ones, perhaps, but as vicious in their hatreds as any on earth.

He shut off the light and went back to get Viola. He found her shivering in the dark exam room, her shirt unbuttoned to the waist. A white bra showed through, cradling her breasts as though for a *Playboy* spread.

"They're gone," he said, averting his eyes. "Let's finish up Jimmy."

Before she could say anything, he went back to the surgery. While Jimmy and Luther peppered him with questions, he did some of the fastest stitching he'd done since his internship at Charity Hospital in New Orleans.

"They want revenge," he told Luther. "They recognized you both, and they're not going to stop looking until they find you. You need to get out of town."

"I ain't runnin' from them cracker motherfuckers," Luther vowed.

"Then you're dumber than you look. They've got more guns and men than you do, and the cops and courts are on their side. You only have one choice. Retreat."

"Dr. Cage is right," Viola said. "Jimmy, please talk some sense into Luther. If ya'll stay in Natchez, you're going to die. That Frank Knox is bad all the way through. He's a killer."

"She's right," Tom concurred, straightening up and surveying his handiwork. "I know the breed. This time, discretion is the better part of valor."

"Freewoods," Jimmy said thoughtfully. "We'll go to Freewoods till things cool down."

"What's Freewoods?" Tom asked.

"Nothing," snapped Luther. "Nowhere. He talkin' crazy."

As Tom washed the blood from his hands and forearms, he noticed Jimmy Revels staring at him. "What is it, Jimmy?"

"You don't mind getting black blood on your skin?"

Tom laughed. "I learned one thing fast as a combat medic: we all bleed the same color."

Jimmy smiled. "You didn't learn that being a medic. You learned that from your parents."

Tom stared back at the serious young man and shook his head. "You're wrong about that." Opening a cabinet, he took out some antibiotics a drug rep had left him and handed them to Luther. "This will keep your wounds from getting infected. Viola can tell you about dosage. Now, you guys get out of here."

"I'll get the car," Viola said. "I'll pull into the garage, then you both get down in the backseat."

"Backseat, my ass," said Luther. "We gettin' in the *trunk*."

Tom waited in a darkest corner of the freezing garage while Viola carried out her plan. He watched the two men fold themselves into the trunk of the Pontiac, quite a feat considering Luther's bulk. After Viola slammed the lid shut, she didn't walk around to the driver's seat, but into the corner where Tom stood. She was only a dark shape in the shadows, but he knew her scent as well as any on earth. She stepped close and took his hand.

"I don't have words," she murmured. "You saved my brother's life."

"Viola," he whispered. "This isn't just dangerous. This could get you killed. All of us."

"I know. And you shouldn't be any part of it."

"What's Freewoods?"

"A place where people don't care what color you are. White, black, Redbone, it doesn't matter. It's safe. Not even klukkers go back up in there."

"Then get those boys there tonight."

He sensed more than saw her nod in the dark.

"Will *you* be all right?" she asked, squeezing his left hand.

"I'm fine. You're the one at risk. You—"

Before he could continue, her arms slipped around him in a hug so fierce that it stole his breath. Unlike the embrace after he'd gotten Gavin Edwards fired, this was no simple act of gratitude. This time Viola's body molded against his from neck to knee. A dizzying rush swept through him, triggering delayed shock from the ordeal they'd just endured. He felt his balance going, and then a wave of desire so powerful that he pulled Viola against him as though trying to merge their bodies through their clothes.

A muffled bang froze them in place—then Viola jerked back as if a spark of static electricity had arced between them. Jimmy and Luther were hammering on the inner lid of the trunk.

"*Be careful,*" Tom said to the darkness. "If a cop stops you, tell him you're making a house call to a Negro place for me. If he gives you trouble, tell him to call me at home."

"I will," Viola assured him. "I'll be all right. I'll see you tomorrow."

As she walked to the driver's door, fear blasted through Tom like Dexedrine. *What if I never see her again?*

"You'd better be here, damn it," he said.

Seven hours later, she was, as perfectly dressed and coiffed as always. Tom, on the other hand, hadn't slept more than a few minutes at a stretch all night. In the span of one hour, by a simple act of decency, he had placed himself beyond the pale of his own tribe and put his job, his life, and his family at risk. Worse, after years of repressing his feelings for Viola, he'd felt something change deep within him, a tectonic shift that could never be undone. By the standards of their ongoing mutual denial, that few seconds' embrace in the garage had been a consummation of sorts, an admission that they shared something so powerful that they lived in constant fear of it, something that could sweep their present lives away.

"*Dr. Cage, is that you?*" asked a muted voice.

Tom blinked in confusion. Then he realized that someone was rapping on the window of his car. A man of about fifty stood on the other side of the glass, waiting for Tom to roll down his window.

"I thought that was you!" the man exulted as Tom pressed the power window button.

The last wisps of Viola's memory were snatched away by the wind that blew into the car when the glass sank into the door frame.

"What you doing down in this part of town, Doc?" asked the man, as though he'd caught Tom in the midst of having an affair. "I'll bet you're thinking about old times, aren't you?"

Could his thoughts be that transparent?

"You don't recognize me, do you?" asked the man.

"Ah . . ."

"Jim Bateman! You used to be my doctor. I grew up around the corner, right over there. Your lab lady used to make me milk shakes sometimes, with that barium drink mixer."

"Oh," Tom said, vaguely recalling a chubby boy who used to hammer at the rear door until someone let him in. "Jim. Of course I remember you."

"I'm right, huh? You were thinking about your old office here. Weren't you?"

"I was," Tom said softly.

"It's just a regular house now," Bateman lamented. "Don't seem right to me. When you were here, this place was *full* of people. The whole block always felt so alive. Now it's just a sleepy old house."

"It is a little disorienting."

Bateman looked at the paint peeling off the old clinic. "You know who I think about sometimes?"

"Who?"

"That black nurse you had. Miss Viola. She was so nice. All these years, and I've never forgotten her."

Tom nodded in amazement.

"Whatever happened to her?"

"She moved to Chicago."

"That right?"

He nodded dully.

"Well, you lost a good one there. You ever hear from her after that?"

Tom swallowed and tried to keep his composure. "She died, Jim."

"Aw . . . don't tell me that. When was this?"

"This morning." For the first time the full weight of Viola's death crashed down upon Tom. Not until this moment had he realized all that had passed from the world with her.

"What?" asked Bateman, clearly confused. "In Chicago you mean?"

"No." Tom looked up at last, into the man's dazed eyes. "Right here in Natchez. She was very ill. She came home to die."

Bateman shook his head in wonder. "I'll be dogged. That just . . . it makes me hurt inside. Kind of like when Hoss died on *Bonanza*. You know?"

"I know."

"No wonder you're out here." Bateman patted him on the shoulder. "I'm sorry I bothered you, Doc. I'll let you be. I talk too damn much. My wife tells me all the time."

"No, I'm glad you stopped. It's good to know Viola's remembered. You take care."

Bateman waved and slowly walked north up Monroe Street, looking from side to side like a man seeing where he lives for the first time.

Tom reached down and put the BMW in drive, then let his crooked fingers fall as he pulled away from the curb, steering with his left hand. For the first time in many years, he began to cry.

CHAPTER 6

HENRY SEXTON WAS sitting at his desk at the *Concordia Beacon* in Ferriday, Louisiana, when the receptionist transferred a call to him and yelled from the front desk that it was important.

"Who is it?" he shouted at the open door of the newsroom.

"The Natchez district attorney!" Lou Ann Whittington shouted back.

Henry frowned and laid his hand on the phone but did not pick it up. In two hours, he was scheduled to do the most important interview of his life. He didn't want to risk anyone sidetracking him, particularly Shadrach Johnson, who never called unless he wanted something—usually publicity.

"Have you got it?" Lou Ann called.

Henry cursed and picked up the phone. "Henry Sexton."

Without preamble, Shad Johnson said, "Mr. Sexton, it's come to my attention that you recently interviewed a woman named Viola Turner. Is that correct?"

Henry blinked in surprise, then looked over at the sports editor, who was making a face at him. "That's right. I spoke to her twice."

"Could you tell me the nature of your questions?"

"I was questioning her in conjunction with a story I'm working on."

"What's that story about?"

Henry felt blood rising into his cheeks. "Without knowing more, I'm afraid I'm going to have to disappoint you there, Mr. Johnson."

"You need to come to my office. Consider that a formal request."

Henry's chest tightened. "I'm a Louisiana resident, Mr. Johnson. You're a Mississippi DA. Why don't you tell me what this is about?"

"Viola Turner is dead. She was killed early this morning."

"*Killed?*" Henry felt the dizzying disorientation that had grown more familiar as he aged; it came with hearing that someone you'd spoken to only a day or two earlier had died. "Are you sure? She was terminally ill."

"I take the coroner's word for that kind of thing, Mr. Sexton. She's on her way to Jackson right now, for the autopsy. This isn't for publication, but it looks like murder."

A bone-deep chill made Henry shudder.

"I'd like you to be here in forty-five minutes, Mr. Sexton. I'll be with the sheriff until then. But I must speak to you. Good-bye."

"Wait! That timing's a problem for me. I've got a critical meeting in two hours. Surely we can talk later this afternoon? I can't see how I can possibly help you, anyway."

"Sheriff's detectives discovered a camcorder at the murder scene, Mr. Sexton. It's marked 'Property of the *Concordia Beacon*.' Did you leave that in Mrs. Turner's sickroom?"

"Uh . . . yes, sir."

"That's one of several things we need to speak about. Should there have been a tape in that camcorder?"

"I would think so, yes."

"Well, there wasn't. Nor anywhere else in the house. The camcorder was lying on the floor, and someone had knocked over the tripod. The remote control was found in the dead woman's bed, however."

Henry looked at his watch. Natchez was twelve miles away, just over the Mississippi River. "How long will I need to be there?"

"We should be able to finish in half an hour."

Henry blew out a rush of air and rubbed his graying goatee. "Okay. I'll be there in forty-five minutes. But I'm leaving a half hour after that. That's nonnegotiable."

"Don't be late. And don't speak to anyone about this. It's a very sensitive case."

Henry cursed and hung up, wishing he'd never answered in the first place. *Why today, of all days?* In two hours, the first Double Eagle in history to grant an interview to a reporter was going to go on the record about the group's crimes. It had taken Henry weeks to set up the conversation, which would be held in secret. He couldn't risk losing this chance. If Viola Turner had indeed been murdered, then today's interview was even more critical than before.

"What's the matter, Henry?" asked Dwayne Dillard, the sports editor. "You look like you saw a ghost."

"It's nothing," he lied, his mind only half under conscious direction.

Glancing around the small newsroom, Henry stood, grabbed his coat off the back of his chair, then hurried out to his Ford Explorer. He couldn't possibly sit waiting in this building for half an hour with so much happening. Having no idea where he was going, he backed into First Street, then headed into Ferriday proper. Little Walter was blowing blues harp on the CD player, wailing with a passion born just fifty miles from Ferriday, in Rapides Parish. Henry sang a couple of lines with the song. He wasn't even thinking, really, just following the half-shuttered streets of his decaying town.

One way or another, Henry had been hunting the Double Eagle group for more than thirty years. His ex-wife claimed that his obsession had cost him their marriage, and she was probably right, yet Henry had refused to abandon his quest. For the past five years, in the pages of the little weekly newspaper he'd once delivered from a bicycle as a boy, he had been publishing stories about the group he considered the deadliest domestic terror cell in American history. And people were starting to pay attention. Henry's successes had embarrassed certain government agencies—the FBI, for example—and they had let him know it. Along with Jerry Mitchell of the *Jackson Clarion-Ledger*, Henry had pushed the Bureau into belatedly forming a cold case squad to revisit unsolved murders from the civil rights era. But though the FBI had infinitely more investigative resources than he, Henry always seemed to stay ahead of them.

The Double Eagle group was a textbook example. Founded in 1964, the Eagles were an ultrasecret splinter cell of the White Knights of the Ku Klux Klan. By Henry's reckoning, they had murdered more than a dozen people, yet they'd evaded capture by the Justice Department at a time when the FBI had saturated the entire Mississippi Klan structure with informants. In forty-one years, only a few members' names had been discovered, and none had been confirmed. No Double Eagle had ever been convicted of a race-related crime, and some had even worked as law enforcement officers. Henry had repeatedly tried to interview reputed members, but they'd always answered with silence or defiance. When he doggedly persisted in his investigations, Henry found himself ostracized by all kinds of people—some racists, others regular citizens who resented him "stirring up the past for no good reason."

One burly redneck had sucker-punched him in the local Winn-Dixie and had to be pulled off Henry by a brave stock boy. But now—

after years of painstaking work to separate truth from legend—Henry had finally done the impossible: he had persuaded a Double Eagle to go on the record. At eleven o'clock this morning, he would meet a seventy-seven-year-old man named Glenn Morehouse. And if Morehouse lived up to his promise—made in the shadow of terminal cancer—he would become the first Double Eagle to break his vow of silence and confess to hate crimes that included assault, arson, rape, kidnapping, torture, and murder.

Like most of his violent brethren, Glenn Morehouse had been raised in a hellfire-and-brimstone Baptist church. Branded on his heart was the certainty that when you died, your soul either flew up to heaven or sank into hell. And by that reckoning, no man could get into heaven without first confessing his sins and honestly repenting them. Henry didn't care what had prompted Morehouse to open up; he only wanted to be there when the truth poured out. For if a Double Eagle ever really told the truth, a dozen murders might be solved in a single hour, a dozen families granted peace after decades of misery.

Since confirming the secret interview at dawn, Henry had been unable to contain himself. Sitting at his desk this morning, the slightest noise in the newspaper office had made him jump. The shocking call about Viola Turner had been the last straw. Before he could even begin to grasp the implications of the old nurse's death, Henry found himself parking before an empty lot that was the barren touchstone of his past, and also of the Albert Norris case.

The weed-choked lot lay between two abandoned buildings on Third Street. Forty-one years ago, Norris's Music Emporium had stood on this hallowed piece of dirt, beating like the secret heart of Henry's hometown. Now empty bottles, paper cups, used condoms, and cigarette packs lay among the dying johnsongrass that covered the mud where Albert Norris's "pickin' porch" had once stood.

As a boy, Henry had first gone into Albert's shop because his mother played a little piano, enough to perform at church or for the Christmas show at the grade school where she taught. Henry's father was a traveling salesman, and rarely home. When he was, he seemed angry, as though he couldn't wait to leave again. He finally died in a car crash in Lawton, Oklahoma, when Henry was seventeen, but by then he was little more than a bad memory. Throughout Henry's boyhood, though, his father had always been out there, like a storm that might blow through town at any time. Albert Norris's store became an escape from all that, and more. It was a magic portal into the mysteries of the universe—not made-up mysteries like the ones his friends read about in books or watched at the Arcade theater, but *real* ones. Secrets so potent that they changed your life irrevocably the moment you were initiated into them.

A month ago, Henry had dug up an old photograph that showed the store during its heyday. He'd been stunned by how small it looked in comparison to the image in his mind. Held off the ground by pyramid-shaped concrete blocks, the Emporium was actually a converted residence built of unpainted cypress and weathered by decades of sun. Albert had cut a big display window into the front wall to show off the pianos and organs he kept in stock.

One of the store's secrets was that it wasn't merely a building, but a musical instrument in its own right, a sound chamber tuned by an accident of construction and played by whoever happened to be jamming inside it: sometimes a leathery old blues shouter thrashing a twangy imitation Stratocaster, other times a first-class pickup band—four or five gifted guys shaking the building with a transformative beat that boomed across the road and out into the little town amid the cotton fields. Often those pickup bands had included Jimmy Revels, Luther Davis, Pooky Wilson, and other local masters of their craft. But the music that people most remembered was Albert himself alone at the piano, playing after hours. That sound was so mournful and exquisitely pure that everyone who lived or worked within earshot—white or black—had asked Albert to leave his doors and windows open when he played. That was Henry's first encounter with the paradox of how music that sounded so sad could lift the soul like nothing else in the world.

The two years he'd spent in and out of Albert's store were the most vivid of Henry's life. Nothing that happened to him afterward ever touched the live-wire euphoria he'd felt within the vibrating walls of that building, or the longing he'd suffered when he was trapped somewhere else, thinking about getting back to it.

Most of the musicians who came through Albert's store were fast-aging boys who would still be boys when they found their graves. Albert himself was a wise man of fifty who'd never let the world beat his dreams out of him. His eyes were deep brown pools set in a darker brown face, and his hands, unlike those of the other black men Henry knew, weren't cracked and broken from backbreaking labor, but soft and long-fingered, like the hands of a surgeon or a classical violinist.

Albert was so well liked in the community that during the nineteen years since the Japanese surrender, a practice unheard-of almost anywhere else in the South had become the norm there. Albert not only served white customers, but white women—white *women* were known to browse his store's extensive library of sheet music—white women *alone,* with Albert the only other person present. Henry's mother had told him this was highly unusual, but she herself bought hymn music in Albert's store. Moreover, in those days, every family that could afford one had a piano in the parlor, and Albert had traveled the parish tuning the instruments for five dollars less than the white tuner charged. Apparently, the white husbands' racism didn't extend to paying extra to have a white man tune their pianos.

Henry's secret odyssey through Albert's store had begun with piano lessons, first with the proprietor, but later with Albert's daughter Swan, who'd been named after a black opera singer from Natchez. Born a slave in 1824, Elizabeth Taylor Greenfield had traveled to London and sung for the queen in Buckingham Palace, where opera enthusiasts christened her the Black Swan. Albert Norris had known all about the Black Swan, of course. Swan's mother had tried to call her Elizabeth, but the child had such beauty and grace that no one ever called her anything but Swan. Like her father, Swan was a musical prodigy, and by seventeen she was handling the majority of Albert's lessons.

One of Swan's pupils was a gangly white fourteen-year-old named Henry Sexton. Despite Albert's strong improvisational style, as a teacher he was a stickler for theory. Henry sometimes felt more bullied by Albert in the teaching room than he did by the redneck coaches on the football field at Ferriday Junior High. But Swan was different. She might run him through a few scales at the beginning of each lesson, but this bored her, and she only did it to please her father. She delighted in teaching Henry to play the songs he really wanted to learn, hits he'd heard on the radio, mostly. Henry lived for the hour he spent with the older girl every Thursday afternoon, confined in the eight-by-ten room with a Baldwin upright and a scent so primally feminine that he could hardly think of anything else.

A narrow vertical window had been set in the door of the teaching room, and Henry had cursed it a thousand times. Albert used the window to keep an eye on Swan when she was teaching boys. Since the store was elevated off the ground, the floorboards always creaked, and Henry used those creaks as a Distant Early Warning System to keep track of Albert's movements. The problem was, some customer was usually playing a piano in the main room, and this masked the sound of Albert's walk. Bass guitars were even worse. To Henry's everlasting gratitude, Albert sometimes taught piano in the display room at the same time Swan was teaching him. And it was one of these afternoons that Swan had given Henry the greatest shock, and the greatest gift, of his life.

He'd been trying to copy her technique on Bach, which was torture when 95 percent of his concentration was on the shapely thigh of the beautiful girl sitting hip to hip with him. He was also praying she wouldn't notice the taut little tent in his lap, which had become a regular feature of the lessons, and which Henry simply could not control. As he struggled to keep his left hand in rhythm, Swan's hand settled on that tent as softly as a butterfly. Then she began to rub it.

"Keep playing," she whispered.

Henry stopped anyway, his heart and lungs expanding like balloons hooked to a high-pressure cylinder.

"Go *on*," Swan urged, her big eyes flashing, "or I'll have to quit."

Sweat poured off Henry's face. He banged his left hand down on the keyboard, and Swan rubbed harder beneath it. Less than a minute later Henry shivered and began to smack the keys like a man with stumps for fingers—but he kept playing. Swan kissed his cheek and said, "Maybe now you can concentrate, *boy*."

After this lesson, Henry ran home and washed his pants in the Whirlpool before his mother could get home from her second job at the church. Then he'd prayed eighteen hours a day for his next lesson to arrive.

When the next Thursday came, Swan made him wait almost the whole hour before doing anything other than what Henry's mother was paying her to do. But fifty minutes into the lesson, Elizabeth Swan Norris got up and moved to Henry's right side, which was not her usual place, then took his right hand and guided it under her dress. Henry gulped when he felt what awaited his fingers. Her wetness confused and terrified him. Still, he let her move his fingers in circles over the hard little berry between her legs while she played piano with her left hand. When Swan finally shuddered against him, the music stopped. When her father looked into the window a few seconds later, he saw two kids on the piano bench and four hands on the keyboard. He did not see that two of the hands were wet.

"Don't you go falling in love with me," Swan warned Henry that day. "If you start talking foolishness, I'll stop these lessons. You hear?"

"But . . . but . . ." Henry stuttered, knowing already that his heart was full of something that felt nothing like foolishness.

"But *nothing*," Swan snapped. "I'm just giving you some special lessons, that's all. Lessons you need."

Five weeks of special lessons followed, each one ending with mutual ecstasy. Twice Swan freed Henry from his jeans and sucked until he almost screamed, and those times he felt what the preachers claimed being filled with the holy spirit was supposed to be like and what a heroin addict had told him it felt like when he'd shot up for the first time.

Once during a "special" lesson, Albert actually left the store to run an errand. Swan didn't waste time with preliminaries. She pulled Henry down to the floor, tugged down his pants, climbed astride him, and unbuttoned her shirt. He'd never seen or felt anything like he did that day, the swelling heat of Swan's chocolate-tipped breasts and the near-religious glaze in her eyes. Swan had known exactly when he was going to finish, and she slid off him and helped with expert hands, laughing as he spent himself across the ebony piano bench. But Henry couldn't laugh. After that day, he *was* in love, or in something even more profound. He was like the drug-addicted musicians Albert spoke mournfully about, the ones who couldn't go more than a few hours without a fix.

Henry could not stop thinking about Swan. His grades plummeted, and his mother noticed. He started riding his bike through the colored section of town, trying to get a look at Swan sitting on Albert's porch. The first time she saw him doing this, Swan knitted her brow in an angry frown and did not wave. The next Thursday, Henry found Albert waiting in the teaching room, saying Swan was too sick to teach. Henry immediately stopped riding his bike on the wrong side of Louisiana Avenue.

The next Thursday he found Swan waiting in the teaching room as though nothing had happened. When Albert started giving a church organist a lesson in the main room, Swan stood up and began playing the piano Jerry Lee Lewis style. As Henry gaped, she reached back with her right hand, flipped up her skirt, and pulled down her panties without stopping the bass line with her left hand. By this time Henry had lost his childish nerves. He dropped his jeans and plunged into her from behind, amazed that she could play so perfectly while he thrust so hard. But on this occasion Swan didn't realize he was going to finish, and neither did he—not until the moment had passed. Suddenly Swan was twice as slippery as before, and she jerked away from Henry as though he'd scalded her.

"I'm sorry!" he cried, yanking up his pants in shame. "It was an accident!"

Swan's face went twice as dark as usual. "Boy, you and your little *thang* gonna get me with *child!*" She sat on the bench and looked down at her little bush while her father played a hymn on a Hammond organ in the next room. "Run up the street to the gas station and get me a pop," she said crossly.

Henry looked blankly at her. "A pop?"

"A Dr. Pepper! A hot one, if you can get it. *Hurry.*"

"What do I tell your father?"

"Tell him . . . tell him you bet me a Dr. Pepper that I couldn't play something."

"Like what?"

Swan nearly swatted him. "What do I care? Charlie Parker. Get going, dummy!"

When Henry returned, Swan took the ten-cent bottle of soda into the bathroom. It was only years later that he learned a fizzing Dr. Pepper had been a primitive method of birth control used by desperate girls in the days before the Pill.

Swan eventually got over her anger, and things continued as before, but most of what came after had been blurred by the passing years. What Henry remembered most was how tense that summer had been, how the sky would pile up each afternoon with slate-gray clouds that looked full of rain but brought only dry thunder. People on the street were grouchy. The white people were tense, the blacks scared or angry.

The air felt so still that noises sounded different than usual. To make things worse, Henry's father came home and stayed for three straight weeks. All he talked about was "nigger trouble" all over the South, and the "goddamn Kennedys twistin' up LBJ." Henry's only escape was the hours he got to spend at school or with Swan.

One August afternoon, while he and Swan sat on the store steps, Albert walked out, looked at the sky, and said, "This drought done turned the ground into a drum." Swan poked a stick in the dust and said, "What you talkin' 'bout, Daddy?" Albert sat down and illustrated his words with his flattened hands. "The ground is the top head, the bedrock the bottom, and precious little water between. Every time a truck goes by, I hear the earth echo. Everybody's prayin' for God to send rain. White and black, they prayin' the same words."

Henry liked it when Albert talked this way, and he wondered why he seemed more in tune with these thoughts than Swan. Swan lived so instinctively that she seemed to care nothing about codifying feelings into language. If it rained, it rained. If it didn't, she'd make do with the heat.

"Is it ever going to rain again?" Henry asked.

Albert did something then that he'd never done in public: he laid a comforting hand on Henry's shoulder and squeezed. "Son," he said softly, "I think maybe a storm's comin' that could wash away everything we know."

Recognizing the anxiety in her father's voice, Swan finally looked up.

"You chil'ren be careful from now on," Albert said. "Don't let nobody see you together. There's good folks and bad in this town, same as everywhere else. But right now the bad ones got the power. You hear me?"

Swan locked eyes with Henry, and they knew then that nothing ever got past her father.

Henry's ringing cell phone startled him so profoundly that his arms flew up defensively. He felt as though he had awakened from a deep, feverish sleep. Shaking his head, he took his phone out of his pocket. The caller was a female FBI agent who often checked in to pick his brain for clues. He wondered if she'd heard about the death of Viola Turner. Henry couldn't let himself think about Viola yet. If he did, he'd lose the objectivity he would so desperately need when he faced Glenn Morehouse. He muted the ringer of his phone and climbed out of his Explorer into the cold wind. Leaving the door open, he walked to the edge of the lot. One of the concrete pyramids that had supported Albert's pickin' porch still stuck up out of the mud. Henry planted his right foot on it. In spite of the coming Morehouse interview, his heart felt as empty as the lot before him.

He looked down the deserted street. A three-legged dog was pissing on a fence, while farther on, a black boy rode a rusted banana bicycle with what appeared to be grim purpose. Forty years ago, this street would have been jumping with the sounds of Albert's piano. People would have been laughing and dancing on their porches, looking forward to the evening, when they would head over to Haney's Big House to hear a name band. Now the druggies Albert used to pity ruled the streets.

The fire that killed Albert Norris had killed more than a man, Henry reflected. It had killed the store, and with the store had passed the magic that flourished there, the living hope of black and white interacting with trust and respect rather than fear and hatred. Henry often wondered why no one had ever built a new business on this site. Some people believed that an evil lingered in this earth after the murderous fire, like a dissonant chord that never faded. The tragic truth, Henry knew, was that bad feelings didn't linger any more than good ones did. There was *no* feeling here. The land itself retained neither Albert's magic nor the horror of his death. All that remained was the memory of an aging reporter and those few survivors who had shared the magic with him.

And the killers, he thought. The Double Eagles who had burned Albert Norris to death—and either flayed or crucified Pooky Wilson— were still walking the streets of Ferriday, Vidalia, and Natchez. Henry was not a vengeful man, but the knowledge that those men lived while their victims lay in the earth ate at him like battery acid. While the Double Eagles watched their grandkids play Little League baseball, the families of their victims mourned grandchildren who had never been born. Worst of all, Henry thought, worse than the goddamned rednecks who had set the fires and wielded the knives and fired the guns, was the privileged millionaire who had ordered many of those murders. But if Glenn Morehouse lived up to his promise this morning, he might just give Henry what he'd craved more than anything else in his life: a weapon to take down an untouchable foe.

Henry wiped tears from his face. Why was he the only pilgrim standing at this place? There wasn't even a memorial marker to commemorate Albert Norris. The man had been buried in his church cemetery, two miles from this spot, and Henry had never found flowers on the grave when he went to visit. Swan lived in Irvine, California. Despite some modest musical success, she'd been married three times and had lost both perfect breasts to cancer. She had a grandson who played in a band with a recording contract. He was the light of her life. After Swan read one of Henry's stories about the fire (sent to her by a local girl she'd gone to school with), she'd sent Henry a picture of her grandson. The boy had Swan's face but Albert's wise eyes. Enclosed with the photo was a note: *"I learned more about my father's murder from your stories than I did in forty years of pestering the FBI. Thank you. Please add my name to your sub-scription list. P.S. You were a good student. XOXO Swan."*

That solitary note would have been sufficient to sustain Henry through his battles with the angry Klansmen, indifferent government bureaucracy, and reluctant or hostile witnesses that waited in his future. But he'd received many more letters like Swan's. That was why the best-intentioned warnings of friends always fell on deaf ears. Swan and Albert Norris had transformed Henry from a timid boy into a man. After being adopted by them, he'd no longer cared whether his biological father loved him or not.

"What you doin' over here, white man?"

Henry turned slowly and saw the black boy on the banana bike sitting a few feet away. He looked about ten, and wore a New Orleans Saints windbreaker, but his eyes had the sullen defiance of a teenager.

"Just lookin' around. There used to be a store on this lot. Did you know that? A music store."

"I need five dollars, man. You got five dollars?"

"What do you need five dollars for?"

"None yo' business. You got it?"

Henry started to walk back to his Explorer, then took out his wallet and handed the kid a one-dollar bill.

"Shit. Gimme that wallet, too," the kid said. "I need that wallet."

Henry put his foot on the running board of the Explorer.

"I said gimme that goddamn wallet!"

Henry turned, half expecting to see a pistol, or at least a knife. But all he saw was the enraged face of a ten-year-old kid who wasn't going anywhere but jail or an early grave. "You can't have it," he said gently. Feeling like Albert must have felt so many times, he said, "Go home to your mama and stay out of trouble."

"Fuck you, old man! Go home to *yo* mama!"

"I wish I had time," Henry said, feeling a stab of guilt. His mother was ill, and probably wouldn't be with him much longer.

He shut the door and started his engine, his mind filled with memories of Viola Turner, an emaciated woman wearing an oxygen mask, her eyes filled with urgency, righteous anger, and concealed fear. Henry had known that Miss Viola was dying, but somehow her actual death seemed counterintuitive. Impossible, even. She had not been ready to die, he was certain of that. But she was gone now. *Another witness silenced.*

"But how?" he murmured. "By time? Or human intervention?" He supposed Shadrach Johnson would tell him when he reached Natchez.

Henry switched on his CD player as he drove past the Arcade theater, and the wail of Little Walter's overdriven harmonica filled the Explorer. After listening for a few seconds, he shook his head and hit the next-track button. Robert Johnson began sawing at rusty old guitar strings with his slide. Today Henry heard only death and sadness in the sound. He hit next again. This time the a capella opening salvo of Kansas's "Carry On Wayward Son" shattered the oppressive silence. It might be cheesy, but Henry didn't give a shit. He was old, he was white, and he needed something to stoke the hope that still smoldered in the darkest recess of his heart. One of the beauties of digital technology was that he could replay the crystalline opening harmonies a hundred times if he wanted to, with one touch of a button. No rewinding, no guesswork. He laid his forefinger on the replay button and hit it one millisecond before the band's instruments kicked in, again and again, all the way to the highway.

"Swan," he whispered, wishing it was still 1964.

CHAPTER 7

SNAKE KNOX STOOD on the tarmac of Concordia Parish Airport and watched Brody Royal's Avanti turboprop scream down out of the gray sky. The fastest private plane of its kind in the world, the $5 million Avanti was one of the quietest aircraft you could buy—on the inside— but to anyone watching it take off or land, it sounded like the devil's fingernails raked over a chalkboard. Touchdown looked a little rough by Snake's standards, but as a crop duster he would likely have found fault with the technique of anyone short of a Blue Angel.

As the Avanti taxied toward the terminal, Snake saw Brody Royal himself at the controls. The old multimillionaire had lost his license due to some deficit on the flight physical, but since his son-in-law was licensed, Royal simply had the younger man perform the takeoffs, then took over the controls and did the flying himself, even the landings back in Concordia Parish.

An hour earlier, Royal's maid had informed Snake that the business-man had made yet another trip to New Orleans. Brody Royal had been flying back and forth three or four times per week ever since Hurri-cane Katrina, and he sure as hell wasn't delivering relief supplies. There had to be money in it—big money—or Brody wouldn't be wasting his time or fuel. Snake gazed covetously at the Italian-built jet with the royal blue *R* on its tail fin and ROYAL OIL emblazoned aft of the seventh window, just above the low-mass wing with its backward-facing pusher props. A machine like that got Snake's blood going quicker than any woman these days. There were women in every damned honky-tonk in America; there were only one hundred Avantis in the whole world.

When the plane stopped, its front door opened and two men with AR-15s slung over their shoulders came down the steps. The chaos of post-Katrina New Orleans had long since been tamped down, but Royal owned a lot of property in the Lower Ninth Ward, and he apparently figured he needed armed security on whatever business he'd been conducting.

After the guards came Randall Regan, Royal's son-in-law, a rawboned, humorless man with the face of a prison guard (which was what he was, in a way, but that was another story). At last the man himself exited the plane: Brody Royal, five feet ten and whipcordtrim, moving with speed and assurance despite his advanced age. His thick silver hair fluttered in the wind as he moved toward the shelter of the terminal with his overcoat folded over his arm. His hawklike face had deep-set eyes that almost never ceased motion, and he caught sight of Snake even before his guards did. When Snake raised his hand in greeting, both guards moved toward him, but Royal called out that Snake was a friend.

Snake lit a Winston and waited for Royal to join him in the lee of the terminal building, watching the businessman's eyes for signs of irritation at his unexpected visit. Royal might be one of the two or three richest men in the state, but thirty-seven years ago, Snake had killed four people at his command, and at this very airport. To Snake's way of thinking, that gave him special access. He saw only frank curiosity in Royal's eyes as the man stepped under the metal awning.

"Surprised to see you out here this time of year," Royal commented, not offering his hand. "What's going on?"

"I thought we might have a word, sir. A quiet word."

"Of course. Well?"

"You may have heard that Glenn Morehouse is dying?"

Royal nodded once.

"Glenn's living out at his sister's place. I've been by there a few times, just to visit, and . . . well, I got a funny feeling. Glenn's all the time reading Henry Sexton's newspaper stories about the Double Eagles and talking about the old times—and not in a good way, either. He's done got religion. Born again."

Royal's eyes had clouded at the mention of Henry Sexton. "Born again, you say? That's never good."

"No, sir. And his sister, Wilma—she's a good girl, old school—Wilma says Glenn made some suspicious phone calls last week when she was out of the room."

Royal watched an airport attendant chock the Avanti's wheels.

"You think your old comrade in arms is thinking about clearing his conscience before he meets his maker?"

"I'd hate to think so, sir. But if you ask me straight out . . . that's what I'm thinking."

"Morehouse was one of the original Eagles, wasn't he?"

"Yep."

"Hard to believe he'd turn traitor."

"The fear of death does funny things to people, I find."

"Religion does, too. Have you spoken to Billy or Forrest about this?"

"Yessir. But they don't seem too concerned about it. At least not enough to do anything ahead of time."

Deeper consternation creased Royal's face. "I see. And you thought . . . ?"

"I just figured you ought to be made aware of the possibility. Considering . . ." *Considering our shared history,* Snake finished silently. "If you wait till the levee breaks, the whole damn Corps of Engineers can't hold back the flood."

"My thoughts exactly." Royal clapped Snake on the shoulder. "You did the right thing coming to me. I'll think about it. Now, I need to get to my bank. There's a lot going on in New Orleans just now."

Snake shook his head in admiration. When Brody Royal said "my bank," he meant it in the literal sense. He owned the motherfucker. *The Royal Cotton Bank.*

"Things are moving fast in the wake of the storm," Royal said. "It's a hell of a mess down there, but there's also a lot of opportunity. The nigras have finally scrambled out of there like rats from a flooded basement, and the old-money boys were caught flat-footed. It's like 1927 in reverse."

Snake wondered how old Brody Royal could have been during the 1927 flood. Just a baby, surely. "I know if anybody can turn a profit out of that bitch Katrina, it'll be you."

Royal looked offended by the coarse language, but then he grinned and slapped Snake on the back. "You're a good man, Knox, like your brother was. Frank was *hard.* Nobody to cross."

"That's a fact, sir."

"Let's keep this visit to ourselves. If anyone questions you, you asked whether I knew of any crop-dusting work over in the western parishes. Meanwhile, keep me apprised of any developments regarding Morehouse, and also what Forrest is thinking. Do you have any problem with that?"

"No, sir. That's why I'm here."

"Good man." Royal glanced down the flight line, toward the ragged crop dusters of Knox's Flying Service. "I noticed the other day that your Pawnee sounds past due for an overhaul."

"She is getting a little loose in the joints, all right."

"Have the mechanic put her on his schedule. On my tab."

"I appreciate it, sir."

"An ounce of prevention's worth a pound of cure."

"You said it."

Royal signaled to the men with the rifles, then made his way toward a blue Range Rover parked in the general aviation lot.

CHAPTER 8

HENRY SEXTON DROVE toward the twin bridges that crossed the Mississippi River at Natchez, a sense of dread perched like a crow on his shoulder. For so many years he'd been investigating on his own, a solitary fisherman dropping his lines into backwaters long abandoned by others. But all the while, time and mortality had been working like rust at the bottom of his boat, eating away at the craft that supported his quest for justice. Witnesses died or fell victim to Alzheimer's disease; hidden evidence sank deeper into the mud below the dark water. Viola Turner was only the latest to die without revealing what she knew.

A month ago, the retired nurse had appeared to Henry like an angel, returning from Chicago after decades away, knowing death was close and struggling with some secret she'd held inside since she left. Henry's most precious hope was that Viola knew the fates of her brother, Jimmy Revels, and Luther Davis. He'd interviewed her twice, and though she hadn't yet built up enough trust in him to speak with complete candor, he'd sensed that Viola was approaching a major revelation. That was why he'd left a voice recorder with her after his first visit, and a camcorder on a tripod after the second. If the mood to talk struck her at 4 A.M., Henry wanted whatever Viola said preserved for the record. Now she was dead, and if the tape from that camcorder was missing, then he had to wonder whether the old nurse had actually used the machine and paid for that act with her life. A wave of nausea hit Henry as he realized that meeting with him might have caused Viola's death.

Her sudden passing was like a replay of another death just five days ago. The two murder cases that most obsessed Henry were those of Albert Norris, the music store owner, and Pooky Wilson, a young musician who'd worked for Albert. Henry had always believed Pooky was murdered for sleeping with the daughter of one of the richest men in Louisiana, a white girl named Katy Royal. Albert had almost certainly died for trying to protect his young employee. Quite a few people in the know had accepted this scenario, even at the time, but Henry had never been able to prove it.

Then seven days ago, Pooky's aged mother had sent word for Henry to come to her hospital bed. Barely able to speak, the desperately ill woman had told him that, after forty-one years of frightened silence, one of her son's boyhood friends had appeared at her bedside and revealed something he'd kept locked in his heart since he was sixteen. Pooky had not only been sleeping with Katy Royal, this friend confirmed, but he had been hiding in Albert's store on the afternoon that Brody Royal and Frank Knox came in and threatened the shop owner's life. Later that night, drawn by the sound of an explosion, this same friend had seen three men leap from the window of Norris's burning store. Two had joined another man, then jumped into a pickup and fled the scene. But the third man had calmly walked to a shiny new car driven by a man the boy recognized as Randall Regan, a brutal roughneck who worked for Brody Royal. At that moment the boy had realized that the third man was Brody Royal himself.

Henry had waited all his life for a source like this. But while Mrs. Wilson had freely given him this information, she'd refused to give up the name of the mysterious witness who'd supplied it. She had wept upon learning the reason for her son's death, and the boy witness— now grown—had hugged her and begged her forgiveness. Then he'd begged her to keep his name secret until he found the courage to tell his story to the FBI. Mrs. Wilson had agreed, and she would not break a sacred promise, especially when she lay on St. Peter's doorstep. Less than twenty-four hours later, she was dead. Cardiac arrest secondary to renal failure, her doctor said. Henry hadn't suspected foul play—not then. But the deaths sure seemed to be piling up. And despite spending much of every day since then hunting for the mystery witness he'd dubbed "Huggy Bear," Henry had so far failed to find him.

He looked down and realized his hands were shaking. If Viola had truly been murdered, then the cases he'd worked alone for so long were about to explode into the spotlight. The FBI agents who always pestered him to share his hard-earned knowledge would seize control of the investigation and subpoena everything he had. No longer would he be the lone crusader for justice, battling federal apathy as well as evil.

Of course, he'd always claimed that he wanted help. He'd pounded on a hundred bureaucratic desks and begged for it. But while he appreciated dedicated college interns and priority treatment for his Freedom of Information Act requests, in reality he had no desire to deal with ego-driven DAs and career-driven FBI agents. Not yet, anyway.

Truth be told, Henry wanted to break these cases on his own terms. He wanted to piece together the missing facts like a jigsaw puzzle, then lay out the sequence of crimes like God looking at history, and only then turn the final picture over to the FBI and the public. He hadn't felt that way in the beginning, but the Bureau had treated him shabbily, and their lack of respect had stung him.

He thought again about the missing videotape Shad Johnson had mentioned. What if Viola's secrets had *not* gone to the grave with her? As Henry neared the Mississippi River, he wondered whether some frightened old Double Eagle with blood on his hands had dumped that tape into the muddy river sometime before dawn. Henry could readily name a couple of cold bastards who wouldn't have had any qualms about killing Viola to keep the past buried.

"Please don't dump that tape," he whispered. "Keep it as a trophy, you sons of bitches."

It would be a stupid thing to do, but Henry had known killers to do dumber things.

As he started up the eastbound span that arched over the red-tinged river, he saw the spire of St. Mary's cathedral standing stark against the clouds. The sight lifted his heart. From this view, Natchez appeared to be the mythical City on the Hill. Sited on a high bluff over the river, the three-hundred-year-old town dominated the landscape for miles around, its churches taller than every other building but one. Natchez occupied the only such high point between Missouri and the Gulf of Mexico, and its citizens had egos to match it—or that's what you believed when you grew up on the Louisiana side of the river. Living in the shadow of that bluff, Henry had felt a mixture of jealousy and resentment toward the people in the antebellum mansions across the water. He just knew that the folks on that hill believed they were better than he was. And from an economic perspective, they always had been.

The cotton barons of the nineteenth century—the "nabobs of Natchez"—had grown most of their crops on the Louisiana side of the river, but they lived on the bluff at Natchez, in palaces that would shame a sultan. High above the yellow fever and the riffraff that plagued the flatboat port at Under-the-Hill, they hunted fox, raced Thoroughbreds, and hosted glittering soirées while only a mile across the river the poor working sods tried to scratch out a living on the margins of the flood-plain. The Civil War had taken the nabobs down a few pegs, but not to rock bottom, since the city had surrendered without a shot, dodging Sherman's fury and remaining structurally intact. Several lean decades had followed the war, but during the Great Depression, a few wily old belles had restored their mansions, put together an annual Spring Pil-grimage, and started fleecing the Yankees and Europeans who traveled south to gawk at plantation palaces that dwarfed Tara from *Gone with the Wind*. Then, around 1940, some lucky redneck struck oil, and within ten years the city was rolling in cash again, selling black gold instead of white and lording it over every town for miles around. This second wave of wealth had brought Brody Royal his fortune, or the seed of it anyway. In the decades afterward, Royal had wisely diversified into a half-dozen other businesses that allowed him to ride out the oil bust of the 1980s like a southern John D. Rockefeller.

As if summoned by Henry's thoughts, an oil field service truck bear-ing the blue legend ROYAL OIL roared out of his blind spot and passed him, headed east toward Natchez.

"I'm coming for you, you bastard," Henry muttered, looking at his watch again and thinking of his upcoming interview. He could not afford to waste time with Shad Johnson.

Henry's tires thumped as his Explorer rolled off the bridge, and he prepared to turn left, into the old downtown. It was during the fifties, he reflected, that a nasty streak of racism had taken root in Natchez. The seeds of that sentiment had come from outside the town proper. Though Natchez had been the slaveholding capital of the South, its leaders were Anglophiles who sympathized with the Union cause. Even those who didn't were wealthy aristocrats who'd educated their sons in the Ivy League and sent their daughters to the royal courts of Europe. Their descendants had a far more enlightened view of race relations than most Mississippians. But by the 1950s, large numbers of poor whites had been brought in to work in the town's new manufac-turing plants, and with them came the extreme and sometimes violent prejudice of the working class. Hailing from places like Liberty, Mississippi, and Monroe, Louisiana—hard-shell Baptist country—these descendants of the archetypal Confederate foot soldier were the disaffected ranks that Klan recruiters found ready for action when the Negro started trying to achieve equal rights in the workplace. Men like Frank and Snake Knox, Sonny Thornfield, and Glenn Morehouse—guys who weren't afraid to get their hands bloody while carrying out the will of the White Citizens' Council members who preferred the status quo but wouldn't risk their liberty or good name to maintain it.

Thankfully, things had changed since those days. Two years ago, the citizens of Natchez had elected Penn Cage mayor, and the former lawyer and author had worked hard to heal the wounds that remained in the city's body politic. Cage's election victory had surprised some, but not Henry. The author had a half a century of goodwill to cash in on— not his own, but that of his father, a beloved physician who'd always treated blacks just as he had whites. That goodwill bought the son more than a third of the black vote on election day, even with Penn running against a black candidate—Shadrach Johnson, the very man Henry was now headed to see.

Henry parked his Explorer in the shadow of the incongruously modern sheriff's department building, retrieved his briefcase from the trunk, and walked across the street toward the DA's office Adjacent to City Hall and the courthouse, the DA's building seemed to crouch under the slit windows of the sheriff's department and the county jail. As Henry trotted up the stairs, his sense of dread intensified. Shad Johnson was a politician with his eye on the main chance. He would undoubtedly ask Henry some pointed questions, and Henry didn't want to say any more than the law required. It would be good practice for dealing with the FBI later in the day, as he would almost surely be required to do.

Henry pushed open the door to the DA's office suite and looked around the anteroom. A slim young black man in a gray suit sat before a modern desk, typing on a notebook computer. The last time Henry visited this office, the secretary had been a woman.

"Can I help you?" the young man asked without a trace of southern accent.

"I'm Henry Sexton."

"Go in. He's waiting for you."

Henry hiked up his khakis with his free hand and walked through the tall door behind the assistant's desk.

Shad Johnson waited behind an antique desk the size of a tennis court. He didn't rise to greet Henry, much less make a move to come around the desk. A light-skinned black man, he regarded Henry with the cool superiority the reporter associated with men who wore their past laurels like social armor. Johnson's dark blue suit probably cost ten times as much as the one Henry wore to church on Sundays. The wall to Henry's right was covered with photographs of the district attorney with various celebrities and politicians, mostly African-American, who had come to Natchez to campaign for Shad in his unsuccessful 1998 bid for mayor. It took a moment for Henry to notice his video camcorder standing on a tripod in the opposite corner of the DA's office.

"Were you surprised to hear that Viola Turner died this morning?" Johnson asked without preamble.

"Yes," Henry admitted.

"Surely you knew she was ill?"

Henry nodded.

"But still you were surprised."

"I was."

Shad pointed to the camcorder on the tripod. "Tell me about the video camera. It seems odd for a reporter to leave a video camera in the house of a dying old woman. What was your reason?"

Henry didn't like the DA's presumptuous tone, especially since Johnson had given him so little help in pursuing unsolved civil rights cases. "I've been a reporter for a long time," he said grudgingly. "Sometimes I can sense when a person is in torment." He thought of Glenn Morehouse, sitting in his sickroom across the river, fearfully facing eternity. "A lot of people from the civil rights era are sick or dying now, and a lot of them are carrying secrets. Something was working on Viola Turner. She wanted to tell it, but she hadn't quite reached the place where she could. That's why I left the camera with her. You never know when the mood to talk is going to strike somebody, and I sensed that Miss Viola didn't have long. So I aimed the camera at her, plugged it in, gave her the remote control, and showed her how to use it. Any time she wanted to, she could make a video recording of herself."

"What do you think she knew, Mr. Sexton?"

Henry had to struggle to bring up the words. "I believe she knew what happened to her brother, Jimmy Revels, back in 1968. And to Luther Davis, of course."

Shad Johnson made a sour face. Henry figured the DA resented his mention of the case because Henry had pushed him for months to look into it. Johnson claimed he could take no action without new evidence, but Henry had pointed out the catch-22 that there was unlikely to be any new evidence until the investigation was reopened.

"Be that as it may," said Johnson, "you seem to be the last person outside the family who spoke to Mrs. Turner, other than her doctor. Did she say anything during your interview that might make you think she was contemplating suicide?"

"Suicide?" Henry felt his cheeks grow hot. His preconceptions about Viola's death went spinning off into space. "No, she didn't. I interviewed her twice, by the way. And she gave me no reason to think she was contemplating something like that. She seemed like a strong woman, despite her illness. Spiritually, I mean. Physically she was very weak."

"Did she say anything about her doctor?"

Henry detected a hostile edge in the DA's voice. "You mean Dr. Cage?"

"Yes, Tom Cage. How did you know Dr. Cage was her doctor?"

"Mrs. Turner reminisced a little about working for him. She seemed very fond of him. She complimented Dr. Cage's dedication to his patients, regardless of their race. Dr. Cage was making daily visits to her home, I believe, trying to ease Mrs. Turner's last days as much as possible. She couldn't breathe very well by the time I interviewed her. Conversation was difficult."

"Did you ever see Dr. Cage at the Revels home?"

"No. But I was only there twice."

Shad suddenly stood, which revealed his somewhat diminutive height. Henry was a gangly six feet two, and towered over the DA, but the smaller man was animated by an energy that more than equalized the difference.

"Can you keep a secret, Mr. Sexton?"

"I've kept some for nearly forty years."

"Will you respect a request to go off the record?"

"That's my bread and butter, Mr. Johnson."

The DA's eyes bored into Henry's with unsettling intensity. "We may be dealing with a case of assisted suicide here. Or even murder by a physician. That's why I'm involved in this matter."

Henry had already accepted the possibility of murder, but this new suggestion floored him. "You mean Tom Cage?"

"That's what the evidence points to at this time."

Henry gulped audibly. "Whoa. Look, I don't even want to hear that. I don't believe it, either."

"Nevertheless, there seems to have been a pact between Mrs. Turner and Dr. Cage to that effect."

Henry felt more flustered than he had in some time. "Well . . . what exactly do you want from me?"

When the DA didn't answer, a horrifying thought hit him. "The camera wasn't on when she died, was it?" he asked, with a macabre feeling that Johnson was going to answer in the affirmative.

"We don't know. The switch was in the on position, but the tripod was overturned and the camera was on the floor. Its cassette door was open, and there was no tape inside. The plug was out of the wall, and the battery was dead as well."

Henry tried to imagine a scenario that could have led to such circumstances.

"Had Viola Turner made any tapes for you prior to last night?" Johnson asked.

"None that I know of. Did you find an audio recorder in the house?"

The DA's eyes narrowed. "No. Why?"

"I left a handheld analog voice recorder with Viola after my first visit, for the same reason I left the video camera a week later."

Johnson wrote something on a piece of paper. "The sheriff's department searched the house, but no tape recorder was found. What brand was it?"

"Olympus."

Johnson noted this. "The killer must have stolen that as well, then. Do you know if Mrs. Turner had recorded anything on that?"

"No idea."

Shad frowned and looked down at his desk.

"How did she die?" Henry asked. "If you don't mind my asking?"

"Morphine overdose, almost certainly. That's off the record. We'll have to wait on the toxicology report to be sure."

Glancing at his camcorder, Henry felt the burn of acid in his stomach. Still attached to the back of the Sony was a rectangle of beige plastic, slightly larger than a pack of cigarettes. This was a Superstream hard drive, an accessory Henry had mounted before he left the camcorder at Viola's house. A filmmaker friend had told him about the drives while working on a documentary about Henry's investigations. The Superstream could be set to record simultaneously with the camera's tape heads, which not only eliminated the laborious process of capturing taped video onto a computer drive before editing could begin, but also made the DV tape a backup of what was on the hard drive. The Superstream could also be set to begin recording when the mini-DV tape ran out, extending available recording time if you were stuck somewhere without extra tapes. Henry rarely kept extra tapes on hand, so he usually left the unit in that mode. He was almost sure the Superstream had been set that way when he left the camera at Viola's house. *Which means there might be something recorded on the hard drive right now—*

"What is it?" the district attorney asked sharply. "Why are you staring at the camera?"

Henry was tempted to say nothing Johnson probably meant to return the camcorder to him; Henry could almost certainly walk out of here with whatever was recorded on the drive. But though he disliked the DA, he believed in the rule of law. If there was something on that hard drive, it might be evidence of a crime. And if he walked out of this office without telling the DA about it, he would probably be committing a crime himself. Woodward and Bernstein wouldn't think twice about filching evidence like that, but Henry couldn't do it. That was probably why he worked at a weekly paper with only five thousand paid subscribers.

"The camcorder might have recorded something," he said in a monotone.

"So what?" Johnson said. "The tape's gone."

Henry almost held his silence, but his sense of fair play pushed him on. "There may be a recording attached *to* the camera. *Now.*"

Johnson's head snapped up. "What do you mean?"

Henry explained about the hard drive. The DA was clearly no com-

puter whiz, but eventually he understood. At Johnson's instruction—
which he barked out like a military order—Henry dismounted the
Superstream from the Sony and laid it on the mammoth desk. Then he
opened his briefcase and took out his PowerBook.

"Can't you just plug the drive into my computer?" Johnson asked.

"No. You have a PC. This drive takes a special program to view,
and I only have the Mac version. If you have a FireWire port and cable, I
can set things up so that a converted copy will be sent to your computer
while we watch the original on mine. You'll be able to watch that copy
on your PC afterward."

"There's no 'we,'" Johnson said firmly. "I'm viewing the tape alone."

"It's not a tape," Henry said patiently. "It's a digital file on a hard
drive. And that hard drive belongs to my newspaper." This was not
strictly true. Henry had purchased the Superstream with his own
money; the *Beacon* didn't have the budget for that kind of equipment,
and if he weren't divorced with a grown child, he wouldn't, either.

"That drive may contain evidence in a murder case," Johnson
argued. "I'll make the decision about what's going to happen to it after
I've seen what's on it."

Henry thought about this. "I don't think you can legally keep me
from seeing what's on my newspaper's hard drive. But whatever you
decide now, I'm taking my computer with me. It's not evidence in a
trial, and all my work is on it. So you'd better let me make you a copy
you can watch on your computer."

While Johnson left the office to find a FireWire cable, Henry made
a fast decision. After opening the program that would play the video file
on the hard drive, he altered its settings so that the file would be copied
to his PowerBook's hard drive at the same time it was being converted
and streamed to the district attorney's computer. In all probability there
was nothing on the drive, but if there was, Henry would leave the office
with his own copy. By the time Shad returned, Henry was standing
beside the DA's Wall of Respect, looking at a photo of Johnson with
Whitney Houston and Bobby Brown, celebrities whose stock had fallen
quite a bit since the days of Shad's mayoral campaign against Wiley
Warren.

"This what you need?" Johnson asked, holding out a FireWire cable.

Henry made the necessary connections, then set the program so that all the DA would have to do was tap the PowerBook's trackpad to play the file.

"Time for you to go," Shad said. "How do I watch the tape?"

It's not a tape, Henry repeated silently. "Just tap the trackpad on my Mac. That'll engage the play button on the screen. Do you want me to start it for you?"

"Yes. But as soon as you hit play, go out to my assistant's office. I'll tell you when I'm done."

Henry touched the trackpad, and the light on the Superstream began to blink. A clattering sound emerged from the Mac's speakers, then something like a strangled wail.

"Get out!" Shad ordered.

As Henry moved toward the door, he glanced down and saw the familiar image of Viola Turner's sickbed. The woman herself was rolling across it as though trying to escape from some predatory animal. His heart leaped into his throat.

"Get out!" the DA shouted.

Henry hurried into the anteroom and shut the door behind him, his pulse still accelerating. The drive *had* recorded something. And whoever had stolen the DV tape from the camera hadn't realized that. *And why would they?* Few laymen would recognize a Superstream video drive, and the idea of old Ku Klux Klansmen recognizing advanced digital technology almost made him laugh. Henry hoped Shad Johnson wouldn't notice the PowerBook's hard drive thrumming as it copied the file from the Superstream. The DA would probably be too absorbed with whatever was on his own screen to notice the whirring of the Mac's drive motor; also, his clunky desktop PC would be droning and clicking like an old washing machine as it copied the video stream.

"Are you all right, Mr. Sexton?" asked the DA's assistant.

Henry wiped his forehead, and his hand came away covered in sweat. He hadn't realized how anxious he was. *What the hell?* he thought with amazement. *I'm copying evidence in a criminal case without permission.* Technically the hard drive belonged to him, of course, but still. Shad Johnson wouldn't hesitate to jail him over something like that. "Do you have any water?"

"Through that door, down the hall."

Henry found a water dispenser down the hall and drank two Dixie cups dry. Even the brief image of Viola Turner in obvious distress had shaken him to the core. Johnson's revelation that he suspected Tom Cage of assisted suicide—or even murder—was too momentous for Henry to focus on now. He felt like an idiot for spending more than four hours with Viola Turner and failing to inspire enough faith for her to confide in him. After a third cup of water, he gathered himself, went back to the anteroom, and sat down.

"Wasn't there a woman receptionist the last time I was here?" he asked distractedly.

"She got pregnant," the young man said with apparent disdain.

Henry checked his watch twenty times before the DA's door opened again, his mind on his upcoming interview across the river. Glenn Morehouse knew enough about the Double Eagles to break a dozen murder cases wide open, and Henry wasn't about to postpone talking to him. If Shad Johnson didn't come out of his office within five minutes, Henry was going to leave. He could retrieve his computer later. More than thirty minutes had passed since he'd started the video player for the DA. That made sense; the Superstream could hold thirty minutes of video at maximum resolution. What had Shad Johnson witnessed in that span of time? An assisted suicide? Or a brutal murder?

Thirty seconds before Henry's self-imposed deadline, Johnson's office door opened. With a sober look, the DA beckoned him back inside. Henry tried to read Johnson's eyes, but he couldn't tell much.

As soon as Shad closed the door behind Henry, he said, "That hard drive is evidence, Mr. Sexton. It'll have to go into the evidence room at the sheriff's department."

"What's on it?"

Shad sat down behind his desk. "You know I can't tell you that."

"That's my newspaper's property, sir."

"It's evidence in a criminal case. End of discussion."

"What about freedom of the press?"

Johnson gave him a thin smile. "In this situation, that and four dollars will buy you a cup of coffee. You can file a protest or hire a constitutional specialist, but that disk drive is going to the evidence room."

Henry considered arguing further for appearance's sake, but he didn't have the time or the energy for a show. As long as he got out of the office with his PowerBook, he would have his own copy of the video file.

"Mr. Sexton," Johnson said, "you're a serious journalist, and I know you care about people. I'm going to ask you not to tell anyone about the existence of this tape. I feel pretty sure you won't do it immediately in any case, because you write for a weekly paper and you don't want Caitlin Masters at the *Examiner* getting the jump on you."

Henry colored but said nothing.

"This case is very delicate," Johnson continued. "I'm going to proceed with the utmost caution and deliberation. Do you understand?"

"You mean it involves the mayor's father, and you don't want your ass hanging out on a limb until you know you're right."

Shad raised his right hand and pointed at Henry. "Don't fuck with me, Henry. I'm not a man you want for an enemy."

Henry believed this, but he'd irritated more frightening people than Shadrach Johnson in his time. "Does the drive show an assisted suicide? Or a murder?"

Johnson turned the question back on him. "Do you know why anyone would want to murder Mrs. Turner?"

Henry swallowed hard, but he held his silence.

"Take your computer and go, Mr. Sexton. I may ask you to appear before a grand jury in the near future."

There it was. All Henry had to do was pack his Mac into his briefcase and leave. Yet he stood rooted to the carpet, like a Cub Scout itching to confess a lie.

"What's the matter?" Johnson asked.

"There's something you should know," Henry said awkwardly.

"What?"

"Members of the Double Eagle group threatened to kill Viola Turner if she ever returned to Natchez."

Shad thought about this for a few moments. "When was this threat made?"

"Before she moved to Chicago."

The DA looked confused. "You mean forty years ago?"

"That's right. Mrs. Turner told me this during our second interview."

"You're talking about the Ku Klux Klan?"

"*Not* the Ku Klux Klan," Henry said, making his annoyance plain. "The Double Eagles. They killed a lot of people, and they probably kidnapped and killed Mrs. Turner's brother."

Shad snorted. "Are you suggesting that some seventy-year-old men went over and killed Viola Turner at five o'clock this morning?"

"I'm just telling you what I know."

"What was the basis of this threat?"

"I believe the Double Eagles knew—or at least believed—that Viola Turner possessed information that could have convicted them for her brother's murder." Henry stopped, then added, "There's also some evidence that the Double Eagles gang-raped Viola Turner back in 1968."

"Did Mrs. Turner tell you that?"

"No. But I think she was just being modest. The rumor was pretty widely believed back in sixty-eight."

"You're talking about hearsay, Mr. Sexton. Even if such a rape occurred in 1968, the statute of limitations would have run out on that crime in 1975. No one could be prosecuted for it today."

"There's no statute of limitations on murder," Henry said doggedly.

Johnson sighed. "I reviewed those case files, what little there was. Nobody ever found Jimmy Revels's body. Luther Davis's, either. You spend too much time living in the past, Henry."

The reporter felt his shoulders sag. "A lot of people say that."

"You can't even see the obvious. If those Double Eagles were still active, they'd have killed *you*, not some nurse already circling the drain." The DA shook his head like a man weary of dealing with a fool. "You're free to go. I need to make some phone calls."

Henry packed his computer into his briefcase and left the office.

CHAPTER 9

AFTER ROSE CLEARED my calendar of all noncritical appointments, I began researching legal precedents in cases similar to the circumstances Shad had described regarding Viola Turner's death. One call to a law school friend in New Orleans confirmed what Shad had told me earlier: Anna Pou, a highly respected EENT physician, might well be charged with murder for organizing the euthanization of eleven patients who couldn't be evacuated during the worst hours of the Katrina flood. While the circumstances of that case and my father's are clearly different, what chilled my blood was my friend's assertion that the prosecution was politically motivated.

Enter Shad Johnson.

The fact that Dad has refused to give me any information about last night's events is disturbing, yet it makes sense if he played some part in a physician-assisted suicide. In most similar situations, when someone makes a stink about the circumstances of death, common sense eventually prevails and no charges are filed. Based on the percentages, I should be able to assume that Viola's son will soon realize that his mother's wishes should trump all else. And yet . . . the longer I sit at my desk, the more intuition whispers that something out of the ordinary is happening. On impulse, I call the Illinois State Bar Association and inquire about Lincoln Turner. The woman I speak to informs me that four months ago, Turner's law license was suspended pending a disbarment proceeding. She won't elaborate on the phone, but a Nexis online search quickly tells me that he's been accused of embezzling funds from a client escrow account. This is the sterling character accusing my father of murder.

So why won't Dad defend himself? He's almost never kept secrets from me, not even in dire circumstances, yet this time something is forcing him out of character. And he's not the only one. Shad Johnson and I share too much history for me to buy into his stated desire to be helpful to my family.

Sure enough, when Shad calls back, I detect a suppressed excitement not present during our first two conversations. It's that excitement that drives me out of my office and onto State Street, making for the DA's office at a fast walk.

The first time someone calls out to me, it barely registers. But when the speaker raises his voice and calls my first name, I turn to see Henry Sexton of the *Concordia Beacon* hailing me from the window of his Explorer. My first instinct is to wave to the reporter and walk on, but the urgency in his voice persuades me to go over to his window. When he tells me he has information concerning my father and Viola Turner, my heart does a double thump before recovering its normal beat. As I climb into the passenger seat, I realize that Henry is truly upset. In fact, he looks like he's been crying.

"Are you okay?" I ask. "What's happened?"

"I only have a few minutes," he says anxiously. "But there's something you need to see."

"What's going on, Henry?"

In a breathless voice, the reporter tells me a disjointed story that starts my pulse speeding, but it's clear that Henry wants to help me, or at least my father. The one fact I've gleaned is that I need to see whatever's on his computer before I speak to Shad Johnson.

"I'd better pull around the corner before I play the file for you," Henry says. "Shad could look out his window and see us sitting here."

"Do it."

The reporter slides his Mac onto my lap, looks furtively up at the sheriff's office, then drives up State Street and turns on Commerce.

I've always considered Henry Sexton to be a modern-day Don Quixote, and for that reason I trust him. I've been accused of having the same complex, but I'm nowhere near Henry's league. The articles he writes about unsolved civil rights murders occasionally attract the odd death threat or flying bottle by way of criticism. The man himself is tall and lanky, with the perpetually sad eyes of a faithful hound. With his wire-rimmed glasses and a goatee, he looks like a cross between a college professor and a biologist you'd expect to find checking the acidity of catfish ponds.

"How about here?" Henry asks, pulling up before the old Jewish temple on Commerce Street. My town house is just around the corner, on Washington, but Shad is expecting me in his office at any moment.

"This is fine, Henry. Let's see it."

He touches his Mac's trackpad, and a three-by-five video window appears on the screen. A hospital bed stands in the corner of what appears to be a dim room in a private residence. First I hear a wail that sets my teeth on edge. Then I make out a skeletal figure thrashing in the covers as though trying to free itself from a knotted sheet. A gasping sound is clearly audible, punctuated by a repeated word that sounds like "Help." The figure half falls off the bed, then reaches for something on the floor. At first I'm not sure what—then I see an empty phone cradle on the bedside table. Suddenly the scene makes sense. The desperate patient has knocked the phone onto the floor and hasn't enough mobility to reach it.

"Help!" comes the strangled cry again. "Cora . . . help me." A few wisps of white hair cling to the patient's skull. In a moment of horror I realize that this emaciated figure must be what remained of the beautiful nurse I remember from my childhood. Viola's right hand opens and closes like a claw, but she cannot twist herself out of the bed. "Lord, he's killing me!" she cries. "Tom . . . *Tom! Why? Where are you?*"

My father's name prickles every hair on my body. Henry's barely breathing beside me. Somehow the old woman struggles back into a supine position in the bed, one hand pulling at her bare throat as though trying to rip away some invisible ligature. Sweat glistens on her face and forehead, and her breath comes far too fast. She's going to hyperventilate, if she doesn't stroke out first. Viola seems to have no idea that the camera is recording anything. But then again, maybe she does.

"Cora!" she screeches, but before she can continue, her gasping stops and her eyes bulge in their sockets. "Hail Mary . . . full of grace," she coughs in a strangled voice. "Hail Mary full of—"

In mid-prayer Viola Turner's mouth locks open, and she sits motionless for so long that I think she must be dead. Then in a final spasm she lurches to her left, throwing herself far enough that her upper torso falls out of the bed. She comes to rest with her lower body still tangled in the bedclothes, her right hand touching the floor near the telephone. I hear no more sounds of respiration. Not even a death rattle.

"She's dead," I say softly.

"I think so," Henry agrees.

"Who else has seen this?"

"Me and the DA. Maybe the sheriff by now."

"Jesus, Henry."

"I know."

Sexton's video isn't the most horrifying visual evidence I've ever seen—not by a long shot. During my years as an assistant DA in Houston, I heard and saw tapes made by narcissistic rapists, torture-killers, and other assorted freaks. But this video would go a long way toward convincing a jury that Viola Turner didn't die by her own choice. Worse, many people might reasonably interpret her last words as a direct accusation against my father. I think the recording is equivocal on that point, but you never know how a jury will read something. If my father were vigorously defending himself on the stand (and had a good explanation for what the recording shows), a jury might believe him. But if he sat silently at the defense table, hiding behind the Fifth Amendment, they might well convict him.

"Is there anything but this on the rest of the recording?"

"Just twenty-eight minutes of her lying there."

"You watched it all?"

"I fast-forwarded through it, but I'm pretty sure."

My right hand is gripping the door handle so hard that my forearm cramps, but I can't pull myself away from the computer screen. For the first time I notice the appointments in Viola's sickroom. On the bedside table stands a white statuette of the Virgin Mary, and hanging on the wall behind the hospital bed are three framed photos: Abraham Lincoln; Martin Luther King Jr.; John and Robert Kennedy standing on the White House Colonnade, looking pensive. The bedside lamp is a faux gas lantern, and it stands on a lace doily—an impractical item to use near a sickbed. I also see a clock-radio, which clearly reads 5:38 A.M.

"Did that look like a morphine overdose to you?" Henry asks.

"No. Is that what Shad thought it was?"

"I think he expected to see a morphine overdose until he saw this." Henry puts his hand on my arm. "Did I break the law by making a copy of this? Or by showing it to you?"

"That's probably open to interpretation. But you don't have to worry about it. I won't tell a soul I've seen it."

"I trust you. I just don't trust Shad Johnson."

"You're not alone in that." I take a deep breath, then rub my eyes until I see stars. "I don't mean to keep you, but you said Shad mentioned my father to you?"

"When I first got to his office, he said he thought he had an assisted suicide situation on his hands. He said Viola and your father had some kind of pact about it. But after he saw this, I got a very different feeling."

"What did he say afterward?"

"Just that the drive was evidence and he had to keep it. But everything had changed somehow. It was more his demeanor than anything else. I had the feeling he was gloating inside. You know?"

"I do." Given the past enmity between Shad and me, this would normally be no surprise, but considering the leverage I have over him—

"This looks bad for your father, doesn't it?"

"Yes. Do you intend to report this in the *Beacon*?"

"Not until I have a much better idea of what's going on."

I look at Henry from the corner of my eye. "A lot of reporters would."

He shakes his head firmly. "Your father took care of my daddy right up to the day he died. Some days, Dr. Cage listened to Mama cry for an hour in his office. Not many doctors would do that. None, these days. I owed you this, Penn. Or him, I reckon."

I lay my hand on his forearm and squeeze it. "Thank you, buddy."

"What does Doc say about all this? Off the record."

"He told me to mind my own business."

"Huh." Henry pooches out his lower lip. "Well . . . I'm sure Doc knows what he's doing."

"Don't count on it. When it comes to the law, he's about as naïve as a seventh grader. He believes the law is about justice."

Henry shakes his head slowly. "It ought to be, but it ain't. I've sure learned that these past few years." He looks over at the door of the public library, where a heavy woman with three small children tries to herd them up the steps. "I hate to say this, Penn, but I need to go. Do you want me to drop you back where we were?"

"You don't need Shad to see you doing that. I'll run from here."

Henry takes the computer from my lap and sets it on the backseat. "I appreciate it. Good luck to you."

As I jog back toward the courthouse, Henry puts the Explorer in gear and roars past me, making for the river.

SHADRACH JOHNSON NORMALLY SITS behind his antebellum-period desk with the condescension of an Arab potentate. Today, however, his customary arrogance is tempered by a watchfulness I've rarely seen in him. Shad's wary demeanor can only be explained by his awareness that I have the power to destroy his political career, and I see no reason to let him forget that during this conversation.

"Before we begin," he says, "I want us to be clear about something."

"What's that?"

"We both know two months ago, you had a certain photograph in your possession. A photograph with me in it."

"Mm-hm," I murmur in a neutral tone, my gaze playing over Shad's jacket, which looks like a Zegna. The DA has always been a clothes-horse. He dresses as precisely as he grooms himself, which is rare among our lawyers and city officials these days. His keeps his hair cut close to his skull and his nails manicured, another unusual touch. The county coroner—an African-American woman with keen observational skills—once quietly suggested to me that Shad is gay, but I've never heard this confirmed. And since Natchez has long been a haven for gays in Mississippi, it seems odd that Shad would remain in the closet.

The photograph that so worries him has nothing to do with sexuality—not so far as I know, anyway. Rather, it shows the district attorney in the presence of a professional football player and a pit bull dog. The dog in question is hanging by its neck from a tree limb, and the football player has a cattle prod in his hand. Both men look fascinated, even excited, by the brutality in which they are taking part.

"You told me you gave me the original JPEG file," Shad goes on, as though each word causes him discomfort. "On that SD card."

"That's right."

"Was that . . . ?"

"The only copy?" I finish helpfully.

"Yes."

I shrug.

His face darkens. "Now, see? Goddamn it, this is just what I expected. A veiled threat."

"Shad, you ought to know me by now. If I make a threat, there won't be any veil. Why don't you just tell me why you summoned me? I thought maybe you were going to introduce me to Lincoln Turner."

The DA barks a laugh. "You don't want that, believe me. That guy's angry enough to punch you out. Your father, for sure."

"If the man's so upset, why did he only get to town a half hour *after* his mother died?"

"Always the lawyer," Shad says drily. "I don't know much about Lincoln Turner yet, and I don't much care to. Right now I just want to make sure things are clear between you and me. Because I'm going to have to move forward in this matter, Penn. I've got no choice."

I expected this, but not quite so soon. "What exactly do you mean by 'move forward'?"

Shad steeples his fingers and leans back in his chair. "When we spoke this morning, I thought we were dealing with a case of assisted suicide. Maybe just plain suicide, okay? I just wanted it to go away. And I believed there was some chance that it would."

"But now?"

"This thing isn't going away, Penn. No way."

"What's changed?"

"We're looking at murder now." The DA's voice is like a wire drawn taut. "First-degree murder."

I have to struggle to hold my face immobile. Even with the video recording, I don't see how he gets to first-degree murder. "What are you talking about?"

"Since we spoke this morning, new evidence has surfaced."

"What kind of evidence are we talking about?"

"You know anybody else sitting in this chair would refuse to answer that question."

"No other DA's future would be hanging by a thread that I hold."

Shad's eyes blaze with frustrated anger. "I can't give you the state's case, damn it! Nobody knows that better than you. And based on the evidence I've seen so far, anybody sitting in this chair would proceed against your father. They'd be negligent not to."

"What's your evidence, Shad?" I ask patiently. "I need to know what my father's facing."

He angrily expels a rush of air. "The sheriff's department took your father's fingerprints off two empty ampoules of morphine and a large syringe found at the scene."

I slowly digest this. Viola didn't appear to have died from a morphine overdose on Henry's recording. "They traced his fingerprints in less than a day?"

"Four years ago, your father registered for a concealed-carry permit. The Highway Patrol fingerprints all applicants for that. When the sheriff's department fed the prints from the syringe into AFIS, Dr. Cage's name popped right out."

"All that proves is that my father held that syringe at some point prior to it being collected at the scene. It doesn't even put him in the house."

"Viola's sister put him in the house. Cora Revels."

"She says she left Dad alone with Viola?"

"That's right. She went to a neighbor's house and fell asleep on the couch."

My mind flies back to Henry's video. "Are you certain that Viola died of a morphine overdose?"

Shad gives a small shrug. "You know we can't be sure of that until the toxicology comes back. That could take weeks."

"Ask the state crime lab to rush it. They'll do that for you on a murder case."

"Are you telling me how to run this case?"

"I'm not convinced this *is* a case. I think you're jumping the gun."

Shad looks genuinely upset. "Penn, you've sat where I'm sitting. No child in the world wants to believe his parent committed a terrible crime. But I have a duty here. If I shirk it, I'll be buried by public opinion as surely as if you published that photo in the *Examiner*."

"I honestly don't see how you get to first-degree murder. But I didn't go to Harvard like you. Help me out here."

Shad clearly wants me out of his office, but so long as he thinks I have the photo, he'll handle me with kid gloves. "Lincoln Turner believes his mother was murdered. The physical evidence supports his assertion. And whether your fiancée chooses to print it in the paper or not, his assertion is likely to become a public accusation very soon. If the past is any guide, the rumor will be all over town long before tomorrow's paper hits the streets."

The mention of Caitlin momentarily derails my thoughts; thankfully, she's out of town for the day, interviewing Katrina evacuees at a FEMA trailer park near the Louisiana state line. "Those were not legal points, Shad."

"But they matter, and you know it. I wish I had better news for you. But the only person who might be able to prevent this situation from getting worse is your father. And you said he wouldn't talk to you. Is he sticking to that position?"

"I haven't spoken to him since our first conversation."

Shad's nostrils flare. "Remember when I told you I didn't think any cop or deputy in town would serve a warrant on your father?"

I nod.

"I've since learned I was wrong."

This tells me that everything Shad knows is leaking through the sheriff's department as we speak. With Billy Byrd wearing the star, that's no surprise. Two years ago, Sheriff Byrd, Shad, and a local circuit judge colluded to try to railroad a friend of mine into Parchman. And while I've never uncovered the basis for that unholy alliance, I know that none of those three will hesitate to use the power of his office to settle personal scores.

"For some reason," Shad goes on, "Billy Byrd has a hard-on to bust your old man. The sheriff seems to be one of the few people who don't worship Tom Cage. In fact, I got the feeling he hates him. You might want to ask your dad about that, as well."

I close my eyes and speak in an exaggerated Eastern European accent. "I'm seeing something in my mind . . . wait . . . yes. It's a picture of . . . a bull? No, a bulldog. The dog is hanging from a tree . . . and there's a district attorney hanging beside it. And people are beating the district attorney with sticks. Now somebody's hanging a sign on his chest. The sign says DISBARRED in big capital letters—"

"Keep your voice down!" Shad hisses, coming half out of his chair. "Goddamn it."

"Only one thing will keep my voice down. Give me whatever you've been holding back."

With the look of a cornered animal, he spits out three words. "There's a tape."

I don't even blink. "What kind of tape?"

He gives me a brief summary of the video I just watched in Henry Sexton's Explorer. The DA clearly interprets Viola's dying words as evidence of my father's guilt.

"That doesn't sound like proof of anything. It sounds like the confused ranting of a person having a heart attack."

"Penn, you might as well save it for—"

"Viola was a trained nurse," I point out. "Why would my father inject her? If she died as the result of an injection of any drug, she almost certainly gave it to herself."

"Save it for the courtroom. I don't have any choice here."

I realize I'm breathing hard. "There's got to be more, Shad. Come on. Murder One?"

The DA shifts in his seat. "I'm not going to let you hold that photo over my head like a sword. Before this is over, you'll want to use it, but you'd better think long and hard before you do."

I hear steel in his voice. "Why is that?"

"Better the devil you know—that's why. You bust me, there's no telling who'll wind up in this chair. The judge could appoint a special prosecutor. And depending on the judge, there's no telling who you might get."

This is a veiled reference to Arthel Minor, the judge who colluded with Shad in the past. "I hear you," I tell him. "But there's something missing from this equation. I haven't heard anything that suggests a motive for murder."

Shad waves this objection away with a flick of his hand. "Malice aforethought is enough to get the state to murder. And in this type of case, intent alone is sufficient to meet the standard for malice."

"By 'this type of case,' you mean an assisted suicide situation?"

"I didn't say that."

Shad tries to look inscrutable, but I see something flickering behind his civil-servant-trapped-by-duty mask. As hard as he's trying to conceal it, Shad cannot hide the fierce joy burning within him. Fate has handed him a chance to pay me back a hundredfold, and by God, he means to use it.

"Are you implying my father killed Viola Turner not to relieve her suffering, but for some other reason?"

The DA blinks once, slowly. "I haven't said that."

You just did. "Shad, what's really going on here? What are you sitting on?"

Shadrach rubs his temples with both hands, like a man in real pain. "As far as your father having a motive to kill Viola Turner, I've got more than you want to hear. But you *won't* hear it in here. Not today. There are some lines I can't cross, no matter what you threaten me with."

He pushes back his chair, rises, and looks down at me with the closest facsimile of compassion he can manufacture. "This case is going to trial, Penn. Even if it was you sitting in this chair, if you knew what I know, you'd go forward and indict for murder. I'm sorry, but there's nothing I can do to change that."

"*Motive,* Shad. I'm not leaving this office without a motive. Where did it come from? The sister? Cora Revels?"

"I'm not saying another word."

"The son, then. Lincoln."

Shad looks down at his desk. Then he raises his eyes and says very softly, "Have you asked yourself why a mother would want to be euthanized a half hour before her son arrived to tell her good-bye?"

As soon as the words leave his lips, I realize I have no answer.

"A mother *wouldn't* want that, would she?" Shad asks gently. "Viola's killer wanted her silenced *before* her son got there. He didn't want Viola to be able to talk to her son face-to-face."

My cheeks are burning. "You're saying my father killed Viola Turner to *silence* her?"

Shad stares at me with the calm certainty of a man who believes he has the full weight of the facts behind him. But surely not even Shad Johnson could actually believe such a thing about my father? *Maybe he doesn't really believe it,* I think. *Maybe he's content to know that others might believe it, or be made to.* But no . . . that's wishful thinking. The look in the DA's eyes is clear: he believes my father committed murder last night.

"What kind of lawyer is the son?" I ask, an unsettled feeling growing in my belly. "Criminal? Corporate? Bankruptcy? Ambulance chaser?"

Shad shrugs as though this is irrelevant, then walks to his window and looks down to the street where Henry was parked only a few minutes ago. He taps the window glass lightly, his brown fingers moving like those of a violinist.

"He's smart," he says. "You sense that right away."

"You didn't know him in Chicago?"

Shad laughs. "God, no. The man went to a night law school."

Our DA has always been quick with contempt. "You said he was about forty?"

"Somewhere around there."

"Did you know he's about to be disbarred for embezzling client escrow funds?"

Shad seems to freeze for a moment, but then he looks back from the window like a man whose mind has moved on to other issues. "You need to get your father a good criminal defense lawyer, Penn. Don't even think about representing him yourself."

"Are you seriously thinking about arresting him?"

"No, but Billy Byrd is."

A current of fear shoots through me. "When?"

"I can probably hold him off until tomorrow morning. If you plan to pull a miracle out of your hat, do it tonight. Life's going to get embarrassing after that."

Shad meets my eye and offers his hand. The guy has balls, I'll grant him that. For him to utter the word *embarrassing* in connection with my father takes unimaginable gall. If Caitlin were to publish the dogfighting photo, Shad would be hounded out of the city by nightfall, no pun intended. Disbarment would follow, and possibly even prison. Yet in spite of all this, I take Shad's hand. My old nemesis has told me more than he should have during this meeting, and even if he only did it out of fear, I owe him something.

"Don't try to see Lincoln Turner," he says in a warning tone. "And don't let your father try, either. You'll only make things worse."

"Where's Turner now?"

"Leave it alone, Penn. Your father is the man you need to find."

CHAPTER 10

AS HIS WRISTWATCH ticked over to eleven, Henry Sexton sat down beside the only admitted member of the Double Eagle group ever to agree to speak for the record. Glenn Morehouse had once been a giant of a man; pictures on the walls of the little den testified to that. One framed snapshot showed him in hunting camouflage beside a dead ten-point buck that looked more like a fawn next to the man who'd killed it. In another he sat behind the wheel of a glittering bass boat that looked like a toy that might not bear his weight. In a third he held two hefty toddlers, one in each huge hand, extended before him like dolls on display. But today, thirteen months after being diagnosed with pancreatic cancer, Morehouse had been reduced to a skeletal figure in a La-Z-Boy recliner, a crocheted comforter on his lap and a bifurcated oxygen hose running from his nose back over his ears and down to a steadily humming machine on the floor. Beside the oxygen machine, a white bucket half covered with a lid read CHEMOTHERAPY WASTE, and a plastic urinal stood beside that. The urine in the wide-mouthed vessel looked like strong tea. Henry could hardly imagine this man beating someone to death with a leather strap with roofing nails stuck through it. But that was the kind of thing Morehouse and his buddies had done in their heyday.

Henry was doing his best to hide his nervousness. He wasn't physically afraid. Morehouse wasn't an immediate threat (unless he had a pistol under his comforter), and nobody knew this meeting was taking place. The house belonged to Morehouse's sister, Wilma Deen, the secretary at a local Baptist church, and Morehouse had sent her out on an errand that should take at least ninety minutes. The house itself sat well back from the nearest pavement, at the end of a washboard gravel road potted with holes, so there were no near neighbors to spy on them. Yet still Henry felt edgy and ill at ease.

In truth, the news of Viola's death had rattled him badly. And with Shad Johnson focused on Tom Cage as a suspect, Henry felt obliged to plumb Morehouse's knowledge of Viola's death as well as the historical Double Eagle crimes. Unless Morehouse mentioned Viola first, however, Henry planned to proceed as though he knew nothing about the nurse's death. Her name would naturally come up when he raised the subject of her missing brother, and at that time he could read Morehouse's face and voice for his true knowledge.

The old man coughed as though his lungs might come up. Henry tried to hide his revulsion at the stench of the room. A small fire crackled in a fireplace on the left wall, but even the burning pine knot in it couldn't mask the stink of salves, urine, vomit, and reheated country cooking—vegetables boiled to a salty mush. In black-owned homes it would have been a sugary mush.

Henry felt unsure how to begin the interview. While he considered the options for his all-important first question, Morehouse said, "Were you ever in the service, Mr. Sexton?"

Henry was tempted to fib, but he never lied if he could help it. He shook his head. "I was One-A during Vietnam, but I got a college deferment. My daddy served, though."

Morehouse silently gauged Henry's age. "Pacific or the ETO?"

"North Africa."

The old man nodded and gave another ragged cough. "Do I have your word not to print anything I tell you until . . . until I've passed?"

"That was the deal." Henry fought the urge to scoot back from Morehouse's chair. The man looked like he had an infection in his left eye, which was inflamed and leaking an opaque fluid. "And I plan to abide by it. Is there anything you won't talk about?"

Morehouse opened and closed the inflamed eye. "There may be a lot I won't say this first time. I'll tell you a bit, and we'll see if you can hold your peace past Thursday's edition. If you can, then we'll meet again. And no tape recorders, remember? I want your word on that."

A murderer asking me to give my word? Henry held up the Moleskine notebook in his hand. Viola Turner had been equally adamant about not recording anything, but she had good reason to fear a reprisal. He wondered who Glenn Morehouse feared during this last stage of his journey to the grave.

"First off," Henry said, consciously dropping into the syntax of his youth, "I'll ask you to provide me some bona fides. How do I know you were really a member of the Double Eagles?"

"Ain't no *were* to it," the old man said. "Once in, never out—that's the rule. Just like the IRA." He lifted the comforter and held out a shaking arm to Henry. When Morehouse opened his hand, Henry saw the dull gleam of gold. The still-huge palm held a twenty-dollar gold piece, minted in 1927. A hole had been drilled or shot through the upper half of Lady Liberty and a leather strap wound through the hole, so that the coin could be worn around the neck.

Henry had heard the legend of the Double Eagle gold pieces long ago, but this was his first glimpse of one. "When did you get that?"

"Frank Knox give it to me in August of sixty-four, the day he founded the Double Eagles. Five days after the FBI found them three bodies up in Neshoba County. Frank's long dead, so tellin' that don't hurt nothin'."

Henry felt his heart skip. He'd always heard that Frank Knox had created the Double Eagles, and now an actual member had given him the exact date: just twenty-two days after the firebombing of the man that Henry had cared most about in the world. Henry wanted the truth about Albert Norris's murder more than anything else Morehouse could give him, but he couldn't let his subject know that. Like all good hunters, Henry would have to be patient. "Will you name the other members of the Double Eagle group?"

Morehouse hacked up some phlegm and spat into his puke bucket. "Not today, I won't."

"Why not?"

"Most of those men have families, for one thing. Wouldn't be right for me to ruin their lives just to ease my conscience. Second, our vow was a rough one, with a specified penalty. I wouldn't want to put my family through that."

"What's a 'rough' vow?"

"Kind of like the Masons' oath, but simpler. We all swore that if we betrayed a brother, our firstborn child would be killed. Whatever else you got was up to Frank. And that weren't no Tom Sawyer bullshit, neither. You ever hear of Earl Hodges, up toward Eddiceton?"

Henry nodded. "A Klan informant. He was beaten to death in

Franklin County. The flesh was ripped off him by a strap with roofing tacks in it."

Morehouse's eyes went cold. "Strap, my ass. We used two-by-fours with nails hammered through 'em. When it was over, you could see Earl's teeth through the back of his skull." A look of pain entered the old man's face. "Frank had no mercy on informants. Which is what I am now, I reckon."

Henry felt a strange numbness creeping through him, as though he'd been bitten by some venomous creature. He'd thought he'd been prepared for this interview, but he was wrong. Morehouse had just confessed to first-degree murder, yet the detachment with which he spoke of human butchery was beyond Henry's experience. The men who'd debriefed Death's-Head SS men after World War II must have felt a similar horror.

Morehouse gave him a disturbingly direct look. "And Earl wasn't even an Eagle, you know? I need to know whether you can keep a secret, Henry, like you promised. At least until I'm gone. Frank always said, 'A man's biggest enemy is his mouth.' And God knows he was right."

"I can keep a secret."

"Well, get on with it, then."

Henry consulted the notes he'd made prior to the interview. "I know the Double Eagle group was founded by Frank Knox. Twenty men, organized into wrecking crews. I'm curious about Frank Knox's younger brother, the one they call Snake. He seems to have been the most violent of all the Eagles, and he's made some pretty fantastic claims in the past three years. About Martin Luther King's assassination, for example."

Morehouse bit his lower lip, and his pale face lost some color. "We won't be talking about Snake Knox today. Move on."

Henry didn't like this, but he decided to go with the flow and return to Snake later. "As best I can tell, the Eagles killed between eleven and fifteen people over the years."

"I don't honestly know. I know about my squad, plus some of the bigger operations by the others."

"Who did your squad kill?" Henry asked in a neutral voice.

Morehouse closed his eyes and breathed in and out several times.

"The first hit I was in charge of was an FBI informant who worked with us at Triton Battery."

Henry felt the thrill he'd felt as a boy in a freezing duck blind when the first mallards came in over the tree line. "Are you talking about Jerry Dugan?"

Morehouse's left cheek twitched. "That's right. Dropped him in a tank of sulfuric acid. The foreman wrote 'accidental fall' on the incident report, but that guardrail was four feet high. Jerry needed a little help getting over it."

Henry had seen Dugan's name in FBI 302s that he'd obtained under the Freedom of Information Act. The Bureau had never been positive that Dugan's death was a homicide. The Natchez police had ruled it an industrial accident. Now, with no more than a facial tic, Glenn Morehouse had not only confirmed the murder but also taken responsibility for it. *Two murders solved in as many minutes.*

"We didn't even want to kill Jerry," Morehouse went on. "We growed up with him, and Frank liked him feeding the Bureau stuff on the regular Klan. But Jerry overheard something about the Metcalfe operation, just a couple of days before we was scheduled to go, so that was that. We had to act quick."

Henry's heart thudded. *The Metcalfe operation?* "Are you talking about George Metcalfe? The president of the Natchez NAACP?"

"That's right."

"You guys planted the bomb in Metcalfe's Chevrolet?"

Morehouse nodded as though confirming some trivial fact.

Henry swallowed and tried to figure the best way forward. "But Metcalfe didn't die. Did the bomb malfunction or something?"

Morehouse shook his head. "We never meant to kill him. If we had, we'd have placed the bomb right under the dashboard instead of under the hood."

"Well . . . what was your motive in that case? To scare Metcalfe? To scare the black population? Or the national NAACP leadership?"

The old man gave Henry a coy smile. "Never you mind, right now. Maybe we'll cover that in our next meeting."

Again Henry hesitated. His usual tactic with hostile sources was to get them into a rhythm of answering questions. The questions themselves weren't critical; it was the give-and-take that counted. Because sources were quick to identify what you most wanted to know, and often held back that information, attempting to use it as currency (or sometimes just out of spite), Henry usually buried his critical queries in a litany of less important ones. But given Morehouse's almost casual confessions, he felt tempted to go straight to the case that meant the most to him. And yet . . . if he somehow let Morehouse see how deeply he cared about Albert Norris, he'd be giving the Double Eagle control over the interview, and that chance he would not take.

"On Valentine's Day in 1964," he said, "a man named Albert Whitley was abducted from the Armstrong Tire and Rubber Company and horsewhipped."

"Shit, Henry. A whippin's small potatoes. Too small for us."

Henry noted this in his Moleskine. "Two weeks later, a black employee of the International Paper Company was shot to death in his car with a machine gun. Were future Double Eagle men involved in that?"

Morehouse made a face as though he'd eaten something bitter. "You're talkin' about Clifton Walker, out on Poor House Road. Flashy nigger. A coupla them shooters eventually wound up in the group, yeah."

A fillip of excitement went up Henry's spine, but he patiently noted the answer in his book. Then, without the slightest change in tone, he said, "Five months later, on July eighteenth, Albert Norris's music store was burned to the ground with Norris inside during the attack. He died four days later from his burns. Was that a Double Eagle operation?"

The old man sucked his teeth and studied Henry in silence.

Henry wondered whether his voice had given him away. He did not fidget. He did not breathe. He gave up nothing.

At length, the former Klansman nodded thoughtfully. "That was a damn shame, there. Albert was a good nigger. A mighty good nigger."

Henry waited, hoping Morehouse would elaborate. But the old man held his silence.

"No mainstream Klan group ever claimed responsibility for Norris," Henry went on. "The FBI thinks the killers used a flamethrower that night. A flamethrower is a pretty exotic weapon, but I'm guessing some World War Two vets might have been able to get hold of one."

The sickly eye regarded Henry with an expression akin to disappointment. "Shit, man. With all the Cuban exiles training in Louisiana back then, my mama could have bought a flamethrower at a garage sale."

Henry wondered why the old man was reluctant to claim responsibility for the Norris attack after he'd been so forthcoming about the other killings. He decided to try a different tack. "The day after the store was burned, an employee of Norris's—a young black man named Pooky Wilson—disappeared."

Morehouse shrugged. "I always thought Wilson robbed his boss's store, then set it on fire and hightailed it out of town. Standard procedure for jungle bunnies. Especially hophead musicians. He's prob'ly livin' on welfare in L.A. right now, with ten kids suckin' on the government tit."

Henry squeezed his left hand into a fist. He'd played a lot of music with Pooky in the summer of 1964, and he'd never known a gentler soul, except Jimmy Revels.

"In 1966," he said in a neutral voice, "a Klan informant told the FBI an interesting story. He was a member of the Brookhaven White Knights. The day after Norris's store burned, his klavern got a call telling them to watch for a black boy who might be trying to make it to the train station over there, to catch the train to Chicago. They found the kid, snatched him right out of the station. A tall kid with one drooping shoulder. That was Pooky Wilson. I know, because Wilson had severe scoliosis. That drooping shoulder made him a natural bass player."

Morehouse stared back at Henry with bovine indifference.

"The Brookhaven Klansmen handed Pooky over to three men they believed were Klansmen from Natchez. But I think those men were future Double Eagles." Henry looked the old man straight in the eyes. "Were you one of those men, Mr. Morehouse?"

Henry saw a flicker of emotion in the man's eyes.

"Klan informants worked for money," Morehouse growled. "They made up whatever their FBI handlers wanted to hear, whatever kept the cash coming. You can't trust a story like that."

"I've heard two reliable stories about Pooky's death," Henry went on. "One says he was flayed alive. The other says he was crucified."

"Oh, bullshit. There were a dozen rumors about that kid. I've heard he was driven out in a field and shot thirty times with a rifle."

Something in the old man's gaze belied his tone of voice. Henry was certain Morehouse knew something about Pooky Wilson's death. As he stared into the rheumy eyes, a blast of intuition told him that Morehouse had *seen* Pooky die. Henry cleared his throat. "I have an FBI report that details a meeting with a different Klan informant. When this man was blind drunk, he told an FBI agent that Pooky Wilson had been crucified at a big cypress tree out in the Lusahatcha Swamp, called the Bone Tree."

The old man's eyes flashed, then went dull again.

"This informant mentioned the names of two men who were there," Henry went on, "but the names were redacted in my copy—blacked out with a Magic Marker. Were you at the Bone Tree that night, Mr. Morehouse?"

Morehouse laughed with derision. "*Bone* Tree? If you believe that old nigger tale, they ought to put you in a rubber room down in Mandeville."

To mask his anger and disappointment Henry looked down at his notebook. "Albert Norris took four days to die from his burns." *Four days of unrelenting agony, you son of a bitch.* "Leland Robb, the doctor who treated him, told the FBI that Norris stated more than once that he'd known his attackers, but he refused to reveal their identities. Even his best friend couldn't get the names out of him."

"Albert wasn't no fool," Morehouse said softly. "Did you talk to Dr. Robb?"

"Dr. Robb died in a midair collision in 1969, when I was in college, along with three other people."

Morehouse smiled strangely, almost coyly again. "Kinda convenient, huh? Doc Robb dying like that? You know who was flying the plane that hit him, don't you?"

"Yes. Snake Knox." Henry had long harbored suspicions about this air crash, but he wasn't going to waste this interview on them. "Let's stick with the burning of the store for now. Albert told Dr. Robb that there were four men involved: three inside and one out, beyond the porch. My understanding is that when Frank Knox formed the Double Eagles, there were four charter members: Frank himself, his brother Snake, Sonny Thornfield, and you. And this was less than a month after the attack on Norris's store. Was it you four who burned Albert out?"

Morehouse returned Henry's accusing stare with surprising calm. "I told you, Henry, I *liked* Albert."

"You probably liked Jerry Dugan, too. You grew up with him. But that didn't stop you guys from killing him."

Fury flashed from the hazy eyes like lightning from a cloudy sky. "Watch yourself, boy."

Henry didn't let his gaze waver. "Why was Albert Norris targeted?"

The old man looked as though he meant to keep stonewalling, but then in a weary voice he said, "You can't be that dumb, Henry. Take your pick. Albert was bootlegging, running numbers on the side . . . he even used that gospel radio show of his to set up adultery and miscegenation. What the hell did he think was gonna happen to him?"

"So the Eagles *were* behind his murder."

Morehouse looked over at the dying fire and said, "Why don't you go outside and get another log for the fire?"

"Why don't you answer my question?"

The old man gave him the stink-eye again, but Henry wasn't going to be deflected. He'd lost too many friends to this man and his kind. "How about we cut the bullshit, Glenn? I know what really happened to Albert Norris, and I know why. In the summer of sixty-four, Pooky Wilson was screwing a white girl named Katy Royal. Her father was Brody Royal, one of the richest men in the parish. Royal killed Pooky to stop the affair and make a point, and he used the Double Eagles to do it. Pooky Wilson was the intended victim all along. Albert just got in the way. He was killed for trying to protect that boy."

Morehouse's eyes had gone wide.

"I told you I knew the truth," Henry said with a rush of triumph. "All I need is confirmation."

Morehouse slowly recovered himself, but he looked a lot less smug than he had before. "Listen to me, Henry. I'm going to tell you this because my mama always liked yours. The stories you've written up to now have irritated some people, but most people can tolerate a little irritation. *But*—if you start messin' with Brody Royal, you won't live long. In fact, you might just beat me to the grave, and that's saying something."

This threat didn't surprise Henry. He'd long known that Brody Royal—the president of Royal Oil and the Royal Cotton Bank, and the

owner of massive farm and timber operations—was little better than a
gangster. "Let's say I'm willing to take that risk."

Morehouse reached out and gripped Henry's wrist with frightful
strength. "If I tell you what happened that night, will you really keep it
secret till I'm feedin' worms? Will you, boy?"

Henry tried to jerk his hand free, but he couldn't. "I *know* Brody
and Frank visited Albert's store that afternoon," he said. "I can prove it."

The old man's eyes narrowed. Then his hand went limp, and Henry
jerked back his own. "How?" asked Morehouse.

"I've got a witness."

Morehouse looked genuinely surprised. "If that's true, what do you
need me for?"

"Because you know everything, and from the inside. You know
exactly who did what, and when. And most important, you know *why.*"

After a long series of wheezing breaths, Morehouse shook his head
in apparent surrender. Then he mumbled, "Frank was there, all right.
He ran that whole operation."

Henry's pulse quickened. "For Brody Royal?"

Morehouse waved this question away. "Leave it, Henry."

But Henry couldn't. "You're never going to be tried for this stuff,
Glenn. Royal won't know you implicated him until you're . . . beyond
his reach. Please confirm that Royal was there that night. And tell me
which others were. Without the names, all this is meaningless."

"Names, names!" Morehouse mocked in a high voice. "You think
it's easy betraying men I fought with through unshirted hell? You don't
know nothin' about it! Those men are my *brothers,* man. The shit we
done and seen, the horrors . . ." He trailed off, breathless again.

Henry wanted to point out that murdering defenseless Americans
had nothing to do with war, but instead he said, "Is Brody Royal your
brother?"

"*Fuck* Brody Royal!" the old man bellowed. "Brody's so far above
the likes of you and me, the devil himself will have to deal with him.
And I'm fine with that."

Henry looked down at his watch. Wilma Deen was due back in
forty-five minutes. If he overstayed his allotted time, she would see
him, and that would quash any chance of further access to Morehouse.
Henry owed it to Jimmy Revels to learn what he could about his fate.

And after what had happened to Jimmy's sister this morning, Henry couldn't in good conscience leave this room without probing Morehouse about that. Yet even a cursory discussion of those cases would eat up the remaining time.

"What's the matter?" Morehouse asked. "You look like you swallowed a bad oyster."

"There's something I don't understand, Glenn. You called me here, okay? You told me you needed to unburden your soul. Well, here I am. We're alone. But the only people you've implicated are yourself and Frank Knox, who's been dead for thirty-seven years. I don't see how you're going to feel any better after this. In fact . . . it's almost like you're just reminiscing about these crimes. *Bragging*, like."

The old man's face drained of blood, and his chin quivered with anger. "I ain't *braggin'*, damn you!"

"No?" Henry felt his own anger rising. "You could end a whole world of misery just by letting me turn on my tape recorder. You could bring peace and closure to a dozen families, justice to this town, and salvation to your soul. Can't you find the courage for that, Glenn? With death so close?"

Morehouse's face darkened. "The things I know wouldn't bring peace to anybody. Take my word for that." He lifted a bruised hand, scratched his scaly arm, and turned bloodshot eyes on Henry. In that moment Henry felt that he was looking at a man being consumed by malignant secrets.

"You ever see a man skinned alive?" Morehouse croaked. "You ever seen a Polaroid of it, even?"

Struck dumb, Henry shook his head.

"A man can live for hours afterward, believe it or not. I'd rather be *burned at the stake* than go that way. I hear the Mexican drug cartels are doin' it now, as a punishment." The old man's eyes were wet. "You can't imagine what some men can do for pleasure, Henry. I promise you that. They make a *hobby* out of that kind of sickness."

Henry clung to his notebook as though it were a lifeline attached to the normal world. "Was that what happened to Pooky Wilson?"

Morehouse didn't answer; he seemed to have slipped into a trance. "I've seen a man crucified, too. Nailed to a cross, just like Jesus. I've seen men drowned . . . every kind of killin' you can imagine. Some during the war, but not all." He squinted like a sailor trying to make out some distant shore. "How can a man get into heaven after seeing those things?"

"By confessing his sins," Henry said. "That's how."

"To who?" The cloudy eyes found him for a moment. "*You?* You can't absolve me of nothing."

Henry had never seen a man so filled with despair. "To God, Glenn. Why would you let scum like Brody Royal stand between you and salvation? You think he's *above* you? Albert Norris was twice the man Royal is. So are you. At least you feel remorse for what you did."

Morehouse's smoldering eyes fixed Henry with bone-deep hatred, but the light of animal curiosity burned there also. "Why is Albert's case so special to you? That's about the only operation we've talked about, and our time's almost gone. Were you related to that nigger or something? Did Albert blacksnake your mama, Henry? I know he tuned up a lot of white housewives after he finished with their pianos." The old man's eyes glinted with wicked delight. "And your daddy spent a whole lot of time on the road, didn't he?"

Henry came out of his chair with both fists clenched, but Morehouse only laughed. "I know Albert had more'n a couple outside kids in Ferriday," he said, still chuckling. "Is *that* why you've spent all these years trying to find out who killed him?" The old Klansman guffawed until his laughter became a desperate coughing jag.

Henry wondered whether Morehouse had any idea how close he'd come to the truth: that Albert had indeed been his father in every sense but the biological one. Henry's heart pounded like a kettledrum. He hadn't been in a fight since the third grade, and most people thought he didn't have a temper. But right now he wanted to jab his pen into Morehouse's swollen eye socket and drive it through his brain.

"You know what?" he said, closing his notebook and stuffing it into his back pocket. "I figure you need me a lot more than I need you. I'm going to walk out of this room and go back to work. I'm going to solve these cases one way or another, with or without you. And when spring comes, I'll smell the flowers and hug my lady and know I'm doing the best I can. But you . . . you're going to sit in this room and rot until they box you up with your sins and bury you. And from the looks of things, that won't be very long."

Henry walked to the door, then turned back and looked at the old man. Morehouse was straining to rise from his chair.

"Wait!" he yelled. "Wait, you son of a bitch!"

Henry felt he was standing on the threshold between life and death. Despite the old man's fury, he could not lift himself out of the chair. While Morehouse sputtered and cursed, Henry walked out into the cold winter light and shut the door behind him.

CHAPTER 11

FLAT ON HIS back beneath a 1998 Camaro, Sonny Thornfield cursed his cell phone, then slid his creeper from beneath the car and dug the phone out of his pocket. The caller ID read DUKE WILLIAMS. Duke Williams was dead—had been for five years—but his wife wasn't. Sandra kept her dead husband's name on the phone listing so that burglars wouldn't target her. Sonny used to stop by Duke's house on occasion to comfort his widow, back when the doctor let him take Viagra. Sonny still took the drug on special occasions, but Sandra Williams didn't rate the risk of death. Her only real utility now was that she lived at the turn that led to Wilma Deen's house.

"Hey, Sandy," Sonny said, grimacing at the leaky ceiling of his automotive shop.

"Hey, Son," she almost cooed. "I'm sorry to bother you."

"No problem, girl. Always glad to hear from you."

"I think I saw something you might be interested in."

"What's that?"

"About an hour ago, Wilma left her house. I was out mulching my zinnia beds, and she spoke to me as she passed. Said she was headed to Tallulah on some errand for Glenn. After she left, as I was going back into my house, another vehicle came up the road—headed in, not out. I figured it was probably a sitter coming to stay with Glenn. But when it got closer, I recognized it. The owner goes to the same church I do."

"Who was it, Sandy?"

"That reporter for the *Beacon*—Henry Sexton."

Sonny rolled off the creeper and sat up with a grunt. "Are you sure?"

"Positive. I shielded my eyes as he passed, and I saw his mustache and goatee. It was Henry, all right."

Sonny's chest had gone tight. "Is he still down there?"

"Mm-hm. I walked out to my mailbox, and I could just see the tail end of his Explorer sticking out from behind Wilma's house. I wouldn't have bothered you, but Snake told me to keep an eye out for anything funny down there. I tried to call Snake, but he didn't answer, so I figured I'd best call you."

"You did right, hon." Sonny steeled himself against the pain in his arthritic knees, then struggled to his feet. "We won't forget you."

He could almost hear Sandra blush. "Aw, ya'll don't need to do anything for me. I'm glad to help. I know Glenn's getting pretty close to the end, and he might not be quite right in his mind, you know?"

"That I do. You call me back when Sexton leaves, and double-check to be sure it was him. Okay?"

"Will do, Sonny. I got nothing else to occupy me."

Sonny ignored the hint. "Thanks, Sandy." He clicked END, then speed-dialed Snake. After five rings, he expected to get voice mail, but then Snake picked up.

"What's up?" he asked in a sleepy croak.

"Did Sandra Williams just call you?"

"Hell, yeah. I'm still half asleep. I didn't have the patience to listen to her bitch about the pickaninnies from that apartment complex walking across her property to get to the Walmart."

"That wasn't why she called. I think we got trouble, pard. Sandy says Henry Sexton is down at Wilma's talking to Glenn, and Wilma's not there."

"*Shit*. Right now?"

"Yep. What you got on tap?"

"I'm supposed to fly down to Baton Rouge and make a pickup."

Snake was referring to a bulk load of ether in transit from Mexico, something Sonny didn't like moving in his cars. "I'm in the middle of work myself. Just had two cars delivered from auction."

Snake grunted to acknowledge that he understood Sonny's actual meaning.

"But I think we'd better go see Billy Knox," Sonny added. "Don't you?"

Snake didn't answer. Sonny knew his old comrade hated taking problems to his son, but that was the procedure, and Sonny hoped Snake wouldn't buck it. Glenn Morehouse knew enough to blow a lot more than Double Eagles out of the water. "Snake?" he said hesitantly.

"I'm thinking."

Sonny looked over at the Camaro. When Sandra called, he'd been trying to open a hidden compartment that concealed two pounds of ephedrine. He'd already retrieved two pounds from behind the coolant reservoir, but the jerry-rigged compartment welded above the exhaust pipe was proving troublesome. He'd ripped his right thumbnail down to the quick, and it hurt like hell. He put it in his mouth and sucked it. "Come on, Snake. We gotta do it."

"Is Sexton still at Wilma's house?"

"Sandra says yeah. She's going to call me when he leaves."

"Goddamn it. I'd like to go take care of that fucker now, before anybody else gets into it. We should've silenced him a month after they diagnosed him. Would have been a mercy."

Sonny gritted his teeth and tried to sound diplomatic. "You know that's not gonna fly. It's been a big enough day already."

"I know . . . I know. All right, Billy's down at Fort Knox. I'll pick you up in my truck and we'll head to Mississippi."

"Fort Knox" was Snake's nickname for Valhalla, the hunting camp that had been in his family for decades. Brody Royal preferred the formal name, but Snake liked reminding people that his family held the deed on all that acreage, regardless of who had paid for it.

"Give me thirty minutes," Sonny said. "I need to secure these cars."

"Works for me. Out."

Sonny pocketed his cell phone, then looked down at his mechanic's creeper with almost spousal resentment. He had a bad feeling in the pit of his belly. He'd had it for some time now. It had started just before Viola came back from Chicago. *And look what came of that,* he thought. *Now Glenn's talking? Jesus.* Trying to keep the past buried was like trying to stop kudzu from growing. Short of pouring gasoline on the ground and killing the earth itself, you couldn't do it. Which is exactly what Snake would argue in half an hour.

"Screw this load," Sonny cursed, kicking the creeper across the floor.

Picking up the tightly packed Ziplocs of ephedrine, he walked into the front office to get some coffee. Bucky Jarrett, an old Double Eagle who worked as his sales manager, looked up from his ten-year-old computer when Sonny dropped the bags on his desk.

"Everything copacetic, boss?" Jarrett slid the Ziplocs into his bottom drawer with a practiced motion.

Sonny shook his head, looking through the broad display window at his little empire of secondhand cars. Just beyond his lot lay Highway

84, thick with midday traffic. A few miles down the road, on the other side of the asphalt, Glenn Morehouse was probably spilling his guts to a reporter. And not just any reporter, either—

"A little short on weight this trip?" Bucky asked.

"I'm having trouble opening the chassis safe."

"Those tamale-heads prob'ly used an air driver to seal it."

"Yep," Sonny agreed. "You been to see Morehouse in a while, Buck?"

"Uh . . . about two Sundays back, I think. Something wrong?"

"How did he seem? Solid?"

Jarrett took a few moments to answer. "Well . . . he cried a bit."

Sonny looked back at his manager. "Cried?"

"When he talked about when we was kids and stuff, you know. Shit, he's dying, man."

"Do you trust him, Bucky?"

Jarrett looked perplexed. "With what?"

"To go quietly, like a man."

Jarrett's eyes bugged. "Shit, Sonny. Don't say that. We got problems with Glenn?"

Sonny clicked his tongue. "We might."

Bucky looked like a tax cheater who'd just opened an audit notice from the IRS. He got up and started rubbing the back of his neck. Getting out from under the Camaro had calmed Sonny a little, and he realized he ought to go back and get the rest of the ephedrine. He didn't need that sitting around the shop while things were popping like this. Bucky could lock up for half an hour and run the stuff out to the warehouse.

"Sonny?" Jarrett asked nervously.

"Yeah?"

"Just before you came in, I heard that old nurse of Dr. Cage's died this morning. Viola something-or-other. Del Richards over at the sheriff's department told me about it."

"Yeah?" Sonny looked back toward the highway. "I hadn't heard that."

"Hell, I didn't even know she was in town. Did you?"

"Can't say I did."

"Del also said he heard Sheriff Byrd say Dr. Cage killed her. Put her out of her misery, like. Don't that beat all?"

Sonny clicked his tongue thoughtfully. "Well . . . Dr. Cage always went his own way. I always liked that about him."

CHAPTER 12

HENRY SEXTON STOOD in the yard of Wilma Deen's house, watching a sparrow trying to stuff itself into a martin house mounted on a pole. He'd walked out of Glenn Morehouse's sickroom with every intention of getting into his SUV and driving away, but once the wind hit his face, he'd felt his rage drain away, leaving behind only a sense of failure. For ten years he'd been working to find a source inside the Double Eagle group. But now that he had one, he'd flung a bunch of righteous bullshit in the man's face and stormed out. *What did I expect?* he asked himself. *A signed confession with a bow on top?* Glenn Morehouse had nothing to look forward to but more suffering followed by death, and Henry had only come here to plunder the dark cave of his conscience. What was more natural than for the old man to gain some pleasure at his expense?

Henry wished he still smoked cigarettes. Fifty yards up the gravel road, a fat black Labrador retriever trudged toward the highway. Beyond the dog, Henry saw movement near the house that stood at the highway turn—Wilma Deen's nearest neighbor. When he focused, though, he lost the impression. After a few seconds of staring, he felt like a deer trying to spot a careful hunter. With four backward steps he carried himself out of sight of the distant house.

What was I thinking? he wondered. Because of his personal obsession with Albert Norris, he'd barely flipped a page in the Eagles' catalog of crime. He hadn't asked about Jimmy Revels and Luther Davis, or even Joe Louis Lewis, the busboy who'd disappeared without a trace. Maybe one or more of those boys was who Morehouse had seen flayed or crucified. Above all, Henry had blown his chance to question Morehouse about Viola Turner's death. Surely he owed his best efforts to Jimmy Revels and Tom Cage, and to all the families who had never learned the fate of their loved ones? He glanced at the clock on his cell phone.

Wilma Deen would return in twenty-five minutes, thirty at the outside. Yet if he walked back into the house now, Morehouse was as likely to curse him as tell him anything further.

Stay or go? he wondered, looking back at his Explorer.

As though in answer, his cell phone rang. The caller ID said G. MOREHOUSE. "Hello?"

"You feel better, asshole?" growled the old man.

"Not really."

"Did you expect me to spill my guts to you the first time we talked? That how it usually goes in your interviews?"

"Not always."

The silence stretched for a bit. Then Morehouse said, "You really don't know what you're dealing with, Henry. Brody Royal didn't start out rich. His daddy was a bootlegger in St. Bernard Parish, and a partner with the Little Man before he ever took over New Orleans."

"The Little Man?" Henry echoed, confused.

"Carlos Marcello, boss of the New Orleans syndicate. Carlos and Brody were in on all kinds of deals together later on. Real estate mostly, but other shit, too. Back in sixty-one, the CIA kidnapped Carlos and flew him down to Central America. They strapped a parachute on him and forced him to jump from the plane at night. That was Bobby Kennedy's idea of a joke. Didn't matter. Two weeks later, Carlos was back in New Orleans. Brody paid the Little Man's hotel bill the whole time he was down there, then helped to fly him back north. That's the kind of crowd Brody Royal ran with, okay? Meyer Lansky, Santo Trafficante, those guys. In 1960, Carlos and Brody gave Richard Nixon close to a million bucks through Hoffa and the Teamsters, trying to beat John Kennedy. That's who you're messing with, Henry. That's who you want to go after with your little pissant newspaper."

Henry looked up the long gravel road that led to Highway 84. The black Lab was gone. "All that was a long time ago, Glenn. And Marcello's dead."

"*Brody* ain't dead. And I'll tell you something that *wasn't* so long ago. You remember when they jailed the state insurance commissioner a couple years back?"

Henry knew the case well. "Ed Schott? Sure. They found two hundred grand in cash in a deep freeze in his storeroom."

"Right. The state claimed that Royal Insurance was paying Schott to rig a state contract. But no company employee was ever indicted."

"A key witness disappeared," Henry said in a casual voice. "Or something."

"Two witnesses. Both women. Do you know who the president of Royal Insurance is?"

"One of Royal's sons, right?"

"Yep. But the CFO is Royal's son-in-law, Randall Regan."

Henry knew all about Regan, who had blocked every attempt Henry had made to interview his wife, Katy. "I've seen him around."

"You know Randall wasn't no real husband to Brody's daughter. He's a watchdog, bought and paid for. He married her less than a year after Pooky Wilson disappeared, after she got back from the sanitarium in Texas. Randall's job was to look after Katy, but he also ran the crooked side of Royal Insurance. About three years back, Randall and Brody were working a sweet deal to rig a state contract—the same kind of deal Governor Edwards went to jail for. The only problem was, Randall was dicking two gals who worked in the office. One was an accountant, married with kids—the other a divorced secretary with a kid. After a while, these two gals figured out Randall was screwing 'em both. So the accountant decided they'd not only get even with him, but get rich doing it. She called some federal whistle-blower line, something the government set up after the Enron mess. You get huge rewards for ratting out corrupt companies now. So, the feds met these gals, but instead of busting Royal Insurance outright, they left the gals in place and ordered them to steal computer files and such. They even wired them up some days, trying to record conversations."

"Go on," Henry said, wishing to God he could tape the cell conversation.

"Around this time, Forrest Knox got wind that Ed Schott was being investigated on the sly."

"Frank Knox's son?"

"That's right. Forrest is a CIB officer in the state police. So Forrest looks into it, finds out about the girls, and passes the word to Brody."

"Oh, God. What did Brody do?"

Morehouse took several wheezing breaths. "One day those gals left work for lunch and didn't come back. Snake and Sonny hogtied 'em, hustled 'em into a Cessna, and flew 'em down to a hunting camp in South Louisiana, close to where Frank used to train Cubans in sixty-one. Brody and Randall were waiting. Claude Devereux was down there, too, for the legal end of things. Those gals started screaming and sobbing the second they saw Randall and the old man, because they thought they knew what was coming. But they didn't have a clue, son."

Henry felt his stomach clench, but he had to know. "What happened?"

"Snake sat 'em down at a table and tied 'em both to chairs. They were facing each other, but he left their hands free. Randall cussed 'em for about five minutes, and one actually had the balls to cuss back. Then Brody asked what they'd told the feds. The girls wouldn't talk. So Brody gave the word, and Randall pinned one woman's arms to the table. Then Brody took out a knife and cut her face up a little. She started talking quick after that. They couldn't shut her up. She was bleeding and slobbering all over the table, and the other girl was sobbing. In about three minutes, they'd spilled everything. Brody went into the next room and talked to Devereux. Claude said it was pretty clear the feds had been told a lot, but without the gals as witnesses, they'd never make a case stick."

Henry knew what must follow, as surely as the feast follows the kill, and it sickened him. But he did what years of experience had taught him he must. "What happened then?"

"Brody told them gals they were going to play a game."

"A game?"

"Yessir. That's Brody, right down to the ground. The winner would get to go back to her kids, but the loser had to die."

"What kind of game was it?"

"Brody's favorite kind. He tells the gals he's gonna give each of 'em a pistol with one bullet in it. Whichever one shoots the other can go home, back to her life. But he's gonna keep a videotape of her killing the other one, to use if she ever tries to tell her FBI friends any of what happened. And if the winner tries to go into witness protection, something like that, he'll do the same thing to a family member or friend. These gals can't believe it at first, right? But then they see old Brody is serious—they see the two pistols—and they freak out. One asks how Randall can let this happen after he's made love to her, to both of them. He just laughs and says he's planning to screw the winner for old times' sake."

Henry felt dizzy. He blew out a lungful of air. "Glenn . . . this is some sick shit. They didn't really do this?"

"You think I could make this up? Brody *gets off* on this kind of thing. He's too old to fuck anymore, so he takes his fun where he can get it. While Snake covered them with a shotgun, Randall gave each woman a .38 revolver. Then the men backed up about twenty feet and told them they could fire when ready."

"Did you see this happen?"

There was a long silence, punctuated by wet breaths. "I ain't sayin'. But I know what happened. Both women were crying, white as death, makeup running down their faces. One put down her pistol, then picked it up again. Pretty soon they're pointing the guns at each other, but real nervous like. The secretary begs Brody to stop the game, to think about their kids. The accountant says the guns probably only have blanks in them. But deep down, they know. They've betrayed the Royal family, and somebody's gonna die for it. Brody says if one or the other don't fire in the next sixty seconds, Snake'll shoot 'em both with the shotgun."

"And Royal was filming this?"

"Yessir. But strictly for pleasure, not leverage. Anyway, as the clock ticked down, the secretary put down her pistol and said she couldn't do it. Or *wouldn't*. She told the other girl, the accountant, that they were going to be killed anyway, and they shouldn't give the bastards the satisfaction. The accountant started shaking like she was trying to pass a kidney stone. But after a few seconds, she shot the secretary right in the face. Hollow-point bullet. Half her head was on the wall, the other half on her blouse, and the rest of her just slumped in the chair. The accountant jumped up with the chair still tied to her and tried to run out of the room."

"Christ, Glenn. Where's this woman now? Don't tell me she still works for Royal Insurance?"

"Nope. Randall took her in the other room and did just what he'd said he would. Then he told Snake to kill her and dump 'em both in the swamp. And that's what Snake did. After Brody and Randall left, Snake cut up the bodies with a chain saw, bagged the parts, flew 'em to a dark hole in the Atchafalaya, and sunk 'em. They were gar crap by the next day."

For a several moments, Henry couldn't find his voice. Obviously Snake had not performed the cleanup duties on his own. But what was the point in pushing Morehouse on this question? Finally, Henry cleared his throat and asked, "What about Commissioner Schott? Why didn't he talk rather than go to prison?"

Morehouse laughed hoarsely. "Is that a joke? Ed Schott knew exactly what Brody was capable of. Seven years in a minimum-security federal prison is a cakewalk compared to what you get for ratting on Brody Royal."

Henry grunted as if in agreement, but inside, his nausea had begun to recede. Filling its place was a familiar emotion, the same one he'd felt for decades at any mention of Brody Royal—an anger almost impossible to contain. "Why did you tell me that story, Glenn?"

"Because it's Brody you're after. But son, if you ever get close to him, you're gonna find yourself playing the same game those girls did, or one like it. And that's no way to die."

Henry heard real concern in the old Double Eagle's voice.

"Shit, my sister just texted me," Morehouse said anxiously. "She's in Waterproof. We ain't got but twenty-five minutes left. I didn't hear your engine. You still out there?"

"Yeah. I'm coming back in."

"You sure you want to, after what I told you?"

Henry knew this was his personal Rubicon. If he walked back into that house, he was putting his life on the line. "I'll bring in a log for the fire."

WHEN HENRY ENTERED MOREHOUSE'S sickroom for the second time, the old man was pissing in the plastic urinal. Henry turned away and set the red oak log on the dying fire, then stirred the coals. Groaning in discomfort, the old man set the jug beside his chair.

"Last case," Henry said, sitting down beside the La-Z-Boy and flipping open his notebook. "March twenty-seventh, 1968. Jimmy Revels and Luther Davis disappeared from Natchez. Neither man was ever seen again. Were they murdered?"

Morehouse nodded reluctantly.

Henry felt a rush of euphoria. He was about to get a truth that had been buried for thirty-seven years. "Before we go any further, would you clear up one thing for me?"

"If I can."

"Between the bombing of George Metcalfe in August of sixty-five and Jimmy Revels disappearing in March of sixty-eight, there were no major Eagle operations that I know about. Snake Knox ran over an old black man who'd registered to vote down in Lusahatcha County, and killed him, but no charges were filed. That seemed more like a crime of passion. Big John DeLillo shot a black man in Babineau's Barbecue, but you told me DeLillo was never an Eagle. So . . . why the time gap?"

Morehouse sighed heavily. "Simple. Frank's boy got killed in Vietnam in July of sixty-six. Friendly-fire incident. A short artillery round blew him to pieces in the shadow of the Rockpile, near the DMZ. Losing his oldest boy messed Frank up something terrible. He stayed drunk for two years, day and night. He didn't snap out of it till right before he died, and even then . . . aw, hell. I don't want to think about that."

Henry felt like an imbecile. How could he have overlooked this? Sometimes you studied a thing so hard for hidden significance that you missed the neon-lit truth staring you in the face. "Frank died just one day after Jimmy and Luther disappeared," he thought aloud. "Was Frank drunk when that pallet of batteries fell on him?"

Morehouse nodded slowly.

"Okay. Why did you guys target Jimmy Revels? Because he was registering blacks to vote?"

"Did you know that boy?" Morehouse asked softly, staring into the fire.

The question prodded Henry like a finger. "No," he lied. "But I know he spent a lot of time in Albert's store, just like Pooky Wilson. I've wondered whether that connection had something to do with why the Eagles targeted him."

Morehouse shook his head. "Ferriday was a small town. All the nigras knew each other."

Henry didn't buy this. He decided to leap off the cliff he'd been avoiding since the interview started. "Jimmy Revels was also Viola Turner's brother. The nurse who worked for Dr. Cage?"

Morehouse just kept staring into the fire.

"You must have met her when you worked for Triton Battery,"

Henry continued, watching Morehouse in profile. "Wasn't Tom Cage the company doctor?"

The old man nodded, but he seemed a thousand miles away. Henry kept talking, trying to prod him. "Viola's husband was killed in Vietnam, just like Frank's older son. She got real close to her brother after that. She worried about the work Jimmy was doing. In February, Jimmy and Luther were attacked by the Double Eagles outside a drive-in. But then you know about that, don't you?"

Morehouse gave a sideways inclination of his head, but still he said nothing.

"People thought Jimmy and Luther had been killed that night, because they vanished for so long. But they were actually hiding out at a place called Freewoods, way out in the county." Henry started to mention the rumor he'd heard about how the Eagles lured Jimmy and Luther out of hiding, but he didn't want to risk alienating the old man further by bringing up a gang rape. "Six weeks later—one day before Frank was killed in that accident—they returned to Natchez. They were seen cruising the parking lots of the redneck bars, and then they disappeared. Viola's convinced that both Jimmy and Luther were kidnapped that night—a Wednesday—and murdered by the end of the week, probably out of revenge or rage over Frank's death. She swore to me that if Jimmy had been alive after that, he'd have contacted her. I believe that."

Morehouse looked at him, suddenly alert. "You talked to Viola?"

"I did." Henry thought of the old nurse, somehow retaining her dignity as she lay in her sister's house with scarcely enough flesh left on her bones to make an indentation on the mattress. "Twice, in fact."

"You flew up to Chicago?"

This question took Henry aback. Would Morehouse have asked that question if he knew Viola had been in Natchez for the last six weeks? "I didn't have to," Henry replied. "Viola was right here in Natchez."

The old man's eyes snapped to Henry, looking more alive than they had all day. "Say *what*?"

"Viola spent the past six weeks in Natchez. Lung cancer."

Morehouse was staring a hole through him. "Viola Turner came back to *Natchez*?"

"That's right." Henry paused before going on, trying to understand the surreal turn the conversation had taken.

Morehouse was staring in disbelief. "She was warned never to come back here!"

"Warned by whom, Glenn?"

"Who do you think? *Us*. If Viola ever came back, she'd be killed. That was the deal. Like a postponed death sentence. Commuted, or whatever."

At some level, Henry realized, he hadn't taken the force of the old death threat seriously enough. He recalled how quickly Shad Johnson had dismissed the idea of Double Eagle involvement in Viola's death, and he felt guilty. "Considering her cancer, Viola probably didn't much care about forty-year-old threats."

"Then she's lost her mind," Morehouse said, plainly speaking in the present tense. "I've got cancer myself, but I ain't *crazy*."

Henry kept silent, afraid of saying the wrong thing. Morehouse seemed to have no idea Viola was dead. Before Henry revealed that fact, he would draw out what information he could. "*Why* was Viola threatened, Glenn? Did she know who killed her brother?"

But Morehouse seemed to have sunk into himself again.

"If she'd known who killed Jimmy," Henry reasoned aloud, "she wouldn't have made it out of Natchez alive. Would she?"

"She damn near didn't," the old man muttered. "If it hadn't been for Ray Presley and Dr. Cage, she wouldn't have."

Henry raced through his mental files: Ray Presley had been a dirty cop in both Natchez and New Orleans. He had strong ties to the Marcello mob and was feared by everyone on both sides of the law. Stranger still, he'd been killed during Penn Cage's effort to solve Natchez's most famous civil rights murder, which had also happened in 1968.

"What did Ray Presley and Dr. Cage have to do with saving Viola?"

The old man touched a knuckle to his forehead as though to ward off some evil spirit. "Ray's dead, Henry. Best to pass over that bastard in silence." A strange urgency came into his eyes. "Are you going to talk to Viola again?"

Henry thought of the emaciated corpse from the video. "I don't know. Why?"

"If you do . . . you tell her I'm sorry. Okay? Tell her I didn't mean her no harm."

Morehouse had to be thinking about the rape. "What did you do to her, Glenn?"

Seeing dread in the old man's eyes, Henry decided to press ahead. "Did you rape her?"

Morehouse winced.

"On March twenty-seventh of sixty-eight," Henry said, "a rumor spread that Viola had been gang-raped by the Klan. I think you guys knew Jimmy and Luther wouldn't be able to keep hiding if they thought Viola was suffering in their place. Was that just a story, Glenn? Or did you guys really rape her?"

Morehouse struck out with one arm, as though to ward off a blow.

"You need to tell it, man. Let go of this thing. That's why you brought me here."

The old man clung to his silence like a shield.

"Viola wouldn't admit the rape to me," Henry said softly, "but I saw the pain in her eyes. You took a turn, didn't you?"

Morehouse's face had gone bone white, and his eyes looked wild.

Henry forced down his disgust and laid a hand on the old man's arm, hoping to appeal to his Baptist fundamentalism. "It's God's judgment you need to worry about, not Snake Knox. God already knows what you did. He wants to hear you own up to what you did, Glenn. That's what matters to Him."

Morehouse jerked his arm away and pulled the crocheted comforter over the lower half of his face. Only his eyes and nose showed, like those of a terrified child after a nightmare. To imagine this pathetic shell of a man brutalizing a proud young woman like Viola Turner sickened Henry; yet he knew now that it had happened.

"You just do what I asked you to do," Morehouse said through the crocheted yarn. "Tell Nurse Viola I never meant her no harm, and tell her to get back to Chicago. *Quick.* I'll pay her airfare if she needs it. She don't deserve what Snake and the others will do to her."

Present tense again. "I'm afraid I can't do that for you, Glenn."

"Why not?"

All Henry's senses kicked wide open, preparing to read the old man's reaction. "Because Viola's dead. Somebody killed her this morning."

The shock in the old man's eyes was so profound that Henry acquitted him of murder on the spot. Morehouse worked his jaw, trying to gum up some spit, but he couldn't seem to do it. The implications of his ignorance spun out in Henry's mind. If the Eagles *had* fulfilled their threat against Viola—and kept Morehouse out of it—then that meant they no longer trusted him. Had the old man realized this yet? Was he gauging the odds of his survival even now? Henry didn't think so. Casting his gaze desperately about the room, Morehouse looked like a man with a terrible sin lashed to his back, one that Viola's death had cursed him to carry into the afterlife.

Henry gently shook his arm. "The Eagles killed Jimmy and Luther back in sixty-eight, didn't they?"

Morehouse nodded like a man struck dumb.

Triumph surged through Henry's chest. He'd toiled for more than a decade to prove this. "Where are their bodies, Glenn? Tell me, man. For the sake of the families."

Morehouse stared into the flames as though hypnotized. The news of Viola's death had pushed him into some kind of fugue state. But Henry could no longer restrain himself. He stood over the recliner and glared down without a shred of mercy in his heart. "You were there when they died, weren't you? *Weren't you?*"

The old man's cheek twitched, but he held his stony silence.

"What did you do to them, Glenn? Is that who you saw crucified?"

"Damn your eyes!" Morehouse shouted, jabbing a fist up at Henry. *"You don't know a goddamn thing. Get out of my house!"*

"Why were they killed, Glenn? Why Jimmy and Luther?"

"They were goddamn Muslims, that's why! They was fomentin' a Muslim rebellion. Snake knew all about it. They was running guns and all kinds of other shit. Hand grenades, dope, you name it!"

Henry would have laughed, were the old man not so enraged. If the Knoxes had given credence to this kind of delusion, they were not only paranoid but stupid. "Jimmy Revels was no Muslim," he said with quiet conviction. "He was Roman Catholic. He sang in local churches. And he sure never ran any guns. He was a pacifist, for God's sake. That's verified in his navy record."

"If he was a pacifist, what was he doin' with a badass nigger like Luther Davis? Davis was a dope dealer and a gunrunner."

"Luther Davis served in Vietnam. Didn't that count for anything with you guys?"

Morehouse looked back at the fire. "I'll tell what it counted for with Snake. Both them boys had tattoos on their arms. Luther's said 'Army,' with an eagle under it. Jimmy's said 'USN,' with the anchor. Neither of them boys was wearing their tattoos when they died," Morehouse murmured. "Get the picture?"

Henry shuddered. He remembered the indigo anchor on Jimmy's arm. He'd seen it when the young vet had taught him R&B guitar riffs in the back of Albert's store. Henry hadn't realized that black skin would show tattoos until he saw Jimmy Revels's arm. "Are you saying Jimmy and Luther were skinned alive? Is that who you saw flayed?"

Morehouse shook his head. "Not like you're thinking. Just the tattoos. Snake said niggers wearing service tattoos was an abomination."

Henry felt like he might vomit. But more than this, he wanted to send Brody Royal to death row at Angola Prison. "Tell me how all this is connected. Tell me about Ray Presley and Dr. Cage. How could they save Viola?"

"It don't matter now," Morehouse whispered. "Not if she's dead. But if you want to prove who killed them two boys, you find those tattoos."

Henry recalled some of the grisly trophies taken by serial killers whose cases he'd followed while working as a reporter. "Are you saying those tattoos still exist? Is that even possible?"

"Oh, yeah. Anybody who knows about tanning can keep a thing like that for a hundred years. Just like a scalp or a hide. It's all skin."

"Damn it, Glenn, think about what I said before. With one taped statement, you could put an end to all this. You could have Snake and the others behind bars by suppertime tomorrow. You could give all those poor victims' families peace. And you could save your own soul. Isn't that why you called me here?"

Desperation shone from the old man's eyes. "I'll think about it. It ain't just myself I'm worried about, you know? I've got family, too. I've got a son, plus two grandkids. They don't live here, and they don't much care whether I live or die. But I care about them. And Snake knows that."

"Glenn, you can defang Snake Knox any time you want. Brody Royal, too. They won't be able to hurt your family."

Morehouse looked at Henry in disbelief. "You ain't heard a damn word I've said, have you? Frank and Snake had *sons*, Henry, and most are on the wrong side of the law. This shit don't die. It goes down through the generations. Look what happened to Viola! Don't assume Snake done it. He would have *wanted* to, but he could've sent any number of guys to do that for him."

Henry thought about Shad Johnson and his quest to convict Tom Cage. "You've got to tell the DA what you know, Glenn. That's the only way to protect yourself. If Snake ordered Viola's death, and he didn't let you know about it, then he already doesn't trust you."

"And why should he?" Morehouse took hold of Henry's wrist. "Listen to me. Ain't no John Law gonna jail Snake. He's got protection."

"What kind of protection? Brody Royal?"

A curtain fell over Morehouse's eyes. "We don't have time to go into that."

"No?" Henry couldn't bring himself to leave the house when there was so much to be learned. Yet his neural circuits felt overloaded. He'd forgotten to ask anything about Joe Louis Lewis, the missing busboy. Yet of all the unanswered questions sparking in his mind, the most fantastic found its way to his vocal cords. "Answer me one question. I know of at least three people that Snake Knox told he shot Martin Luther King. I always assumed that was bullshit. Just a drunk redneck talking. But the FBI won't comment one way or the other. And photographic evidence from the scene suggests that the shooter fired from the mechanical penthouse above the elevator shaft of the Fred P. Gattis Building, not the bathroom of the rooming house across the street, where James Earl Ray was. Before I go, I want you to look me in the eye and tell me Snake Knox is full of shit."

Morehouse's eyes had grown round and white. "I'm only going to tell you one thing about Snake, Henry. The motherfucker is crazy, but crazy like a fox. What he's done or ain't done, nobody knows but Snake and the devil himself. And in case you didn't know, he served as a sniper in Korea."

A chill ran along Henry's arms.

"You watch your ass after you leave here," Morehouse said, in the tone of a fellow soldier. "Don't stray far from cover."

Henry glanced anxiously at his watch. "Please give me the bodies, Glenn. Without the bodies, Jimmy and Luther stay a kidnapping on the books."

The old man shook his head. "Not today. You ain't proved I can trust you yet. And I don't want to read all this in the *Beacon* on Thursday. You prove I can trust you, I'll tell you some things that'll scorch your eardrums."

Henry's frustration finally boiled over. "I won't print a damned thing you've told me! I swear it."

Morehouse glanced at the wall clock. "Wilma's gonna come up the driveway any minute. If she does, we're both dead."

Henry stood up and looked down at the old man. "No, *you're* dead. Where did you dump those boys? I've heard the Jericho Hole, by Lake St. John, and I've heard the Bone Tree. Which was it? Or was it someplace else?"

"I don't know where they are, Henry. I never did. The Bone Tree ain't even a real thing. Don't do this, man. Wilma would sell me out to Snake in a minute." Every passing second was pushing Morehouse deeper into panic. "I'm *beggin'* you," he pleaded. "Get out now."

The cell phone in the old man's hand pinged. He peered at the LCD and his face went blotchy with panic. "Wilma's down at the end of the road! Her dog got loose while she was gone, and she's trying to get him into her truck. She'll be here any minute!"

Henry wanted to push the old man to the wall, but if he did, he'd never get another interview with him. "I'll go. But only if you'll call me later."

"It's too late!" Morehouse wailed. "You can't get out without her seeing you now!"

Henry thought about the topography outside the house. "Are you sure there's no other way out? I came in a four-wheel drive."

Relief washed over the old man's face. "Drive right through the ditch at this end of the road, then head for the tree line. Park behind the trees until you see Wilma come in. Then you can work your way east toward the river. There's a dirt track over that way that'll get you to the levee road. But you gotta go *now*."

Henry stuffed his Moleskine in his pocket and trotted to the door. "If you don't call me before midnight, I'm coming back here."

"I will, if I can. Otherwise tomorrow. *Go!*"

Henry opened the door and glanced up the gravel road. Seeing no vehicles, he ran to his Explorer. Ten seconds later he was nose-down in a ravine, fighting mud and gravity. With a lurch the Explorer slammed to a stop. For thirty awful seconds, his worn tires spun and whined in vain, and Henry sweated like he was being chased by a demon, not a leather-faced old woman. As his heart thundered in his chest, he realized that what he'd heard during the past hour had altered his life forever, as it would soon alter the world. He hadn't even begun to process all that Morehouse had told him. Henry was no conspiracy theorist; he was the opposite, in fact. But the look in Morehouse's eyes when he'd asked about Snake Knox and Martin Luther King had sunk into the marrow of Henry's bones. With a squawk and a stink of burning rubber, the tires finally caught and carried Henry over the lip of the ditch. After one last glance at his rearview mirror, he gunned his motor and made for the tree line across the empty field.

CHAPTER 13

FORTY MILES DOWN the Mississippi River, Billy Knox waited in the study of the Valhalla Exotic Hunting Reserve, which his father stubbornly insisted on calling by its original name: Fort Knox. The massive compound straddled the boundary between Lusahatcha County, Mississippi, and West Feliciana Parish, Louisiana, both of which lay on the eastern bank of the Mississippi River. Though much of Valhalla was surrounded and protected by impassable swampland for part of the year, a fourteen-foot-high fence kept trespassers out and valuable game species in. Trophy heads of African antelope, Canadian moose, and whitetail deer jutted from every wall in the lodge, while grizzly bears and alligators guarded the corners with lifelike menace. Behind Billy's chair, a seven-hundred-pound hog with a spear in its back prepared for a charge. The Teddy Roosevelt décor pegged Billy's cheese meter, but he hadn't gotten up the nerve to take any of it down. His cousin Forrest liked the lodge exactly the way it was—the way his father Frank had liked it—and Billy didn't fancy the consequences of desecrating the memory of Frank Knox.

Billy liked to think of himself as a redneck renaissance man. From humble beginnings, he'd raised himself to a plane where he was able to contemplate spending $250,000 to hire Jimmy Buffett to perform at his upcoming forty-fourth birthday party. Not many men could do that. The fact that he'd broken a multitude of laws to attain his present position was of no consequence. The lesson of history was that every great fortune was built upon a great crime, and great men from medieval popes to modern philanthropists had succeeded by taking this maxim to heart, just as Billy had done.

The drug trade had been Billy's primary engine of success, but over the past five years he'd expanded into real estate, oil, timber, and hunting equipment. He also produced a reality hunting show for television,

one carried on five separate cable channels. Top NASCAR drivers, NFL
players, and country music stars had appeared on the show with him,
hunting everything from alligators and razorbacks to the prize bucks
that roamed the wooded hills of Valhalla. More than a few admirers
had observed that Billy fit right in with that elite: with his dirty blond
hair and ice-blue eyes, he looked like the lead singer of a 1970s southern
rock band. He exuded a daredevil aura, much as his father once had,
and society women found his charm irresistible.

At bottom, Billy thought of himself as a modern-day buccaneer,
using his wiles to circumvent onerous, puritanical laws passed to keep
red-blooded Americans from enjoying themselves. An avid reader of
the maritime novels of Patrick O'Brian, he'd bought a thirty-five-foot
sloop and christened her *Aubrey* to fulfill his most cherished fantasy.
Thanks to Hurricane Katrina, however, the *Aubrey* now lay on her side
in a pine barren north of Biloxi, wrecked beyond salvage. But today
that was the least of Billy's problems. For he shared more than his blond
locks with Captain Jack Aubrey. Like Jack, whose Radical father caused
him no end of problems by intemperate behavior in Parliament and in
private life, Billy Knox had been cursed with a father who bowed to no
authority but his own.

When Snake Knox finally walked into the study and sat across from
his son's desk, he wore a look of sullen resentment. That look had been
his default expression ever since Billy ascended to the alpha position (at
least nominally) in the Knox organization. Billy preferred to focus on
Sonny Thornfield, who sat to Snake's right and maintained an expression
of sober deference, despite being more than thirty years older than Billy.

"We gonna discuss this?" Snake muttered. "Or we just gonna sit
here and waste the fuckin' day?"

Billy sighed with forbearance. At times like this, he wondered why
he and Forrest bothered with geriatric crew leaders. Managing them
often felt like riding herd on a bunch of old women, except old women
didn't generally kill people who backtalked them. On the other hand,
old men made excellent managers for the front businesses required to
keep a successful drug empire running. As a rule, the suspicion of cops
and DAs operated inversely with the age of the men they encountered.
The unprecedented expansion of the meth trade was starting to change
this built-in biological bias, but on balance, geriatric family members

beat the hell out of any punks Billy could hire on the open market. Besides, the trust factor alone was worth whatever hassle working with family brought with it. The loyalty of his father's old Klan crew could not be questioned. Yet paradoxically, it was the fanatical loyalty of the Double Eagles that had created Billy's current dilemma.

"Tell me again why you think the only solution is to kill poor old Glenn Morehouse," he said.

"Glenn swore an oath," Snake snapped. "Same as we all did, he knew the penalty, and that's what he's got to pay."

Billy smiled enough to show his white teeth. "I hear you, Pop." Pride meant a lot to these old men, so he tried to tread carefully around their feelings when he could. On the other hand, he couldn't let antiquated notions of honor put his livelihood at risk. "Tell me more about this woman who told you Morehouse is talking."

"Sandy's a neighbor of Glenn's sister," Sonny said. "She lives at the head of the gravel road that runs over to Wilma's place. She's Duke Williams's widow. Reliable."

"And Wilma wasn't at the house," Snake repeated. "Glenn sent her on an errand so he could meet Sexton without her there."

"That's pure supposition," Billy observed.

"Huh?"

"For all you know, Henry was staking out that road on his own hook, and when he saw the sister leave, he ambushed poor old Glenn."

"You've got a point," Sonny admitted.

"Bull*shit*," Snake hissed. "Henry's never spoke a word to Glenn in his life before today, far as I know. And he's had a thousand chances. I'll lay you a hundred to one Glenn called him. And if Glenn spills what he knows, you can kiss all this good-bye." Snake waved his arms around to take in their opulent surroundings. "Jimmy Buffett won't be out on the deck playing 'Margaritaville' while you rub some LSU cheerleader's ass. You'll be sweatin' in your bunk under a big buck nigger in Angola."

Billy took a deep breath and tried to rein in his temper. Opening his desk drawer, he took out a tin of Copenhagen and stuffed a pinch under his bottom lip. The two old men watched as he let the glass-infused snuff abrade his lip and release calming nicotine into his blood. "And you're so sure that you're willing to kill your childhood buddy without giving him a chance to tell his side?"

"Oh, I'll give him a chance," Snake said. "Just before I slice his cods off."

"Why would Glenn betray you guys after all these years? He did some killing himself, didn't he?"

"Damn straight," said Snake. "Worse than that."

Billy knew Snake's taste for sadism all too well; he didn't want any details.

"Glenn drowned an FBI informant in acid," Sonny said. "Out at the Triton plant."

Billy shook his head in amazement. "And you really think he would admit that to a reporter?"

Snake cut his eyes at Sonny, and Billy saw some meaning pass between the two older men. Then Snake said, "When a man starts feeling death's cold breath on the back of his neck, that sets him thinking. The sins he's been carryin' suddenly seem to weigh twice as much as before."

"You speaking from experience?" Billy asked skeptically.

"Kiss my ass, boy. It takes some intestinal fortitude to walk tall all the way to the grave. And Glenn was always short in that department. If Frank was there to give orders, Glenn would beat his way through a brick wall with nothing but his fists. But leave him alone, you was liable to find him huddled in the corner crying about the dark. He's like a big baby."

"Sonny?" Billy prompted.

Sonny cocked his head and spoke softly. "I've been thinking about what you said earlier. That Henry might have ambushed Glenn. How would Henry know to go to Glenn on his own? We didn't exactly advertise our membership."

"Damned straight," Snake said. "There it is."

Billy laughed, though he knew his father would hate him for it. "Bull*shit*. How many times did I see you show that JFK coin of yours around when I was a kid? The one with the bullet holes in it. How many gold pieces got flashed around at family gatherings like Super Bowl rings?"

Snake averted his eyes, but Billy went on mercilessly. "Twenty men in your damn outfit. How many kids did they have? How many wives and ex-wives? You think they didn't know any names of other members?

A guy like Henry Sexton—a guy who grew up around here—I'll bet he could get every Eagle's name inside of six months, and maybe quicker. I'll bet he's had most of your names for years."

"No way," Sonny insisted, his chin quivering. "If he did, he'd already have printed 'em in that rag of his."

Billy shook his head. "Not necessarily. I've done my own checking into Henry Sexton. He's playing a long game."

Sonny leaned closer.

Billy spat dip juice into an empty shot glass. "Henry's in constant contact with the FBI. Field agents call him for regular updates on the stories he's working. And the stories he's working are *your* old glory cases. Albert Norris, Joe Louis Lewis, Jimmy and Luther. Now, that's not the end of the world—not so far—but we don't want the Bureau digging any deeper than they already have. Not while you're on *my* payroll. And not when the attorney general's putting eighty-year-old men away for murders that happened when I was in diapers."

"Preacher Killen was a dumbass," Snake grumbled. "That's why Frank never brought him into the Eagles. Ernest Avants wasn't much better. We got to shut Glenn up *ASAP*, Bill. And he's not the only one. That goddamn reporter—"

Billy held up his hand to silence Snake. "Don't even go there, Pop."

Sonny said, "How do you know about Henry Sexton's contacts with the FBI?"

Billy smiled. "That's my business, Uncle Son. But take it as gospel."

Billy wasn't related to Sonny by blood, but Sonny appreciated the term of affection.

"As I was *about to say,*" Snake muttered with a glare at Sonny, "it ain't only Glenn we need to take care of. It's time to shut down Henry Sexton, too."

Billy looked sharply at his father, but Snake pushed on regardless. "We shoulda done it five years back, before he printed half the shit he has already. And you know it, William."

Billy laid his palms on the desk with restraint. "Are you going senile or what? The *Beacon* is a pissant weekly that people forget as soon as they wrap the garbage in it. But if you kill Henry Sexton, the goddamn lid will blow off this place. Penn Cage's girlfriend will fill up the *Natchez Examiner* with Double Eagle stories. Then we'll get Jerry Mitchell down from the *Clarion-Ledger*. That bastard got the Medgar Evers case reopened, and he'll jump on your asses with both feet if you give him an excuse. We've got too much to hide for that!"

When Snake opened his mouth to argue, Billy rotated his chair and looked at the huge razorback mounted on a polished stand of swamp ash standing behind him. The kids in the family called it "Hogzilla." His cousin Forrest had killed that hog; the spear he'd used still jutted from the monster's back like the sword of a matador. The taxidermist had done a superb job: the hog's eyes blazed, and its tusks gleamed like the deadly weapons they were. Billy often wondered at the courage it must have required to take on such an animal with only a spear and a horse. *Seven hundred pounds of pissed-off razorback—*

"Hey!" Snake barked. "You gonna just sit there with your back to us, like Elvis?"

After a deep breath, Billy turned, carefully spat tobacco juice into the shot glass, then looked up at his father with startling coldness. "Before we dispense with your insane proposition, I want to know something." He jabbed a finger at his father. "And I want a straight answer."

Snake regarded his son with some emotion between suspicion and malice, but Sonny nodded like a faithful lieutenant.

"When I heard Viola Turner died this morning, I thought of you first. So I made a couple of phone calls. And Sheriff Billy Byrd told me that Dr. Cage is going to be charged with that murder."

Snake nodded, a little smugly, Billy thought. "That's what we heard, too."

"I know you guys went out to see Viola a couple weeks back. A friendly reminder, you said, that she needed to stay quiet until the end."

"That's right," Sonny confirmed. "That's all we done, Bill."

Snake glared at his comrade.

Billy let the silence drag, but his father gave up nothing. "Be that as it may," Billy went on, "I'm asking you two, here and now, *did you kill that woman?*"

Snake almost came up out of his chair. "You just said they're charging Dr. Cage for murder! You think they'd do that for the hell of it?"

"They might do it for some reason of their own," Billy said calmly. "That black DA hates Penn Cage. And Billy Byrd's got no love for the doc. But you didn't answer my question, Pop. Did you two have anything to do with that old woman's death?"

Sonny started to speak, but Snake shushed him with a hiss.

"Talk to me, Uncle Sonny," Billy commanded. "Don't pay Daddy no mind. This is too important."

"We'd been watching her some," Sonny admitted. "And we might have done it, Bill. She talked to Henry a couple of times, you know. But he didn't print anything about it, and you'd told me you had a way of knowing ahead of time if Henry was going to print anything too bad. So we laid off."

Snake got to his feet, reached into his shirt, lifted a leather cord from around his neck, and dropped his JFK half dollar onto Billy's desk. Billy saw the two familiar holes in the coin that had fascinated him since childhood. For Billy, the sharp, circular rim of that bullet hole in JFK's pristine profile always evoked the horror of the Zapruder film.

"I'd have damn sure killed Viola," Snake said, "if Dr. Cage hadn't done it first. And I wouldn't have asked your permission, neither. That's Eagle business, and it's got nothing to do with you."

Billy shook his head wearily, wondering why his father hadn't mellowed with age, like most older men he knew.

"That bitch made a promise," Snake said, as if reciting holy writ. "She knew the penalty if she broke it, and she came back to Natchez anyway. She called down her own punishment, same as Glenn. They took the choice out of our hands."

Billy leaned forward and flipped up the half dollar with a fingernail. "You're damned lucky Dr. Cage did you that favor," he said softly. "*If* he did."

"He did," Sonny said. "I swear it, Billy."

"Good. Because if you two killed that old woman without clearing it first, Forrest would drop the hammer on you." Billy looked pointedly at his father. "It don't mean a thing to Forrest that you're blood, either. You know that."

"Did Forrest call you about Viola?" Sonny asked anxiously. "Did he say something?"

"No discussion of Forrest," Billy said. "Not even here."

Sonny nodded quickly, but Snake looked furious. "I *came* here to ask permission, goddamn it—on Glenn and Henry—and all you've done is sit there and jabber about being careful. And now you threaten us?"

Billy wondered if his father's posturing was a front, if Snake had actually killed Viola and simply lucked out that Dr. Cage had somehow been implicated. But unless Sonny betrayed Snake and told Billy the truth, he'd never know for sure. It didn't matter now. So long as Dr. Cage went to jail for Viola's murder, the threat to his organization would be neutralized.

"Uncle Sonny," Billy said, returning to the reason for their meeting. "No Double Eagle has ever talked to any reporter. Do you really believe Glenn Morehouse wants to be the first?"

Sonny made a point of not looking at Snake. "God help us, Bill, but I'm afraid your daddy's right. Glenn's done got religion. He's scared. What does he care about prison? Or us? He's tryin' to get right with God. Wilma says he's been ravin' when he's on his medication. I think he'll probably spill every gol-dern thing he knows before he's done. He might've already done it. We're liable to read our whole life stories in this Thursday's *Beacon*."

"If we don't have FBI agents knocking on our doors tonight," Snake added.

At this prospect, the first worm of anxiety burrowed into Billy's gut. He fished a Xanax from his pocket and crushed the bitter tablet between his teeth.

"I wish I felt different," Sonny concluded, "but there it is. Glenn could put us all in Angola, Bill. You and Forrest, too. Even Mr. Royal."

"All right," Billy said, swallowing the powdered pill with a grimace. "All right. What do you old outlaws want to do?"

"An oath is an oath," Snake declared. "There's rules. *Pre*scriptions and *pro*scriptions, as Frank used to say."

Billy stirred at the mention of the blood oath his uncle had created back in 1964. "Let me get this straight. Poor Glenn has one foot in the grave, but you two want to carry out some medieval penalty on him? One that'll make the front page of every paper from here to Los Angeles?"

"That's the law," Sonny said with imperious certainty. "That's what Frank laid down for traitors, and everybody agreed."

"Well, that's not gonna happen. *If* Glenn is a traitor, he's got to die. But dead is dead, no matter how you get there."

"Of course it matters," Snake argued, shaking his head with exaggerated passion. "Glenn was *one of us.* Don't you see?"

"No. I don't."

Snake's eyes widened in indignation. "What about *honor,* boy?"

"Honor don't cover the payroll, Pop."

Snake's face had gone so red that Billy feared he might burst a blood vessel. "We've *got* to make an example for everybody else."

Billy thought this over. His father had a point, but on balance, the risk wasn't worth it. "The goal here is survival. However Glenn dies, the people who matter will get the message. But he's not *going* to die unless you can confirm you're right. I'll do some checking on my end. You guys can confront Glenn directly. But"—Billy pointed at Sonny—"he only dies if *you* believe he's betrayed us. Got it?"

Sonny gave him a casual but sincere salute.

"And even if Glenn *has* crossed over, you've got to forget all that code-of-silence crap. He needs to go gently into that good night."

Snake looked perplexed. "What the hell are you talkin' about?"

"He needs to choke to death on a Hall's Mentho-Lyptus, or fall down in the shower. He doesn't need his throat cut by two guys who think they're costarring in a sequel to *Goodfellas.*"

Snake gritted his teeth, then said defiantly: "This ain't the way Frank would have handled it."

Billy was glad he'd eaten the Xanax. "Uncle Frank's dead," he said mildly. "Been dead thirty-seven years."

"That don't matter," Snake said softly. "You know it don't."

"*Forrest* isn't dead," Billy said more firmly. "You want to take this up with him?" Billy slid his chair to the right, opening their line of sight to the big razorback. "'Cause I can tell you exactly how he feels about it."

Sonny swallowed audibly, his Adam's apple bobbing in his wrinkled throat.

"This ain't right," Snake said, but the defiance had gone out of him.

"Are we clear on what's going to happen and not happen?" Billy asked.

Sonny nodded. Snake took longer, but he eventually nodded his assent, as Billy had known he would. These men had had their time in power, but that time was long gone. Mentioning Forrest to them was like a Wehrmacht officer mentioning the Gestapo to a German line soldier.

Billy pushed back from the table with a frustrated sigh. "We're done here, boys. Let me know how it goes."

Snake slid his half dollar off the table, slipped it back over his head, then gave his son a sullen glare. "You figure Brody feels the same way about this as you and Forrest?"

Anger flashed through Billy like a stroke of lightning. He stood and looked down at his father. "What the hell does Brody Royal have to do with any of this?"

Snake said nothing, but Billy saw more smugness in the curl of his father's lip.

"Not a damn thing," Sonny said, grabbing Snake's arm and pulling him to the study door.

Billy stayed on his feet and watched them go. He hoped to hell Brody Royal wasn't under the delusion that he was free to whack people on his own anymore. That era had come and gone, only some men refused to see it. And the more power they had, the longer it seemed to take them. When the main door banged shut, Billy sat down and pulled up the Web page of Jimmy Buffett's agent. But his mind was no longer on his birthday party. It was on Viola Turner, and all the men who might have had a motive to kill her.

CHAPTER 14

THOUGH MOST OF the staff had left the *Beacon* office, Henry had stayed at his desk, working patiently at his computer. The Morehouse interview had forced him to rethink his entire view of the Double Eagle cases, and also to rejigger his priorities. The old Klansman had confessed to or described at least ten murders, and he'd hinted at others, but one confession had left Henry in a dilemma. He needed to inform the FBI that Jerry Dugan, a Bureau informant, had been murdered at Triton Battery in 1964. But doing so would instantly create problems. The Bureau would want to know Henry's source, and that he could not reveal. Also, he usually published new information within a day of talking to the FBI, yet he'd promised Morehouse that he wouldn't publish anything until death took him. Who could predict when that would occur? Morehouse appeared to be at death's door, yet Henry had known many cancer patients to far outlive even the most optimistic prognoses.

Then there was the question of missing corpses. Of the dozen-odd murders Henry was investigating, four involved missing men, and without a corpus delicti, a murder case was stillborn, almost without exception. He'd never doubted that Pooky Wilson, Joe Louis Lewis, Jimmy Revels, and Luther Davis were dead, and today Morehouse had confirmed his instincts (with the exception of Lewis, whom Henry had forgotten to ask about before time ran out). Yet Henry still had no clue to the location of the bodies. The Jericho Hole and the Bone Tree had always been rumored dump sites, yet Morehouse had discounted both. Dragging the Jericho Hole was beyond Henry's resources, and while he had a fresh lead on the Bone Tree, finding this near-mythical totem had eluded everyone who'd tried it since the 1960s.

Something about the murders of Revels and Davis haunted Glenn Morehouse in a way that the other killings did not, Henry was sure. He suspected it was the gang rape of Jimmy's sister Viola, in which

Morehouse had almost surely participated. The old Eagle had exposed the depraved brutality of the Revels-Davis murders by revealing that the boys' military tattoos had been cut from their bodies (after death, Henry hoped) and might even have been kept as trophies. More disturbing still, Morehouse had mumbled half coherently about witnessing deaths by flaying, burning, drowning, and crucifixion. Yet he hadn't specified who had suffered these fates. Henry had always heard that Pooky Wilson and Joe Louis Lewis had suffered the most cruel treatment, but now he wondered whether Revels and Davis had endured equally horrific deaths.

More germane to the present, Glenn Morehouse seemed absolutely sure that Snake Knox had murdered Viola Turner to fulfill their decades-old threat, or else had ordered it done. But as for why this threat had originally been made, the old Eagle had refused to speak. It might simply be that she could identify the men who'd raped her, but Henry suspected that Viola had specific knowledge about her brother's death. Most puzzling was Morehouse's assertion that Viola never would have made it to Chicago alive had it not been for Ray Presley and Dr. Tom Cage. *How had a dirty cop (and inveterate racist) teamed up with a beloved physician to save Viola Turner from the vengeance of the Double Eagles?*

All told, today's interview had generated enough leads to keep an FBI field office busy for six months, and Henry felt overwhelmed. Simply reviewing and prioritizing his notes would take a full night's work, and he was exhausted already. But the more he reflected on the day's revelations, the more certain he became that he should call Penn Cage. After only twenty minutes with Shadrach Johnson, Henry had sensed that the Natchez DA intended to try to convict Tom Cage for Viola's murder. And that Henry could not let stand.

He was about to call Penn from his desk phone when his cell phone rang. The LCD read: G. MOREHOUSE. Scarcely able to believe that the old man had fulfilled his promise, Henry hit the answer button with shaking hands.

"Hello?" he said, filled with irrational fear that he would hear the voice of Wilma Deen (or God forbid, Snake Knox) checking to find out whom Henry had called earlier.

"It's me," whispered Glenn Morehouse.

"Are you okay?" Henry asked. "Can you talk?"

"Wilma's back in her room watching TV. I think she took a sleeping pill, so I took the chance."

"What's on your mind, Glenn?" He was half afraid that Morehouse would try to deny everything he'd said this morning.

"I been thinking about all we said today. About Viola, mostly. It pains me something fierce to look back on all that. I know you don't understand, but . . . things was just different then."

"I know," Henry said, thinking Morehouse sounded different than he had face-to-face, smaller and less imposing. He wondered if the old Klansman had taken a pill himself.

"You asked me about the bodies," Morehouse said. "Where they might be."

"Do you know?"

"Them places you mentioned? The Jericho Hole and the Bone Tree? You won't go far wrong if you check them out."

Henry's pulse picked up. "Are you saying the Bone Tree really exists?"

"I wish it didn't." Morehouse wheezed, then burped. He sounded drunk. "But it does. At least it did about fifteen years ago. That was the last time I saw it."

The hair rose on Henry's neck and forearms. "Can you tell me how to get there?"

"Naw. The times I went there it was night, and I was in a boat. I ain't never been good at directions like that. Everything looks the same in the swamp. Frank or Snake always took me out there. Sonny might remember the way."

"Sonny Thornfield?"

"Shit, Henry. You got me talking too much."

"You're doing the right thing, brother. You know it. Surely you can tell me something about where that tree is."

"Lusahatcha Swamp. But tellin' you to hunt for a cypress tree back in there is like telling you to go outside on my five acres and find one blade of grass that has my initials wrote on it."

"Not quite. Death leaves traces, Glenn. Skeletal remains. Corpses put out gases caused by decay, other things."

Morehouse gave a hollow laugh. "Even if they dumped a corpse in there yesterday, you wouldn't have a prayer. That swamp bubbles out methane twenty-four hours a day. All manner of creatures been killin' and dyin' in there every minute for a million years. And forty-year-old bones have either rotted or been shit out by hogs and alligators. Can't nobody show you that tree except somebody who's been there. And anybody who's been there who *would* have showed it to you . . . they died there."

"Does anyone besides the Double Eagles know where it is?"

"Some of the nigras down in Lusahatcha County, supposedly, but they wouldn't go there for a million bucks. If you go down there a-lookin', watch yourself. Because they'll know. Nothing moves down there that those boys don't know about."

"I went down there once with a guide, but I didn't find anything."

"Then you were lucky. If you go back, take the National Guard with you."

"What about the Jericho Hole? Over the years, I've heard rumors that ten different bodies were dumped in there."

"Might have been. That's a deep old hole."

"Were Luther and Jimmy buried together?"

"Who said anything about *buried*? They're not together. I can tell you that much."

Henry forced himself to think back to the interview. "You wanted to tell me something about that plane crash this morning. The midair collision. Do you think Snake risked his own life to kill Dr. Robb by flying his plane into Robb's? Crazy or not, no pilot can control the physics of a midair collision."

Morehouse laughed. "Man, I once saw Snake jump off a two-story building because somebody offered him fifty bucks. You hear me? But think about that so-called collision, Henry. Nobody saw it but Snake and his nephew. There was heavy fog. Weren't no tower at all. How do you know there even *was* a collision?"

"I've thought of that. Snake could simply have sabotaged Robb's plane, then banged up his own wing with a hammer after the other plane crashed. Snake's plane was hardly damaged. As long as his nephew confirmed the midair collision, nobody was going to question their story."

"Yessir. That's about the size of it."

"Four people died in that crash, Glenn. One girl was only twenty-one years old. Would Snake really have murdered three innocent people just to kill Dr. Robb?"

"If Snake thought Lee Robb was gonna put him in jail, he'd have machine-gunned the man in a crowd of nuns on Sunday morning. Look at who was on that plane when it went down. Then look at who was *supposed* to be on it. Hell . . . I done give you enough to work it out, Henry. I need to go."

"Wait!" Henry felt an almost hysterical reluctance to let Morehouse off the phone. His panic was irrational; surely they could talk again tomorrow. But his years of experience were telling him one thing: *Your source is talking. The faucet is flowing, and it might never flow this way again.* "Just a couple more questions—please."

"Wilma's program goes off in five minutes. Make it fast."

Henry checked his watch: six minutes to the bottom of the hour. "The Natchez DA seems to think Tom Cage killed Viola Turner."

"Dr. Cage? Bullshit."

"What about a mercy killing?"

"Well . . . I can see that, I guess. If Dr. Cage would pay me that kind of visit, I might be obliged. A painless end ain't the worst thing in the world. Just like a loyal old dog. Only I ain't been so loyal."

"Do you know of any reason Dr. Cage would kill Viola to keep her quiet?"

"What? Hell, no. Dr. Cage couldn't do that, even if he had a reason. It was Snake, I tell you. Prob'ly Sonny, too. They still run together, you know. They're in business together."

Henry had heard rumors that some former Eagles were involved in the local meth trade, which had been exploding over the past few years. "Really?" he said, feigning ignorance. "I thought Snake had his crop-dusting service, and Sonny has a used car lot."

Morehouse barked a drunken laugh. "That's rich, boy. Their real business is dope. You didn't know that?"

"I've heard some rumors. I didn't put much credence in them."

"Snake's son Billy is the biggest goddamn meth dealer in the state."

"Snake and Sonny work for Billy Knox?"

"Yep. They're in the transport end of things. Airplanes and a car lot. Don't take a brain surgeon to figure that out, does it?"

"So Snake and Sonny would have the knowledge to try to fake a suicide with drugs?"

Another inebriated laugh. "I'd be surprised if they ain't done that a bunch of times in their line of work."

"Where does Billy live?"

"Billy's got houses all over, man. Land, too. And he ain't never even been *arrested* in this state. Which there's a reason for, you know. Those guys are protected. You gotta be, to stay in that business. Just like whores."

"Who protects them, Glenn? Brody Royal?"

"No. Billy's cousin. Forrest shields their operation and thins out their competition every few months."

"Forrest Knox? The state policeman?"

"Forrest ain't just a trooper, Henry. He's the director of the goddamn Criminal Investigations Bureau. And every man who works for the Knoxes knows the law, same as we knew with Frank. You threaten the group, you die. Law of the jungle."

Henry checked his watch. "When can we speak again, Glenn? Face-to-face?"

"That depends on Wilma. And on how long I live."

"How long do the doctors give you?"

An awkward silence stretched into black emptiness. Then Morehouse spoke in a cracked voice. "A month, maybe, my oncologist said."

Henry wrote "30 days?" on the pad beside his computer. Looking down at the note, it struck him for the first time how devastating was Morehouse's plight. The empty silence between them—which a moment ago had seemed like the vast reaches of space—contracted until Henry felt like a boy holding a tin can on the end of a wire stretched between two tree houses. And the boy holding the other can was on the verge of losing whatever grip he still had on himself.

"Are you there?" Henry asked tentatively. "Are you okay, Glenn?"

A single wracking sob came through the phone.

"What's the matter, man?"

"They made me do those things, Henry," said a childlike voice.

"What things?"

"They made me hurt Jimmy. And Viola. I *hated* it."

"Who made you do that?"

"Snake, mostly. But they all pushed me. To scare people, and hurt 'em. Ever since we was kids. Just because I'm big. But Snake knew I couldn't stand up to him. Nobody could."

Henry swallowed hard. "What did Snake make you do, Glenn?"

"I can't say it."

"Yes, you can. Let it go, brother."

Another sob. Then the old man croaked, "Unnatural things. Sins against God. Like in Leviticus."

Henry shuddered at the images this conjured, but also at the raw pain in the man's voice. "Did you kill Jimmy Revels, Glenn?"

"No. I couldn't of done that. That boy was different. Whenever Snake hit or cut Luther, Jimmy acted like it hurt him worse than it did Luther. Which was crazy, cause Revels was a skinny little thing, and Luther was a damn gorilla. And—when we had our way with Viola . . . Jesus."

The stunned numbness of the earlier interview had returned. "Wait a second. Are you saying Jimmy and Luther saw Viola raped? How could that be?"

"Don't you know *anything,* Henry? Snake went crazy after Frank died. He sent some boys to grab Viola again. He claimed it was to make them boys talk, and then to shut her up, but he just wanted her again. And them boys didn't *know* nothing, Henry. Nothing Snake wanted to hear, no ways."

Henry was "gobsmacked," as an English reporter he knew would say. "If Viola witnessed so much, why on earth did Snake let her live?"

"I already told you that."

"Ray Presley and Dr. Cage?"

"Yeah. Jesus . . . I took too many pills. I ain't used to this pain patch they got me on."

Henry sensed that he was going to have to wait until the next inter-view to get to the bottom of this story. They'd already passed the time limit Morehouse had set on their conversation. But he had to make one more stab at the case that meant the most to him—

"Wilma?" Morehouse said sharply.

Henry's breath caught in his throat. The silence lasted so long that Henry thought Morehouse had hung up. But after some indeterminate delay, Glenn whispered, "Did you hear that?"

"I didn't hear anything."

"You didn't hear a click?"

"No. I think we're fine. But we'd better go. Her show must be over."

"Wait . . . I still hear her TV. Listen to me, Henry. You're a good ole boy. I know you mean well. But you need to start paying attention. They know where you live, and where your mama lives, too."

Henry's face and palms went cold. "My mother?"

"How you think they operate, son? They hit you where you're soft."

"Who exactly are you talking about? Snake?"

"All of 'em. Snake, Sonny, Billy, Forrest . . . even Brody and his son-in-law. Don't kid yourself. You were right about that flamethrower, too. They've still got it. You hear me? It still works. And that's a shitty way to die. I wouldn't wish it on a Jap."

"Glenn—"

"There's one more thing. Something I need to clear up. I lied to you about something today. Something big."

Henry's heart thumped. "What's that?"

"About Jimmy and Luther. I told you Frank picked them because they was black Muslims, running guns."

"I knew that wasn't true. I always knew Jimmy was the real target, because of his civil rights work."

Morehouse wheezed into the phone. "If you think that, you're just as dumb as I am."

"What do you mean?"

"Jimmy Revels wasn't the real target."

Henry felt like he'd been punched in the gut. "Then who was? Luther Davis?"

"*Hell*, no."

"Glenn . . . what the hell are you tryin' to say?"

"The real target was Bobby Kennedy."

Henry gulped. "*What?*"

"Senator Robert Francis Kennedy."

"Glenn, that's crazy. You must be drunk. That's *nuts*."

"You think so? You ever hear of the Ben Chester White case?"

"You know I have."

"Well, this was like that."

Henry's mind raced over the White case, which involved the brutal murder of a sixty-seven-year-old black handyman just outside Natchez. In June 1966, some Klansmen had offered White two dollars and an orange soda pop to "help them find their lost dog." Then they drove him out into the woods and shot him close to twenty times. Out of a hundred details of that crime, one lit up like fireworks behind Henry's eyes: *Ben Chester White was murdered to lure Martin Luther King to Natchez, so that he could be assassinated.*

In a quavering voice, Henry said, "Say it plain, Glenn. I don't want to make assumptions."

"The whole damn operation got FUBAR, but it started with Frank, way back on the sandbar, the day he founded the Eagles. Then Brody Royal and Carlos Marcello got into it. Nobody hated Bobby Kennedy like Carlos. . . ."

Henry took out a pen and started writing as fast as he could.

CHAPTER 15

EVERY DOCTOR EVENTUALLY commits murder.

All physicians make mistakes, both of commission and omission, and sooner or later one will be fatal. But some doctors kill more directly. When certain patients near death, these physicians walk the legally sanctioned road of withdrawing nourishment or mechanical support, allowing a "natural" death to occur. Others kill more purposefully, by actually providing the drugs for patients to make a permanent end to their suffering. But a few physicians—the brave or the mad—walk the last mile and administer the lethal drug themselves, usually for those too ill to do so. To some people, those few doctors are criminals; to others—to the gravely ill and their families—they can be angels of mercy. My father has probably done all of the above. And now, barring a miracle, he, unlike so many of his colleagues before him, will be charged with murder.

I'm no expert on assisted suicide, but murder is another matter. Eight years as an assistant DA in Harris County, Texas, lifted me into the major league of murder trials. I tried many of Houston's highest-profile cases, and as a result sent sixteen people to death row at the Walls Unit in Huntsville. Then a slow accretion of events and realizations convinced me that I had not been divinely ordained to punish the guilty. I had seen inexcusable mistakes made in capital cases—by cops, lawyers, pathologists, crime labs, and juries—and this weighed heavily in my decision to leave the prosecutor's office. I never convicted an innocent man, but I worried I'd seen it done by colleagues, and nine months ago a burgeoning scandal in the Houston crime lab suggested that my sickening premonitions were all too accurate. Having my own father charged with murder is a sobering prospect, especially in a small Mississippi town. If there's anything Dad can do to head off his arrest tomorrow, he needs to do it—for my mother, for my daughter, and most of all for himself.

Seven weeks ago he almost died, I remind myself, as I park my car and walk to the side door of his medical office. *Keep that fact at the forefront of your mind.* It's easy to dismiss a heart attack, once the critical danger has passed, but something tells me that the psychological fallout of Dad's near-death experience is affecting his assessment of his present jeopardy. Of course, he doesn't yet grasp the full magnitude of that jeopardy. He still believes that the district attorney views Viola's death as assisted suicide. I almost called him several times today to correct that perception, but I wanted to be sure I had a clear understanding of the situation first. More important, I wanted to speak to Dad alone. This isn't easy to manage, since at home my mother always seems to hover within earshot, and when he's in his office, his longtime nurse, Melba Price, is forever at his side.

Before I could even attempt such a meeting, I had to spend three hours with the superintendent of schools and three dozen angry parents. I came into office promising to reform education in the city. Two years later, 50 percent of the kids in our public schools drop out before graduating from the twelfth grade, while only 2 percent in our private schools drop out. The city's public schools are 95 percent black, the private schools 85 percent white. This problem is easy to diagnose but virtually impossible to cure, and even basic treatment is one of the most contentious issues in the county. This afternoon's meeting brought zero progress.

After leaving that meeting, I drove past my parents' house and saw that my father's car wasn't in their driveway. On a hunch I drove by his office and found his old BMW parked in the back. That car was a gift from me, bought with my first big royalty check, and he's kept it perfectly maintained ever since. Dad developed a love for German cars when he served in Bonn as an army doctor during the early 1960s, and he's shown no inclination to trade in the old 740 for anything newer. With dusk falling and only one other car parked in the lot, I decide to brace him on his home turf.

I try not to get impatient as I bang loudly on the side door. Dad's too deaf to hear the knocking, and anyone else will assume I'm an after-hours patient or a drug salesman. But after repeated efforts, a key rattles in the lock and the dark face of Melba Price appears in the crack. The nurse's expression instantly morphs from a glare to a welcoming smile of relief.

"What's he doing, Melba?"

"What you think he's doin'? Goin' over charts on the patients Dr. Elliott been seein' for him." Melba points down the hall. "Just follow the cigar smoke."

A former schoolmate of mine, Drew Elliott is now one of my father's junior partners. Drew has taken on as many patients as he can during Dad's recuperation, but no full-time doctor—not even an athletic forty-two-year-old—can keep up with my father's workload on top of his own.

I start down the hall, then stop and lay my hand on the nurse's arm. "Melba, have you been going out to treat Viola Turner for the past few weeks?"

She takes a deep breath and tries to pull away, but I hold her arm. "I'm trying to help him, Melba. You know that. And I'd never hurt you to do it."

The nurse sucks in her upper lip, and her eyes flick nervously toward the ceiling before finally settling on me. "I went out there a few times. Drove Doc out there a few more. Miss Viola was in a bad way, Penn. She really should have been in a hospital, but she said she'd seen too many folks die in hospitals, and she didn't want any part of that."

"Thank you. Don't tell me any more."

I squeeze her wrist, then follow the smoke down the hall. Turning right, I see my father through a cloud of blue haze rising from the Romeo y Julieta burning in an ashtray on his desk. His concentration is absolute as he pores over a patient's medical record. Through the obfuscating cloud, I recognize the familiar clutter of his office, a room so packed with books and other objects that not even Melba's constant labor can keep it in order.

At first glance, Dad's inner sanctum looks like an exhibit at the Smithsonian: *The Small-Town General Practitioner's Office, Circa 1952.* From the meticulously hand-painted Napoleonic soldiers in a glass cabinet to the 1/96th scale model of the USS *Constitution* on a bookshelf, from the red Dinky double-decker London bus on his desk to the P-51 Mustang suspended from the ceiling by fishing line, this room exudes the scent of history. On a credenza to my left sits a set of pistols that date to the Revolutionary War, and a Civil War surgeon's kit with the long, gleaming knives used for countless amputations in the days before antibiotics and helicopters.

A casual observer might take the occupant of this office as something of an antique himself—the white beard and sagging flesh make it easy to do—but that would be a grave mistake. For the shelves of this room are lined with books that have kept my father's mind sharper and more vital than those of colleagues half his age, who haven't read a biography or literary novel since they left college. Skipping the medical library on the lower shelves, one quick perusal of the spines reveals biographies spanning three centuries of American history, weighted to the Civil War; a sprinkling of philosophers from Aristotle to Wittgenstein; a set of the Greek tragedians; a treasured shelf of nineteenth- and twentieth-century novels, mostly by Russian and American authors; a dozen back issues of *Foreign Affairs;* a shelf covering the Middle East, with a focus on Islam and Iran; and assorted volumes on subjects from counterterrorism to Seymour Cray. Sadly, this office holds but a tiny fraction of his original collection. In essence, this room is a twelve-by-fifteen lifeboat containing the survivors of the fire that destroyed my parents' home in 1998, and with it a library fifty years in the making.

"Melba?" Dad says, his eyes still on the chart. "This note says Drew put Jeanne Edwards on five hundred milligrams of Cipro b.i.d. She had a little reaction to Cipro the last time I put her on it, didn't she?"

Expecting to see his nurse, Dad looks up and blinks in confusion. "Penn? Is it five thirty already?"

"Quarter to six."

"Has Melba gone?"

"No. She's still out there."

I sit on the worn leather sofa Dad brought here from his downtown office against the fervent protests of the decorator who did the new office building. Whenever I sit on this smoke-cured artifact, I think of the secrets confided by the thousands of patients who sat here before me, and the prognoses, both hopeful and terrible, that my father gave them. Today, though, I'm wondering whether this familiar sofa is old enough that Viola Turner sat on it as a young nurse.

"Tell me about Viola," I say softly.

Dad sighs heavily, then leans back in the leather chair behind his desk. No matter how aged and battered his body gets, his blue-gray eyes, like his mind, remain incisively clear. But this evening the bags under them tell me that he hasn't slept for many hours, maybe even days. Fifteen years ago his face developed a healthy roundness over his bones. After his beard went white, children sometimes mistook him for Santa Claus in December. But now, seven weeks after a heart attack, he's become gaunt and angular again. With his hollow cheeks and eyes, he reminds me of Mathew Brady's photograph of Robert E. Lee, taken shortly after the surrender at Appomattox. The civilian clothes Lee wore in that photo could not disguise the solemn gaze of a man who'd endured loss of a magnitude known to only a few men throughout history. A shadow of that look darkens my father's face now.

"I'm not going to talk about last night," he says.

Stonewalling is no longer an option, but I'm going to wait a few minutes to tell him that. "I'm not asking about last night. I'm asking about Viola herself."

His chair creaks as he leans farther back (at least I hope it was his chair; it might have been his joints). "Viola was a Revels, originally. That's a famous name across the South. Hiram Revels was the first black U.S. senator, seated during Reconstruction. He represented Mississippi. I never knew whether or not Viola was descended from him, and she didn't either, but I always suspected she was. Revels was a brilliant man, and Viola was pretty sharp herself."

"Was she a trained nurse?"

"Not formally. She wasn't an RN, or even an LPN. Back in those days, the docs would take on some of the smartest girls and train them right in the hospitals. And I'll tell you, some of the nurses who came out of those programs knew more medicine than those I see getting out of the schools today. That's how Esther was trained. Same program. It was hands-on from the first day, the way it was in the army."

Esther Ford worked for my father longer than any other nurse, nearly forty years, and by the time she retired last year she was a physician assistant. Four months after she retired, Esther died of a stroke in her sleep. I'd give almost anything to have her around to question about Viola's relationship with Dad.

"Viola had worked at Charity Hospital before Dr. Lucas hired her," Dad goes on. "Young as she was, she'd done some of everything. Delivered babies, assisted with all kinds of surgery—you name it, she'd helped do it. More than I had, in some areas. Her Creole grandmother was a midwife in New Orleans, and Viola had spent several years with her as a girl. That's where she picked up her French, and a lot of hard-earned medical knowledge besides. Most days, Viola and Esther could have run this clinic on their own."

I start to ask another question, but Dad says, "I imagine the licensing requirements were stricter in Chicago than in Mississippi, though. I don't think Viola had an easy time getting work when she got up there."

"Did you stay in contact with her after she left Natchez?"

"No. She sent a couple of letters to the clinic, but I don't think she put much truth in them. I saw her sister as a patient, and Cora told me things weren't going too well for Viola 'up north.' Viola got married soon after she got there. Too soon, as it turned out. Women tend to do that during hard times. The pretty ones, anyway. She married some kind of con man. A hustler."

A con man? "Do you know if he was the father of the son who's down here? This Lincoln Turner?"

"I assume so. They have the same last name. But on the other hand, I don't understand how he could be. Turner was the last name of the man Viola married down here, the one who was killed in Vietnam. It's hard to believe she'd move to Chicago and marry a different man named Turner. But she didn't talk to me about any of that, and I didn't push it. He's in jail now, by the way—the father."

In jail? "That gives us something to think about."

Dad arches his eyebrows.

"If Lincoln Turner was raised by a con man," I say, "maybe he's down here looking for money. This afternoon I called the Illinois State Bar Association and found out Lincoln is about to be disbarred."

"Really? What for?"

"He apparently embezzled money from a client escrow account, and I got hints of a deeper scandal. Possible bribery of a judge. Maybe the apple didn't fall far from the tree. I'll find out more soon, but for now, what else can you tell me about Viola's life in Chicago?"

"Only what I learned these past weeks. I gather the husband was a charming rogue. He did all right in the beginning, so it took her a while to discover his crooked streak. But before long, Viola was doing all the work and he was spending all the money. He drank it up or gambled it away. After a while, she started drinking to help herself deal with *his* drinking. It's an old story. Viola gained weight, started smoking, got depressed. She aged fast. The North could be as cruel as the South to blacks in those days. More cruel, in some ways. Things went steadily downhill. The husband looked elsewhere for sex. He'd probably been cheating on her from the start, Viola said."

Dad shakes his head with a mixture of sadness and incomprehension. "I think it hurt Viola's pride when she lost her looks. She was never vain, but I don't care how selfless a woman is, she still cares about her looks. And Viola had been a beauty. I think between the drinking, the no-'count husband, and working hard to raise her son, she just wore herself out."

"I sure hate to hear that. What I remember of Viola is like a dream. In my mind she looks like a TV star."

Dad smiles wistfully. "I don't think anybody who ever knew her down here would believe her fate. That's why she never came home. Viola wanted people to remember her as she had been. And they did. She only worked here for eight years, but people still ask about her thirty-seven years later. She had a life force that made you want to be close to her. One lady told me that a smile from Viola Turner could warm you up on a cold day. She could give a child a shot without a tear being shed, and that was something in the days of screw-on needles you had to sand the burrs off of."

I can't help but laugh. "You're right."

Dad starts to smile, but the expression dies a-borning. "Penn . . . if you'd seen Viola in her sickbed yesterday, you'd have cried. I did, after the first time I saw her. Time is a terrible thing. And lung cancer's worse."

"I did see her," I confess, wondering at the irony of the smoke filling this office.

Dad blinks like an old man awakened from an accidental nap. "You what? What do you mean?"

"Today I saw a video recording of the last minute of Viola's life."

His eyes narrow with suspicion. "What are you talking about?"

As deliberately as I can, I explain about Henry Sexton and the hard drive mounted on the camera left in Viola's sickroom. "The mini-DV tape was missing," I conclude, "but the hard drive was still there.

Viola must have rolled over the remote control in her death throes. And that's what got recorded. Shad Johnson has no idea I've seen the recording, of course."

Dad is staring at me with an inscrutable expression. "What did you see?"

"Viola dying. But it sure didn't look like any morphine overdose."

"Why do you say that?"

I pause before answering. "If you have to ask me that, you weren't in the room."

Dad's gaze seems locked on some obscure title in the bookshelves to my left. *A defense mechanism.* "Penn, please just tell me."

"It looked like some sort of heart attack to me, or maybe a drug reaction. Possibly a stroke. She was short of breath, gasping, sweating. She was trying to reach a telephone that had fallen onto the floor. Whatever the underlying problem was, she called out your name twice. And the district attorney thinks that's tantamount to an accusation of guilt. A dying accusation, in fact—which carries more weight, legally speaking."

Dad appears not only lost in thought, but strangely untroubled by my words. Part of me wants to shake him until he faces up to the looming danger, but another wants to spare him all the stress I can (as my mother begged me to do) and minimize the chance of another heart attack.

"Shad's full of shit, of course," I say.

Dad cuts his eyes at me. "Why do you say that?"

"Because if you'd helped Viola to die, she would have died painlessly. And you would have held her hand to the very end."

He looks back at me without blinking. "Are you sure you know me so well?"

"Yes. Dad, a lot has happened since we spoke this morning. That video isn't your only problem. The sheriff's department has a syringe with your fingerprints on it, and also two prescription vials of morphine sulfate, with you listed as the prescribing physician. Worse, Viola's sister has stated that you and Viola had a euthanasia pact, and I gather she's willing to testify to that. Cora Revels will establish that you've been treating Viola for the past few weeks. I don't know what other physical evidence they have, but they'll get toxicology back from the medical examiner in Jackson before long. If they rush it, we're liable to know what killed her in two or three days."

"That should make interesting reading."

"You don't already know what it will say?"

Dad shrugs noncommittally. "I'll tell you something about death: it's infinitely variable. A twenty-year-old Olympic athlete can trip over a curb and die instantly, and a ninety-year-old woman with three kinds of cancer can live to be a hundred."

"Your point?"

"Drug interactions are unpredictable."

His enigmatic tone makes me wonder if he's caught in some transition stage between shock and grief. I should have recognized it immediately, based on my experience with murder victims' families in Houston. But all that seems a long time ago now, and despite the nearness of Viola's death, I need Dad to snap out of it. I need his self-preservation instinct to kick in.

"The DA isn't thinking about drug interactions. He's not even thinking about assisted suicide anymore. Shad intends to charge you with murder."

After a brief grimace, Dad takes a brown bottle from his inside coat pocket and places a tiny white pill under his tongue.

"Is that nitro? You're having angina now?"

He nods distractedly. "I'm fine. Go on."

"I wish I could spare you this, but I can't. At first I assumed that Shad's idea of murder was you giving Viola the morphine injection, which is technically murder but much less serious than what we're facing now. This afternoon Shad told me that he's planning to charge you with first-degree murder. He won't give me details, but he claims to have strong evidence of motive on your part—a motive for premeditated murder."

Dad looks incredulous. "What kind of motive?"

"Shad believes you wanted to silence Viola before she could reveal some information you want kept secret."

"That's preposterous."

"That's the contention of Viola's son."

"Johnson wouldn't tell you what this information was?"

I shake my head. Part of me wants to ask the brutally blunt question about Viola and my father, but for some reason I can't bring myself to do it. Confronting him about a possible affair with Viola feels like challenging Dwight Eisenhower about his wartime mistress.

"Dad," I say instead, "I have something on Shad that would destroy his legal career, and he knows it. He wouldn't risk moving against you unless he felt he had no other choice. Whatever Lincoln Turner told Shad, or showed him, Shad genuinely believes it was a motive for murder."

My father ponders this revelation like a monk parsing contradictory passages in the Bible.

"Given what I just told you, is there anything you want to tell me now?"

He grunts and shifts position like a man with upper back pain. "No."

Leaning forward, I speak with all the conviction I can muster. "There is nothing you could tell me today that would alter my opinion of you, or make me judge you. *Nothing*. You understand?"

He closes his eyes for a moment. "Are you so sure?"

"Yes. If you and Viola were closer than you should have been . . . I've got no problem with that."

Nothing in his expression changes.

"If you and Viola had a euthanasia pact, I've got no problem with that, either. You ought to know that." I look meaningfully to his left, where a portrait of me with Sarah and Annie sits framed. "Maybe something went wrong, or something unforeseen occurred. Whatever it was, you're the only person who can shed light on that event. And if you don't, you're going to wind up on trial for murder."

Dad's face hardens. "If that's true . . . then so be it."

I groan with frustration. "Dad, the trusty old doctor-patient privilege defense isn't going to fly in this case. You understand?"

"You're mighty quick to make light of that. Penn, you once told me about a journalist who went to jail for three weeks to protect a source, and you couldn't stop telling me how much you admired the man."

"That's different."

"You're right. This is far more serious. Do you realize how sacred the doctor-patient privilege is? I have patients secretly suffering from HIV, patients fighting suicidal depression, wives who've secretly had abortions, mothers who suspect their husbands of abusing their children, women who've been raped and never told the police, prominent drug addicts . . . the list is endless. If I were forced to reveal any of that in court, incalculable suffering would ensue. Yet you act like fighting to protect that secrecy is some quaint gesture. Do you expect me to raise a white flag at the first sign of danger? Surely you know me better than that. I'm seventy-three years old. If I choose this hill to make my stand, that's my lookout."

His righteous passion silences me, but only for a few moments. "I'm sorry if I sounded glib. But I'd understand your position a lot better if you only had yourself to worry about. What about Mom? Do you think she can stand waiting at home while you die slowly in Parchman Prison? Hell, in the shape you're in, you might not even make it to Parchman. You could die in the county lockup awaiting trial. Think about the reality of that for Mom."

"I *am* thinking of your mother," Dad says in a tone somewhere between reverence and shame.

I shake my head. "I don't believe it. You're wracked with guilt about something. Fine. We've all done things we regret. But I don't care what you might have done, and neither does Mom. Nothing on this earth could push us away from you."

He slowly shakes his head. "You don't know that. You can't."

"You think you've committed a sin so terrible that you could never be forgiven?"

"No. But there are some things so—so *complicated* that it's a man's duty to work them out for himself. Not to depend on others to do it for him."

"Dad . . . I'd never say this to a client. But you're not going to be my client beyond tomorrow, not if you're going to trial, and—"

"You won't defend me if this goes to trial?"

"A lawyer who represents himself or his family has a fool for a client."

He seems to take this philosophically. "Go on, then."

"Tell me what happened at Cora Revels's house last night. Just the facts, in sequence, as best you can remember them." I hold up my right hand. "Before you say no, let me tell you why you should confide in me. Maybe what happened was assisted suicide. Or maybe it *was* murder. But it might have been manslaughter, or even plain suicide. We won't know until I hear the facts. Because even though laymen use those terms, each one has a strict legal definition."

For a moment I think I've convinced him. Then he says, "I'm not sure I know myself what happened last night."

"What do you mean? Can you prove you weren't there? Or what time you left? With an alibi, this whole mess can magically go away. According to the clock-radio beside Viola's bed, she died at five thirty-eight A.M."

He lifts a small, desert-colored replica of a Tiger tank from a shelf behind him and toys with its scaled-down 88 mm gun. After slowly turning the turret a few times, he sets the tank back on the shelf. "That's not what I meant. I *was* there. But I'm still not sure what happened. Or why."

"Did you do anything to assist Viola to die? Did you inject her? *Was* there some kind of unexpected drug interaction?"

Dad blinks twice, then seems to shake himself out of a trance. "We've come full circle, Penn. I've told you I can't discuss what happened last night. Let that be an end of it."

"You mean you *won't* discuss it."

He turns up his palms, exposing his arthritically deformed fingers. "Semantics."

"I know you didn't murder Viola. I know that. You're trying to protect somebody. Nothing else makes sense. You can't be trying to protect yourself, because you're about to destroy yourself. So it must be someone else. Tell me who you're trying to save, and I'll do all in my power to protect them. I swear it. Your life is on the line, Dad."

"I've been on borrowed time for quite a while, son. You know that."

At last my frustration boils over, and I get to my feet. "Why won't you let me help you?"

"Because you can't," he says calmly. He picks up his dead cigar from the ashtray, puts it in his mouth, and relights it with a high-pressure butane lighter that roars like a miniature welding torch. "Penn, let me tell you something: I thought I knew *my* father. He lived to be eighty-six, remember? Died of colon cancer. Do you remember how religious he was?"

"He never missed a Sunday at church. Or a Wednesday night."

"That's right." Dad exhales a raft of blue smoke. "Well, near the end, I found him staring out the front window of his house, crying. *Crying*. Can you see Percy Cage doing that?"

My grandfather was as hard as a Salem judge. "No, I can't."

"When I asked why he was crying, Dad told me he was afraid. Afraid of dying. I can't tell you how shocked I was. I asked whether his religious faith didn't give him some comfort—his belief in the after-life. He turned to me with a stare that made me shudder, and he said, 'There's nothing after this life, Tom. This world. Nothing.' Then he looked back out the window."

Dad studies the glowing tip of his cigar. "I felt like the earth had cracked open at my feet. Even though I believed basically the same thing. Dad had been going to church his whole life, professing faith, teaching Sunday school, saying and doing all the right things. But when it came to actually staring into the void, all that went out the window. All those years, he'd never been the person I thought I knew. Never. I'm not judging him. I'm just saying that I had no idea who my own father really was."

My palms tingle as I stare back into my father's eyes. Do I have similar blind spots when I look at him? Is that what he's telling me? I've sometimes wondered whether human beings are like the universe itself, where 95 percent of what surrounds us is dark matter, and cannot be seen. The only way black holes can be detected is by the behavior of what's around them—light and matter being distorted by immense forces within the collapsing star. Have I seen and yet not seen certain events that hint at deep, invisible forces within my own father? Could Viola's flight from Natchez in 1968 have been one of those events? What about my sister's decision to leave America and live in England? Or Dad's decision to help my wife die peacefully rather than in agony? *You may be right,* says a voice in my head, *but this isn't the time or place for speculation.* Gathering myself as best I can, I sit back on the sofa and try to punch through his defenses.

"I've been thinking back to the day of your last heart attack. I was on the river with Caitlin, spreading that waitress's ashes. When Mom called me, she said you were in terrible pain, but you were asking to see me, that you were desperate to tell me something very important."

He stares at his cigar like a primitive tribesman entranced by fire.

"Mom said you were afraid you would die before you could tell me whatever it was. Then, when I got to the hospital, you acted like you had no memory of that."

"Wasn't I unconscious when you got to the hospital?"

"Pretty much."

"You asked me about this last month. My answer is the same. When I woke up, I had no memory of what you're talking about."

"But Mom confirmed that you said those things."

He shrugs. "I was out of my head. Obtunded, we say in medicine."

"Uh-huh. Or maybe once you woke up, you realized you were going to survive, so you didn't feel compelled to confess whatever it was."

He suddenly looks too exhausted to argue further. If Mom were here, she would tell me to stop warting him. But I can't. He's risking his life by forcing Shad to proceed with an arrest. The last time Dad was involved in a trial was during my senior year in high school—a malpractice case. That stress caused his first heart attack, and he was only forty-six. Tonight he's thirty years and several surgeries down the road.

"Let's back up a second," I say. "When you were telling me about Viola, you skimmed over why she left town."

He shrugs. "That's no mystery. The KKK had kidnapped and murdered her brother. Also a friend of his. The bodies were never found, but I never had any doubt that the Klan killed those boys. How could Viola stay here after that?"

"Which Klan guys? Do you have any idea?"

"Probably the same bastards behind the rest of the killings around here. The rednecks who worked out at Triton and Armstrong and IP. Or those Double Eagles that Henry Sexton writes about."

I don't want to reveal my contact with Henry yet. "Do you know that for sure?"

"Who else could it have been? Everybody knew who'd done it, in a general way. But nobody knew *exactly*. That's how it was all over the South. That's why the violence continued. Nobody was willing to look too deeply into it, for fear of being targeted themselves."

Dad takes another pull on his cigar, then sets it in the ashtray. "Did you ever hear about the Heffner family in McComb?"

"No." McComb, Mississippi, is only sixty miles east of Natchez.

"Red Heffner was an insurance man. Ex–air force. He invited a northern civil rights worker and a liberal preacher to his house for dinner. Next thing you know, the men in his neighborhood formed a vigilante association and started terrorizing his family. Red had to move them out of town. And his wife's daughter by her first husband—who'd been killed in the Battle of the Bulge—had been elected Miss Mississippi that year. Can you imagine? Miss Mississippi was like *royalty* back then. Compared to the Heffners, we were nobody, in the social scheme of things. I wish I'd had his moral courage, the courage to get involved, but I was fresh out the army, and you were only four years old."

I sense that Dad is leading me away from the central subject—cleverly, but doing it all the same. My patience has almost evaporated when my cell phone rings in my pocket. The screen reads HENRY SEXTON.

"I need to take this, Dad. Hello?"

"Penn, it's Henry. We need to talk." The reporter's voice quavers with fear. "I've learned a lot since this morning. You need to know about it, and the sooner the better."

My pulse picks up. "What is it?"

"Not on a cell phone. It's too easy to eavesdrop on these things, or so my FBI friends tell me."

"Where are you?"

"At the *Beacon* office. Is there any way you can drive over here? I wouldn't ask if I didn't think it could help your father."

My heart thuds in my chest. "My father?"

Dad looks up with interest.

"That's all I can say on the phone. I know Dr. Cage is in trouble, and this can help him. But you've got to come here to hear it."

I look at my watch. Annie has a basketball game in half an hour. If I drive to Ferriday, I'll miss it. But what choice do I have? At least her grandmother will make the game. "I'm on my way, Henry. Give me twenty minutes."

"Call my cell when you get here. The door's locked."

"Was that Henry Sexton?" Dad asks as I pocket my phone.

"Yes. He says he may be able to help you. I'm glad somebody wants to, since you refuse to help yourself."

Dad gives me an unpleasant look. "How could Henry possibly help me? What does he know about any of this?"

"I don't know. But he interviewed Viola a couple of times in the weeks before she died. By the way, do you have any idea what happened to the videotape that was in Henry's camera?"

Dad just stares back at me, saying nothing.

Oh, Christ . . . this is bad. After rubbing my temples for a few seconds, I stand and reach for the doorknob. "Don't kid yourself about this. If you don't give me more than you have, Sheriff Byrd is going to arrest you for murder in the morning."

"Nothing can stop that, son. I've already accepted it."

"Are you telling me Shad would arrest you even if he knew all that you know?"

"I didn't say that." Dad sighs wearily. "Is there any chance that Johnson would ask for the death penalty?"

"I don't see how Shad could stretch this into capital murder. Even if you killed Viola, it wasn't during the commission of a separate felony, so the felony murder rule doesn't apply."

Dad exhales with relief. "I just don't want your mother to have to contemplate that."

"Have you told Mom about *any* of this?"

He gives me a sheepish look. "Not yet."

I drop my hand from the doorknob. "Dad, for God's sake. If you're charged with assisted suicide, we can almost certainly plead it down to probation. Even if a jury found you guilty, we'd have a shot at a suspended sentence, or maybe just losing your license. So far as I can discover, no physician in Mississippi has gone to prison for assisted suicide. But several have gone to Parchman for murder."

"Penn . . . we're going in circles again."

My impassioned argument has made no impression. "I suppose so. Well . . . the sheriff's deputies could come as early as six A.M. Hopefully, they'll wait until eight or nine, but you never know. I'll be ready to bail you out. That's *if* the judge sets bail, of course."

"I can't control the district attorney or the sheriff," Dad says with the resignation of Mohandas Gandhi. "What I told you this morning is what I'll tell the judge tomorrow. What happened between Viola and me happened between doctor and patient, and that's where it's going to stay. I owe her that much. At *least* that much. Shad Johnson and his ilk can go spit. They're dogs barking at a passing hearse."

My face colors. "And Viola's son? Is Lincoln Turner a dog barking at a hearse?"

"I'm sure that boy is grieving. But time can work wonders with grief. I've seen it ten thousand times. A night's sleep just might change his mind."

I doubt it.

"Will you call me if Henry Sexton has new information?" he asks.

"I will, if you'll tell me what you're hiding from me."

He looks away like a caged animal turning from a door it knows is locked. Then he picks up the medical record he was reading when I walked in and lifts the phone to resume his dictation.

MELBA PRICE IS LEANING against the wall by the back door, her big purse slung over the shoulder of her white uniform, her dark eyes watching me for clues. She looks like a middle-aged version of Esther Ford, and again I wish the old nurse were alive for me to question about Viola.

"Is the word out yet?" I ask.

"What do you mean?" Melba is playing dumb, which she most assuredly is not.

"About what Dad might have done. Is it spreading in the black community?"

"There's a little talk. Nothing bad yet."

"What do they think about Shad Johnson these days?"

"My people?"

"Mm-hm."

"Old Shadrach might not have a lot of black friends, but I will say this. He's stuck around town enough years now that he's earned some respect. He's done a lot for black boys busted on drug charges, and that buys some gratitude."

"How do they feel about Dad?"

"Lord, you know that. Dr. Cage is a saint on the north side of town."

"Do you think anything could change that?"

Melba looks thoughtful. "They say that in Natchez people will forgive you for everything except going bankrupt. But that's on the white side of town. On the black side, it's something else people don't forgive."

"What's that?"

"Breaking faith."

"That sounds like a long conversation."

Melba taps me in the middle of the chest. "You just do whatever you got to do to keep Doc out of jail. That man don't deserve jail, no matter what he's done. Not one day."

"Were you listening at the door?"

The middle-aged nurse's perfectly plucked eyebrows pantomime childlike innocence. "Wouldn't dream of it, baby."

"The only person who can keep Dad out of jail is Dad himself. Why don't you convince him to talk to me?"

She gives me a mocking laugh. "I don't control that man! He's my boss, not the other way around."

"I'll bet forty years ago, Viola Turner would have told me the same thing."

Melba's face instantly turns sober. "You hush, boy. Get out of here, so he'll finish those records and I can get home."

"Do what you can, Melba."

She watches me forlornly as I back down the hallway.

"I'll try."

CHAPTER 16

TOM CAGE GOT slowly up from his chair, then locked his office door. Melba would panic if she turned that handle and found it locked, but he didn't want her coming in for at least a couple of minutes. Going to the bookcase behind his desk, he took down a signed first edition of *The Killer Angels* by Michael Shaara, a treasure that survived the house fire only because he'd had it on his office shelves at the time. None of his nurses would open this book, not even if they were desperate for something to read, because it was set during the Civil War. Tom fanned the pages to the three-quarters point, then reached in and slid out a Polaroid photograph he'd kept since 1968.

The faded snapshot, which still had the primary-color saturation of a Technicolor movie, showed Viola Turner standing in front of a cabinet in Tom's private office in the old clinic on Monroe Street. She wasn't smiling. She was looking directly into the camera with a candid vulnerability that no one at the clinic had ever seen. Gone were the professional smile and practiced deference. In this picture, Viola was not the perfect ambassador for her race that her parents had raised her to be, but merely a woman in her late twenties, her defenses down, her eyes unguarded, her carefully straightened hair askew. Tom had shot the photo on a rainy afternoon one week after he patched up Jimmy Revels and Luther Davis, following their brawl with the Double Eagles. By that afternoon he was as different from the doctor who'd treated those boys as the Tom Cage who left Korea had been from the eighteen-year-old version of himself who'd arrived there in 1950.

What had changed him was Viola Turner.

The day after their midnight surgery, Viola had opened up the clinic as usual. By the time Tom got there, the surgery room was spic-and-span again, the bloody towels gone, the instruments autoclaved and ready for a new patient. The room where Tom had treated the Eagles was just as clean. Dr. Lucas didn't notice anything out of order, nor did the clinic's female staff. But Tom and Viola could no longer carry off the act they'd been perfecting for the previous four years. Their frantic embrace in the corner of the garage had shattered some boundary between them, and every instant of eye contact now communicated hidden significance. Tom was certain everyone in the clinic could sense the new intimacy between them, like a magnetic field made visible. He'd sensed the same thing whenever Gavin Edwards had been involved with one of the office girls. Edwards had never gone out of his way to hide his affairs, but even if he had, it would have been pointless. Once certain levels of intimacy have been reached, they simply cannot be concealed within a small group.

During stolen moments that day, in quick snatches of conversation, Tom learned that Viola had gotten her brother and Luther Davis to the relative safety of Freewoods, a backwoods sanctuary for bootleggers, criminals, and people of all races who needed protection from the law. So long as Jimmy and Luther stayed there, they would be safe from Frank Knox and the Ku Klux Klan. The problem was, Jimmy was too committed to his civil rights work to stay hidden in the forests south of town while his brothers in the movement fought to change America. Viola's anxiety about Jimmy made her quieter than usual, and the other girls commented on it. But beneath Viola's worry Tom sensed something else, like a powerful motor spinning ceaselessly inside her, throwing off an energy that seemed directed at him. If he was alone in an examining room, he sensed her approach even before he heard her footfalls. When they worked together—when she passed him an instrument, say—any accidental touch sent a startling current up the nerves of his arm. He hardly slept that night, and Peggy noticed. But hardest to take were the gazes of the office girls, which followed him like the eyes of watchful informers.

This heightened state of tension was shattered by the most commonplace of office events. Dr. Lucas had owned his X-ray unit for fifteen years, and the new developing machine he'd bought for it was temperamental. The X-ray tech could sometimes repair it, but when she couldn't, Tom had proved the most adept at getting the unit back into operation. (Tom had a photographic darkroom at home, and he was much more mechanically inclined than Dr. Lucas.) Two days after the midnight surgery, the X-ray developer broke down yet again. Since the X-ray tech was on vacation, Tom had no choice but to take on the task of repairing the machine. And since Viola was Tom's nurse, it was she who would be helping him get the unit back online.

The developing room was hardly bigger than a closet; it had, in fact, been a closet in the original house. The old metal developing tanks stood against the wall opposite the door, still serving as back-ups when the automatic developer couldn't be coaxed into action. The new machine sat on a stand against the right wall, and a metal cabinet for storing film stood against the left. The middle of this U contained barely enough room for one person to work; with two it was like being shoehorned into a crowded elevator. Separation was impossible.

Tom first thought the problem was a jammed sheet of film, but he'd checked the path under the red glow of the safelight and found it unobstructed. Then he fed an already developed X-ray through the machine; it went through fine. The next step was to shut off the lights—even the safelight—and run an undeveloped X-ray through the machine.

Standing with his stomach pressed against Viola's back, he reached over his shoulder and shut off the overhead safelight. Utter darkness enveloped them. He heard her sliding open the bars of the rectangular cartridge that protected the X-ray film from light, then the rattle and pop of flexing film as she extracted it. Tom shifted back against the door so that she could turn and feed the film sheet into the machine. In the confines of the closet, her scent was even stronger than on the night she'd hugged him, strong enough to declare itself over the acrid bite of the developing chemicals. Tom felt his breath go shallow when her shoulder dug into his chest. She was trying to feed the film into the machine's narrow slot.

"Sorry," she said, as her shoulder prodded him again. "Got it."

It would take ninety seconds for the exposed black sheet to pass through the chemicals—developer, stop bath, fixer—and finally the machine's dryer. Even with his back flat against the door, there was no way to avoid physical contact. Viola's upper back was flat against his chest, her hair brushed his face, and her rump pressed against his thighs and crotch. Tom's mouth felt parched, but his palms were coated with sweat. Within thirty seconds his heart was pounding. He could feel her chest expand with each breath. To his alarm, his penis shifted, then grew steadily against her tight skirt. He didn't know whether to apologize or to try to move away; any movement would only aggravate the problem. He was acutely aware that the rest of the office staff were outside the door, not to mention the twenty or so patients in the clinic. Yet in the cavelike darkness of the X-ray room, it was as though the two of them had stepped from a mother ship into deep space.

When Viola began to turn in place, Tom experienced something between panic and exultation. When she was halfway around, her hand slid up his arm, her fingers searching along his shoulder, his collarbone, and then his neck, like the hand of a blind woman. When her fingers found his mouth, she probed it with a fingertip, then rose on tiptoe and pressed her lips to his. Tom's back flexed against the door as the shock went through him. Then he recovered himself, and the wood behind him creaked as he wrapped his arms around her. He squeezed hard enough to crush the breath from some women, but Viola only slid her fingers up into the hair behind his head and pulled his mouth harder against hers.

The sharp taste of her stunned him, so different was it from what he'd known most of his life. Her tongue and full lips sucked his own, and her teeth bit his flesh. Despite the cramped quarters, they were not still. Their bodies slid, twisted, and probed, pressing together until no pocket of air remained between them. Their movements had a frantic quality, driven by the knowledge that after years of denial they might only have a few moments in this protective darkness. Tom wanted to squeeze her breasts, but he held back until he heard her skirt slide up her stockings. Thus encouraged, he unzipped the back of her white uniform dress and pulled it from her muscular shoulders. A low-pitched purr rose from her throat, then she reached back and unhooked her bra. Tom wasn't sure how to proceed in the confined space. Viola solved his dilemma by entwining her arms behind his neck, pulling herself up, and closing her thighs around his waist.

Even through her stockings, the heat from her pubis felt like the coffee mug he sometimes set between his legs as he drove to work. Despite being married for four years, Viola had never borne children, and her breasts were firm and high. As Tom kneaded them, he noticed they felt made of muscle rather than fat. He bent his neck and sucked a swollen nipple into his mouth. She moaned deep in her throat, then choked off the sound as though suddenly remembering the danger.

"There's not enough room," he whispered. "The door's going to break open."

"Let me down," she said. "Scoot back. It's locked."

Tom pressed his back against the door so hard that the wood groaned.

As Viola slowly turned away, she said, "There's not enough room to take my stockings off."

"It's all right," he replied, not meaning it. "We can wait."

He heard a swish of polyester against nylon, then a sharp ripping sound. Blood throbbed in his veins.

"Are you ready?" she asked.

He reached down, seeking out her hand in the dark. His fingers slid across her bare behind, found her grasping fingers. He pressed them against the swelling in his pants. She deftly unzipped him with a nurse's confidence. When she closed her hand around his penis, he sucked in his breath, afraid he would lose control then and there. He felt her rise on tiptoe, tugging him forward, under her rump.

"Jesus," he whispered, bending his knees. "Will they hear us?"

"They'll think we're working on the machine. Just push."

He pushed.

She sucked in her breath sharply. "Lower down."

"Sorry."

"*Oh,*" she groaned, much too loudly.

He'd plunged into her virtually without resistance. When her weight settled back against his pubic bone, she shuddered along the length of her body. He took hold of her hips and began to thrust into her by flexing and unflexing his knees, gently rocking in the confined space. Almost no other motion was possible.

"This won't be good for you," he said.

"Rub me," she whispered, pulling his right hand from her hip and guiding it to the rip she'd made in her hose.

As his fingers slipped between her thighs, Tom received one of the most profound shocks of his life. Viola's pubic hair was softer than any he'd ever felt. Even after years of giving pelvic exams to Negro women, he'd unconsciously assumed that their pubic hair was coarser than a white woman's. With Viola, at least, the opposite was true. He was still pondering this when he discovered her swollen clitoris. She jerked as though he'd shocked her, then flung her head to the right and bit his upper arm as though only this could keep her quiet.

In the claustrophobic darkroom, they developed a slow but effective rhythm, a primitive, serpentine dance, slowly building toward ecstasy. Tom felt as though they were suspended in water, intertwined like nether creatures fulfilling some ritual that had sustained their species for millions of years. The experience transcended anything he'd ever felt with a woman. Apart from his wife, Tom's sexual experience was limited to two prostitutes in Japan during the war. But even so, he sensed that if he'd coupled with a dozen gifted courtesans, this experience would surpass them all. There was no color in the darkroom—and barely any form, it seemed—yet his senses had never felt more alive to every stimulus. The enforced silence of their coupling drove them deeper inward, until only the oceanic pounding of blood in his ears competed with the electrical hum of the developing machine against the wall. Deprived of light and visual cues, his inner ear became confused, and the sense of being in water gave way to something still more surreal. He felt as though they were making love on some distant planet that dwarfed the earth, their bodies twenty times as dense as normal, his penis harder than it had ever been, her breasts as resilient and hard-tipped as those of a woman who'd lived in this environment all her life.

He cursed the fact that he was behind her. He longed to kiss her mouth, her neck, her breasts again—he hadn't even seen them!—but with the gift for anticipation she'd always possessed, Viola tilted back her head and opened her mouth to his. As he explored this alien space with his tongue, her clitoris grew so hard that it felt masculine under his fingers. He kissed and rubbed her, kissed and rubbed. At last she tore her mouth away and bit into his arm, her body convulsing in the dark. His back slammed against the door, and for a moment Tom feared it would burst open, but then his own spasms began and he abandoned all fear of being caught.

When he finally sagged against her, Viola leaned back and nuzzled her hair in the hollow of his neck. The feeling of heightened density slowly faded. Now they were levitating in the dark, floating inches above the floor, hovering in their sealed capsule while outside the world moved in barely controlled chaos.

"Can you reach the safelight?" he asked, still inside her.

Viola extended her long, slender arm and pressed the switch that bathed the closet in a soft red glow. He slipped out of her then, and she slowly turned until she faced him. Her eyes were black pools in the eerie glow, but her face radiated happiness.

"That's the first time I've done this since James died," she said softly.

He hugged her gently. "This is the first time I've ever done anything outside my marriage."

Viola closed her eyes, and he realized what a stupid thing that was to say. "Do you think anybody heard?" he asked.

"They'll think we were banging on the machine to make it work."

When at last she opened her eyes again, he felt a mixture of unreality, guilt, and euphoria that would not diminish for many weeks. More than one boundary had been crossed in that room. The sin of adultery paled in comparison to the tribal law they had broken. Only one taboo was greater—a white woman sleeping with a black man. Viola was forbidden fruit in more ways than one, and Tom wondered how much of the intensity he'd experienced might be attributed to that fact.

"I've got a problem," she said, her voice disturbingly practical.

"What?"

"One of those witches from up front is liable to be waiting right outside this door."

"What's the problem?"

Viola took his hand and guided it along her inner thighs. Her panty hose were soaking wet.

"Don't worry," he said, taking down a refill bottle of developer for the machine. He removed the cap and splashed some of the chemical across his shirt and trousers, more onto the floor, and some onto Viola's panty hose.

"We'll tell them I was on the floor working under the machine, and you spilled this in the dark. You can go home to shower, and I'll do the same."

"What about fixing the machine?"

Tom lifted the black sheet of film from the tray atop the developer and held it up in front of the safelight. He saw the white outlines of a hip joint, its ball and socket clearly visible. "I think we fixed it the old-fashioned way."

"That chemical's stinging me," Viola whispered. "Ohh. I need to get to the bathroom."

Tom swallowed hard. This was the kind of moment Gavin Edwards would handle with the suave detachment of Hugh Hefner, but Tom felt only confusion and guilt.

"It's all right," Viola said. "I don't know what to say, either. But I do need water down there."

He kissed her forehead. "I just want you to know this meant something to me."

She smiled and touched his cheek. "I wouldn't have done it if I didn't know that."

He took a deep breath, then opened the door and let in the harsh light of the real world.

What followed this incident was a forty-five-day period of mutual obsession that oscillated wildly between panic and bliss. Sleep was impossible, but Tom realized that the euphoria he experienced during the hours he spent with Viola somehow made up for the deficit. Yet that euphoria was punctuated by paralyzing episodes of fear. They tried not to make stupid mistakes in the clinic, but it was impossible to endure a day without one at least closing a hand around the other's, and most days they did more than that. Thanks to clever sabotage by Viola, the X-ray developer broke down frequently during this period. They spent so many hours "repairing" it that even Dr. Lucas—a noted skinflint— offered to buy a new machine. Four times during those weeks they met at the clinic after hours: twice to "inventory surgical instruments," once to "make a purchasing plan" for a new autoclave and instruments, and once with no excuse at all. Craziest of all, three times Tom went to Viola's home while pretending be on late-night house calls.

Those hours in Viola's house were the most revelatory of Tom's life. Viola had always seemed modest in the clinic, but in the privacy of her home she shed her modesty with her clothes. She had no difficulty granting Tom's desire that she sit or stand and be stared at from all sides, while he tried to take in the profound simplicity of her beauty. Her skin was soft and without blemish. This perfection was partly youth, he knew, but even with young white women, whom he saw unclothed on a regular basis, he had the impression that no limb was quite aware of what the others were doing, that the whole was very much a collection of parts. Viola was all of a piece. Each part flowed into the next with seamless fluidity, so that medical terms like *ventral, dorsal, medial,* and *distal* blurred into meaninglessness.

Her abandonment of modesty extended much further than nudity. In her daily role as a nurse, Viola was a model of self-possession, politeness, and rectitude. With some adult patients she spoke only when spoken to; with others she was as intimate as a family member, providing comfort while moving things along without the patients becoming aware they were being "handled." Throughout, her rich voice remained carefully modulated, like a cello being played by a master of control. In her own house, though, Viola spoke without restraint. She purred, keened, groaned, shrieked, *sang*—all without a trace of self-consciousness. The first time Tom heard her laugh with complete freedom, something in his heart leaped, as it had when hearing the trilling of a bird in the forests of his youth. It was then that he understood something of what those children must have felt when she focused all her attention upon them in the clinic, chanting softly, entrancing them with the Creole language of her girlhood.

It was only the second time that he visited her house that he began to notice his physical surroundings. Viola made the most of her modest salary, saving and spending wisely, so her home was much better kept and decorated than the Negro houses Tom had visited on house calls. But compared to the furniture and fabrics that filled his house, her possessions were almost junk. Ironically, Peggy Cage had started life as poor as Viola Revels (and Tom hadn't had it much better). But the institutionalized obstacles that had blocked Viola's upward path were monumental compared to the difficulties that he and Peggy had perceived as hardships. And that, Tom realized, was an injustice of immeasurable magnitude. Because Viola was as smart as he was. That was a fact, yet she would never be given an opportunity to prove it. Thankfully, she seemed less troubled by this situation than he was. The practical impossibility of a colored girl born in 1940s Mississippi becoming a physician meant that Viola had discounted such a future from the beginning. But Tom knew the truth: in every way she was his equal, yet accidents of birth had separated her from him as surely as a French peasant from Louis XIV.

Viola displayed only two photos of her husband in her house. One showed James Turner in his army uniform, looking confident and proud. The other appeared to have been taken at a high school dance. James looked as uncomfortable in a rented tuxedo as Tom had felt in his own in 1950; Viola, on the other hand, looked so serene in her gown that she seemed destined for a red carpet somewhere. Gazing at that picture, Tom realized how little he knew about the dreams of the woman whose bed he now shared. Yet he didn't ask. For to hear the disparity between the dreams of that gowned girl and the uniformed reality that Viola lived every day might have been unbearable.

But one night, without any prompting, Viola told him that she'd once yearned to be a rhythm-and-blues singer. Not a diva, she said, like Diana Ross, but one of the girls behind her, with matching satin gowns that swayed to perfectly choreographed dance moves. Tom couldn't have been more surprised. Until then, he had only heard the French lullabies she sang to keep children calm while he sutured them. But when she ripped out a verse and chorus of "You Can't Hurry Love" while dancing a trademark Motown routine, he believed. When Viola asked about *his* childhood dreams, Tom was embarrassed to confess that as a boy he had longed to be an archaeologist, poring over maps in the Valley of the Kings, searching for temples and tombs not yet plundered by grave robbers. Smiling, Viola had taken his hand, pressed it between her thighs, and said, "This temple hasn't been plundered yet."

"It's certainly been discovered," he replied.

"Has it?" Her eyebrows arched. "That's what all the white explorers say. They stumble over some supposedly 'lost' city and then claim to have discovered it, when the natives have known about it for centuries."

"How many explorers know about this treasure?" he asked, rubbing her steadily.

She lay back on her elbows. "Mmm . . . let me see. There's you . . . and my husband . . . and a very pretty boy I went to school with . . . and—"

"That's two too many," Tom said.

Viola pretended to pout. "What do you expect, when you took so long to show up? What was I supposed to do all that time?"

"You're only twenty-eight."

"That's *ancient* in my country."

This kind of playfulness, Tom reflected, was entirely absent from his marriage. He didn't blame Peggy for their rather perfunctory sex life. He blamed her parents, and the long line of ancestors who had blindly embraced repressive strains of Christianity, with their puritanical separation of body and spirit, the equation of pleasure with shame, and the near deification of guilt. All that had led to generations of frustrated, lying men and guilt-ridden women. Tom knew those women well. He'd been reared by one, and he'd married another. Even when almost every fiber of Peggy's being cried out for release, her relentlessly conditioned mind short-circuited her desire, burying the ancient urge with destructive consequences that no one had yet evolved a system to calculate. Tom had heard countless similar stories in his medical practice, and he saw the pernicious results. He sometimes wondered whether the myriad of vague female complaints he encountered—"nerves," "vapors," "hysteria"—might not be cured by a few nights of guilt-free sex. But for many of those women, that cure could not be accomplished without a pharmacological guillotine that would sever the body from the cerebral cortex. Until that existed, true sexual fulfillment for those patients would remain unattainable.

In the previous century, when laws governing doctors were much less stringent, his professional forebears had approached this problem directly. Tom had read medical histories that described doctors using electrical vibrators of various types to treat women suffering from "hysteria." The cure was simple: orgasm. Many female patients had never experienced orgasm, at least not with their husbands, who were frequently inattentive, ignorant of the existence of the clitoris, or both. Tom suspected that most of those long-suffering women had been the "beneficiaries" of a repressive religious upbringing, and thus could not bring themselves even to masturbate for relief. This sexual deprivation had obviously persisted into the 1960s, especially in the Bible Belt, but across the nation, too. One only had to look at the sexual primers and self-help books starting to climb the bestseller lists to find proof. Peggy had actually purchased a couple of these titles, but she'd yet to put any of their suggestions into practice. Tom almost dreaded the day that she would try. Watching someone struggle to break down rigid barriers in their personality was a difficult thing to witness—much less help with—after one had stepped into a world where sexual intimacy was effortless.

In Viola Turner's bedroom, shame had no place. Body and spirit were one. Viola might be a devout Catholic, but she made love without a trace of guilt. In Peggy's world, desire *was* guilt. In Viola's, desire was action. In Viola's bed, the word *no* did not exist. If Tom asked her why she did a certain thing, her answer was always the same: "Because it feels good." Viola would gaze steadily, almost tauntingly back at him, certain that her answer was true and irreducible. "Does it feel good to you?" she would ask. Such childlike simplicity, Tom realized, was the essence of sexual love. There was a darker side to sex, of course; sexuality had as many facets as the human personality. But the darker sides, he was coming to believe, grew out of repression rather than from the natural openness that Viola personified.

In this atmosphere, sexual epiphanies occurred almost daily, and Tom felt alternately foolish and empowered by them. Never had he experienced the kind of protracted pleasure Viola gave him, nor had he seen a woman experience such heights of arousal and release. He tried to believe himself free of prejudice during these encounters, but ultimately he couldn't fool himself on this score. At the deepest level, he felt as though he were coupling with some exotic creature brought from a distant land, or even another planet. When Viola rode him, single-minded in her focus, he saw clearly that "guilt" and "shame" were man-made constructs that, however deeply ingrained they had become in the Calvinist lineage of his people, had only been lightly grafted onto the surface of Viola's tribe, and had never really taken. Tom knew such thoughts were inherently racist, but they were his thoughts nonetheless, and could not be denied.

He didn't speak of love with Viola—not in the beginning. And on the first day he found the word forming in his mouth, she read his mind and put a finger to his lips. When he tried to move the finger away, Viola shook her head and closed her eyes, squeezing tears from beneath her lids. She had never blocked out the truth that Tom denied like a little boy pretending he could fly from the roof of his parents' house. The laws that precluded the two of them from having a future together were as absolute as the laws that would break the legs of the boy who leaped from a roof with only a red cape to hold him aloft. Yet despite this awareness, not even Viola could make herself stop the affair.

For six weeks they courted disaster, dancing along a precipice that skirted a bottomless void. Thankfully Viola had no one to answer to, since she lived alone, and Peggy assumed that Tom was simply working harder than usual. During the sleepless nights beside his wife's softly snoring form, Tom would lie stiff and sweating, his mind under assault by dangerous fantasies. But having tasted Viola, who could say what was sane or mad? After discovering portals to new worlds through an almost miraculously feminine woman, what man would not dream of a future with her? Of running off to a place where skin color meant nothing? Viola swore that no such place existed, not even in Paris. That might be, Tom admitted, but the real obstacle to fulfilling that dream was his children. How many times did he rise from bed and pad into the rooms of his son and daughter? Jenny was sixteen then, Penn only eight. To look down at their innocent faces and imagine leaving was impossible. Yet Tom could not stop his mind from fleeing to that fantasy realm where he would awaken to Viola every day, to her liquid eyes, her effortless smile, and the fluid grace of her body.

That dream ended forty-five days after it began.

Nearly seven weeks after they consummated their desire in the X-ray room, Viola suddenly changed. The previous day, Tom had rendezvoused with her as usual, and her eyes had shone with boundless love. The next morning, when he saw her in the clinic, the light had gone out of her eyes, and impassable walls had been raised around her. When he tried to question her, she only shook her head and hurried on to the next patient. Without saying anything, Viola made it clear that Tom Cage was as irrevocably part of her past as her dead husband. At first he thought she must have received some bad news about her brother. But during a tense coffee break she told him that Jimmy was still hiding in Freewoods, though chafing to return to Natchez and "the struggle." After two hours of dazed disbelief, Tom finally cornered Viola in an examining room and demanded an explanation for the distance between them.

"You have a family," she said with lacerating formality. "If we'd kept going, we would have destroyed that. We have no right to do that. You can't build happiness on someone else's pain."

Before Tom could answer, she brushed past him and went back to work. As the day wore on, Tom rehearsed a thousand arguments in his mind, but the more he tried to argue with her premise, the more right he realized she was. He'd been in denial from the beginning, and Viola had simply chosen to force him out of it. There were only two possible endings for their relationship: in Scenario One, Tom would keep his family and Viola would be alone, at least until she found someone new; in Scenario Two . . . well, Scenario Two was unthinkable. If Tom tried to possess Viola, he would destroy his family, his career, Viola, and possibly even himself.

In truth, both scenarios seemed unendurable. To lose Viola would be agony, yet to give up his family would mean betraying his deepest convictions. Then, like an unexpected blow, the full weight of the first possibility struck Tom: to see Viola in love with someone else . . . that might well shatter him. After this realization, every moment of that day became a struggle to maintain control of himself. He was trying to figure out some Solomonic solution when Dr. Lucas called him into his office and told him that Viola had asked to be assigned to Dr. Ross, a GP Lucas had hired two months earlier. Ross was only two years out of medical school, and Dr. Lucas told Tom that both Ross and the clinic would benefit from Viola's experience. Tom sat in shock before his senior partner's desk, unable to find credible words of protest.

"It's for the best," Lucas said in a stern voice. "Viola's close to a nervous breakdown. And you're not thinking straight, Tom. If you were, you wouldn't be putting your family at risk. The clinic, too, to be honest, with the way the goddamn Klan has been going at it these past couple of years."

"The Klan?" Tom said dully.

"Let's just leave it at that, all right? Viola will be working under Dr. Ross from now on. You'll get Anna Mae."

Tom swallowed hard, trying to find his voice.

"That's all," Dr. Lucas said. "Go home and see your kids. I saw Penn's name in the newspaper yesterday, didn't I?"

"Penn?"

"Your son, goddamn it! He hit a home run at Duncan Park. *Go home!*"

Somehow Tom rose from the chair and found his way down the hall to his office. He buzzed the receptionist and asked to see Viola, but the receptionist told him all the nurses had gone for the day. He was certain he'd heard a note of triumph in the woman's voice. He waited until everyone had left the clinic, then called Viola's house. She didn't answer.

He found a stack of charts and began dictating, but between each record he dialed Viola's house. She never answered. As the tension in him grew to an unbearable pitch, he swept the files onto the floor, then ran out to his car and drove to the colored side of town. Whenever he'd gone to Viola's house before, he'd always been in her car, lying on the floor of her backseat. Now he drove right up to her frame house, his eyes scanning the carport, which was empty. He wanted to park out front and wait for her, but even unhinged as he was, he knew that would be crazy.

That night he lay clenching and unclenching his sweaty fists beside his sleeping wife. In the hour before dawn, he felt closer to madness than he ever had in his life—even in Korea. The seed of that madness was the knowledge not only that he had to give up Viola, but that one day—perhaps not long from now—she would be lying in the arms of another man. Nothing could mitigate the horror of this prospect, or assuage the anger he felt—not even the thought of his wife and children, happy and carefree in a bountiful future. For the price of their happiness was Viola.

But even if he were willing to pay that price, how could he work in proximity to a woman he loved but could no longer touch? How could he treat her as merely an employee? How could she ask that of him? And how could she endure it? Unless . . . no—she loved him still. Of that he was certain. Viola would keep her job because she needed it to eat. Any merciful separation would have to be provided by him. That meant finding a new clinic. Maybe starting his own practice . . .

By the next morning, Tom had fallen into a state of near catatonia. He didn't shower before driving to work, and he moved like an automaton when he got out of the car, not speaking to anyone he passed on the sidewalk. He knew no other way to face the lie he would now be living, one that slowly starved the soul rather than nourishing it, one that snuffed out hope rather than kindling it. What Tom did not know was that behind the door of the clinic that morning waited a future of blood and violence that would surpass even the war—

"Dr. Cage?" called a panicked voice. "Dr. Cage, the door's locked!"

Tom heard a harsh rapping at his office door. How long had it been going on? "Just a damn minute," he said under his breath. With a last look at the Polaroid of Viola, he slipped the photo back into *The Killer Angels* and reshelved the book.

"Dr. Cage!" Melba cried, her voice insistent. "Are you all right?"

"I'm fine! I'm coming!" He took a deep breath, then opened the door and stepped back so that Melba could enter. "I must have locked it by mistake."

"Don't do that!" said the nurse. "I didn't know what might have happened in here."

"Melba . . ." He shook his head and opened his palms. "I'm not going to kill myself or anything."

"Of course not. I just . . . your *heart*. Anything could happen, and at any time. That's what your cardiologist said."

"I locked it by mistake," Tom said gently. "But listen . . . if it's my time, there's not much we can do."

Melba gave him a sisterly glare. "Don't you say that. Don't talk like that."

"All right."

"Well, then. The reason I needed to talk to you is that someone's been calling on the phone for you. He's waiting on the line now."

Tom looked at the phone on his desk. "I didn't hear it ring."

Melba squinted in puzzlement. "You didn't?"

Over the years, so many thousands of patients had called Tom that he'd developed the ability to tune out the telephone altogether. "Lost in thought, I guess. Who is it?"

"He wouldn't say. The caller ID said 'pay phone,' but all the man will say is that he served in Korea with you."

Tom felt his heartbeat quicken.

"Thanks, Mel. I'll take it."

She hesitated, then went out. As soon as the door closed, he picked up the phone. "Walt?"

"You bet," said a Texas drawl.

"Don't say anything until my nurse hangs up."

They waited for the click of the receiver. Tom had e-mailed Walt Garrity a few hours earlier, instructing the old Texas Ranger to call him at home using a pay phone.

There was a clatter in Tom's left ear, then Melba said, "Dr. Cage? Have you got it?"

"I've got it," he said, waiting for the click.

It was slow in coming, but at last it did. "Okay, Walt."

"Jeez, pardner. Could you make it any harder on a fella?"

"What do you mean?"

"You just about can't *find* a pay phone these days."

"Sorry."

The old Ranger chuckled. "I finally found one in the lobby of a hotel. I think mostly hookers and drug dealers use it. Anyway, what's going on? Not your ticker again, is it?"

"No. This is worse."

"Shit. Fire away."

"I'm in trouble, buddy. I need help."

"What kind of trouble?"

"The law."

Garrity took a moment to process this. "That sounds like your son's line of country."

"Normally, it would be. But I have to keep Penn out of this. This is . . . different."

"Different how?"

"This is like Korea."

"Which part?"

Tom hesitated, wishing he didn't have to raise any ghosts for Garrity. "Like the ambulance."

"Oh, God. How do you mean?"

"Similar situation."

This time the silence dragged for a long time. "I think I've got you. Tell me what you need."

"I hate to ask this, Walt. I hate to ask you to leave Carmelita." Garrity had found his true love late in life, a Mexican woman who put up with nothing but took wonderful care of him. "But I need you to come to Natchez."

"Keep talking."

"I may be in custody soon. Probably not tonight, but possibly as early as tomorrow. If that happens, I'm going to need you on the outside, doing what I can't from jail."

"I hear you."

"This could be dangerous. I won't lie to you."

"Imagine that," said the Ranger.

"Before you say yes, I want you to know—"

"I'll tell you what *I* know, Corpsman Cage. Medics stick together. Right? Whatever you need, you've got it. You know that."

Tom felt an unexpected rush of emotion. "Thanks, buddy."

"Can you be more specific about your situation?"

"Not on the phone. Let's just say I've got a target painted on my back."

"Just like that ol' red cross in the snow, huh?"

"Yep. A lot like that."

"What goes around comes around, I reckon."

"Walt—"

"Put a sock in it, Corpsman. Remember what we told the wounded. 'Lie still. Play dead. Help's a-comin'.' I'll be there tomorrow, if not sooner."

The connection went dead.

Tom raised his arm and wiped tears from his eyes for the second time that day.

CHAPTER 17

MY KNOWLEDGE OF FERRIDAY, Louisiana, is so limited that I only recently realized that the town lies within Concordia Parish. I always thought the *Concordia Beacon* was printed in Vidalia, the little town just across the river from Natchez. I'd never confess this to Henry Sexton, of course. The man has done some amazing journalism from this farming village. I won't be surprised if Henry brings a Pulitzer back to Ferriday someday, if only he lives long enough to accept it.

Dusk is falling as I roll into the town proper, its main drag a hodge-podge of gas stations, convenience stores, and small repair shops. The newest-looking building in sight is a Kentucky Fried Chicken. For most of my life, I thought of Ferriday only as a town I had to pass through to get to Lake St. John. During the *Urban Cowboy* craze, I'd hear it mentioned as the birthplace of Mickey Gilley, and later as that of Jimmy Swaggart. Both men are cultural footnotes now, and favorite son General Claire Chennault is as unfamiliar to anyone under fifty as the crank telephone. It's local boy Jerry Lee Lewis—the Killer, by his own proclamation—who wrote his name in the brightest lights on the world's stage. Jerry Lee may have tarnished his legacy by marrying his thirteen-year-old cousin (something that wouldn't have shocked the homefolks nearly so much as it did the London reporters who first broke the story), but John Lennon kissed his feet twenty years later, and the Killer is still going strong. My clearest memory of Ferriday is driving over to sit in the decaying old Arcade theater in 1978, because unlike Natchez's conservative theaters, the Arcade was showing Michael Cimino's *The Deer Hunter*. To this day, I believe the Arcade owners booked the film because they thought it was a movie about deer hunting, not Vietnam.

The *Concordia Beacon* is housed in a shockingly small building on the north edge of town. No bigger than a successful dentist's office, it stands at the border of an empty cotton field that stretches off toward a distant tree line. The sickly sweet smell of some chemical poison rides the chilly breeze as I get out and walk to the glass front door.

I hold my breath until I get inside.

A woman of sixty-five stands behind a high receptionist's desk, her hair done in a style that would have looked fashionable in the late 1950s. She looks as though she's gathering up her things to leave. I hear a radio playing in the back, but when the woman calls "Henry?" over her shoulder, the music stops.

"Send him on back!" comes the reply. Then the music starts up again.

The woman laughs and shakes her head. "Same old Henry. I worry about that boy."

She comes around the desk carrying a big purse and a cake box. "I sure like your books, Mayor Cage. My husband does too. And he don't hardly read nothing anymore, so that's saying something."

"I appreciate it, Mrs. . . . ?"

"Whittington," she says. "I used to be a Smithdale, ages ago. I only say that 'cause Dr. Cage treated me when I was a teenager. They don't make 'em like Dr. Cage anymore."

I give the obligatory smile I always do in these situations.

As Mrs. Whittington passes me, I feel her hand close on my wrist, and she looks into my eyes with the disarming sincerity of country people. "I mean it," she says earnestly. "You take care of your daddy."

I promise that I will, realizing as I do that the rumors must already be spreading outward through landlines and the cellular airwaves like vibrations through a spiderweb.

"We'll be praying for you," Mrs. Whittington says, and then she's gone.

I hear the glass door being locked as I pass through the doorway into a larger room containing several small desks, a photocopier, and tall shelves holding big bound volumes filled with back issues of the *Beacon*. Seated behind one of the desks, playing an old National guitar with a shining silver resonator, is Henry Sexton, the lanky, unassuming baby boomer who has stirred up more trouble for ex-Klansmen than almost any reporter in the South. Henry nods when he sees me, but he keeps on playing, using a gold cigarette lighter as a slide, filling the room with crystalline wails that soar over droning low notes that ebb and flow like the moaning of a grieving man. With his gray-ing mustache and goatee, he looks more like an old musician than a journalist.

"Come on in and sit down," he says, scrunching up his mouth as he plays a particularly difficult passage; then he tosses out a flurry of blue notes that vanish into a shimmering harmonic at the twelfth fret.

"Sounds good," I say, as he lays the National flat in his lap.

"I try to keep my hand in. Calms me down when I'm stressed out. Playing this guitar always makes me think of Albert Norris."

As Henry takes his hands from the strings, I notice his hands are shaking. "Did you know him personally?" I ask, quickly looking up at his eyes.

A deeper sadness comes into Henry's perpetually sad eyes. "I knew him well. As a boy, of course." His face brightens a little. "As a matter of fact, I bought that guitar off a man Albert sold it to back in the fifties. Albert was a pianist by training, but he could play a mean guitar when he wanted to. But it was Jimmy Revels who taught me to play the slide like that—with a cigarette lighter instead of a bottleneck. Steve Crop-per did the same thing on some big records. But you didn't come here to learn about the blues."

"I didn't realize you knew Jimmy Revels, either. You've never men-tioned that in your articles, have you?"

"No. I try to keep my writing as objective as possible. But I knew Jimmy pretty well. Luther Davis, too. I was close to Albert's whole fam-ily, and most everybody who hung out in the store. That's one reason I've never let those cases rest. Maybe the main reason."

"Well, I admire you for it."

Henry shakes his head. "I respect you more for taking on the Del Payton case. It's easy to work hard at something when you have a per-sonal stake in it."

I don't want Henry thinking I'm a better man than I am. "Honestly, when Payton's family first came to me, I turned them down. They sort of embarrassed me into taking the case. You could say I took it out of white guilt."

Henry goes still, his eyes smoldering in his mild face. "Don't knock white guilt. Let me tell you something. There's a PBS crew filming a documentary about my work. They're covering a few other investigative journalists, too. And the question people always ask when the director shows them footage is 'Where are the black reporters in this story? All you're showing us is white men trying to solve these civil rights murders.'"

"How do you answer them?"

"With the same question. Where *are* the black reporters? I need all the help I can get. But it's white men working these cases, almost exclusively. And I'm not sure why. Is it guilt, like you said? I'll tell you this: when I read my list of black murder victims from the sixties, hardly a black person in America recognizes a name. There's something wrong with that, brother."

Henry leans back and flicks his fingernails across the open-tuned strings on the National. "Albert Norris was like a father to me, Penn. But Jimmy Revels broke my heart. And he never even knew it. Ain't that something?"

Jimmy Revels broke my heart? This strange lament stops me cold. For a moment I wonder if Henry is telling me he's gay, but he reads my mind and snaps this delusion with a laugh. "No, not like that. But we don't have time to go into that story. Did you tell Shad Johnson I made a copy of what was on that hard drive?"

"No. I promised you I wouldn't, and I keep my promises."

"Thank you. I need favors from Shad from time to time."

"Has he helped you in the past?"

"No. But he's all I've got to work with over there right now."

"My fiancée would tell you you've got nothing, then."

Henry looks strangely uncomfortable.

"Do you know Caitlin?"

"I've met her a couple of times," he says quietly.

His tone doesn't sound favorable. "But?"

"Well . . ." He looks at the floor between us. "She's big-time, you know? Pulitzer Prize and everything. I just work for a little weekly paper."

"Don't underestimate what you're doing, Henry. I've heard Caitlin compliment your stories many times. She has tremendous respect for you."

He actually blushes at this. "I appreciate that."

Henry probably thinks I'm just being polite, but the truth is, Cait-

lin has sounded almost jealous when she's mentioned Henry's work.
I've occasionally wondered whether she's followed up some of the leads
he's unearthed, without telling me about it. Maybe that's what Henry's
worried about. He doesn't want to reveal hard-won information to me,
when it might wind up in Caitlin's hands an hour later.

"Henry, let me put your mind at rest about something. Caitlin
Masters is no threat to you—not through me. She and I keep a high
wall between our careers. We have to. You may find that difficult to
believe, but as Natchez's mayor and her one newspaper publisher,
we've been through enough conflict-of-interest situations that we've
learned to compartmentalize. And that arrangement has been tested,
believe me. It's caused serious stress in our relationship. But we've
stuck to it. *Nothing* you tell me will get to Caitlin. Okay? Not without
your permission."

Henry sighs with obvious relief. "I appreciate it."

"So, tell me why you called me."

Henry raises the National into playing position again, almost like
it's a shield. "Penn, do you believe your daddy killed Viola?"

"Are we alone in this building?"

"We are now."

"And we're off the record?"

"You're not even here, brother."

"He might have, Henry. I don't know. You saw the tape. We may
have seen a botched attempt at euthanasia. An unexpected drug reaction. I can't see my father screwing up such a thing, but he might cover
for someone else who did. A family member, maybe. I just spent half an
hour talking to Dad, and he stuck to the doctor-patient privilege pitch
like the Maginot Line. What do you think happened?"

"I think it was straight-up murder, and the Double Eagles did it."

This assertion hits me like cold water in the face. "The splinter
group of the Klan you've written about?"

Henry nods. "In 1968, the Double Eagles warned Viola that if
she ever returned to Natchez, they'd kill her. They kidnapped and
murdered her brother, Jimmy Revels, and I believe Viola saw enough
to put some Eagles behind bars. She may even have seen them kill
Jimmy, or Luther Davis."

"How do you know this? I've never read it in your stories."

"Viola told me about the old warning two weeks ago, but she wouldn't go farther than that. But today, right after I talked to you, I interviewed the first Double Eagle ever to go on the record about any of their crimes. He's positive that some of his old brothers killed Viola to fulfill that threat."

My breath comes a little shallower. "Does he know that for a fact?"

"No. He's out of the loop these days, as far as they're concerned. But I believe he's right."

"Do you have any evidence?"

"Only circumstantial, I'm afraid. But that'll change soon."

Not what I'd hoped for, but . . . "Who is this Double Eagle?"

"I can't tell you that. Not yet."

Henry's refusal hits me with delayed effect, like the pain of a puncture wound. "Are you serious? We need to get this guy in front of a district attorney. Or some FBI agents, at least."

"That'll never happen. He only talked to me on the condition that I not print anything until after he's dead—which from the looks of him won't be long."

"Henry, Shad means to charge my father with murder tomorrow. First-degree murder."

"I was afraid of that. But you don't have to worry. Your father's innocent. There's no way he'll even go to trial for this crime. A week from now, I'll have nailed the Eagles for it."

"A week in the county jail could easily kill my dad. Please tell me who this guy is. I'm a former prosecutor. I have a lot of experience persuading reluctant witnesses to turn state's evidence."

"Maybe so. But you're not the prosecutor here or across the river. You can't offer immunity in exchange for testimony."

"A district attorney can."

"The DA hates your guts."

"Shad Johnson hates my guts. But what about the Concordia Parish DA?"

Henry folds his arms over the face of his guitar and looks hard into my eyes. "No one can offer a man immunity against death. And death is the only thing motivating this source. Fear of Hell with a capital *H.*"

Ever since I talked to Dad, the simmering anxiety in my chest has threatened to boil into panic. Henry's refusal to confide in me isn't helping matters. "Henry . . . with all due respect, are you being honest about your reason for holding back this witness? Are you afraid I'm going to tell Caitlin about him? Because I absolutely won't do that."

"I believe you. But your sole priority right now is your father. You desperately want to save him. And I can't risk you scaring off this source by trying to rush him. You might even accidentally expose him to the Eagles and get him killed. We can't blow the chance to solve a dozen murder cases just to get your father clear of trouble a few days faster."

I have to admit that Henry is making sense. It's not his fault that Dad won't speak up in his own defense. But something about Henry's thesis *doesn't* make sense, though I can't quite put my finger on it.

"Did any of this come up with Shad today?"

"I told him about the 1968 threat."

"How did he respond?"

"Wasn't interested. Shad said if the Eagles were still active, they'd have killed me a long time ago, not some old nurse who was already dying."

"That actually makes sense."

The reporter gives me a sour look. "Not really. Until about a month ago, I didn't really know enough to hurt them. Not seriously. Unlike Viola Turner."

I grunt noncommittally.

"I'll tell you something Shad doesn't know," he says. "The Eagles are no stranger to drugs. I'd heard rumors, but today my source confirmed it. The Eagles are heavy into the crystal meth trade statewide. They could easily have gotten ahold of something that would kill Viola."

"Why haven't you told Shad this?"

"Because I promised I wouldn't reveal anything my source told me until after he's dead. And because he'd deny it, if I did."

"They're into the drug trade *now*?"

"Yes, with their sons. And they would be far more likely to make a mistake with them than your father."

The idea of the Double Eagles dabbling in the drug trade tickles something deep in my mind, but Henry's mention of my father blanks out all intuition. The logical flaw in Henry's theory of Viola's murder is flashing like an electrical scoreboard behind my eyes.

"Henry, we're missing the forest here."

"What do you mean?"

"If the Double Eagles killed Viola, then why is my father acting the way he is? If he's innocent . . . *why is he acting guilty?*"

This stumps the reporter. He reaches out and gives one of the National's tuning pegs a twist, then answers in a thoughtful voice. "What if the Eagles framed your father? They knew Dr. Cage was treating her, they saw a chance to blame him for their hit, and they seized their chance."

"Then why isn't Dad screaming from the rooftops that he's innocent?"

Henry's sad eyes move from the tuning pegs to my face. "They must have something on him. Something from the past that your father doesn't want exposed."

"Something he'd go to prison over? No way."

Henry doesn't look convinced. "Are you sure? Such things certainly exist, depending on a man's concern over how people see him."

"What could be that bad, Henry?"

The reporter clucks his tongue. "Let me tell you something my source said today. First, he inadvertently let slip that Viola had witnessed the torture of her brother and Luther Davis. When I asked why on earth the Eagles would have let her live after that, guess what he told me."

"No idea."

" '*If it hadn't been for Ray Presley and Dr. Tom Cage, she wouldn't have lived.*' "

A chill of presentiment races along my back and shoulders, and I can see Henry knows I know the significance of Presley's name.

"Ray was the dirtiest cop who ever set foot in Natchez," he says, "and maybe even New Orleans. I know from your book that Presley was up to his neck in the Del Payton murder. And from other sources, I've gathered that Presley had a long-standing relationship with your father, which has always puzzled me. I can't imagine what that was based on."

My thoughts and memories swirl without coherence. Ray Presley was one of the worst human beings I've ever known, and I've met some deeply disturbed men in my career. Presley not only disgraced his badge and murdered men for money; he also raped my high school sweetheart, something I didn't discover until almost twenty years after the fact.

"Henry . . . I can't give you details, but when I was a kid, a woman in our family was in real danger. This was in another state, and the police refused to help. In fact, they were part of the problem. In desperation, Dad turned to Ray Presley. Ray took care of the problem, but as you might guess, he went outside the law to do it. And he held that over my father's head until his own death."

Henry thinks for a moment. "I see. Well . . . if your dad got Ray to help him in that case, then I guess he could have turned to Presley when Viola was in trouble. There's no way Ray would have intervened to save Viola on his own hook."

"Would my dad really have gone that far to save Viola?"

"She was his nurse for five years."

I give Henry a searching look. "And maybe more than that?"

"I didn't say that."

"But you've been thinking it. I have, too, ever since this morning."

Henry sighs and taps the shining metal face of the National. "Was Dr. Cage the straying kind?"

"Not that I know of. But God knows every man's capable of it, if the right temptation comes along."

"Granted. But even if he and Viola were lovers, I don't see how it would alter cases. I think your father cared about Viola and wanted to protect her, whether he'd slept with her or not."

I can no longer keep my darkest fear buried in my brain. "It might alter cases quite a bit if it turns out that Dad fathered Viola's child. That Lincoln Turner is his son. *That* might be a secret worth going to prison to keep hidden. In my father's mind, anyway."

Henry sits as still as a stone Buddha, watching me cautiously. "Maybe," he concedes finally. "But I've already gone down that road, and I don't believe it. I do believe Lincoln Turner is the son of a white man—but not your father. I checked Lincoln's age, and he was surely conceived around the time Viola left Natchez."

I'm actually trembling. "And?"

"I staked out Shad Johnson's office for a while this afternoon, and I got a good look at the man himself. Lincoln, I mean."

"Lincoln was at Shad's office again?"

"Yes. And he's a very dark-skinned fellow. About three times as dark as Shad Johnson, I'd say, and twice as dark as his mother. Your father is Scots-English, a very light-skinned man."

"Is that scientific proof?"

Henry looks at the floor, then seems to take some silent decision. "I want to show you something, Penn." He looks up, his face vulnerable. "But before I do, I need one promise. I've worked too long and too hard on these cases to hand it all over to other people now."

"I know you have, Henry. Nothing you tell me will leave this building. And I expect the same discretion from you."

"That's good enough for me." Setting down the guitar and taking a set of keys from his desk drawer, he leads me down a narrow hallway to a metal door at the back of the building. He opens two locks, then pushes the door open with a screech and flips on a fluorescent light.

Following him inside, I find a ten-by-twelve room whose walls are plastered with maps, photographs, a bulletin board, a whiteboard, and pushpins connecting various names, photos, and locations on the walls. Three worktables form a U with its open end facing the door, and the lower half of each wall seems to be braced with banker's boxes spilling files. The room instantly hurls me back to the days when I was prosecuting capital murder cases in Houston. Our workrooms were larger than this, but the atmosphere was the same.

"The nerve center of your investigations?"

"Yep. Almost totally analog, I'm embarrassed to say."

"Nothing wrong with analog, buddy."

"An intern I had from Syracuse called this my war room. I call it the cooler, because it holds the cold cases from the last forty years. I'm working twelve unsolved murders from the 1960s alone, and those are just the ones I'm sure were murder. The FBI would kill to see inside this room."

The first thing that really catches my eye is a poster advertising a Ku Klux Klan rally to be held at Liberty Park in Natchez, which was less than a mile from the house I grew up in.

"As far as the paternity issue," Henry says, "less than a week before Viola fled Natchez, she was gang-raped by several members of the Double Eagle group. I don't know the etiquette of gang rape, but I'm guessing none of those bastards wore condoms. And if I had to guess who was there, I'd pick Frank and Snake Knox, Sonny Thornfield, and the guy I interviewed this morning. I have pictures of all those men."

He takes my elbow and leads me to a rogues' gallery tacked to the wall opposite us. "Here," he says, tapping the black-and-white snaps with his right forefinger. "These four sterling citizens here. Tell me what you see."

My mind is too consumed by fear to make much of the faces. I see a blur of pale-skinned, hollow-eyed men of the kind you see in Civil War photographs. Except . . . one. One man is darker than his comrades— *much* darker—almost as though he has a deep tan or sunburn. But when I look closer, I see that the color is part of his biology, perhaps a sign of Creole or even Indian blood, like a Louisiana Redbone.

"Who's this?" I ask, touching the photo.

"Walter Stillson 'Sonny' Thornfield. And in my opinion, Lincoln Turner's father."

Despite the horror implied in this statement—for Viola, and for Lincoln, if he knows the truth—I feel a flood of relief. "Do you think Lincoln knows about his mother's rape?"

"I hope not. But even if he does, what bastard child doesn't pray that he's the son of the lord of the manor, and not a lowly peasant?"

"So Lincoln may believe that my father is his father, even if he's not."

"Yes. And that would certainly explain his level of anger, given the situation. I doubt any African-American mother would want to tell her son that he was fathered by a white-trash ex-Klansman who'd raped her. Much less, one of many. Especially since Viola got married soon after she arrived in Chicago—in the time-honored tradition of so many girls 'in trouble' during that era. Viola probably told Lincoln he was the son of her husband. At least for most of his life."

I remember my dad telling me about Viola marrying a con man in Chicago. "Well, somebody needs to tell Lincoln the truth, before he pushes this thing any further."

"Shad Johnson is the man pushing the murder investigation. Lincoln is just his excuse. It's no secret Shad hates you, and your father has given him a golden opportunity for revenge."

Without warning, my view of the entire case makes a tectonic shift. "Holy Christ, Henry. *Shad* thinks Lincoln is my father's son. If Lincoln told him that, Shad might easily believe Dad would kill Viola to keep it secret."

This realization stops Henry cold. "I hadn't thought of that."

"I've got to talk to Shad."

Henry holds up a warning hand. "Think hard before you do that. Come back over here and let me show you something."

He leads me back around the table to the poster advertising the Ku Klux Klan rally near my childhood home.

"That was the biggest Klan rally ever held in the South," he informs me. "Thirty-seven hundred people attended—men, women, and children." He turns to his worktable, fishes through a stack of photographs, chooses two, and steps back toward me. "I was looking at these before I called you."

The photo on top is in color. It shows my father, aged about thirty-five, standing in front of a single-engine airplane in bright sunlight with a man a little older than he. Both men sport the long sideburns fashionable in the seventies.

"Who's that?" I ask. "He looks familiar."

"Dr. Leland Robb. He treated Albert Norris for the four days that he lay dying from his burns in 1964. He and your father were friends."

"I don't really remember him."

"You were only nine years old when he died in a midair collision a few miles from here."

"Wait a minute! I remember that. I went out on a couple of dates with the daughter of the pilot who died in that crash. She never really got over that."

Henry nods soberly. "I'm not surprised. I believe Dr. Robb was murdered, Penn."

"What?"

"Bear with me." He slides the photo under the one beneath it. The second shot is black-and-white, and as soon as I comprehend what I'm seeing, the hair on my neck stands up. A rush of scents and images fills my brain: the smell of horses and barbecue and burning kerosene; clouds of pink cotton candy; wild-eyed men standing in the beds of pickup trucks, yelling about God's wrath while women sell embroidered sheets from card tables nearby. In this photograph, my father is standing amid some Ku Klux Klansmen wearing white robes and hoods. Dad's wearing street clothes, as is another man beside him, but everyone else in the photo, except the children, is dressed in full Klan regalia.

"Where was this taken?" I whisper.

"At the Klan rally advertised on that poster. Or just outside it. July 1965. This was shot by an FBI agent. Do you recognize anyone in the picture besides your father?"

"The man standing with Dad looks like . . . holy shit. Ray Presley."

After an awkward silence, Henry says, "Ray was never in the Klan. He kept his hand in everything, though. This could have been a chance meeting."

"Who's the Klansman talking to Dad?"

"Frank Knox," Henry says evenly. "The founder of the Double Eagle group."

My face feels numb. "Goddamn it, Henry. What is this?"

"Frank Knox was a patient of your father's. All the Double Eagles were."

"They must have worked at Armstrong Tire or Triton Battery."

"They did. Recognize anybody else?"

I study the photo more closely. "Yeah . . . me."

"*What?*" Henry leans down over the photo.

I point to a little towheaded boy with a flattop, talking to two other kids. "That's me, right there. Age five. And that kid is Jackie Steele. He pitched for my Dixie Youth baseball team a few years later. Dad took me to this rally when I was a kid. I didn't realize it was this one until now. All I really remember is that the horses were wearing robes and hoods, like the people. They reminded me of the horses in *Ivanhoe*."

"Why would he take you to that rally?"

"I think he wanted to show me history while it was happening, even if it was terrible. Do you believe there was more to it?"

Henry stands with his hands on his hips, looking like a man who just climbed out of a ditch after digging for twelve hours straight. "I don't know, Penn. This is a rough group he's talking to. But I'll tell you this. These sons of bitches here"—he sweeps his hand to his right, taking in a row of photos on the wall that looks like a mug book of convicts culled from 1950s-vintage chain gangs—"they murdered the man who was more of a father to me than my own blood. They burned him alive. These same bastards would love to send your daddy to Parchman for

killing an old woman that they did terrible things to—*terrible* things—
and almost certainly killed last night." He fixes me with a single-minded
stare. "I mean to take them down, Penn. I mean to make them pay."
Henry's jaw quivers from the force of his passion. "If it's the last thing I
do on earth, I'll make them face their just punishment."

"I believe you, Henry. Why are you showing me all this?"

The reporter wipes a tear from the corner of his eye. "If you stay
to hear the rest, you'll understand. I think I've been on my own too
long. People are dying so fast . . . too fast. I don't know who I can trust,
or whose life I can justify putting in danger. These are some bad boys.
There's young ones involved, too. I called you because I know you've
been in this kind of scrape before. You've got connections I don't. You've
fought the FBI before, and won. You can keep them off my back while
I walk the last mile of this thing. But more than that, you've got a stake
in this. One way or another, your father is involved in every important
murder case I've been working these past years."

"What?" I break in, another chill racing along my skin.

Henry nods soberly. "And Dr. Cage has consistently refused to let
me interview him. Your daddy knows things about this time, Penn.
Things he's afraid to talk about. And I imagine some of them have to do
with Viola." Henry waves his hand around the room again, taking in
the artifacts of a more troubled decade. "This is our legacy, brother. It's
not easy for me to do, but I'm asking for your help."

I lay my hand on his shoulder and squeeze tight. "I'm with you, bud.
Tell me what you know."

CHAPTER 18

SNAKE KNOX AND Sonny Thornfield stood beneath a leafless oak, dripping cold water from a brief shower they'd endured with the grim silence of old soldiers. The pin oak stood beside a gravel drive that led to the house where Glenn Morehouse was dying. Sonny wore a camouflaged nylon shoulder pack slung across his chest. Snake's hands were empty, but he had a pistol tucked in his waistband at the small of his back. They'd driven in from the dirt road back by the levee, then parked behind the trees and walked in, so that no one would see their truck. For twenty-five minutes they'd been waiting for a signal that had not come. The porch light of the solitary house should have gone dark long ago.

"What the hell?" Sonny whispered. "We're gonna have dogs barking in a minute."

"That's why I brought my pistol," Snake said.

"You fire that hogleg, they'll hear it all the way to Frogmore."

Sonny wondered what a passerby would think if he saw two white men in their seventies standing under a tree after an icy rain, not even smoking cigarettes. Of course, there were no passersby out here. Even if there were, he supposed nobody would think twice about two old men standing by the road. Once you passed seventy, no one really saw you unless you put yourself in their way. This rankled Snake, especially where women were concerned, but Sonny didn't mind. He liked anonymity.

"You think the dumb slut forgot?" Snake asked, pointing toward the lone yellow porch light of the small ranch-style house.

"Not Wilma. Maybe Glenn won't take his pill or something."

Snake hiked up his jacket collar to dry his neck. "This is bullshit. Let's just go in there and do it."

"Wait," Sonny said nervously. "Are you sure we shouldn't call Billy first? I'm pretty sure he didn't want us to go ahead until he okayed it."

"Wrong. What he said was, make sure *you* were convinced Glenn was ratting us out. Shit. Him and Forrest'll never get past that Martin Luther King thing. Frank always said a man's biggest enemy is his mouth." Snake spat. "Well, boss man? Are you convinced?"

Snake's eyes were menacing in the dark.

"Yeah, I believe it," Sonny said nervously. After all, Wilma Deen had told them she'd walked in on the tail end of a call that she was almost sure had been to Henry Sexton. But still . . . "What about Forrest? You think he's cool with this?"

Snake snorted. "I *don't give a shit*. All Forrest is thinking about is moving up in the state police and whatever power play he's got going with Brody in New Orleans. I don't plan to move down to that hell-hole, even though God did the world a favor and washed all the welfare trash out of there. I'm staying right here, and I ain't lettin' Morehouse or Henry Sexton send me to Angola to live out my days. Brody Royal's okay with this, and that's all I need to know."

Sonny didn't want to think about Snake trying to exploit tensions between the two most powerful men in their universe.

"Billy's mama ruined him," Snake muttered. "Thinks he's the god-damn king of everything now. One of these days I'm gonna tear that boy a new one."

I'll lay odds you won't, Sonny thought, but what he said was "I got some Skoal. Want a pinch?"

"No."

Sonny was fishing for his tin when Snake tensed beside him.

"The light's gone," Snake said. "Let's move."

Sonny followed him silently across the road, as silently as you could move over packed gravel anyway. When they reached the front porch, Sonny pulled back the screen door with a slow screech and tapped lightly against the wood.

Someone turned the knob and drew the door inward. The repellent odors of a sickroom wafted out of the darkness. As Sonny drew back, a pale, hollow-eyed face appeared in the crack of the door, hovering like an apparition. Wilma Deen, Glenn Morehouse's sister.

"How many of you?" she asked, her wrinkled face pinched with suspicion.

"Just me and Snake."

She opened the door wider and drew her flannel housecoat tight.

"Glenn sleepin'?" asked Snake.

"He's woozy, but he ain't down yet. Which is odd, because I doubled his usual dose."

"Well, I need to talk to him anyway. Let's go. I'm soaked to the skin already, and I don't fancy bein' here longer than we got to be."

The three of them gathered inside the tiny foyer. Wilma had the indurated skin of a lifelong chain smoker, and her eyes held a weariness that made Sonny tired.

"Has he talked to Henry Sexton any more since that last phone call?" Snake asked.

"I don't think so. I've hardly left him. I went to the bathroom earlier, but he was dozing. What ya'll gonna do? You ain't gonna hurt him, are you?"

"Not like we oughta," Snake said. "Not like what the oath says."

Wilma gave him a mistrustful look. "Well, we've got a problem, anyway."

"What problem?"

"Glenn's got a gun in there."

"*What?*" Snake whispered. "In the bed with him?"

She nodded. "His old .45. First time I've seen it out of the closet. He's been acting paranoid for a few days. The doctor calls it 'hypervigilance.' He says people get that way sometimes when the end is close."

"It's closer than he thinks," Snake muttered. "But we didn't come for no shoot-out. Besides, it wouldn't look right." He looked hard at Wilma. "You got to go in there and get that gun, Willy."

She reddened at this childhood nickname. "How'm I s'posed to do that?"

"Hell . . . you're his sister. You'll figure something out."

"Wait a second," Sonny said. "Even if we get that gun, if Glenn's all paranoid, he could fight us. That won't look right, either."

"He can't fight you," Wilma assured them.

"Shows what you know," Snake said. "I saw Glenn break a Jap sergeant's neck while he had two bullets in his back."

Wilma shook her head as though exhausted. "He ain't what he was no more. There ain't much left now."

Sonny felt weak with grief and regret.

"What am I supposed to do when you're finished?" Wilma asked.

"Swallow a coupla Glenn's sleeping pills," Snake advised. "Then go in your room and go to sleep. When you wake up in the morning, call his doctor and give the news. Glenn was feeling poorly when you put him to bed, and he was dead when you woke up. That's all you know."

Wilma's eyes had gone wide. "You want me to stay in the house all night with his body?"

Snake shrugged. "It ain't as bad as you think. I spent all night in a foxhole with two dead buddies, and one was in pieces. Remember, Billy's gonna take good care of you for this."

Wilma's thin lips communicated skepticism. "What about the funeral?"

"Pay that out of your own money," Sonny advised. "Billy will take care of you on the back end, plus some."

"You'll do fine," Snake said, giving her a brittle smile. "You always was a good old girl, Willy."

"I wasn't always old," she murmured. "Ya'll are asking too damn much, you know that?"

"I know," Sonny said, earning a glare from Snake.

She folded her age-spotted arms in front of her and gave them a disgusted look. "But I guess there's no other way. Just swear you'll leave me in peace when it's done. And keep that damned Forrest off my back."

"Don't worry about Forrest," Snake said. "He's gonna make sure you get a nice piece of change out of this."

"Bullshit. Nothing's changed since high school, Snake. Five minutes after you screwed me, you're were kickin' me out of the car. Forrest fooled around with my grandniece a few years back, and he's no different than you."

Snake stared back at her without remorse. "All right, well . . . you'd better go get his gun."

Wilma shook her head, then turned and walked down the hall toward the bedroom that held what was left of her brother.

CHAPTER 19

HENRY SEXTON AND I sit facing each other in the tight U created by the worktables that line three walls of his "war room." I feel like I've been transported to the hotel room of some obsessed FBI agent in Mississippi circa 1964.

"I've been working these cases on and off for twenty years," Henry says. "Hard for the last ten. Have you read many of my articles?"

"Most of them, I think."

"Do you feel you have a working knowledge of the facts?"

"I'm a former criminal prosecutor, Henry. Just tell me what you haven't put in the paper."

He nods with relief. "I've connected the Double Eagle group to at least a dozen murders between 1964 and 1972, but five cases mean more to me than the others."

"Albert Norris and Pooky Wilson are the top two. Right?"

"They were until this afternoon. Those killings happened in 1964, and I've known what happened and why for damn near twenty years. I couldn't print a lot of it, but everything I've learned since has borne out my theory. Proving it all is another matter, of course. Still, I'm a lot closer than I was two weeks ago."

"And the other three deaths? Is one Dr. Robb? The guy in the picture with my dad, by the airplane?"

"Yes. Five years after Albert died, Robb was murdered because he knew who'd killed Albert and Pooky. Forget everything you ever heard about that midair collision. It's bullshit."

"Well, you've got me curious, I'll say that. What about the last two cases? Jimmy Revels and Luther Davis?"

Henry smiled sadly. "Am I that obvious? Well . . . you know Revels and Davis were kidnapped in 1968 and never found. I've always been certain they were murdered, and they were. But I thought I understood the dynamic of that crime as well. This afternoon I found out that I was wrong—so wrong that my mind is still blown by the scope of it."

Something in Henry's voice quickens my interest. "Can we skip right to that case?"

"No. We need to start in sixty-four."

"Which case was my dad most involved in?"

"All of them. *All* these murders are connected, Penn. First, because the Double Eagles carried them out. Second, because a far more powerful man than any Eagle gave the kill orders in almost every case."

I start to interrupt him to ask who, but he waves his hand and says, "I'll give you the name in sixty seconds. Third, your father is connected to all five of those critical homicides in some way."

"I've never seen Dad's name in any of your articles."

"I leave a lot out of my articles, just as your fiancée does, I'm sure. Forget whatever you've read. I'm going to tell you what I think really happened in those cases."

"Fire away."

"Albert Norris was murdered because Pooky Wilson—one of his employees—was having sex with the daughter of one of the most powerful white men in this parish. When that man found out what his daughter was doing, he decided to have Pooky killed. He enlisted the Double Eagles to do that. Albert tried to protect the boy, and he died for it."

"Is this powerful white man still alive?"

"Yes. His name is Brody Royal."

The name takes my breath away. Almost no one else Henry could have mentioned would have surprised me more. "As in Royal Oil? The Royal Cotton Bank? Royal Insurance?"

"The same."

"Jesus, Henry. Royal's one of the richest men in the state."

"He's also a sadist and a killer. In 1964, he had the Klan and the Eagles comb this parish for Pooky Wilson, but they couldn't find him. Royal knew that Pooky worked for Albert Norris, so he and Frank Knox went to Albert's store and threatened him. Albert refused to give Pooky up. Later that night, they came back and burned him out, probably with a flamethrower."

I've long known the details of this crime, but I can scarcely get my mind around the idea of Brody Royal being involved. But if his daughter was having sex with a black boy in 1964, anything is possible. "I didn't hear my father's name in there."

"You're about to. It took Albert four days to die. He was treated by Dr. Leland Robb, the man in the snapshot with your father. Norris was only really clearheaded for the first day. He told the FBI—and also his best friend—that he'd recognized his attackers, but he refused to name them. Dr. Robb confirmed this to the press, and he stuck to his story for years."

"I remember that."

"The day after the firebombing, Pooky Wilson vanished. I now know that he tried to reach the Brookhaven train station to flee north, but he was captured by Brookhaven Klansmen. They delivered him to four Natchez Klansmen who less than one month later would become Double Eagles. At that point Pooky was taken out into the woods—possibly the Lusahatcha Swamp—and either crucified or flayed alive."

"Aw, man. Don't tell me that."

"I wish I didn't have to. Even though most of the FBI's attention was on Neshoba County, searching for the missing civil rights workers, the Bureau started working the Norris case. But on August fourth, the Neshoba bodies were discovered in that dam. All the FBI's focus shifted north. Five days later, Frank Knox formed the Double Eagle group on a sandbar south of the Triton Battery plant. Within a year, the fledgling Eagles had murdered several people, among them an FBI Klan informant named Jerry Dugan—something no one ever confirmed was murder until today. Your father was the company doctor for Triton, and he signed Dugan's death certificate."

"That sounds like pure chance. Nothing you've said ties Dad to the Norris case."

"Just wait. Let's jump ahead five years. On November first, 1969, Leland Robb climbed into the airplane you saw in that photo to travel to Arkansas for a fishing trip. At least that was the story put out afterward. With him were a charter pilot and two young ladies of what used to be called easy moral disposition."

"Hookers?"

"No. Sorority girls who liked to party. Sisters from Tennessee. Twenty-one and twenty-seven. Dr. Robb was forty-two and married. He could fly, but he liked to drink on his fishing trips, so he hired a local charter pilot. According to the sole witness, shortly after takeoff in heavy fog, Dr. Robb's plane unexpectedly returned to land and collided with a second plane that was attempting to take off from the same strip. Everyone on board Robb's plane perished. But the pilot of the other plane, a crop duster, walked away without injury. Do you know who that pilot was?"

I shrug my shoulders. "No idea."

"Snake Knox, Frank's brother."

"No."

"Yes. He'd taken over leadership of the Double Eagles on the day of his brother's death."

While I ponder this, Henry says, "Do you know where Frank Knox died?"

"No."

"In the surgery room of your father's office."

"*What?*"

"Industrial accident. A pallet of batteries fell on him in the spring of sixty-eight. But that's part of the Revels-Davis case. Let's stick to the crash for now."

Henry's revelations have left me speechless. This is the kind of thing you can never put into a novel, because it stretches credibility too far. Yet history is filled with such unbelievable coincidences. "Who was the sole witness to the crash?"

"Snake Knox's nephew, Forrest. Forrest was Frank Knox's son, sixteen at the time. Frank had been dead for a year. Forrest's and Snake's statements were accepted at face value, and that was the end of Dr. Robb and his friends."

"I see where you're going. Before Albert Norris died, he revealed the identities of his killers to Dr. Robb. And you think the Double Eagles murdered Robb to keep him quiet."

"One way or another, Penn, Snake Knox brought Dr. Robb's plane down. But the Eagles didn't give the order."

After a puzzled moment, my mind leaps ahead to close the logical loop. "Brody Royal?"

Henry nods with utter certainty.

"But Dr. Robb was killed five *years* after Albert Norris. Why wait so long to silence him? And a midair collision? Not even a topflight crop duster could engineer that with any hope of survival."

"I don't think there ever *was* a collision. I think Snake sabotaged Robb's plane, then banged up his own wing with a sledgehammer just after Robb went down beyond the runway. This was an isolated, unattended airport. Heavy fog, no control tower. Snake lied to the police and the FAA, his nephew backed him up, and that was it. No one could contest their story."

Despite his intensity, Henry hasn't sold me. "There's lots easier ways to kill people, Henry, and without the collateral damage. Do you have any evidence that the crash was murder?"

"My Double Eagle source as much as told me it was murder today. I didn't want to use up my time with him going into detail on that. But I've got circumstantial evidence. You decide how strong it is."

"Go on."

"Think about Albert Norris after the firebombing. He's dying in agonizing pain, third-degree burns over ninety percent of his body. Dr. Robb can't do a thing for him. Albert doesn't tell the FBI anything, or even his best friend. But before he slips into a coma, he names Brody Royal and Frank Knox as his killers. Probably two others as well— Sonny Thornfield and Snake Knox. The second that Dr. Robb hears those first two names, his blood runs cold. He knows he's a dead man if he ever reveals them. So he publicly supports the story that Albert never named his killers. But *privately,* that knowledge is eating him up. Robb treated Albert's best friend for years, and that poor man never stopped mourning his buddy. All that time, *Dr. Robb knew who had killed Albert.* He ran into the Double Eagles almost daily in the community. And Robb was even closer to Brody Royal than that."

"How do you mean?"

"Along with a lawyer named Claude Devereux, Robb was partners with Royal in a big hunting camp down the river. Robb often flew them down there to hunt or work on the land."

The first name pings on something in my memory. "Is Claude Devereux the old Cajun who practices law in Vidalia?"

"That's him," Henry says with distaste. "And he's a piece of work. Devereux represented not only Dr. Robb, but also several Klan members and Double Eagles over the years. I don't think Robb knew that, though. Because when he couldn't stand keeping the secret anymore, it was Devereux he confided in. I'm sure Devereux told him Brody

Royal couldn't possibly have been involved in Albert's death—poor old Albert had surely been ranting on morphine, out of his head. Devereux probably promised to make discreet inquiries about Frank Knox, even though he'd represented Knox in court before."

"What happened?"

"Nothing. Years passed. At that point, either guilt finally overpowered Dr. Robb's fear, or Robb started to suspect that Brody Royal was screwing his wife."

"*What?*"

"Are you really surprised? This is Louisiana, man. I'll explain that in a minute, but whether that was true or not, Dr. Robb decided to confide his secret in someone besides Devereux—someone he knew he could trust." Henry straightens up and looks hard into my eyes. "I think he chose your father. Tom Cage, M.D., the well-known paragon of rectitude."

Of course. Who else? "How well did Dad and Robb know each other?" I ask, looking down at the photo of my father by the plane.

"Robb and your father attended several antique gun shows together around this time. Robb would fly them there in his plane."

"Henry, are you suggesting that my father has known for forty years who murdered Albert Norris? And he's never told anyone about it?"

The reporter holds up his palms. "You're here talking to me because your father is keeping secrets from you. When you first came in, you told me you thought he might have killed Viola."

"*Technically.* Under the law." My cheeks are burning. "But I don't consider mercy-killing murder. This is something else altogether."

"Let me finish my story. Then make up your own mind. I think that when Dr. Robb came to him, your father instantly realized how dangerous the information was. He probably urged Robb to talk to somebody with real authority. I think Robb chose Orrin Dixon, a young congressman from Tennessee. Robb and Dixon had been fraternity brothers at Vanderbilt. Dixon had recently started voting moderately on race, and he'd also become close to President Johnson. Plus, Robb and Dixon had kept up their friendship over the years, and they'd been on several fishing trips in various states."

"Accompanied by young women?"

"Let's just say that the girls who died in the crash had both worked as interns for Congressman Dixon in Washington in the past."

"Democracy in action."

"On *this* occasion," Henry goes on, "the girls were already in Louisiana. Dixon was scheduled to fly in on another plane, then the whole party would leave for Arkansas the next morning. A private camp up in the Ozarks."

"Five people, total?"

Henry slowly shakes his head. "No. One other person was scheduled to fly that morning."

My mind races to fill in the blank. "Brody Royal?"

"No." Henry is fairly bursting to enlighten me, but at last the picture is starting to come clear.

"Claude Devereux."

"Right. After the crash, Devereux claimed that Congressman Dixon had a last-minute scheduling conflict, so Robb had decided they'd fish in Tennessee instead. So Dixon could still get in some fishing, right? Devereux told reporters that he'd had no desire to fish in Tennessee, so he begged off, and that decision saved his life."

"How did he explain the girls?"

"Claimed they'd been doing PR work for the congressman down here and were simply being given a plane ride back to Knoxville as a favor. Dixon's office denied this, but it supported the rest of the story, and the FAA wasn't concerned with who was sleeping with whom, only the mechanics of the mishap."

I take a minute to mull this over. "Claude Devereux's a sharp lawyer. You think that when Robb changed their flight destination at the last minute, he figured Robb was planning to spill his guts to Dixon?"

"I do." Henry's perpetually sad expression has morphed into the alert stare of a hunter closing on his prey. "And Claude couldn't let that happen. Frank Knox was dead by this time, but Brody Royal was still Devereux's richest client—not to mention the source of his political power."

"Do you think Devereux ordered the hit? Or that he told Royal about Dr. Robb, and Royal ordered it?"

"Devereux would have told Royal about the danger, to keep the blood off his own hands. He knew what Royal would do. We're talking about a man who'd ordered the crucifixion or flaying of an eighteen-year-old boy." Henry's face has flushed with emotion. "All Royal had to do was call Snake Knox and tell him how things stood. Snake was always at the airport, because of his crop-dusting business. Snake probably laughed and told Devereux he'd better find an excuse to get off that plane—which he did. Eight hours later, Dr. Robb was dead."

"Along with a pilot and two young girls."

"Snake wouldn't have hesitated a second over that. Unlike Ku Klux Klansmen, he was all cow, no hat."

"No hood, you mean. I'm still not hearing proof, Henry. But I did hear several unsupported suppositions. What did the NTSB find at the crash site? Anything suspicious?"

"I told you, they accepted Snake's story at face value."

"You also said Snake sabotaged the plane. Any proof of that?"

"Three different pilots have told me the surest way to bring down Robb's plane undetected would have been to put water in the fuel tank. It wouldn't take much, and the evidence would burn away in the fire."

"Can't a pilot check for water in his tanks?"

"There's a sump they can check, but some pilots don't. Snake Knox knows everything there is to know about small planes. If he wanted to use water and be sure it wouldn't be picked up in the sump, he could have filled a few condoms with it and dropped them into the tank. It would take the fuel a while to eat through the rubbers, but once it did, that plane was coming down. And remember—Dr. Robb's plane had already taken off, then unexpectedly returned to land, which caused the accident. Nobody ever explained why that plane came back so fast. Robb's pilot had thousands of hours of experience. I think he felt his power going and tried like hell to make it back. He almost did, too."

Henry is making this murder sound plausible, but as an assistant DA, I learned that you can almost always construct a scenario to fit a preconceived result. "Do you have anything else to make this case? Do you have your source on tape?"

"No." Henry looks embarrassed. "He wouldn't let me record him during our first session. But goddamn it, Penn. First principles, right? *Cui bono?* Who benefited from the crash? Dr. Robb's death didn't simply remove the threat of exposure from Brody's life. Six months after the plane went down, Brody Royal married Dr. Robb's widow."

And the circle closes. Gooseflesh has risen on my arms. "Royal had a double motive for wanting Robb dead."

Henry gives me a silent nod, knowing that this last piece of informa-

tion has convinced me. "She was a stunning redhead. I wanted to interview her, but she died of a stroke before I could get her to agree to talk."

"Have you talked to Congressman Dixon?"

"Same story. Dixon died two years ago, abdominal aneurysm. But I
don't think Robb ever told him anything. Dixon wouldn't have sat on that."

Again the heat rises to my face. "But my father did? Damn it, Henry,
you want me to believe that the most ethical man I've ever known withheld critical murder evidence for forty years?"

Henry nods slowly. "I'm not saying I blame him. There's a lot you
don't know about Brody Royal. What could your father have gained by
revealing what he knew? A clean conscience? The moral high ground?
That doesn't mean anything if you're dead."

I've made this point myself before, specifically to my fiancée. But
even so, it's hard for me to see my father making that choice.

"Your father's a good man, Penn. But he's probably carrying burdens that no man should have to carry alone. There's no telling what
he saw and heard back in those days. What he might have done with
the best of intentions, and yet caused terrible consequences. I'm not surprised he doesn't want to talk to Shad Johnson. He won't talk to me, and
he loved my parents. He won't even talk to *you*, his own son."

"But *what does* he know, Henry? The identity of Albert's and
Pooky's killers? Is that really enough to explain his self-destructive
silence about Viola?"

Henry shakes his head. "No. But we still haven't covered the most
disturbing part of this story. The murder of Viola's brother. The gang
rape, all that. Once I've finished, you won't have much trouble understanding why your father is reluctant to talk about that time."

A chill of presentiment makes me feel nauseated. "What are you
saying, man? Would you cut to the fucking chase?"

The reporter holds up his hands, trying to get me to be patient. "I'm
going to make a cup of coffee. Do you want some?"

I reach out and take hold of his arm, but he gently disengages, then
takes a carafe from a stained old Mr. Coffee machine and fills it at a
small sink. He's clearly deep in thought, and his thoughts seem to be
causing him pain. He measures out some Eight O'Clock brand, then,
once he has the coffee going, returns to his worktable and slides another
photograph from a manila envelope.

"I wasn't sure whether I should show you this," he says, passing me the three-by-five print.

The photo shows four men standing in the stern of what looks like a deep-sea fishing boat. I recognize my father and Ray Presley standing together, facing two other men who look only vaguely familiar. Seeing Dad with a crooked cop I was glad to watch die gives me a surreal sense of foreboding.

"I recognize Dad and Ray. Who are the other two men?"

"That's Claude Devereux," Henry says, pointing to a dark-skinned man on the right side of the photo. The camera apparently caught Devereux telling a humorous story, because the other men are smiling or laughing. Dad, Ray, and Devereux look to be in their mid-thirties in this image, but the fourth man looks older, maybe forty. Even laughing, his hawklike face and wiry build give him a powerful presence.

"Who's that?" I ask, pointing at him.

"That's Brody Royal."

"Jesus, Henry," I breathe, feeling dizzy.

"He looks like a shorter Charlton Heston, doesn't he?"

"Where the hell was this taken?"

"No idea. I found that photo in the *Beacon* morgue. The man who likely shot it is dead, and no one seems to know where it was taken. It could be the Gulf of Mexico or the South China Sea. I'm hoping you can get the answer from your father, among other things."

I nod slowly. "I intend to."

"Was I wrong to show it to you?"

"No. I want to know everything you do. I need to know."

"Are you sure?"

"Yes."

Henry takes several photocopied pages from the manila folder. They appear to be heavily redacted FBI surveillance reports from the 1970s. Much of the typing that hasn't been blacked out is scarcely readable.

"What's this stuff?"

"Three FBI reports detailing trips taken from New Orleans to Natchez for medical treatment."

"By whom?" I ask, my chest tightening.

"Members of Carlos Marcello's Mafia organization. In each case, they were followed to the door of your father's office on Monroe Street.

Twice during normal office hours, but once at about eight P.M., and Ray Presley also showed up on that occasion."

Sour bile rises into my throat. "Goddamn it, Henry. What are you telling me here?"

"I don't know what it all means, Penn. I just want you fully informed when you finally speak to your father."

While I stare at the reports in disbelief, Henry fills a Northeast Louisiana University mug to the brim with coffee and takes a scalding sip. "Damn, I needed that."

After pouring me a cup, he takes the reports from my hand and looks into my eyes. "How far would your father go to protect his family? Would he go to jail for the rest of his life?"

To my surprise, tears well in the corners of my eyes. "Without a second's hesitation. Dad doesn't have much time left anyway. He's already outlived every prognosis he's been given."

"I figured as much. When you first came in, you told me you thought your dad might be trying to protect somebody. What if that somebody is you, Penn?"

"Me?"

"Not *just* you. Your mother, your daughter, your fiancée, your whole family. What if the Eagles simply exploited the chance to frame your father, then threatened to kill members of his family if he fought it? No one knows better than Tom Cage what the Double Eagles are capable of, and there's no Ray Presley around to protect you anymore."

I nod slowly, weighing the odds. "If someone made that threat, and Dad believed they'd carry it through . . . yes, he might sacrifice himself without a fight."

"Today I heard a story that I wish I'd never heard. The man at the center of it was Brody Royal. I've heard some pretty horrible things in my time, but this . . ."

"You already told me Royal was involved in horrific murders."

"That was back in the sixties. This happened only two years ago."

Two years ago? Again Henry has stunned me. I look down at the photo of my father in the boat with Brody Royal. "Do you have anything stronger than coffee?"

He opens a drawer and takes out a half-empty bottle of Wild Turkey. Unscrewing the top, he pours double shots into paper cups.

"Confusion to the enemy," he says, raising his cup.

CHAPTER 20

SONNY THORNFIELD STOOD in the hallway of Wilma Deen's house, peering through a crack in the door of the room where Glenn Morehouse lay on a motorized hospital bed, his torso raised at a thirty-degree angle. The flickering blue light of a television washed over his shockingly skeletal form. His sister had carried in a cup of ice chips, and Wilma alternated between placing these on his tongue and sponging off his sweating forehead. Glenn's head was to Sonny's left. Wilma had placed herself on the far side of the bed. Sonny couldn't see any pistol from where he stood, but he believed it was there. Glenn might have it in his left hand, under the covers. *It would be a damned .45,* Sonny thought, recalling men he'd seen knocked down by the Colt cannon.

"Jesus," Snake whispered from behind Sonny. "Ain't been but a month since I last saw him, and he done shrunk to half of what he was."

Sonny nodded. It was hard to believe that anything, even cancer, could change a man so much. Like a half-drowned man, Morehouse sucked in a deep breath. Then his eyes opened wide, as if something had frightened him.

"Take it easy," Wilma half sang, like a doting grandmother. "Everything's fine. You were almost asleep. You fell off that sleep cliff."

"Something's wrong," Glenn said. "I can feel it."

"No, everything's fine. You remember what the doctor said. Everybody gets that feeling when they get this poorly."

Morehouse strained upward, squinted around the room, then finally settled back against the mattress. Wilma fed him another ice chip. After a minute or so, his eyelids began to fall again. Sonny wondered whether she meant to wait until he was completely unconscious to go for the gun.

Ten seconds later, she laid her left hand on her brother's arm and began to stroke it. She sponged his forehead with her right hand, then moved it away as if to dip the rag again. But this time her hand disappeared behind his leg, and a moment later Morehouse cried out in terror.

Wilma backed away from the bed, a Colt .45 automatic in her hand.

While her brother gaped at her, Snake shoved Sonny into the room and moved quickly around him the bedside.

Morehouse turned his skull, his eyes going wide in recognition. "Snake! Sonny!"

Snake smiled with a cobra-like expression suited to his namesake. "Surprised, pardner?"

"What are ya'll doin' here?"

"You know." Snake's eyes glittered in the television light.

"What do you mean? What do I know?"

"You've been jawin' to people you shouldn't. Tryin' to get your name in the papers."

Morehouse's mouth opened, but he did not speak. He raised his hands and covered his eyes like a child trying to pretend that the horror in front of him wasn't real. "I ain't done nothin'!" he cried.

"That's a lie."

The big hands slowly fell from the anguished face. "Oh Lord," Glenn said in a slurred voice. "Ya'll done come to cut my throat, ain't you?"

"We damn sure ought to."

"Wilma!" Morehouse cried. "Call the sheriff! They've come to kill me!"

Snake laughed. "Wilma ain't callin' nobody 'cept the coroner."

Glenn froze, his eyes on the doorway. His sister stood there like an avenging angel, as silent as a witness to an execution. Morehouse started to speak, but she held up a warning finger, and he began to sob.

"We know you've been talking to Henry Sexton," Sonny said. "We need to know what got said, Glenn."

"I ain't told that bastard nothing! He ambushed me. How was I supposed to stop him?"

"Come on," muttered Snake. "At least you can be a man and admit what you done. The question is why. Did you get to thinking 'bout hellfire or some such nonsense? You scared of that Baptist *Hay-des* that Preacher Gibbons was always rantin' about?"

Morehouse shuddered in his bed.

"Remember the oath you swore? Same one we all did."

"I was just a kid," Morehouse said, almost crying. "Just a stupid kid without sense to know right from wrong."

"Bullshit! You were thirty-five and proud to swear it. And if it was up to me, I'd do just what the oath says to do. But lucky for you, it ain't."

Glenn cut his eyes at the phone on the table beside his bed. "Who's it up to?"

"You know." Sonny lifted the cordless phone from the bedside table and tossed it onto a chair across the room. "Billy said give you a choice."

Glenn's eyes ping-ponged from Snake to Sonny and back again. "What kind of choice?"

"I'll tell you," said Snake, smiling again. He drew a deer-skinning knife from a scabbard on the side of his belt. "On one hand, I've got this blade, which'll take off your nuts before you even feel the sting. You know a man can bleed to death after that, 'cause you've seen it."

Morehouse shut his eyes.

"But in Sonny's backpack, there's a vial of fentanyl that'll send you off to fairyland as sweet and easy as Rip van Winkle."

Snake had chosen fentanyl because Glenn's doctor had prescribed the fentanyl patch once his pain became intractable.

Morehouse was praying, Sonny realized, a droning murmur of indistinct words.

"Glenn!" Sonny said sharply. "Snap out of it!"

The drone only grew more insistent.

"You know how easy morphine is," Snake said in an oily voice. "You saw it in the war. Fentanyl's a hundred times more powerful. If I had to meet St. Peter tonight, no question which route I'd pick."

Morehouse's eyes opened, looking suspicious. "How do I get the fentanyl?"

"Tell us everything you told the reporter. You hold back, you die a gelding."

Morehouse was struggling to swallow. Sonny picked up a glass of water from the bedside table and helped him take a sip.

"There you go," Sonny said. "All primed up now. Spill."

"I didn't tell Sexton nothin', boys. I didn't trust him."

"He was here for a whole hour this morning," Snake said. "You must have told him something."

Morehouse shook his head.

Snake held up the knife and turned it in the lamplight. "I've only got three questions, Mountain." Stepping forward, he slid the point under Morehouse's inflamed eye. "First, did you say the name Forrest Knox? Did your lips form those two words?"

"Jesus, no. I ain't crazy!"

"You're lying, Glenn. I'm gonna cut this eye out."

"No!" Morehouse wailed.

"What about Brody Royal? Did you say anything about Brody?"

At the mention of this name Morehouse lost his color. "I swear before God, boys. I wouldn't do that."

"Did Sexton *ask* about Brody or Forrest?"

"Neither one. He just wanted to know about . . ."

"Us?" Snake finished.

Morehouse nodded, then pulled up the covers and hugged himself beneath them.

"How much did you tell him?"

"Nothin' about ya'll. I talked about the war mostly. All he cared about was Albert Norris. I think him and that nigger was related or something. I told him I thought Pooky had killed Albert and run off with whatever whiskey and cash Albert had stashed in the store. Or reefer, that he kept for them musicians."

"Did Sexton tape any of this?"

"Hell, no. I wouldn't let him. I told him that, straight up."

Snake gave Sonny a sidelong look. Glenn actually sounded convincing.

"I can't sleep no more, Sonny!" Morehouse cried. "Every time I close my eyes, I see the things we done. I can't get no peace. It's like when I got back from the war. I keep seein' Jerry Dugan down in that acid tank, and that Lewis boy a-bleedin' under that tree. That alone's enough to send us all to hell."

"Do you see Jimmy Revels?" Snake asked in a perverse voice. "I figured you'd see him most of all. Considerin' what you done to him. And how much you liked it."

"Ya'll made me do that! I didn't know what I was doing. That still don't make it right, I know. Not to God."

"That's between you and God," Snake said. "Not you and some newspaper reporter."

Glenn's shallow respirations sounded like a breeze blowing through dry leaves. Sonny saw tears running down his pale cheeks. He seemed to struggle on the bed, his movements spastic.

"You drugged me," Glenn said, his accusing eyes searching out Wilma in the darkness. "You . . . you helped them kill me. *God sees you, Sister.*"

Wilma's slippers hissed on the parquet floor. "I'm gonna wait in the kitchen," she said. "Ya'll don't hurt him no more'n you have to."

"Can't stand to see your handiwork?" Glenn cried, his eyelids falling, rising, falling again.

Sonny motioned for Wilma to leave, but she leaned over her brother with bitter anger in her eyes. "You broke faith. You didn't leave me any choice."

"Not with God, I didn't!" Morehouse bellowed.

"Blood first, Glenn," she said with utter conviction. "God after."

Wilma gave her brother a glare of challenge, but he said nothing. As she turned to go, Sonny caught her arm and whispered, "When was the last time a nurse stuck him for blood?"

"The home health nurse pulled some this morning. They poke him all the time now."

"Where? Has he still got a good vein in the elbow?"

"He's got a PICC line in." She slid her arm from Sonny's grasp. "You can inject whatever you want in there."

"I didn't tell Henry half of what I should have!" Glenn cried with newfound strength. Sonny heard righteous anger, and saw the fear draining from Glenn's face like life from a dying body.

"I didn't tell Henry nothin' about Forrest," Glenn vowed. "Or Brody. But I'll say it now. The hell I'm going to tonight is nothing compared to what awaits you two with *them.*"

"I've had enough of this," Snake growled. "He's gettin' off easy, you ask me."

"Let's just get it over with," Sonny said. Unzipping his camo shoulder pack, he drew out a syringe prefilled with a lethal dose of fentanyl. "You want me to do it?"

"No. Just hold it till I'm ready." Snake walked around the hospital bed and took hold of Glenn's forearm—an arm once strong enough to snap a man's cervical spine—to examine the PICC line. When Glenn started to struggle, Snake passed his knife over the bed to Sonny. "He keeps fightin', sever his jugular."

"Don't fight it, baby," Wilma said from the doorway, shocking Sonny. Apparently she meant to stay to the end. "You're just making it worse."

Glenn stopped struggling at the sound of his sister's words, but his eyes had taken on a sudden alertness. They had been dull before, but now they glinted with . . . what? *Triumph?*

"Something's wrong," Sonny said, and Snake looked up sharply.

"His hands!" Wilma yelled. "Check his hands!"

Sonny ripped back the coverlet. One of Morehouse's fists was clenched around a chunk of plastic with a chain on it.

"Shit!" Snake cursed. "That's one of them Live Alert things!"

Snake tried to wrench the necklace from Morehouse's clawlike grasp, but Wilma cried, "Don't worry about it! That thing don't even work! I quit paying the bill after he moved in with me."

Sonny couldn't take his eyes from Morehouse's face. His old friend wouldn't look so proud of himself unless he'd foxed them somehow.

"Make him give it to you," Sonny said, passing the knife back to Snake.

Snake followed the catheter line to where it disappeared under Morehouse's boxer shorts. The knife vanished under the shorts.

"I'm counting to three," Snake said. "After that—"

Morehouse hurled the Live Alert necklace across the room, where it caromed off the wall and rattled on the floor.

"I oughta cut 'em off anyway," Snake said, "just for the aggravation."

The ringing telephone froze them all where they stood. When it rang the second time, Morehouse began to laugh.

"I called 'em with my credit card last Friday!" he cried. "What you gonna do now?"

Wilma snatched up the cordless phone and checked the caller ID. "Oh, God. He really did. It's the Live Alert people."

"God*damn* it!" Snake shouted.

"I'll tell them it was a false alarm," she said, moving quickly to the door.

"You need a password for that," Morehouse told her, giving Snake a defiant glare.

The phone kept ringing in Wilma's hand.

"False alarm's no good," Sonny said, thinking aloud. "Not if he turns up dead in the morning."

Something changed in Snake's demeanor. He looked like a big buck realizing he was being watched from a tree stand. Turning to Wilma, he said, "Tell the dispatcher Glenn just died."

Wilma's mouth fell open.

Glenn began to scream.

"Hurry!" Snake shouted. "Go in the other room. Tell 'em it looks like a stroke or a heart attack. No breath sounds, no heartbeat. He's already going gray."

Wilma scuttled through the door on her macabre errand.

Sonny saw Snake looking at him the way Frank used to look at him when they were about to assault a hostile beach. "Take his right hand, Sonny," Snake ordered. "Don't bruise him any more than you have to."

Without a word, Sonny laid the fentanyl syringe on the bedside table, then grabbed his old friend's thick wrist and held it against the mattress. Snake had already done the same on the opposite side. Sonny was surprised it was that easy, even after the cancer. Glenn Morehouse had been physically stronger than any man he'd ever known.

"Pass me that syringe," Snake ordered.

"Wait!" Wilma cried from the doorway. "They're sending an ambulance anyway, just to be sure. It's already on the way."

Fear bloomed in Sonny's chest, and his mouth went dry.

"You son of a bitch," Snake said, looking like he wanted to stab Morehouse in the heart. "Give me that syringe, Son."

"Will it kill him in time?"

"If you'd hurry up it will!"

As Sonny reached for the syringe, Morehouse yanked both arms up off the mattress with such power that Sonny's head crashed into Snake's. It was all Sonny could do to cling to the big wrist.

"Watch out!" he cried, stunned by the strength flowing through Morehouse's arm. His old comrade's eyes were nearly white with panic, like the eyes of a coyote trying to rip itself out of a trap.

"This ain't gonna work!" Sonny shouted, as Morehouse slung him against the bedside table with almost superhuman strength. The impact knocked the syringe to the floor. "What do we do?"

"I heard a siren!" Wilma shouted. "Jesus, do something!"

"You've gotta do it, Willy!" Snake told her. "Grab that syringe and shoot it into the port!"

Wilma had gone white. "I can't do that!"

"It's got to be done, and we ain't got enough hands."

Morehouse howled like a senseless brute with no power of speech. He had become fear incarnate. Wilma stood shaking like a child pushed beyond its limits. Sonny heard the siren now; its distant scream turned his bladder to stone.

"Do it!" Snake roared at Wilma. "Do it now, or we're all going to jail!"

Morehouse was still fighting, but Sonny felt the great strength waning at last. Wilma's eyes sought him out, silently asking permission for this act of blood betrayal. Sonny had done many things he regretted, and this might be the worst sin of all, but they had no choice anymore. As Snake cursed and Morehouse bellowed like a steer going to slaughter, Sonny nodded.

Wilma closed her eyes, her lips moving in silence. Then she picked up the syringe off the floor and moved quickly to the far side of the bed.

"Don't fight me, Glenn," she said softly. "It's time to go see Mama."

CHAPTER 21

I'M NO STRANGER to perverse crimes, but Henry's tale of Brody Royal's revenge on two female whistle-blowers has sickened me.

"Royal's son-in-law forced one woman to kill the other?" I ask in disbelief. "And then he killed the other one anyway?"

"He had Snake kill her. That's the story I got today. And I believe it."

I gulp the rest of my bourbon and hold out my cup for a refill. "You hate him, don't you? Royal, I mean."

"Yessir, I do."

Henry's hatred for Brody Royal is obviously proportional to his love for the Norris family, but I don't have time to plumb that connection now. "There's no way my father was friends with a man who could do that," I tell him. "No way."

"I'm sure you're right," Henry says, but he sounds less than sure.

"My daughter's going to be wondering where I am. Tell me about the Revels case. No offense, but I came to find out about Viola Turner. I came to help my father."

"I know. And though I don't quite understand how yet, I believe that whatever saves your father is going to be what destroys Brody Royal."

This idea has an appealing symmetry, but I have yet to be convinced. "Jimmy Revels and Luther Davis. Go."

"Jimmy and Luther were last seen in Natchez, Mississippi, on March twenty-seventh, 1968. After that, they dropped off the planet. Two months earlier, they'd gotten into a brawl with three Double Eagles at a whites-only drive-in that resulted in a highway chase and a fight on the road. Shots were fired, but no one sought treatment at any area hospital. I suspect your father may have patched them up, but I can't prove that. The FBI never classified these cases as murders, because they had no bodies. But everyone knew they'd been killed by the Double Eagles. I always assumed Jimmy was the main target, because he was a civil rights activist. He'd worked hard to register black voters, he played a role in the Natchez boycott, he led marches, and he played music at civil rights rallies."

"Why did people assume the Double Eagles killed them, rather than the Klan? Because of the brawl?"

"Mostly. After the brawl, Jimmy and Luther went into hiding at a place called Freewoods, a kind of outlaw sanctuary. Nobody knew where they were. When the Eagles couldn't locate those boys after six weeks, they decided to rape Viola."

"To draw Jimmy out of hiding."

"Exactly. The rumor started spreading on March twenty-seventh. I wasn't sure it was more than a rumor until today. My Eagle source confirmed it."

"So how were you *wrong* about the Revels case?"

Henry's basset hound expression returns. "I was wrong about the most critical part—the motive behind it. *Jimmy Revels wasn't the real target.*"

"Who was?"

Henry takes a long pull of coffee. "Hold on to your ass, bubba. The target was Robert Kennedy."

I set down my cup and stare at him in shock. "You're kidding, right?"

"No. Are you familiar with the Ben Chester White case?"

"I think so. Three Klansmen murdered a harmless old black man in the Homochitto National Forest."

"Do you remember their motive?"

My mind races back through endless case summaries. "The Klansmen asked the old man to help them find a lost dog. But . . ." The answer hits me like an unexpected blow. "They wanted to lure Martin Luther King to Natchez. To assassinate him."

Henry's cheeks have flushed red, and not from the whiskey. "They weren't the only guys to have that idea."

"But *Robert Kennedy*? Why would the Eagles want him dead?"

"The Double Eagles didn't initiate the operation."

"Who did? Brody Royal?"

Henry shakes his head. "Someone who hated Bobby Kennedy more than anyone on earth, and that's saying something. Can you guess? This guy was the last son of a bitch you wanted to be on the bad side of."

"Enough with the games, Henry. Who was it?"

"Carlos Marcello."

The Little Sicilian. Mafia boss of New Orleans from the fifties through the seventies. "Ray Presley used to work as a bagman for Marcello while he was a cop in New Orleans. Was Presley Marcello's connection to the Double Eagles?"

"No." Henry takes a piece of paper from the table and hands it to me. It seems to be a real estate deed for a Metairie, Louisiana, motel, titled in the name MarYal Corporation. "MarYal?" I ask. "Marcello-Royal?"

Henry smiles. "Their relationship dated back to Royal's days as a bootlegger in St. Bernard Parish. Marcello was clawing his way to the top of the New Orleans underworld at that time, and he was tight with Royal's old man. Once Brody struck it rich in oil, he got into quite a few real estate deals with Carlos. Marcello sometimes used the Double Eagles as muscle in Florida deals. And listen to this: three years before he founded the Double Eagles, Frank Knox worked as a combat arms instructor at a South Louisiana training camp for Cuban cadres going into the Bay of Pigs. Carlos was helping to fund that camp. Frank was officially listed on the JMWAVE, Operation Mongoose payroll."

"I wish I could say this sounds nuts, Henry. But it sounds all too familiar to an ex-prosecutor from Texas. So . . . Jimmy Revels was bait for Robert Kennedy. Obviously the RFK plan went ass-over-teakettle somehow. What went down?"

"Carlos's motive for killing Bobby wasn't just business. Bobby had aggressively pursued the mob since the mid-fifties, at a time when J. Edgar Hoover said there was no organized crime in America. As attorney general for his brother, Bobby went into high gear. Even JFK thought he was a zealot."

Henry's story is old news to me. "It's no secret that the Mafia wanted Bobby Kennedy dead. Carlos Marcello was named by the House Select Committee on Assassinations as one of the men most likely to be involved in the conspiracy to assassinate JFK, along with Santo Trafficante and Sam Giancana. Two witnesses verified that while Carlos wanted Bobby dead, he said, 'If you cut off a dog's tail, he'll keep biting you, but if you cut off its head . . . no more.'"

"You knew all that?" Henry asks. "I had to look it up."

"A steady parade of JFK crackpots visited my office in Houston. Finish your story."

"JFK was killed in November 1963. By sixty-four, Bobby was out on his ass. LBJ hated him. Bobby ran for senator in New York and won, no big deal. But in March of 1968, Eugene McCarthy entered a primary against LBJ and damn near *won*. There was blood in the water. Everybody knew Johnson was vulnerable because of Vietnam. Four days later, on March sixteenth, Bobby announced he was running for president. Can you imagine how Carlos Marcello reacted when he heard that?"

"He probably shot a hole in his TV, Elvis-style."

Henry can barely contain his excitement. "Carlos vowed RFK would never be president. Then he talked to his old buddy Brody Royal. I can just hear the classic Sicilian line: *Will someone take this stone from my shoe?* According to my source, Marcello was thinking of a patsy setup, like with Oswald. But Frank Knox had been thinking about this kind of hit ever since he founded the Double Eagles. When Brody told Frank what Carlos wanted, Frank said instead of an individual patsy like Oswald, a collective one would work better. The Mississippi Ku Klux Klan, for example. The Ben Chester White case was a perfect setup for it. Those idiots had just chosen the wrong victim, a harmless handyman. Frank knew that if they killed the right black man, Bobby Kennedy would come back to Mississippi to make a campaign speech and commiserate with the widow. Bobby had just visited the Mississippi Delta on his poverty tour the year before."

This wakes me up. "What made Jimmy Revels the right black man? He was only about twenty-five, wasn't he?"

"Twenty-six." Henry gives me a strange smile. "Listen to this. Even though Jimmy and Luther had been in hiding, from the day RFK announced his candidacy, those two had been crisscrossing the state, tirelessly persuading black Mississippi voters to register to vote. He used the chance of voting for John Kennedy's brother as inspiration, and it was working. Mississippi blacks hadn't forgotten Bobby holding those sick and starving Delta babies in his lap. Penn, one hour ago, an old NAACP officer informed me that in late March of sixty-eight—probably Monday the twenty-fifth—Bobby Kennedy placed a personal call to the Jackson headquarters of the NAACP and spoke to Jimmy Revels to thank him for his work. They talked for two and a half minutes."

This I believe. "Henry, when George Metcalfe survived that Klan bomb in 1965, Bobby Kennedy called the Jefferson Davis Hospital in Natchez to talk to Metcalfe personally. I know that because my father was his doctor, and he heard one side of the conversation."

Henry shakes his head in amazement. "And the hits just keep on comin'. By the way, that was no Klan bomb. The Double Eagles planted that bomb in Metcalfe's car, and they weren't even trying to kill him. They were trying to wound him and lure Martin Luther King down here."

It takes me a second to remember to breathe. "To assassinate him?"

Henry nods, his eyes bright with excitement. "That was the template for the later attempt with Kennedy. Only King didn't come here. If he had, he'd have died three years earlier than he did."

"Shit, Henry. Run the timeline on the RFK operation."

"It's early sixty-eight. Jimmy and Luther brawl with the Eagles on February seventh. They go into hiding at Freewoods. Kennedy announces for president on March sixteenth. Jimmy and Luther start crisscrossing the state in secret, speaking to blacks in their homes and churches. Kennedy calls Jimmy to thank him on the twenty-fifth. When Frank Knox hears about this, he picks Jimmy as their victim. Viola is gang-raped the night of March twenty-sixth. The rumor starts to spread. Within twenty-four hours, Jimmy and Luther were seen in Natchez and Concordia Parish, cruising the parking lots of joints like Mildred's and the Emerald Isle. This was a Wednesday night. That night they vanished for good—just like Pooky Wilson and Joe Louis Lewis before them."

"If the goal was to lure RFK to Mississippi," I reason, "I'd expect some kind of semi-public atrocity, like a lynching or a bombing."

Henry nods, his face taut. "I think that was the plan. They were probably surprised to have gotten Jimmy and Luther so fast. I'll bet Frank meant to hold them over the weekend, then kill them Sunday, so that the murders would make the network news on Monday. But fate dealt a joker out of the deck. The day after Jimmy and Luther disappeared was the day a pallet of batteries fell on Frank Knox. I think he was probably drunk when it happened. Jimmy and Luther were being held captive at a machine shop out in the county. Frank had only gone in to work to keep up appearances. Coworkers took him to your father's office, and that's where he died."

A tingling sensation runs along my forearms, then settles in my palms.

Henry's eyes radiate almost electric energy. "Instant karma, man. Frank Knox died while being treated by your father and Viola Turner—a woman he'd raped only two days earlier. What are the odds of that?"

"A billion to one. Are you positive about this? Dad's never mentioned any of it to me."

Henry's ominous look returns. "Viola was your father's trauma nurse. She always assisted him in his surgery. And get this: nobody can remember seeing Viola in Natchez after the day Frank died. They figured she split town with her brother and Luther, or else split after they were killed. Weeks later, Viola was found in Chicago, alone. Jimmy and Luther were never seen again."

"Where had she been in the meantime?"

"Nobody knows. It was a blank spot in her life, and she refused to fill it during our interviews. The FBI worked Jimmy's and Luther's disappearances pretty hard, but on April fourth Martin Luther King was assassinated in Memphis. Then on May fourteenth—"

"Del Payton was murdered with a truck bomb," I finish. "And that consumed whatever local FBI resources were still in town."

"Exactly. What would become *your* most famous case thirty years later grabbed all the headlines. After that, Jimmy and Luther were virtually forgotten. No one found any bodies, and the Bureau only located Viola much later."

"What about the plan to lure Kennedy down here?"

"I think Brody Royal scrapped it after Frank died. He didn't trust Snake to carry out an operation of that magnitude, or keep his mouth shut if he did. Brody ordered Snake to kill Jimmy, Luther, and Viola, and make sure their bodies would never be found, no matter how hard the FBI might search for them."

"Then how the hell did Viola survive?"

"According to my Eagle source, Ray Presley and your father saved her."

My frustration is compounding every minute. "How the hell could they have done that?"

"I don't know. Remember the machine shop? Snake went nuts when his brother died. He started torturing those boys out of grief.

At some point they kidnapped Viola again and brought her out there, and she was brutalized some more. I'm afraid even Jimmy might have been molested. But that was probably trivial compared to his ultimate fate."

"How the hell could Viola escape? You think Ray got her out?"

"My source didn't give me the details of that. We got cut off. And since Ray is dead, probably no one but your father and the Double Eagles know the answer."

I take another drink of bourbon, but I can hardly taste it. My mind is well and truly blown. "Two things I don't understand. One, if all this happened the way you said, then Viola knew enough to send serious criminals to the gas chamber. Why would she keep her mouth shut, after they'd killed her brother? The Bureau had agents in Natchez in 1968. Why didn't she talk to them?"

Henry sighs. "That's like asking why a Sioux squaw didn't go the U.S. Cavalry for help in 1880, after white settlers had terrorized her and killed her family. Viola knew exactly what Snake Knox and his buddies were capable of, and she knew the FBI couldn't protect her from them."

"They killed her brother, Henry. They gang-raped her. Do you really believe she would have kept quiet about that?"

The reporter's eyes smolder with an emotion I can't quite read. "Maybe. By the time the Eagles found her in Chicago, she was pregnant. What if they threatened her child? Her brother was already dead. Would a mother risk her infant's life to put her trust in white men who'd failed to convict the Klan in almost every single murder case in Mississippi up to that time?"

Henry has a point. "But if the kid was a result of the gang rape?"

The reporter shrugs. "We don't know enough to guess, Penn. What's your second objection?"

"If Brody scrapped the RFK assassination plan, how did he square it with Marcello? Godfathers don't generally take 'no' for an answer."

"My source didn't tell me. Maybe Brody told him straight: 'Without Frank Knox in charge, we can't take the risk.' But the timeline suggests another answer. Del Payton was blown up just weeks after Revels and Davis disappeared, right? What if I told you that Brody Royal and Judge Leo Marston were occasional business partners back in the sixties?"

"I picture two rattlesnakes in a sack." Leo Marston is the father of a woman I once thought I would marry. He now resides in Parchman Penitentiary.

"Brody and Leo lived on opposite sides of the river, but they had greed in common. Brody was far wealthier than Marston, but Leo had more political clout. He also had the blood pedigree that Royal didn't. Leo invested in quite a few Royal Oil wells, and he made some real money. I think they were pretty tight."

"Del Payton was murdered to intimidate black union members," I think aloud. "You're thinking Brody Royal had advance knowledge through Leo that a crime like that was about to happen? If he did, he could cancel the Revels hit and claim Del Payton had been killed to lure Kennedy down here."

"Exactly."

"And three weeks after Payton died, Sirhan Sirhan made the whole question moot. Any real chance of another Kennedy taking the White House died at the Ambassador Hotel in Los Angeles."

Henry looks pleased that his story led me to the same conclusion.

"The Viola angle still doesn't play," I argue. "From what you've told me, Brody Royal is a monster. Even if Viola didn't know about his involvement in all this, the Double Eagles did. If Viola was a threat to the Eagles, then she was a threat to Brody Royal through them. I can't believe anything would have stopped Royal from killing her."

Henry taps the photo of my father in the boat with Brody Royal. "Which brings us right back here. Maybe your father pledged something in exchange for Viola's life. Maybe he guaranteed her silence. I don't know. You'll have to ask him."

"I will," I mutter, trying not to give rein to the anger I feel at Dad's silence earlier today. "You said the FBI found Viola in Chicago?"

"One agent questioned her. I've got his 302 in my files. According to him, Viola believed Jimmy and Luther had been murdered, but she offered no proof. The agent noted that she behaved like someone in shock, or perhaps even sedated by drugs. He also noted that she was pregnant."

I lean back and consider this. "Given all you've told me, it's pretty hard to believe that Viola had the nerve to come back here, even to die."

"I think she knew she could trust your father to give her a painless death. To her, that was worth the risk of retaliation by the Eagles. It's about as sad as anything I ever heard."

"But she didn't get a painless death," I point out. "And that's how I know my father didn't kill her. We've *got* to explain all this to Shad, Henry."

Henry's skepticism is plain. "Without proof?"

"We have to get him proof. A statement from your Double Eagle source. Did you tape *any* of the stuff he said today?"

The reporter shakes his head. "I took good notes."

"Christ, man. You should have taped the bastard on the sly. That may have been a once-in-a-lifetime chance."

"No. He wants to talk to me again."

"When?"

"As soon as he can get his sister to leave the house again."

I stand and pace around the table, trying to control my anxiety. What I would give to be a prosecutor again, with subpoena power. A suffocating sense of foreboding has taken hold of me. "How careful were you today, Henry? Where did you interview this guy?"

"At his sister's home. He sent her out of town on an errand. It's a pretty isolated place. He doesn't think the Eagles are onto him, but they've clearly cut him out of the loop on sensitive stuff. I think it's going to be fine, Penn. He—"

A loud, old-fashioned ringing stops Henry in midsentence. He digs for an office phone buried under some loose papers. "That's probably Sherry, my girlfriend. I'm way late getting home." He lifts the black receiver to his ear. "*Concordia Beacon* . . . Oh, hey, Lou Ann." Henry covers the mouthpiece with his hand and looks up at me. "It's Mrs. Whittington, the lady you met when you came in."

My mind is ranging through all Henry told me, searching for moral pressure points that might induce my father to open up to me before tomorrow.

"When?" Henry asks in a shocked voice. "Just now? . . . Who told you that?" He fishes a cell phone from his front pocket and checks its LCD. "I had my ringer off. Damn it!"

I give the reporter an inquisitive look, but he turns away to concentrate on the conversation. "What do they think happened? . . . Okay, do me a favor and call Sherry back. Tell her I'm with a source and I'll call her as soon as I can. . . . Thanks, Lou Ann. . . . I know. . . . I sure will. . . . You, too. Bye."

When he turns back to me, Henry looks five years older than he did only a minute ago. "That was about my Eagle source. Paramedics just brought him in to the Mercy Hospital emergency room. He was DOA."

A blast of neurochemicals blanks my mind. Where before I had anxious thoughts, only fear courses now. "Henry, Viola Turner and your secret source just died within twelve hours of each other. What do you think that says about your future?"

The reporter blinks as though he doesn't quite comprehend my point.

"Do you have a gun here?" I ask.

"A gun? No. I've never carried one."

"You're working day and night to send ex–Ku Klux Klansmen to Angola, and you don't carry a gun? Angola is filled with pissed-off black convicts. Those old white men would kill almost anybody to stay out of there."

Henry shrugs, looking dazed. "My girlfriend carries a pistol, and my mother keeps a shotgun at her house. The PBS guys making the film about me think I'm nuts for not carrying a gun. Do you carry one?"

"I'm licensed, but I don't have one on me now. Not in the car, either."

A stubborn defiance creeps into the reporter's eyes. "I promised myself when I started that I wasn't going to change my way of living because of these lowlifes. The fact that I've pursued these cases without fear, publishing things as I go, living unafraid . . . that makes a statement. Even to scum like Snake Knox and Brody Royal. It says that I know what I'm doing is right, and what they did was wrong."

While Henry preaches, I move to the war room's metal door and lock it. The *Beacon* stands on the very edge of town, across the road from an empty cotton field. "We need to get out of here. Does that phone still have a dial tone?"

"The office phone?"

"The landline! Check it."

Henry lifts the black phone from its hook and puts it to his ear, then nods with relief.

"Dial 911 and ask for Sheriff Dennis."

The reporter looks uncomfortable. "Walker Dennis isn't exactly a fan of mine."

"I'll do the talking."

CHAPTER 22

"SLOW DOWN, GODDAMN IT!" Snake ordered. "Ain't nobody chasing us."

Sonny Thornfield eased off the gas as he approached the shore of Old River, where he maintained a fishing camp that almost no one in the world knew he owned. Though it stood only a few miles from where Glenn Morehouse had died, no one could find them here in ten years of searching.

The clammy sweat of panic still soaked Sonny's shirt, which made it miserable inside his coat. He and Snake had been only halfway to the tree line behind Wilma's house when the ambulance came barreling up the gravel road, red lights flashing. Sonny worried that in the chaos of the death scene, Wilma might break down and tell the paramedics everything. Snake disagreed.

"She handled it pretty good, I thought," he said. "Wilma's a tough old girl. You wouldn't think it to look at her now, but she was a fine-lookin' thing back in her day."

"I remember," Sonny said dully. "I can still see her in her bathing suit out by Lake Bruin."

Snake grunted. "She was a decent piece of ass, in a pinch."

"I never got to find out."

"You're about the only one." Snake stuffed his hands into his pockets and sucked at the cigarette clamped between his teeth.

"I wish I hadn't seen Glenn that way," Sonny said, peering into the darkness to the left of his headlights. All the camp houses here were built on thirty-foot stilts to escape the perennial flooding from the backwaters of the Mississippi.

"Yeah," Snake said, toying with his heater vent. "But damn, he fought like a demon at the end, didn't he? Sumbitch picked me right up off the floor!"

Sonny tried to suppress the awful memory. "Remember back in the summer of sixty-four, when we tested that C-4 during those family picnics?"

Snake laughed. "Hell, yeah! I'd wrap that Primacord around a stump and cut the top right off, like slicing sausage for jambalaya. The kids loved it."

"Glenn loved that even more than they did. He was like a kid himself."

Snake nodded in the dashboard light. "He always was the weakest of us, though. But he's gone now. Best forgotten."

Sonny wished this were possible. All he could see was his old friend's last moments on earth. After his sister injected the PICC line's port with fentanyl, Snake and Sonny had held the emaciated giant down for another twenty seconds. Then his arms had gone limp, and he'd sagged back against the mattress, breathing only once every fifteen seconds or so.

"Can he hear me?" Wilma had asked in a cracked voice.

Snake leaned over their old comrade, then stuck a finger under his jaw. "If you've got anything to tell him, you better say it quick."

She shoved Sonny out of the way, then climbed onto the bed and lay beside her brother. Cradling Glenn's head against her breasts, she began to sing, so softly that Sonny couldn't recognize the tune. He thought it might be a hymn, but the more he heard, the more it sounded like a children's song. Snake was shouting from the door that they should go, but Sonny couldn't pull himself away.

"Get out," Wilma said coldly. "Get out, you bastards."

After a last look at the eerie tableau, Sonny bolted and followed Snake through the back door at a run. He could still hear the screen door slam in the night, its screeching spring like the howl of a tortured soul.

"Looks like the water's rising," Snake said, staring out over the moonlit backwater. "Temperature's dropping, too. Might be good fishing tomorrow."

Sonny had always known he was different from Snake, but in that moment he wanted to leap from the truck and run until he'd forever separated himself from this man who had led him into so much violence. But it was far too late for that. He was bound inextricably to Snake, as surely as to his own blood.

"Might be," Sonny said, his throat parched with fear. "Maybe we'll go out early."

CHAPTER 23

HENRY SEXTON AND I sit locked in his war room, waiting for an escort from the Concordia Parish Sheriff's Office. It took me a couple of minutes to reach Sheriff Dennis, who sounded as amazed as the 911 operator to get a call from the mayor of Natchez. I said nothing to him about the possible murder of one of Henry's sources, but I did tell him I was concerned for Henry's safety. The sheriff agreed to send a cruiser around to escort us home within ten minutes.

"They really killed him, didn't they?" Henry says in a dazed voice.

"I'd say so. After decades of silence, this guy decides to open up to a reporter investigating unsolved murders in which he was involved. Then he dies that very night?"

"His cancer was terminal," Henry says halfheartedly. "Maybe the stress of today pushed him into some fatal event. I mean—"

"Henry, wake up. They killed him."

The reporter looks at me like a sailor who doesn't want to admit that a hurricane is headed his way. "They must have found out he talked to me today. Which means *I* killed him."

"Don't even start down that road. He lived by the sword, he died by it."

He squints at me as if trying to decide whether we're two different kinds of men.

"Do you have any idea who might have blown your source to the Double Eagles?"

Henry stares blankly at the cracked tile floor. "I know Glenn didn't trust his sister."

"Glenn?"

Henry shakes his head at the absurdity of trying to keep a dead man's name secret. "Glenn Ed Morehouse." Rising from his chair, he stabs the heaviest of the men in the group of pictures he tapped only a few minutes ago. In the photo beneath his finger, a man with the corn-fed build and flattop haircut of an offensive lineman from the golden age of Ole Miss football stares out with irrepressible good humor.

"One the four founding Double Eagles," Henry says. "Frank Knox gave him his gold piece five days after the Neshoba County bodies were found. I saw that coin this morning, Penn. The man was in torment over the things he'd done."

"Well, he's at peace now. You need to think about yourself for a change."

"There was so much I still needed to ask him."

Don't go there, either, I say silently, cursing Henry's failure to record the answers to the questions he did ask.

"Are you sure we can trust Sheriff Dennis?" he asks worriedly. "Ever since Huey Long's time, the sheriffs have run this parish like a third-world dictatorship. At one point, there were no jury trials for nine years straight. And the Kiwanis types didn't care, so long as the country club stayed white and blacks moved to the other side of the street when a white man walked down it. Things have changed on the surface, but that *Magnolia Queen* mess you exposed back in October makes me wonder."

"You're being paranoid, Henry. The old sheriff and six deputies have been indicted. Walker Dennis was the one deputy that everybody in this parish agreed was clean. That's why they appointed him."

Henry doesn't look convinced. "But they're all out on bail right now. And all that dogfighting and prostitution . . . how could Walker Dennis not have known about that?"

"Maybe he did," I concede. "A lot of people probably knew about it, on both sides of the river. But it's pretty hard to fight the current when everybody else is swimming downstream."

"And the meth stuff?" he asks, looking far from reassured. "How could the Knoxes be moving that much stuff without Sheriff Dennis's knowledge?"

"I don't know. Tell me more about their operation."

"Morehouse said it's a big-time drug ring. They supply dealers state-wide, and possibly in Arkansas and Texas as well. Crystal meth is their main product, but God only knows what else they're into."

"Meth trafficking carries heavy mandatory sentences. A DA could pressure the hell out of the Double Eagles by offering immunity on the trafficking charges in exchange for information on the old civil rights crimes—not to mention Viola's death. We need to keep that in mind as we go forward."

Henry nods skeptically.

"Who leads the Knox organization now?"

"Morehouse said Billy Knox runs the drug ring."

"Who's Billy Knox?"

"Snake's son. About your age. He's a legitimate businessman, according to his 1040. He's into everything from timber to TV production. He uses old Eagles in the meth operation, probably because he knows he can trust them. Guys like Snake and Sonny Thornfield own front businesses that shield the operation. Car dealerships, Snake's crop-dusting operation, that kind of thing."

"Perfect for laundering drug profits. Also for purchasing and moving precursor chemicals. We might just have to give this operation a little scrutiny, depending on how things go."

Henry shakes his head like a man trying to come to grips with a new world. "We'll have to be damn careful. Morehouse said the drug operation has powerful protection."

"From whom? Brody Royal?"

"In part, maybe. You may not know this, but the district attorney of this parish is married to one of Brody Royal's nieces."

"Oh, God. Have you checked the court record for any signs of corruption on his part?"

Henry shrugs. "He seems pretty clean. I don't think he's the heavyweight protection for the meth trade. The Knox people are never even arrested."

"Who's shielding them?"

Henry's eyes lock on to mine. "Remember Forrest Knox?"

This takes me a minute. "The kid who witnessed the plane crash? Frank's son?"

"Right. You know what he does for a living now?"

"No idea."

"He's a lieutenant colonel in the Louisiana State Police. Director of their Criminal Investigations Bureau."

This seems too absurd to believe, yet it must be true. Henry's eyes are shining with perverse satisfaction. "How the hell could Forrest Knox rise so high in law enforcement with his family pedigree?"

"This is Louisiana, brother. The land of Edwin Edwards and David Duke."

"It can't be that simple."

"No. Forrest was a war hero, for one thing. Vietnam, Silver Star. For another, he worked his whole life to distance himself from his relatives—at least in public. The Double Eagle connection always dogged him, but his political instincts are so good that he managed to rise above it. Forrest and Snake supposedly hate each other, and have no recorded contact except at family funerals. But Billy and Forrest sometimes get together at a fancy hunting camp they own in Lusahatcha County. And it seems awful coincidental that a big-time drug dealer never seems to get arrested in a state where his cousin is chief of the most powerful criminal investigative agency."

"Bottom line, if we push the Knox family, they'll push back."

Henry nods slowly.

We sit in demoralized silence for a bit, but beneath my disappointment about Morehouse's death, I can't help but feel anxious to speak to both Shad Johnson and my father. If Henry is right, and Lincoln Turner mistakenly believes he's my father's son, then I know what Shad is using as motive to make the case for premeditated murder. He actually believes my father killed Viola to hide Lincoln's paternity. This theory has more than one hole in it, but I can see how Shad would latch on to it. I need to explode that notion as soon as possible.

"You're thinking about your father, aren't you?" Henry says, almost accusingly.

"I am. You've been a tremendous help to him tonight, Henry."

"Are you still going to confront him about the Brody Royal connection?"

"Absolutely."

"And will you tell me what you find out?"

"If it bears on any of these murders, I will. I promise you that."

He gets up and pours what's left of the coffee out of the carafe, his right hand trembling. "The sheriff sure seems to be taking his time sending that deputy. You think we're okay?"

"I'd feel better if I had a pistol. But I think we're all right."

He nods dispiritedly.

"Henry, I'm not going to abandon you on these cases. Not even if I get Shad to drop the case against my father."

No response.

"Tell me something," I say, trying to distract him. "If there was one thing you could have tomorrow, as if by magic, what would it be? I don't mean Glenn Morehouse brought back to life. I'm talking about the realm of the possible. What would be most valuable to you? Nonredacted FBI files?"

The reporter pooches out his lower lip, then rubs his mustache. "Anything?"

"Anything."

"I'd want the Jericho Hole drained. Or dragged, anyway."

This surprises me. "Tell me why."

"If we had the missing bodies, the FBI would be forced to reopen all the cases and go at them full bore. The political pressure would be unbearable if they didn't. I consider two dump sites ground zero for these cases, forensically speaking. One is the Jericho Hole. The other is a place called the Bone Tree, in the Lusahatcha Swamp. The Bone Tree is probably the better spot, and there's some chance that it might stand on federal land."

"That would mean federal jurisdiction. That's always the better path in these kinds of cases."

"I know, but we won't find the Bone Tree without a battalion of National Guard troops. And today Morehouse told me I'd hit pay dirt at both places."

"Who do you think was dumped in the Jericho Hole?"

"Luther Davis's Pontiac was never found after he and Jimmy vanished. I've often wondered if the Eagles didn't sink one or both boys somewhere in that car. Why not the Jericho Hole? Joe Louis Lewis could be down there, too. Given the mineral content of the water, I wouldn't be surprised if those bones had stayed preserved all these years. We might just get lucky. The problem is, the Jericho Hole's on private property. But why did you bring this up? Do you think you can get the FBI to search that hole?"

"Not without more concrete evidence. But I know a guy who used to work as a commercial diver. An ex-marine. He's got some sonar-type equipment. I'll see what he can do for us. But we're not going to mention this to anybody. Not unless we find something. Then I think we're obligated to share it with the Bureau."

"I'm fine with that, so long as we can get a good look at it first. Take some pictures."

"You'll get all the time you need, Henry."

Rather than look relieved, the reporter splays both hands on the worktable and leans over it, his face pale. "Penn, I need to tell you one more thing."

My stomach clenches in dread. "About my father?"

"No. You may think I'm crazy, but I have to say this. Glenn Morehouse told me something else about the Robert Kennedy operation. He said that Snake refused to stand down when Royal ordered him to. Snake still wanted a public death for Jimmy Revels, something that would bring RFK or Dr. King to town for the funeral. He said that if the Eagles stood down, then Frank had died for nothing. Snake refused to toe the line until Ray Presley delivered a personal ultimatum from Carlos Marcello. Whatever Ray said did the trick, but Snake still didn't like it. That's why Jimmy and Luther suffered so terribly before they died. Anyway, according to Morehouse, Snake never let Frank's plan drop. He swore he was going to finish the job for his brother. We know Sirhan killed Bobby two months later, like you said. That was a close-range hit, and even conspiracy theorists agree on who was in that kitchen that night. And that was L.A., of course. Another world."

"But . . . ?"

"Martin Luther King died just four or five days after Jimmy and Luther did. Snake Knox was in a homicidal rage. And Dr. King was one of Frank Knox's original targets, dating back to 1964."

I can't keep the incredulity out of my voice. "You're not seriously suggesting that Snake Knox killed Martin Luther King?"

Henry gives me a look that brings a rush of heat to my face. "Hear me out, will you? I know of three different people Snake told that he fired the fatal shot in Memphis that day."

"Oh, that's just whiskey talk."

"That's what I've always figured, too. But it's not like Snake has been bragging about this all his life. The first time he claimed it to anyone but an Eagle was only three years ago. But he told Morehouse a long time before that. After Glenn called me back, I did a quick read-up on the James Earl Ray case. Dr. King's own family doesn't believe Ray killed him. And I took a look at some of the crime scene evidence before you came over. There's a real possibility that King was shot from the roof of the nearby Fred P. Gattis Building."

"Jesus, Henry. And?"

"Well . . . Memphis is only six hours from Natchez by car—two by air. Snake was a crop duster. He could have flown up there and back with no one the wiser. And he was a trained sniper."

I'm shaking my head even before he finishes speaking. "All circumstantial. Do you have anything concrete?"

"Nobody knows where Snake was that day. He didn't report to work at Triton, but nobody made a fuss because Frank's funeral had been the previous Sunday. Everybody figured he was laid up drunk somewhere."

"Have you asked the FBI about Snake's claims?"

Henry shakes his head. "They wouldn't tell me anything even if they knew. And if they don't know, they'd think I'm a nut job."

"You're right."

"So? What do you think?"

"I think this is a distraction. And it's unprovable. Even if Snake confessed, you'd never know whether he was telling the truth or just trying to get on TV. Besides, my gut says the time window is too short. For two gunmen to have been there implies a conspiracy. Snake couldn't have thrust himself into a conspiracy in four or five days, no matter how angry he was. The alternative is coincidence, and I *hate* coincidence."

Henry looks like he wants to let go of the idea, but can't quite do it. "What if Snake had hoped to lure King down to Jimmy's funeral as well as Kennedy? When it all went bad, he decided to take revenge on the closest target of opportunity."

I shake my head. "Look, you've made real progress on terrible murders whose victims deserve justice. Focusing on the King assassination at this point is like hunting for unicorns. Snake Knox killed quite a few people in his time, and you're going to nail him for one or more of those murders. That's good enough."

Henry holds my gaze for a few seconds longer, then nods as though he's taken my words to heart.

As I check my watch, my cell phone pings with a text message from Walker Dennis:

Cruiser wating outside w deputy in it. u guys coming out or what?

"Our carriage awaits," I tell Henry, who tenses instantly. "Do you feel good enough about this to walk out there unarmed?"

He shrugs. "What choice do we have?"

"I could call the Natchez police chief and ask him to ride over here and get us. But I don't think that's necessary."

"Screw it, then. Let's go."

I slide the picture of my father and Brody Royal off the table. "May I take this?"

"Sure. I've got a copy."

Henry unlocks the door of the war room and leads me down the hall to the main office. Red lights are flashing in the parking lot, and their distorted refraction through the glass door lends a cinematic sense of danger to the scene. As Henry gathers papers into his briefcase, I touch his shoulder, and he jumps like a man who thought he was alone.

"I really need to be able to tell Shad Johnson a little of what you've told me tonight," I say. "Not much, and I won't tell Caitlin anything. But if I can't slow Shad down, he's going to have my father arrested in the morning. Will you give me your blessing for that much?"

Henry looks like a man being asked to lend out his life savings.

"I wouldn't ask if I had another option. But Dad nearly died from that last heart attack. I'm not sure he can survive an arrest, much less jail."

To his credit, Henry hesitates only a moment. "Do whatever you have to, Penn. I don't want Doc to suffer for something he didn't do."

"Thank you." I edge up to the glass door. A white Ford Crown Vic with a bubblegum light waits in the dark parking lot to my left, gray smoke puffing from its tailpipe. "Okay. We're going to walk out there like we own the town. Right?"

"If you say so."

"I'll go first."

"Won't argue with that."

Turning my back to the door, I take hold of his arms. "Before we go, is there anything else you want to tell me?"

Henry's eyes widen. "Are you saying you think I'm about to get shot?"

"I hope not. But you never know."

Henry seems to waver. Then he says, "There's a witness who can take down Brody Royal. I haven't found him yet, because I don't know his name. He was a childhood friend of Pooky Wilson's. I call him 'Huggy Bear.' He went to Pooky's mother a week ago, just before she died. He wanted forgiveness, after forty years of silence. He saw Brody leave Albert's store that night, just as the fire started, and get into a car with his future son-in-law, Randall Regan. I think Mr. Huggy Bear left Ferriday a long time ago. He's the only eyewitness who wasn't one of Albert's killers. Find him, and we'll nail Brody."

"Thank you, Henry."

He nods once. "If I don't make it, you find him. And talk to your father. I hate to say it, but I think Doc has known about Brody Royal from the beginning."

With that, the reporter turns away and, forgetting our plan, walks through the glass door like a man striding onto the red carpet at a world premiere.

CHAPTER 24

LIEUTENANT COLONEL FORREST Knox was lying on his sofa watching the Baltimore Ravens demolish Brett Favre and the Packers on Monday Night Football when the text message came in. Forrest had always loved Favre. Number 4 was a tough Mississippi boy from the old school, the last of the gunslingers. But lately Favre had been tanking, and tonight the coach had replaced him with some punk named Rodgers late in the third quarter. When Forrest's secure cell phone pinged, he actually welcomed the interruption.

The text was from Al Ozan, a captain who served in his Criminal Investigations Bureau. Forrest had been expecting Ozan to update him on a load of precursor chemicals from Mexico later on, but not yet. The body of the message brought Forrest bolt upright on the couch.

G. Morehouse DOA at Mercy Hospital. Please advise.

A faint thrumming began in Forrest's chest, a gift of intuition that told him when action was imminent—a gift that had carried him through Vietnam and countless lethal confrontations in civilian life. He took a plug of Red Man from the bag on the coffee table, stuffed it into his cheek, and waited for the shock to wear off.

His wife had gone to bed at the end of the first quarter, and he'd been thinking about getting Ozan to call him out on a fake emergency so he could run over and pop the wife of a young moron in Patrol. Cherie Delaune had sent Forrest the all-clear signal an hour ago—meaning her husband was on patrol and her daughter was spending the night out—but Forrest hadn't been able to summon the energy for the trip. If he could have snapped his fingers and been in Cherie's bed, he'd have done it. But ever since Katrina hit, work had been steadily grinding him down. Tonight was only the second time since the storm that he'd gotten home before 9 P.M.

"Good ol' Glenn," he said, ruminating about his father. "Poor bastard. Rest in peace, Mountain."

Forrest reached down to the floor for his black leather boots, pulled them on with a groan, then stood and buckled on his gun belt. Walking into the kitchen, he spat tobacco juice into the sink, then unscrewed the top off a prescription bottle and dry-swallowed four Adderall, which had been given to him by a detective-sergeant in the narcotics division. The Adderall helped him focus. Then he opened a second bottle and swallowed a 50 mg Viagra. Even with the Morehouse development, he had time for a quick stop by Cherie's house. He needed to hit it fast, or he'd risk her husband going off shift. Forrest didn't need a confrontation with a fellow state cop, even if he was just in Patrol. He called Ozan on his secure cell. The captain answered on the first ring.

"What you think, boss?" Ozan asked by way of greeting.

"Was it the cancer, Alphonse?"

"Don't know yet. I just called Billy, but he didn't answer. I know Snake has been nervous as a cat since that Viola Turner got back to Natchez, and I think he may have got Brody Royal stirred up."

"Brody? What makes you say that?"

"I ran into Royal's son-in-law, that Randall Regan, buying a muzzle-loader over at the Bass Pro Shops. He mentioned the Turner woman dying. So Brody's obviously been thinking about her. I been thinking that her and Morehouse dying on the same day seems a little funny. Don't it?"

Forrest glanced at the flickering television as Baltimore put another nail in Green Bay's coffin. He was waiting for his instinct to tell him something, as it always did during times of danger. Maybe Favre himself was the message. Gifted quarterbacks sometimes stayed in the game too long, and it was looking more and more like Brett should have left the league a couple of years back. Forrest was older than Favre, yet he was only now coming into the prime of his earning potential. His playing field was the state of Louisiana, and he had it wired from Shreveport to New Orleans. About all he really had in common with Favre, other than geography of birth, was being his own worst enemy. Keeping his primal impulses in check chafed Forrest's spirit. Men with outsized appetites and abilities ought to get some sort of exemption from the rules of common men. In a way, of course, Forrest had exactly that—the badge he wore every day, the mantle of authority that kept most potential troublemakers at arm's length.

"Call Snake, Al," he said. "Get it straight from him. All that blood-oath bullshit Daddy started is one big pain in the ass."

"Any personal message?"

"Tell Snake to stay away from Henry Sexton. I see Henry's stories within an hour of him drafting them, so Snake should just calm the fuck down. I know Billy's told him already, but that's not the same as it coming from me."

Ozan laughed. "Not by a damn sight, boss. I just hope it's not too late. Snake's been wanting to kill that reporter ever since I've known him."

"That is absolutely the last thing we need. I sure wish Billy could control his daddy."

Alphonse laughed again. "You think if your old man was alive, you could control him?"

Forrest's mind filled with the forbidding image of his father roused to anger, something no man had ever faced without fear. "You got a point there, Al. How's that other thing coming? The Mexican run?"

"Unloading in Barataria Bay right now."

"And the cash?"

"Our runner's bringing it up to Fort Knox tonight."

Forrest glanced at his Breitling and calculated how long a stop at Cherie's might take him. The Valhalla Exotic Hunting Reserve lay fifty miles north of Baton Rouge. "I'm gonna make a cooter stop before we go."

"Shit. Where?"

"Where do you think?"

Ozan groaned. "Where's that husband of hers?"

"On patrol over near Lafayette. I had the dispatcher check his twenty."

"What if he doubles back without reporting in? You been hitting that a little too often for comfort. Not to mention longer than usual."

"Why you think I'm taking you with me?"

Ozan chuckled. "All right. Just remember, Ricky ain't the sharpest knife in the drawer, but you don't need that kind of trouble—not with Colonel Mackiever crawling up your backside."

The mention of the superintendent of the state police sent a flood of acid into Forrest's stomach. Ozan himself had originally been assigned to Forrest's division as a plant by Colonel Mackiever, after Internal Affairs had failed to get any dirt on Forrest. Mackiever had figured a Redbone like Ozan would never allow himself to be corrupted by a man with the Ku Klux Klan in his lineage. But Forrest had learned long ago that blacks and Indians craved money and power every bit as much as white men, and within four months, the only reports Ozan sent back to the colonel were being scripted by Forrest himself.

"I can't help it, Alphonse," Forrest said, as the Adderall hit his system like a blast of pure oxygen. "I crave that girl's kink. But you're right: she's starting to get ideas above herself."

"Don't they all, eventually?"

Forrest grabbed a coat, locked the house, then walked out to his supercharged cruiser. "I guess. Men grab the low-hanging fruit, but women always want to trade up to the next branch. This better be my last trip." As he climbed behind the wheel, a perverse idea struck him. "Hey, maybe you ought to take her over. You're moving up in the world."

"I doubt she'd be into me, boss. I'm an acquired taste."

That's the damn truth. Forrest laughed, thinking of the big Redbone. Ozan was like a modern version of Injun Joe from *Tom Sawyer.* "Maybe you can educate her palate. Expand her horizons."

"Not with her husband in the troop. After she spent one night with me, he'd know she was different. Ruint. I've seen it too many times."

Forrest suppressed laughter as he backed out the driveway. "We'll see. You just let me hit it one more time before you ruin her."

"Consider it a Christmas gift. Unmarked ride for the pit stop?"

"Always. Pick me up outside headquarters."

Forrest felt his face flush from the Viagra, and his cock stiffened as he thought of his immediate destination. "I'm serious about Snake. Tell him if he kills Henry Sexton, I'll lock him and Sonny in Angola myself. They'll be wearing Depends twenty-four hours a day after that. Maybe Snake'll pass that message to Brody Royal."

Ozan's laughter carried a cruel edge of pleasure. "Happy to pass that on, boss."

CHAPTER 25

THE CONCORDIA PARISH Sheriff's Department cruiser peels off my tail after Henry Sexton and I reach the Pizza Hut at the western edge of Vidalia. Driving ahead of me, Henry Sexton turns off the main highway into a residential neighborhood, while I continue toward the twin bridges that span the Mississippi River, five miles to the east. The lights of Natchez glimmer on the bluff high above them, calling me back home.

The moment we left the *Beacon* office, I called a retired cop named James Ervin to set up security for Henry and his loved ones, but for the last few miles I've fought the urge to use my cell phone again. I don't like making decisions in the heat of the moment, especially after absorbing an information dump like the one Henry laid on me tonight. In the span of sixty minutes, the reporter gave me the results of twenty years of painstaking investigation, and the full ramifications aren't easy to grasp. For the time being, I don't intend to try. What matters now is my father's plight, and whether or not he's willing to try to extricate himself from it. With a preparatory tensing of my stomach muscles, I dial Dad's cell phone. He doesn't answer until I've nearly despaired of getting him.

"Hello, Penn," he says in a softer voice than usual.

"You told me to call you if Henry had any new information that was relevant. Well, he had a lot. We need to have a very different conversation than the one we had this afternoon."

"Son . . . I can't talk now. Peggy is upset."

"I imagine she is, if you've just told her about this mess. Is she right there?"

"No, but close enough."

"Hold the earpiece close to your head, then." I lower my voice. "I'm going to ask you one question, and I want a yes-or-no answer. I need you to answer it, because before I can make a move, I need to know where you stand."

"I will, if I can."

"Will you take a DNA test to establish whether or not you are Lincoln Turner's father?"

There's a stunned silence. "Penn—"

"Yes or no, Dad. Please."

More silence. I could have asked whether or not he'd fathered a child by Viola, or whether it's even possible, but what would be the point? Though I've never known him to lie to me, in the end this question will only be answered by scientific evidence.

"I will," he says at length.

My relief is palpable. Passing into Vidalia, I adjust my brights for oncoming traffic. "All right. I'll see you later tonight."

"Make it late, after Peggy's asleep. Midnight."

"Okay."

I hit END and squeeze the steering wheel until my knuckles ache. I'm not even sure what his answer meant. But from a legal standpoint all that matters now is his willingness to take the test. Before I can second-guess myself, I call Shad Johnson's cell phone. It rings several times, but just as I expect to be kicked to voice mail, the DA's smooth voice comes on the line.

"I've been expecting you to call back all day."

"My father didn't kill Viola Turner."

"Do you have exculpatory evidence I don't know about?"

"I know how you convinced yourself you could win a case for premeditated murder. You believe Lincoln Turner is my father's illegitimate son, by Viola."

The line goes silent.

"If that's your case, Shad, you'd better slow down. Because Tom Cage is not that man's father. Dad just told me he's willing to take a DNA test, at your pleasure. I'm sure Lincoln spun you a heartbreaking story, but there are some biographical details of which he's blissfully unaware—the first being that his mother was gang-raped by ex–Ku Klux Klansmen just before she fled Natchez. And not once, but twice, a few days apart. Henry Sexton believes one of those men is Lincoln Turner's father."

"What does Henry Sexton have to do with this?"

"He's an expert on the Double Eagle group. So, before you call a press conference making charges about my father and his 1960s love child, I'd verify my soon-to-be-disbarred client's story. You don't want to be charged with defamation and false arrest."

"He's not my client. I'm the district attorney."

"Call it what you will. But if you arrest Dad in the morning, you'll be stepping into serious trouble. Don't let Lincoln Turner and Sheriff Byrd drag you into something you'll regret."

The phone stays silent, but I know Shad is thinking furiously. Rather than push him further, I let him stew in his anxieties awhile.

"What do you expect me to do with this?" he asks finally. "Throw out a murder case based on a phone call from the mayor?"

"It shouldn't even *be* a murder case. Not against my father, anyway."

"Penn, listen. This thing has taken on a life of its own. Lincoln's pushing every political hot button he can in this town. You know I've got to deal with my own community in a case like this."

"Your *community* wouldn't even know about this if you weren't stirring it up."

"You're wrong! Black deputies worked that crime scene, man. Plus, Billy Byrd's not about to lay off without proof that Dr. Cage wasn't involved."

"Everybody's pushing this thing but you, huh? I don't buy it, Shad."

"Your father hasn't even tried to defend himself! What are people supposed to make of that?"

There's no denying this problem. "I know that looks bad. But this is a complex situation."

"Not from where I sit. You have the luxury of dealing in theories; I'm stuck with what I can prove. I've got your father's fingerprints on morphine vials and a horse-sized syringe. I've got a suicide pact between your father and the victim, and the victim's sister puts him at the scene just prior to death. Lincoln's paternity angle is just the cherry on top."

"Don't bullshit me, Shad! Lincoln's assumed paternity is what took you from assisted suicide to murder. Nothing else. Are you seriously fucking with me? Because I know *exactly* how to handle that."

"No—Penn, wait."

Gripping the wheel fiercely, I try to rein in my anger. "A man named Glenn Morehouse was murdered near Vidalia tonight. You need to look into that. He was spilling his guts to Henry Sexton, and the Double

Eagle group killed him for it. The same reason they killed Viola four-teen hours earlier."

"Can you prove that?"

"Talk to Henry Sexton."

"I will. But meanwhile, I don't have control over what Billy Byrd does."

"You're the DA. He's the sheriff. Muzzle that son of a bitch."

"I'll try, but it's not going to be easy. If anything goes down in the morning, you call me before you do anything crazy."

"I might not have time, Shad. The *Examiner* has that Web edition now, and Caitlin's always hungry for a good story."

"Penn . . . please, man. I'm not doing anything that any other DA wouldn't do."

I slam my hand against the wheel, outraged at having to resort to blackmail. "If Sheriff Byrd goes forward with an arrest, you make damn sure he does it late enough that I can post bail immediately. Because if Dad sees the inside of a cell, you're going to be packing your bags before lunch."

"I hear you. But you're assuming that the judge will grant bail."

Fury blazes along every nerve in my body. "The only way Dad *won't* get bail is if you argue that the judge should deny it! And if you do that, you know what to expect. Some pictures are worth more than a thousand words, bud. Some are worth a career and a law license."

"I've told you about the political pressure. I can't believe you're threatening me like this."

"Karma's a bitch, Shad."

This time he says nothing, and I cut the connection.

Without noticing, I've crossed the apex of the eastbound bridge and started descending toward the cut in the Natchez bluff. A hundred feet below the span, two floating casinos disguised as nineteenth-century steamboats glitter on the black water. A third was put out of commission eight weeks ago, in what would have been the greatest river catastrophe since the *Sultana* exploded in 1865, had not luck intervened. The refitted casino boat is scheduled to go back into operation eleven weeks from now, and many of our local citizens are waiting anxiously for their paychecks to resume.

As I pass through the cut, my heart pounds from my exchange with

Shad. But rather than dwell on what he said, my mind turns to my session with Henry Sexton, and to action. Glancing down from the highway, I search my phone's contacts list for Kirk Boisseau.

Kirk graduated from St. Stephen's Preparatory School four years ahead of me. After a truncated career in the Marine Corps—a Force Recon unit—he spent several years working as a commercial diver, both in the Mississippi River and the Gulf of Mexico. Kirk owns an earthmoving company now, but he devotes much of his time to kayak racing on the Mississippi River. Guys like Kirk never quite adjust to civilian life, and thus are usually open to pushing the envelope, especially in a good cause.

"Mayor *Cage*," he says by way of answering his cell phone. "Don't tell me—research question for a novel. Could I really cut somebody's throat with a Visa card?"

"Not this time."

"You've finally found the funding for my white-water park?"

"Uh . . . no. Sorry."

"Then what the hell are you bothering me for?"

"Are you in the mood to break the law?"

There's a brief pause, during which I hear Susan Werner singing "Barbed Wire Boys" through the phone. Then Kirk says, "What you got in mind?"

"A little creative trespassing."

Kirk grunts. "Sounds mildly interesting."

"With some diving at the end of it."

"Now I'm getting a chubby."

"Are you familiar with the Jericho Hole?"

"I've studied it on maps. That's private property."

"I'm aware."

"What you looking for, Penn?"

"Bones. Human."

"A body?"

"Just the bones."

"How old we talking?"

"Forty years."

Kirk gives a skeptical grunt. "That hole was created when a levee crevasse opened up long ago. The river's probably swept through there several times over the last forty years during flood stage. That would have scoured any bones out of there."

"From what I understand, quite a few corpses have been dumped in that hole over the years. But the guys we're looking for may have been wired to something before they got thrown in. An engine block, for example. They might even be locked inside a car."

"Well, that would certainly help."

"Do you know how deep that hole really is, Kirk?"

"No. Maybe forty to sixty feet."

"Can you search it for me?"

"When you need it done?"

"Yesterday."

"Why did I ask? I've still got my lights and equipment. How close can I take my truck without being detected?"

"No idea."

"Hang on . . . I'm checking a topo map. I know a crop duster who works that area. He can tell me the lay of the land. Is the property owner the type to shoot first and ask questions later?"

"Again, no idea. But I'd suggest treating this more as a Force Recon mission than a commercial diving job. This is beyond the call of duty."

"You know what I say to that."

"What?"

"Oo-*rah,* motherfucker! Beats the shit out of pushing dirt all day. Who's the dead guy?"

"Two civil rights activists. Vietnam vets."

"Even better. Let's haul those ground-pounders up and make somebody pay."

My sense of relief is so strong that laughter almost bubbles out of my chest. "Thanks, Kirk."

"Thank me after I've found the guy."

"Gratitude's one of my strong suits. You know that."

"That I do, Mayor. Look, I'm going to need somebody standing post on the bank while I'm down hole. Do you have time to back me up?"

"I'm afraid I'll be spending tomorrow in court, defending my father."

"What?"

"It's a long story. Can you get somebody else?"

"Yeah, my girlfriend can cover it. Just tell me you've got my back, legally speaking."

"Absolutely. I'll pay any fines and keep you out of jail, no worries."

"Good enough. Hey, if I do find the guy, what exactly do you want me to bring up?"

"Two or three bones, the bigger the better. I want a DNA match, if possible. I need probable cause for the FBI to come in and drain the whole lake. A bone with barbed wire around it or crushed under an engine block would be fantastic. Photos *in situ* would be the jackpot."

"I read you. I'll see what I can do."

"Thanks, Kirk. Be careful."

"Way of life, bro. Out."

Turning right on State Street, I press END and head away from the river, wondering whether Shad will really force me to go public with the dogfighting photo.

As I park by the old carriage step in front of my town house, I feel a powerful urge to talk to my mother. Where our family is concerned, she's always known all secrets great and small, though she's carried most in silence. But before I take that irrevocable step, I need to give Dad one more chance to come clean on his own.

Getting out of my car, I stand in the cold wind blowing up Washington Street and bask in the yellow glow emanating from the first-floor windows of my house. For the past seven years, Caitlin Masters and I have lived in separate houses on opposite sides of this beautiful street. Her Acura is parked in her driveway now, but this living arrangement is soon to change, though not in the way Caitlin expects. I have a breathtaking surprise for her, a wedding present she will not quite believe, and it involves our future home. But today's events have raised a specter of uncertainty in that regard, one I've not yet decided how to handle.

As I start up my steps, a big V-8 engine revs loudly, rumbling between the houses. Headlights flash out of the darkness to my left, streaking through the street in front of my house. Washington is a one-way street that runs toward the river, but these lights are shining *from* the river. Before I can think further, a big white pickup truck blasts out of the line of cars parked beside the Temple B'nai Israel and roars toward me.

Backpedaling up the steps, I stare into the pickup's open window,

searching for the glint of a gun barrel. To my surprise, the truck screeches
to a stop, its diesel engine idling low and heavy, like that of a tank. A dark
face hovers in the driver's window; I can just make out the whites of eyes
in its upper half.

"You the mayor?" asks a voice that's not quite James Earl Jones deep,
but very nearly so.

"That's right," I answer, still wary of an attack.

"I want to talk to you."

"I have an office."

The lips part enough for me to see yellow-white teeth. "I ain't gonna
hurt you none."

"You're going to hurt somebody, driving like that." Edging down off
the steps, I move warily toward his window. "You're going the wrong
way on a one-way street."

"That right?" The man laughs without humor. "Well, I'm new in
town."

"Where are you from?"

The eyelids blink once, slowly. "You don't know who I am?"

His face is darker than those of many local blacks, and squarer than
most, as well. There's a grayish cast to his skin, or perhaps even a blue
tint, but it's hard to tell by the dashboard lights. He has a strong jaw and
nose, but I can't tell much about his eyes. Up close, the sclera are more
yellow than white, giving him a jaundiced look. I'm about to say I don't
recognize the face when I realize I must be looking at Viola's son—
Lincoln Turner.

"Does this truck have Illinois plates?"

Lincoln grins. "Give that man a see-gar!"

"What do you want here?"

"Your daddy killed my mama," he says, all humor gone from the
bass voice. "I'd say we're overdue for a meeting."

An emotion I'd like to call something else but which is in fact raw
fear has scrambled my nerves. I suddenly need to piss—badly.

"Why are you here at my house?"

"I wanted to see your face. And to tell you something. There was a
time when your daddy could have done what he did to my mama and
have nothing happen behind it. But that time's past. Even in Mississippi."

"Are you so certain about what happened to your mother?"

"My auntie doesn't lie, Mayor."

Turner must be referring to Cora Revels. I consider raising the question of his paternity, but a dark street doesn't seem like the best place to bring up a gang rape. Better to let Shad broach this subject with Turner.

"This isn't the proper venue to discuss these matters, Mr. Turner."

He grins again. "A lawyer, even now? Out here?" His voice is taunting. "Are you inviting me into your house? With your fiancée and your little girl?"

My chest goes tight and his mention of Caitlin and Annie. The subtextual threat is clear. "Maybe another time."

As I turn to go, Turner's voice rumbles in his chest like distant thunder. This must be his version of a chuckle. "Are you going to be defending your father in court?"

"I'm not a defense attorney, Mr. Turner."

"Call me Lincoln." He revs the big engine twice, and I resist the urge to cover my ears. "That's not what I asked you," he reminds me. "I asked, are *you* gonna be defending *him*?"

I turn back and give him a level stare. "I don't think this case is going to reach a courtroom."

The luminous teeth shine again in his dark face. "Oh, yes it will. You can bank on that, my brother."

"I was sorry about your mother. I only knew her when I was a boy, but I remember her. I liked and respected her."

The teeth vanish. "You didn't know shit about her."

My fear that he might be carrying a weapon returns. "I didn't mean to presume anything. You have a good evening," I say absurdly, backing away from the truck.

I'm already on the sidewalk when he shouts, "All that fancy legal education you got? All those years you spent in the courtroom? They're not going to help your daddy one bit!"

We'll see about that. "Aren't you an attorney yourself?" I call.

"Not like you. I didn't go to a high-dollar law school with a world-class library and scouts from the big firms waiting for the graduates. I went to a night school, the kind 'real' lawyers joke about. Until I hand them their asses in court, that is. I've been scrapping out a living since the day I was born, Mayor. I've seen things white-shoe lawyers like you

can't even imagine. So don't be thinkin' we've got anything in common. Just remember what I told you: your daddy's going down—all the
way down—like he should have done a long time ago."

This guy just lost his mother, I remind myself, but she was terminally
ill for nearly a year. His fury is clearly based on a perception of insult
much older than that. Could he have some idea that he was likely conceived during his mother's rape by Mississippi rednecks?

"What do you really know about my father?" I ask.

The eyes narrow to slits. "More than you, I'll bet. I know what my
mama knew. Your daddy might have shut her up last night, but I'm still
vertical." Turner thumps his big chest with his fist. "I'm the chicken
come home to roost, brother, the cat that got thrown in the river but
finds his way back home. I'm the *avenging motherfucking angel*. A *black*
angel! Men reap what they sow, Mr. Mayor. You'll find out the details
when reaping time comes."

"When will that be?"

The low thunder rolls in his chest again. "When the judge and jury
are listening. When all the cameras are switched on, and the lights are
shining bright as noontime." Turner jams his truck into gear with a
lurch. "You take care now."

The big wheels spin with a scream that makes me shudder, and the
truck reverses up Washington Street to the intersection, where Turner
executes a stunt maneuver that spins his vehicle 180 degrees. Gunning
the engine, he fishtails up Washington, narrowly missing sedans parked
on both sides of the crape myrtle–lined street. I stare after the pickup,
recalling a night two months ago when a man far more frightening
than Lincoln Turner ambushed me on my porch. But fear and danger
aren't always directly proportional. We're all terrified by rattlesnakes,
but the spider we brush off our sleeve with hardly a thought is far more
likely to hurt us.

CHAPTER 26

HENRY SEXTON'S GIRLFRIEND lived in a leafy neighborhood near the western end of one of the two bridges spanning the Mississippi River from Vidalia, Louisiana, to Natchez. As per Penn's instructions, Henry had gone straight there and loaded her shotgun, then waited for a retired cop that Penn had hired to pick up Henry's mother and deliver her to Sherry's house. He'd told Penn that the two women had never gotten along and never would, but Penn had persuaded him that twelve hours of constant fighting between Sherry and his mother would be preferable to both of them being killed. Of course, Henry had the much harder job of making the women understand what was at stake—without sending them into total panic.

Sherry cottoned on pretty quick. She'd always insisted that Henry was courting disaster by probing old Klan murders, and she'd often tried to dissuade him from pursuing potentially dangerous leads. His mother, on the other hand, believed that since nothing had happened to Henry up to now, nothing was likely to in the future. The white-haired old lady perched in a club chair in Sherry's den like a dowager countess being forced to accept the hospitality of a peasant, while Sherry made futile offers of coffee, biscuits, fried chicken, and even banana nut bread.

"For the life of me," sniffed Mrs. Sexton, "I don't see how someone expects to host *anybody* without a drop of sherry in the house. No pun intended."

Henry announced that he was running over to McDonough's package store to buy a bottle of Dry Sack, but James Ervin, the heavy-jowled old cop that Penn had hired to watch over them, told him they'd better make do with what they had. After Henry got his mother to accept some Chardonnay, Ervin led him and Sherry into the guest room to give them a quiet refresher course on handling her shotgun. Unlike 98 percent of the boys he'd grown up with, Henry had little experience with guns, but the 12-gauge Ithaca was pretty simple to operate, and after some dry-firing, he felt he could repel an intruder if necessary. The wisest course in that circumstance, Ervin suggested in a kindly voice, would probably be to let Sherry handle the shotgun.

Once the ladies had settled into an uncomfortable truce, Henry retreated to the kitchen, took out his Moleskine notebook, and pretended to work on an article at the Formica-topped table. The fact was, he could barely keep his thoughts in any kind of order. The knowledge that Glenn Morehouse now lay on a slab in the hospital morgue, after they'd talked intimately only hours ago, was disorienting enough; but to be nearly certain that his interview had triggered the old man's murder had given Henry a far more visceral appreciation of the dangers of his quest.

While Sherry guessed answers on a game show in the den, he opened his briefcase and removed an envelope containing several photographs. One was the original photo of Tom Cage with Brody Royal and his cronies in the fishing boat. But another Henry had decided against showing Penn, at the last moment. He slid it out now, keeping one corner under a page in his notebook so that he could easily cover it if someone entered the kitchen.

This photo showed a blurry image of Henry himself, shot with a telephoto lens as he walked out of the Ferriday Walmart. A rifle scope reticle had been perfectly superimposed over his face, with a bull's-eye on his forehead. He'd received this photo in the mail, and he'd duly turned it over to the FBI, but the Bureau had been unable to trace it. All they could verify was that it had been mailed from Omaha, Nebraska, which Henry could see from the postmark. What Henry didn't tell the FBI was that he'd spent the week prior to receiving this threatening photo in New Orleans, investigating the real estate dealings between Brody Royal and Carlos Marcello. The old Mafia boss had died in 1993, long after Alzheimer's claimed his mind, but the MarYal Corporation still had extensive holdings in New Orleans and South Florida. Throughout his investigations of the Double Eagles, Henry had ignored all threats. But investigating Brody Royal and his ties to the Mafia was apparently different, and something had told him he ought to back off, at least for the time being.

"Baby?" Sherry said softly from behind him.

Henry started at the sound of her voice, but it was too late to hide the picture. Sherry already knew about it, anyway. He jerked when she laid her hand on his shoulder. A working nurse, Sherry had an amazingly gentle touch, but tonight Henry was as jumpy as he'd ever been in his life.

"Did you show Penn Cage that picture?"

He shook his head.

"Why not?"

"I got it months ago, and nothing's happened since."

"Nothing quite as bad, you mean."

He turned in his chair and squeezed her hand. "Look, Mama won't have to be here more than a couple of days, if that."

"Oh, I'm fine with her," Sherry said with sincerity. "She's your mother, and she's welcome. I only hope she doesn't try to make it as hard on Jamie as she does on me."

Jamie was Sherry's fifteen-year-old son.

"She likes Jamie," Henry assured her, hoping he was right.

"Mmm." Sherry poured herself a cup of coffee and sat at the table, her gaze as penetrating as any he'd ever faced. "If this situation is so dangerous, why haven't you called the sheriff's department?"

"Because I'm not sure we can trust them."

Fresh concern furrowed her brow. "What about the FBI, then?"

"I am going to call them tonight. But I don't expect they'll send anyone to protect us."

"They might, if you told them everything you know."

Henry stared at her, then slowly shook his head. "I can't do that, babe."

"Why not? Because you want an exclusive story?"

"No. Because they never tell me a damn thing, yet they expect me to give them everything I've spent my life uncovering. I'm doing their jobs for them, and—by God, it's just not right."

Sherry stared into her coffee cup for a while, then laid a hand on his forearm and squeezed it softly. "What if you get hurt because of that stubbornness of yours? That's not right, either. I love you, and I need you."

Henry acknowledged her concern with a nod, but he knew he wouldn't change his mind. "That's a risk I've taken from the beginning. It's just something I've got to do."

"What if Jamie gets hurt, Henry? What then? These men you write about have used *bombs*. They've shot blindly into houses. I remember that stuff from when I was a little girl."

They've done a lot worse than that, he thought. "I don't think that's going to happen, Sher. But even if I gave everything to the FBI, they wouldn't send us a protective detail tonight. That's not how they work."

"So it's you against the world?"

"No. I have Penn Cage helping me now."

She made a sour face. "Oh, Penn Cage. What can he do?"

"Penn knows a lot of people. When he tried the Del Payton case, he fought the director of the FBI, and he won."

Sherry lowered her voice to a whisper. "Then why does he send one old colored man to guard us when people are dying left and right? He's rich—he can afford to get you a real bodyguard. I'm sorry, Henry, but how do you know he's not trying to steal your story for that Caitlin Masters he lives with?"

Henry shook his head resentfully. "He's not doing that. Penn's just trying to help his father."

"Who may have murdered one of his own patients, according to the reports I heard at the hospital. His own nurse!"

"You know better than that. You're talking about Tom Cage, for God's sake."

Sherry laid a hand over one of his. "All I know is, they're from the high side of the river. They've got money. They're different from us, and I don't think you can afford to—"

"I get the message," Henry snapped, pulling his hand from beneath hers. "But I believe they're honorable men, as honorable as any I've ever known, and I trust them."

She shrugged to show how little appreciated she felt. "Well, I hope you're right. That's all I can say."

"Time will tell. I need to get back to work. I've got some calls to make."

Sherry huffed and went back to check on his mother.

Henry slid the original photo of the four men in the stern of the fishing boat out of the envelope. He'd studied this image for countless hours, and he'd gleaned a lot from it. What most struck him was how profoundly Brody Royal dominated the group. Dr. Cage and Claude Devereux were highly intelligent men, even brilliant, while Presley possessed animal cleverness. Yet Royal's eyes held an awareness of the other men, and of the camera, that the others' eyes did not. And while Ray Presley was feared by all who knew him (and was known to be a killer), it was Royal who exuded the aura of a predator. The hawklike face with its gray eyes and proud beak of a nose made a statement, but there was more to his charisma than this. An invisible field seemed to surround the older man, creating a buffer zone that the others would not enter. This deference might have been due to Royal's wealth, of course, but on balance Henry didn't assign much weight to that. It was more that in any group of men, a natural hierarchy always established itself, and in this one—despite the presence of some very strong personalities—Brody Royal sat atop the ziggurat.

Henry slid the photo aside and rubbed his forehead. He'd revealed far more to Penn tonight than he'd originally intended, but he hadn't told him everything. The rifle scope photo was one omission. Another was the story of Brody Royal's daughter, Katy, the girl who'd triggered the deaths of Pooky Wilson and Albert Norris, by inviting Pooky to cross a line that meant death to him but not to her. *Not to imply that the girl didn't suffer,* Henry thought. Because she had—terribly. After Pooky vanished, Katy Royal had gone a little crazy, by all reports, so crazy that her father had forcibly committed her to a private sanitarium in Texas. The Borgen Institute no longer existed, but after dozens of phone calls, Henry had managed to track down a nurse who'd worked there during the sixties and seventies.

He soon learned that electroshock therapy had been a staple of treatment for Dr. Wilhelm Borgen, who'd founded the hospital. Five minutes' research told Henry that "electroshock therapy" could mean a lot of different things, so he'd called the nurse back with specific questions. All her answers were discouraging. By the 1960s ECT, or electroconvulsive therapy, had begun to move away from the bilateral sine-wave method that caused so many terrible side effects, but when Katy Royal resided at the Borgen Institute, they had yet to embrace any of those advances. And while informed consent was today a prerequisite of ECT, at the Borgen Institute prior to 1971, patients were routinely administered electroshock therapy against their will. The side effects of such treatment ran the gamut from broken bones to long-term cognitive degradation and even amnesia.

Four days ago, Henry had seen the results firsthand. After years of fruitless attempts to get past Katy's husband and interview her about Pooky Wilson, Henry had done something he almost never did: scheduled an interview under false pretenses. Under the pretext of doing a human interest story on breeding bichons frises (Katy's main hobby), Henry had visited Mrs. Regan at home while her husband was at work. After making her comfortable with some puffball questions, he'd segued into her childhood in Ferriday. At first Katy spoke glowingly of those years, as most adults tended to do of rural childhoods. But when Henry brought up Albert Norris, a glaze had come over the woman's face. When he pushed on and mentioned the name Pooky Wilson, Katy denied any knowledge about the boy. At first Henry had been sure she was hiding something. After all, following her return from Texas, her father had married Katy off to Randall Regan, the brutal roughneck who had chauffeured his boss away from the Albert Norris murder scene. One of Regan's jobs had been to insulate Katy from reporters like himself. But when she insisted that she recalled nothing about either Pooky or Albert Norris, Henry began to wonder whether the doctors at the Borgen Institute had turned those sections of her memory to mush. When he left the house, Mrs. Regan had politely thanked him for coming and invited him to return anytime he wished. Henry felt so guilty about what he'd done that he actually went back to the office and wrote a story about Katy Regan and her dogs.

But later that night, lying in bed, the nagging thought had returned that she must remember *something*. As a young girl, Katy Royal had made love to Pooky Wilson many times, and she must have been as heartbroken by his disappearance as Henry had been by the realization that Swan Norris would never be his. How much had Katy known at the time? Surely some trace of the intense pain she'd felt as a young girl must remain in her cerebral cortex.

As the volume of the den television rose to compensate for his mother's increasing deafness, Henry realized that with Viola and Morehouse dead, Katy Royal's importance as a potential witness against her father had dramatically increased. Next time he got access to her, he decided, he would confide to Katy his love for Swan, and the heartache he'd suffered at losing her. Maybe that would summon an echo from the white space that supposedly lay in Katy Royal's traumatized memory banks.

Without warning, Henry suddenly saw a vision of Glenn More-house fighting for his life in his sickbed, struggling against friends who saw him as a traitor. *He knew he was going to die,* Henry thought. *He knew talking to me would cost him his life, and he still did it.* Henry closed his eyes and said a silent prayer for the murderer who'd chosen him as confessor. When his cell phone rang, it took a few seconds to register that it was his, not Sherry's. He didn't recognize the number, and he almost decided not to answer. But in the end, he did.

"Henry Sexton," he said, holding his breath.

First he heard only staticky silence. Then a voice he placed as belonging to a rural man of African-American descent began to speak. He hardly met men who talked this way anymore.

"Yassir. I heard you lookin' fuh dat tree wha all dem boys died at."

Henry's belly clenched. Unlike so many would-be tipsters before, this caller was the real thing. "Where did you hear that?"

"Man I know told me tha might be some money in it, if a body could show you that awful place."

"That's right."

"How much you payin', suh?"

Henry's personal finances were modest, and always stretched to the limit. He was willing to pay up to five hundred dollars, but he didn't want to pay more than he had to. "How much do you want?"

"A thousand dollah. Cash money."

Henry felt a cold sweat break out on his face. *A thousand dollars?* Most black folks he knew around Ferriday would do a hard month's work for that sum.

"That's a lot of money. How can I be sure you know what you claim to know?"

"I guess you can't. But I knows everything they is to know 'bout that ol' swamp, and that be my price. I's liable to need some luck just to live to spend it."

Henry couldn't argue with this logic. He was trying to think of a way to bargain with the man when it struck him that Penn Cage would probably be glad to subsidize the discovery of the Bone Tree. And Penn wouldn't hesitate to pay that sum. "All right," Henry said in a voice just above a whisper. "One thousand dollars, cash. But not a dollar more."

"Aiite, den. When you wants to go?"

"When can you take me?"

"*Not till Wendsy, mebbe T'ursy. I call you back in a day or two.*"

"That's fine. Could I ask what you do for a living?"

Low, rich laughter came down the line. "*I helps people find game when it be's scarce. Mebbe take a little out o' season, sometimes, you know.*"

A *poacher*, Henry thought. A poacher might well know the secret paths of the Lusahatcha Swamp. "Will you tell me your name?"

"*Toby,*" said the poacher.

"Toby what?" Henry asked, grabbing a pencil and flipping over the photo of Tom and the men in the fishing boat.

"*Toby Rambin. But don't axe around about me. I don't exist, hear? I call you back in a couple days. You jus' get that cash ready.*"

The connection went dead.

As Henry scrawled on the paper, he thanked God that Sherry hadn't heard this conversation. He looked down at the phone shaking in his hand.

"Who was that?" Sherry asked from the doorway.

"Nobody, babe. Just another dead-end lead."

CHAPTER 27

WALKING UP MY front steps for the second time in fifteen minutes, I pause before the door to gather myself. I was unable to catch up to Lincoln after he disappeared over the hill on Washington Street. I cruised the parking lots of the hotels on the bluff—the casino lots, too—but I saw no white pickup with Illinois plates. On my way back, I called Don Logan, the chief of police, and asked him to have his patrolmen keep an eye out for Lincoln's truck. Not a legitimate use of power, exactly, but the office of mayor comes with some perks.

I feel a little odd hesitating before my own front door, but on the other hand, I feel like I'm bringing home a kilo of heroin that must be hidden from a drug addict. Caitlin would give almost anything to possess the information Henry confided in me tonight. Armed with that, she would begin a newspaper crusade that would blast open those cold cases, eventually solve the murders, and probably win her a second Pulitzer Prize. But that honor is reserved for Henry Sexton, who worked the cases when nobody else gave a damn, and who's now living under the threat of harm to himself and his family. When Caitlin demands to know what I'm doing to help my father—as she will when she learns that he's in danger—I will have to edit myself very carefully.

She's been working south of town all day, but she may already have heard about Dad's trouble. On the other hand, if she had heard something, she probably would have texted me. I'm only thankful that neither she nor Annie noticed Lincoln Turner's truck rumbling outside the house.

Taking out my key, I let myself into the foyer and bolt the door behind me. The laughter of my eleven-year-old daughter rings down the hallway from the kitchen. "Annie?" I call. "I'm home!"

The laughter stops, and a rush of feet heralds the appearance of my dead wife's avatar in the hallway. I probably shouldn't think of Annie that way, but anyone who knew her mother shares this perception. My tall, willowy daughter is almost the reincarnation of Sarah. Sometimes I wonder if this impression is a trick my mind plays on me, but then I'll see an old photograph and realize the resemblance is growing stronger with each passing year.

"What's the matter, Daddy?" she asks, stopping in mid-stride and staring at me with the preternatural perception that also descended from her mother. "You look scared."

"No, I just missed you today."

She comes forward and wraps her arms around me, in a single gesture draining away half the anxiety that Lincoln Turner caused in me. "Come in the kitchen," she says. "Caitlin and I are cooking pasta primavera."

"You mean *you're* cooking it." I know from experience that my fiancée never cooks anything more complicated than a Lean Cuisine.

"Caitlin's helping," Annie says with a wink.

She pulls me down the hall and into the kitchen, where Caitlin is standing over a pot with a frown knotting her brow.

"This is why I don't cook," Caitlin snaps. "I can't even boil effing *water.*"

Annie snickers and checks the pasta pot. "Those noodles have definitely been in there too long. Let's get them out."

Caitlin wisely stands aside for Annie to rescue the noodles, and I'm glad to see the twinkle of a smile in Caitlin's eyes, though her lips are tight with frustration. Caitlin still has two or three inches on Annie, but it won't be long before my daughter catches up to her. Despite both being tall beauties, they could not be more different in type. Caitlin has pale skin and jet-black hair, with startling green eyes that shy away from nothing. Her build is angular and almost masculine from some perspectives, but she's curved where it counts. Annie is dark blond with light blue eyes that radiate kindness, not calculation, and her skin glows with the bloom of youth.

"See?" Annie says, carefully dumping the noodles into a colander in the sink, while boiling water steams around her head.

"I'd already have third-degree burns," Caitlin says. She once tried to make her mother's lasagna, but that effort is best forgotten. That's the level of domestic bliss you get with a newspaper publisher.

"You know what Ruby used to say." I laugh, hugging Caitlin to my waist. "If you ain't burnt yourself, you ain't cookin'."

Ruby was the black maid who raised me, and very much a second mother to me. Annie laughs at my remark, and Caitlin pinches my behind while Annie deals with the noodles.

I was thirty-eight when I met Caitlin, and I'd been a widower less than a year. She was ten years my junior and out to win a Pulitzer before she turned thirty. Her chosen venue was the *Natchez Examiner,* one of twenty-odd newspapers owned at that time by her father, a North Carolina businessman who cares more about profits than changing the world. During the Delano Payton case, Caitlin and I formed an unlikely partnership that brought us closer than either had expected, and we quickly fell in love.

Looking back on that time, it seems hard to believe we've let seven years pass without getting married. The fact is, when you're both working full-time and enjoying the benefits of marriage without the burdens, it's easy to let time slip by without looking too closely at things. During those years we suffered one or two periods of cool distance, when Caitlin took extended assignments in Boston and even farther afield, but those were exceptions. Yet no matter how close we grew during the years prior to our engagement, Caitlin kept one last wall between herself and my daughter—probably to protect them both from heartbreak, should things not work out in the end. But ever since we made the decision to get married, Caitlin and Annie have become inseparable. Annie has insisted on helping with the wedding preparations, from the shower and the flowers to choosing the band for the reception. I've done little, of course; my most important contribution has miraculously remained secret. But after the events of today, I'm not sure it can remain so.

I must not be doing a very good job of concealing my worries, because before Annie can serve the pasta, Caitlin pulls me into the hallway.

"Where are ya'll going?" Annie asks, obviously annoyed.

"We need to talk upstairs for a few minutes," Caitlin explains. "Grown-up stuff."

"And when exactly do I become a grown-up? Every grown-up I meet tells me how grown-up I am already."

"When you're thirteen!" Caitlin calls from the foot of the stairs.

"*Twelve!*" Annie retorts.

"How about twenty-one?" I shout.

"How about *now*? This sucks!"

"We'll hurry!" Caitlin promises.

"Ya'll better!"

UPSTAIRS, CAITLIN CROSSES HER legs Indian-style on my bed and fixes her luminous eyes upon me with the disturbing concentration I've come to know like a third person in our relationship.

"What's the deal?" she asks.

"What deal? You haven't told me anything about *your* day."

"FEMA trailers suck, end of story. What's eating you?"

Knowing it would be useless to try to withhold the main story, I give a heavy sigh and prop my ass on the top of my dresser. "Dad's in trouble."

Caitlin draws back her head to brace for bad news. "Not another heart attack."

"No."

"Thank God. What, then?"

"Legal trouble."

"Malpractice?"

"I wish."

She brushes a strand of black hair from her eyes. "Penn, you're scaring me. What is it?"

I summarize the day's action with the precision of a legal brief, and Caitlin doesn't interrupt. This is the upside of living with a brilliant woman. She may not be much of a cook, but she can digest information in a fraction of the time it takes most people. I begin with Shad's call to my office this morning and edit myself on the fly. I tell her there's a video recording of Viola's death, and that Henry Sexton made it, but not that he kept a copy for himself. I explain that Viola died brutally and that a botched mercy killing seems possible, but Shad Johnson is contemplating murder charges against Dad. After quickly outlining the crime scene evidence, I tell her that, according to Henry, the Double Eagle group had a standing hit order on Viola if she ever returned to Natchez, probably because Viola knew things that could send surviving

Double Eagles to prison—things related to the kidnapping and murder of her brother, a local civil rights activist. I also explain that the murder charge is being driven by Viola's son, who only appeared in Natchez this morning. Caitlin pays particularly close attention here, but I distract her by moving quickly past the subject.

I sketch Henry's theory about Double Eagle involvement in the local meth trade but elide Henry's belief that my father had suspicious ties to Brody Royal or individual Double Eagles. I also leave out the murder of Glenn Morehouse, the fact that Morehouse was one of Henry's sources, and everything about the murders of Albert Norris, Pooky Wilson, and Dr. Leland Robb. (No Brody Royal avenging his daughter's "honor," no "Huggy Bear" who could put Brody Royal in jail, and most of all, no plot to assassinate RFK. Those items are the heroin that Caitlin could not bear to resist.) Most damning (should Caitlin discover the truth), I say nothing about Henry and me working together to nail the Eagles, or Kirk Boisseau covertly diving the Jericho Hole tomorrow. I've become adept at the self-editing process over the past few years with Caitlin, and the only reactions I see are an occasional raised eyebrow and some added color in her cheeks.

As soon as I finish my summary, though, she says, "You're not telling me everything about Henry Sexton. Not by a damn sight."

"I promised him I'd keep some things confidential. Henry's pretty sensitive about the work he's done on those old cases."

She smiles with more than a hint of envy. "Rightfully so. He's done good work, and he doesn't want me to steal it."

"So, now you're up to speed. Back downstairs?"

"Not quite yet. Your father's silence worries me. Why the hell won't Tom talk to you about his nurse's death?"

"I'm not sure."

"But you have a theory."

After several seconds of hesitation, I outline the possibility that Lincoln might believe that Dad is his father, and that this—more than forensic evidence—may be what pushed Shad toward a murder charge.

"Did Tom have an affair with Viola?" she asks bluntly.

"I don't know."

"You haven't asked him?"

"No. I'm going to see him again later. But he already told me he's willing to take a DNA test to establish paternity. He sounded confident."

Thankfully, Annie calls up the stairs to tell us supper is getting cold.

Caitlin closes her eyes, inhales deeply, then exhales slowly. Then she opens her eyes and says, "We're going to have to postpone the wedding."

I walk to the bed and take her hand. "Are you sure?"

"Yes. We have to make sure Tom is safe. We're not getting married with that cloud hanging over our heads. The wedding's going to be everything we planned, and your father sitting in jail is *not* part of that picture."

"Annie won't like it."

"Let me handle Annie. That's a girl thing." Suddenly Caitlin's hand goes to her mouth. "Does your mother know any of this?"

"I think Dad's telling her about it now."

"Ahh. I talked to her just a few minutes ago, and she didn't say a word about it. She must not have known."

"Not necessarily. Mom could put on a perfect bridge party with a riot going on in her backyard."

Caitlin nods thoughtfully. "Whatever Tom's hiding, he's more afraid of it than of being arrested for murder. That can't be good."

She slips off of the bed, takes my hand, and pulls me toward the stairs. "Come on. You tell Annie about the legal trouble, and I'll explain the wedding."

At the top of the stairs, she stops suddenly, her jaw set tight.

"What is it?"

"Shad Johnson," she almost spits. "What's his fucking problem? Doesn't he realize what you could do to him with that dogfighting photo?"

I give her a sheepish look. "Actually, I gave him back the original. In exchange, he promised he wouldn't run for reelection."

Caitlin lowers her chin and raises her eyebrows, peering into my eyes with irresistible intensity. "Bullshit. If you did, you kept a copy."

I try to play out the bluff, but she sees through me.

"*Where are you guys?*" Annie calls from downstairs.

"Coming!" Caitlin yells down the stairwell.

"Getting Shad disbarred could be counterproductive," I tell her. "Better the devil you know, you know? There's no telling who might be appointed to take his place."

"I don't care. Shad hates you. And given what he knows you could do to him with that photo, I'm stunned that he's gone as far as he has with this. There's something going on that we're not seeing."

A fleeting image of Lincoln Turner's burning eyes flashes through my mind. I'm glad I didn't tell Caitlin about his impromptu visit outside.

"*Da-ad!*" Annie yells.

"We'll talk about it later," Caitlin says, trotting down the stairs and leaving me feeling like a fool standing at the head of them.

SUPPER IS IN OUR bellies, the dishes are in the sink, and the three of us were sitting comfortably around the oak table by the large kitchen window until I gave Annie a PG-13 summary of Dad's problems and Caitlin broke the news about postponing the wedding. My daughter is far from the "fine" state that Caitlin predicted, but it's her grandfather she's worried about.

"So did Papa do something wrong, or not?" she asks, her chin quivering. "What do you mean by laws *on the books?*"

In the matter of assisted suicide, she seems to be having trouble with the idea that written laws don't always ideally reflect right and wrong.

"Well," I temporize, thinking how the simplest things can sometimes be the most difficult to explain, "laws are legislated by men and then recorded in books. But—"

"By men *and* women," Caitlin interjects.

"That's right. But those laws don't always stay the same. We've talked before about how the Supreme Court changes laws from time to time, on things like capital punishment. Remember?"

Annie nods.

"Well, Congress sometimes changes the laws, as well. Back in the 1920s, they made it illegal for anyone to drink alcohol. Then they repealed that law in 1933. So, written laws aren't always permanent. And they're not perfect expressions of what's right and wrong."

"That's where I'm confused."

"At one time it was illegal for women to vote," Caitlin says. "Does that seem right to you?"

"No way. But what does that have to do with Papa?"

"Have you heard the word *euthanasia?*"

"Sure. Mrs. Bryant talked about it in school. She talked about when people want to be taken off life support and stuff. And she talked about Dr. Kevorkian."

Jesus. "Annie," I say as gently as I can, "Papa is probably going to be accused of something similar to that."

Her face goes white, and Caitlin strokes her shoulder. "Of *murdering* somebody?"

"Some people may say that. They might say that he helped somebody to die, and others might say he committed murder."

"But Papa wouldn't hurt anybody."

"No, he wouldn't. The person who died was a nurse who used to work for Papa a long time ago. She moved away from here when I was only eight years old. Then she came back because she was dying of cancer, and she was in a lot of pain. Terrible pain."

"So she wanted to die?"

"I believe she did. Before the pain got too bad, and before she couldn't do anything to take care of herself. Sometimes people in that situation want a shot that will put them to sleep, so they won't have to hurt anymore. That's where the term *mercy killing* comes from."

Annie's cheeks and brow are scrunched tight. "Well, they do it for dogs and cats. They did it to Margaret's dog, because he was too old and had cancer."

"You're right. But humans and animals are different, and some people believe that nobody has a right to shorten a person's life, no matter how much pain they're in."

"What do *you* think?"

I glance at Caitlin, who gives me the slightest of nods. "Boo, I think that a very sick person, as long as they're in their right mind, ought to have the right to decide for themselves how much suffering they should have to endure."

Annie transfers her gaze to Caitlin. "What do you think?"

"I believe the same thing your father does. The law is wrong. And in some states, like Oregon, they have a special law that allows sick people to decide for themselves about dying."

One tear streaks Annie's face. "But we're not in Oregon. We're in Mississippi. What will they do to Papa? They won't put him in jail, will they?"

I hug her to my chest. "If they do, it'll probably only be for a few minutes. But there's a small chance there might be a trial."

"That's why we need to postpone the wedding," Caitlin says. "Just in case."

Annie's crying full-on now. "Dad, you can't let them do that! Papa wouldn't ever hurt anybody. He wouldn't *ever* do anything wrong!"

The faith of children is an awesome thing to behold. If only we could all be worthy of it. "I think you're right, baby. And I'm going to do everything I can to keep Papa safe at home."

"You *have* to," she cries with sudden fervor. "You're still a lawyer. You need to stop doing everything else and just take care of Papa."

"What do you mean?"

"I mean stop being mayor and writing books and everything else. None of that matters now. You're the best lawyer and you have to take care of Papa!"

Caitlin stands and rubs Annie's shoulders.

"I'll be representing him tomorrow," I assure her. "But I'm not the best lawyer to defend him in a trial. He'd need a criminal lawyer for that."

"You *were* that!"

"I was a prosecutor. Papa will need an expert at keeping people *out* of jail."

Annie is shaking her head. "Who could do that better than someone who knows all the ways to put people *in* jail?"

Caitlin gives me a look that I have no trouble translating: *Out of the mouths of babes* . . .

"I want you to trust me on this, Annie. I promise I'll be working on it night and day."

She studies me in silence for several seconds. "If we postpone the wedding, when are ya'll going to get married?"

Caitlin smiles, then leans down and kisses the top of her head. "We'll just have to see how quickly your father can make this trouble go away."

Both of them train their eyes on me, and the resulting ache in my belly must resemble what a soldier feels when standing before a military tribunal.

How's that for motivation?

CHAPTER 28

FORREST KNOX GOT up from the house trailer's queen-sized bed and fastened his belt. He hadn't even taken off his boots. The auburn-haired woman lay stomach-down across the sheets like a wrung-out dishrag, red welts rising from her naked hindquarters. Forrest didn't know why some women liked pain, but he'd learned long ago that many of the ones who did seemed to marry cops. It wasn't the prospect of pain that attracted them, but power—not the power of money and status, but of immediate physical domination. And women like that tended to get bored quickly. They couldn't push the edge with the same man again and again, because the edge was always being rounded off by experience. Once that kind of woman knew a man's limit, she lost the thrill she'd initially sought.

Cherie Delaune was a perfect example. Thirty-three years old, she had one teenage daughter and a husband with sawdust for brains who spent most of his time patrolling highways on the state dime. Forrest had no doubt that she'd prayed more than once for her husband to die in a traffic accident, which was the widowmaker in their business. Most of the men on the memorial wall at state police headquarters had died in highway accidents of various types. A shoot-out was rare; more guys had killed themselves with their own guns than had bought it in Hollywood-style gun battles.

"Why do you want to rush out of here?" Cherie drawled. "Ricky ain't gonna be back till dawn."

"Got business to tend to," Forrest said.

"What kind of business?"

"My business."

Cherie raised her middle finger, but her lips parted in a smile behind it. "Why don't you talk to Ricky's boss and get him some extra duty? He needs the overtime. Me and Crystal need a break from his crap, too. Not to mention, you could come around more often."

Forrest thought briefly of Crystal Delaune, Cherie's flirtatious sixteen-year-old, then banished the image. "Patrol isn't my division, I told you that."

"You could still do it if you wanted. You just don't want to come over any more than you do now."

Forrest buttoned his shirt and shoved the tail beneath his belt. "If I came any more often, you'd be as bored with me as you are with Ricky. Unless I marked you up good, and then he'd know about it. Which is what you want, deep down, isn't it? To blow all this shit up?"

"You're the one who shaved my coochie. Nothing subtle about that. Ricky's already asked me about it like five times. Maybe *you're* the one who wants to blow up my marriage."

Forrest laughed. "Like you couldn't lie your way out of that little dilemma with about four brain cells."

Cherie pouted and pulled the covers over her rump. "You think you know so much. You really think I'd get bored if we was together?"

"Doesn't matter," Forrest said, strapping on his gun belt. "You ain't gonna get the chance."

Cherie scrabbled onto her knees and grabbed his belt buckle. "One more time before you go. I know you can do it. I can tell when you've taken a pill."

Forrest shook his head. Now that he'd relieved his need, the prospect of collecting cash up at Fort Knox far outweighed that of a second round with Cherie. *Now, if she was willing to bring Crystal into it . . .*

Forrest's secure cell phone rang in his pocket. Taking it out, he saw that the caller was Billy Knox. His cousin only called in cases of extreme emergency.

"What's up?" he answered, and Cherie gave an exaggerated pout.

"Henry Sexton met with somebody else tonight."

"Put me out of my misery."

"Dr. Tom Cage's son. The mayor of Natchez."

This took Forrest off guard. "Where did this happen?"

"Over at the *Beacon* offices. They were together quite a while. Then Cage called the Concordia Parish Sheriff's Office for protection on the way back to Natchez."

Forrest's threat-detection instinct went on high alert. His mind raced through possible explanations for this turn of events.

"I got that from our mole in Walker Dennis's HQ," Billy said. "What you want to do?"

"Doing nothing is usually best, William."

"'Usually' don't cut it this time. Penn Cage hasn't always been mayor of a one-horse town. He was a big-time prosecutor in Houston, and he knows people in Washington. I think we've reached the point of no return on Henry Sexton."

Forrest looked over at Cherie's breasts, which hung heavily over the sheet. She was watching him like an expectant hunting dog. "You mean you think Snake had the right idea."

"Maybe so, yeah. I don't want to wake up and see our names splashed across the front page of the newspaper."

"The *Beacon*'s only published once a week, and the next edition's three days from now. So stay cool. I'll think about this and get back to you."

"Okay, but the *Natchez Examiner* runs every goddamned day. And Penn Cage's girlfriend would *love* to run with a story like this. There's no telling how much Glenn Morehouse told Sexton, or what Sexton told Cage tonight."

Cherie reached out toward Forrest's belt again, but he slapped her hand away. He never worried about Henry Sexton, because he'd had a state police tech specialist plant a monitoring program in the *Beacon*'s intranet that gave him access to every story being drafted at the newspaper, often days before publication. That tech had also installed a keystroke recorder in Henry's home computer, one that secretly transmitted everything Henry had typed in the past twenty-four hours to another cop who sifted through the reports every day. But Billy was right: Henry's involvement with Penn Cage had opened a conduit to his girlfriend, and Forrest had no mechanism in place to monitor her.

"What's the mayor's family situation?" he asked.

"You remember his old man, Doc Cage. The mother's still alive, and Penn's sister lives in England."

"Kids?"

"One girl, about twelve, I guess. And I think he's engaged to the Masters girl."

Forrest smiled with satisfaction. "Plenty of pressure points, then. I'll get back to you."

"Please don't take all night, cuz. I need to make some decisions."

"I hear you. Did you get that Buffett show arranged?"

"No. His management's squeezing me hard on the money, and my plate's a little full right now anyway."

"It's your birthday, man. Chill. I'll chip in a quarter of the fee."

"Seriously?"

"Talk to you later, Parrothead."

Forrest ended the call and slid his phone back into his pocket.

As he stared at Cherie's breasts with renewed interest, she said, "Did I tell you I saw your wife at Esplanade mall the other day?"

Ice instantly coated Forrest's heart. He picked up his coat from the chair, knowing she hadn't finished with this subject.

"She looks a lot better than you told me," Cherie went on. "I was downright jealous." She gave him a chiding look. "I couldn't help wondering what she would do if she knew what we get up to over here."

The ice on Forrest's heart climbed up his throat. *How can these bitches be so goddamned stupid? Like possums running toward a spotlight on a varmint rifle . . .*

Cherie gave him a girlish come-hither look, then spoke in a teasing singsong: "Come on and stay. I'll give you what you're always begging for."

Forrest stepped closer to the bed. He knew some truly kinky women down in New Orleans, but nothing could compare to a housewife so bored she would scratch scars into her arms to keep from going out of her mind every day. "Next time," he said. "Alphonse is waiting for me."

"Oh, screw that ugly Redbone," Cherie said, and then she giggled. "On second thought, you couldn't pay me to screw him."

Forrest didn't laugh. He took her by the wrist and squeezed hard enough to make her wince. "Next time I may bring Alphonse in here to take a turn. And he won't be paying you. You think about that while I'm gone."

Cherie looked at him as though he'd broken some unspoken rule. "You don't mean that, Forrest."

He walked to the door, opened it, and looked back with utter seriousness. "Alphonse, come in here a second."

Cherie Delaune's face drained of blood. She'd had no idea that Ozan had been sitting out in the trailer's den, waiting to run interference if her husband showed up. But when the big Redbone walked through the door, she understood quick enough. If Ricky had come home while she was doing Forrest, he probably would have died in front of his own television.

"Ya'll get out of here," Cherie said in a small voice. "This ain't funny."

Ozan laughed, his copper-colored face alight with anticipation.

"You sure you don't want to take a turn, Al?" Forrest said. "She's all ready for you. And we can spare twenty minutes."

Like a cornered animal, Cherie Delaune searched desperately for an exit, but both men were blocking the only door.

"Ya'll can't make me do this!" she cried, pulling the covers over herself.

"No?" said Forrest. "Who you gonna tell?"

"I didn't mean what I said about your wife, Forrest."

Ozan walked toward the bed.

"Get away from me!" Cherie shouted. *"I ain't no whore! Forrest!"*

But Forrest was already in the hall, headed toward the trailer's kitchen, a wicked smile on his face.

He took a jug of milk from the refrigerator, then sat down on a cheap sofa, laid his pistol beside him, and thought about Penn Cage and his family.

CHAPTER 29

CAITLIN AND I are lying in the claw-foot tub in my bathroom, steam filling the air and fogging the mirrors. The tub is wide enough that she can lie nestled in my left arm, her cheek on my shoulder. The only light comes from a lamp in the corner, throwing strange shadows across the walls and the hardwood floor. Annie has been asleep for an hour, so we decided to risk a bath. Prior to our engagement, Caitlin never spent a whole night here; she was always gone by the time Annie awakened. Now she occasionally stays until morning. Often, though, she leaves after making love, to work late at the paper or simply to pay her staff a visit as the next day's stories start going up on the website and the print edition gets put to bed.

"How are you going to cover Dad's arrest?" I ask. "If it happens."

She takes her time answering. "We'll have to print it in the police record section. But other than that, I don't think we'll do anything."

"That will probably upset a lot of people. Even if Shad doesn't press for coverage—"

"He'd better not press for anything. I'll publish that dogfighting snapshot so fast he won't have time to get dressed before splitting town."

I run the fingers of my right hand through her damp hair. "I'm just saying that Viola's son is likely to make a stink, if his intention is to make it as hard on Dad as he can. Not to mention some black community leaders, and my political enemies among the whites. You won't be able to keep it out of the paper altogether."

"Let me ask you something," she says in a tone that makes me catch my breath. "Do you think Tom slept with Viola back in the day or not?"

"I honestly don't know."

"How attractive was she?"

"In my memory, she was pretty."

"One to ten."

"Uh . . . eight? Maybe nine."

"Plus the forbidden-fruit thing, you can't ignore that."

"Well . . . I'll find out tonight."

"You'd better assume it's true, no matter what he says."

"Why? This is Dad we're talking about."

"Yes, but until a DNA test proves otherwise, Shad is going to proceed as though it's true. I think he must believe it; otherwise he wouldn't risk you destroying his career."

"I know."

"If Tom *is* arrested, will the judge set bail? Do you know which judge it will be?"

"The initial appearance will be before the Justice Court judge, since Viola died in the county. That's Charlie Noyes. Charlie won't see Dad as a flight risk, and he'll be skeptical about the crime, so I'm hoping for a decently low bond. Also, Shad promised try to arrange the timing of the arrest so that if the judge does set bail, we can process Dad through the system without him actually having to spend time in a cell."

"Thank God. With all the drugs he needs just to keep going, I wouldn't feel comfortable with him spending even an hour in jail."

"Imagine him spending *years* in one."

"I can't. Annie's right. That simply cannot happen."

"If he doesn't start talking to me tonight, it could."

"We need more hot," Caitlin says, extending one toned leg and turning the hot water tap with her toes. "Can you imagine any reason other than this paternity thing to explain Tom circling the wagons without you?"

"All I can work out is that he's protecting someone. That's all he's ever tried to do, so why should he change now? The other option is that the Double Eagles have threatened our lives. The family, I mean. Possibly even Annie. You know Dad would take a bullet to protect her."

"Any of you," she says, squeezing my hand. "That's why we have to protect him. Even from himself. As much as I love Tom, he has one major flaw. He's from the Humphrey Bogart, Ernest Hemingway school."

"He's a stoic, all right. But that may not be the whole explanation. I know he has some secrets. There are definitely chapters of his life he's never told me about."

"Like?"

"Korea, for one. I know he was wounded there, but I don't know how. I know he has a couple of medals, but only because my mother told me. Dad seems almost ashamed of them."

"Didn't he save Walt Garrity's life over there?"

"Yes, and Walt saved his. But they've never told anyone how that happened—not even my mother."

"That's definitely weird." Caitlin lifts her leg again, then hooks her big toe around the lever and pulls the tap closed. "I can't stop thinking about Tom and Viola. Your mom certainly never gave me the idea that Tom ever cheated on her."

"She wouldn't, even if he had and she knew about it."

"Oh, she'd know," Caitlin said with certainty. "Peggy is smarter than all of us."

This is a truth known only to our family, but none of us doubts it.

Caitlin runs her fingernails along my forearm. "If this somehow went as far as a trial, would you really not defend him?"

"Absolutely not. I've been thinking about Quentin Avery."

She looks up in surprise. "The civil rights lawyer?"

"That's right."

"Didn't he die?"

"No. He just lost his other leg. Diabetes."

"Christ, that's an epidemic down here. Surely he must be retired?"

"Quentin lost his legs, Caitlin, not his brain. But he is retired, as a matter of fact."

"How old is he?"

"A little older than Dad, probably. Dad's been his personal physician for most of his life. If Quentin Avery would come out of retirement to defend anybody, it would be Dad."

"I've heard some mixed things about Quentin over the years."

"You could say the same about me. Quentin is my first choice, hands down."

A black Mississippian who left his native state in the early 1950s to go to law school, Quentin Avery fought on the front lines of the civil rights movement, wherever those lines happened to be. More than once, he tried landmark cases before the Supreme Court of the United States, and won. In the latter part of his career, Quentin drew criticism for taking on lucrative plaintiffs' cases, but even then he always did a certain amount of pro bono work for the cause.

Caitlin rises into a sitting position, then slides to the other end of tub, so that she's facing me, her breasts half submerged in the water. Intuition tells me she's about to probe me about Henry Sexton's work. I need to distract her. As casually as possible, I say, "Didn't you tell me the other day that you were late for your period?"

She waves her hand as if dismissing the most trivial of issues. "Oh, you know me. Too much exercise, probably. I'll get it this week."

My digression has thrown her off balance, but only for a few seconds. She jabs my chest with her toes and says, "I know you made Henry a promise, but you need to give me something to work on. There's no way I can sleep after what's happened. Give me some way to help Tom."

"I wish I could. But I really need to go see him now."

"What about Annie? I was planning to go back to the paper."

"What for? It would really help me if you stayed with her. Just for an hour. I could take her with me, but Mom's probably already in bed."

Caitlin doesn't even try to hide her frustration. "I'll stay. But if you find out about the paternity thing, you've got to tell me the answer. You didn't promise Henry anything about *that*."

"I know. You're right." I touch her knee and squeeze gently. "But there's something you need to know."

Fear flickers in her eyes. "You don't think Tom killed her?"

"No. But I honestly don't know. Dad might well have had a euthanasia pact with Viola."

Caitlin fans steam away from her face like a garden-club matron at a summer tea. "Come on, out with it."

"He helped Sarah at the end."

Caitlin looks toward the ceiling and closes her eyes. Then she says, "You don't have to tell me."

"Do you want to know?"

Taking my hand, she squeezes softly. "Yes."

"Sarah's breast cancer was particularly aggressive. We were living in Houston then, so she got cutting-edge care, but it wasn't enough. She had a lot of mets—that's metastases. Her brain, her bones. Intractable pain. She fought hard, but in some ways that was as much a curse as a blessing. The harder she fought, the worse it got. Her parents had been living with us, but even that got too hard. Her father had to move to a hotel nearby. He couldn't take the strain. At the end, the doctors couldn't control the pain without knocking her out. Sarah wanted to be at home with Annie, and she wanted to be conscious."

I pause for a moment, trying to come to grips with the memory. It's one I don't allow out of my subconscious very often.

"Was Tom treating her also?"

"Not up to that point. But when things reached that pass, Dad drove out from Natchez with a black bag. He talked to Sarah's doctors, then got rid of the nurses we had working at the house. From that point on, he and Mom and Sarah's mother took care of her. I don't know how he did it, but Dad managed to give Sarah extended lucid periods without pain. She spent almost every minute of that time with Annie."

"And you," Caitlin says softly.

I nod, trying to finish the story without remembering too vividly, or even fully engaging with my thoughts. "That lasted about three days. Then one night, Dad came in and relieved me from my shift beside Sarah's bed. I went out to the couch and fell asleep. He woke me about five hours later."

"She was gone?"

I nod again. "He just squeezed my shoulder and said, 'She was a trouper, son.'" My voice cracks, and I take a moment to regain my composure. "I can't tell you what that means when Dad says that about somebody. He's seen a lot of death."

"Oh, Penn . . . I'm sorry it was so bad."

"It's over now. Long over."

"Not really. It never will be, not completely. I'm just glad Annie wasn't old enough to know how bad it really was."

"Me, too. The treatments are a lot better now, just seven years later."

"Are you positive Tom helped her at the end?"

I shrug. "He never said he did. But looking back . . . yeah, I'm sure."

"Did her parents know?"

"Her mother did. But all she ever said was that Sarah was lucky to have Dad treating her at the end."

"They were right."

"I hope she still feels that way. Because a trial like this will drag a magnifying glass over Dad's entire career."

"Oh, God." Caitlin's green eyes fix me with laserlike intensity.

"You've got to kill this thing in the cradle, Penn. I'm dead serious. Your father won't survive this kind of stress."

"I'm working on it. But I don't think there's any way to prevent an arrest tomorrow."

She raises her eyebrows like a schoolteacher silently reprimanding a student.

"You're thinking about the photo. The nuclear option."

"I'm thinking about *survival*," she says.

"Let's wait and see what Dad says tonight. An arrest isn't the end of the world. The charge is more important. I already let Shad know the stakes, and I think he got the message."

Caitlin makes it clear that this answer doesn't satisfy her. Suddenly the heat is too much for me. "I need to get out."

"Me, too," she says, almost in surrender.

She waits for me to stand and then pull her to her feet, which is our habit. Afterward, we hug for a few moments, but soon the chill is too much. Lifting towels off a nearby chair, we dry off in front of the gas heater.

"Stop staring at my butt," she says, whipping her towel behind her to block my view. "As soon as you get back from your parents', I'm going back to work. And I'm going to search all my databases while you're gone. Isn't there something you can give me to work on that might help Tom? You know what I can do, Penn. Exploit me, for God's sake."

As I close my eyes in forbearance, a little voice says, *You'd better use every resource you have on this.* Even if I give Caitlin nothing, she'll be an expert on the Double Eagle group within two hours. Taking hold of her shoulders, I look hard into her eyes.

"I'm going to give you two names. Don't ask me *any* questions. Not whether they have any relation to each other, or even to these cases. But if you can find out everything there is to know about them—without them knowing you're digging—it will be a big help."

She smiles with her eyes. "Deal."

"The first is Brody Royal. The second is Forrest Knox."

She's already committed the names to memory. "That's it?"

I nod. "Go do your thing. And stay below the radar. This case is more dangerous than you know."

"Have these guys really threatened your family?"

"I don't know for sure. I do know that one is a ruthless killer. The other may be a corrupt cop."

Caitlin slowly shakes her head, her eyes burning with desire to strike back at anyone who would threaten us. Her fierce resolve gives me more inspiration than Henry's noble but slow-burning commitment. Caitlin stirred to action is an unstoppable force. Two months ago, she was compelled to listen to a woman being raped in a room next to the one in which she herself was being held captive. Since then, she has become a tireless crusader for victims of sexual violence, raising money and awareness on a national scale.

"There's one more thing," I say softly. "I'm breaking my word to Henry to tell you, but this bears on Lincoln's paternity."

"I understand."

"Viola Turner was gang-raped by the Double Eagle group just before she left Natchez. On two different occasions. Henry thinks one of those rapists is Lincoln's biological father. I just thought you should know. For Dad's sake."

Caitlin opens her mouth but says nothing. Her chin is quivering like Annie's did an hour ago, and her eyes blaze with a hatred I can scarcely imagine. "Anything else?" she asks hoarsely.

I shake my head. "I'll see you when I get back."

She drops her towel to the floor and walks stark naked into my bedroom to get dressed. Paradoxically, I'm reminded of nothing so much as a soldier girding herself for war.

CHAPTER 30

DRIVING TO MY parents' house, I call Henry Sexton to let him know Kirk Boisseau will be diving the Jericho Hole at dawn. The reporter sounds beside himself with excitement. He's already informed the FBI of Glenn Morehouse's death and relayed the Double Eagle's confirmation of the murder of Bureau informant Jerry Dugan in 1965. As a result, at least one Bureau agent has promised to look into the Morehouse case immediately, and Henry believes he meant what he said. Before he lets me go, Henry apologizes for calling my father's honor into question, and I tell him I've never developed the habit of shooting the messenger. By the time we hang up, I'm nearing my parents' house, so I call ahead.

"Dr. Cage," says the confident baritone that's greeted every late-night caller for the past forty-three years.

"It's me."

"The garage door's open. Come in that way. I'm in the study."

"Is Mom all right?"

"More or less. You know your mother."

Yes. Her picture is in the dictionary under "steel magnolia." "I'll see you in a minute."

I park behind his old 740 and quickly make my way through the dark garage. This house has never grown familiar to me—the house I grew up in was burned to the ground by Ray Presley in 1998. Once I gain the hall, I spy a faint glow beneath Dad's study door. Walking softly, so as not to wake my mother, I find him sitting at his study desk, smoking a Partagas and poring over a thick book, his trifocals gleaming in the light of the reading lamp.

"Dad?" I say softly.

He looks up and smiles. "Come in, son. I tried to sleep earlier, but it was no use." Closing the book on a brass marker, he sets it aside. "I've been reading Shelby Foote."

Naturally. My father's future hangs by a thread, and he's reading Civil War history.

"Did you know he died this past June?" he asks, as though we have nothing more urgent to discuss. "Heart attack, secondary to a pulmonary embolism."

"I didn't know that." I take a seat in the more comfortable of the two chairs that face his desk. Behind him, his shelves are filled with rare books sent by dozens of friends and dealers who felt compelled to offer some tangible expression of solace after his library burned. Only now do I realize that Dad is wearing a multicolored robe that my sister and I gave him for Christmas thirty years ago.

He's not going to change his mind, I realize. *He's really going to make my mother watch him walk to a sheriff's cruiser in handcuffs.*

"Dad, Billy Byrd is going to arrest you tomorrow morning."

His smile fades but doesn't quite disappear. "He'll enjoy that."

"What's the deal there? Shad says Sheriff Byrd has some kind of personal grudge against you."

"Oh . . . well, I treated Billy's wife for years. She had a long history of suspicious bruises and lacerations, plus one fracture. Need I continue?"

"Sheriff Byrd is a wifebeater?"

"That's about the size of it."

"And he knows you know that?"

"Yes."

"The wife told him?"

"No. Billy came in for a physical, and I told him that if his wife showed up in my office with another suspicious injury, I'd swear out a warrant against him with the chief of police."

I sit back and try to process this. "Well, given that history, don't you think you'd do well to stay out of the county jail?"

Dad lays his hand on the volume of Foote and sighs. "I've treated most of those deputies down there, or their parents. I think that will probably balance the sheriff's ill will. Billy finally divorced that wife, by the way, to her everlasting good fortune."

"Dad, from what I know, the physical evidence at the death scene is against you. The facts as I know them are against you. That doesn't bode well for your legal prospects."

He puts the Partagas between his teeth, and a blue nimbus of smoke floats out of his mouth as he speaks. "Old Shelby said something interest-ing about facts: 'People make a grievous error thinking that a list of facts is the truth. Facts are just the bare bones out of which truth is made.'"

How do you respond to a guy who talks like this? He should write a book: Zen and the Art of Evading Questions, *by Tom Cage.*

"You said you spoke to Henry Sexton," he reminds me. "What did he tell you?"

I want to probe Dad about the extent of his relations with Viola, but I can't quite bring myself to open with such an invasion of his privacy. "Do you remember a man named Glenn Morehouse?"

"I think so. Big fellow? Hypertensive."

"That's him. He was murdered tonight, for talking to Henry Sexton."

Dad's eyes widen slightly behind his glasses. "I see. I imagine More-house knew a lot about . . . Henry's special areas of interest."

"That's an understatement." I can't temporize any longer. "Dad, forgive me, but earlier you told me you'd take a DNA test regarding Lincoln Turner's paternity. I have to go one step further. Could you conceivably be Lincoln's father? Is there *any* chance of that?"

He takes the cigar from his mouth and sets it in his ashtray. "No," he says, his voice and eyes steady.

Thank God, I say silently, trying not to show my relief. "Well, Lincoln seems to believe you are. He was parked outside my house tonight when I got home."

Real alarm comes into Dad's face. "Did he threaten you?"

"Only with exposure of the truth, which he said would destroy you."

After a few moments, Dad waves his hand. "Don't pay any attention to that."

"Could Viola have told him he's your son?"

Dad sighs. "If you'd asked me two months ago, I'd have said no. But after what I saw these past weeks . . . it's possible. Viola was depressed, even desperate. And considering the alternative story . . ."

So Dad knows about Viola's rape. "All right, then. We need to get the DNA test out of the way as soon as possible, so both Shad and Lincoln can start seeing this thing more objectively."

"Is Lincoln Turner all Henry spoke to you about?"

"No. He told me a lot, but we both need to get some sleep soon. Based on what Henry told me, there are three questions I'd like to ask you."

He sits back and laces his fingers across his belly. "Go ahead."

"Did Dr. Leland Robb tell you who killed Albert Norris and Pooky Wilson before he died in that plane crash? Have you known for all these years and kept quiet about it?"

Dad shifts forward and sits straighter in the chair. "What's the second question?"

"You can't answer that one first?"

"I'd prefer to hear all three before I answer."

This is like questioning a guilty client. "All right. Glenn Morehouse told Henry that Viola would have been killed in 1968 if it hadn't been for you and Ray Presley."

This time he remains motionless, but something subtle changes in his eyes.

"I assume I know why you saved her," I go on. "But *how* did you do it? When she was on the wrong side of the Double Eagles and . . ."

"And what?"

"That's my third question." I lean forward and slide the picture of Dad on the fishing boat with Brody Royal, Claude Devereux, and Ray Presley across his desk. "I think she was a threat to Brody Royal as well."

"My God," he breathes, leaning over the photo. "Where did you get this?"

"From Henry. Tell me about Brody Royal, Dad. According to Henry, he was behind the deaths of Albert Norris, Pooky Wilson, Jimmy Revels, Luther Davis, *and* Dr. Robb. This morning I'd have said this guy was a typical Louisiana businessman, only richer. An upper-echelon Rotary type. Now I hear he's a sociopath who plotted with Carlos Marcello to assassinate Robert Kennedy."

Dad looks up, obviously startled.

"In this photo you seem to be deep-sea fishing with Royal and two other world-class bastards." Mindful of my mother, I prevent myself from raising my voice. "What's the deal?"

He leans back and regards me with what looks like regret. "Penn . . . why are you digging into all this?"

I want to lean across the desk and shake him by his shirt. Instead, I take a deep breath and force my voice lower. "The moment I saw Henry's video, I knew you didn't kill Viola. But since you wouldn't tell me who did kill her, I set out to find the answer myself. I now believe the Double Eagles killed her, either for their own reasons or to protect Brody Royal. After what Henry told me today, I think that no matter what happens with your case, I'm going to have to help him solve those cases he's been working. In fact, tomorrow morning, I'm having a friend dive the Jericho Hole to search for bodies."

I pause to let Dad absorb what I'm saying. "The past is coming up to the surface, one way or another. I've come here to give you a chance to warn me if we're likely to find something that implicates you in any way."

He looks around his study as if searching for something. "Penn," he says finally, "this isn't like the Del Payton case. As important as that was, it was basically a case of greed. The race angle was only incidental."

I feel my face flush with frustration. "You're avoiding my question. This picture isn't all Henry has, you know. I saw FBI surveillance records that document Marcello's hoods driving up from New Orleans to visit your office in the 1970s. Can you explain that?"

To my surprise, he shrugs as though he has nothing to hide. "I probably did treat some of Ray's friends from New Orleans. God knows I treated enough Ku Klux Klansmen among the workers at Armstrong and Triton and IP. But there's nothing evil in that. Assholes need doctors, too."

"But why would mobsters drive the three hours from New Orleans to see you? In at least one case, a visit was after hours, and Ray Presley showed up at your office at the same time."

Dad looks confused for a few moments, but then he seems to recover his composure. "I remember that! Some of Ray's old cronies tried to bribe me to write fraudulent prescriptions for amphetamines. That was the big-demand drug back then. I said no, and that was that. Honestly, I didn't see it as any different from Natchez lawyers asking me to pad my bills to fatten up their personal injury lawsuits. Human beings are avaricious, Penn. You know that."

He's responded to all my questions with calm assurance, yet amid all the words I sense a different kind of concealment. "Dad . . . so far as I know, in all my life, you only refused to open up to me about one thing—Korea. But today I discovered there's a whole other chapter you kept back. This afternoon you lamented not doing more to help during the civil rights struggle, but it sounds like you were neck-deep in it.

Henry says he's been trying to interview you about that era for years, yet you've constantly put him off. Why?"

He focuses in the middle distance for a few silent seconds. Then he looks at me and answers in a low, earnest voice. "I never told you about the war because you can't *tell* anyone about war, any more than you can tell a virgin what it means to go through labor. But make no mistake: what happened here during the 1960s was a war, too. A civil war." He thumps Shelby Foote's thick history. "Maybe the true end of this one. And as in any war, there were casualties. Viola was one of them."

"Viola was gang-raped in 1968. I'm thinking you already know that."

His jaw tightens and flexes. If there's such a thing as an offended silence, that's what I'm listening to now. "I'm not going to discuss that," he says. "Viola's gone, and she's finally out of pain. That's all that matters now."

I lean forward, my eyes accusing. "Is it? A lot more people who survived that era need peace just as badly as she, and preferably while they're still alive. Many of the men who committed those crimes are still walking around. They're still hurting people. Do you think men who gang-raped Viola twice deserve to live out their days in peace?"

Dad looks up sharply, his face pale. Then he closes his eyes, and his head sags forward. I start to go on, but he raises a hand to stop me. "Don't say any more. I'll answer your three questions. Then I want you to drop all this."

"I can't promise that."

He sighs heavily. "Leland Robb was a good man. He was a good physician, too, and he died badly. Aircraft fires are always terrible. They called me to identify his body. I had to use X-rays."

"I don't think Henry knows that."

"A month before that crash, Leland came to see me. He was upset and needed to get something off his chest. He mentioned Frank Knox being at Albert Norris's store on the afternoon Norris died, but Frank had been dead over a year by this time. Leland wanted to tell me about another man who'd been there, but I stopped him. Something in his manner told me how explosive that information was." Dad shakes his head and picks up his cigar. "I wish now that I'd responded differently, but at the time . . . Leland was truly terrified. I urged him to confide in someone who could actually do something about what he knew—the

FBI, or a moderate politician—but he didn't. After he died, I wondered whether there might have been some sort of foul play involved, but the FAA didn't find anything suspicious about the crash. What could I do?"

The tone in my father's voice is both alien and familiar; it's the voice of witnesses who stood by while someone else was being robbed, beaten, or killed. "You could have told the FBI about Frank Knox threatening Albert Norris. You could have told them that the man who collided with Dr. Robb's plane had probably murdered Norris along with his brother!"

Dad's unblinking gaze silences me. "If I'd done that," he says softly, "you and I might not be sitting here now. Your mother might be a widow. You don't know what those men were capable of. It's not very honorable, I know, but that's the choice I made."

I want to argue, but who am I to question my father about decisions made during a time I lived through as a little boy under his protection?

Before I can remind him of my other questions, he says, "As for saving Viola . . . all I did was send a request through Ray Presley to Brody Royal and Claude Devereux."

"You knew that they had ties to the Double Eagles?"

"Yes."

"How?"

"I'll tell you in a minute. But as for your question, I simply told them I was sure that Viola had no intention of speaking to the authorities. I think Royal or Devereux or someone up the line believed me, and they knew I understood that if she talked, Viola wouldn't be the only one to pay a price. In any case, they let her live. That's all I can tell you about that."

"And this photo? With Royal and the others?"

Dad slides the image back toward me, but his eyes remain on it. "Leland took that picture. It was 1966. I don't know how Henry Sexton got hold of it. Lee used to fly us to gun shows back in the sixties. That one was in Biloxi. You know I hate the water, but Lee had committed us to go deep-sea fishing with Royal and Devereux, who were down there on business. Dixie Mafia business, probably. Anyway, we'd run into Ray Presley at the show, so he joined us. The whole cruise only lasted five or six hours. I hadn't known Royal at all before that. But afterward . . ." Dad is looking at me but seems not to see me.

"What?"

"Another man came along on that trip. A tall, lanky fellow—ex-military. At first the cruise was fun and games. We caught a few mackerel, and drank enough beer to pretend we were extras in *To Have and Have Not*. That's when Lee shot this picture. But Royal and the lanky fellow were serious drinkers. And the more they drank, the more they talked. The more they talked, the more frightened I got. Lee, too."

"What did they talk about?"

"Paramilitary operations, mostly. The military guy turned out to be ex-army, but on the CIA payroll. He'd worked down at a camp training Cuban expatriates for the Bay of Pigs. He knew Frank and Snake Knox from there, and I gathered that he already knew Ray, too. They talked about Guatemala, Chile, Cuba, even Eastern Europe. Coups d'état, past and present. When this guy went to the head, Brody told us he was some kind of CIA trigger man. Royal was tied in with all this somehow, politically. He was a big anticommunist, I guess. He seemed to be a link between Marcello and the CIA, anyway. I thought about all this a few minutes ago, when you said something about Royal being involved in a plot to kill Robert Kennedy."

"Did Royal talk about Kennedy on that trip?"

Dad sighs, then answers in a reluctant voice. "Not Bobby. But Jack . . . yes. When the CIA guy and Royal were the drunkest—when we were finally headed back to the marina—they started talking about Dallas. That's all the CIA guy called it: *Dallas*. But it was the way he said it that chilled me. Like he'd been there. He was furious at whoever had planned the operation, and kept saying how unprofessional it was. Now and then he'd cuss up a storm in French. When I tried to move away from them, Devereux cornered me in the bow and started trying to involve me in a personal injury lawsuit he had going."

Dad laughs bitterly, and the result is like a painful cough. "That voyage turned into a damned nightmare. By the time we got back to Biloxi, the CIA guy was ready to fight somebody—anybody. Brody apologized and asked whether Leland or I could sedate him. He was serious. But we didn't have any drugs with us. We got the hell off that boat as fast as we could and took off."

"Why would Dr. Robb go into business with Royal after that?"

"Lee was already partners with Brody by that time. I think the next day he told himself he'd imagined most of what we'd heard. But I'd recognized the edge in that guy's voice, from Korea. I'd run across a few intelligence types over there, guys nobody wanted to mess with. There's a dark undercurrent to American power, Penn, and Royal and his friend were part of that. And since we're showing each other old snapshots . . . let me show you one."

He turns and reaches back into the bookshelf behind him and pulls out a worn copy of *Lanterns on the Levee: Recollections of a Planter's Son*, by William Alexander Percy, the Mississippi soldier and poet who raised his second cousin Walker Percy. Fanning the pages, Dad pulls out a faded color photo and slides it slowly across his desk.

"I only have this because Percy's book was in my office the year of the fire," he says with ineffable grief. We almost never speak of the event that destroyed the priceless library my father spent most of his life amassing, or the human cost that dwarfed the loss of those treasured books. Yet on this night, when Ray Presley's name has already been spoken, it seems more than apropos.

Examining the picture, I see a little boy who looks like me standing beside a seesaw on the now-vanished playground of St. Stephen's grade school. Back then St. Stephen's was still an Episcopal school, and our classes were held in an antebellum mansion downtown.

"I remember this picture," I tell him. "I was in first grade. I thought you used it as a bookmark."

"I did," Dad says, his eyes hard. "For a specific reason. One week after that Gulf fishing trip, Ray Presley visited my office. He told me that Carlos Marcello had heard Brody's CIA guest had gotten drunk and said a little too much. Marcello wanted me to know the guy was a nut job, and that nothing he said should be believed."

"If that was true, why would Marcello bother sending Ray to tell you that?"

Dad nods slowly. "Exactly. And here's the thing: Ray was close to Jim Garrison's investigation of the JFK assassination in New Orleans. He said witnesses were vanishing, and some had already been murdered. Making yourself a potential witness in the investigation of the JFK assassination was the equivalent of suicide. Ray was telling me this as a favor, believe it nor not. Then he gave me that picture of you. He apologized, and he swore he hadn't taken it himself, but the implication was clear."

"I'll bet Ray shot this himself."

"I imagine so. And now you know why, when Leland Robb came to me in 1969, I didn't want to hear his story. They'd already let me know what crossing Brody Royal or Carlos Marcello would cost me. You."

Me? Only a few hours ago, Henry Sexton suggested as much—though he figured it was the Double Eagles who'd threatened my life. The truth is even more disturbing. Without knowing it, I once functioned as a hostage to the Mafia, not the Ku Klux Klan, and to prevent my father from speaking out, not about the atrocities of Brody Royal but the drunken boasts of a CIA operative.

"Is there a particular reason you kept this picture in Will Percy's book?"

Dad looks away, his jaw tight. "Perhaps. But that's a conversation for another night."

"So that fishing boat picture with Royal . . . it's just a fluke?"

"Essentially, yes. I never had any kind of relationship with Brody Royal. If there was justice in the world, that bastard would be dying of ALS, instead of the sweet young mother I diagnosed three months ago. But that kind of justice is a child's dream. The evil prosper, and the innocent pay the bills for them. I've seen it all my life, and so have you."

"Why haven't you told Henry Sexton any of this?"

Dad holds up both hands, as if raising an invisible wall between us once more. "I have my reasons, and I've said my piece. I want you to keep all this between us, Penn. I admire what Henry's done these past years, but I'm afraid that if he continues, he'll end up like Glenn Morehouse. I worry about you, too," he says, his voice thickening. "Don't start poking into the Double Eagles or Brody Royal. That's not your war."

Unreasonably upset, I find myself on my feet. "So that's it? This is your cross to bear alone?"

"I'm afraid it is. I've got a path to walk, and there's no turning off it. Not yet, anyway."

"Why won't you let me walk it with you?"

"Will you be in court tomorrow if they arrest me?"

"You know I will," I say grudgingly.

He turns up his palms. "Then I won't be alone, will I?"

"You're not the only one who's going to pay for this martyr act! Annie's scared out of her wits, and God only knows what this is doing to Mom."

He nods, his lips tight. "I realize the next few days may be tough. But I've given this a lot of thought. If the state chooses to jail me for my silence, then so be it."

I pace away from his desk, then back, trying to put my incredulity into words. "How long can you survive in jail? A week? A month?"

Dad looks to his right, where a bust of Abraham Lincoln stands beside his window. "You know, few people remember that Lincoln offered Robert E. Lee command of a Union army when the war began. Lee wanted to hold the Union together. His family's sympathies lay with the Union. But he was a Virginian, and in the end, he couldn't take up arms against his home state. He tried to sit out the war, and they wouldn't let him. He knew it would end in defeat for the South, but he fought to the limit of his abilities in spite of that. He fought with honor and brilliance, despite the wrongness of his cause."

What is he trying to tell me? "What's your point, Dad?"

"Fate doesn't let men choose their wars. Or even their battles, sometimes. But one resolute man can sometimes accomplish remarkable things against overwhelming odds."

Why is he speaking in code? Did my father commit some great evil in the past to protect our family? Or keep silent about one? Or is he doing that now?

"Dad . . . this afternoon, when I asked you about the videotape missing from the camera Henry left at Viola's place, your reaction made me think you might have it. Or know where it is."

He studies me in silence for a few seconds. "I don't think anybody's going to find that tape. I wouldn't worry about it, if I were you."

Jesus. "Has somebody threatened our family? Please tell me. Is that why you're walking willingly into this buzz saw?"

He stares at me a long time before answering. "Not overtly, no."

"But a threat is implicit in the situation. Look, if that's it, we can handle this. We can protect ourselves against Royal and the Eagles. Don't let any threat dictate your actions."

He looks at me the way I've looked at people who have little understanding of the true workings of the justice system. "There are only two ways to protect yourself against people like that. One is to go into witness protection—permanently. Do you want to yank your mother out of her present life? Walk away from the mayor's office and never come home again? Do you want to pull Annie out of school and

Caitlin away from her newspaper? All to live in Kansas under false names?"

He's right about this, at least. "Of course not. What's the second way?"

After watching me in silence for several seconds, he rolls his chair back from the desk and gets slowly to his feet. "I've already forgotten what I was thinking." He gives me a forced smile. "I'm exhausted, son. It's time for bed."

I feel a miserably familiar emotion, one that parents have felt since time immemorial when trying to help a stubborn child. The reverse, I find, is even more excruciating. Fighting my father all day has left me spent.

"I'll walk you out," he says, taking his cigar from the edge of the desk and getting to his feet with a cartilaginous creak. Then he leads me up the hall with a shuffling gait that's painful to watch. When we reach the door to the garage, he squeezes my arm.

"I know you don't understand my actions, but that's only natural. More of my friends are dead than alive. You're in a different stage of life. Don't forget what I said about Royal and the Knoxes. That's not your war."

"How much danger do you think there is?"

"That depends on what you do over the next few days. If you're really going to drag the Jericho Hole, maybe you ought to get some protection. Have you thought about calling in Daniel Kelly on this?"

"I tried to reach him earlier. He hired on with another security firm, and he's back in Afghanistan."

"Well . . . then arm yourself and keep your eyes open. I'd put a guard on Henry, too. They say the Lord watches over little children and fools, but I think Henry's about used up his allotment of grace."

Without quite meaning to, I reach out and hug my father, tight. "Good night, Dad."

"Good night. I hope I haven't disappointed you too much."

I want to tell him I love him, but the lump in my throat prevents it. My mind spins with memories of Will Percy, a Mississippian of legendary accomplishments. A hero of the Great War, a Princeton-educated poet, a graduate of Harvard Law School and founder of the Yale Younger Poets, Will Percy represented everything that was best in an educated southerner. Yet in the crucible of the Great Flood of 1927, after being placed in charge of flood relief for Washington County, this man of honor had utterly failed the black population he hoped to save and done irreparable damage to race relations in Mississippi. Does my father see himself in Will Percy? Were the 1960s my father's Great Flood? I seem to remember that Will Percy's greatest mistake was failing to stand up to his own father when it mattered most. I can't afford to make the same mistake.

As I turn away from him and make my way back to my car, I realize that I don't know much more than I did before I arrived. But I do know this: today Shadrach Johnson, Sheriff Billy Byrd, and Lincoln Turner declared war on my family.

The first casualty of that war will be Shad Johnson.

CHAPTER 31

TOM LAY IN bed beside his wife, who until a few minutes ago had been reading a novel whose plot she would forget in a week. Peggy Cage read more than two hundred books a year, her way of coping with the troubling transition from wakefulness to sleep, an insomnia that worsened a little each year. Now she snored softly beside him as she had for more than fifty years.

After Penn left, Tom had stood in the darkness for several minutes, smoking silently. He suspected that Partagas might be the last he would smoke for a long time, maybe forever. Strangely, this didn't concern him much. Lying to his son had altered something inside him, and not for the better. The moment he'd denied being Viola's lover, he'd felt as though some deep part of him had generated malignant cells that would proliferate until they killed him. Yet how could he answer such questions? Did he have a duty to confess to his son every last sin of his life? He didn't think so. Penn would learn the most painful of laws in his own time: If a man lived long enough, his past would always overtake him, no matter how fast he ran or how morally he tried to live subsequently. And how men dealt with that law ultimately revealed their true natures.

Tom stuffed a pillow between his arthritic knees, then turned on his side and listened to Peggy snore. Her regular breathing comforted him. Viola's death had shaken him so profoundly that he felt detached from the material world, like an astronaut drifting away from his mother ship. This sense of dislocation reminded him of those sleepless weeks forty years ago, when he and Viola had stolen every private moment they could. But he was no longer the man he'd been then. A quarter century ago, surgeons had cut vessels from his legs and grafted them into his coronary arteries, allowing him to survive into his late fifties. Since then, various stents had been inserted to keep him alive, and they'd held up pretty well. But now his heart itself was failing. He sometimes had to take seven or eight nitroglycerine tablets simply to get through the day. If tomorrow morning brought the sheriff to his door . . . what then?

He'd always known it would come to this. As Penn had said, the past was fighting its way to the surface, like a sunken corpse filling with the gases of decay. Knowing what tomorrow might bring, Tom had allowed himself two shots of bourbon along with his evening cigar, then sat up reading *The Official Records of the War of the Rebellion*. Tonight he had reread the order, given at Gettysburg, that had placed the "University Greys" of Ole Miss—Penn's alma mater—in the first wave of Pickett's Charge. Lee's fatal mistake had doomed every last boy in that unit, and the Confederacy with them. To Lee's everlasting credit, after he was beaten, he had forbidden any guerrilla activity that would extend the conflict, and had supported Reconstruction.

Tom thought about the Lost Cause myth, and how Jim Crow had grown out of Reconstruction as surely as World War II had grown out of Versailles. In so many ways, the primary issue of the Civil War had never truly been settled, and both North and South were complicit in this tragedy. A hundred years after the dreadful sacrifice at Antietam, President Kennedy had been forced to call out the National Guard to get a single black man admitted to Ole Miss. Kennedy's assassination a year later had set LBJ on the road to the Civil Rights Act of 1964 and the Voting Rights Act of 1965, which opened the way for black leaders to carry their struggle onto Main Street, USA. And God, how white America had fought back—both North and South.

Tom's life was inextricably bound up with the tumultuous events of that era. His seven-week affair with Viola had begun two days after they had patched up Jimmy Revels, Luther Davis, and the Double Eagles after that highway brawl, and it had ended—truly ended—on the day Frank Knox died. One day prior, Viola had asked Dr. Lucas to switch her to Dr. Ross, leaving Tom crazed with longing and emotionally adrift. When he arrived at the clinic the next morning, he'd been thinking only of himself, with no idea what fate had in store for him. Within sixty minutes, Viola Turner would teach him just how blind a man could be to the world around him, and even to those he loved.

As per Dr. Lucas's orders, Viola began that day working under Dr. Ross, who was elated by the new arrangement. Tom got Anna Mae Nugent, an older white nurse, as a substitute. He went through the motions with his first five or six patients, then told Anna Mae that he needed to make some calls from his office. He'd just closed the door and removed his stethoscope when he heard a shout from up near reception. A moment later, Anna Mae came barreling up the hall.

"They just brought a man in from Triton Battery!" she cried. "A pallet of batteries fell on him. He's tore up bad, Doc. Looks like a hospital case, but he was already here, so I told them to put him in the surgery."

Tom grabbed his stethoscope and walked calmly toward the surgery, his grief over Viola easing with every step. Dr. Lucas was performing an appendectomy at the Jefferson Davis Hospital, but even if he'd been in the clinic, Lucas would have expected Tom to take this case. Dr. Lucas liked nice, clean surgeries scheduled far in advance. Surprise traumas weren't to his taste. The upshot of all this was that Tom wouldn't even have to ask for Viola; it was understood that she assisted on all trauma cases that came to the clinic.

"Do you need help, Tom?" Jim Ross asked from a doorway to his right. "Anna Mae said the guy looks bad."

"No, I'm fine," Tom said quickly. "I'm just going to stabilize him, then get him transported to the emergency room. I'd appreciate it if you'd call an ambulance for me."

"Done."

"Anna Mae?" Tom called. "Pull the man's record."

"I'll have it down there in a second."

Tom turned the corner and almost plowed into Viola, who was hurrying up the hall from the direction of the surgery.

"What are you doing?" he asked. "Who's with the patient?"

"Two of his friends."

"No nurse?"

"No." Viola's face was taut, her eyes dead. "I'm not treating him."

"What?"

"You heard me. I'm not treating that man."

"Who is it?" Tom asked, stunned by her defiant tone.

"Frank Knox."

Suddenly Tom thought he understood. It was Knox and two Klan buddies who had assaulted Jimmy and Luther seven weeks earlier. It was only natural for Viola to hate the man. But refusing to treat him was unacceptable.

"Viola, you have to get in there."

Her eyes flashed fury. "Anna Mae can do it."

"How badly is he hurt?"

"Bad enough. Head injury. Cracked ribs, maybe a pneumothorax."

"Anna Mae can't handle that! I need you."

Viola closed her eyes, and he saw then that she'd probably slept as little as he—maybe less.

"I'm sorry," he said, "but you don't have a choice. I don't, either. Get back there."

She averted her eyes and muttered something that sounded like curses in French. Then she set her jaw and looked him dead in the eye. "I won't work with his friends in there," she said through gritted teeth.

"Kick them out, then! Hell, I'll do it."

After another moment, Viola turned and hurried back toward the surgery. Tom was starting after her when Anna Mae tapped him on the shoulder and passed him a manila file labeled BENJAMIN FRANKLIN KNOX. The label had a blue border, indicating the patient was an employee of the Triton Battery Corporation. Tom flipped open the file and walked slowly back toward the surgery.

As he passed through the little waiting room near the lab, he saw Sonny Thornfield and Glenn Morehouse, the two other men involved in the assault on Jimmy and Luther, pacing the room like expectant fathers. Thornfield was still limping from the bullet wound Luther Davis had given him two months earlier.

"Hey, Doc!" Thornfield called. "Is Frank gonna be okay?"

"I haven't seen him yet. I'll let you know as soon as I know something."

"He's tore up bad," Morehouse said. "Half a pallet of batteries hit him."

"That colored nurse kicked us out," Thornfield griped.

"That's what she's supposed to do. You guys were in the service. You know to stay out of the way. There's an ambulance coming now, and we'll be moving him to the hospital right away."

"Okay, sorry," Thornfield said. "Do whatever you can, Doc. You can't let Frank die."

Tom waved them off and went on to the surgery.

When he opened the door, he froze, stunned by a scene so unexpected that it paralyzed him for a few critical moments. Frank Knox lay on the floor, half propped against a cabinet, his mouth gaping, his face blue. Viola stood five feet away, staring down at Knox like a vengeful goddess watching the death of a mortal who had offended her. In her hand was a 60 cc syringe, one of the big ones Tom used to drain swollen knees, far too large to be of any use in Knox's situation.

"What the hell's going on here?" Tom asked in a shocked whisper. He shut the door behind him. "What's he doing on the floor?"

"Dying," Viola said in a monotone.

"*Fuck!*" He shoved her out of the way and knelt beside Knox, holding his stethoscope to the man's chest. He heard no heartbeat or breath sounds. "Help me get him up, Viola!"

"No."

"*What!*"

Tom frantically examined Knox's head and torso, searching for the most serious injury. The airway seemed to be open, but Knox had a massive contusion on his skull, which almost certainly meant a concussion. As Tom felt his way along Knox's chest, he realized that the falling batteries had not only crushed ribs on his left side, but had also torn open his chest wall. Morehouse and Thornfield had no business bringing this man to a clinic. He should have gone straight to the hospital.

"Go check on the ambulance," Tom ordered.

"No," Viola said again, her voice almost lethargic.

Tom scrambled to his feet, enraged by her lack of professionalism. He might be an emotional wreck due to their affair, but he wasn't about to let a patient die because of it, no matter who the man might be.

"*Go check on the ambulance!*" he repeated.

Viola didn't even look at him. Like a little girl who'd pulled the wings off some insect, she just watched Knox turning blue.

Tom slapped her face. "What the hell's wrong with you?"

Viola didn't respond.

He slapped her again, hard.

At last she looked up, her eyes cold and dead. "He raped me."

Something curdled in Tom's stomach. "What?"

"He—raped—me." Viola's eyes seemed to focus at last, and they held an accusatory fire that cut through Tom's bewildered anger. "That man there," she said. "He raped me. His friends helped. The ones outside. Plus one more. They had a fine old time . . . yes, sir."

Tom suddenly felt as though he were trying to think and move underwater. The man on the floor seemed far less important than he had only a moment ago. "When was this?"

"Two nights ago." Viola cocked her head as though trying to discern some detail of Knox's mortal suffering.

Tom almost staggered under the rush of awareness that resolved every question that had been torturing him since yesterday. "*Why?*" he asked.

"They couldn't find Jimmy," she said in the same monotone. "They did it to flush him out of Freewoods. This one did, anyway. The rest of them just wanted me. You know what that feels like, don't you? To want me?"

Tom looked down at Knox, who was gaping like a landed fish on the floor. To his surprise, he felt no urge whatever to save the man. Not even in Korea had he felt this emotion, or lack of it. Indeed, in Korea he had helped to save wounded North Korean and Chinese soldiers, despite seeing horrors they had inflicted upon American prisoners. But if what Viola said was true—and Tom had never been more certain of anything—then he wanted Frank Knox to die where he lay.

The sound of a distant siren pulled Tom out of his trance. He took hold of Viola's wrist and held up the oversized syringe. "What's this for?"

"Air," she said. "Like those dogs you told me about, in medical school."

Tom went dizzy for a moment. One of his worst memories from medical school was having to euthanize dogs with air injections after medical experiments. About a month ago, he had told Viola about that experience, and she had just used the information to murder Frank Knox. Tom wondered how much air it had taken to cause a vapor lock in the Klansman's heart. At least 200 ccs, and probably more.

"We've got to get him up on the table," he said in a detached voice. "I'm not touching him."

"We're going to the gas chamber if you don't help me get him up." "I don't care."

"Your brother will. Help me!" Tom was trying to communicate the idea that he was no longer working to save Knox, but Viola. "It has to look right when the ambulance men get here."

At last Viola seemed to grasp the import of his words. Together, they wrestled Knox's limp body onto the examining table. Tom put the stethoscope to his heart again. There was no heartbeat, not even a whisper of a pulse.

"He's gone," Tom said, grabbing the syringe from Viola's hand and removing the needle. "Where did you inject him?"

"Twice internally. Once in the antecubital vein."

"Christ." Tom stuffed the syringe into the bottom corner of a cabinet. "Which arm?"

Viola pointed to the crook of Knox's right elbow.

Tom opened a fresh syringe, drew two milligrams of adrenaline from a vial, then carefully injected it into the hole where Viola had injected the air.

The drug had no discernible effect on the prostrate man.

The siren was screaming now, just outside the clinic. Then the crew cut it and the wail began to drop in pitch, like a child's top spinning down to stillness.

"When they come in," Tom said, "we're going to be working our asses off. Get a blood pressure cuff on him, and I'll be treating him for a tension pneumothorax. Do you hear me?"

Viola made no sound, but she did turn and get the sphygmomanometer.

What happened next unfolded with the unreality of dreams. Anna Mae screamed when she opened the door for the ambulance crew. The two attendants shook their heads and said Knox should have been taken to the hospital. Anybody could see the man was mortally wounded. Sonny Thornfield stood in the door and cursed the forklift operator who'd spilled the load of batteries, then himself for not taking Knox to the hospital, and finally the ambulance men for not getting to the clinic sooner. Glenn Morehouse cried like a little boy who'd lost his father until Thornfield cursed him for being a baby and dragged him out of the clinic to take the news back to the boys at the plant.

Eventually—after Dr. Ross had put in his two cents and all the office girls had glommed all the details they could spread later as gossip—Tom was left in his private office with Viola, who sat on the couch like the rape victims he'd treated during his internship at Charity Hospital at New Orleans. It was as though whatever the Klansmen had done to her had happened only an hour ago, not two days earlier.

"Tell me," he pleaded.

"What's the use?" Viola asked.

"Why didn't you call the police after it happened?"

She closed her eyes, and by this simple gesture communicated that

Tom might be the stupidest man on the planet. At length she said, "You can't rape a black woman in this state. Not if you're white. Ain't no such thing. Don't you even know that, Tom Cage?"

The coldness in her voice startled him. "I guess I thought—"

"*Thought?* You didn't think. You're walking around with blinders on! That's what you're doing."

"But—"

"No, Tom." The face that had always seemed so serene was now distorted by pain and grief. "You've got to face how things *are.* They came at me to get to Jimmy. They couldn't find him, so they hurt the only thing they knew would matter to him. And if Jimmy finds out what they done to me, he's as good as dead. Pacifist or not, he'll do just what they want—go after them—and they'll kill him. I'm worried he may already have heard." Viola's eyes blazed suddenly, and she leaned forward, stabbing the air with her forefinger. "So you can't ever tell him! Swear it."

"Viola—"

"Swear it, before God!"

"I swear, Viola. I'll never tell Jimmy."

"Or Luther!"

"Luther, either. I swear."

She collapsed against the sofa back.

"Are you all right?" he asked. "Physically, I mean?"

Viola turned her head and wiped tears on her sleeve. "I don't really know. They beat me. Everywhere but where it would show. I had to come up here and steal some antibiotics. You reckon Dr. Lucas will fire me for that?"

"Viola, please don't—"

"You can't help me, Tom. You want to, but what can you do? You've got a wife and kids to take care of. You want to fight the Ku Klux Klan for me? I know you're brave. But are you that kind of hero?"

Until that moment, Tom had never quite realized how high the risks of becoming involved with Viola were. She seemed to want an answer to her question. Her unblinking gaze probed him like an X-ray beam.

"I don't know what to do," he said. "You're probably right about the police not believing you. It would be your word against Knox's buddies, and they'd all give each other alibis."

She gave him the most cynical look he had ever seen.

"To be honest," he said, "about the only thing we could do . . . is kill them."

Viola nodded slowly. "I got one of them."

Tom shuddered as the magnitude of what they had done hit home. "There'll almost certainly be an autopsy," he thought aloud. "An experienced pathologist might discover the true cause of death, but this post will probably be done by Adam Leeds. With Knox's massive injuries, Leeds won't be looking for anything exotic. I doubt he'll notice the air escaping when he cuts open Knox's heart."

Viola seemed unconcerned by the risk of being found out.

"Where's Jimmy now?" Tom asked. "Still in Freewoods?"

"I don't know. I've stopped calling him, in case the klukkers on the police force are tapping my phone."

Viola was right about the police department having Klansmen in its ranks. "What do you want to do now? Do you want to go home?"

Her eyes had been flat and lifeless for so long that it stunned Tom to see some depth come back into them. "What do I want?" she asked softly. "I want you to take me away from here. I want you to take me to a place where we can have children and grow old together. A place where my brother can come live and be safe, and play music all day long. A place where I can love you like you ought to be loved, and you can love me the same."

Tom felt himself shaking.

"What's the matter?" she asked. "Don't I look the same to you anymore? Do I look different to you, now that you know them rednecks used me?"

"No."

"Do I look different now that I killed somebody in front of you?"

"No. I'm as guilty as you of that crime."

She stared relentlessly at him, as though waiting for him to admit that he could not give her what she wanted. But she was only waiting for him to face what she'd known all along.

"You finally see, don't you?" Viola said. "It was just a dream. Every time we made love, we were just children pretending. *This* is the truth, right here. My torn genitals. That dead man on his way to the morgue. My brother running for his life. And you going back to Peggy and your

babies. That's the truth, Tom. There ain't no place for me in that picture. I'm on my own. I always have been."

"Please tell me what I can do," he said uselessly.

She stood, wavered on her feet, then straightened up. "Nothing.
There's nothing in your power."

He walked around his desk, but she held up a warning hand, just
like a traffic cop. "A hug won't help."

"What do we do now?" he asked.

She shook her head. "I don't know. Pray, I guess. Can murderers pray?"

"That bastard deserved what he got. Don't think about him anymore."

"He deserved *worse*," Viola said with venom. "I won't lose no sleep
over that trash. I just . . . I guess I don't know what to do next, either."

"One day at a time," Tom said, hating the impotence in his voice.
"That's all we can do. And pray the worst is over."

But it wasn't over. Not by a damn sight—

"*Tom?*" Peggy moaned, sitting up in bed, then shielding her eyes
against the reading light she'd left on.

"What's the matter, honey?" he asked.

Peggy rubbed her eyes until she was more than half awake. "I had
a nightmare."

"Are you all right?"

"I don't know." She felt along the bedside table for her water glass,
then took a gulp. "We were at a funeral."

"Whose funeral?"

Peggy blinked, still bleary with sleep. "I don't know. I saw the casket there, and I was holding Annie's hand, and she was crying."

"That doesn't mean anything. It was just a dream."

"It felt so real. I'm trying to remember who was sitting with us. I
want to know."

You want to know who was in the casket, he thought. "You said 'we'
when you woke up. Was I sitting with you?"

Peggy's eyes widened suddenly. "Oh, Tom. I think it was one of the
kids. Penn or Jenny. Dear God."

He laid his hand on her forearm and squeezed. "It doesn't matter
who it was, Peg. That was just a dream."

She stared at him with almost frightening intensity. "I'm telling
you, it felt *real*. Like it *means* something. It couldn't, could it?"

"No. It's just the stress of today, and tomorrow. Premonitions of death are a normal human feeling during times like this."

Peggy took his hand and fixed her eyes on him with solemn deliberation of a priest. "Tom . . . I want to talk to you about last night."

He felt his defenses go up. "Peg—"

"I know you don't want to talk about it," she said quickly. "But I feel like we should. We have to, don't we? I'm not sure I can go on if we don't."

He met her gaze but said nothing.

"I know sometimes it's better to leave some things unsaid," she went on. "And maybe this is one of those times. But I truly feel like something terrible is coming toward us."

Tom closed his other hand over hers. "If you really want to talk about it, we can. But I think this is one of those times where it's best to move forward, and not look back. Remember Lot's wife."

As Peggy gazed back at him across fifty years of experience, he knew that she understood him better than anyone ever had—better even than Viola, in most ways. Her hazel eyes moved across his face, missing nothing. Then she said, "I'm going to try to go back to sleep."

He gave her an encouraging smile. "Everything's going to be all right tomorrow. You'll see."

"You don't think you should listen to Penn? About hiring Quentin?"

"There may come a time for that. But right now I think I'm better off following my own counsel."

She patted the quilt over his thigh. "All right. Do you want to take one of my pills?"

"Better not. I'm fine, Peg. Go back to sleep."

She stared sadly at him for a few moments, then patted his side and lay back down. Seconds later she began to snore again.

Tom thought of all the years that had passed since he'd given up Viola, years drifting down upon each other like leaves settling on a forest floor. Over time those leaves had hardened and begun to petrify. The young Tom Cage—the man who had loved Viola with soul-searing ardor—lay somewhere beneath those leaves, entombed in ash like an ember after a wildfire. And Viola . . . whatever had remained of her younger self was long gone. That person existed only as a memory that occasionally flickered to life in the minds of those she had treated decades ago. There were probably patients she'd touched similarly in Chicago, hundreds of them, but Tom knew nothing of those people, or those years. And he suspected that the Viola they had known was not quite the same enchanted spirit who had so blessed the people of Natchez.

A fearful ache went through him as he thought of his impending arrest. He had already laid out his clothes on a chair, in case the sheriff came early. Peggy had helped, never once questioning him about anything deeper than his choice of shirt and tie. Rebuffing Penn all day had been more difficult than dealing with his wife. It was a tempting proposition to simply put himself in his son's hands. Penn had the legal talent and experience to do as good a job as anyone alive defending him. But to do that, Penn would need the truth, and Tom was not prepared to burden him with that. Not yet. He might never be.

For now, Walt Garrity would be his ally. The old Texas Ranger wasn't a lawyer, but he had other talents. More to the point, Walt had shared horrific trials with Tom. Together they had endured things that young men should never be asked to witness, much less take part in, and they had survived them together. They had literally saved each other's lives. If Tom was going to be confined in jail, he couldn't ask for a better second pair of eyes and ears than those of Walt Garrity. At least that had been the reasoning that prompted his earlier call to Walt.

Yet tonight Penn had unknowingly brought Tom a glimmer of hope. For the death of Glenn Morehouse offered Tom a chance he hadn't dared hope for: a chance at true deliverance. As Peggy snored beside him, Tom pondered the Greek and Hebrew legends of the scapegoat. *Pharmakos* to the Greeks, *Azazel* to the Hebrews. A shameful human practice, he'd always thought, one born from guilt and superstition. But most human behavior had grown out of necessity, and he now understood the empirical value of the rituals for which he had felt only contempt before.

He thought about Morehouse, the hypertensive battery assembler who'd committed unspeakable atrocities as a young man. Like so many guilty souls, Morehouse had desperately sought redemption through confession before the end. Had cancer claimed him? Or had his fellow Eagles finally stepped out of the shadows to stop his mouth forever, before he could unburden his conscience? Tom didn't care one way or the other. All he knew for sure was that if he walked down the path that had opened to him now, Viola would surely forgive him.

CHAPTER 32

"MR. ROYAL, SNAKE Knox is at the gate."

Brody Royal looked up from a set of aerial photos he'd commissioned of the flooded Lower Ninth Ward in New Orleans. "I'll see him, Hargrove."

"Yes, sir."

Brody set aside the flood photos, picked up his glass of whiskey, and got up from the sofa. More and more frequently over the past year, he'd spent his leisure hours in the basement of his home on Lake Concordia. Most of this vast underground floor was occupied by a state-of-the-art firing range, but Brody had also added a display room for his collection of antique weapons. Over the years, this room had taken on the look of a gentlemen's club, with comfortable furniture occupying the rectangular space between the glass-fronted cypress display cases. Here Brody entertained senators, governors, CEOs, sports stars, and country singers, allowing them to fire weapons they'd only seen in Hollywood movies. He loved watching citified ego-freaks turn into jelly as the BAR came alive in their hands, chewing up a fifty-five-gallon drum placed against the wall of railroad ties at the end of the shooting lanes.

The staircase leading to the house's main floor was decorated with photographs that made Shad Johnson's Wall of Respect look like a bulletin board in a teenage girl's room. Anyone ascending those stairs saw Brody's father and Governor Huey P. Long standing behind a balcony rail draped in campaign bunting. After that came Brody Sr. and a grinning young Carlos Marcello sitting in the bed of a tomato truck loaded with slot machines. Signed photos included Brody himself with President Lyndon Johnson, Mercury astronauts Alan Shepard and Gus Grissom, President Richard Nixon, and Ronald Reagan. Candid shots showed Brody playing poker with John Stennis and Big Jim Eastland, eating catfish at Jughead's with Senator Earl Long, drinking with Ernest

Hemingway in the Carousel Bar in the Hotel Monteleone, and singing with Al Hirt on the roof of the Eola Hotel. Brody's favorite image, shot in 1952, only showed him in the background, while in the glare of a flashbulb General Douglas MacArthur danced with Natchez belle Pythia Nolan, whom Brody had once pursued with all his will but had failed to bring to the altar.

Hearing an engine upstairs in the driveway, Brody walked over to the fieldstone fireplace, where a large framed display above the mantel held pride of place. The left-hand photograph in the frame showed the levee at Caernarvon, Louisiana, being dynamited in 1927. The photo on the right showed an aerial image of St. Bernard Parish, Brody's childhood home, flooded from end to end as a result of that levee breach. The two photos bookended a cashier's check in the amount of twelve dollars and fifty cents. Drawn on a once-renowned New Orleans bank, this sum had been issued in 1928 as "full reparations" for the loss of his family's land, home, and two mercantile stores. Brody's father had never cashed this check, which he'd considered absolute proof of the baseness of the human spirit. Brody himself had spent decades working to avenge his father, and now, near the end of his life, God and nature had conspired to grant him his wish.

"Mr. Royal?" said a familiar voice from the foot of the stairs.

Brody turned and motioned Snake Knox to come deeper into the room.

"What can I do for you, Snake?"

The crop duster beamed with pleasure, his eyes taking in the gleaming weapons behind the glass. He'd only been down here a few times, and he clearly felt awed by his surroundings.

"Glenn Morehouse has sung his last song," he said.

Brody acknowledged the news with a nod. "Any problems?"

"No, sir."

"Good work."

Randall Regan came down the stairs, nodded to Snake, then poured himself a Stella Artois from a small Viking refrigerator and watched Knox the way a hawk watches a serpent in a field.

"There's another problem, though," Snake said. "Henry Sexton met with Mayor Penn Cage tonight. For a good while, too. Over at the *Beacon* office."

Royal glanced at his son-in-law, whose eyes went cold. "I don't like that."

"I didn't figure you would," Snake said. "When Penn Cage gets a burr up his ass about something, he don't quit. Remember when he put Judge Marston in prison? And that cunt of his with the newspaper . . ."

"Yes." Brody sipped his whiskey. "You know, Leo Marston was a friend of mine. Also a business partner. His incarceration caused me considerable difficulty. I always felt like I owed Penn Cage for that."

"Yes, sir. Is there anything you want me to do?"

"Do Forrest and Billy know that Sexton spoke to the mayor tonight?"

Snake nodded. "Billy's pretty worried about it, actually. But Forrest don't seem too concerned."

"So you came to me."

"I figured you'd want to know."

For the first time, Randall spoke. "You figured right."

"I'll take this under advisement and get back to you tomorrow," Brody said. "Keep me apprised of any developments."

"Yes, sir."

Brody smiled. "That's all."

Contrary to expectations, Snake didn't turn to go. The crop duster was staring into the display cases behind Brody, as though looking for something in particular. Brody had a feeling he knew what it was.

"Can I help you, Snake?"

"Is my rifle still down here?"

Brody smiled and pointed to the display case closest to the shooting stations of the firing range. Every case in this room featured polycarbonate glass for security, but the last case was unique in that it could be sealed with a wooden insert that concealed it altogether. Broader than the others, it held two scoped rifles mounted horizontally at chest height, and below them a German Flammenwerfer 41, the most advanced flamethrower of World War II.

Snake walked over to the cabinet and gazed at the rifles. As Brody stepped up behind him, Snake shook his head and whistled long and low.

"What you figure these beauties would fetch on eBay?" he asked.

The top rifle was a 1959 Remington 700, chambered for a .243 cartridge and mounted with a 7x Kahles scope. Beneath it was a 1962 Winchester Model 70, chambered for .30-06 Springfield and mounting a 5x Leupold scope. The Winchester was "Snake's rifle."

"Two million apiece?" Brody guessed. "Hell, maybe five. But we'd never see the money." He chuckled at the thought. "Our kids would be spending it while we rotted in jail."

Snake shook his head again. "You've got balls, Mr. Royal. Damn . . . I'll give you that."

Brody's chest swelled. Before he turned back to the sofa, he read the engraved brass plaques mounted beneath the rifles. Each was decorated with a small, full-color American flag. The plaque beneath the Remington read: *November 22, 1963.* The one beneath Snake's Winchester read: *April 4, 1968.*

OUT ON THE NARROW lane outside Brody Royal's house, a sixty-seven-year-old black man wearing a Detroit Tigers baseball cap drove his pickup truck along the shore of Lake Concordia. He saw a guard with a rifle slung over his shoulder standing a few yards down the driveway. Sleepy Johnston waved happily with his right hand, playing the part of an elderly fool, and kept driving with his knee. His right hand held a Glock .40-caliber pistol. He'd have to go around the lake now, and drive out the other way. But at least he'd gotten a look at the pickup truck parked before Brody Royal's garage door.

It belonged to Snake Knox. *One of Albert's killers . . .*

Sleepy had made his usual rounds tonight, which was how he'd recently gotten reacquainted with the characters from the bad old days of his youth. It was also how he'd discovered the Audi S4 parked outside the *Concordia Beacon.* While he waited to see who would come out and claim that car, a sheriff's cruiser had pulled up and scared him off. By pulling around to Main Street and waiting a couple of minutes, Sleepy had managed to follow the Audi back to Natchez, to a town house on Washington Street. There the car's owner had gotten into some kind of confrontation with a black man in a white pickup truck with Illinois plates. By rolling down his window at the nearest intersection, Sleepy had heard the truck's driver refer to the white man as "Mayor."

Then he'd understood. Henry Sexton had been meeting with the mayor of Natchez, the son of a doctor who had sewed up Sleepy's right knee when he was a little boy. Rumors were already circulating that Dr. Cage had killed his old nurse as part of some suicide pact, but most folks seemed to think that she had been ready to die. All Sleepy knew was that Viola had been the prettiest girl he'd ever seen, before or after he left the South. And her brother Jimmy had been one hell of a musician— far better than Sleepy or Pooky would ever be.

Sleepy turned on the radio and searched for an R&B station. The sound of rap drove him crazy. He finally settled on Sly and the Family Stone playing "If You Want Me to Stay," circa 1973. As the bass guitar pumped sinuously around him in the closed cab, Sleepy lit a Salem and wondered at the tragedy that, of Jimmy, Pooky, and himself, only one had survived to hear this song on the radio.

If God has a plan, he thought, *it's a piss-poor one.*

TUESDAY

CHAPTER 33

SHERIFF BILLY BYRD personally arrested my father at 8:45 A.M. Dad was sitting at the breakfast table when the law arrived. Mom sat opposite him with a cup of coffee and a Dopp kit filled with prescription drugs in front of her, while I talked to her on the telephone, reassuring her that I would be waiting at the sheriff's department. A strangled sob came over the line.

As I sped toward the sheriff's department, my mother called my cell phone and told me that a deputy had handcuffed Dad before they put him in the backseat of the cruiser, with all the neighbors watching. She was terrified that he would develop chest pain on the way to the station; his nitro tablets were sitting in a Ziploc bag on the passenger seat of her car. *Surely,* I thought, *Dad kept a couple of tablets in his pocket for the ride downtown.*

To my relief, Shad Johnson had arranged things with Sheriff Byrd so that, after being booked, Dad would be taken directly before the Justice Court judge, and not spend any time in a cell. Shad apparently remains intimidated enough by my possible exposure of the dogfighting photo not to push too hard. Still, being photographed and fingerprinted like a common criminal always takes a toll on a man of my father's integrity. When Dad finally emerged from the bowels of the station, his face already looked haggard. *What,* I wondered, *would a month in a cell do to him? Or six months while awaiting trial?*

It would kill him.

THE ADAMS COUNTY JUSTICE Court stands across the street and half a block down from the sheriff's department. It's housed in the same one-story building as the county coroner and the sheriff's department's investigators. The low structure is fronted with squat, cream-colored Doric columns that look like a giant compressed them to half their intended height.

Judge Charles Noyes has obviously been awaiting my father's arrival. A man of sixty-plus who spent most of his life selling insurance, Charlie Noyes made the transition to this new career about ten years ago. In Mississippi, Justice Court judges aren't required to be lawyers, a strange reality that isn't as rare in America as one might think. The same rule applies in New York State and several other supposedly enlightened jurisdictions. Law enforcement officers tend to resent this state of affairs, and often blame the legal ignorance of Justice Court judges for lowering charges against defendants, thus sabotaging prosecutions before a "competent" judge even becomes aware of the case. At least Charlie Noyes has a hardwood desk, a secretary, and a court reporter. In some Mississippi counties, Justice Court consists of a card table in the storeroom of the judge's house.

Few defendants in this court are represented by lawyers, since most appear to contest traffic tickets and DUIs—the minor league of the legal system. But Justice Court judges sometimes handle initial appearances in criminal felonies, which is why today I stand at my father's side, ready to deal with the issues of bond and whatever other surprises Shad Johnson might have in store. I never believed Shad's claim that he wouldn't be here today, and Shad quickly validates my skepticism by walking into the modest courtroom at one minute before nine.

Plainly saddened to see my father standing before his desk in handcuffs, Judge Noyes looks surprised to find the district attorney exhibiting the body language of a lawyer about to argue a major case. My mother's outfit gives the proceeding an even more formal air. She's dressed for a ladies' bridge party in 1962, and Judge Noyes seems flustered by her presence. After running his hand over his balding pate, he begins the hearing with an unexpected comment.

"I see no reason that this defendant should be handcuffed. Everybody knows Dr. Cage has terrible arthritis. Look at his hands. Take those restraints off, Wilbur."

The deputy standing behind my father instantly complies. Dad's wrists look red and inflamed after only a short time in the chafing cuffs. That's what psoriatic arthritis will do to you.

Taking refuge in routine, Judge Noyes reads the charge against my father and asks if he understands it. When Dad answers in the affirmative, the judge recites his rights, concluding with the promise that if he can't afford an attorney, one will be appointed for him. At this point, I state that I'm representing my father in this matter, at least for the time being. Judge Noyes gives me a smile of appreciation, as if this is only as it should be.

When the judge moves his gaze to Shad Johnson, he looks like an artilleryman bringing a cannon to bear. "On the matter of *bond*," he says, a note of challenge in his voice. "Does the district attorney have anything to say?"

"Yes, Your Honor." Shad steps forward, compensating for his diminutive height with hidden insoles, a bespoke suit, and his naturally powerful voice. "I realize that Dr. Cage is a long-standing resident of this county. But this was a particularly heinous murder, and life imprisonment is a possibility. The defendant is wealthy by local standards, he has a passport, and he could easily flee the jurisdiction if he so chose. To ensure that he appears at trial, I respectfully ask that bail be denied in this case."

Shad's request stuns me speechless. Granted, the charge is murder, but he could easily have covered his ass with his primary constituency by asking for a one- or two-million-dollar bond.

Judge Noyes's gaze hardens into a basilisk stare. "Mr. District Attorney, are you suggesting that Dr. Cage be held in the county jail for up to nine months while he awaits trial in the Circuit Court?"

Under Mississippi's laughable "speedy trial" rule, the state is allowed to wait 270 days before a defendant must be given his day in court. This long delay pleases most defendants, who are in no hurry to accelerate the wheels of justice. But this case is different.

"The charge is first-degree murder, Judge," Shad says with quiet insistence.

"It is, indeed," says Noyes. "And here's my thinking on that. Tom Cage has been practicing medicine in this town for . . . how long?"

"Forty-two years," my mother says softly.

"Forty-two years!" the judge exclaims. "Forty-two years taking care of the people of this county. And so far as I know, Dr. Cage has never even spit on the sidewalk, much less broken a law. Now, Mr. District Attorney, you surely know that this town has a serious shortage of primary-care physicians. And I see no reason why a doctor of Tom Cage's exemplary reputation should languish in jail when he could be providing desperately needed health care to the citizens of Adams County."

In an almost apologetic tone, Shad says, "Judge, if I may? I understand your logic. But if—and I say if—this defendant were to flee this jurisdiction prior to his trial, we would all find ourselves with a great deal of egg on our faces."

Judge Noyes nods slowly. "Of course, of course. The political argument. Let's all be sure to cover our behinds. Mr. District Attorney, I seem to recall you once telling me how you and a friend spent the year between high school and college traveling around Europe on a Eurailpass. Do you recall that?"

Shads blinks in confusion. "Yes, but—"

"When Tom Cage got out of high school, he didn't take a year off to go gallivanting around Europe. He spent a year fighting Chinese communists in North Korea, repelling human-wave attacks in weather that would freeze the hooves off a bighorn sheep. Machine-gun barrels melted from firing for hours without a break. Can you wrap your steel-trap mind around that, Counselor?"

Shad is still blinking like a man who finds himself unexpectedly staring into a blazing spotlight.

"Dr. Cage was taken prisoner in that war, Mr. Johnson, and only by exceptional personal fortitude did he escape with his life."

This statement leaves me flabbergasted. Never in my life have I heard that my father was a POW. But one glance at his solemn profile tells me it's true. When I look back at my mother, she nods once.

"So—here's my thinking on the matter of bond," Judge Noyes concludes. "If Tom Cage didn't run then, he won't run now. Do you have any further argument, sir?"

Shad controls his notorious temper with difficulty. I can only imagine what kind of restraint it must take for a black graduate of the Harvard Law School to stand silent while a white man who never attended any law school lectures him from the bench.

"Your Honor, the defendant's military record has no bearing on—"

"*Hush,*" says Judge Noyes, using what could only loosely be described as local courtroom argot.

Shad is quite right in his argument, but as every attorney knows, it's the judge's courtroom, whether that judge ever passed a bar exam or not.

"Your Honor," Shad says in a rigidly controlled voice, "I ask that bond be set at an amount commensurate with the seriousness of the crime, and one sufficient to assuage the community's choler."

Confusion distorts the judge's smooth face. "*Color?* Just what color community are you talking about assuaging here?"

"*Cho*-ler," Shad says, trying to clarify his intent. "Displeasure."

Judge Noyes looks like he'd like to throw his gavel at the district attorney. "What amount would you recommend, Mr. Johnson?"

"Two million dollars."

The judge grimaces like a constipated bulldog. At length he gives a sigh of resignation and says, "All right."

A deputy against the wall, probably the one who cuffed Dad at the house, nods with satisfaction.

Two hundred grand in cash, I note silently.

"Bond is set at fifty thousand dollars," says Judge Noyes.

A choked sob of relief breaks from my mother's throat. Shad stands openmouthed in a theatrical display of shock. Judge Noyes has sent a very loud message with this ruling. He clearly believes something is amiss in this case, and he's willing to take political heat for his faith in my father.

Before Shad can protest, a new voice comes from the back of the room, taking us all by surprise: "*All right. All right, I see how it is.*"

The voice is soft but resonant—far deeper than any other man's in the room—and my chest tightens at the familiar sound. Turning in my chair, I see Lincoln Turner standing at the back of the small room. His suit hangs loosely on his large frame, as though he's recently lost weight. My first wild thought is that the Justice Court door has no metal detector. Men whose mothers have been murdered have been known to execute the alleged killer in the presence of a dozen deputies. A millisecond after this thought rises in my mind, I stand and interpose myself between Lincoln and my father.

"Who is that man?" Judge Noyes asks irritably.

"Your Honor," Shad says, obviously discomfited by Lincoln's appearance, "this is Mr. Lincoln Turner, the victim's son."

Noyes's eyes narrow. "I see." He directs his next comments to the back of the room, which is less than twenty feet from his desk. "Sir, you have my deepest sympathy, but I must ask you to refrain from interrupting this proceeding."

"This is a public hearing," Lincoln growls. "And I ain't what you're used to up in here. I ain't some field nigger, Judge, or the son of one. I'm a lawyer."

"Public it may be," Noyes says, squinting. "But as a lawyer, you surely understand contempt of court."

Despite his warning tone, Noyes is clearly uncertain about how to handle this unexpected confrontation.

Shad moves toward Lincoln, motioning for him to calm down, but Turner raises a big hand to stop him. "Get out of my face, Johnson! I've come to say one thing, and then I'll go. If the sheriff hauled *me* up in here on a murder charge, I'd be lucky to get a million-dollar bail. But I guess white doctors get a free pass. Man, you people don't even try to *hide* this shit. It's right out here for everybody to see. Ain't nothing changed down here in a hundred years!"

Judge Noyes bangs his gavel. "That's it. Mr. Turner, you are now in contempt of—"

"I hold *you* in contempt!" Turner shouts, but by then the DA has gotten to him and started pushing the larger man toward the door.

"I'll take care of this, Judge!" Shad calls, making a pleading motion with his right hand.

"You'd better!" Noyes shouts back. "Or he's going straight to jail!"

When the door closes, all of us stand like stunned witnesses to a bar fight. My father and mother look shell-shocked, but Noyes and his staff are scarcely less rattled. "Wilbur," Noyes says to his deputy, "are you tits on a boar hog or what?"

The deputy reddens and looks at the carpet.

"I'll be damned if that's ever happened in here," Noyes mutters. "I think I'd better put that fellow in jail for one night, just on principle. Hell, as a matter of public safety."

I step toward the bench and speak quietly. "Judge, with respect, this might be one of those times where the less that's done to exacerbate matters, the sooner grief can run its course."

Noyes clearly thinks my suggestion presumptuous, but after he glances at my father, who also nods, the air seems to go out of him.

"Where's the district attorney?" he asks, glaring at the deputy.

As Wilbur moves toward the door, Shad reenters the courtroom, smoothing his lapels. "Judge, I apologize for that outburst. I advised Mr. Turner not to come to court, and he chose to ignore my counsel. The man is distraught over his mother's death, and as you know, in murder cases emotions can run very high."

"That's no excuse, Counselor."

"No, Your Honor. Now, as to the matter of bond—"

Judge Noyes holds up his right hand. "Before you start gabbling about special treatment, I'm going to set stringent conditions on this bond. Dr. Cage is not to leave the state. He's to continue practicing medicine, unless prevented by illness. He's not to contact any member of the victim's family. He may not consume alcohol or drugs, other than prescription drugs, and he cannot handle firearms." Noyes looks from Shad to my father. "Is that clear, Dr. Cage?"

"Yes, Your Honor."

"All right, then. I hope the powers that be get this mess straightened out before it goes any further." Noyes looks at me. "Are you prepared to post bond?"

My mother's voice comes from behind me, quavering with emotion. "We're prepared to write a check immediately, Judge."

"Good." He looks at the deputy. "Dr. Cage is not to be handcuffed again. And make sure that fellow outside doesn't bother him on his way to his car. You hear me, Wilbur? If that man assaults anybody, use your weapon."

Wilbur's face goes pale. "Yessir."

"Next case."

Shad says, "But Judge, the state—"

"Next case, goddamn it!"

OUT ON THE SIDEWALK, the sun has banished the cold morning wind and is now heating the concrete to a temperature more suited to spring than December. Thankfully, I've seen no sign of Lincoln Turner or his white pickup. Mom, Dad, and I stand before the Justice Court building with tangible awkwardness. Though we are linked by blood and by a palpable sense of relief, the reason for our being here has not been discussed by more than two of us at a time.

"Thank you, Penn," Mom says softly.

"I didn't do anything. Judge Noyes is obviously a fan of Dad's."

"But it was important for you to be here. Families have to stick together in times like this. Everyone needs to see that."

I'm anxious to discuss the logistics of getting Dad to a clinic to be swabbed for a DNA paternity test, but my mother has not left his side. Asking her to give us some time alone would not be taken well just now.

"I never knew you were taken prisoner in Korea," I say to Dad.

He shrugs as though this is nothing of consequence, his eyes seeming to contemplate something far away. "It was Walt and me. We escaped after a few days. We were lucky. Few did. I don't know how Charlie Noyes knows about it. Another vet must have told him. The upside is, I doubt the Adams County jail could be worse than North Korea in late November."

"Did Caitlin send that photographer?" Mom asks.

"What photographer?" I ask.

"The one at the back. He slipped in while Shad was talking to the judge. He took some notes, and then he shot pictures during that man's outburst."

I try to conceal my alarm. "I didn't see any flash."

"He wasn't using one."

A pro. I can see the headline now: DID WHITE DOCTOR MURDER BLACK NURSE IN MISSISSIPPI? That kind of story sells a lot of newspapers, even in the twenty-first century. "Shad must have invited a reporter down from Jackson."

"It's freezing out here," Mom says. "Let's get home, Tom. I have your medicine in my purse."

"I need to get to the office," he protests. "You heard the judge. I have to keep working."

"You can mind the judge later. Right now you're minding me. We just endured enough excitement for the next ten years. And I want the neighbors to see you coming right back home where you belong."

"All right," Dad says, a note of surrender in his voice. "Jack Kilgard sure stood up for me, didn't he?"

"What's he talking about?" I ask.

A warm smile lights my mother's face. "When the deputy hand-cuffed your father and started walking out to the car, Jack blocked Sher-iff Byrd's way and gave him a piece of his mind."

A transplanted Yankee, Jack Kilgard is a retired naval engineer who worked for fifteen years at the Triton Battery plant. He probably knew all the Double Eagles personally.

"All six foot five of him," Dad says. "Jack cussed up a blue streak, and I don't think I've heard him cuss in the forty years I've known him."

Mom shakes her head. "He told Billy Byrd he'd be out of office as soon as the next election came around."

Dad laughs. "He kept calling the jail the 'pokey.' I honestly think he scared Billy."

"Come on, Tom," Mom says, knowing that all this bravado counts for nothing in the sausage grinder of the legal system. "We won a battle, not the war. Let's get home."

As they walk away, Dad glances back at me, and I signal that he should call me as soon as he gets a chance.

He nods and continues on.

As I watch my mother's Camry pull away, one thing comes clear. By asking that my father be held without bail, Shad Johnson has obliterated any residual illusion that he means to cut me a break in this case. He is, as Caitlin predicted, going after my father with everything in his arse-nal. What I don't understand is *why,* when he knows I can end his legal career by e-mailing one photograph to the bar association.

"Penn?" says a voice from behind me.

I turn and find Shad looking up at me, a faint cloud of condensation coming from his mouth with each breath.

"I guess my bond request took you by surprise in there."

"You could say that."

He turns up his palms like a man dealing with events beyond his control. "I had to do it. This is the most racially charged case I've han-dled since taking office."

"That's why you want my father to sit in a cell for nine months? What the hell, Shad? You know there's zero risk of him trying to flee."

"I *don't* know that. But I did know Judge Noyes would deny my request. That's why I made it. I didn't think he would burn my ass like that while doing it, but that's not your problem. Penn . . . there are angles to this case you don't know about yet. Once you do, I think you'll understand why I have to pursue this without concern for my own career."

I turn away for a moment, trying to hold my anger in check. "You never do anything without considering your career. Nobody does, but you're worse than most. You invited a photographer down here for this appearance, didn't you?"

"Hell, no! Lincoln must have invited him to witness that little floor show. You think I wanted to be spanked like that in front of a reporter?"

"No." As I think about this, the truth driving Shad's strategy hits me in a revelatory flash. "In fact, you wouldn't have come to Justice Court if you had a choice."

"What do you mean?" he asks, but he knows.

"The grand jury's in session. You could have gone straight there for an indictment, even without an arrest. Then you could have got an arraignment in circuit court. But you didn't, because this is Judge Elder's month."

Shad's blank look is almost comical.

Normally, he would want Judge Joe Elder to be assigned my father's case. Elder is a fine judge, and impartial, so far as I know. But he is African-American, and Shad would much prefer him to the other circuit judge, sixty-three-year-old Eunice Franklin, a white female who is known to admire my father. But last month, Joe Elder announced that he planned to resign and move to Memphis, where his physician brother can treat him for his worsening liver disease. If Shad had gone to the grand jury today, Dad's murder case would have been tried by an unknown replacement for Elder, six months down the road. Given local demographics, that replacement judge is likely to be black, but that doesn't mean he or she won't be a fan of my father.

"What's your game?" I ask. "You trying to find out who Joe Elder's replacement will be?"

Anger fairly sparks from Shad's eyes.

"That's it, isn't it?" I decide. "Judge Elder has been at the Mayo Clinic for the past week. You're hoping to dodge Judge Franklin and get someone assigned that you can play like a fiddle."

"That sounds downright paranoid, Mayor."

I lean toward him and speak low. "Shad, I never thought in a million years that I'd use that photograph against you. I never thought you'd force me to. But you're going after my father. That's like going after my *child*. Do you hear me? I will not spare you."

"Don't act like I'm the one in the wrong here," he snaps, pulling back and looking up the street. "Your father is refusing to assist the coroner with a legal obligation, and you're trying to blackmail the district attorney. Any objective listener would brand you the bad guy here."

I know Shad too well to let this bother me.

"Penn," he continues gravely, "have you considered the possibility that your father might actually be guilty?"

Of course I have. "Of murder?"

"Yes."

"No."

The ping of my cell phone alerts me to a call. My first instinct is to ignore it until I'm clear of Shad, but then I remember that Kirk Boisseau is diving the Jericho Hole this morning. While Shad watches, I dig out my phone and check the screen. Sure enough, it reads KIRK B.

"Hey, buddy," I answer. "I'm in a meeting. What's the situation?"

"I found what you wanted."

My heart quickens, but I keep my face impassive. "What would that be?"

"Bones."

"The ones I mentioned?"

"I'm pretty sure."

Shad looks impatient. "That was fast," I say casually. "What makes you think so?"

"There was a car sitting on them. Some were handcuffed to a steering column. If they hadn't been, they'd have washed out into the river back in the flood of seventy-three."

My heart stutters, and I turn away from the DA in hopes of concealing my excitement. "Where are you now?"

"On Highway 84. We had to tear ass out of there. The landowner was riding a four-wheeler around the hole when I came out of the water the last time, and that hole ain't exactly a lake. It's more like a big pond."

Shad points at his wristwatch, a platinum Rolex.

"Thank you, Rose," I say with all sincerity. "I'll call you back in a few minutes."

Again I give Shad my full attention. "You and I need to arrange a DNA test," I remind him. "Immediately. I want this paternity bullshit settled before rumors hit the street."

"Okay by me," he says. "But the usual procedure isn't going to cut it. Lincoln Turner doesn't trust any local lab to send the right swab to New Orleans or Jackson. He doesn't even trust the cops down here. We're going to have to get an out-of-town lab to send a tech."

"Christ, Shad. Well . . . get on it. The sooner Turner knows the truth, the sooner sanity might prevail. Have you spoken to him about his possible parentage? And by that, I mean the gang rape."

The district attorney looks up and down Wall Street again. The stately old thoroughfare is empty, but pedestrians are moving along Main Street to his left. "Penn, you've been laboring under some misconceptions for a long time. It's not really my place to enlighten you—especially not out here—but maybe we need to clear the air. Why don't you come to my office a little later?"

"I'll stop by when I finish with some business. I need to get an old photo album out of my safe."

The DA shakes his head the way he might at a charity case. "Don't do anything without talking to me first. I'm telling you that for your sake."

As he strides off down Wall Street, I call Kirk back and promise to meet him in twenty minutes, in the parking lot of a music store owned by a friend of mine. Then I call Caitlin. I asked that she not come to the initial appearance this morning, so that no one present would feel they were playing to the media. She only agreed on the condition that I call her as soon as court adjourned.

"Did the judge grant bail?" she asks by way of greeting.

"Fifty grand. Dad's out."

"How much did Shad ask for?"

"He asked that bail be denied."

"I told you! The gloves are off. Shad thinks this is his golden chance to get back at you. You've got to go nuclear. You should have done it last night."

"I pretty much did. But he chose to ignore the threat." A tick of worry is biting at me. "I'm concerned that he's got the photo covered somehow."

"How?" she asks, incredulous. "How could he possibly protect himself from that picture? He could go to jail over that, right?"

"Probably not. But he'd definitely be disbarred."

"Are you sure the image is safe?"

"I've got the flash drive in my pocket now. But Shad would be crazy to proceed this way unless he's figured a way to cover his ass."

"Maybe he thinks he has equally damaging material on you. Or on Tom. Is that possible?"

A cold shiver goes through me. "Not on me. But something's not right about this. Shad just spoke very cryptically to me outside the courtroom, and he didn't sound like a man who's afraid. He asked whether I'd considered whether Dad was really guilty, then suggested I come up to his office later to discuss it."

"Then what are you doing talking to me?"

"You'd have had a stroke if I didn't call you first."

"Granted. Now get up there and find out what cards he's holding."

I would, but I have some bones to look at across the river. I start walking toward my parking space at City Hall. "I will. But I want to be sure I've thought through every angle before I confront Shad again."

I give her a quick summary of Lincoln's unexpected appearance and outburst, then tell her about the photographer.

"That bastard," she says. "Shad probably asked the *Clarion-Ledger* to send someone down."

"Shad claims Lincoln did it, and he may have. I'm afraid the media storm is about to hit."

"That's all right. I'm a good sailor. I'll come by City Hall after lunch. I love you."

The instant I hit END, a female voice calls out from behind me, "Mr. Mayor?"

I turn, ready to politely brush off a constituent, but I find myself looking at Jewel Washington, the county coroner. Jewel's office is two doors down from the Justice Court.

"I saw you out here talking to the DA," she says, beckoning me toward her office door.

"I don't have much time," I tell her.

"You have time for this."

Jewel is an African-American woman of about fifty-five, and a former surgical nurse. Just as Justice Court judges don't have to be lawyers in Mississippi, coroners don't have to be M.D.s. But in Jewel's case, her lack of a medical degree has proved no impediment to the efficient running of her office. A perfectionist in all things, she has an unerring sense of justice. Jewel also happens to love my father, having known him for many years.

"I heard Shad asked for no bail," she whispers, opening the door to her office suite, which leads into a small, empty reception area.

"News travels fast in this building."

"You know it, honey. Thank heaven Judge Noyes feels the same way about your daddy that I do."

"I appreciate that, Jewel. What's up?"

"Shad's getting on my last nerve about Miss Viola's autopsy. He wants me to try to rush the pathologist up in Jackson, and also to use my contacts at the state crime lab to rush the toxicology. He wants everything done yesterday."

"What does he most want to know?"

"You know. Cause of death. The *exact* cause."

"Do you know yet?"

Jewel raises her eyebrows and clucks her tongue once. "She didn't die from any morphine overdose."

"I didn't think so," I reply, recalling the recording on Henry Sexton's hard drive. "How sure are you?"

"Miss Viola had a PICC line in place for receiving meds, but she'd developed complications with it. Her sister said she'd been getting direct injections for pain the last couple of days. Whoever injected Viola with morphine pushed the needle right through her antecubital vein. Would have been easy to do, because that vein was shot. Some morphine probably got into her system, but most of it went into the soft tissue beneath the vein. No way that killed her. The home health nurse told me she had a huge tolerance built up."

"Then what killed her?"

"It's looking like an adrenaline overdose. But they're not positive yet."

I squeeze the coroner's wrist. "Thank you, Jewel."

"Wait, baby. That's not what I came to tell you."

Glancing through the small windows that frame her office door, I watch an ancient Chrysler trundle down Wall Street with a white-haired woman at the wheel. "I'm listening."

"Two things. One, I worked alongside Dr. Cage long enough to know he wouldn't push a needle through nobody's antecubital vein."

"Not even under stress?"

Jewel scowls. "He wouldn't have wasted time trying to hit that old thing. I've seen Doc find a deep vein to draw blood from a four-hundred-pound man. He's got the best touch I ever saw. Either somebody without medical training gave that injection, or Viola tried to inject herself, and she was so far gone that her nurse's training was useless."

"Good. What's the second thing?"

"News flash. Shad Johnson *hates* yo' ass, boy. You made him lose one election and beat him yourself in another. Add to that the Del Payton case, Dr. Elliott's trial, and that casino mess a couple months back . . . that's a big account coming due, from Shad's point of view. That Negro ain't playing. He means for Doc to die in jail."

"That's what Caitlin thinks, too."

Jewel's eyes gleam like the precious stones she was named after. "I always said that girl was smart." She takes hold of my hand and squeezes. "If you need help, call my son, not me. He's staying in town for a while. Your fiancée can find out his phone number."

Before I can respond, Jewel pulls open her door, pushes me outside, and shuts it again. The lock turns behind me.

After a stunned couple of seconds, I hear Kirk Boisseau's excited voice in my head: *Bones . . . There was a car sitting on them.*

After a paranoid glance at the sheriff's department, I start running for my car.

CHAPTER 34

KIRK BOISSEAU DRIVES a scarred Nissan Titan with kayak racks mounted over its bed and roof. His truck is parked in the side lot of Easterling's Music Company, a family-owned music store that's surely connected in spirit to Albert Norris's long-vanished emporium. The owner, a man nearly my father's age, is a gifted musician and a country philosopher in the mold of Will Rogers. His store sits right beside Carter Street, the busy main thoroughfare of Vidalia, Louisiana, and thus makes a convenient but unobtrusive place to pick up the bones Kirk found in the Jericho Hole.

When I pull my Audi to the far side of the Titan, I find Henry Sexton standing beside the truck's passenger window, where Kirk's girlfriend, Nancy something, is sitting. Henry's Explorer must be parked behind the store. The reporter's face is bright with excitement, but Nancy's is lined with concern.

By the time I climb out of my car, Kirk has gotten out and come around to my side of the truck. The ex-marine's face shines like that of a boy who just dug up a dinosaur bone. An inch taller than I, Kirk has a waist no bigger than a woman's and the shoulders of a mountain gorilla, the result of good genes and kayaking miles every day on the Mississippi River.

"Where's the fossil?" I ask.

He grins and reaches through the passenger window, down between Nancy's legs, then brings up a foot-long object wrapped in wet newspaper. When he unwraps the soaked paper, I see a dark brown cylinder with a rounded head at one end. I've visited the burial sites of many murder victims, and in seconds my brain categorizes this artifact as the distal end of a femur.

"Human for sure?"

"It's no chimpanzee," Kirk says.

If the bone is in fact a human femur, then I'm looking at what must be the lower three-quarters of it. Below where the hip should be—the trochanter and other protuberances—the bone appears to have been crushed.

"The water mineralized this?" I ask.

"Obviously!" Henry Sexton exults, shivering with excitement. "Do you realize what this means?"

"Is this all you brought up?" I ask, trying to stay focused.

Kirk reaches into the truck and brings up more wet newspaper. "Three more in here. I think the whole skeleton is down in the Jericho Hole, but it's got a car sitting on it."

"What make of car?" Henry asks sharply.

Kirk purses his lips. "I'm not sure. I was focusing on the bones. It was a convertible, I know that."

Henry's eyes bug halfway out of his head. "Luther Davis drove a 1957 Pontiac Bonneville convertible!"

"Did it look like a Pontiac?" I ask.

Kirk snorts in derision. "It looked like a big hunk of rust lying upside down."

"Were the bones just loose on the bottom?" asks Henry.

"Hell, no. The river would have scoured any loose bones out long ago. The only reason I found these is because they were in the car. The femur was fastened to the steering column with barbed wire. I had to dig my hand up from under to reach it."

"Oh, man," Henry breathes. "Oh, shit. After all this time."

"Check this out," says Kirk, his eyes flashing. From the new bundle of paper he brings out another brown piece of bone. This one is long and thin, with a rusted piece of barbed wire still embedded in it.

A rush of adrenaline flushes through me.

"Jesus Lord," Henry breathes. "Morehouse was telling the truth. That's Luther Davis."

"Maybe," I say with caution born from experience. "Boys, we are in dire need of expert help."

Henry gazes reverently at the find as though at a perfect new specimen of *Australopithecus*. "Were there enough bones under that car to be two people?"

"You'll have to move it to find out. But you guys haven't seen the showstopper yet." He removes what looks like a fossilized vertebra from the newspaper. "This was buried under a couple of inches of mud. Looks like part of a backbone to me."

"What's special about it?" Henry asks.

Kirk rolls the bone over in his fingers and points to a small, dark protrusion with his other hand. "See this?"

Henry squints at the bone like an orthopedic intern. What is it?"

"A bullet."

The reporter's hand flies to his mouth.

"Can you tell what caliber it is?" I ask.

"No, but it's small."

"Nine millimeter?"

Kirk scrapes the encrusted projectile with a fingernail. "Closer to seven, I'd say. Hard to tell with the mineralization. But the owner of this vertebra was definitely shot in the spine."

While Henry looks stricken, Kirk says, "You want me to go back down there and try to bring up some more? With that landowner on the lookout, I'd have to make a night dive."

"No!" his girlfriend snaps from the passenger window. "You heard Penn. It's time to bring in the law."

"I didn't say that exactly," I point out. "But we probably don't have any choice."

Henry appears torn. "I don't like the idea of turning this over to Sheriff Walker Dennis."

"I know, but this parish is his jurisdiction, first and foremost. We ought to give Walker a shot at doing the right thing."

"Even if Sheriff Dennis is honest, I worry about leaks in his department. He's got some deputies with family connections I don't like. I know an expert down at LSU that even the FBI consults in murder cases. They call her the Bone Lady. Nobody in the world could tell us more about these bones than she could, and we wouldn't have to show the sheriff anything until we were sure."

Henry's past experiences with law enforcement have obviously left him cynical. "Let's talk about the FBI for a second. Last night you said you needed me to run interference for you. What's your relationship with the Bureau?"

Henry cocks his head like a man who can't make up his mind. "For a long time they ignored me. Then they started warning me about talking to witnesses in what they called 'open' cases. I laugh at that now. If the public ever finds out how the Bureau dragged its feet on those murders, there'll be hell to pay. Now, of course, field agents call me every week. They basically want to use me as a de facto investigator."

"Who's your main contact with them?"

"I've dealt with a dozen different agents. The FBI has jurisdictional problems within its own agency. Different field offices or resident agencies handled the various original cases, so the records are spread out, and each agent only has a few pieces of the puzzle. They've got a cold case squad, but not even those people have access to all the data. It's ridiculous."

"Do you trust any of them?"

"There is one guy I like," Henry concedes. "He works out of the New Orleans field office now, but he's no suit. He's a Vietnam vet named John Kaiser. That's who I called about Morehouse last night."

The agent's name tweaks something in my memory.

"Kaiser's not officially responsible for any of these cases, but he's got a personal interest. He trained under some of the agents who originally worked the murders, and he'd like to solve them, if he can. He's helped get me in touch with old-timers when I needed to. If we're duty bound to share information with somebody official, I'd prefer to deal with Kaiser."

"I'm glad you're open to somebody in the Bureau, but we've got to at least give Walker Dennis a chance."

"What if the bones disappear? More than bones disappeared out of that office in the old days."

Henry is referring to several ice chests that reportedly held the decomposing flesh of two civil rights murder victims in 1965. Like a lot of other evidence from that era, those coolers vanished without trace.

"We'll only show him one," I promise. "Remember, Walker was probably in kindergarten during the bad old days."

Kirk Boisseau's eyes have been moving back and forth between us like those of a grunt watching two officers argue strategy. "Don't worry, Henry," he says, "there's a lot more bones where those came from."

"After you talk to the sheriff," Nancy interjects, "where will *we* stand? Kirk and me? We took these bones off private property."

"If these bones are what we think they are," I tell her, "that won't matter. You might be asked some questions to establish exactly where you found them, but no one's going to press trespassing charges. They'll be too busy trying to keep out of trouble themselves."

"What if they're *not* what you think?"

"Then your names will never come up."

Nancy breathes a little easier after this, but her jaw remains set.

Henry tugs anxiously at his mustache. He's clearly afraid to let these bones out of his personal custody, and after all the work he's done on these cases, I can hardly blame him.

"Sheriff's an elected position," Kirk reminds us. "Walker Dennis won't want any part of this tar baby."

"I don't want you to say a word to him about my sources," Henry says.

"No chance," I promise. "And Kirk is probably right. Walker will want to punt this to the feds to protect his own ass. But at least we'll know where we stand with him."

Henry slaps the side of Kirk's truck. "Screw it. It's been thirty-seven years since those boys disappeared. Let's find out what the sheriff's made of."

I take the carefully wrapped bones from Kirk and give him sober thanks, but the marine just laughs and shakes his head. "Beats the shit out of working for a living."

Nancy clearly has a different opinion.

Twenty seconds later, the parking lot is empty again.

THE CONCORDIA PARISH SHERIFF'S Office occupies the lower floor of the parish courthouse, an incongruously modern building constructed in the 1970s. Partially faced with brown reflective windows tilted back at an angle, the stucco building looks onto the junky sprawl that lines Highway 84 from Vidalia to Ferriday. The presence of the sheriff's department is evidenced by clusters of white cruisers to the left of the courthouse, augmented by rescue boats and a mobile command post parked under metal shelters at the rear.

I called Sheriff Dennis as soon as Henry and I pulled out of the music store parking lot, and he agreed to meet us with the understanding that I would explain why we needed a deputy to escort us out of Ferriday last night. When we arrive at the basement motor pool, we find a brown-uniformed deputy waiting to lead us up to the sheriff's office.

After walking a gauntlet of good old boys in uniform, we find Walker Dennis seated behind his desk, watching CNN on a TV mounted in an upper corner of the room, as in a hospital. Like Sheriff Billy Byrd, Walker wears a Stetson, but he's younger than Byrd (maybe forty-seven) and in slightly better shape. In my youth, I played a few baseball games against Vidalia teams that starred Walker Dennis, but unlike me, he went on to play college ball. Walker's default expression is a smile of private amusement, as though he's in possession of information others are not. As Henry and I take the seats he offers us, I note the usual artifacts of political office around the room: framed photos with local dignitaries and sports stars, memorabilia from notable cases, and citations from various civic and professional groups.

I know nothing of Sheriff Dennis's politics, but no sheriff in North Louisiana gets elected for being liberal. This is hard-shell Baptist country, as red as Mississippi when it comes to political litmus tests. On the other hand, 40 percent of this parish is black, and the city of Ferriday has a much higher black-white ratio than that. Walker couldn't do his job if he didn't know how to walk the tightrope between the races.

Before he speaks, the sheriff leans back in his chair and gives us an expansive smile, distorted by the dip of snuff packed beneath his lower lip. "I'm mighty honored to have the mayor of Natchez over here," he says, obviously meaning to begin with small talk, the Vaseline of political interaction in the South. "Must be important business."

"It is," I say flatly.

The sheriff's smile vanishes like smoke. "Let's hear it, Penn."

I lay the wet newspaper on his desk and open it to reveal the dark bone with rusted barbed wire set in it.

"What's this?" Dennis asks, leaning over his desk.

"Looks like a piece of ulna to me."

"A what?"

"An arm bone."

The sheriff clears his throat. "Who'd it belong to?"

"Luther Davis, probably," Henry says.

The sheriff's cheeks lose three shades of color.

"Luther was a big man," Henry says, "much bigger than Jimmy Revels. We also found a leg bone, and it's big, even for a femur. These bones were found underneath a convertible, which is what Luther Davis drove before he disappeared. Those bones almost certainly belong to Luther Davis."

A sheen of sweat has formed on the sheriff's scalp and forehead. "And where is this convertible?"

"At the bottom of the Jericho Hole," Henry says with a touch of resentment. I'm guessing he's asked Walker Dennis to investigate that body of water before. "We didn't even have to look hard."

"Sweet Jesus," Dennis almost moans. "Did you have a federal warrant or something?"

I shake my head. "We didn't find this bone, Walker. A local scuba diver did. A recreational diver. Under a rusted convertible, as Henry said."

Walker Dennis closes his eyes and shakes his head. "That's not a bone. That's a stick of dynamite. And it could blow us all to hell." He gives me a sharp look. "Especially you and me."

"Well, we're not putting it back under the water. And there are a lot more where this came from. We've even got one with a bullet embedded in it. This is a very important find, Sheriff. A major discovery, both historically and legally."

Dennis takes off his hat and rubs his thinning hair. "Jesus H. Christ, Penn. What do you propose I do with this?"

"Drain the Jericho Hole," Henry says, as though proposing that the sheriff empty a horse trough with a sump pump.

"*Drain* the . . . ? Shit, you're crazy."

"It's probably going to have to be done," I tell him. "Unless you bring an expert team of divers in here, and heavy salvage equipment. The only question is, will it be done under a state warrant or a federal one?"

Sheriff Dennis lifts an Ole Miss coffee mug off the desk and spits tobacco juice into it. "I like spitting on the Rebels," he says distractedly.

"I have a feeling I know which warrant it's going to be," Henry says. "Let's go, Penn."

"Damn it, Henry," the sheriff says wearily. "Take it easy. You boys sure know how to screw up a pretty day."

"We just wanted to give you the chance to take the lead on the investigation," I tell him. "If you wanted to."

Walker stares at the bone another few seconds, then looks up with rueful eyes. "I sure appreciate it, Mayor. But I wouldn't want to take all the credit for something like this. Besides, my office isn't equipped to handle it. The logistics alone are overwhelming. And then the forensic side . . . No, I think the FBI is the proper outfit for this case. This is right up their alley. I'll be glad to lend all the support they ask for, but they definitely ought to be the lead agency on this."

In any other circumstances, this answer would be stunning. For a local sheriff to voluntarily cede jurisdiction to "the feds" is almost unprecedented. But the subtext here is plain: *civil rights murder.* In a parish with these demographics, Sheriff Dennis's decision is the prudent one Kirk Boisseau predicted.

I give him a knowing smile. "I hear you, Walker. But there's one other thing I'd like to discuss with you. Henry already knows about it, so consider this a private conversation. This problem is a lot more suited to your . . . outfit."

Dennis looks downright afraid now. "What's that?"

"You've got a serious meth problem in this parish. Not just users, but meth labs. Major labs, and suppliers, too."

Sheriff Dennis stares warily back at me, and even Henry looks puzzled by my digression. "What's the local meth trade got to do with these bones?"

"More than you might think."

After glancing at his office door as if to make sure it's completely shut, Walker speaks softly. "What the hell's going on here, Penn? You walk in my office out of the blue and start talking about *our* meth problem? You think you don't have crystal meth over in Natchez?"

"Of course we do. I'm not interested in the meth. I'm interested in the men who make and sell it."

Walker's eyes narrow, then go wide with comprehension. "And what exactly do you want me to do?"

"Clamp down on every meth dealer in the parish. I mean hit them hard. Shut down the supply for at least a month, maybe two."

"To what end?"

"To what *end*?" Henry echoes, almost shrilly. "How about enforcing the law of the land? Is there some reason you don't want to arrest local meth dealers?"

A pained expression comes into the sheriff's face. "Henry, we're off the fuckin' record here."

I hold up my hand to restrain the reporter. "I want you to hit the Knoxes," I say evenly. "I want them to feel some heat."

Dennis licks his lips, but he gives me no clue to his inner reaction. "I've actually been working up to a big bust for a while."

Henry snorts, but the sheriff ignores him.

"That's how we do it over here," Walker goes on, "like it or not. We build up tips from our informants, then hit a big load of dealers all at once."

"Is Billy Knox on your hit list?"

Sheriff Dennis shifts his weight in his chair. He looks even less comfortable than he did when we were discussing the bones. "Penn, I've heard all kinds of rumors about Billy over the years, but so far as I can tell, he's a legitimate businessman. And a damn successful one."

"Too successful," Henry mutters.

The sheriff expels a long rush of air, like a deflating balloon. "How exactly do you define that, Henry? Making money ain't a crime yet, is it? If you boys have some hard information, I'll be happy to follow up on it."

"We have information," I tell him, "but not the kind you need. I'll just say this: if you hit the meth dealers in this parish hard enough, Billy Knox is going to feel it."

The sheriff squints at me for several seconds, then gestures at the bone on his desk. "You still haven't told me how that connects to this. How 'bout you tell me why you and Jimmy Olsen here needed an escort home last night? What were you afraid of?"

I look at Henry, but the reporter shakes his head.

"So that's how it is," says the sheriff. "Then I guess neither of you can tell me why the FBI showed up at the hospital morgue and took possession of Glenn Morehouse's body this morning?"

Henry and I look at each other in shock.

"Yep," says Dennis. "They transported that corpse to the Belle Chasse Naval Air Station, on Lake Pontchartrain. Which is strange, because last time I checked, murder was a state crime."

Henry and I solve this mystery simultaneously: his call to Special Agent John Kaiser must have produced this result.

"You want to know what we were afraid of last night?" I ask softly.
Dennis nods.

"The Double Eagle group. Snake Knox and Sonny Thornfield, for
example."

"And Forrest Knox," Henry adds.

Dennis sits up straight, both hands held in front of him. "Hold it
right there. Listen to me, men. Forrest Knox is the director of the Criminal Investigations Bureau of the state police. If you've got a problem
with him, you need to take it up with him—not a lowly sheriff in a poor
parish like this one. I've been in this job exactly five and a half weeks.
I've spent day and night trying to put this department back together
after the explosion that Penn here caused when he busted that casino
boat, or gambling syndicate, or whatever it was. And that's almost more
than I can handle."

Before Henry can say anything, I ask, "Have you heard that my
father's been charged with murder?"

The sheriff gives me a sober nod.

"He's being framed, Walker."

"That, I believe."

"The victim was the sister of Jimmy Revels, who died with Luther
Davis. Jimmy's bones may be down under that convertible with Luther's,
not five miles from here. Henry's not going to give up his sources, but
I'll tell you this: the Double Eagles killed Revels and Davis, and they
killed Viola Turner, too. My father's not going to jail for those bastards.
I'm going to squeeze until one of them pops and gives up Viola's killer."

I stand and lift the bone fragment from the desk. "If you won't help
me, I'll go to the DEA and the FBI. But I'd prefer to work with you. I told
Henry you're a stand-up guy, and I still believe that. This is your chance
to make a difference, Walker. To show people they were right to put
you in this job. And all you have to do is enforce the law."

Breathing hard, I sense more than see Henry nodding at my side.

Sheriff Dennis looks flustered by my passion. Leaning toward him,
I add, "This is personal, Walker. I'm going to pull every string I can
reach on this case. And I know some people."

The sheriff ducks his head and spits into the Ole Miss cup again. "I
know you do, buddy. And I've got no problem rousting out every meth
cooker in this parish at the crack of dawn, if that's what you want. But

if you're after Billy Knox, jailing the local fuckups won't hurt him none. Billy's way too slick for that."

"I thought you said he was a legitimate businessman," Henry comments.

Dennis cuts his eyes at Henry; he's losing his patience with the *Beacon*'s intrepid reporter. "I said I can't *prove* different. But legit or not, Billy's made a shitload of money in about five different businesses while everybody else has been watching their bank accounts shrink to nothing."

"What does that tell you?" Henry asks.

"One, he's smart. Why don't you call the IRS on him, Henry?"

"Some people," Henry says in a quavering voice, "think Billy Knox isn't the smart one in that family. They think a certain cousin of his might be running interference for him in this parish."

Sheriff Dennis's face goes slack for a couple of seconds, like a man who can't believe you just called his wife a slut.

"*Nathan Bedford Forrest Knox,*" Henry says defiantly.

Dennis looks at me to see whether I share Henry's apparent lunacy. Then he rises, his face bright pink, and splays his big hands on his desk.

"Nothing personal," Henry says, far too late.

"*Nothing personal?*" Dennis shakes his head as though he can't decide whether to kick us out of his office or throw us into a cell. "Henry, you're saying I'm either a crook or a fool, and I don't care for either choice. So, why don't you *get the fuck out of my office?*"

"All right," I say, pulling the reporter up out of his chair. "Henry should have phrased that better, Walker. He didn't mean it the way it sounded."

"The hell he didn't!" Dennis's face has gone scarlet, and a thick vein bulges in his forehead. He used to look exactly this way when he charged aggressive pitchers from the plate. "For your information, Forrest Knox *hates* his cousin, and most of the rest of his family. He's had to fight that Klan history all his life. The only time I've ever seen *Lieutenant Colonel* Knox in Billy's presence was at a family funeral, and they didn't even shake hands!"

Every deputy outside this office must have heard the sheriff's rant. *And maybe he meant for them to.* Henry starts to say something, but I silence him with a shake of my head.

"Sorry we bothered you, Walker. At least this way you won't be surprised when the FBI comes into your parish to check out these bones."

Sheriff Dennis's eyes burn into Henry's back as I hustle the reporter out the door. "Hold on, Penn."

I stop and turn back.

"Shut the door."

After I do, he grimaces again, then looks up with man-to-man intimacy. "Are you sure you want to stir up all this old trouble? In my experience, the only thing that happens when you do that is everybody gets covered in shit."

"Maybe. But in my experience, you usually have to dig through a lot of shit to find the truth. Whether it's old shit or new makes no difference to me."

Walker studies me for a few silent seconds. "And you realize who you're screwing with?"

My breath stops in my throat. "They've left me no choice, Walker. From what I can see, the Knoxes killed Viola, and they want my old man to pay for it. I'm not going to let that happen. Anybody gets in my way, it's their lookout."

Dennis nods slowly. "All right, then. Good luck to you, brother. I'll think on what you've told me."

"Don't take too long." I open his door. "Have a nice day, though."

"Fat chance."

"I went to Ole Miss, by the way."

Dennis spits into his cup again. "I know."

STANDING BETWEEN OUR VEHICLES outside the sheriff's department, Henry gives me a look of contrition. "Guess I didn't help much, huh?"

"It didn't go too badly."

"What did he say after I left?"

"Walker knows what's going on in this parish."

Henry gives me a suspicious look. "Did he admit that?"

"As much as he could, yes. He tried to warn me how dangerous this could be."

"It would be a lot less dangerous if people like him did their jobs. We *gave* him the damn bones, and he wouldn't lift a finger to investigate them!"

"Not even the FBI has done its job in these cases, Henry. Walker's a rookie sheriff. Give him a few hours to absorb this. He may come through yet."

"I'm not waiting around for that."

"No, you're not. You're going to call John Kaiser and tell him about the bones."

After an initial moment of shock, Henry grabs my forearm, his eyes bright with excitement. "Could you believe what Dennis said about the Bureau taking Morehouse's body? That has to be Kaiser behind that, right?"

"Must be. I don't know how Kaiser swung that, but he's clearly jumping on this case in a big way. Let's see how fast he moves on the bones."

The reporter nods thoughtfully. "Can I mention your name when I call him?"

"You can tell him I'm involved, but for now you should stay point man with the Bureau. I'll check out Kaiser as soon as I can."

Anxiety clouds Henry's eyes again. "What was all that about the meth stuff? Asking Dennis to bust the Knoxes? I wasn't expecting that."

"Just a test. I wanted to see how much pushback I'd get."

"And?"

"Don't know yet. Walker's one of those country boys who's hard to read."

Henry looks like he's about to crawl out of skin from excitement. "I hate to ask, but did you speak to your father last night? About the photo with Brody Royal, all that?"

"I did, but there were no great revelations. Dr. Robb shot that photo on a deep-sea fishing trip off Biloxi that lasted five hours. My father hated Royal. He did overhear some drunk talk about the JFK assassination, but let's save that for another time. I keep thinking about what you said about Pooky Wilson's friend, the one you call 'Huggy Bear.' You said he could put Brody Royal away for the murder of Albert Norris. Why has it been so hard to identify him?"

Henry's eyes cloud again. "Albert opened his store in 1949. When he died, it had been open fifteen years. During that time, he employed or trained between forty and fifty young men. And that doesn't count the musicians who hung out there for extended periods. I've busted my ass to track them all down, and I've been amazed to learn how many of them are dead. But I still haven't managed to find him."

"But didn't you say he visited the deathbed of Wilson's mother? Surely some family member remembers him?"

"Mrs. Wilson didn't have much family. One home health nurse remembered a black man in his sixties who came for a short visit, but she didn't hear his name, and he wasn't there for long. He was wearing a black baseball cap. I'm thinking that might be my man."

"Well, keep looking. The sooner we can apply pressure to Royal and the Eagles, the sooner we can make one of them give up Viola's killer."

Henry says nothing, but I can read his response in his eyes: *Is that our main priority here?*

Whatever Henry may think, it's certainly my priority. "Keep your eyes open. Walker Dennis is no coward. If he's scared, there's a reason for it."

"You, too."

Henry offers me his hand. I shake it, then climb into my Audi and head for the Natchez bridge. As I arc over the river, my cell phone pings, and I find a text message from Rose, my secretary, whom I asked to find out all she could about Judge Joseph Elder's health and job situation. The LCD reads:

> *Judge Elder will be back at work next Monday. Still planning to resign and move to Memphis so far as I can find out. No word on his replacement. Putting out feelers everywhere I can—on the DL, of course. Good luck.*

"Next Monday," I say aloud, as pain hits high in my stomach. If Shad decides to take my father's case before the grand jury and have his case placed on Judge Elder's docket, then Elder could arraign Dad and revoke his bail, even if he won't be the judge who actually tries his case down the road. And as I realized yesterday, for my father, jail almost certainly equals death. Whether Shad follows this course is a purely political decision, and I haven't enough information to predict what he might do. But the relief I felt this morning at hearing Judge Noyes's low bail has vanished. Depending on Judge Elder's mood and philosophy, Shad could take my father's freedom at any time.

CHAPTER 35

LIEUTENANT COLONEL NATHAN Bedford Forrest Knox sat at his desk in Louisiana State Police headquarters in Baton Rouge, writing an assessment of the need to maintain a permanent state police presence in the city of New Orleans. State police SWAT teams had deployed there the first day after the storm and operated 24/7 for eight weeks before returning to normal duties. No one had doubted the need then. In the immediate aftermath of Katrina, three hundred New Orleans Police Department officers had deserted their duties, and the Crescent City had become a free-fire zone in which criminals roamed at will, homing in on the drone of generators to rob citizens struggling to survive amid the floodwaters. So far as the public knew, such crimes had been checked by Lieutenant General Russel Honoré, the so-called Ragin' Cajun, an appellation that made Forrest laugh. Honoré was a Creole by birth, not a Cajun.

While the army had played an important role post Katrina, the tide of anarchy loosed during those first seventy-two hours of the flood had been stemmed by snipers operating under wartime rules of engagement. That story could never be told, of course. Rumors had leaked out, as they always did. Police officers on loan from other states had reported encountering significant numbers of corpses with unexplained gunshot wounds (wounds that a Navy SEAL sniper had described as "180 grains of due process")—but the biblical scale of the destruction had made it easy to write off most of those deaths with only superficial inquiries. Where the public was concerned, Forrest Knox didn't mind anonymity; it was the foundation of his strength. But a small cadre of powerful men knew that it was officers like him who'd stepped up to provide the last line of defense against chaos, and they were working hard to show their gratitude by having him moved into his boss's job: superintendent of state police.

At issue now was the future of the city. Unlike most of America,

Forrest's political patrons saw Hurricane Katrina not as a natural disaster but as divine intervention. In less than a week, the apocalyptic storm had purged New Orleans of the human filth that had infected and almost killed it. The flooding caused by levee breaches had triggered the largest forced resettlement of a minority population in America since the surviving Indians were moved onto reservations. The benefits of this mass exodus were plain to see: prior to the hurricane, New Orleans had perennially posted the highest murder rate in the country, as well as the lowest standard of living of any major American city; after three hundred thousand residents fled (among them nearly all the city's poor blacks), the city's homicide epidemic disappeared along with them. New Orleans's murder rate was now lower than it had been in decades. But no one was under any illusions. If those poor blacks were allowed to return to the once-teeming hellholes of the St. Thomas, St. Bernard, Desire, Florida, Calliope, Lafitte, Melpomene, and Iberville housing projects, the blight of violent crime would return with them.

Forrest's patrons meant to make sure that this did not happen.

Already they were pushing hard to have the housing projects demolished to make way for "mixed-income" developments, which would profoundly alter the demographic landscape of the city, skewing it whiter and more affluent. Any black tenants who did return to the city would be forced to find housing on the periphery, far from tourists and the new breed of citizen. This transformation wasn't easy. Since the 1940s-vintage projects had been built in the brick barracks style, they were some of the few buildings to survive Katrina with only minor damage. But politics could work miracles: many of the public housing developments had been chained against returning residents, and the wheels were already in motion to condemn most of them.

The economic incentive was enormous. The Iberville housing project alone—which stood on priceless land between the French Quarter and Tremé—would over time be worth hundreds of millions to the right developers. And the old housing authority projects weren't the only targets. Six weeks ago, Governor Blanco had lifted the ban on evictions, and landlords lost no time using "unpaid rent" as an excuse to kick out "undesirable" tenants who had fled the city for safer ground. With New Orleans's poorest residents relocated to other cities, black leaders had lost the heart of their constituencies. With luck, regulations would soon be passed that would focus rebuilding efforts on those areas that fell in line with the vision shared by those who would own the future. Areas like the Lower Ninth Ward would initially be left to rot, while those with immediate "gentrification" potential would be exploited by eager developers. Eventually the dead zones would be bulldozed flat and the wreckage hauled away. Sparkling new homes would rise from the ruins, homes that attracted the kind of people who knew how to work and live in harmony with each other.

But for this vision to be made real, America would have to buy into the notion that New Orleans was safe—and open for business. The NOPD was about the last agency on earth capable of accomplishing that objective. Historically, the city had always accepted a certain amount of police corruption (the French Quarter's reputation as a den of iniquity being one of its main attractions), but since the 1970s the city had descended ever farther and faster down a slope from whence there seemed no return. By 1993 New Orleans led the nation in homicides, and its police force had become so ineffectual that the Justice Department considered federalizing it. Two years later, after four NOPD officers were charged with murder, a black female cop had executed her former partner and two Vietnamese children during an armed robbery. As the sickening details of that crime emerged, Louisianans began to realize that this sordid affair was only the tip of a submerged volcano. Yet it would be another ten years before Katrina swept in like the wrath of God and accomplished what mortal men could not.

Forrest looked back at those years as literally the antediluvian period of the city. A new future was coming, one very different from that envisioned by the black and mixed-race "leaders" who'd controlled the city's political machine Before the Deluge. He would put none of this in his report, of course. He would cite studies by conservative think tanks and bleeding-heart liberal groups alike, all of whom agreed that the city was in danger of dying. The stinger would come in the tail of his assessment, where he would quote U.S. Drug Enforcement Administration officers who'd reported that young black thugs were already returning to their old haunts, trying to stake out new turf before their rivals in the drug trade could get back to the city. You didn't have to lay it on very thick for that kind of story to scare the living hell out of white corporate types.

Forrest's secure cell phone vibrated in his pocket. He usually didn't answer it while at headquarters, but with the problems back in his home parish, he felt he needed to. Sure enough, the code name on the LCD screen told him the call was from an informant in the Concordia Parish Sheriff's Office.

"What you got?" Forrest said by way of an answer.

"Mayor Penn Cage and Henry Sexton came to Walker's office a little while ago. They had a bone with them. They said it came out of the Jericho Hole."

Forrest felt a seismic shift, as though the floor had rumbled beneath his feet. "What was the result of their visit?"

"They got their nose bumped. I heard Sheriff Dennis yelling at them from my desk. They looked unhappy when they left, but they were talking about the FBI."

"I see." Forrest heard footsteps approaching his door. By the sound of them, he was about to receive a visit from the only man in the building who outranked him. "I'll have to call you back."

He clicked END and barely got the phone back in his pocket before Colonel Griffith Mackiever opened the door and took a seat in the chair opposite Forrest's desk. Five foot ten, with iron-gray hair, Colonel Mackiever had the grip of a lumberjack. A former Texas Ranger, he seemed to believe he knew everything there was to know about law enforcement, and for the time being, Forrest had to act as though he agreed.

"How you coming on that report?" Mackiever asked.

"It's slow going. But I'm making some headway."

"I'd just as soon you slow it down some more."

"What do you mean?"

Mackiever raised one eyebrow. "We've got no business trying to act as a municipal police force within New Orleans. It's still a mess down there, but we aren't the answer."

"Isn't that exactly why they need us in there, sir? We all know they've been fudging their crime stats for twenty years; it's only a matter of time before the drug gangs move back in. There's no way the NOPD is going to be able to handle them."

Mackiever watched Forrest closely as he spoke. "Ninety-eight percent of the criminals who left are still gone," he said, "and with the projects locked down, they haven't got much to come back to."

"They'll be back, sir. Most of them went to Houston, and the Texas justice system is a whole new reality for them. They screw up over there, they get serious prison time. No . . . they're coming back."

"Well . . . that's a matter to be worked out between the NOPD, the FBI, the DEA, the BATF, and the district attorney's office. We cover the state, not New Orleans. I want your assessment to make the case for us staying *out* of there, and I'm going to review it as soon as you're finished."

"Sir, I wonder if your chief of staff wouldn't be better suited to write this report."

Mackiever had a strange expression where he scowled with the lower half of his face while his eyes told you he was just playing with you. He used that expression now. "I know your feelings, Knox. And I wouldn't have chosen you for this, if it was up to me. But the governor asked specifically for your opinion, as chief of Criminal Investigations, so I'm going to give it to her."

"*My* opinion?" Forrest echoed, feigning ignorance.

"That's right. Some heavy hitters in this state seem to think you might make a good replacement for me after I retire. But until that day, I'll treat you as any superior officer would."

"Which means?"

"When I want your opinion, I give it to you."

The colonel got to his feet and walked out, leaving the door open behind him.

"Bastard," Forrest muttered. He got up and closed the door, then returned to his desk and lit a Marlboro in violation of regulations.

In truth, Mackiever was right. The drug gangs hadn't yet started to return, and if Forrest had his way, they never would. He'd already taken advantage of the storm to eliminate a few dangerous witnesses and business competitors. He'd been well paid for some of those actions, while others he'd carried out to settle personal scores. His cousin Billy's meth operation, for example, would run unchallenged for at least a year in the southern half of the state. But Forrest had far bigger plans, and if his patrons wanted state troopers patrolling the streets of New Orleans, he'd do his best to give them that.

Thinking of Billy brought the informant's phone call back into his mind. Taking out his secure cell phone, Forrest called Alphonse Ozan.

"Talk to me, boss," the Redbone said.

Ozan's voice brought back a memory of last night: pulling away from Cherie Delaune's house trailer, after giving the Redbone thirty minutes alone with her. "How'd it go?" Forrest had asked. "You ruin her?" Ozan had laughed and said, "Oh, yeah, boss. Next time Ricky try to hit that, he gon' fall in."

Forrest forced the lurid scene out of his mind. "I want you to find out everything there is to know about the mayor of Natchez, Mississippi. Especially people with grudges against him. A former prosecutor always has a shitload of enemies rotting in prison. You need to check Texas, mainly."

"No problem," Ozan said, sounding enthusiastic. "I bet Huntsville is full of guys who'd like to carve his liver for him."

"If we're lucky, some of his old pals have wound up in Angola in the past few years."

Ozan laughed. "True dat, boss."

"Call Snake, too. He's gonna hear that Henry Sexton and Cage went to see Sheriff Dennis with some bone they pulled out of the Jericho Hole, and I don't want him to panic. Reiterate what I said last night: nobody touches Henry Sexton unless I give the word. Got it?"

"Got it."

"Find out about Cage's fiancée, too. The newspaper publisher."

"Lookin' forward to it, boss. She's a hot one, that girl. I seen pictures."

Forrest ended the call there, but Ozan's predatory laughter echoed in his ears for a long time.

CHAPTER 36

"I CAN'T BELIEVE you kept this from me!" Caitlin snaps, her eyes flashing with anger. "What else have you held back?"

She's talking about Glenn Morehouse and his interview with Henry Sexton. There's nothing quite like confronting an angry and intelligent woman who also happens to be your lover.

"You obviously figured out Morehouse was a Double Eagle on your own," I point out. "I didn't need to tell you."

"But the *time* I lost."

"Are you in a race?"

"Oh, come on. That's all journalism is, and with Shad or Lincoln tipping out-of-town papers, this story's going to break fast."

"You want to take over Henry's story, don't you? And you swore to me that you wouldn't."

Caitlin is one of those rare people who never seem to blink, and now she focuses on me with the eerie intensity of a serpent watching a bird it intends to devour. "I didn't know how big this thing was when I made that promise. I want to know what else hasn't been made public."

I shouldn't answer, but Caitlin has already begun to work her way into the story. Overnight she's become an expert on the Double Eagle group. And while she's been unable to discover anything incriminating on Brody Royal or Forrest Knox, she's focused on the fact that the female whistle-blowers from Royal Insurance who disappeared two years ago vanished in exactly the same way that Jimmy Revels and Luther Davis did in 1968: without a trace—just like several other Double Eagle victims. Caitlin is already convinced that Brody Royal has been the directing power behind the Double Eagles since the murder of Albert Norris, and she doesn't know a fraction of what I do.

"Who do the Jericho Hole bones belong to?" she presses. "Jimmy Revels?"

"The bones Kirk brought up probably belong to Luther Davis. He was the larger of the two men by far."

She mulls this over with a resentful frown. Despite all I've confided to her, she seems to believe that I'm trying to sabotage her career in favor of a man I barely know. It's clear that nothing less than full disclosure will satisfy her, and on that point I must disappoint her.

"Caitlin, I told you about Luther's bones because it's only a matter of time before the story gets out—from Sheriff Dennis's office, probably. I gave you Brody Royal and Forrest Knox in spite of promising Henry I wouldn't. But that's it, at least for now. And you can't print *any* of that, remember? Not until Henry does."

Two pinks moons appear high on her cheeks. "Henry Sexton is a fine investigative reporter, but he works for a *weekly* newspaper. A tiny shop in the middle of nowhere. It's read by five thousand people, many of whom would prefer he didn't delve into the things that obsess him."

"You can't take over Henry's story. And I won't help you try."

She leans forward, and I feel myself pulling away from her. "Penn, this story is *big*. Bigger than Henry. Bigger than you or me, bigger even than your father. There's a secret history here, and yesterday's deaths are going bring it roaring back into the headlines."

"It's the murder charges against Dad that will do that. Viola's death would hardly rate a mention in your paper."

She winces at this but doesn't argue. Nor does she address my central point. "The FBI taking possession of Morehouse's body is unprecedented," she says. "John Kaiser is treating this like a terrorism case."

"I suspect he is. Otherwise, he wouldn't have had the power to do that."

Ninety minutes ago, Henry called and informed me that Special Agent John Kaiser had dispatched a car from the FBI's New Orleans field office to collect the bones Kirk Boisseau discovered this morning. Kaiser refused to comment on his decision to take possession of Glenn Morehouse's corpse, but he assured Henry that he intended to take unprecedented measures to bring the surviving Double Eagles to justice. Since I initiated Kirk's dive, I felt I could report that much to Caitlin without breaking faith with Henry. But beyond that . . .

"You can't hold me to a promise I made in ignorance!" she insists.

I lean back in my chair and let her reflect on the absurdity of her statement. "I'm more worried about Shad's plans for Dad than I am about those bones."

"Have you figured a way to expedite that DNA test?"

"The timing of that's basically up to Shad, I'm afraid."

"Are you going to tell Tom your worries about Shad trying to find a way to get his bail revoked?"

"Not until I can get him away from Mom. He was going home before heading to the office."

"So what about the dogfighting photo?" she asks, jarring me back the present. "Isn't it time to give Shad another look at it, so he can watch his career pass before his eyes?"

"He knows what I have, and that hasn't stopped him. I'm missing something, and that worries me. Plus, using that image *is* the equivalent of going nuclear. There's no way to predict what the ultimate result might be."

She nods as though in agreement, but I can tell her thoughts aren't really on my father's problems. She's thinking about the Double Eagles, and Henry Sexton's secret knowledge.

"Go on," I tell her. "Get it out."

"Penn, a weekly paper simply *can't* cover a case like this. It's a matter of inadequate staff and resources. And this story's too important now to let—"

"This story has *always* been important," I cut in. "And Henry has always treated it that way, even when no other journalist in the country gave a damn about these murders."

That dart went deep, but Caitlin knows I'm right. Still, I can't deny her point. She leans forward, elbows on her knees, her green eyes bright with excitement. "The *Beacon* is a fine vehicle for providing historical perspective, for unearthing backstory and doing patient investigation. But this is *breaking news*. And the *Examiner* can't ignore it."

My internal radar goes on alert. Given the risk of libel inherent in this kind of story, Caitlin must figure Henry has reams of information that he hasn't made public. She would probably perform sexual favors for a chance to break this story nationwide. She would for me, anyway.

The phone on my desk buzzes, drawing our eyes to it. I press the lighted button. "What is it, Rose?"

"Henry Sexton is out here. I told him you couldn't be disturbed, but he says it's an emergency."

Caitlin's eyes shine with anticipation, and she doesn't offer to leave. "Send him in, Rose."

"Yes, sir."

Five seconds later, my door opens and Henry walks in wearing corduroy pants, a flannel shirt, and John Lennon glasses. He must have been wearing contacts last night. The moment he sees Caitlin, he looks like a college professor flummoxed by a question he can't answer. Caitlin has actually sunk down in her chair in the vain hope that Henry won't see her until he's blurted out whatever is on his mind. The woman is shameless.

"Henry, you know my fiancée."

He moves awkwardly around the chair and shakes hands with Caitlin, who straightens in her chair and smiles like an actress auditioning for a coveted role. But Henry doesn't return the expression. He looks back at me with utter sincerity and says, "We need to talk, brother."

"Does Caitlin need to leave? If this visit has to do with your investigations, don't hesitate to kick her out."

Henry gives this question grave consideration, his face hardening with something like territorial instinct. "Under any other circumstances, I would. But if she'll promise not to print what I'm about to say, or post it online, I'm willing to say it in front of her."

"Henry, what the hell is going on?"

"Do you know about the grand jury?"

My diaphragm flattens like that of a boxer about to take a body blow. "No. What's happened?"

"Shad took your father's case before them right after lunch."

For a few seconds I stop breathing. The work of grand juries is supposed to be confidential, but I sense that Henry already knows what happened in that chamber today. "Tell me."

He gives Caitlin a mistrustful glance, then says, "They returned a true bill half an hour ago. I'm sorry, Penn."

"Mother*fuck*," Caitlin curses, anger making her eyes blaze like klieg lights. "An Adams County grand jury indicted Tom Cage for murder?"

"They sure did," Henry confirms. "I can hardly believe it myself."

Henry and I share a look: last night he assured me that he'd nail the Double Eagles for Viola's death long before my father could be indicted.

"How the hell do you know that when I don't?" Caitlin asks.

Henry lowers his chin and gives me a look that says: *Does this girl have her priorities straight?*

"Who's the judge?" I ask.

"Joe Elder."

I shake my head with something close to despair. "How certain are you of this?"

Henry's cheeks redden a bit. "One hundred percent. That's all I can tell you, with or without Caitlin here, so don't ask me more. I just thought you ought to know."

"Damn it! Shad must have some serious evidence to sway a Natchez grand jury against Dad."

"Do you think it was my video? I'd sure hate to think that."

"If so, it wasn't your fault. What that tape means is open to interpretation. And since the accused can't have a lawyer in the grand jury room, Shad could put whatever spin he wanted to on every frame."

Henry's eyes are welling up, and I can sense just how much he cares about my father.

"Shadrach Johnson," Caitlin says with contempt. "It's time to nuke him, Penn, I swear to God."

I signal for her to keep quiet, but she's too angry to pay attention.

"Say the word," she hisses. "I'll have that photo up on our Web edition in ten minutes. Front page, bigger than VJ Day. Shad won't even reach the city limits before PETA is screaming for his hide."

"What photo?" Henry asks, blinking.

"Sorry, Henry," she says with a hint of irony. "Privileged information."

He gives her a look that a teacher might give an arrogant student.

"Damn it all!" I yell, getting up and pacing around the room. "Shad must really believe Dad is guilty. Otherwise, he's gone insane."

"Bullshit," says Caitlin. "This is a vendetta, nothing else. He proved that this morning, when he asked that bail be denied."

I'm still not sure of this. These tactics aren't Shad's usual Clausewitz strategy. This is a blitzkrieg, and the risks to Shad are considerable, all of which begs the question of what's really going on. But if I don't respond immediately, my father could be overrun by a legal offensive that could kill him before he even gets to trial.

When Caitlin walks to the window looking onto the oaks in front of City Hall, I can tell by her posture that she's thinking hard. After a few moments, she turns back to us, her eyes focused on Henry. "May I ask you a question, Henry?"

"I can't wait."

"When does your next edition come out?"

"Thursday."

"Two days from now. And the next edition after that?"

"Next Thursday. We come out every Thursday."

"I see."

God, she's shameless.

"Henry, may I be blunt with you?" she goes on.

He meets her eyes with steady calm. "I thought you already were."

"Do you think a weekly paper is capable of covering a story that's breaking as fast as this one?"

Henry works his mouth around in silence for a few seconds. "Well, yes. Not the way you could with your daily, of course. But we've got our Web edition up and running, and I can post articles to that all day long."

"True. But that's not quite the same thing, and more to the point, you're really a one-man shop over there when it comes to these cold cases."

Henry takes his time parsing her words and tone. "What are you saying, exactly?"

"She wants to know everything you know about the Double Eagles," I tell him. "She wants to take over your story."

"*Not* true," Caitlin snaps. "That's not what I'm asking for at all." She walks over to the reporter and lightly touches his arm, taking back his attention. "I have a proposal for you, Henry."

Last night Henry's worst fear was having his story stolen. But Caitlin isn't going to steal it from him; she's going to convince him he has a journalistic duty to give it to her. "A proposal?" he asks.

"Yes. I'd like you to start working for me."

He draws back in puzzlement. "For you?"

"For the *Examiner*. I'm the publisher, you know, not a reporter or even the editor. I don't have any business trying to write this story myself. But unless I have you working for me, I'm going to have to take it on, the way I did the Del Payton story."

This statement is disingenuous. We all know she won a Pulitzer for her Del Payton coverage.

"I'd much prefer to have *you* covering this story for us," she continues. "With our media group's considerable resources backing you up. We'd publish under your byline, naturally."

To my surprise, Henry's face goes red, then darkens with anger. Even Caitlin takes a step back when she sees the frustration in his eyes. After all his painstaking work, I can only imagine the personal affront he must feel her overture to be.

"You can tell her to go to hell, Henry," I say. "I mean that."

Caitlin gives me a sharp glare, but then she takes two steps closer to him. "I realize what I'm asking. And I admit that I'm partly motivated by self-interest. But you can't deny that I can bring considerable firepower to what until now has been a solo quest—albeit an impressively successful one."

Henry looks up at her at last, then turns to me like a man seeking sanctuary, as if he's only able to stand the intensity of Caitlin's expectant gaze for a few seconds. I know the feeling well.

"This is complicated," he says. "Because Dr. Cage's case is one part of the story, and the cold cases are another. And I've been covering those just fine in the *Beacon*."

"I believe all those stories are about to become one," Caitlin says with unerring instinct. "One explosive story. The kind of story that comes along only once in a career."

Henry looks genuinely surprised. This must be the last thing he expected when he walked through my door. He's always known Caitlin was a threat to his monopoly on this story, but he probably never realized that the nature of his own newspaper might be a serious weakness. "I'll admit the validity of your argument," he says. "But even if I wanted to do that, I don't know that my publisher would agree."

Caitlin gives him another high-wattage smile. "I'm not trying to steal you away. You'd be a guest reporter—and a well-paid one. We'll credit each story: 'Special to the *Examiner,* by Henry Sexton of the *Concordia Beacon.*'"

Henry nods sharply. "You bet your ass you would."

He rubs his palms down his thighs as though to flatten his corduroy pants, then looks to me as though for guidance. "What do you think, Penn?"

"I think it's hard to say no to this woman. But that's no reason to say yes. Not unless you're sure."

Caitlin maintains her smile, but her eyes flash fury at me.

"What do you think about her argument?"

"She has a point about the weekly-versus-daily issue, especially with my father's case. You could cover it on the Web, but there's no question that her father's media group would give you massive exposure on a daily basis. On the other hand, you've been covering the Double Eagle story for years. That's yours, and I think you'll win a Pulitzer for it someday. The problem is, the past has crashed into the present. Look what happened with the bones this morning. The two stories are already tangling together. If the Eagles killed Viola, which you believe, then by sticking to your old methods you run the risk of other reporters catching up to you, and fast."

"You think I should take the offer."

"No. I'm saying every proposition has good and bad points. But I will tell you this: Caitlin's very good at her job, and she can have your stories running coast to coast by tomorrow."

Henry turns away from us and studies a framed photograph on the wall. It shows me with Willie Morris, my former lit professor, who edited *Harper's Magazine* during the 1960s. In the photo we're drinking a beer at the Gin, an Oxford, Mississippi, bar that, like Willie himself, no longer exists except in memory.

"This would take some serious negotiation with my publisher," Henry says.

"Whatever you want, you've got it."

He looks at Caitlin like a suspicious man dealing with a car salesman. "If we did it, I'd still want to be able to publish in the *Beacon* on Thursdays."

Caitlin smiles, sensing victory. "Absolutely."

Henry looks to me again.

"She's never broken a promise that I know about," I tell him. "You don't have any worries on that score."

"Let me talk to Mr. Fraser, my publisher. Then I'll get back to you. But even if you meet his conditions, I'll still have one of my own."

"Anything you want," Caitlin insists.

"The deaths of Viola and Glenn Morehouse have convinced me the danger is very real. I've been thinking about publishing most of what I have this Thursday, as a kind of neutralizing attack."

My senses sharpen at this, and Caitlin gulps audibly.

"If I did that," he goes on, "then the Double Eagles would have nothing to gain by killing me or my loved ones, because the information would already be public. And the FBI would have the information, too, which I'm going to have to give them pretty soon anyway."

"That's a damn good idea, Henry," I say, knowing I'll pay a domestic price for this later.

"It's also a very big step," Caitlin says cautiously. "I'm not saying you shouldn't do that. But if you fire at the Eagles and miss, you've told them what you have and what you don't, and maybe made yourself look foolish in the process. You might also risk a libel suit."

Henry nods soberly. "I've considered that."

"There are other ways to handle the security issue. Penn and I have dealt with death threats more than once."

The reporter takes off his glasses and carefully wipes the lenses with his shirt. "I'm not bending on that point. Too many people have died already."

Caitlin's triumph quickly vanishes into concern over the next skirmish in her crusade. "Can you call your publisher from here? I'd like us to get started right away."

Henry holds up his hands. "Oh, no. Mr. Fraser lives right across the river in Vidalia. I need to speak to him about this in person. He's gone way out on a limb for me, letting me upset folks like I have. He's gotten a lot of nasty remarks these past years, and a few threats besides. But he's stuck to his guns and backed me all the way. He's a good Christian man, and he did some brave reporting back in his day. I owe him a personal visit."

"Go see your publisher, Henry," I tell him. "Caitlin will be waiting for you with open arms if you decide to share your talents with the *Examiner*."

Henry gives me an uncertain nod, then moves toward the door.

"And make her pay you like you're Bob Woodward!" I call as he turns the handle. "Her father can afford it."

I expect Caitlin to cuss me when the door closes, but after waiting a few seconds, she whoops and pumps her fist in the air. "I thought you'd screwed me," she says. "But then you sold him for me!"

"I gave him my honest opinion. You're right about the weekly paper issue. He can't cover this story week to week, not like he could with a whole media group behind him. This thing is going to unfold by the minute."

She walks up and lays a cool hand on my cheek. "I haven't forgotten about your father. If for some reason Shad doesn't cave because of the photo, I'll take his case apart piece by piece in the paper."

"That sounds a little biased."

"This is war," she says. "And he started it."

I sigh heavily. "I'd better call Dad and tell him about the grand jury, before anyone else does."

"Do you mind if I stay?"

"No," I reply, but part of me is angry. If Henry had been willing to leave with her a few moments ago, Caitlin would not be staying for this.

I try Dad's private office line first, but Melba picks up and tells me he came in for an hour, then went home to lie down after lunch. When I call home, Mom says he hasn't been there since he left for the office after his court hearing. With my pulse accelerating, I try Dad's cell phone, knowing that he almost never answers it. This time, though, he picks up on the fourth ring.

"Hello, Penn," he says in an almost buoyant voice.

I look at Caitlin and shrug. "Dad? Where are you?"

"Just taking a drive. I couldn't concentrate at the office, and I didn't want to sit at home with your mother asking me questions all day. I needed some time to think."

I'll bet. "Are you okay? You having chest pains or anything?"

"I took a nitro earlier, but I'm fine now. Really."

"Exactly where are you?"

"Sitting in the mall parking lot. I went to the bookstore, just looking. They didn't have anything. You know me."

"You probably spent a hundred bucks."

"Close," he says with a chuckle. "What is it, son? You must have some news."

"All bad, I'm afraid. Shad Johnson took your case to the grand jury a couple of hours ago. They indicted you for murder."

The silence that follows seems to roar like an approaching wind. "Dad? Are you all right?"

"Yeah." More silence, but this time it doesn't last as long. "I guess I knew this would happen. I figured it would take a few days, though. If not weeks."

"Me, too. I know it seems bad, but we'll deal with it. I just didn't want you to hear it anywhere else."

"Thanks. Will the news be all over town?"

"It's not supposed to be, and grand juries are usually pretty tight-lipped. It probably depends on what Shad said in there. If he brought up any paternity issues . . . there's just no telling." While Dad digests this, I add, "I think it's time I give Quentin Avery a call."

Now the silence is so profound that I wonder whether the connection has gone dead. "Quentin's having a pretty bad time," Dad says finally. "He's lost both legs, and he's having trouble with infections. He's even had pneumonia. Then there's his retinopathy, neuropathy, and just about everything else that can go wrong with diabetes."

"Dad, this is the rest of your life we're talking about."

"Yes, but it's early days yet, even if the DA is moving fast. You can easily handle this phase of things. Let's give it a day or two and see what develops. Then we'll call Quentin, if you still think we need to."

"We don't have that luxury. If Quentin's too sick to handle a big-league murder trial, I need to know now. You're going to need a big gun for this case. The best criminal lawyer money can buy."

"As far as I'm concerned, that's you."

"You're wrong. Seriously. We also need to get that DNA test done. That's probably the best chance we have at defusing this prosecution, but Shad is delaying things. We're going have to use an out-of-town lab."

He grunts in surprise. "All right. Well . . . you schedule it and let me know where I need to be."

"I will. There's one more thing. Now that you've been indicted, you're on Judge Joe Elder's docket. He won't be the judge who tries you down the road, because he's resigning soon. But if Shad can persuade him, Judge Elder could revoke your bail."

"How soon?"

"He could actually do it today from the Mayo Clinic, which is where he is now. But I doubt Joe would do that without an arraignment. I'm thinking Monday at the earliest."

"All right, then. Don't worry about me, son. Hey, did you turn up anything out of the Jericho Hole?"

"We did, in fact. I think we found Luther Davis's bones, wired to the steering wheel of his car."

"My God. I remember that boy. You keep after the bastards, Penn. Just remember what I told you last night. The Knoxes are bad, but Brody Royal is no one to mess with. You protect yourself. Henry, too."

"I will."

As he clicks off, I feel a strange presentiment that the real danger is to my father, not to Henry and me.

"How did he take it?" Caitlin asks.

"Remarkably well, considering."

"When Shad went before the grand jury, could he have told them that Tom is Lincoln's father?"

"He shouldn't, but a DA can do pretty much anything he likes in that room. It's a one-man show. A Natchez grand jury would have been damned reluctant to indict a respected physician for murder. To sway them, Shad probably had to play at least one ace from his sleeve."

Caitlin paces across the room, tapping the groove between her upper lip and nose. This habit, a stagy gesture she makes when thinking purposefully, is so distinctive that I actually looked up the anatomy one day. That groove is called the philtrum.

"Do you have any pictures of Luther Davis's bones?" she asks.

"Yes."

"Where?"

"In a safe place. Patience, please."

Her eyes flash with anticipation. *"Where?"*

I look down at my hands for a few seconds, then meet her gaze again.

"Not here." I touch the page button on my desk phone. "Rose, please find Quentin Avery's home number for me."

"Washington, D.C., or Jefferson County?"

"I've been trying both his cell and his D.C. number without any luck. Try his Jefferson County place."

"Tom doesn't want to hire Quentin?" Caitlin asks, as I mute the intercom.

"Not yet. But we can't wait for reality to sink in. You said it: this is war. Shad needs to be reminded that actions have consequences, and that we're not without resources." Opening my desk drawer, I lift out a Baggie that contains a small USB flash drive and press my intercom again. "Rose, get me Shad Johnson, too, please."

"Will do. Just a sec."

"Are you going to hit him with the photo now?" Caitlin asks.

I nod once, my jaw tightening.

"God, I wish I could go with you." She sits on my desk and touches my wrist. "Tell me one thing. Are we going to treat this case like every other? In terms of the wall we keep between our jobs?"

"I don't know. What do you think?"

"With your father's life at stake? No way. But I suppose we might need to keep some things compartmentalized. I guess we can negotiate each development as it comes up."

I look hard into her eyes. "I made Henry a promise."

She smiles. "You won't have to keep it long. He'll be working for me by tonight." She looks pointedly at her watch, then slides off my desk. "I need to get back to the paper."

"You're going to wait until you hear from Henry before you publish anything, right?" I'm thinking of the Web edition. "Even online?"

While Caitlin glares, my intercom clicks. "Shad Johnson on One, Mayor."

With a quick surge of adrenaline, I put Shad on the speakerphone.

"I'm accepting your earlier invitation," I tell him. "I need a couple of minutes of your time."

"You'll have to wait forty-five minutes. I've got somebody coming in."

"Not a campaign consultant, I hope?"

The DA chuckles, and his voice doesn't sound even slightly anxious. "Still got your sense of humor, I see. That's good, considering. Later, Mayor."

Shad's confident tone unsettles me, but when I hang up, Caitlin gives me the pitiless stare of a warrior's wife. "No mercy," she intones. "I mean it. You show that arrogant prick a future working as a goddamn paralegal."

"I intend to."

She gives my hand one last squeeze, her eyes burning into mine. "You know what's thicker than water."

I nod once.

After a light kiss on my forehead, she's gone.

I look down at the nearly weightless stub of plastic and metal in my hand. Can this harmless-looking object keep my father out of jail? For two months I've believed that the digital image stored within this USB flash drive represented Shad Johnson's career. But today I have an unsettling feeling that my old nemesis is a step ahead of me.

CHAPTER 37

TOM CAGE STOOD over his office desk, packing a leather weekend bag with necessities. After a brief stop at home, and a not-so-brief disagreement with Peggy, he'd returned to the office and seen quite a few patients. He'd worked on his records through lunch, trying not to dwell on the possibility that he might be making the last written notes of his medical career. Then he'd driven to the mall bookstore, a minor rebellion against the strictures of his bail agreement, and also a journey meant to gain time alone, where he could reflect one last time on his plan. After returning to the office and seeing a few more patients, he'd retired to his private office and begun packing the things he'd secretly brought from home.

Melba knew not to disturb him when the door was closed. Already in the bag were two changes of clothes, a Ziploc containing a month's worth of prescription drugs, a prescription pad, and a short-barreled Magnum .357. To these Tom added a plastic case containing diabetic syringes, two packs of insulin vials, and his first edition of *The Killer Angels,* which contained the fading Polaroid of Viola he'd shot in 1968. After compulsively looking up to be sure the door was closed, he opened the bottom drawer of his desk and removed another Ziploc bag. This one contained two vials of adrenaline, a syringe exactly like the one stored in the evidence room at the sheriff's department, some powerful narcotics, a vial of local anesthetic, and six pairs of latex gloves. It also held a small pewter box that concealed three baby teeth belonging to Lincoln Turner. Tom tucked this Ziploc carefully into the weekend bag, then closed his desk drawer.

On impulse, he turned to the shelf behind his desk and picked up a framed family photo. A neighbor had taken it in 1988, before Jenny left for her teaching job in England. In it, Tom, Peggy, Jenny, Penn, and Sarah stood before their old house—the one the kids had grown up in, the one that had held Tom's beloved library. That library was gone now, up in smoke, just like Penn's first wife. Annie had not yet been conceived when this picture was shot; nor had the first malfunctioning cell in Sarah's breast begun to fulfill its terrible destiny. Tom closed his eyes and thought of his daughter-in-law for a few moments, a penance for the relief he'd felt when Penn finally proposed to Caitlin Masters.

For some years, Tom had worried that part of his son had died with Sarah, the way part of Tom had perished when Viola left for Chicago. But Caitlin had not only proved stronger than Penn's grief; she'd also brought some light back into Tom's life. The medical books on Tom's shelves described no clinically measurable "life-force," but after more than forty years of practicing medicine, he was certain that some people were born with an extra ration of it. Caitlin certainly had been, as had Viola Turner. A few boys in Korea had possessed this special quality, the ones who'd survived wounds that would have killed any ordinary soldier. Viola's thirty-seven years in Chicago had all but killed her unique vitality, and Tom knew now that he'd had more to do with that premature death than he ever suspected.

Taking a wooden tongue depressor from a jar, he pried the back off the picture frame, then slipped the family portrait into *The Killer Angels* alongside the snapshot of Viola. All that remained on his desktop now was a Sony videotape cartridge, the tape he'd removed from Henry Sexton's camcorder on the morning Viola died. Tom stared down at the tape but did not touch it. After some reflection, he walked to the window and looked out at the office parking lot. For the past quarter hour he'd been watching for a tall, silver conversion van called a Roadtrek. The only silver vehicle in the back lot now was a Natchez city police car. The cruiser appeared to be empty, but Tom's heart began laboring every time he looked out at it.

Returning to his desk, he fixed his gaze on the tape, an artifact of one of the stupidest decisions he'd ever made. Rubbing his eyes hard, he turned to another framed photo on his shelf. This one showed two shirtless young men of eighteen standing in front of a snow-covered mountain. Both men wore army fatigues, both held cigarettes, and both were grinning despite the fact that dried blood covered their hands and forearms.

Tom jumped at a loud rapping on his office door. Before he could say anything, the door opened and Melba Price leaned in, her face somber.

"I just got a strange call on the main office line," his chief nurse said softly. "A man. He gave me a private message for you, but he wouldn't say who he was."

Melba's view of the videotape was blocked by the weekend bag on the desk. Closing his hand over the tape, Tom picked it up and dropped it into the bag, then zipped the bag shut. "What did he say?"

"He said, 'I was at the Frozen Chosin.' Then he said to tell you he was parked on the south side of the office."

It took a few moments for Tom to orient himself. In all the years he'd practiced medicine here, he'd never had occasion to think about how the building lay in relation to the cardinal directions. Thinking about the sunlight in the late afternoons, he realized that the rear of the office faced east.

"Dr. Cage," Melba said, stepping fully inside and closing the door. "You're free on bail, right?"

"You know I am."

"And there are conditions to the bail, you said."

"That's right." He glanced down at the zipped bag. "And I've already broken at least one of them."

Melba sighed, her eyes clouded with sorrow and anxiety. "Where are you going?"

Tom avoided her gaze. "I'm going home to lie down. I'm having some angina. Just as you told Penn I was."

She shook her head with regret. "You mean that's what I'm supposed to tell the police."

Tom finally looked into her eyes. "That's all you know, Mel. I went home to lie down, and I never came back. And you never got that phone call."

The nurse waved her hand dismissively. "I just want to know *you* know what you're doing. You're not about to try anything crazy, are you?"

He gave her the most confident smile he could manage. "Have you ever thought I was crazy?"

"All the time, thank goodness." The nurse smiled, but the worry lines remained around her eyes.

Tom went to the window and pulled back the curtain. The police car was still there. And still empty, or so it appeared.

"Who you going to meet out there?" Melba asked.

Tom let the curtain fall, then turned and picked up his bag. As he moved to the door, he reached out and squeezed his nurse's warm hand. "A friend, Mel. A very old friend. You take care of yourself."

She reached after him as he departed. "You call me if you need help. I mean it. I'll do anything you need, Doc. You know that."

Tom felt wetness in his eyes. *If only I were the man everyone seems to believe I am.*

TOM FOUND THE SILVER conversion van exactly where Walt had told Melba it would be, on the south side of his office building. Framed in the open driver's window was a face tanned so deeply that even in December it looked like varnished wood. Walt Garrity had spent thirty years as a Texas Ranger, and every hour in the sun showed on his face. But Walt's eyes still smoldered with the fire that had driven him to hunt men across trackless wastes in the days when Sputnik was still on the drawing board and the only computers in America were in the Pentagon. In more recent years, the retired ranger had worked as an investigator for the Houston DA's office, where Penn had first met him.

"*Itty-wa deska,* Private!" Walt snapped.

Tom found himself grinning. *Itty-wa deska* was phonetic Korean for "Get the *hell* over here!"

"Police car scare you?" Tom asked, walking up and slapping his hand against the van's side.

"It didn't reassure me."

"City cop," Tom said. "Probably here as a patient."

Walt shrugged. "Will that nurse I talked to be any problem?"

"No. Mel's good people."

"Get in, then. There's a full-size door on the other side. Good for crips like you."

Tom scanned the parking lot, wondering if Sheriff Byrd had anyone watching his office. This side of his office bordered an apartment complex, and he saw no one between the buildings. Cars were passing on the boulevard to the east, but too fast for their drivers to notice anything back here. He walked around the Roadtrek and found the door Walt had described. Tom had to stoop to get through it. As he pulled the door shut behind him, he found himself in a spotlessly clean RV, small but laid out with supreme efficiency.

"We'll stow your bag later," Walt said. "Sit behind me till we get out of here."

Garrity was sitting in a captain's chair, but another seat lay directly behind him. Tom collapsed onto cushy leather and felt the van lurch as Walt put it in gear. A police radio turned down low chattered in the background.

"I've run down a lot of bail jumpers in my time," Walt said. "This is the first time I ever helped one skip."

"Thanks for getting here so fast."

"Hell, I'm just glad for the chance to make up for last time."

Two months earlier, the old Ranger had tried to help Penn with some dangerous business, and he'd failed in a way that left Walt thinking that age had finally robbed him of the ability to do what he'd done so well for so long.

"Glad to accommodate you," Tom said. "Get this kimchee cab moving."

He expected a belly laugh, but instead, Walt rotated his captain's chair and looked intently at him. "You know they can try you in absentia if you skip bail, right?"

Tom's stomach rolled. "I didn't know that."

Walt nodded. "I only mention it because they indicted you so fast. The DA obviously has a burr up his ass about you."

"We'll be done with our work long before this ever gets to trial. Hopefully before they even know I'm gone. Let's go."

Walt slapped him on the knee, and Tom winced as the Ranger turned back toward the steering wheel. Fifteen seconds later, Walt drove past the empty police car, turned onto Jefferson Davis Boulevard, and joined the traffic moving toward Highway 61.

"Did you bring the things I asked for?" Tom asked.

"That and a lot more. We could track a whole terror cell with this van, and wipe 'em out anytime you say."

Tom nodded with relief. "Good."

"You gonna tell me who we're after?"

"All in good time, *compadre*. Let's get the hell out of town."

CHAPTER 38

WAITING IN MY office for my confrontation with Shad Johnson, I plugged the USB flash drive into my computer and opened the JPEG that has hung over the DA like a sword of Damocles for the past seven weeks. The fresh sight of it still engenders disbelief. I can't quite get my mind around the fact that a calculating manipulator like Shad would put himself in a situation that could destroy his career overnight. On the other hand, he certainly wouldn't be the first.

In the photo, a blood-soaked pit bull hangs by its neck from a rope tied to a tree limb while three men look on. The dog appears to be jerking its hindquarters away from something in the hand of one of the men. It's an electric cattle prod, and the man holding it is Darius Jones, an All-Pro wide receiver. Standing to the left of Darius is Shadrach Johnson, his face shining with something like rapture. Few things in life have shocked me more than seeing Shad in this context, but it only proves the lesson I've learned time and again: none of us truly knows anybody. How Shad could possibly try to use my father's plight to get revenge on me is unfathomable, given the existence of this image. I recall former Louisiana governor Edwin Edwards's campaign boast that the only thing that could keep him from retaking the governor's office was "being found with a dead woman or a live boy." But Governor Edwards hadn't seen this picture. In this day and age, being seen torturing a dog is political suicide.

As the screen trips over to my screen saver, my mind turns to Quentin Avery. Among trial lawyers, Quentin is known as "Preacher" for his awe-inspiring ability to sway juries. But even in dry history books, his name figures prominently in some chapters. During the 1960s and '70s, Quentin argued four cases before the United States Supreme Court—one a landmark civil rights case—and won them all. He became a hero to many, and his name was mentioned in the same sentences as Thurgood Marshall and James Nabrit. But by the mid-

1980s, the young firebrand had turned his mind to lucre rather than to justice, taking on high-profile (and very profitable) drug cases. In the 1990s he moved on to personal injury cases, two of which made him genuinely wealthy. Throughout those years, Quentin did enough pro bono work that the people who mattered maintained their respect for him, but the image of a black knight on a shining steed had been forever tarnished, and his name was never again spoken with the same reverence as those of the men with whom he'd rubbed shoulders during the most dangerous years of the movement.

"Mayor?" Rose says over my intercom. "I haven't been able to reach Mr. Avery, but I have his wife on the phone."

"Thank you, Rose. I'll pick up."

Though in his seventies, Quentin is married to an attorney in her early forties, a woman very protective of her husband. When Quentin and I worked a case together two years ago, it took Doris Avery some time to warm up to me. I like to think that she and I ended up in a state of mutual respect, but from what Dad told me about Quentin's health, Doris has probably been under immense strain in recent months.

"Doris, this is Penn."

"Hello," says the weary alto voice I remember.

"Thank you for taking my call. I know things have been difficult for Quentin lately, and I wouldn't call unless it was an emergency."

"*Emergency* is a relative term. I know why you're calling. A friend from Natchez told me Tom was arrested this morning, and why."

"Does Quentin know?"

"No. He's a sick man, Penn. Very sick. I will tell him after he wakes up, but only because he'll be angry if he finds out later that I kept it from him."

"Are you guys in D.C.?"

"No, Jefferson County. Your father has actually been treating Quentin, despite his heart attack."

Yet another fact Dad has kept from me, and possibly from my mother as well.

"Tom has been a godsend," Doris continues. "But I have to tell you this: Quentin can't handle a murder trial. Not a case he'd be as personally invested in as this one. If they lost, and your father went to jail, it would kill Quentin. He can certainly give you advice, but *please* don't ask him to handle the trial."

"I hope there won't be a trial, Doris. But Dad's already been indicted. It happened only a couple of hours after his initial appearance, and I think Shad's going to try to have his bail revoked."

"Hmm. That sounds fishy."

"It is. Joe Elder is the judge, at least for now. And unless I'm mistaken, Joe clerked for Quentin back in the day. I'm hoping Quentin can help me get the charges reduced, if not dismissed altogether."

"I hope that's possible. You're right about Joe Elder working for Quentin. I've met him several times socially. He's a fair man. I have your phone numbers, Penn. We'll get back to you after Quentin's awake and up to speed."

"Thank you, Doris. I mean it."

"I know."

And then she's gone.

A cold emptiness settles in my chest as Doris's voice echoes in my mind: *Quentin can't handle a murder trial.*

I run through a mental short list of the most gifted defense attorneys I faced during my courtroom career, and even jot down a couple of names. But in the last analysis, not one measures up to Quentin Avery. And yet . . . all that talent and experience is contained in a body that is falling apart. The parallels with my father are downright eerie.

"It's after five," Rose says over the intercom. "Do you need me for anything else?"

"Go home, Rose. I'll see you tomorrow."

"Should I lock the door?"

"No, I'll be right behind you, and I've got files to carry. Tomorrow is my meeting with the selectmen about the Forks of the Road proposal, right?"

"I'm afraid so."

The political controversy that surrounds this racially charged project would be enough to sink me under normal circumstances, but right now it seems only a peripheral annoyance. That said, I'll have to spend at least an hour tonight prepping for tomorrow's meeting. I'm gathering up the relevant files when the door to my office opens. I jerk my head up, half expecting to see the angry face of Lincoln Turner, but instead I find the kind eyes of Jewel Washington watching me.

"Jewel! What are you doing here?"

"Sorry to sneak up on you. I was waiting for Rose to leave."

"What's going on?"

She crosses to my desk and hands me a manila envelope. "I'm going to be asking the supervisors for a budget increase for my department at the next meeting. I need an assistant. I wanted you to be aware in case there's anything you can do to help me."

"Well . . . I'd like to help, but you know I have no vote on that board."

"I know that." Jewel looks over her shoulder as though someone might walk in at any moment. "But your opinion carries a lot of weight."

"I'll do what I can." I shake the envelope. "Is this the budget?"

She smiles. "The budget's in there. And if anyone asks later, that's all you found. But you study the last few pages real close, all right? In fact, I think you ought to look at them now."

Jewel is my favorite city employee, but right now I'm not sure I can focus on any routine matters. "Jewel—"

She reaches out and squeezes my hand. "Read it, baby."

Setting down my files, I open the folder and flip through what looks like the usual appeal for assistance from a bureaucratic department. As I reach the end, though, the typeface changes, becoming much smaller, and I see handwritten notes and diagrams—some of the human body. Flipping back one page, I read a boldface title: PRELIMINARY POSTMORTEM RESULTS. VIOLA REVELS TURNER. Michael Winton, M.D., F.C.A.P. I nearly swallow my Adam's apple.

"More interesting than you thought?" Jewel asks with a sly look.

"I'll definitely give your request my fullest attention."

She lowers her voice to a whisper. "I'll give you the short version now. Miss Viola died from an overdose of adrenaline."

"Was it an amount that might be reasonably given in a code-blue situation?"

Jewel shakes her head. "Massive overdose. If it was administered by a health-care professional, it almost had to be intentional, unless they picked up the wrong-dilution syringe by mistake. If it was a layman . . . who knows? I can imagine a lot of different scenarios, but none of them look particularly good for Dr. Cage."

"Does Shad have a copy of this yet?"

"As of about ten minutes ago."

So you were Shad's appointment. I sag onto my desk. Despite the help that so many people seem prepared to offer, and their faith in my father's good character, I have a sense that, like the _Titanic,_ we're on a stately but unalterable course toward disaster. Somewhere in the darkness ahead lies a submerged berg that will tear a hole beneath the waterline of all our hopes.

"Hey," Jewel says gently, coming forward. "You don't look good."

"It's been a truly crappy day."

She gives me hard-earned smile of empathy. "I've seen a few myself."

"Any advice for getting through them?"

The coroner snorts with something like contempt. "You wantin' some of that magic Negro advice? The mystical secret for getting through times of trial and tribulation?"

"I'll take anything you've got."

"The best advice I ever heard came from a white man. A fat Englishman with his back against the wall and the wolf at his door."

I raise my eyebrows, too tired to ask.

"Never, _never_ quit." Jewel smiles. "Winston Churchill smoked a cigar, just like your daddy."

"You really believe in Dad, don't you?"

Her pupils seem to dilate in their dark irises. "I know men, baby. I've seen enough bad ones to recognize the good. And your daddy's in a class by himself. If you have any questions about the autopsy, call my son's cell, not mine."

I hand her my cell phone and ask her to enter the number for me. As she does, I say, "I've always felt like you do about Dad. But the way he's acting about Viola has shaken my faith. I hate telling you that, but it's true."

Jewel hands the phone back to me, and then her eyes seem to go out of focus. She's looking inward. "I don't know what happened to Miss Viola that night. All that autopsy can tell you is what happened _inside_ her body. But Tom Cage wouldn't hurt a soul unless it was to relieve pain. And sometimes . . . Lord, that's all you can do. Every nurse knows that." She takes me by the hand, her grasp warm and maternal. "Whatever decision your daddy made that night, I'll stake my job it was the right one."

This heartfelt vow pierces me to the quick. Caitlin's easy reassurance barely scratched the surface of my anxiety, but Jewel's faith has sunk into me like a harpoon. "That means a lot, coming from you."

The coroner's eyes harden. "My faith doesn't buy you anything, Penn. You've got to steel yourself for what's coming. You're too much like your father. That's your weakness. You always look for the good in folks. But in Billy Byrd and old Shadrach, you'd be lookin' in vain."

Her warning tone sobers me. "Jewel . . . let me show you something. Come around to my side of the desk."

As she does, I hit a button on my keyboard, banishing the screen saver and summoning the obscene photograph of Shad Johnson and the bloody pit bull back to the screen. Jewel's hand flies to her chest when she realizes who and what she's seeing. Then she shakes her head like a devout Christian being forced to look at the devil's work.

"What are you going to do with this picture?"

"I'm about to show it to Brother Shad."

She shakes her head again, then looks up at me with new eyes. "I was wrong, wasn't I? You're not quite as naïve as your daddy, after all."

"I hope not."

"Lord, I'd give a month's salary to see Shadrach's face when you show him this."

"A lot of people would. Jewel, do you know anything about Lincoln Turner?"

She cuts her eyes at me. "Not yet. But I've been asking around, quiet like. I've already seen him twice today, hangin' round the courthouse like the ghost at the feast. Don't worry, I'll get to the bottom of *him*."

"Thanks. What about Judge Joe Elder? He's not another Arthel Minor, is he?" Minor is a recently retired hack who in the past colluded with Shad to go after one of my father's partners.

"No, no. Judge Joe's a good man, and smart as a whip. But he did grow up over in Ferriday. I'm sure he took his share of abuse from the rednecks over there. He's no reverse racist or anything, but—" Jewel appears to be blushing. "Joe probably wouldn't find it hard to believe that your father took advantage of Viola back in the old days. Even though I do. I can see why Shad would want Joe over Judge Franklin."

"Thank you, Jewel."

She turns back to my monitor and clucks her tongue three times. "My grandbaby fair *worships* that Darius Jones. But Lord, Shadrach Johnson . . . pride surely goeth before destruction."

"I hope it doesn't come to that."

She looks up, her eyes showing confusion. Then she shakes her head and says, "My daddy told me politics was dirty business. I guess he was more right than I knew. I'd tell you good luck, but I don't want any part of this."

"Thank you, Jewel." I hold up the autopsy report. "For this."

She nods once, then hurries through my door, pulling her coat around her like a woman going out to face a storm.

Reaching down to my mouse, I move the cursor to the File menu, and press PRINT.

CHAPTER 39

"THE DISTRICT ATTORNEY is expecting you, Mr. Mayor," Shad Johnson's male assistant says. "Go in."

When I open the door, I freeze. As expected, Shad is waiting behind his enormous desk, but I didn't expect to find Sheriff Billy Byrd's bulk wedged into a chair to Shad's left, watching me with a smirk.

"Come in, Mr. Mayor," Shad says with apparent deference. "Close the door."

Shad motions me to the chair before his desk, but I don't sit. Instead I walk forward and grip the chair back, bracing myself for whatever these two have cooked up. They're the unlikeliest allies I've ever seen—a Harvard-educated, liberal black lawyer and a redneck sheriff who barely escaped high school with a diploma—yet they have colluded before, so I shouldn't be surprised.

"What's the deal, guys?"

"No deal," says Shad. "Congratulations on your father getting bail. He obviously has a lot of support in the community."

Sheriff Byrd gives a porcine snort, his eyes barely visible beneath the brim of his Stetson.

"After the initial appearance," I say, ignoring Byrd, "you told me there were some things I didn't know. You said you thought we ought to clear the air. Then you ran straight to the grand jury for an indictment. Have you cut some kind of deal with Joe Elder to revoke Dad's bail?"

Shad and Billy share a fast look. "Judge Elder will not only be handling the case for now. I can also tell you in confidence that he's considering staying on the bench through its conclusion."

A wave of nausea loosens my bowels. Shad wouldn't have asked Elder to stay through this trial unless he were confident of some kind of bias.

"Don't look so frightened, Penn. Joe Elder's the most impartial judge to sit in this county for decades. He's firm but fair. Your father won't get a free pass, of course, but then he shouldn't. Nobody should."

"Is Elder going to revoke Dad's bail?" I ask in a barely controlled voice.

Shad sniffs and looks over at a window. "That's unlikely without an arraignment. But I'd expect that Monday, when the judge comes back to work. Now, let's move on to more pressing matters—"

"What did you say to the grand jury?" I demand. "Did you repeat Lincoln Turner's allegations about his paternity? Because if you did, and it gets out, you're going to find yourself—"

"Whoa, there, Mayor." Shad glances at Byrd again. "What did I tell you? He can't speak three sentences without threatening me."

"You can't say you haven't asked for it."

The DA shakes his head with what looks like forbearance. "I told you, you've got the wrong idea about me. But I'll let the sheriff explain."

Sheriff Byrd has a set of keys in his hand, and he works each key through his fingers as he speaks. "Couple months back," he says, "when all that shit broke loose about the casino boat? With the dogfighting and such?"

I give him a faint nod, hyperconscious of the photograph in the inside pocket of my sport coat.

"Back when your girlfriend was putting your picture in the paper every day, saying what a big hero you were?"

"The police chief was in there quite a bit, too," I remind him. The jurisdictional disputes between the Adams County Sheriff's Office and the Natchez Police Department are legendary.

"My *point*," Sheriff Byrd says, "is that you and Chief Logan seemed happy to take all the credit for the dogfighting and prostitution busts. And I let you. *But*—I only done that so's I could protect my sources."

It takes restraint not to laugh at this. "Sources? What the hell are you talking about?"

The sheriff raises his hat brim a few millimeters, letting light into his puffy little eyes. "I'm talking about the dogfighting and whoring that was going on, on both sides of the river. I'd been investigating that for quite some time when all hell broke loose in October."

An incredulous laugh escapes my lips. "This is a joke, right?"

"Hell, no, it ain't. You wouldn't know nothing about my operations, of course, living up in your ivory tower."

"I don't recall you making any arrests, Billy."

"That's 'cause you and your army buddy busted right up into the middle of my investigation. Committed a few crimes of your own in the process, too. That's why your buddy left here in such an awful damned hurry, ain't it? Had the feds all over his ass."

Righteous anger floods through me when I think of Daniel Kelly and the service he did this town. "You're full of shit, Billy. What's that got to do with the price of oil?"

Byrd shifts on his seat, but every inch of his blubber exudes confidence. "Anyhow, it's come to my attention that you've been threatening the district attorney with some sort of blackmail. Something about a compromising photograph?"

"Is that what Shad told you?"

"Don't matter who told me what, Mayor. But I sure hope that's not the case. Because the fact is, District Attorney Johnson here was one of my main confidential informants throughout my dogfighting investigation."

As their scam comes clear, my blood pressure plummets, and I waver on my feet. "Do you seriously expect anyone to believe that?"

Byrd's lips widen into something like a leer. "I surely do. That was a pretty high-toned bunch running that dogfighting ring, and I needed somebody who could mingle with the upper crust. Plus, them Irishmen was bringing in pro athletes and rappers and such, most of 'em black. When I told the DA my problem, he offered to make out like he was into that kind of thing, and get me some inside information."

"And that's how there came to be a photo of our district attorney and a star athlete torturing a pit bull?"

"That's exactly right." Sheriff Byrd's dull eyes twinkle. "You know the lengths CIs have to go to, to get credibility with their targets."

Both men are watching me carefully, awaiting my response.

"Gentlemen—and I'm using that term facetiously—I've heard some bullshit in my day. But I have never heard such unadulterated crap as that."

Sheriff Byrd's face darkens. "That's the way it is, bud."

Ignoring Billy, I walk up to Shad's desk, take the photo out of my coat pocket, unfold it, and lay it on the polished wood.

"Imagine that under a thirty-point headline, Shad. And I'm not talking about the *Concordia Beacon* or the *Natchez Examiner*. I'm talking about *USA Today*. The *New York Times*. The *Trib*, back in your old stomping ground."

Shad's throat clicks as he swallows.

"Look at your face, Shad. It would take one hell of a lawyer to sell that look as *duty*."

His eyes remain on the picture for several seconds. Then he slowly composes himself and looks up at me. "You heard the sheriff."

"Does revenge on me really mean that much to you? You'll risk everything for it?"

Without lowering his eyes, he turns the photo facedown on the desk.

"Billy," I say softly, "will you swear to your story in court?"

"You're damn right I will."

At last I look at him. "Perjury. Is that a new low for you? Or just an old habit?"

Byrd comes halfway out of his chair, then slowly settles back into it. He's not used to being talked to like that. *Not twice in one day, anyway,* I think, recalling Jack Kilgard's tirade on my parents' sidewalk.

"Your day's comin', son," he growls. "I've got all the records I need to prove what I told you."

"I'll bet you do. I'll bet you worked on them all last night, over a fifth of Jack Daniel's. You and Shad both. Only he drank pinot noir, right?"

The sheriff stands and steps toward me, but Shad stops him with an upraised hand. Some power dynamic exists between these two men that I don't fully understand.

"The upshot of all this is simple," Shad tells me. "The photograph you brought with you is merely a record of activities I undertook as an undercover officer for Sheriff Byrd—and for myself, obviously, as the senior law enforcement officer in the county."

"You're a disgrace to this office. That's what you are."

But Shad has regained his unruffled mien. "I know it's a shock to find out that we're back on a level playing field, but that's politics, isn't it? Change is the only constant."

Byrd snickers, then says, "Your daddy shoulda wore a rubber when he screwed that hot chocolate back in the day."

A white-hot flash of anger almost causes me to whirl and hit him, but at the last second I compose myself and turn to leave. As I near the door, the sound of Byrd's smug laughter stops me in my tracks. I turn back to him and speak with utter contempt.

"You wife-beating son of a bitch. Jack Kilgard was right. Come the next election, you're going to be looking for a job."

Byrd's eyes glint in his pocked face. "Maybe. But either way, your daddy's gonna be rotting on Parchman Farm. He's gonna die there, with all the . . ." The sheriff searches for a word, then falls silent.

"All the what, Billy? Go ahead and finish, so your partner can hear you. '*With all the niggers he loves so much.*' That's what you were going to say, wasn't it? Your mind's like a neon sign, man. You fat fuck."

Byrd's face twitches. Then he drops his right hand to the butt of the pistol in his belt.

"No!" Shad cries, jumping up and interposing himself between us. "Penn, get the hell out of here!"

Shaking with rage, I back slowly toward the door, my eyes on Shad. "What's driving you, Shad? This asshole has to stop himself saying 'nigger' ten times a day, if he bothers at all, and you've climbed into bed with him!"

Shad gives me his *Mona Lisa* smile. "Politics and bedfellows, my brother. Sometimes I'm amazed myself."

I stab my right forefinger at Billy, and though I say nothing, the subtext is clear to two Mississippi boys.

In a voice laced with malice, he says, "You better pray your daddy's bail ain't revoked. And you'd better make sure he don't break one condition of his bond. If he does, I'll own his ass until the last day of trial. And I can make it mighty rough on a prisoner in my jail. Think about that tonight when you're laid up with your dyke girlfriend, trying to get to sleep."

The prospect of my father in this man's custody sends a shudder down my back, and Billy Byrd doesn't miss it. He smiles like an arrogant prizefighter first sensing fear in his opponent.

"Don't forget your picture," Shad says brightly, walking to his desk and retrieving the printout, which he holds out to me.

"Keep it. Put it on your Wall of Respect, since you're so proud of it."

My right hand tingles as I grasp the doorknob, and something makes me turn to the DA one last time. "Stop this while you can, Shad. Before it gets so big you can't stop it."

Almost imperceptibly, the district attorney shakes his head.

"*Hubris,* Shad. Remember the word?"

Like a black Leonard Nimoy, he raises one chiding eyebrow. "That's a question better asked of your father, I think. Don't you?"

CHAPTER 40

BACK ON THE STREET, the full import of what happened in Shad John-son's office finally sinks in. For a few seconds I think I might actually vomit. I've been through many tense confrontations in my career, but not with my father's life hanging in the balance.

"This thing's going to trial," I murmur. "Christ."

Until a couple of minutes ago, I believed that the photo of Shad torturing that pit bull was my weapon of last resort, like Israel's nuclear stockpile. Now I've opened my arsenal and found my plutonium replaced with baking powder. The realization that nothing can hin-der Shad from going after my father with maximum intensity—from exploiting every sordid detail of this situation in the media—is almost paralyzing.

"Afternoon, Mayor," says a lawyer's secretary, hurrying past, her coat wrapped tight against the wind.

The temperature is dropping fast. To avoid further human interac-tion, I back into a recessed doorway and gaze at the wall of the sheriff's office and jail, whose high slit-windows give it the look of a Stalinist prison. Huddling in the nook while people stride past, I try to get my bearings and make a plan.

Nothing comes to me.

Taking out my cell phone, I dial Quentin Avery's house in Jefferson County. His cell phone rings eight times, and then a sterile female voice informs me that the AT&T customer I've called has not set up his voice mail. "Of course he hasn't. He's a fucking fossil."

Slowly it comes to me that in this town that once nurtured me—the town that, in theory, I rule—I have no power to alter the course of events. *Mayor Penn Cage*. What a joke. The title is meaningless. My Mis-sissippi law license grants me more power than my political office. As I consider heading to the City Hall parking lot for my car, one of Billy

Byrd's growled taunts comes back to me with cutting power: *Your daddy shoulda wore a rubber when he screwed that hot chocolate back in the day.*

Why do so many people seem ready to assume that my father and Viola were lovers? I'm almost certain that Shad painted this scenario for the grand jury this afternoon, and their true bill proves they believed it. Last night, even Caitlin told me I should assume that Dad had made love with Viola, given her beauty and the closeness of their work relationship.

Am I the only fool involved in this mess?

For the first time since Shad called me with the news of Viola's death, I feel utterly directionless—a ship without a rudder. Stranger still, I feel a temporal dislocation that's almost dizzying. Some passing pedestrians clutch Christmas packages in their hands, but that makes no sense. Caitlin and I were supposed to be married on Christmas Eve, which can't be many days from now, yet the idea seems absurd. I don't even have a firm grip on the *year*. The last definite event in my mind is Hurricane Katrina, which must have been . . . four months ago? Everything since seems a blur, with my father's face at the center of it. Leaning out of the doorway, I blink against the chill wind, and whatever grip I still had on the present falls way.

I am eight years old. My father has dropped me off at the hospital to visit a friend who broke both his legs in a motorcycle accident. Dad promises to return by 9:30 P.M., when visiting hours are over. *If I'm late,* he says, *walk outside and wait under the light pole by the flower bed in front of the hospital.* I do what I can to amuse my friend, who's in constant agony from the traction cables attached to pins through his femurs, and I silently resolve never to get on a motorcycle. At nine thirty, the nurses tell me I have to go.

As instructed, I take the elevator down and walk out into the humid night, then make my way down to the empty flower bed. An hour passes. Dad doesn't come for me. I have no change for a pay phone. The hospital doors are locked. Standing under the humming streetlight, I watch the cars roar past; I'm fighting tears, afraid to do anything, until my father finally drives up sometime after eleven. He tells me he's been on a house call (his all-purpose answer for every late arrival, one that is never questioned). For some reason, though, I don't believe him this time. Something in his voice, or maybe his averted eyes, tells me that he's lying. This realization terrifies me. From this moment forward, some part of me knows I cannot completely trust my father. I know only this: *My mother would never have left me alone beside the highway with no idea where to go or what to do.*

As the years passed, no similar incident occurred, yet this one stayed with me. Something about that night opened the door to a darkness that less fortunate children lived with every day and night: the horror of abandonment. And now . . . thirty-seven years later, the terror of that night has returned with paralyzing intensity. Though all the years since have reinforced the belief that my father is the paragon of virtue everyone believes he is, my certainty about that deception remains clear. *Why did he lie that night? Where had he been?*

"I was eight," I murmur, rubbing my arms to stay warm. "That means it was 1968. Spring or summer of sixty-eight."

The year Viola Turner left Natchez, I realize. *What month did she leave? April? Yes . . . soon after Martin Luther King was killed.*

My mind returns to the friend who broke his legs on the motorcycle. He lives on the West Coast now; I haven't seen him for years. Surely he would remember when he was hurt, and how long he was in the hospital. That accident changed his life. But do I really need to call him? One thing I remember for sure: his stay in the hospital caused him to miss weeks of school. So it wasn't summertime. Nor was it cold outside, while I waited for my dad. It had to be . . . spring. The spring of 1968.

"Jesus," I whisper, realizing what this might mean.

Last night Dad denied the possibility that he could be Lincoln Turner's father. I took this denial as an assertion that he'd never slept with Viola. *But was it?* He also told me that his only connection to Brody Royal had been incidental, and that the photo of them together had been a fluke.

"What if he was lying?" I murmur. "And not just about Viola, but all of it? About Royal, Leland Robb . . . *all* of it?"

The wind snatches away my words, but not before they open a chasm at my feet. I feel that if I take one step forward, I'll tumble into a blackness that has no bottom. *What now?* Should I track down my father and try to shake the truth out of him? What would be the point? If he lied last night, he'll only lie again today. I could question my mother, but that would only rip open a chasm at *her* feet, and force her to ponder the possibility that her life isn't what she's always believed it to be. I can hardly imagine a more painful or pointless course of action.

As I stand frozen in the doorway, another voice rises in my mind. It's not mine, or my father's, or any other that I've heard in a long time. This voice is soft and feminine, yet filled with conviction. It belongs to my wife, Sarah, dead seven years now. She has spoken to me only in times of great travail, and then almost too softly to hear. But tonight her words come clear to me: *If you want the truth . . . you know what to do.*

"I don't," I say to the empty street, wondering if I'm going mad.

Do what you do best, she says.

"What's that?" I mutter.

Solve the crime.

AROUND THE BLOCK FROM Shad's office, in the City Hall parking lot, I climb into my Audi and start the engine, my heart pounding from the run from Shad's office. All the way around the block, my wife's voice echoed like a mantra in my head: *Solve the crime, solve the crime. . . .*

The preliminary autopsy report Jewel Washington passed to me (in violation of the law) lies on the passenger seat beside me. I analyzed hundreds of such documents during my years as an assistant DA, but right now I can't bring myself to wade through a pathologist's report. That work is more suited to the deep of the night, when no interruptions will break my concentration. Besides, that report can only tell me so much. Without access to the crime scene evidence—all of it—I can only make deductions based on part of the picture, and that's asking for trouble. Beyond this, all my instinct tells me that Viola's murder won't be solved by deconstructing the crime, Sherlock Holmes–style. In fact, I believe I already know who actually robbed Viola of her last few days of life. According to Henry Sexton, Glenn Morehouse believed that his Double Eagle comrades murdered Viola, to bury her knowledge about the murders of her brother and Luther Davis. But the murder of Jimmy Revels was actually *ordered* by Brody Royal, in an effort carry out the will of Carlos Marcello, who wanted Bobby Kennedy dead before he could be elected president. Though that plot was ultimately aborted—due to the accidental death of Frank Knox—Jimmy and Luther were killed and "disappeared" to obliterate all trace of the plan. *How much could Viola have known about any of that?* According to Morehouse, Viola was held prisoner in the machine shop where and while her brother and

Luther were tortured, but by then the RFK hit had been canceled. Is it possible that Snake Knox and his buddies—knowing they were about to kill Jimmy, Luther, and Viola—spoke freely about Royal and Marcello's planned operation in front of their prisoners?

No. If they had, they'd never have let Viola live, no matter what my father promised them in return.

As I ponder this paradox, I realize how little the Double Eagles interest me. Their motive for murder was one-dimensional. There's no mystery in atavistic racism. But the Double Eagles almost never operated autonomously. Even before Frank Knox died, they took their cues from Brody Royal. It was Brody who wanted Pooky Wilson dead (for consorting with his daughter), and Brody who authorized killing Albert Norris. It was Brody Royal who lifted Frank Knox out of his drunken grief to try to lure Bobby Kennedy into Carlos Marcello's sights, and Royal who ordered Snake Knox to make sure Dr. Leland Robb's plane never reached its destination three years later.

"Goddamn it," I whisper. "Royal is the key."

The only real mystery in all this is my father's stubborn silence. He hasn't spoken one word about Viola's death, and he's flatly denied an intimate relationship with her. To my amazement, he seems as opaque as Brody Royal to me now. All my life, my father has seemed a model of virtue and humility, yet today a childhood memory returned to whisper that he's also a liar. Caitlin spent most of last night and half of today researching Royal, yet she discovered nothing incriminating on the multimillionaire (who Henry insists is a homicidal monster). How can I resolve these contradictions? If Royal is the sadistic sociopath Henry Sexton believes he is, how could he have concealed it for so long? And if my father isn't the medical version of Atticus Finch that we all believe him to be . . . *then what is he?*

To answer these questions, I need the kind of source that Caitlin couldn't access with all the power of her father's media empire, that the police couldn't match with all their informants and all the information petrifying in dusty file rooms across Mississippi and Louisiana. I need information that lives not on hard disks in remote servers, but in the soft tissue of aging human brains.

And one brain in particular.

Putting the Audi in gear, I back out of my parking space and pull into

Commerce Street, driving almost in a trance. A few hours ago, Caitlin said something that's resonated ever since: *"There's a secret history here . . ."* That phrase always makes me think of Donna Tartt, the Mississippi-born writer, though that title originated with Procopius and his exposé of the crimes of the emperor Justinian. Every small town has its *historia arcana*, and in Natchez, our secret historian is a woman whom few people have seen in the past ten years. A fabled recluse, she lives with her three servants in one of the finest antebellum mansions in the city. Her name is Pythia Nolan—"Pithy" to her friends—and she's probably one of the few Natchezians who could read Procopius in the original Attic Greek.

Born into one of Natchez's oldest families, Pithy was widowed in 1943, when her husband was shot down over the Pacific. She never remarried, but she lived a full and varied life, and as a result knows everything about anyone who matters in Mississippi over the age of forty, and most things about their offspring. I've used Pithy as a secret source for three of my novels, and her disguised anecdotes invariably delight or shock my readers, even those on the other side of the world. As per our agreement, her name has never appeared on my acknowledgments pages, a distinction that some locals point to with pride. Pithy operated by some personal code that I suspect made her an instrument of karma. Through what she revealed through me, she dispensed a sort of stealth justice, even if the only people who recognized themselves were those who had committed the sins for which she believed they should pay.

About a year ago, to my dismay, Pithy stopped taking my phone calls. She claimed that I hadn't sufficiently disguised information she'd given me for my last book. No amount of apology or obeisance has proved sufficient to reopen the gates of her famed mansion to me, but today I must risk rejection once more. For no one is more likely to know what secrets lie behind the public faces of Brody Royal and Tom Cage.

Pithy is probably older than Royal, and while her wealth may not be as liquid, the widowed belle probably owns more land than the Louisiana magnate. She was my father's first patient when he moved to Natchez (as she never tires of reminding him), and Dad continues to make regular house calls at her mansion, though he's almost as sick as she is. I say "almost" because Pithy is dying of emphysema. She coped well with the disease for some years, but over the past six months she's deteriorated rapidly, or so Dad tells me.

Dialing her number from the contacts list on my phone, I wait two rings; then a rich African-American voice, says, "Mrs. Nolan's residence."

That voice belongs to Flora Adams, Pithy's maid since 1956, and the daughter of her mother's maid.

"Flora, this is Penn Cage. I need to talk to Pithy, in person if you think she'll see me. It's very important."

"Mayor, if you'd called yesterday, you wouldn't have stood a chance. But if talking to you can speed up Dr. Cage coming back out here, you've got a magic key to her sickroom."

"That's exactly what I'm coming to see her about. Dad's in trouble, and I think Pithy may be able to help get him out of it."

"Come on, then. Doc Cage was s'posed to see Miss Pithy today, but he didn't show up. She's about to die for one of his cortisone shots."

"I'll be out front in five minutes."

"I'll have Darius open the gate."

Flipping the S4 into Tiptronic mode, I roar down Homochitto Street and blow through the yellow light onto Lower Woodville Road, which blurs into background as I drive. How small and helpless Henry Sexton must have felt all these years, pursuing Brody Royal—a multi-millionaire who counts senators, governors, judges, and business magnates among his close friends. A man who could with impunity order the murders of two federal witnesses and go on as though nothing had happened. If any man in this area is untouchable, it's Brody Royal. Yet the despair I felt in the doorway outside Shad's office has faded. If Shad told me the truth up in his office—if Dad's bail won't likely be revoked until Judge Elder returns next Monday—then I have six days to prove that someone else killed Viola, or at least to raise reasonable doubt. And if anyone can illuminate the hidden chapters of my town's history, it's the old woman dying in regal splendor in her cloistered mansion, the keeper of our collective secrets. . . .

Pithy Nolan.

CHAPTER 41

WALT GARRITY'S SILVER Roadtrek hummed northward on Highway 61 in the diffuse glow of the setting sun. He and Tom had been making mile-long laps on a stretch of Highway 61 while Snake Knox and Sonny Thornfield ate supper at a nearby Ryan's Steakhouse.

Tom had told Walt enough to convince him of the tactical soundness of his plan, but thankfully his old friend had not pressed him for more information. Even with the bond of shared combat—and worse—Tom was not sure he could tell Walt everything. There was no risk of losing their quarry, because earlier Walt had affixed a GPS tracking device beneath Knox's pickup, which could be monitored on a screen he'd plugged into his cigarette lighter. Walt had done this at the Concordia airport, while Knox visited the service hangar. When they traced Snake to Ryan's to test the GPS tracker, Tom had recognized Sonny Thornfield getting out of another pickup truck nearby. Apparently, the two men had met for an early supper. Walt intended to attach a tracker to Thornfield's pickup as well, but he was worried he might be seen from one of the restaurant's broad windows.

Walt drove with a plastic Coke cup between his legs, while Tom munched on a Wendy's cheeseburger in the passenger seat. Every now and then Walt's police scanner chattered—too low for Tom to make out the messages, but Walt apparently missed nothing. The codes meant nothing to Tom anyway, except for a few he remembered from his days staffing the St. Catherine's ER.

"Food all right?" Walt asked.

"Good," Tom said, reaching for iced tea to wash down his cheeseburger. "Peggy would kill me if she knew I was eating this."

Walt gave an obligatory chuckle. Then his voice dropped, and he said, "I know you don't like lying to your boy."

"It's better this way," Tom said, trying to believe it. "Penn's got too much weighing on him already. And I don't want him worrying Quentin to death."

"Does that old lawyer know how to keep his mouth shut?"

Tom nodded. "When Quentin Avery goes to his grave, a lot of people will rest easier."

"From what you said, it doesn't sound like that'll be a very long trip."

Tom looked out at what remained of the little town of Washington, which had been the capital of the Mississippi Territory until 1802. "None of us knows the length of that trip, do we?"

Walt slowed and began a careful U-turn near the entrance to Jefferson Military College, where John James Audubon had once taught as a professor. "Some are closer than others. A grunt walking through a minefield is likely to buy it a lot sooner than a Remington Raider."

"Remington Raider" was what they'd called rear-echelon typists in Korea. Tom tapped the window absently, his mind on other things. He'd missed a house call earlier that day, on one of his favorite patients, an elderly woman dying of emphysema. "Brother, at this age we're all in the minefield."

"Speak for yourself. I intend to be keeping Carmelita just as happy ten years from now as I am today."

Tom watched his breath fog the window glass. He hoped his friend would be that lucky. He'd watched so many friends and patients die over the past ten years that life seemed the most fragile and tenuous state imaginable. Korea had taught him that lesson early, but somehow he'd blinded himself to it in the intervening years. You basically had to, to function in the world. But the steadily lengthening list of the dead—Viola's only the latest name to be added—had forced him to confront the fact that he had little time left himself. That was tough enough from an existential perspective; but to have his perception of his whole history shattered, and with it his legacy, as had happened in the past two days, had pushed him into uncharted territory. Tom had never felt so alone and isolated.

Jumping bail on a murder charge was probably the most extreme action he had taken in his life. Had he followed the mildly restrictive terms of his bail, he would have been entitled to the presumption of innocence by all men and women of goodwill. But now he was a fugitive, his flight a tacit admission of guilt. Any cop who recognized him could use deadly force to take him into custody, and if he died in the process, no one would ask too many questions. Tom had actually been counting on that. But that didn't make the reality easier. Walt Garrity was risking his life at this moment. Tom had already let so many people down, Viola and Peggy first among them. Penn, after that. But there were others, and the tragedy was that he might never be able to explain his behavior to them.

"Screw this," Walt muttered. "I'm going to plant that tracker when we make this next pass. You keep lookout."

A ripple of fear went through Tom's chest. "Are you sure?"

"Hell, yeah. Those two are in there digging into a couple of T-bones, not watching the parking lot."

This time, when they reached the steak house, Walt turned into the big lot and parked two spaces away from Sonny Thornfield's pickup.

Tom popped a nitro under his tongue, hoping to head off his angina.

"Two minutes," Walt said, holding the magnetized device in his hand. "I'm gonna wire this baby into his electrical system, just like the other one. We're not gonna risk having dead batteries when it comes to the action. If you see those assholes coming out of the restaurant, start the engine. I'll hear it."

Tom started to warn his friend to be careful, but Walt had already left the van.

CHAPTER 42

PYTHIA NOLAN'S PALATIAL antebellum mansion stands on eighty-eight forested acres in the middle of Natchez. Called "Corinth," it's one of the few great houses still in the hands of the family that built it. As a rule, I don't like Greek Revival mansions—especially the local variety, bland boxes with columned porticos—but Corinth was built on the scale of an authentic Greek temple, and its craftsmanship is beyond replication in our era.

The estate's wrought-iron gate stands twelve feet tall and is usually closed, but today I find it open, with Darius Stone, Pithy's driver, waiting for me in a fifteen-year-old Bentley. After I drive through, Darius closes the gate and follows me up the paved private road to the house. The driveway is probably half a mile long, and it winds through acres of oak and elm trees bearded with Spanish moss. Half a dozen Hollywood production companies have begged to use Corinth in their films, but Pithy has never allowed it.

As the mansion comes into sight, I see Xerxes, Darius's aptly named son, operating a truck-mounted auger near a line of shrubs. His dark muscles ripple in the fading light, but because of the roar of the tool's motor, he doesn't look up until I'm almost past him. Recognizing me, he waves, then goes back to work.

Flora Adams awaits me at the front door. One of the few maids in town who still wear a uniform, Flora has the imperious manner of an exiled queen. She's always driven a Lincoln Town Car—one that belongs to her, not her employer—and her three sons all graduated from college, courtesy of Pithy Nolan. Flora also owns a fine two-story house in town, which Pithy gave her twenty years ago. After Pithy fell ill, Flora chose to live in Corinth's renovated slave quarters for convenience's sake.

"She said bring you right up," Flora says, holding open the door.

"She's had a rough couple of days. She misses Dr. Cage something terrible. I believe she misses you, too, though she'd never admit it."

As Flora leads me to the grand staircase, I recall a story my mother told me about Pithy Nolan. Pithy achieved fame—or infamy, depending on one's prejudices—in the late 1960s, during a historic Garden Club meeting. The issue in question was whether to terminate the practice of serving refreshments during the annual Spring Pilgrimage tours, since new federal laws would allow "people of color" to actually tour the great southern mansions—homes they had previously been allowed in only as slaves or paid servants. Carried to its logical conclusion, this practice might result in southern ladies of good family actually waiting upon "Negroes" at table. ("Oh, the horror!") This discussion, prickly at first, quickly became heated, with the majority clamoring to do away with refreshments altogether. After twenty minutes of squabbling, Pythia Nolan stood up and cleared her throat.

As a "homeowner," she enjoyed special status in the Garden Club. But unlike many homeowners who were "house poor," Pithy Nolan still had wads of cash. And not only did she own one of the city's crown jewels, but she also had an impeccably blue bloodline dating back to the Revolutionary War. Pithy was a past president of the Daughters of the American Revolution, a summa cum laude graduate of Bryn Mawr, and the widow of a war hero. Furthermore, she had the brass of any five ladies present. So when Pithy Nolan cleared her throat, the room fell silent.

She cast her icy gaze about the room and said, "Heaven spare us from all this *jabbering*. There's not one woman here who hasn't served her own maid supper a hundred times, waited on her hand and foot, and eaten from the same set of utensils. The refreshment service brings much-needed money to this club. So put an end to all this *hysteria* and move on to something that actually matters. I'm starving."

The tinkle of a china cup boomed like a thunderclap in the silence that followed Pithy's radical statement of the obvious. But sixty seconds later, the assembled ladies voted in a landslide to continue the refreshment service, regardless of who might show up. On the outcome of such quotidian skirmishes hinges the march of Progress. Pithy Nolan did more for racial equality that day than a hundred CORE workers marching the streets of Natchez could have managed in a month.

Now, forty years later, she lies in her upstairs bedroom, chained to the oxygen tank that gives only partial relief from her advanced emphysema. Facing imminent death, Pithy finally quit smoking her beloved cigarettes last year. According to Dad, it was Flora who finally cut her off, enduring repeated firings during the process. Pithy eventually rehired her, of course, being unable to subsist without Flora's ministrations.

I remind myself not to look shocked when Flora opens the bedroom door. Pithy has a regal bearing, even in her sickbed, but she looks much thinner than when I last saw her, and her eyes are frighteningly hollow.

"It's not *you* I want to see," she says in a weak voice. "It's your father. But come closer. Let's see if you've aged as much as I have."

Tensing my stomach against the sickroom smells, I move to Pithy's bedside. Flora motions me to the chair she sits in throughout the day. Half a crocheted comforter lies draped over the table beside it, a gleaming blue needle left in the yarn. Near Pithy's bed, a heavy funk of old urine, flatulence, and medicinal creams simmers beneath a welcome breath of fresh eucalyptus. Then I see crushed leaves scattered on her bedside tables.

"Don't stand on ceremony!" she says. "Take a seat. You've always been a gentleman, even if you don't know when to stop writing."

"Pithy, I—"

"Water under the bridge. Tell me where my doctor is. I'll tell you every secret I know for ten milligrams of cortisone."

I can't help but smile. Dad has probably injected Pithy's arthritic joints with ten times the legal limit of steroids over the years. Today her skin—which in the oil portrait downstairs glows like fresh cream—looks as thin and fragile as rice paper. Her brilliant blue eyes are clouded, and they look wet, as though someone just administered eyedrops.

"I'm sorry, but I don't know where Dad is," I confess. "That's why I'm here."

"Well, you must think I can help, or you wouldn't be here. Start talking. I'll need to get back on my oxygen soon."

"Dad's in trouble, Pithy."

"I've heard some things. Enough trouble to postpone a wedding?"

I can't help but smile again. "You heard that, too?"

She rolls her eyes. Pithy's telephone is her lifeline to the world, and even in her present condition she doesn't miss much. "You go on and marry that girl, even if she is half a Yankee. She's got spunk, and you've dawdled long enough."

"I'm going to. Postponing the ceremony was Caitlin's idea."

"Well, don't let her get away. You're ten years older than she is. Remember the old adage: 'Don't keep a girl guessing too long, or she'll find the answer somewhere else.' "

Flora chuckles behind me. "Sho' will."

"Bring Penn a cold drink, Flo. I think we still have one or two cans of Tab down in the icebox. And bring me some sherry to go with this nasty ginger tea."

"All right."

As Flora's steps fade, I say, "They indicted him, Pithy. For murder."

"I heard. But darling, there's a world of difference between that and being convicted. Some of the best people have been indicted for one thing or another. And anyone worth knowing has been arrested at *least* once."

"Have you?"

She vouchsafes me a smile. "What Mardi Gras anecdote is complete without a night in jail?" Pithy fans her face with her hand. "Enough repartee. What do I know that you don't?"

"Tell me about Brody Royal."

Pithy inclines her head slightly, and I can almost see the flash of synapses behind her eyes. "What do you want to know?"

There's no point trying to hide anything from this woman, and I haven't got time anyway. "Brody almost certainly killed some people a while back, mostly black men. Albert Norris and Pooky Wilson to start. He also ordered the deaths of Jimmy Revels and Luther Davis. Probably Dr. Leland Robb, too, which caused the deaths of three other innocent people."

My bald assertion has managed to impress a woman not easily shocked. "Well, well," she trills. "You said a mouthful there. If Brody Royal did all that, why didn't the high sheriff hang him in the court-house square? Why is he roaming free?"

"That's what I've come to find out."

"Dear me. Sooner or later, everything comes to the surface, doesn't it?"

"Talk to me, Pithy. Please. And don't hold anything back."

Without my saying it, she knows that her answers will somehow bear on my father's fate. "Most people think Brody came from wealth," she begins. "Nothing could be further from the truth. His father was a storekeeper and bootlegger in St. Bernard Parish. When Stanley Duchaine and his banker friends dynamited the levee in 1927 to save New Orleans, St. Bernard and Plaquemines parishes were wiped out. Brody's father lost everything. He—and eventually Brody—rebuilt his business from nothing, and they didn't worry about which side of the law they were on. They were in thick with those Italians who ended up running the city."

"The Marcello family?"

"That's right. The ones who put the slot machines into Concordia Parish when Huey Long was governor, then later when Noah Cross was sheriff. My husband despised Brody, for getting his mob connections to fix it so he could avoid military service during the war. Anyway, Brody did a little bit of everything until 1948, when he struck oil near Natchez. One of the biggest early fields, I believe, and it's still producing. That staked him, and he never looked back. Before you could shake a stick at a snake, he owned a bank, an insurance company, and thousands of acres of timber."

"You sure know a lot about him."

She gives me a secretive smile. "Brody courted me for a while. Although *pursued* might be a better word."

"What?"

"He and I are exactly the same age. The year I was queen of the Confederate Pageant, Brody tried everything he could to get me to marry him. But I'd just lost my husband to the war, and I was no fool. I saw what he was after."

"What? Sex?"

"Lord, no. He got that from half the floozies on both sides of the river. Brody wanted respectability. My family was everything his wasn't. He'd never forgotten where he came from, and he never wanted anyone to be above him again. He *hated* those haughty New Orleans bankers who'd ruined his father, and he'd made up his mind to become one of them. The biggest of them. And he's done it, though it took decades. He got his revenge, too."

"What do you mean?"

"One of the richest of those New Orleans moneymen was originally from Natchez. His daughter Catherine spent a lot of time here as a child. Cathy was in my court when I was queen, and once Brody found out who she was, he went after her with a vengeance—literally. She didn't know enough to see through his charm. She married him—pregnant—and her father nearly disowned her for it."

"That was Brody's revenge?"

"Only the beginning, I'm afraid. Marrying Catherine opened the doors that had always been shut to him, doors no amount of money could open. The right Mardi Gras krewe, the Yacht Club, the second-best gentlemen's club. And once he had that . . . Brody didn't need her anymore."

"What happened?"

"A lot of private suffering, I know. Some of it terrible, if rumor can be believed. In the end, Cathy drowned in her own bathtub. That was, oh . . . 1962. Her blood alcohol level was off the chart, so nobody looked too deeply into it. But her father was still alive, and I imagine he knew the truth. Brody had been cheating on Cathy from the beginning. That was no secret. And he'd got control of quite a bit of the family money by managing their investments. In the end, he virtually broke the father."

"It sounds like *The Count of Monte Cristo.*"

"Not far from it. Revenge never brought Brody happiness, though. Nothing could. He's gotten steadily richer, but his family . . ."

"What?"

"The sons are lazy. They're from his second marriage. The daughter was his hope, I think. Katy was a pretty thing, and all the local beaux chased her. But something happened after her mother's death. Katy disappeared, and everyone assumed she'd gotten pregnant. Back in those days, they sent girls to relatives to have the babies. But it turned out that Brody had committed her to an asylum in Texas. A private sanatorium—very tony, but still. A year later, Katy came back without any baby. If there ever was one, I suppose it was given up for adoption."

"What about abortion?"

"Very difficult in those days, dear. Anyway, Brody married Katy to one of his workmen, an awful Black Irishman. A jumped-up roughneck, basically." Pithy shook her head with poignant sadness. "I don't know what they did to that girl in Texas, but all her spark was gone. And with that chapter closed, Brody turned his hand to making money again."

"Until he married Dr. Robb's wife in 1970."

The old woman gives me a sharp look. "Something tells me that for once, you know more than I do about something."

"I'm pretty sure Brody arranged for that plane to go down."

"Because he wanted to marry Sue Robb?"

"That was probably half the reason," I tell her. "But Dr. Robb also knew about earlier murders Brody had committed."

Pithy taps her fingers on the coverlet, trying to absorb this. "You don't think Brody killed all these people himself, surely?"

"No. Some ex-Klansmen helped him. Knoxes from across the river."

Pithy twists her lips so angrily that I think she's about to spit. "I curse the day the city brought in outsiders to work at those factories after the war. Most were decent working people trying to better themselves, of course. But others . . . that's where the Klan recruited their rank and file. They were *trash*. Low, unadulterated white trash. Back-shooters and bombers."

Decades ago, David L. Cohn, a well-known Mississippi intellectual, made this case in the pages of the *New Yorker* (echoing Goethe from a century earlier). For all I know, Cohn used Pithy as his source. "Did you ever have any contact with the Knoxes and their cronies?"

"Why, they accosted me right on Main Street! Outside the H. F. Byrne shoe store. Some workers from that battery plant told me I was 'messin' in nigra business.' Said I'd better keep in line or else there'd be trouble. I said, 'Jody McNeely, if Major Nolan wasn't lying at the bottom of the Pacific, he'd knock you to the curb this instant. I can't do that, but if I see you dragging one of those timber crosses onto my property, I'll shoot you down and sort it out with the sheriff afterwards.'" Pithy lowers her head, cold fire in her eyes. "And don't think I wouldn't have done it. I shot my first deer when I was ten."

"How did they take that?"

She laughed softly. "It plumb stumped them! The ringleader nearly swallowed his Adam's apple. Their kind always was easily intimidated. They're peasants in their bones, and they jump at the crack of a whip."

"Brody Royal won't."

Her smile vanishes. "No, he won't."

"What about his attorney, Claude Devereux?"

Pithy makes a sour face. "Comparing that shyster to a snake would be a slander to the serpent." While I try to think of how to segue into the question of my father's past, maternal concern flows from the old woman's eyes. "Penn, you're your father's son, and I love you for it. You're a knight in shining armor, and most of the time, that's a fine thing. But fights with men like this aren't won in court. Snakes as old as Brody and Claude have already been trampled by most beasts of the field, and lived to tell the tale."

I lay my hand over her cool, dry fingers and squeeze gently. "I've been in darker places than you know, Pithy. I can handle myself."

She gazes back at me with unnerving intensity. "So has your father, dear. Tom was in combat, the same as my husband, and no man comes through that unscathed."

"Pithy . . . do you think there's any chance that Dad could have been friends with Brody Royal? Even a long time ago?"

She draws back her head, her opinion clear. "Absolutely not. The only man I even remember being close to Brody was Leo Marston, and Leo *hated* Tom. You know that."

I remember Henry saying something about Brody and Judge Marston being partners. Leo was one of the cruelest sons of bitches I knew among the parents of kids I grew up with, and if he and Royal were friends, then I can't imagine my father spending any time at all with Brody—which squares with what Dad told me.

Pithy's face tightens with sudden urgency. "Why aren't the two of you working together on this? Where *is* Tom? Is he hurt? Has someone kidnapped him?"

"No, no," I reassure her. "He's fine."

But Pithy isn't fooled. With oracular vision, she sees right through me, all the way down to my deepest fears. "Poor darling. Every son and daughter learns a heartbreaking truth someday. I only hope that in this case it's something you can live with."

"Since you were Dad's first patient, you must have known Viola Turner."

The old woman takes a deeper breath than she has up to now, then lets it out very slowly. "Of course I did. But don't ask me anything you don't want the answer to."

Her warning chills me, but this is half the reason I've come. "Did Viola and Dad have an affair, Pithy?"

"I can't speak to that. But your father loved that girl—that I do know."

"How do you know?"

"Men are simple creatures, but they're not all the same. Many from your father's generation, doctors especially, went a little crazy in the 1960s. They'd grown up in the corseted thirties and forties, studied day and night, married as virgins. Then suddenly the world changed. They were making money, they were respected, and women threw themselves at their feet. A lot of them rogered everything wearing a skirt. They never considered leaving their wives, of course. They just wanted sex."

"And Dad?"

"Your father wasn't one of those. Tom was a fine and faithful fellow. But *that* kind of man is susceptible to a different kind of temptation. You see, the women of that period—women like your mother—grew up with the biggest dose of Calvinist guilt and shame any American women ever got. And it gave them problems in the boudoir. Even faithful husbands couldn't help wondering what it would be like to be with a woman who didn't carry that crippling burden."

"A woman like Viola?"

Pithy shrugs. "Who knows? She was part Creole, and those girls were wise in the ways of love. Although not all black women were the unfettered carnal creatures of myth. Negro girls got a heavy dose of guilt in their churches, too. But some women, black or white, are just different. You've heard the expression 'old soul'? Well, some women are born with a *free* soul. A soul that all the fire and brimstone in the world can't hem in. I knew a girl like that in college. When women like that give themselves, they give everything, even if it kills them. And I don't think any man alive can resist that."

"Was Viola like that?"

Pithy focuses on some invisible point in space. "Yes. I felt it before I saw it. Viola was beautiful, but there was something hidden beneath her beauty. 'Still waters run deep,' the saying goes. And your father wasn't the kind to miss that. No one could ever say Tom Cage was slow."

"Did Viola love him?"

Pithy looks at me like a disappointed tutor. "Viola recognized Tom the same way he did her. One man in ten thousand. Lord, I was half in love with him myself. Still am, and I'm old as dirt."

Just as I smile again, Pithy brings me back to reality with a kick in the gut. "Are you afraid he really killed her, Penn?"

I look deep into her watery eyes. "If I told you he did, would you doubt me?"

"Not if it was done from mercy. For any other reason, yes. I'm counting on Tom to help me when my time comes. When the oxygen stops working, and all that's left is to lie here suffocating . . . I'll know it's time."

I squeeze her hand again. "Has he told you he would?"

"He doesn't have to *tell* me. He'll do the right thing when the time comes. Your father's got more courage than any man I've met since my husband, the consequences be damned."

"Viola's death wasn't a mercy killing."

"Then Tom didn't do it. I heard she died terribly, but I didn't know what was true. If that's the case, then don't waste a minute worrying about it."

"How can you be so sure?"

"Because I know Tom. Murder's not in him."

I look at the floor. "I'm not sure what's in him anymore."

Pithy flicks her left hand as though at a fly. "Pooh. Not in any universe could Tom Cage murder a woman he loved. But having an affair . , , any man can do that. Woman, too." Pithy draws her fingers from beneath my hand and takes hold of my wrist. "Let me tell you one of *my* secrets. When I was twenty-one, my father seduced my best friend. My mother had no idea, of course, but it happened."

Pithy hasn't often revealed family secrets to me—at least not those of *her* family. "You knew this at the time?"

"I found out. My friend was so despondent that she attempted suicide. Always more dramatic than efficient, was Emily. But still . . . the damage was done."

"Did you tell your mother about it?"

"Don't be obtuse, dear. I didn't have to tell her."

"I thought you said she didn't know about it."

Pithy gives me a sidelong glance. "For God's sake. On some level, mothers know *everything*."

"Mama knows," I murmur.

"What's that?"

"Something a friend of mine used to say. _Mama knows_. It implies a sort of maternal extrasensory perception, I think."

Pithy smiles. "A wise friend. But my point was, you can't give this sexual nonsense too much weight. Did the fact that Martin Luther King diddled all those women change what he did for his people? Or Franklin Roosevelt? General Eisenhower? Not one whit. Men are men, and gods are for storybooks. And if you've read your Edith Hamilton or Jane Harrison—or the Old Testament, for that matter—you'll know that gods acted like men most of the time, or worse."

"I realize Dad's as human as the next man."

"No, you don't. And that why this hurts so much."

I try to pull my hand back, but Pithy holds me with surprising strength.

"Lord, I wish you could get me a shot of cortisone. My joints are red-hot."

"I'm going to call Melba as soon as I leave and get you taken care of."

She frowns, afraid to get her hopes up. "Melba can't prescribe, can she?"

"I'll get Drew to order your shot."

The china-blue eyes widen with gratitude. "You're my _angel_, dear. You have _made my day_."

I'm your fix, I reply silently, but I say nothing. Who could deny a dying woman a little comfort?

"I need my oxygen now," she says. "I'm going to buzz Flora."

As she touches a button, I reach down to the portable cart by her bed and retrieve the mask, then carefully fit it around her head. It feeds oxygen to her nose but keeps her mouth free to talk.

"I met Edith Hamilton at Bryn Mawr," she says wistfully. "Did I tell you? She gave the most wonderful lecture: _The Greek Way_." Pithy shivers suddenly, then takes a sip of cold tea from her bedside table. "Ugh . . . this would give a billy goat indigestion. Don't leave yet, Penn. Let me get settled. This talk about Tom has me _frazzled_."

"I'm not going anywhere."

She takes several deep breaths as though trying to quell panic. "You know, sometimes . . . when I get oxygen-deprived . . . I hook up the machine, and then the gas hits my lungs . . . and I _see_ things."

I suppress a smile. Pithy Nolan has always been conscious that she was named for the priestess of the cave at Delphi. She's the third Pythia in her family, and it's long been said that the women in the maternal line possessed "second sight," a colloquial term for the gift of prophecy. A hundred years ago, women in New Orleans and Baltimore quietly sought out her grandmother in matters involving family decisions, believing that she had foreknowledge of the future. Pithy has told me of cases where she predicted the illnesses or deaths of certain people.

As Flora pads into the room, I reflect on the irony of a woman of rigorous intellect believing in the idea of precognition.

"Flo," Pithy says. "Go down the hall to that cabinet where I keep my old jewelry and look in the bottom drawer. Bring me what's folded up in tissue paper at the back. You know what I'm talking about?"

"Yes. I'll get it."

Flora gives me a curious look as she departs, but I can't read her meaning.

"I knew Albert Norris," Pithy says dreamily. "That man had a way with white people. In those days, colored men would stand off and let whites get comfortable before they approached. Albert didn't do that. He didn't have to. White people just naturally warmed to him. He was always in and out of white homes. Folks were mighty upset when he died. That went a long way toward turning people against the Klan across the river."

"I've heard that. You just breathe, Pithy."

"No . . . I want to talk. I've missed our little confabs."

"Have you heard from your son lately?"

"Oh, Robby's still up in Boston. He'll never come back south again, except to bury me. He'll sell Corinth off to some greedy carpetbagger."

She chuckles to keep from crying, and then her eyes close. Time passes, marked by the soft rush of labored breathing, and then Flora silently appears beside me.

"I got it, Miss Pithy," she whispers, as though hoping the old woman won't hear her.

Pithy's eyes blink, then open and focus on me. "Give it to Mayor Cage."

Flora unfolds the tissue paper and hands me what appears to be a small straight razor with a sterling silver handle. I recognize the razor from seeing my father receive old-fashioned barbershop shaves as a boy, but also from more than one crime scene in Houston. Some older black and Mexican criminals tended to use them, and I knew cops who used straight razors as throw-down weapons, because they're so easy to conceal.

"Brody Royal gave me that as a present when we were courting," Pithy says, as though still shocked by the idea. "Can you imagine? He said it was for my protection. In case I ever got into a tight spot. Look at the engraving on the handle."

Examining the silver handle, I make out the faint inscription, "A Lady's Best Friend," in fine script.

"Could anything say more about the man than that?" Pithy asks. "A straight razor is a pimp's weapon. Or a prostitute's. Maybe a professional gambler's, if you want to be charitable. But Brody didn't know any better, you see? *That was the world he'd grown up in.*"

Carefully opening the blade, I realize what a perfect weapon of last resort this razor would be. Far slimmer than a pocketknife, it could easily hide behind the seam of any garment.

"Take that with you," Pithy says, lifting a hand to silence my protest. "To remind you who you're up against. Don't expect fair play. Don't expect chivalry."

"I won't forget."

She grimaces in pain. "I need a Valium, Flo. My heart is racing."

Flora goes to the bedside table and takes a small white pill from its bottle, then holds it up to Pithy's mouth with a cup of water. The old woman shakes her head, and the maid pulls back the mask and places the pill under her tongue.

"Your daddy taught me this," Pithy whispers. "Hits the bloodstream faster."

Flora and I stand silently beside the bed for a couple of minutes, and in that time Pithy's eyelids slowly fall.

"Is she asleep?"

"I never know," Flora whispers. "Sometimes I think she is, and then she'll raise up when a car passes a mile out on the highway." The maid steps closer to the bed and studies her employer's face, then turns to me. "I think you can go now. I'm so glad you came. It did her a world of good."

"I'm going to send Melba out to give her a shot."

"Good. Her joints have given her the devil this week."

"How are *your* joints doing?"

Flora's smile broadens. "Did Doc tell you about me?"

"Tell me what?"

"Sometimes, when my ol' Arthur gets bad, Doc gives me a little shot, too. On the way out to his car, usually."

It suddenly strikes me that when my father dies, it's people like this who will mourn him most deeply. In shotgun shacks and mansions alike, people like Flora and Pithy will sit and remember the doctor who came to their bedside, and listened, and did what he could to make their lives a little better.

"You be careful, Mayor," Flora says.

My hand is on the doorknob when Pithy calls, "Wait!" in full voice. When I turn, the old woman is propped up on one elbow, her face tight with pain.

"What's the matter?" I ask, hurrying to her side.

The old dowager shakes her head, her eyes wide in terror.

Flora looks as shaken as I am by Pithy's sudden fervor. "Settle down, now," she says, but this does no good. Pithy is staring beyond me as though at some spectral presence, but there's only wallpaper there. "Remember what Aristotle said!" she cries. "*Undeservedly you will atone for the sins of your fathers.* And Horace!"

Horace? "What did Horace say, Pithy?"

"*Mothers are fonder than fathers of their children, because they're more certain they are their own.*"

This sends a shock through me. I feel a strange dread, perhaps even a presentiment of some approaching calamity. Suddenly the old woman grabs my hand, looks wildly into my eyes, and cries, "If all the girls who attended the Yale prom were laid end to end, I wouldn't be a bit surprised!"

Flora takes hold of Pithy's shoulders and gently forces her down onto the pillows. "You'd better go, Mayor."

"No!" Pithy insists, still wide-eyed. "Something's burning!"

Flora sniffs the air. "No, Miss Pithy. Ain't nothing burnin'."

"*Don't lie to me! The fires of hell are God's love, scalding torture to the sinner.*" The old woman's head bobs up and down for emphasis, and then she sags back into the covers.

Flora turns to me, stricken with grief.

"Does this happen often?" I whisper.

The maid shakes her head and crosses herself. "You go on. We'll be all right."

I lean over the bed and look down at Pithy's half-closed eyes. "What do you see, Pithy?"

The old woman squints like a sailor staring into a storm, then collapses as though drained of all energy.

Flora takes my hand and pulls me away from the bed. "I'll take care of her, Penn."

"I think Drew should examine her."

"She'll be all right. This, too, shall pass."

Honoring Flora's request, I back slowly out of the room. When I reach the door, the maid turns from the bed and looks at me. "Don't pay her no mind. I think when you asked about her son, it upset her. That's all it was. Miss Pithy's strong, but she never got over her husband being killed like that, while she was with child. That's why she never remarried."

"Thank you, Flora."

"Go take care of your daddy. The Lord has more work for him to do yet."

Slipping the straight razor into my inside coat pocket, I descend the grand staircase and walk out into the filtered light of the setting sun. As I take out my cell phone to call Drew's office about the cortisone, an adamantine certainty settles in my heart. I was right to come here. Though Pithy Nolan didn't know one fact about how Viola died, she's convinced me that Brody Royal and the Double Eagles murdered the dying nurse. Whatever else my father may be guilty of, he's held his silence only to protect our family from those men. The only mysteries are how to prove this, and how to do it without getting killed.

CHAPTER 43

DARKNESS FELL FAST over Ferriday, sweeping across the delta as the sun fled westward, covering the empty fields and farm roads with shadow, then darkness. The ragged parade of dilapidated businesses along Highway 84 turned into a twinkling line of lights, like a convoy of ships sailing between the islands of Ferriday and Vidalia. That string of lights stretched all the way across the twin bridges linking Vidalia to Natchez on its high bluff, but the proud old city was a world away from Henry Sexton, who sat before his computer in the offices of the *Beacon*, on the dark northern edge of Ferriday.

All afternoon he'd been moving boxes of files into his Explorer, preparing to transport them to his girlfriend's house, which was much closer to Natchez. If he was going to be working for Caitlin Masters (his publisher had graciously given him permission a few hours earlier), then he needed his files closer than twelve miles away. He didn't trust Masters enough to store his files in her building—not yet anyway—but he was excited, and nervous, too. Filing stories for a media group with more than twenty newspapers was a foreign concept to him after all his years at the *Beacon*. But Penn was right: the murders of Viola Turner and Glenn Morehouse would require that, as would the bones coming up out of the Jericho Hole.

Henry hadn't yet told Caitlin that he'd decided to work for her. She'd called his cell phone four times in the past two hours, but his pride demanded that he leave her in suspense a bit longer. *Maybe tomorrow morning*, he thought. *What could it hurt?* Besides, he had a few more leads he wanted to run down before he was working on Caitlin Masters's dime.

He'd been working to set up a meeting with Toby Rambin, the poacher in Lusahatcha County who claimed to know the location of the Bone Tree. Henry had held back that information from Penn both last night and today. (You couldn't give a man everything you had right off, even if you did like him.) He'd also made another phone call to Katy Royal Regan, after confirming that her husband was at the Royal Insurance office. This time the courtesy that Katy had shown during Henry's previous visit was nowhere in evidence. His call had plainly terrified her, and she screamed that he should never contact her again. Her last words still echoed in Henry's ears: *Pooky's dead! I'm not! What do you expect me to DO?* However upset the woman was, her words certainly seemed to confirm that she remembered *something* about Pooky Wilson.

This tantalizing development had brought Henry more anxiety than satisfaction. Until that call, he'd pretty much convinced himself that the smartest thing to do was run a front-page story on Thursday that would cover his theories about all the murders he'd been working, even if he couldn't cite all his sources. Once he did that—if he wrote it right—the Double Eagles would stand to gain nothing by hurting him or his loved ones, and the FBI couldn't accuse him of holding back evidence. Better still, printing a comprehensive story in the *Beacon* would assuage his guilt about moving over to the *Examiner* to cover the more recent developments. Mr. Fraser would have the pleasure and pride of publishing the story that would cap Henry's years of investigation, and Henry felt he owed the man that. But the idea that Katy Royal might remember enough about the events surrounding Albert's and Pooky's deaths in 1964 to convict her father and the Double Eagles made Henry reluctant to jump the gun.

"It's always something," he muttered. "Damn."

He stared at his old Compaq computer with dread. Moving boxes of files was easy compared to trying to copy all the data on his hard drive. But he needed it. He had never used a notebook computer, and now he was going to pay the price for being behind the times.

"Dang," he muttered, realizing he'd left the external hard drive he'd bought at Walmart in the front seat of his Explorer.

He sighed, then got up and walked past the front desk to the door.

"Did you get finished?" Lou Ann Whittington asked from the desk.

"Not even close. I've still got to copy my hard drive."

Lou Ann was only ten years older than Henry, but she smiled like a proud mother. "Well, don't sound like that. You're moving up to the big time."

Henry grinned. "I don't know about that. I feel pretty guilty about it, actually."

"Don't, hon. It's the story that matters. Getting it out to the most people. Right?"

"Right."

"I'm going to leave in a couple of minutes. I've got to get home and make supper for Sam. You be sure and call for a deputy before you go. It's pitch-black out there now, and the last cruiser passed about five minutes ago."

Henry's smile vanished. Walker Dennis had kept one or another of his patrol cars sitting outside the *Beacon* office for most of the day. Henry figured he was doing this as a favor to Penn Cage, or maybe because he didn't want the embarrassment of Henry being injured on his watch. But there was also the possibility that Dennis was creating a false sense of security in order to set him up. Henry didn't really believe this, but he also knew that he'd been naïve in the past. That was why he'd agreed to let Lou Ann lend him her pepper spray, which was now attached to his key ring.

"I will," he promised. "Tell Sam I hope his gallbladder surgery goes well."

Lou Ann smiled again. "I will. You knock 'em dead over in Natchez."

Henry thanked her and went out to his Explorer. The air was cooler than it had been before sundown, but it still wasn't truly cold. He walked around to the far side of his vehicle to retrieve the new hard drive from his passenger seat. He was putting his key into the lock when he noticed that the Explorer's rear window had been smashed. As his eyes narrowed, he heard a scratch of gravel on asphalt, then a rush of feet.

Whirling, he saw something fly at his head. He threw up his hands out of instinct, and felt his left forearm break to the musical ring of metal. *Baseball bat,* he thought, as pain blasted through his body.

"Grab his arms!" someone shouted. "Get him in the truck!"

Adrenaline surged through Henry, turning his heart into a runaway engine. He saw three vague shapes in the darkness, two grasping at him, the third holding high a shining blue bat. Pale faces lunged toward him, eyes blazing with hatred.

They're just kids, he realized. *What the hell?*

Powerful hands closed on his broken arm. He brought up his key ring with the other, mashed his thumb on the canister of pepper spray, and waved his arm wildly. The boys began to scream and curse, and then the bat crashed down on his right wrist. He heard his keys hit the cement. He could hardly see through the pain arcing through his head.

"My *eyes!*" yelled a boy. "*I can't see!*"

"Get him in the goddamned truck!"

Groping along the edge of his Explorer, Henry tried to move toward the *Beacon* building, but the bat glanced against his skull, knocking him nearly senseless. Blood ran into his eyes. He wanted to scream, *Why are you doing this?* But he barely had the breath to stay on his feet.

The powerful hands grabbed his arm again, and searing agony almost brought him to his knees. Only the blood in his eyes distracted him from the pain. As they dragged him away from his SUV, Henry kicked out as hard as he could with his right leg. He connected with something. A man screamed, and one pair of hands fell away.

"*My knee!*" shouted a voice. "*Oh, goddamn—*"

Henry kicked again but this time only felt air.

"By God, that's *enough*," someone grunted.

The bat clanged into Henry skull again, just above his left ear. Fireworks exploded behind his eyes. Then it crashed into his jaw. *If I fall, I'm dead,* he thought dimly. Yet he was too dazed to defend himself any longer.

"Hold him still!" said another voice.

Two boys grabbed his arms and held him up against the Explorer while the third drove the end of the bat into his solar plexus, again and again. The air in Henry's lungs burst from his throat in agonizing jets.

"You're gonna kill him! We're s'posed to take him for questioning first!"

"Screw that! This nigger lover's said all he ever needs to say. We got his shit. This ends right here."

Through a curtain of blood, Henry saw the flash of steel at his waist. He tried to beg for mercy, but his throat had locked shut.

A bright blade plunged into his belly.

Henry felt it slice sideways, severing vital tissue, and fire filled his torso. He sucked in one gasp of air, then the knife flashed to his throat.

"*Last words, Mr. Henry? Before I shut your mouth for good?*"

The boy with the knife looked about twenty, with a bland face and cruel eyes. The knife danced before Henry's face, its blade black with blood. *His* blood—

"Speak up, Mr. Henry! You ain't run out of words, have you? That can't be!"

"*Get off him!*" screamed a woman's voice. A familiar voice. It was Lou Ann, the *Beacon*'s receptionist. "*Leave him alone!*"

The boy pinning Henry's right arm laughed with amazement.

"Run, Lou Ann!" Henry coughed. "Get back inside!"

The cold blade lodged against his jugular vein, and Lou Ann Whittington yelled again. "*Don't make me shoot you boys! I swear to God I'll do it!*"

The boy holding the knife looked left.

Henry followed his eyes. Lou Ann stood by the hood of the Explorer, all five feet four of her, her purse in one hand and a nickel-plated .38 revolver in the other.

"This ain't none of your business, lady," one boy said in a voice devoid of fear.

Lou Ann aimed her pistol over his head, and a crack of flame rent the darkness. "You let Mr. Sexton go!"

"Stay out of this, you old bitch!" shouted one of the others.

Through ringing ears Henry heard the receptionist's shaky voice echo off the wall of the building. "*Let him go right now, trash! Or I'll kill you.*"

"Cut his fucking throat, Charley," said the boy on Henry's left, moving toward Lou Ann.

She fired again. This time the bullet dug a divot out of the cinderblock wall behind the boys.

Henry tried to twist free, but all he managed to do was collapse on the pavement. All three boys were moving toward Lou Ann now.

"*Run!*" Henry tried to yell, but only a whisper emerged.

As the first boy reached Lou Ann, she shot him point-blank in the stomach.

He fell to his knees and looked down at his bloody shirt.

"*Shit!*" screamed one of the others, stopping in his tracks and holding up both hands.

The wounded boy fell facedown on the cement.

"Don't make me kill you," Lou Ann said in a shaky voice.

After a second's hesitation, the other two grabbed their fallen comrade and dragged him around the corner of building. Henry heard car doors slamming. Then Lou Ann Whittington's tear-stained face appeared above his. Her mouth was moving, but all he heard was squealing tires.

"Henry?" She slapped his face. *"Can you hear me?"*

He coughed and spat blood. "Thank you, Lou. That was . . ." He couldn't remember what he'd meant to say. Then he caught it, like a soap bubble flying on the wind: ". . . a brave thing."

"Don't you die on me, Henry Sexton!"

"I'm not . . . just resting my eyes."

"Henry!" Lou Ann was fumbling with her cell phone. "This is Lou Ann Whittington over at the *Beacon*! Mr. Sexton just got stabbed! He's beat half to death. We need an ambulance over here right away. The law, too. Hurry!"

A dark veil was descending over Lou Ann's face. Henry heard other voices but couldn't make sense of them. People were gasping and barking around him, but he couldn't make out their faces, or even their bodies. He thought of Katy Royal, who was probably sitting in a room with her husband somewhere, scared to death that he'd find out she'd once loved a black boy, or that she'd been in an asylum, or God knew what else—

"Stay awake, Henry!" Lou Ann slapped his face again. "Oh, God, roll over. Can you turn your head? Your mouth's full of blood."

He screamed as she rolled him, but at least the hot fluid drained from his throat, and he got one good breath. He spat out some more blood, and then she let him down onto his back again.

"Don't let them get you like this," she said, sobbing. "Not after all you've done."

To Henry's amazement, Lou Ann looked skyward and began to pray, appealing directly to Jesus in a voice that sounded as though it would break any moment. He wanted to give her a message for Sherry, but no words would come. His stomach and sides were wet. His balls, too. *They must have hit an artery,* he thought. *Or I pissed myself . . .*

"My files!" he cried suddenly, trying to rise from the asphalt. "Did they get my files?"

"Whoa, big fella," Lou Ann said, gently pressing him back to the ground. "You've got a lot of stories to write yet. The ambulance is nearly here."

"Keys," Henry whispered. "Ya'll need my keys."

Tears poured from Lou Ann's eyes, and her chin quivered like a child's. She cradled his head in her hands. Henry wanted to tell her not to worry, but all he could do was gasp for air.

The wail of a siren rode to him on the night air. The wail rose in pitch, then became a horn, a solo saxophone, bobbing on the current of Ray Charles's piano, the last show Ray had played at Haney's Big House. Out of that divine music swelled the earthy yet ethereal voice of Swan Norris, singing alone in a blue spotlight, her timbre dark and true as Billie Holiday's, giving voice to ineffable suffering: "... *blood on the leaves,*" she sang. "... *blood at the root.*"

"Hear that siren, Henry?" Lou Ann asked, palpable relief in her voice. "They're almost here. It's not your time yet." She wiped his brow with the tail of her blouse.

As a wind of reverent applause swelled around Swan, Henry's mind flickered, then winked out.

CHAPTER 44

ANNIE AND I are doing our "homework" together in the den. She's working on a paper about Benjamin Franklin, while I pretend to work on the proposal for the restoration of the Forks of the Road slave market site. Jewel's smuggled preliminary autopsy report sits beside me, and the lines I'm writing in my notebook have more to do with criminology than history. Even so, having this shared time with my daughter is one benefit of being mayor that I never anticipated. In my previous jobs—writing novels and preparing capital murder prosecutions—I had to be alone while I worked, but being mayor doesn't require nearly so much concentration. In fact, the job has been done by men with less intellectual power than my daughter has at age eleven.

The despair I felt outside Shad's office dissipated further after my visit to Pithy Nolan, but I still haven't figured out how to free my father from Shad Johnson's net of vengeance. The Double Eagle group's sole vulnerability seems to be their involvement in the meth trade. To exploit that, I'd need the power I once wielded as a prosecutor: the authority to subpoena witnesses, make arrests, and offer plea bargains. As Henry pointed out last night, I don't have that. Brody Royal's vulnerability—if he has one—remains unknown. All I know at this point is that Royal has far more to lose than the Eagles (at least in terms of wealth and reputation), and he won't hesitate to violently defend those assets. I feel certain that, through the Eagles, Brody has already threatened our family, and I've been pondering ways to protect us—thus freeing my father to reveal what he knows about them. But again, I'll require official help to accomplish this.

More disturbing, I still haven't heard from Quentin Avery, Dad's best hope for a first-rate legal defense. With Shad moving so aggressively on the legal front, and bail revocation possible at any moment, we should already be planning Dad's defense. My father himself is no help in this regard, of course. And though I still have no proof of physical intimacy between them, instinct tells me that I cannot trust him where Viola is concerned. Before I can ponder the significance of this, Annie looks up from her work and snaps her fingers with a loud pop.

"I need a break," she says from the sofa. "How about some Blue Bell?"

"I don't need ice cream," I tell her, rubbing my thickening middle. Once December arrives, I find myself running less and less.

"Caitlin doesn't care about your tummy."

If only that were true . . . As I set aside my files on the Forks of the Road project, our home phone rings beside me. I pick up the cordless and check its LCD, which reads: CONCORDIA PARI.

"Penn Cage," I answer.

"Mayor, this is Walker Dennis. I've got bad news. Real bad. Henry Sexton was just attacked outside the *Beacon* offices. Stabbed, and beat half to death with a baseball bat. He's in critical condition."

I grit my teeth to stifle a cry. "Where is he now?"

"Mercy Hospital in Ferriday."

Exquisitely sensitive to any mood change, Annie is staring at me like a baby antelope watching its mother for a signal to flee.

"'Half to death' is a pretty vague term, Walker."

"He was stabbed in the belly. He's got a couple of broken bones, a severe concussion, scalp lacerations, a bruised heart. His mouth is busted up, and his face is so swollen I can hardly recognize him. He looks like he was in a car crash."

All I can think of is Henry standing in my office today, looking flustered by Caitlin's offer to hire him at the *Examiner*. "Is he conscious?"

"In and out. They were gonna chopper him out, but Henry kept mumbling that he wanted to stay where he was, and now the doctor thinks they can probably handle it here. The bone doctor's on his way to the hospital."

"Who's staffing the ER over there?"

"That new doctor, Waheed-something. Foreigner. Henry doesn't have a doctor of his own. His mother doesn't think he's been to see one since your father treated him as a boy."

Typical male. "Walker, I'm going to ask Drew Elliott to drive over there. Tell the ER doctor that Drew is Henry's doctor of record. Unless they have a board-certified ER doc, we want Drew in charge of Henry's care."

"I hear you, buddy. And thanks. I'll take care of it."

"Do you have any idea who attacked him?"

"Just a vague description. Three white males between twenty and thirty."

"That young?"

"That's what Lou Ann Whittington said. She's the secretary over there. It was just luck that she walked outside to leave for the night. She carries a .38 in her bag. She told the bastards to stop hitting him, and when they didn't, she started shooting. She hit one, and they took off. That lady saved Henry's life, no question about it."

"I thought Henry was going to call you for an escort at quitting time."

"He was supposed to. The dispatcher was waiting for his call, and I had a man ready to go at a moment's notice. Apparently Henry went out to his Explorer to get a computer drive, and they jumped him. He managed to Mace them, and that stalled things enough so that Lou Ann came out in time."

"Did Henry recognize any of them?"

"He thinks he might have known one of them, but he couldn't give me a name. Seems like they meant to kidnap him, but when he resisted they decided to kill him. I've got to wait to question him again. Poor guy's out of his head."

Annie reaches out and takes my hand. Her skin is cold. I squeeze tight.

"They stole a bunch of Henry's files, too," the sheriff adds. "Busted out his back window."

"What files?"

"Mrs. Whittington thinks it was all his old Klan stuff. He was going to take it all over to his girlfriend's house. Makes you wonder, doesn't it? Anyhow . . . tell Dr. Elliott to hurry. I'll let you know if they decide to medevac Henry down to Baton Rouge."

"Okay," I say dully. "Thanks."

When I set down the phone, I realize Annie is scared to death.

"What happened, Daddy? Your face looks white."

I sit beside her on the sofa and put my arm around her. "Somebody I work with just got hurt. Don't be afraid. He's all right. Everything's going to be okay."

"Who was it?"

"A reporter. You've never met him, but he's a really good man." Despite my reassurances, the realization that somebody tried to kill Henry tonight has shaken me to the core. I hug Annie, then stand so that she won't feel my anxiety. "I'm going to have to make some calls, Boo. Maybe you should go in the kitchen and fix that ice cream."

Annie stays put. "You said you didn't want ice cream."

"I said I didn't *need* it. I'll eat some when I'm done with my calls."

"I'd rather stay here. I'll just keep doing my homework."

Sure you will. "Okay. But don't let this stuff upset you."

As I dial my parents' house, Annie nods and puts on a brave face, but she's faking. Ever since my wife's death, my daughter has been unable to witness me losing any degree of control without freaking out. In the first months after Sarah's death, Annie literally couldn't leave my side. She had to be touching me, even in sleep, or she would experience night terrors. The road from that place to where we are now has been a long one, and Caitlin—along with the move back to Natchez and proximity to my parents—did much to bring us down it. Sudden crises like this one sometimes trigger severe anxiety in Annie, but unless I'm going to wait for my mother to drive over here, my choices are to keep her with me or banish her into a separate room, where she'll feel even more anxious.

"Hello?" says my mother. "Penn?"

"Mom, is everything okay there?"

"Yes, I think so. Your father's sleeping. Today was just too much for him, I think."

"Is the cop still outside?"

"Yes, I've seen him several times, walking around the house."

"I'm going to have Chief Logan send a squad car over to stand guard."

"Is that really necessary?"

"Yes. Henry Sexton was just stabbed and beaten."

"Oh my God."

"You and Dad stay inside. Don't go out for any reason. I'll call back in a while. I need to talk to Dad before tomorrow."

"All right. But—"

She tries to go on, but I beg off and call Chief Logan, who's just heard of the attack on Henry. He's happy to send a squad car to my parents' house, and says he's sending one to mine as well. I thank him and hang up, then glance at Annie, who's pretending to work. A protective instinct of almost frightening intensity swells within me as I watch her, but I force my fingers to text Caitlin at the newspaper.

> *Henry Sexton just assaulted outside the Beacon. In bad shape. In Mercy Hospital ER. Nothing u can do there for now. My home line will be busy. Perps stole some of Henry's files. Come here if u need to talk. Sorry.*

As soon as the "Message Sent" confirmation appears, I call Drew Elliott, a local internist and one of my father's younger partners. I dial his cell phone to circumvent the answering machine that, along with his wife, screens his home calls.

"Hey, Penn. Been a while. Tom okay?"

"I think so. Do you have privileges at the Ferriday hospital?"

"I do, actually. Why?"

"A good friend of mine was just stabbed and beaten. He's over there in the ER. I just told Sheriff Walker Dennis you were his doctor."

"You what?"

"Dad treated him when he was a boy, but now he doesn't have a doctor. But he needs help, and I'm asking you to see him, as a favor to me."

"He's in the Ferriday ER, you say?"

"Yeah. It's Henry Sexton, the reporter."

Drew takes a few seconds with this. "The guy who writes those stories about the KKK?"

"Yep."

Drew grunts like a man getting to his feet. "Okay, I'm on my way. I'll give you a call as soon as I've assessed him."

"Thanks. Do whatever you think is necessary. I don't know if he has insurance, but I'll cover any costs he can't pay."

"I hear you. Let me get going."

"Just a second, Drew. How did Dad seem to you at the clinic today?"

I hear Drew breathing as he walks. "Same as ever, I guess, considering. I didn't see that much of him. I rarely do, unless I make a point to walk down to his end of the office for a consult. That murder mess isn't really going to trial, is it?"

"I hope not, but it could. I'll tell you about that another time."

"Okay. I'll let you know how Henry is."

Before I have time to second-guess myself, I hang up and call Information for the number of the New Orleans field office of the FBI. Using the automatic connect option, I watch Annie as I await the first ring. She's still watching me so intently that I wonder if she's blinked even once.

"FBI," says a female voice. "New Orleans Field Office."

"I'm trying to reach Special Agent John Kaiser. The situation is urgent. My name is Penn Cage."

"Agent Kaiser is not in the building, sir."

"Can you get him a message? This could be life or death."

"What was your name again?"

"Penn Cage. I'm the mayor of Natchez, Mississippi. Three men just tried to kill one of Agent Kaiser's confidential informants. Please take my telephone number."

After she does, I decide to make sure my message gets through. "Tell Agent Kaiser I'm the Mississippi lawyer who forced the resignation of Director John Portman in 1998."

I'm pretty sure I hear a gulp at the other end of the line.

"Do you have that?"

"Yes, sir."

As soon as I hang up, I rise and start pacing, trying to think of the most efficient moves I can make while I wait for Kaiser's callback, which could take hours.

"Life or death?" Annie echoes. "Is your friend going to die?"

"I hope not, Boo. But he's hurt pretty bad."

"Is Dr. Drew going to take care of him?"

I smile and nod, tying to convey confidence. "Drew's going over there now. If anyone around here can fix Mr. Henry up, he can."

"What about Papa?"

I considered calling Dad to check on Henry, but it's been years since he treated trauma cases in the ER. "Papa's under too much strain to be dealing with a trauma case right now."

"Do they have a CAT scan machine across the river?"

"Uh . . . I think so."

"Do they have a neurologist?"

My eleven-year-old daughter is a huge fan of both *Grey's Anatomy* and *House, M.D.* Initially, I tried to keep her from watching these shows, but after a while I gave up. Annie has an almost morbid interest in cancer, which killed her mother, and she's told me repeatedly that her ambition is to become an oncologist and cure the disease.

"I don't think so," I admit. "But Drew knows how to read a scan. If Henry has bleeding in his brain, they'll airlift him to Baton Rouge."

"Why not Jackson?"

"The Louisiana doctors have connections in Baton Rouge and New Orleans, not Jackson."

"That's weird, since Natchez and Vidalia are only a mile apart."

I walk over and lay my hand on her shoulder. "Boo, in a lot of ways, the Mississippi River is like a locked gate."

The slam of the front door tells me Caitlin must have run right out the door of the *Examiner* when she got my text. The newspaper office is less than a mile from our houses as the crow flies, but she must have driven fifty or sixty miles an hour through the maze of one-way streets that is downtown Natchez to get here so fast.

"What do you know about Henry?" she asks, almost skidding into the room.

Annie jumps up and hugs Caitlin's waist.

Before I can answer, the telephone rings. The LED says UNKNOWN NUMBER. I hold up my hand to Caitlin and answer.

"Penn Cage."

"Mayor, this is Special Agent John Kaiser. What's happened? Is it Henry Sexton?"

"How did you know?"

"Just a feeling. Is he alive?"

"Right now he is."

"Thank God."

CHAPTER 45

AS CONCISELY AS POSSIBLE, I summarize what I know about the attack on Henry for Special Agent Kaiser, while Caitlin memorizes every word. Halfway through my account, I notice Caitlin staring at the preliminary autopsy report for Viola Turner, which lies on the back of the sofa. I was stupid to leave it out.

"What's Henry's present condition?" Kaiser asks with military succinctness.

"He's in and out of consciousness. I've sent the best doctor I could get to check him out. I called you because I know you've been in contact with Henry about the Jericho Hole bones, and tonight's assault was probably related to the cases he's been working."

"Henry told me you put some security on him last night," Kaiser says.

"Just an ex-cop. The Concordia Parish Sheriff's Office was watching him today. They were supposed to provide an escort when he finished work, but the wires got crossed. I should have hired somebody to stay with him every second. I guess I didn't think they'd go for him at the newspaper."

"I assume the sheriff's covering Henry at the hospital now?"

"Yes, Sheriff Walker Dennis. He's hoping to question Henry some more."

"Do you know Sheriff Dennis personally?"

"Sort of. I played Little League ball with him as a kid."

"Do you think he could have set Henry up?"

A chill runs along my arms. "My first instinct says no. But I honestly don't know him well."

"Well, it's something to consider. By the way, I'm expediting the DNA analysis on the Jericho Hole bones, and we've sent the bullet up to the crime lab in Washington. That was good work going into that lake. Sometimes the shortest route between two points doesn't involve a search warrant."

"As long as the guys breaking the rules can be trusted."

"Amen. Henry told me a little about your father's case, too."

"Did he?" I say coolly.

Kaiser is silent for a few seconds. "Would it surprise you to learn that I know quite a bit about you, Mayor?"

"Because of my battle with Director Portman, you mean?"

Kaiser chuckles softly. "No, though I was no fan of that elitist asshole. I'm actually a friend of Dwight Stone."

This name hurls me back in time. Dwight Stone was one of more than a dozen FBI agents assigned to Natchez during the 1960s. When I was persuaded by distraught family members to look into the murder of civil rights activist Delano Payton, the trail eventually led me to Dwight, who'd retired to the mountains of Colorado. He did more than help me solve the cold case; he ended up saving my life.

"That says a lot for you," I tell Kaiser. "What are you going to do about Henry? *Can* you do anything?"

"You bet your ass I can. I'm going to add some men to his guard detail, and I'm coming up there myself, first thing in the morning."

"First thing" means different things to different people. New Orleans is three hours south of Natchez, but Kaiser sounds like the crack-of-dawn type to me. Before I can ask for clarification, he says, "If Walker Dennis is bent, or he has a mole in his department, the discovery of those bones in the Jericho Hole might have triggered Henry's beating."

"Couldn't it just as easily have been Henry's interviews with Glenn Morehouse and Viola Turner?"

"Of course. Can you keep something absolutely between us?"

"Absolutely."

"Morehouse died of an overdose of fentanyl, which he was taking by prescription. But the dose was too high to have come from his patch, or even two of them. He was murdered, no question."

Kaiser's openness is startling after years of dealing with close-mouthed FBI agents. "I figured as much. One thing strikes me as strange. Henry described his assailants as being between twenty and thirty years old. That doesn't sound like Double Eagles to me."

"All those bastards had sons and grandsons. Keep an open mind as we move forward."

I'm surprised to hear Kaiser use the plural pronoun. "What's your idea of moving forward?"

"Getting the rest of those bones up, ASAP."

My heart is pumping faster. "How are you going to do that?"

"I'm not sure yet, but I've got a couple of ideas. The Double Eagles have crossed the line this time. I'm coming up there loaded for bear."

Kaiser doesn't talk like most FBI agents I've worked with. Around laymen, Bureau people tend to speak like fighter pilots and accountants—without emotion. "Agent Kaiser, I'm going to take a shot in the dark here. I think my family may be in as much danger as Henry Sexton was. I believe Brody Royal and the Double Eagles have threatened us, to make my father take the blame for a murder they committed. Are you with me?"

"Keep going."

"I don't exactly have a private army up here. I was wondering whether you might be able to protect my father as a federal witness. I believe my dad knows who murdered Albert Norris, and probably Dr. Leland Robb and three other people as well."

Kaiser grunts but offers nothing.

"And this may sound crazy," I add, "but Dad might also have information about the major assassinations of the 1960s. A man named Brody Royal definitely does. Do you know that name?"

"I know who Royal is. He barely evaded prosecution in a state insurance fraud case."

"That's the one. I think if you could assure my father that our family is safe, he could help you quite a bit."

After a few seconds, Kaiser says, "Let me make some calls. I'm just getting up to speed on some of this. I probably won't know for sure what I can do until tomorrow morning. Can you protect your folks until then?"

"I think so. And anything you need on my side of the river, let me know. I'll get it done."

"Do you have a lot of influence with Shad Johnson?" The lightest touch of irony colors Kaiser's voice.

"I can still make things happen here when I need to," I assure him.

"Good." The FBI agent gives me a 504 cell number, which I enter into my contacts list, and then I let him go.

"Was that John Kaiser?" Caitlin asks, her face strangely flushed.

"Yes. He's coming up here tomorrow."

Her face lights up as though I've announced that Robert Redford is coming to town.

"What's the deal?" I ask. Annie, too, looks curious.

"Don't you know who Kaiser's wife is?" Caitlin asks.

"No."

"Jordan Glass!"

I shake my head, perplexed. Then it hits me. "The war photographer? From Oxford, Mississippi?"

"Yes. Holy *shit*."

Annie is bemused by Caitlin's schoolgirl excitement.

"Jordan Glass has won two Pulitzers," Caitlin informs us. "Maybe three. Not to mention the goddamn Robert Capa Gold Medal. Not that it matters. She's past all that. Glass is like Nachtwey, or even Dickey Chappelle, for God's sake! She's on that level."

"You have a Pulitzer," I remind her.

Caitlin dismisses this with a flick of her hand. "I was lucky. Jordan Glass is the *shit*. She's a freaking legend."

Annie is shaking her head in amazement.

"Are you sure she's married to *this* John Kaiser?" I ask, motioning for Annie to leave the room.

"I'll stop cursing," Caitlin promises, signaling Annie to stay. "I read all of Henry's stories last night, remember? He mentioned Kaiser several times, so I checked him out. He's married to her, all right. They met while working a big murder case in New Orleans." Caitlin shrugs. "You know me."

That I do. No stone left unturned, no matter how far off the main path it may be. "Well, the assault on Henry really upset Kaiser. I think we're finally going to see some federal action on the Double Eagle group."

"Based on the bones Kirk Boisseau found?"

"That'll be the legal justification."

"Can I print anything about the bones yet?"

"Not until you clear it with Henry."

A shadow flits across her features. I hope it's guilt for being so ready to exploit the misfortune of a colleague. When a story gets hot, Caitlin instantly reverts from publisher to reporter, and in that mode she operates with the ruthless dispassion of a surgeon.

"You said 'I figured as much' to Kaiser," she observes. "What did he tell you?"

Christ. "I can't tell you. He made that very clear."

She makes very little effort to conceal her frustration. "Something about Glenn Morehouse, right? They've had his body since this morning."

She's like a hunting dog that never gets distracted from the scent. "Next time I talk to Kaiser, I'll ask if I can pass it to you, off the record."

Caitlin grimaces but doesn't argue. "Do you think it would be all right for me to visit Henry at the hospital?"

"Not tonight. You'd just be in the way."

"But he may have already decided to work for me! He may be my employee *now*."

"He hasn't signed anything. You can call Sheriff Dennis for any details you need, or Mrs. Whittington, the secretary who chased away the assailants."

"Did I hear you say someone stole Henry's files?"

"Sheriff Dennis said the assailants took some files from his vehicle during the attack. He was apparently moving them to his girlfriend's house."

Caitlin gives me a triumphant look that says, *Come on*. "Why would Henry be doing that unless he'd decided to change his work circumstances?"

Thankfully, the house phone rings again before I can answer.

"This is crazy," Annie says, looking much happier to be watching this circus than researching Benjamin Franklin. "This is like during Katrina."

"Penn Cage," I answer.

"*Hizzoner the Mayor*," says a warm baritone filled with the character imparted by fifty years of whiskey and tobacco. "This is Quentin. How they hangin' today, Counselor?"

The shocks are coming almost too fast to process. "Just a minute, Quentin." I cover the mouthpiece, but Caitlin's already nodding that she understands.

"I'm heading back to the office," she says. "Call me as soon as Drew calls you."

"Do *not* go over to that hospital," I tell her. "Security's a major issue now. Stay at your office, and call me when you're ready to come home. I'll drive over and follow you back."

It takes a few seconds, but she finally nods.

"Wait—could you take Annie in the kitchen for a couple of minutes before you go?"

She hesitates, then pulls Annie up from the sofa. "Come on, squirt. Your dad needs to take this call alone."

As Annie disappears into the kitchen, Caitlin nods at the autopsy report on the back of the sofa, then raises her eyebrows—an obvious request for permission. Though I know I'll pay for it later, I shake my head. She glares at me for two ominous seconds, then turns and follows Annie into the kitchen.

"Sorry, Quentin," I say, trying to gather my thoughts. "Thanks for getting back to me." *At last,* I add silently.

"I've been sleeping a lot lately. Apparently, I missed some of today's action."

"I wouldn't bother you if we didn't have a desperate situation here."

"Let me stop you right there," he says, and I brace myself for protests that his declining health prevents him from being able to help me. "I've already talked to your father."

"*What*? When was this?"

"That's neither here nor there, Brother Penn. Like everything else relating to this matter, that falls under the attorney-client privilege. But I know most of the details of the case, and there's no need for you and your mama to get worried. Not yet, anyway."

After I get my wind back, I ask, "Are you telling me you've agreed to represent Dad in the murder of Viola Turner?"

"Obviously."

"But Doris said—"

"My wife don't run my practice, boy! Your father needs a lawyer. I'm it."

"But . . . he told me not to call you, not to bother you. Had he *already* called you by then?"

"That's a family matter, son, not a legal one. But I wouldn't press him too hard right now. What matters at this point—and what I got directly from Tom—is that he wants me handling this case. *Alone.*"

"Alone" in this case means only one thing: without me. "Why, Quentin?"

"You'll have to ask your daddy that. But again, I wouldn't yet. He's carrying a heavy load just now."

"What the hell does that mean?"

"It's not my place to tell you."

"Jesus, man. Did he confess or something?"

An incredulous laugh makes me pull back from the receiver. "Boy, you know I'd never ask a client that. Not even Tom Cage."

"I know. I just . . . I *don't* know. It's like Dad has become someone else overnight."

"Well," Quentin says in a sage voice, "that happens to everybody sooner or later. Every son eventually learns his daddy has feet of clay. You just happen to have a father of singular rectitude, so it took until you were forty-five. That doesn't make it any less painful."

Echoes of Pithy Nolan. "I need to tell you something, Quentin."

"I'll just sip this glass of whiskey while you do."

"Doris must have gone out to the store."

He laughs softly. "Speak on, brother."

I tell him what happened to Henry Sexton, then give him a quick summary of Shad Johnson's moves, news of the FBI's pending involvement, and the findings in the preliminary autopsy report. As I conclude, I get up and take that report from the sofa back, then sit back down.

"Good work getting hold of that report," Quentin says. "You haven't lost your touch, I see. And we could have got a lot worse judges than Joe Elder. The Sexton thing is disturbing, though. Makes me think the Double Eagles are night-riding again."

"Are you familiar with that group?"

Quentin's chuckle is a low rasp. "I knew some of those crackers all too well, my boy. This is like Old Home Week for me. You just keep me apprised of any developments in that line. If I'm unavailable, you can tell Doris anything you would me. Almost anything, anyway. I'll trust your judgment on that."

Quentin is a lot like the traditional FBI; he prefers a one-way flow of information, with him on the receiving end. Feeling like I've surrendered to fate, I start to hang up, but concern for my father overrides my decorum. "Quentin, I have to ask you a hard question."

"They're the only ones worth asking, most times."

"I know you haven't been doing well. Can you handle a major murder trial, if it comes to that?"

There's a long pause, during which I hear the high wheeze of an old man breathing. "I won't lie to you," he says finally. "The Lord has taken a lot from me since my prime. I've had some low days. I can't walk, can't eat anything worth eating, and I can't give my woman what she needs. And no matter what a woman tells you to comfort you, that eats you up inside. It's enough to make a man lie down and never get up again."

I hear the sound of careful sipping, then the pained groan of an old man shifting position. "But they'll have to lay me out dead on the courtroom floor before I let anybody put Tom Cage behind bars."

For the first time since yesterday morning, I feel the burden of defending my father partly lifted from my shoulders. The relief of having a lawyer with Quentin Avery's gifts in Dad's corner—even if his powers aren't what they once were—is enough to bring tears to my eyes. I want to say, "I never doubted you," but Quentin knows better. "Thank you" is all I can manage.

"Don't feel bad for asking what you did. There's no room for sentiment when family's on the line."

"I appreciate it, Quentin."

"Get a good night's sleep, brother. Do whatever you need to about the Double Eagles, but leave Shad Johnson and Joe Elder to me. Those boys don't want no part of my bad side. Now, Doris just opened the front door, and she'll beat me like an egg-suckin' dog if she catches me with this bourbon. You'd hear me holler all the way to Natchez."

I hear a click, and then a female voice says, "Hello, Penn." Before I can respond, Doris Avery continues in a voice that holds many emotions: regret, fear, foreboding. "I pray to God we make it through this trial."

"I do, too," I tell her, meaning all of us, but most of all, Quentin and my father.

After she hangs up, I get less than twenty seconds of silence to reflect on the conversation. Then Caitlin is standing in front of me with her eyebrows arched and her hands on her hips.

"Today we talked about our old deal," she reminds me. "I thought we'd decided to throw it out the window in this case. How can I help Tom if I don't know everything that's going on?"

She's talking about my father's needs, but her eyes tell me that her hunger for a major story is already overriding all other considerations. My recognition of that hunger unsettles me. I'm about to reply when her gaze lights on the sofa back where Jewel's file lay a minute ago.

"You moved that autopsy report so I wouldn't pick it up?" she asks with disbelief.

I feel like I'm talking to an addict who's rationalizing her need for vodka or pills. "I'm not even supposed to have that report. Jewel Washington put her career on the line to pass me that."

Caitlin's incredulity changes into anger. "You think I'd do something that could hurt Jewel?"

"No. But you might well find yourself on the witness stand before this is over. I don't want you committing perjury to protect me or anybody else, even if you're willing to do it."

The familiar pink moons have appeared on her cheeks. Before she can attack, I add, "We're in unmapped territory, Caitlin. I tried to use the picture on Shad today, but he and Billy Byrd had already figured a way to defuse that particular bomb."

This gets her attention. "How?"

"Billy will swear Shad was working undercover for him when that photo was taken. I could still release the photo, but it won't stop the case against Dad."

"I still think Shad would be run out of office."

"Maybe. But I'm not sure I want that."

She's grinding her teeth now, which isn't good, but it's better than yelling. God only knows what she told Annie to keep her in the kitchen. "You don't trust me," she says flatly.

"That's not it. You know it's not."

"Henry was going to come to work for me. You keeping this stuff from me is just—insulting."

I toss the autopsy report onto the sofa. "The preliminary report pegs Viola's cause of death as adrenaline overdose, but all that really does is muddy the water. And you obviously can't report it."

She stares at me for several awkward seconds. Then she nods once. "Thank you."

"Why do you think Henry was going to say yes to working for you?"

"I just know it. You'll see." She shakes her head again, as though words have failed her. "I'm going back to work."

"Can't you stay and eat some ice cream with us?"

I only asked this out of courtesy. There's no way Caitlin will sit in this room after what just transpired—not until she's had time to vent her frustration.

"Too much to do," she says. "I'll text you later."

I'd normally give her a hug, but tonight she would be stiff to my touch. Thankfully, Annie sails in with a bowl of Blue Bell vanilla in each hand. Before she can speak, Caitlin kisses the top of her head, then heads for the front door.

"Bye!" Annie shouts, looking perplexed.

"Bye," comes Caitlin's halfhearted echo.

"What happened?" Annie asks me, staring worriedly after her future stepmother.

"The attack on Mr. Henry has upset everybody."

My daughter shakes her head slowly, then turns anxious eyes on me. "Don't you and Caitlin want the same thing? Aren't you on the same side?"

I reach out and squeeze her forearm. "Yes. Sometimes it gets complicated, Boo, that's all. But down deep, we are."

Annie thinks about this for several seconds. I expect her to say, "I know ya'll are," or something like that. But when my daughter's eyes find mine again, she says, "I hope so."

TEN MINUTES AFTER WE finished our ice cream, I sent Annie to her room to work on her paper before bed. My conscious intention was to study Viola's autopsy report, but not long after I picked up the photocopied pages, my mind was consumed by resentment that my father decided to confide his secrets—whatever they might be—to Quentin Avery. *Why has Dad chosen to leave me in the dark? Is he that ashamed of having an affair with an employee? Is he afraid of something else? Or is he simply trying to protect our family?* At this point, that's about the only scenario I'd be willing to forgive. With Viola and Morehouse dead—and Henry Sexton close to death—there's clearly information in play that people are willing to kill to suppress. The question is, does my father also possess it?

As I reflect on this possibility, the obvious implication of my earlier deduction hits me like a stitch in the side. If Dad is lying about his relationship with Viola . . . then everything Lincoln Turner contends could be true. And Shad Johnson could be prosecuting Dad in the legitimate belief that he killed Viola to silence her about Lincoln's paternity.

Despite Quentin's injunction against bothering Dad, I feel an almost irresistible compulsion to do just that. The old lawyer might be content to let matters proceed at a glacial pace, but I can't do that while Henry's life hangs in the balance. For while the attack on the reporter *might* have been triggered by his interviews with Viola and Morehouse, it might just as easily have been caused by his meeting with me, or the visit we made to Sheriff Dennis's office. And none of those contacts would ever have occurred had my father come clean about Viola's death from the beginning.

Holding my compulsion in check, I walk down to my basement office and take a manila folder from the bookshelf. It contains dozens of snapshots and mementoes I used to make a short video for Dad's seventy-second birthday. Shuffling through the photos, I find the image I'm looking for: Christmas Eve at Dr. Wendell Lucas's office, December 1963. John F. Kennedy has been dead just about a month. Dad and Mom have just moved Jenny and me to Natchez, in the midst of a harrowing blizzard.

Why have I come for this photograph? What can it tell me?

Dr. Lucas's waiting room has been decorated with red poinsettias, and four bottles of champagne stand open on a coffee table. The clerical staff are big-bosomed country girls with bouffant hairdos. Dr. Lucas and my father stand center stage, their white coats open to reveal the suits and ties they wore to work every day. To their right stand two elderly white nurses I remember vaguely, and beside them the dark-skinned Esther Ford, whose kind eyes remain indelibly alive in my memory. Behind these three women—taller, younger, and so strikingly beautiful that, once your eye falls upon her, she dominates the entire photograph—stands Viola Turner.

Most of the women are grinning and toasting the camera, and even Esther's smile is wider than usual. Viola's expression is more remote, her wide brown eyes alert as those of a doe in an open field, her perfect teeth not showing at all. Her beauty is simultaneously earthy and ethereal. It's also a special pass, of sorts. Viola stands easily among these mostly white people, as Esther does, but she is not *of* them. She's an interloper, a silent scout for an army that would soon be fighting a bloody war for equality. Less than a year after this picture was taken, the first skirmishes would break out on both sides of the river, and Albert Norris would die. Pooky Wilson, too.

As I try to decipher the reality behind Viola's façade, a sudden association tugs deep in my brain. *What is it?* Maybe the longer I study her face, the more powerful my childhood memories become, like embers in a breeze being fanned into flame. Yet the harder I focus on her, the more whatever I'm trying to remember recedes. I shouldn't be surprised. This photograph is only a frozen slice of the past: two-dimensional, opaque, easily deceptive. My visit with Pithy was more penetrating, like a medical history, facts enhanced by a temporal context and by Pithy's insight—yet still insufficient. What I need now is the psychological equivalent of an MRI, a three-dimensional scan of the relationships between these characters I'm only just coming to know: Viola Turner, Brody Royal, the Knox family, even Lincoln Turner. For only with the deepest knowledge can one diagnose that most elusive of conditions: the truth.

Touching my fingertip to Viola's face, I realize that one question must be answered before all others: *How far did Dad go with you?*

Walking to my desk, I lift the phone and dial my parents' house again. I'd rather speak to Dad in person, and away from my mother, but the only way I could pull that off would be to take Annie with me to distract Mom, and Mom would instantly see through my ploy.

"Penn?" says my mother, her voice surprisingly alert. "Has something happened? Did Henry die?"

"No." I'd expected the reassuring "Dr. Cage" that usually greets night callers. "I was hoping to talk to Dad, remember?"

A shuffling sound comes through the phone. "He's still asleep."

This surprises me. Despite the emotional toll that today's events must have taken on him, my father is a night owl, and always has been. Almost nothing can force him to sleep during what most people consider reasonable hours. Maybe being arrested and handcuffed in his own yard pushed even Dad past his limit. "I really need to talk to him, Mom."

"You don't want me to wake him, up, do you? Not after today."

Yes, I do. And then I want you to go into the other room and watch television while we talk. "I guess not. But I *must* speak to him before nine tomorrow morning."

"Do you think that attack on Henry Sexton had anything to do with your father? Henry's been writing about the bad old days for years now, and he's never hesitated to name names. That's courting disaster if I ever saw it. He probably just pushed somebody too far in his last article."

"Mom, I think . . ." I falter, searching for some nonthreatening way to explain my concern. "Dad is somehow caught up in this old Double Eagle mess. He used to treat all those guys from Triton Battery, and he's refusing to talk about it to the police."

This time her answer is longer in coming. "Your father's no fool, Penn. He knows what he's doing."

"You didn't look so sure of that in court this morning."

"Well, that was upsetting, naturally. But Judge Noyes did the right thing in the end."

"The situation has changed now. Dad's bail could be revoked at any time."

"Oh, no."

"Don't panic, Mom. But I need to ask you a simple question."

"Oh, Penn . . . I don't like this."

"I've never known you to lie, and I need to know the answer to this." Silence.

Before anxiety can stop me, I ask what I've withheld up to now because of my reluctance to upset my mother. "I need to know what time Dad got home on the night Viola died."

The silence that follows this lasts longer than it should.

"What are you really asking me?" she says softly.

I close my eyes, already regretting my question. "Just a fact, nothing more." *Tell me it was before 5:38 A.M.*

"You don't really believe your father could have killed Viola, do you? Tell me you don't believe that."

"I don't. But I'd like to be able to *prove* that he didn't."

A long, pained sigh comes down the line. "Is this just between you and me?"

Oh, God. "Yes."

"I don't know *what* time Tom got home that night. It was very late, and I'd taken a second pill by that time."

I've never known my mother to be so out of it that she didn't know when Dad got home—especially during the past few years. She waits up for him like a helicopter mom praying for a teenager to get in. "Best guess, Mom. What time was it?"

"I don't know for sure. I really don't."

"You said it was very late, so you obviously have a general idea."

"After three," she says at length. "I was dead to the world, honestly."

After three . . . "Mom—"

"Could anybody be taping this call?" she asks sharply.

My stomach does a little flip. "No. That's just on TV." This isn't exactly accurate, but Shad will assume that I've warned Dad against any dangerous discussions on the telephone, and Judge Elder isn't likely to authorize a wiretap from the Mayo Clinic. "Why do you ask, Mom?"

"Because whatever time your father needs to have gotten home that night, that's what time I remember him getting home. He was right beside me in this bed. You hear me?"

My heart thumps, hard. *No. I didn't hear that.*

"Just make sure I know the right time. Before it's life-or-death."

I close my eyes and swallow hard. Only hours ago I realized my father may have been lying to me for most of my life. Now my mother has told me she's willing to lie under oath to protect him. "Mom, I really need to talk to Dad tonight."

"I'll have him call you when he wakes up. You know he hardly ever sleeps through the night."

"If he doesn't call me before midnight, I'm going to drive over there and wake him up."

"What about Annie? You can't wake that child on a school night, and you're certainly not leaving her there. Is Caitlin staying over?"

"No. Mom, *please* just make sure Dad calls me."

She sighs with irritation. "All right."

"I'm sorry if I woke you up."

The intensity drains out of her voice, which suddenly becomes almost casual again. "You didn't. I was reading."

"Did you take a pill tonight?"

"After what happened this morning, that pill might as well be a placebo."

"Try a different book. A bad book is the best sedative. And leave Dad a note to call me, in case you fall asleep. He's bound to get up to pee soon."

"I will. Good night."

After I hang up, I collapse into my most comfortable chair, my mind across the river with Henry. Hopefully, Drew will call to update me soon.

Though I still mean to go over the autopsy report in detail, my hand picks up the Christmas party photo once more. *Why does it haunt me so?* Dad would have been thirty-one when this was shot, Viola . . . twenty-three. Both are looking directly at the camera, and Dad appears tired, as he often did when I was a boy. Beneath Viola's beauty (which is obvious despite what almost seems an effort to conceal it), I sense something else, as Pithy Nolan once did. Something withheld. Perhaps a black woman with Viola's power of attraction had already learned that she must conceal that power in the presence of others, or at least around whites.

This afternoon, Pithy Nolan told me it would be impossible to work in close quarters with a woman like Viola and not fall a little bit in love with her. And what did Dad tell me about the 1960s last night? *What happened here was a war, too.* I can't help but think of Yuri Zhivago working on the Russian battle front with Larissa Antipov (who is forever Julie Christie in my mind). How could Dad not have been smitten by Viola?

Leaning back in my chair, I close my eyes and let the picture fall on my lap. Before a half-dozen breaths fill my lungs, I sit bolt upright, my heart pounding. Snatching up the picture, I study Viola once more, my heartbeat still accelerating. As soon as I stopped trying to figure out what I was missing in the photograph, an epiphany flashed through me. What I've been searching for isn't visible in the picture. Nor was it ever visible in Viola's presence.

It was her smell.

Even now, I remember it with startling clarity. When Viola sat me down to prick my finger or to give me a tetanus shot, then reached into the glass jar to give me a peppermint, her scent teased my nose in a way I've never forgotten. There was perfume in it, one whose name I'll probably never know. But there was something else beneath that fragrance, something as clean as fresh-turned earth or newly mown grass. The perfumed fraction of that complex scent smells expensive in my memory, something a nurse would not likely have been able to afford. But whether I'm right or wrong about this, one thing I know with certainty: The night my father picked me up so late from the hospital, and told me he'd been on a house call, his imported cigar wasn't the smell that struck me as I climbed into the car.

It was the tantalizing scent of Viola Turner.

CHAPTER 46

BILLY KNOX SAT at the oak desk in the study of the lodge at Fort Knox, a Walther pistol before him. Two of the three young men who had attacked Henry Sexton stood across from him, their eyes pinned as though flying high on speed. Fear had done that: raw, gut-churning fear. Their wounded friend—the one the old lady had plugged in the belly—lay on a bench against the wall opposite the desk, a tarp folded under him to stop him bleeding onto the upholstery. His name was Casey Whelan. Sonny had injected him with something that was supposed to stop the pain, and Snake had wrapped two turns of camouflage-pattern duct tape around his mouth. Though the tape had slipped a bit, the screaming had finally subsided, but Whelan was still moaning.

Snake Knox stood behind Billy like an older ghost of his son. Beside Snake crouched the seven-hundred-pound razorback Forrest had killed with a spear, the shaft of which still jutted from the hog's back. And near the hog, concealed behind a partly open door, stood Forrest Knox himself.

"Why do you think Brody chose you guys to kill Henry?" Billy asked.

"It was Randall Regan give us the job," answered Charley Wise, the braver of the two boys. The other boy, Jake Whitten, had said nothing since their arrival. "Randall's my uncle, Mr. Knox. I don't even think Mr. Brody knows us by name. He'll come around to wells when we're drillin' sometimes, even had a drink with us once. Told us stories about chasin' pussy and getting into brawls and such. But it was Randall who called us with this."

"And what did he say?"

"He asked us to come out to Mr. Royal's place on Lake Concordia. He told us he had a job for some tough boys, and there was good money in it."

"How much?"

"Five grand apiece."

Sonny whistled, and Billy and Snake shared a look. "What did he tell you to do?"

"He said to grab Mr. Henry and bring him to Mr. Brody's house on the lake. To that basement room out there. They wanted to question him about something."

"Did they mean to kill him?"

The two boys looked at each other. "I'm pretty sure they did," Charley said. "Uncle Randall hates Mr. Henry. Always did. But he didn't want us to take any guns on the job, in case a cop stopped us. He also told me that if Mr. Henry had anything in his Explorer, like a computer or anything, to bring it with us. That's why we brought them files along."

Charley pointed at a stack of banker's boxes on the floor to his left.

"That's the only smart thing you did tonight," Billy said. "And what brought you to us?"

"Mr. Royal, I guess you could say. Once that old bitch shot Casey, we hauled ass and called Uncle Randall. He cussed up a storm and told me he'd call me back. I figure he must've called Old Man Royal at that point, because he called back and told me he couldn't help Casey. He told me not to go to any hospital within a hundred miles, and that if his or Brody's name got mentioned, we'd be dead by sundown the next day. I called Mr. Thornfield because I know some guys in the meth business, and I always heard your crew had a first-class operation. Cops on the pad, and even a doctor for emergencies."

Snake grunted behind Billy. Billy and Sonny shared a worried look. From the moment Sonny called Billy about the three boys, Billy had figured the only choice was to liquidate them (and then decide how to handle Brody Royal going rogue). But to Billy's surprise, Forrest had wanted to hear out the boys first. He thought it might be possible to let two of them live. Billy saw no sense in taking this risk, but he'd humored Forrest by giving the boys a chance to tell their side of the story. He wondered what Forrest was thinking now.

Casey Whelan gave out a long, guttural moan. Billy looked over and saw a froth of blood on the duct tape covering the boy's mouth. He shook his head with distaste. Raiford Prison in Florida, where he'd served a stretch for dealing coke in the early eighties, had been filled with hapless would-be criminals like these.

"I know we messed up, Mr. Billy," Charley admitted. "But we'll make it right. Let me run over to the hospital. I'll finish the job right now. That son of a bitch won't ever write another line in that newspaper."

Billy toyed with the Walther on his desk, then glanced over his shoulder. "What do you think, Daddy?"

Snake replied in a dry voice, like palm fronds rattling in the wind. "You send boys to do a man's job, you get what we got now. A clusterfuck."

"That hospital's crawling with cops now," Billy thought aloud. "Sheriff Dennis is over there, and maybe even the FBI by now. If they caught you, you'd spill everything you know before an hour passed."

"No, sir!" Charley practically yelped. "I know how to keep my mouth shut."

"Yeah. What about you, Jake? You're mighty quiet."

The burly young roughneck standing behind Charley shook his head like a confused little boy. Fear had rendered him physically unable to speak. He couldn't keep his eyes off Casey Whelan, who appeared to be dying on the bench.

"Well, Pop?" Billy said, mostly for the sake of his father's pride. The real decision belonged to Forrest.

"They look like talkers to me," Snake rasped.

Charley looked like he was straining not to pee down his leg.

"Ya'll stay here," Billy said. "I'll be back in a second with somebody who knows about gunshot wounds. Don't say a word while he's in here. You understand?"

Jake and Charley nodded anxiously.

Billy pushed open the door behind his desk and went out. Forrest was already walking down the hall to the master bedroom, where a Steve McQueen movie was playing on the flat-screen.

"Did you hear all that?"

Forrest nodded. He'd changed out of his state police uniform, into jeans and a *Who Dat?* New Orleans Saints sweatshirt.

"What do you think about their story?"

"I think Brody must be getting Alzheimer's."

"He's got professional security. Why would he use those idiots?"

Forrest snorted. "His pros are legit. He can't ask them to go kill a reporter."

"Huh. Well, I say we drop them in the swamp. Have Daddy dump their truck in Dallas or somewhere even farther."

"They're locals," Forrest pointed out. "All of them going missing at the same time would draw attention." He reached into a dresser drawer and brought out a camouflage balaclava mask, one of dozens the club kept for hunting during the coldest months. Forrest stretched out the neck opening, then pulled the mask over his head, taking care over the lump of scar tissue that marked his missing ear. Walking to a mirror, he chuckled as he centered the mask over his mouth.

"Reminds me of the A Shau Valley," he said.

Whatever, Billy thought, turning to lead his cousin back to the study.

When he opened the door, he saw Casey Whelan flailing in agony, and Sonny trying to hold him down on the bench. The other boys looked frightened, but their faces went white at the sight of the masked figure behind Billy.

"Is he the doctor?" asked Jake Whitten.

Billy raised a finger to his lips.

Forrest walked to the bench and knelt beside Whelan's squirming body. Taking a small flashlight from his pocket, he studied the boy's bloody abdomen, then palpated it with two fingers. Whelan screamed. Forrest held his bloody fingers in the light beam and checked them. Then he stood.

"Liver," he said. "Nothing anybody can do for him."

Whelan moaned in despair.

"Not even at a hospital?" asked Charley.

Forrest shook his head, then walked to the door behind the desk and left the study.

Billy held up his hand to prevent questions, then followed Forrest.

He found his cousin sitting on the bed, watching Steve McQueen drive a green '68 Mustang GT Fastback hell-for-leather down a crowded street.

"You still say let the other two go?" Billy asked.

Forrest nodded without taking his eyes off the movie.

"Do you really think those two chickenshits can keep their mouths shut about this?"

"I do."

"Why?"

"Because the two healthy ones are going to finish off their buddy. Go back and explain that's the only way they get to walk out of here alive. That way, instead of three dead roustabouts, we get two expend-able grunts who'll do anything we tell them to."

It took Billy a few seconds to grasp Forrest's reasoning, but once he did, he realized that his cousin had been thinking two moves ahead of him, as always. "What if they won't do it?"

"Not an option." Forrest's eyes tracked the Mustang across the screen. "This kind of plan sells itself, William."

Realizing the conversation was over, Billy walked back down to the study, then sat behind his desk. "You two boys want to keep on breathing?"

Charley nodded first, and his eyes told Billy that he sensed the price of survival might be high. Billy reached into his desk and took out a Buck knife with an eight-inch blade. Too big to be a practical deer-skinning knife, it looked more like a bayonet. "You'll have to prove it."

"How?" Charley asked, his eyes locked on the knife.

"Shut your friend up. For good."

Behind the boys, Sonny Thornfield blanched. Charley's mouth fell open, but no sound emerged. He swallowed, then turned to Jake, who was shivering.

"That guy in the mask said Casey's dying already," Charley pointed out. "Can't we just let him pass in his own time?"

"You're missing the point, son," Billy said, not unkindly. "Think about it."

While Charley tried to do that, his friend Jake seized the knife from Billy and moved toward the bench.

"Not in here!" Billy snapped. "I don't want blood spraying all over the damn wall. And we'd never get it out of the rug. There's a deck right outside this room. Take him out there. The door's behind that curtain."

Sonny pulled back the curtain and opened the door. Cold air drifted into the study. Jake Whitten motioned for Charley to help him lift Whelan. After a moment's hesitation, Charley walked to the bench, grasped Whelan's legs, and helped carry him out onto the deck.

Five seconds after Sonny closed the door, a shriek pierced the air. Whelan screamed so loudly that Billy knew the duct tape had come off his mouth. Snake walked to the door and peered out at the slaughter. Billy pulled a *Pro Video* magazine from his top drawer and rotated his swivel chair toward the stuffed hog behind him. He'd never derived pleasure from this kind of thing, as his father did. He heard Sonny slowly counting aloud: *"One-Mississippi, two-Mississippi . . ."* By the time Sonny reached ten, the screaming had stopped, and Billy turned back toward the door.

Still wearing the balaclava, Forrest stood beside Sonny, one of the Valhalla camcorders in his hand, filming the murder through a window beside the deck door. He must have slipped in through the study's side entrance. Forrest lowered the camera, then turned and walked to the door behind Billy's desk.

"Dead?" Billy asked as he passed.

"Finally. Those boys don't know beans about killing. Make them hose off the deck before they leave."

As Forrest closed the door, Charley and Whitten came back inside and stood unsteadily before Billy's desk, their chests heaving. Both had been covered by arterial spray: Charley looked like he'd been hit in the head with a paint-filled balloon.

"What do we tell Uncle Randall?" Charley panted.

"Nothing. You guys may work for Royal Oil during the day, but I'm your boss now. I'll let Randall know how things stand." He looked from Charley to Jake. "Do ya'll know who the publisher of the Natchez newspaper is?"

Charley shrugged.

"I do," said Jake, using his shirttail to wipe the blood from his face. "I've seen her, I mean. At the health club in Natchez, when I was pumping iron. She's hot, for an old chick."

Billy shook his head. "She's thirty-five, dipshit."

Jake nodded. "That's what I meant."

"A thirty-five-year-old woman is better in bed than anything you ever had, numbnuts."

"You want us to do something to her?" Charley asked, sensing they still had ground to make up with Billy.

"I'll let you know. Right now, carry your boy to the skinning shed and leave him there. Then hose off the deck, go to the mudroom, and clean yourselves up. Leave your clothes there. Sonny will bring you fresh ones. Then go home and think about how you screwed up tonight. Say a prayer, and thank the Lord your dipstick is still connected to your body."

"Yessir," said Jake Whitten. "We'll do that. Thank you."

"Get out of my sight."

Sonny pulled back the curtain once more, and the boys disappeared onto the deck.

Snake laughed softly. "I'll be damned. Those punks ain't *ever* gonna talk about what happened tonight. Did you think of that, son?"

Billy inclined his head toward the door through which Forrest had disappeared.

"They shit their pants when Forrest walked in with that mask on," Sonny said.

"The only problem with all this," Snake reflected, "is that Henry Sexton's still breathing. I don't blame Brody Royal for what he done, only that Randall picked a crap crew to handle the job. Now Henry's spilling his guts to the FBI, and he's probably being guarded around the clock. I could have shot him from four hundred yards out, from that cotton field across from the *Beacon*."

"Henry may die yet," Billy reminded them. "The last report I got said critical condition."

"What does Forrest say?" Snake asked.

Billy gave his father a warning glance. "He'll tell you what you need to know."

"What about the Masters girl?" Sonny asked. "You're not thinking of going after her? Her old man owns a shitload of newspapers."

Billy shrugged. "Again, Forrest's decision."

"Well, where the hell is he?" Snake asked. "We need to talk about this. Is he already gone?"

"Ozan was waiting for him outside. I imagine they've gone to see Brody."

"Whoa," Sonny whispered. "That's one face-off I'll be happy to miss."

"Forrest won't do nothing," Snake said. "Deep down, he knows Brody was right to hit Henry, and Brody's the man with the power in his pocket."

Billy was amazed by his father's lack of perception. He couldn't count the times he'd thanked his dead mother for her genetic blessings. "Don't be so sure," he said. "Forrest has his breaking point, like anybody else."

"Well, I ain't seen him hit it for a lot of years now."

"I have," Sonny whispered. "You'd better pray you never do. Forrest is his daddy made flesh again. Frank Knox come to life, only smarter."

Snake smiled strangely. "Now *that's* something I'd dearly love to see."

Billy got up from his desk. "Before this mess is over, I'm afraid we're all going to see it." He turned to the door, then looked back. "Get those boys some clothes, Sonny. Camo jumpsuits are fine."

Sonny walked to the side door, but Snake held his ground, staring at his son in silent reproach. Billy shook his head, then walked back to the bedroom, hoping to find Forrest still there.

He was.

Forrest stood before the dresser mirror, buttoning the double-pocketed shirt of his state police uniform. He spoke to Billy without looking at him.

"Brody's gone off the reservation. We're liable to get the FBI down here over the attack on Sexton. We're going to Al Qaeda rules."

"Al Qaeda rules" meant radio and phone silence. All messages from this point forward would be passed in person, face-to-face. "Okay," Billy said, worried by the anger in his cousin's voice. "When are you going to talk to Brody?"

"Tonight." Forrest quickly tied his tie and cinched the knot tight. "I'll send word to you later, let you know how it goes."

"Brody must be pretty worried to have done this. You going to go easy on him?"

Forrest looked back at Billy, his eyes dark and cold. "What do you think?"

Then he placed his Stetson on his head, adjusted it in the mirror, and walked out without another word.

Billy sat on the bed, turned up the sound on *Bullitt,* and tried not to think about the future. His father worried him. Because as hard and cunning as Snake was, he somehow failed to grasp a central fact about his life: if Forrest ever decided that "Uncle Snake" was a threat to his plans, he would kill him with no more remorse than he'd felt killing VC cadre leaders in Vietnam or crack dealers in New Orleans. The same logic applied to Brody Royal, regardless of the older man's money and power. Billy wondered whether Brody understood that any better than his father did. He hoped so. If he didn't . . . the consequences didn't bear thinking about.

CHAPTER 47

TOM AND WALT sat in the rear cabin of Walt's RV, drinking chicory coffee and waiting for Sonny Thornfield and Snake Knox to leave their hunting camp in Lusahatcha County. It was tight quarters inside the Roadtrek, which was more a customized van than a conventional RV. Fitted out in Canada, its high-tech interior held a gas cooktop, a microwave oven, a marine toilet, a pullout shower with hot-water heater, a refrigerator, a flat-screen TV, and beds enough to sleep four, if you folded down the two captain's chairs. Later Walt would stow the table and convert the U-shaped couch on which they sat into a six-foot-long bed, but for now they hunched over the table as they'd once hunched over campfires in the snow of Korea.

Walt had parked in a KOA campground near the old entrance to the Natchez Trace, on Highway 61 North. There were about thirty other RVs in the park, so it was a good place to avoid police attention. RV-owning tourists weren't generally the perpetrators of crimes in the Natchez area, or any other. Every few minutes Walt would walk forward and check the screen that monitored the GPS position of the trackers he'd placed on the Double Eagles' vehicles. After leaving Knox's vehicle in a Natchez parking lot, both Snake and Sonny had traveled southward out of town in Thornfield's pickup. At first Tom had been confused about their destination, but then he recalled Ray Presley telling him about a hunting camp that the Knox family maintained in Lusahatcha County, which they called Fort Knox, predictably. Soon enough, the GPS tracker confirmed his theory.

While waiting for the Eagles to move again, Tom had been telling Walt the story of his relationship with Viola, which the Ranger had known nothing about before tonight. Despite their close bond, the two men had rarely seen each other face-to-face after Korea—probably only seven or eight times in the past fifty years. A chance meeting between

Penn and Walt in Houston had rekindled their friendship, but despite some good conversations since that time, Tom had never felt the need to confide what had happened between him and his nurse so long ago. But now he had no choice. If Walt didn't know enough background, he wouldn't be able to make good judgments during the present crisis.

Walt remained silent throughout the tale, and had even turned off his police scanner so as not to be distracted from Tom's soft words. He occasionally raised his eyebrows, as when Viola stood over the dying Frank Knox in Tom's office. But Walt had seen and heard most everything during his years as a Texas Ranger, and now, nursing his coffee, he prompted Tom for the end of the story.

"Is that when she left town?" he asked. "After Knox was dead and the two of you had talked it out?"

Tom shook his head. "I wish to God she had, because things went to hell right after that. Viola thought her brother was still hiding out in Freewoods, but the rape rumor had already done its work. Jimmy and Luther had come out of hiding the previous day, and the Eagles kidnapped them late that night."

"Shit."

"Viola got word that her brother had left Freewoods, and when he didn't call her, she just about went out of her mind. She was sure the Klan had them. She didn't know what to do. How could she go to the police, when she'd just committed murder herself? She knew the cops wouldn't do anything anyway. She begged me to help, but I didn't know what I could do."

"I'm glad you didn't call me," Walt said. "I was caught up in the same kind of mess over in Texas. Nothing but Klan trouble for a few years, seems like. For once the Mexicans actually got put on the back burner. Anyway . . . what happened next?"

"The Double Eagles took Viola."

Walt had been toying with a cold french fry, but he stopped and looked up. "What?"

"The very night we killed Frank Knox, they grabbed her right out of her house, about two in the morning. I didn't know any details then, of course. But when she didn't show up for work, I went straight to her house and saw the signs of a struggle."

"Did you call the police?"

"*Hell* no. You know I couldn't do that. I called Ray Presley."

A hard smile cracked Walt's wrinkled face. Ray Presley was one chapter of Tom's life that Walt did know about. More to the point, Presley's reputation as a crooked cop and former New Orleans Mafia enforcer stretched all the way to Texas. "You wanted her back," Walt said. "What choice did you have?"

"None that I could see. I told Ray to find her, no matter what he had to do. I told him I'd pay any price."

"And?"

"He did."

Walt smiled. "How long did it take him?"

"Less than twenty-four hours. He called in a lot of favors to do it, but he found her in a machine shop out in Franklin County, north of where we are now." A wave of heat crossed Tom's face. "It was bad, Walt. Snake Knox was enraged over his brother's death. Sonny Thornfield and a couple of others were with him. They'd been torturing Luther and Jimmy out of anger, but also out of pure sadism. The worst torture, of course, would be to hurt Viola, so they kidnapped her."

"What did they want from the boys?"

Tom hesitated, but then he told Walt about Carlos Marcello's plan to lure Robert Kennedy to Natchez by murdering Jimmy Revels. Walt's eyes went wide, and he opened a beer when Tom began describing Brody Royal's part in the plot.

"But it was all for nothing," Tom concluded. "When Frank died, Royal or Marcello called off the operation. Ray didn't think they trusted Snake to handle it professionally."

Walt nodded, then gave Tom a piercing look. "You're not telling me everything you know about the Marcello angle, are you? The Kennedy stuff?"

"Maybe another night," Tom said. "That had nothing to do with me."

"Well. Did those bastards torture your girl at the machine shop?"

A flush of heat came back into Tom's face as the killing fever rose again. "Ray told me that when he first approached the machine shop, he heard a woman screaming, then a man screaming for them to stop. I figure that was Viola and Jimmy. Ray took out his pistol and went in. He was ready to kill them if he had to."

"Which he'd done before."

Tom nodded. "Plenty of times. Ray was a bad customer, but he didn't lack guts. He found Viola half naked and blindfolded. He told the Eagles he was taking her out, but that he'd leave the two boys behind. He hadn't been paid to get them out, see? And he told them that."

"Smart," Walt said. "That's probably the only way he could have got out alive."

"I'm sure of it. Ray said Viola was shrieking like a madwoman when he dragged her out of there, begging him to go back and get her brother."

"I imagine she was."

"Ray called me from a pay phone. Twenty minutes later, we met down an oil field road and he put her in the backseat of my car. I had my black bag, and I sedated the hell out of her. Didn't have any choice."

Walt opened a tin of Skoal and tucked a pinch under his bottom lip. "Don't tell me you took her home to Peggy."

Tom snorted. "I wasn't that desperate. Not then, anyway. I couldn't make up my mind where to hide her, though. I knew the Klan would be combing the city for her, not just the Double Eagles. That meant cops and deputies in those days. I needed somewhere they'd never think of looking. And this was the middle of the night, for Christ's sake. Then it hit me."

"Where?"

"Nellie Jackson's place."

Walt's eyes narrowed. "The whorehouse?"

Tom nodded.

Amazement and admiration showed on Walt's face. Nellie's was a Natchez institution that lasted from the late 1920s until 1990. The internationally known brothel operated in the downtown area without interference from police for its entire history. Among those in city politics, it was generally believed that Nellie had maintained an extensive photo collection of her clients—many of whom were politicians—and this made her remarkable business run possible. But in fact, what had allowed Nellie Jackson to flourish was the fact that Nellie was based in Natchez, a city with a long history of libertinism, more spiritually akin to New Orleans than to the corrupt but conservative parish across the river.

"I figured the last place in the world they'd go looking for a church-going girl like Viola would be Nellie's," Tom said. "And I didn't even tell Ray where I'd taken her."

Walt grinned. "I knew I taught you something in Korea."

"I'd been treating Nellie for five years when this happened," Tom continued. "She brought her girls in regularly for VD checks. New girls every few weeks, most times. Anyway, I went back to the pay phone and called Nellie about Viola. Nellie told me she'd be happy to help. The first night Viola stayed in a back room at the whorehouse, but the next day Nellie moved her to a rent house she owned on the north side of town. She stayed there six days."

"And they never found her?"

"Nope. I found out years later that Nellie had worked as an informant for the FBI. She kept girls of every race, but they entertained white clients only. Nellie took the rednecks' money, listened to their conversations, filmed them in bed, and reported everything of interest back to the Bureau. She did more for the civil rights movement than most fine, upstanding church people ever did."

"Whatever happened to Nellie?"

Tom closed his eyes and tried to vanquish the horror that always followed that question. "In the late eighties, some drunk college kid she wouldn't let in the door got angry. He went across the street, filled up an ice chest with gasoline, and rang the doorbell. When Nellie answered, he dumped the gas all over her and threw a match. She was eighty-seven years old then, and she died in agony."

"That's always the way with whores," Walt said with fondness and regret. "Never ends well. Some no-'count customer always does something stupid, or the whore does something stupid to save some no-'count. Same difference."

Walt reached into a drawer and brought out a flat bottle of Woodford Reserve bourbon. "How 'bout we take a snort of this, buddy?"

"You go ahead. I've got to watch my sugar."

Walt did, closing his eyes as the fine whiskey slid down his gullet.

"At least that punk spilled gas on himself, too," Tom said. "He had enough third-degree burns to see his life pass before his eyes before he went to prison."

"So how did you get Viola out of town?"

"I didn't. After Ray saved her, it was all I could do to keep her from going to the police. I knew those boys were dead. Viola was so upset, she didn't care if she went to jail for murdering Frank Knox. She just wanted her brother found. The Eagles were still looking high and low for her, but she didn't care. I'd give her elephant doses of Valium, and they'd hardly put a dent in her. Just as she was about to snap, Martin Luther King was assassinated. The whole town went crazy then. The FBI turned all its attention to that case, and the Double Eagles went to ground. I got Reverend Walter Nightingale, a black patient of mine, to go by and talk to Viola. Somehow, he got her to see reason. The next day, she left Natchez and went to Chicago, just like thousands of Mississippi blacks before her." Nearly overcome with guilt, Tom reached out for the whiskey bottle and took a slug that burned all the way down. "And until the other night, I didn't even know whether she rode the bus or the train."

Walt shook his head with empathy. "Which was it?"

"Bus." Tom took another slug of bourbon. "You know why so many blacks from Mississippi ended up in Chicago?"

"Why?"

"It was the cheapest bus or rail ticket they could get to a major northern city."

"I'll be dogged. It's simple, when you think about it."

"Most things are, once you understand them."

Walt took back the bottle and let it hang from his weathered hand. "When did you next talk to her after she left?"

"Six weeks ago." Tom lowered his head and wiped tears from his eyes. "I loved that woman, Walt. And I didn't see or talk to her for thirty-seven years."

"Goddamn, son. That's rough."

"I know you know it."

Walt took a deep breath, then gave a long sigh. Tom knew he was thinking about a Japanese girl he'd fallen in love with during an R&R in Japan. She had haunted Walt for the rest of his life.

"I've got no right to say I loved her," Tom said, filled with anguish. "How can you say you loved a woman you didn't try to talk to for thirty-seven years?"

"Easy," Walt said angrily. "Did you ever go a day without thinking about her? One goddamn day?"

Tom thought about it. "Not for the first ten years or so. But after that . . . yes, I did. I don't think I could have survived otherwise. Not sober, anyway."

Walt grunted with empathy. "How did it go for Viola in Chicago?"

"Not good."

"That's what I figured. The land of peace and plenty up north wasn't all it was cracked up to be." Walt took a sip of lukewarm coffee. "Did she ever try to contact you?"

"Not that I know of."

Walt's eyes glinted in the dim light. "You think maybe she did, and Peggy put the quietus on it?"

"Maybe. But I don't think so. Viola had too much pride for that."

"Pride don't last long when you're tryin' to survive."

"It wasn't like that," Tom said. "I sent her money."

"How'd you know where to send it?"

"Viola sent a few letters to the office. Not to me, but to the girls, you know. I sent money to the address those letters came from. Enough to buy staples and pay the rent. She cashed the checks. It was her signature on the back. I knew her handwriting, but I checked it against one of the letters to be sure."

"How long did you do this?"

Tom looked down at his coffee. "Thirty-seven years."

Walt reached out and patted his shoulder. "Partner, you haven't changed a bit, have you?"

"Does anybody?"

Walt smiled sadly. "Not in my experience. Did you ever tell Peggy about all this?"

"No."

"She never found out you were sending the money?"

"I don't think so. She handled our money, but I always kept one account for myself that nobody ever saw but me."

"Jesus, buddy. This reminds me of some of the World War Two vets who looked after women they met while they were overseas."

"Yeah. Gregory Peck played in a movie about that. *The Man in the Gray Flannel Suit*."

"I saw that!" Walt smiled. "Damn, we're old, ain't we?"

Tom took the whiskey bottle and looked at it, contemplating

another swig. "Walt . . . when I first saw Viola after all those years, my heart seized in my chest. Literally. I remembered her as a perfect beauty of twenty-eight, and what I saw was an old woman a few steps from death's door." He took a sip of whiskey, but now it tasted like acid. "It wasn't just the cancer that had done it. It was time and gin and cigarettes and God knows what else." A lump rose into Tom's throat, and he heard his voice break. "She didn't have any *teeth*, Walt. Just dentures, and bad ones at that. I felt sick for two days afterward, every time I thought of her."

"But you treated her."

Tom nodded. "Hardest thing I ever did."

Walt took the bottle and slipped it back into the drawer above the microwave. "You helped her, buddy."

"I wanted to. I wanted to save her. But there wasn't any way to—not by that time."

Walt squeezed his shoulder. "I know. You know I know."

Tom felt himself shivering. "That's the only reason I can tell you."

"Tell me, then. Get it out."

"I'm tired, Walt."

"Screw that. Get the monkey off your back. This is me, son. We squatted in the mud and the blood and shit together. You can't get no closer than that."

Tom began to speak in spite of himself. "It was like I told you on the phone. When I first called you. It was like the ambulance. Exactly like it."

"Goddamn it," Walt whispered. "I knew it."

Tom jumped when his cell phone vibrated in his pants.

"What is it?" Walt asked.

"My cell," Tom said, digging the shaking phone out of his pocket with difficulty. The LCD read QUENTIN AVERY.

"I told you to keep the damned thing off! They can track you with that."

"I know. I turned it back on at the Sonic to check for messages, and I guess I forgot to turn it off."

"Jesus." Walt thumped the side of his head. "Radio silence!"

"Quentin?" Tom said, holding the phone tight to his ear. "Are you there?"

"I'm here. Penn called me, and he knows I'm your lawyer now."

Tom swallowed. His throat was dry. "What else does he know?"

"Nothing."

"Does he know I'm gone?"

"*I* don't know you're gone."

"Okay . . . okay. Good."

"But I need to ask you about something."

"What?"

"The Double Eagle group." Quentin Avery said the name the way a German Jew might say "Schutzstaffel." Hatred and contempt dripped from his tongue, but there was a trace of fear, too, even after all these years. "They attacked Henry Sexton tonight. He's barely hanging on."

"Oh, God." Tom felt nausea in the pit of his stomach. The cheeseburger was trying to come up. "What happened?"

Quentin had hardly begun his story when Walt tapped Tom on the shoulder. "They're moving, Tom. Snake and Sonny are headed back toward Natchez. I'm going to drive to the bridge and pick them up when they cross back into Louisiana."

Tom nodded and motioned for Walt to start the van. "Sorry, Quentin. Are you still there?"

"Yeah. And I'm concerned that you seem to have forgotten your age. You and your buddy both."

"We're all going to have to forget that for the duration, Quentin. You included. Finish your story about Sexton."

While Quentin told his tale of the assault on Henry, Tom saw an image of a worried little boy who'd stood by while Tom stitched up his mother's arm after an accident with some kind of farming implement. Tom had met Henry several times as an adult, of course, while treating his parents, but for some reason Tom tended to remember members of the generation behind his own as children.

Unlike Tom, who had spent most of his life trying to distance himself from the 1960s, Henry Sexton had tried to resurrect them, and he'd paid for his efforts tonight—possibly with his life, if he succumbed to his injuries. As the Roadtrek jounced out of the KOA park and onto Highway 61 South, and Quentin Avery's mellifluous voice filled his ear, Tom said a silent prayer for the reporter. It was an atheist's prayer, a foxhole prayer, but that was the only kind Tom had been able to manage for fifty years or more.

He put his thumb over the mike on his cell phone and turned toward Walt. "Have you still got them on your scope?"

The old Ranger nodded, his eyes glued to the screen mounted on the dashboard. "Still coming north. You still think Sonny Thornfield is the one to hit?"

When Walt turned, and Tom met his old friend's eyes, no words were necessary.

"Turn that damned phone off when you're finished with your lawyer," Walt grumbled. "I don't fancy spending the rest of my days in Parchman."

"I will. You watch the damned road."

CHAPTER 48

BRODY ROYAL POINTED through the windshield of his son-in-law's pickup toward a small building at the end of the street.

"Dark as a damn speakeasy," he said. "I doubt they even have crime scene tape up."

Randall Regan braked, then tensed as the squeal of rotors echoed down the street. "I don't see a soul. I figured after what happened to Henry, the sheriff would have posted a man outside."

"Amateurs," said Brody. "Just like your nephew and his crew. Jesus, Mary, and Joseph. They couldn't drag one fifty-year-old man into a truck?"

"They didn't figure on a secretary packing a pistol."

Brody grunted and peered down the dark street. "This town's dying. There's nobody on this side, this time of night. Not during the winter, anyway. It was different back in sixty-four. That night we burned Norris's store, the signal was the end of the last shift at the King Hotel. That meant Ferriday was shutting down for the night."

"When did the King close down?"

"Oh, hell, thirty years back."

"There's not even a crack dealer back here," said Regan, chuckling as he rolled toward the *Concordia Beacon* building. "They're all over on the main drag. They sell their shit right on Wallace Boulevard."

Brody shook his head with disgust. "We'd have strung them up from the lampposts in my day. One on every block. Slow down, Randall. Just ease right up to the door."

Regan craned his head over the steering wheel.

"Nose your fender up there and just push the door open."

Regan drove over the glittering shards of Henry Sexton's rear windshield, then turned his wheel to the right and slowed the truck to a crawl. The weight and momentum of the fender shattered every inch of glass in the door, like putting a finger through a sheet of ice.

"Back up," Brody said, reaching for his door handle.

Regan did.

"Get the Flammenwerfer."

Regan moved quickly. He'd been practicing with the flamethrower for the past two hours, and he'd become quite adept with the heavy unit. He strapped the two cylinders on his back, then took the firing pipe in his hand and walked through the door of the newspaper office.

Brody followed him, his pulse quickening.

"Computers first?" Regan asked.

"No. We need to get his private workroom first, then work our way backward. My source tells me he calls it his 'war room.' If he taped Morehouse, that's where the tape will be. Unless he had it at home."

"War room?" said Regan, heading down a hallway. "I'll give him his war."

He tried a couple of doors but found only storage rooms. The third, however, opened into a small room with maps and photographs covering every wall. Brody stepped inside and whistled. He recognized most of the Double Eagles in the first few seconds. Other photos showed Dr. Robb, a Ku Klux Klan rally, and charts of various kinds.

"Pay dirt," he said, searching for his own face among the photos taped to the wall.

You think Forrest is gonna be okay with this?" Randall asked.

"You think I care?" Brody caught sight of his daughter's face, tacked to the far wall. He almost crossed the room for the picture, but then he backed out of the doorway. "Burn it, Randall," he said in a strangled voice. "Burn it all."

"Yes, sir."

Brody heard a clank and a hiss, followed by a roar that sent chills racing over his body. A jet of liquid flame reached out from the pipe in Regan's hand, like Lucifer pissing fire on the world. Henry's Sexton's war room became an inferno, driving Brody back from the breathtaking heat.

Randall shouted with exultation at the destruction, but Brody just stared into the flames, recalling a time before he'd lost his daughter, when the life he'd always wanted still seemed possible, and his hands had held something more than money and power. Across the room, his daughter's face curled and turned to ash. Brody stumbled back, his nostrils stinging with the petroleum reek of battle, and staggered out toward the truck.

TWO HUNDRED YARDS UP Tennessee Avenue, Sleepy Johnston sat behind the wheel of a GMC pickup, his Detroit Tigers baseball cap pulled low over his face, and stared at the truck parked against the *Beacon* building. Squinting through the dim light thrown off by the streetlamp, he saw a sign on the truck's door: ROYAL OIL, INC.

Sleepy hadn't been sure what the old man and his son-in-law were up to at first, not even after he saw the big man put on the heavy backpack and walk into the newspaper office. But Sleepy recognized the deep red glow coming from the shattered door well enough. He'd seen that same glow on the night they burned out Albert Norris. A small crowd had gathered to watch the landmark shop collapse into itself while the firemen vainly played their hoses over the ruins, and Sleepy had been among them.

A lot of grown men and boys had cried that week. Others had cussed a friend, punched a stranger, or spat in some cracker's mashed potatoes before they served his plate. But despite this anger, a deep and shameful fear had been born in the hearts of many black men in the parish that night. That fear had ultimately driven Sleepy away, all the way to Detroit. For if the Klan could kill a respected businessman like Albert Norris and get away with it, what chance did he have?

Sleepy thought about Albert as he watched the red glow rising in the *Beacon*'s door. Albert had given Sleepy his nickname because of the perpetual haze in his eyes—a haze induced by the reefer Sleepy and his cousins regularly ferried up from their auntie's house in New Orleans. Sleepy had always wanted to work for Albert, like Pooky did, but Albert didn't tolerate drug use among his employees, even though it was epidemic among the musicians he served. Still, Sleepy had loved the old man ("old" to the boy he'd been then, anyway—Sleepy was now ten years older than Albert had been when he died). Somehow, Albert had sensed that Sleepy had a tough home life, and always had a kind word for him. He'd also made sure that Sleepy stayed employed as a musician, usually with road bands.

When he wasn't on the road, Sleepy had lived part of the year in

New Orleans and part over in Wisner, a few miles from Ferriday, but
he often slept in the attic of a cousin who lived near Albert's store. That
was where he'd been on the night he heard the explosion that changed
his life. Running out into the empty road, he'd seen three white men
leap from the window of the burning store. One had been the man
whose name was now painted on the door of the truck parked in front
of the burning newspaper building. In 1964, talking to the police was
not an option for a black boy, and Sleepy had left town as soon as he
could. But not before the next afternoon, when Pooky had come to
him wild-eyed with terror, crying that the Klan was combing the
parish for him with dogs. Sleepy had known Pooky was fooling with
a white girl, and he'd warned him about it, but Pooky wouldn't listen.
The fool had pussy on the brain and couldn't think straight. And back
in those days, white pussy was a powerful drug—a lot more powerful
than the weed Pooky filched from Sleepy's stash when he thought his
friend wasn't looking.

The furnace glow from the *Beacon*'s door pulled Sleepy's gaze like
the fires of hell. Waves of heat distorted the air above the building. *Why
are they doing this?* he wondered. *They already stabbed poor Henry Sexton.*
Guilt made Sleepy squirm in the seat of his truck. He knew the reporter
had been looking all over the parish for him. He thanked God Pooky's
mother had kept her promise and held his name back.

Sleepy looked down at his cell phone and thought about dialing 911.
It would be so easy. All he'd have to do was report that a Royal Oil truck
had smashed open the door of the *Beacon*, and some men had set the
building on fire. He wouldn't even have to mention Old Man Royal. But
he *could*. . . .

"And then what?" Sleepy wondered aloud. He could still see the
hawk-eyed white devil he'd known as a boy. And if Brody Royal could
order a hit on a famous white reporter like Henry Sexton—even today—
what chance did a retired electrician's helper have?

"Ain't nothing changed down here," Sleepy mumbled. "That
motherfucker still owns this town. That's why he's burnin' up the newspaper like he don't care who comes along. He *don't*. He don't have to."

At bottom, this was the reason Sleepy hadn't contacted Henry
Sexton. Because in spite of all the progress since the bad old days,
nobody could protect you from bastards like Brody Royal. Henry Sex-

ton couldn't even protect himself. Oh, they'd sing your praises at your funeral for doing the noble thing, but you'd still be dead.

Sleepy touched the baseball card he'd taped to his dashboard before driving down from Michigan. The card bore the image of Gates Brown, one of the black stars of the 1968 Detroit Tigers team, which had won the World Series. Sleepy had actually made it to three of those games, and not much in life had come close to the joy he'd felt there. Feeling a part of that season was what had finally enabled him to tolerate living in the North. Ever since, he'd carried the Gates Brown card as a good luck charm, and it had often brought him peace during tough times.

"I could throw my cell phone in the river," he thought aloud. "After I called 911."

Then Sleepy realized that he knew too little about technology to feel safe even if he did that. Brody Royal probably knew people who could backtrack a 911 phone call and tell him exactly who'd made it. Sleepy was still arguing with himself when Royal stumbled out of the burning building and leaned against the side of the truck. The sight of the old man in such a vulnerable position made Sleepy want to drive down the street and squash him between the two trucks. His hand was rising to his ignition key when Royal's son-in-law ran out of the building and pulled off his heavy backpack. Sliding down low in the seat, Sleepy watched the two men from beneath the arc of his steering wheel until the truck backed away from the burgeoning fire and disappeared down the dark street.

With shaking hands, Sleepy cranked his own truck and followed them.

CHAPTER 49

WALT GARRITY CRUISED slowly up the gravel road in pitch darkness while Tom studied the scope monitoring the GPS tracker on Sonny Thornfield's truck. A hundred yards down the slope to their left lay Old River, once a great bend in the Mississippi River but now a lake created by a cutoff dug by the Army Corps of Engineers in 1932. You could still access the Mississippi from Old River, through a channel a half mile east of here, and that's why all the fishing camps along Old River were built on thirty-foot-high stilts. When the Mississippi flooded, Old River did, too, and the only way in or out was by boat. But the people who owned camps here loved that isolation, and that, Tom figured, was what Sonny Thornfield had come here to find.

"Let's hope he's alone," Walt said.

Tom had made house calls down here before. A few of the camps were luxurious, but most were little more than shacks on stilts, with three flights of iron steps for access. All had makeshift elevators, metal cages hauled up and down a metal track system by a truck winch mounted at the top.

"Shouldn't that one be it?" Walt asked, pointing up into the darkness, where a faint yellow light burned.

"I think so," Tom said, still trying to decipher the screen.

Walt made a sharp left into an empty driveway next door to the camp where Thornfield had parked, and cut his engine. "No point wasting time," he said, touching the derringer that hung on a chain beneath his shirt. "Same signal as the steak house, okay? If you see anything strange, start the engine."

"I will. You be careful."

Walt saluted, then got out of the van and silently closed the door.

Tom quickly lost sight of him in the darkness, but he felt confident that Walt would succeed in his mission. A seasoned hunter of men, the old Ranger wouldn't hesitate to use force if things got dicey. Walt had given Tom a handheld radio to monitor, and reiterated that Tom must leave his cell phone switched off. Tom felt exposed sitting in the empty driveway, even in the dark. But at least most of the camp houses had RVs of various types parked beneath them. As he waited in the van, alone but for the ticking of the cooling engine, his mind began to wander.

All day, he had been quietly contemplating a biblical tale his father had despised. On the Day of Atonement, the priest of the temple had chosen two goats by lot. One would be sacrificed on the altar for the sins of Israel, the other cast out into the desert, bearing the sins of the people on its head. The first goat was known as the Lord's Goat. The second—the *Azazel*—became known as the scapegoat. Because the scapegoat was sent away to perish, it came to represent any person blamed or punished for the sins of others, or to distract attention from the real cause of a crime. The Bible was replete with examples: Eve blamed for original sin, Jonah for a storm at sea. Barabbas, the thief, was allowed to live while Jesus, the Lord's Goat, died for the sins of man. In the New Testament, Satan had become the scapegoat for God's harsher side.

Tom's father, a man of rigid moral rectitude, had condemned this practice as an expression of man's basest urges. He'd recounted countless historical examples: Alfred Dreyfus rotting on Devil's Island; royal whipping boys beaten bloody; medical patients scapegoated for epidemics; Jews being led to the ovens as Tom approached puberty. Percy Cage had ingrained in his son the conviction that a man of honor admitted his mistakes, took responsibility for them, and stoically accepted his punishment. Evading responsibility for sin was cowardice, plain and simple. Yet in the present circumstance, Tom thought, he had no choice. Not if he wanted to live with his family for the final year of two of his life, and not in a locked cage.

He thought of Glenn Morehouse, the simple-minded factory worker he'd treated so long ago. Morehouse was probably the least guilty of all the Double Eagles, because he'd had the least free will. He'd also possessed some remnant of a conscience, because he'd been murdered for trying to unburden his soul before death. But Glenn Morehouse, too, had committed murder. He'd participated in Viola's rape, and probably countless other acts of brutality. Few tears, if any, had been shed at his death. And since Morehouse *was* dead, what more fitting scapegoat could there be for Viola's murder?

Tom's radio crackled in his lap. Then Walt said, "He's moving around inside."

Tom's chest tightened. He reached down into his bag for his short-barreled .357 and laid the heavy pistol in his lap.

"Get ready," Walt said. "I think he's coming out."

Tom got to his feet—he had to stoop inside the van—then opened the side door and stepped out into the night. The smell of dead fish and rotting vegetation assailed him. He stuck the .357 into his waistband and crunched up the gravel driveway, then crossed over into some shadows thrown by the light beneath Sonny's camp house. He'd barely found a place to wait when he heard a screen door bang against its frame high above him.

A new sound puzzled him for a few seconds. Then he realized that Thornfield was pissing off the deck high above. By the light of the moon, Tom saw urine falling in a thin, irregular stream to his right. *Old man's prostate,* he thought. Tom had little doubt that Walt would make use of Thornfield being indisposed to get control of him. Sure enough, he heard a squawk of surprise, and the trickle of urine abruptly stopped.

Angry words passed above him, and then, as Walt had predicted, someone started down to the ground in the makeshift elevator. Walt had told Tom to expect Sonny in the cage, and ten seconds later, the old Double Eagle appeared, clinging to the bars of a flimsy metal elevator as the winch groaned and whined high above him.

Tom heard Walt descending a metal staircase on the other side of the elevated shack, but he seemed in no hurry. As Walt had predicted, Sonny seemed to think this was a chance for escape. Wearing only pajama pants and a wifebeater T-shirt, he peered back at the staircase, gauging Walt's rate of descent, a sly smile on his lips.

When the cage hit the ground, he jerked up the safety bar that held him inside and started toward his pickup truck. Either he kept a spare key inside, or there was a gun under its seat. Tom stepped out of the shadows, directly in his path. The old Eagle's eyes went wide, then narrowed when he recognized Tom.

"What you doin' here, Doc?"

"Waiting for you, Sonny."

Thornfield looked back up at the staircase. Walt was only about halfway down and he hadn't increased his pace. "I need to get somethin' out of my truck, Doc. I'll be with you in a sec."

Tom took the Smith & Wesson out of his waistband and pointed it at Thornfield's potbelly. The T-shirt that covered it was stained with fried egg and something dark, maybe jelly. "You wait right where you are."

"Hey, Doc, take it easy with that. There's a guy upstairs tryin' to rob me."

Tom couldn't help but smile. "He's not here to rob you. He's here to help me. We need to ask you some questions, Sonny. We've got a proposition for you."

Walt's boots clanged on the metal steps as he neared the ground. Thornfield seemed to understand that once the man in the cowboy hat reached ground level, he would lose all chance of escape. Without another word, Sonny started running toward the next house over.

"Stop!" Tom shouted.

Sonny looked back over his shoulder but didn't stop.

Tom raised his pistol, aimed between Thornfield's shoulder blades, and cocked the hammer. The old man turned, trying to decide whether Tom had the nerve to fire.

"I'll kill you, Sonny," Tom said, surprised by his desire to pull the trigger. "You deserve it, for what you did to Viola."

Thornfield stopped backpedaling and stood uncertainly between the camp houses. Tom walked toward him, still aiming the pistol. "You raped Viola when she was a happy young woman. You and Frank and the others. You ruined her life. If I kill you now, I could pin Viola's murder on you, along with whatever else your buddies need to take off the books."

Sonny's eyes widened, and then his face took on the cast of the eternal loser who feels put upon by the world. "What do you guys want with me? I ain't nobody. And I ain't done nothin' to you. I didn't hurt that Viola none, neither. You got the wrong idea, Doc. Way wrong."

Walt took a couple of steps past Tom. "If that's the case," he said, "I'm sure we'll find a way to make it up to you. But right now, you need to step into that van over there."

"No way," Sonny said, glancing at the Roadtrek. "I ain't gonna. I ain't no fool. And Doc ain't gonna shoot me."

Walt raised his derringer and touched the barrel to Thornfield's forehead. "Maybe not. But I'll blow your damn brains out and never lose a moment's sleep over it. So, you can take your chances in the van or you can die where you stand. Make your choice, bub. I need some coffee."

"Who are you?" Sonny asked.

"Captain Walt Garrity, Texas Rangers."

Sonny's mouth worked around as though trying to raise a plug of spit. There was a lot of white showing in his eyes.

"Life or death, Sonny?" Tom said. "Life is in the van."

"Shit," Sonny said. Then he started walking toward the Roadtrek.

CHAPTER 50

IF A MAN *is forced to choose between the truth and his father, only a fool chooses the truth.* That quote rings in my head like a mocking mantra as I pull into my parents' driveway. Annie sits puzzled beside me. I woke her from a dead sleep an hour after realizing why I'd sought out the old photograph of Viola. After my epiphany about the night my father left me stranded at the hospital, I struggled to understand what might have resulted from their relationship, and I quickly came to the conclusion that Lincoln Turner was one possible answer. This realization must have overwhelmed me, because I quickly slipped into a dreamless coma. But while I slept, a key of some kind turned deep within me, for I started awake with my second revelation of the night. To my surprise, it concerned my mother, not my father.

When I called my mother earlier tonight—my second call of the evening—she told me my father was still asleep. The wrongness of that answer should have hit me instantly. Had this not been one of the most stressful days in all our lives, it would have, but I assumed that Dad was exhausted from the day's events, and from grief over Viola. But when I snapped awake in my chair the second time, I knew how mistaken I'd been.

I can't remember ever being at my parents' house at night with my father asleep and my mother awake. Invariably, my mother lay in bed while my father dictated medical charts by phone, painted lead soldiers, read in his library, or watched movies in bed while Mom snored under the influence of her sleeping pills. Only during the day would I find my father asleep and my mother awake. As soon as this realization hit me, I knew I had to go to my parents' house. I calmed Annie as much as I could after waking her, but during the drive over, she quickly sensed my anxiety. I took her hand in mine and told her everything would be fine, but I'm not at all confident of this.

Together we get out of the car and walk hand in hand to the carport door. On the way over, I called Chief Logan and told him to warn his patrolmen that I would be coming, but I didn't call my mother. Ringing the bell at this hour might frighten her, but I'm unwilling to let her manipulate me any longer. If I must choose between the truth and my father . . . I choose the truth.

"Who is it?" Mom calls through the door.

"Penn."

"*Penn?* What on earth? Why didn't you call?"

"Mom, it's cold. And I have Annie with me. Open up!"

After five seconds of silence, she flips the bolt and opens the door. I see many emotions in her face, but fear is dominant. I also see one hand hidden in the pocket of her housecoat. Whatever she's holding there looks heavy—probably the .38 Special my father gave her decades ago.

"Why don't you make Annie some hot chocolate?" I say, slipping past her and into the kitchen.

"I don't need any hot chocolate," Annie says. "Gram? Are you okay?"

I walk into the den and toward the hallway that leads to their bedroom.

"Penn!" Mom calls after me. "Your father's exhausted. Please don't put any more stress on him today."

With a last look back at her, I enter the dark hall and move along it, my heart pounding with dread. Her hurried footsteps rush up behind me.

"Penn, please don't wake—"

I whirl on her, my face hot. "He's not in there, is he?"

She takes a deep breath and looks at the floor.

"Mom?"

When she looks up, her eyes are red. "No."

For a few seconds the world seems to shudder on its axis. A couple of hours ago I learned my mother would lie on the stand to protect my father. But now I realize she's been lying to *me*. How could that deception possibly help Dad? Who could it protect him from, other than me? But then the answer comes to me: my parents believe they're protecting me by keeping me ignorant of my father's insanely desperate act.

"Daddy?" says a small voice.

Annie stands watching us from the end of the hall. I want to comfort her, but I can scarcely get my mind around what's happening myself. "Where is he, Mom? Tell me."

"I don't know," she says, hurrying to Annie's side.

"Is that the truth?"

She looks back at me in surrender. "Yes."

"Do you have a way to reach him?"

"No."

"I don't believe you."

She hugs Annie and whispers something in her ear.

"Why do you look so mad, Daddy? Is Papa okay?"

"I'm not mad, baby. Please go back to the kitchen for a second. We'll be right there."

After my mother whispers something else, Annie reluctantly obeys.

I step closer to my mother so that I can keep my voice low. "He's jumped bail?"

She nods.

"How long ago?" I ask, trying to compute how much time has elapsed since I called earlier. "Two or three hours?"

"I think he left just after lunch. I'm honestly not sure."

I feel like a man blinded by some injury, suddenly having his bandages ripped off. I spent the second half of this day working on the assumption that I'd have the opportunity to try again to persuade Dad to save himself, and that Quentin Avery might help me do that. But the truth is that my father jumped bail hours ago, and probably fled the city. *Maybe even the country.*

A primal blast of fear surges through me. Two days ago, Viola Turner was murdered in her sickbed. Last night Glenn Morehouse was murdered almost the same way. Tonight someone tried to kill Henry Sexton. Right after that, Special Agent John Kaiser asked me if I could protect my "folks" until the FBI arrives tomorrow. I said I could. What the hell was I thinking?

"Mom, pack a bag. Right now. Clothes for three days."

Her eyes go wide. "What?"

I take her arm and start leading her up the hall. "We're in danger. All of us. When was the last time you talked to Dad?"

"Around noon," she says, trying to hold her ground. "Wait!"

"We can't. Pack the bag and bring your pistol. Don't take more than five minutes. Annie and I will be in the kitchen."

She stops. "Penn, I can't leave this house."

"Why not? Is Dad going to call you here?"

"No, but . . ." She doesn't know what to say. "Where are we going? To your house?"

"Only long enough to get Annie packed. We've got to go into hiding. At least you and Annie do, until I can find out what's really going on. The FBI will be here tomorrow, and things should be safer then."

"Penn, this is crazy. Why are you saying this?"

"Because Dad's put us all in danger! Maybe more than he understands. I hope so. But either way, I'm going to need your help with Annie."

Mom shakes her head, reflexively resisting me. Gripping her shoulders, I lean down and look hard into her eyes. *Annie needs you.* Now, go. *Go!*"

She hesitates five or six seconds, but then her resistance crumbles. Annie is the future of our family, and my mother cannot contemplate exposing her to danger. The decision made, she takes her pistol from her pocket and darts through the bedroom door.

CHAPTER 51

TOM SAT IN the back of Walt Garrity's Roadtrek van, looking into the flat, uncommunicative eyes of Sonny Thornfield. They'd sat him on the edge of the six-by-six-foot bed in the rear of the van. The old Double Eagle's hands and feet were bound with a pair of flex-cuffs that Walt had brought from Texas.

"What the hell am I doing here?" Thornfield asked.

Neither Tom nor Walt answered. Walt had explained to Tom that for their plan to work they must instill genuine terror in Thornfield. If they had more time, a different approach might work. But under the pressure they faced now, they couldn't afford gentleness. Sonny Thornfield had to believe that they didn't care whether he lived or died. Only then would he grasp at the only escape route they offered him.

To ensure privacy, Walt had parked the Roadtrek on the river side of the levee, near the edge of the borrow pits—the long trenches left behind where earth was "borrowed" after the 1927 flood to build the levee system that protected Louisiana from the wrath of the Mississippi River. In the decades since, those huge pits had filled with black water, cottonwood trees, and scrub vegetation, a perfect environment for snakes, fish, and alligators to thrive. More than one corpse had been found in the borrow pits over the years, and at this time of night, the only people likely to drive down here would be poachers or teenagers looking for a place to have sex. They would give the polished silver RV a wide berth.

"You guys just kidnapped me," Sonny said resentfully. "That's a fucking felony."

Walt backhanded him across the face, just to set the tone of the occasion.

The old Klansman let out a screech of anger. "What the hell are *you* up to?" he asked Tom. "You aren't supposed to leave Mississippi."

Tom reached into his weekend bag and brought out his .357 Magnum. "I'm not supposed to be handling firearms, either. But I'm making an exception tonight."

Thornfield's demeanor hardly changed. He didn't seem to believe he was in lethal danger, even after they'd driven so far from town. The low chatter of the police scanner seemed to puzzle him, but he hadn't asked about it yet.

"You did kidnap Viola Turner in 1968," Tom said. "You helped gang-rape her, and then you helped torture her. I know, because I'm the one who sent Ray Presley to take her back."

For the first time, fear flickered in Thornfield's eyes. Even dead, Ray Presley scared most people more than a live man could.

"I ain't sayin' shit to you," Sonny said. "Either one of you. You might as well take me back home."

Walt punched him in the gut, driving the wind from his lungs. Drool rolled down the old man's chin as he straightened up.

"Are ya'll taping this or something?" he asked, coughing violently. "The statue of limitations has run out on rape, you know. A *long* time ago. It's like it never happened, far as the law's concerned."

Tom spoke patiently, as though he had all day to make his points. "You also murdered Viola's brother, and a man named Luther Davis. There's no stat*ute* of limitations on murder, Sonny."

"You can't prove that. The FBI doesn't even think those two were murdered."

"We're not concerned with what the FBI thinks. Do you remember the night you got shot in the leg? The night Frank and Glenn brought you to my office? February 1968?"

Thornfield glanced down at his left leg. "What about it?"

"Viola was there that night. Her brother and Luther Davis, too. You'd gotten into a brawl with them, and I was patching them up when you got there. I know you were looking to get revenge on them. But they hid out in Freewoods, so you raped Viola to smoke them out."

A little more of Thornfield's defiance evaporated.

Walt squatted before him with surprising flexibility. "If you think we snatched you and drove you down here because we give a flying fuck about the law, you're dumber than I figured."

This time Sonny held his silence. Like Ray Presley, Walt gave off an aura of impending violence, and Sonny recognized it.

"We know you tortured them boys," Walt said. "Presley told Tom all about it. You sliced off their service tattoos, which I take personally, you no-'count son of a bitch."

Sonny swallowed and drew back a couple of inches.

"I'm no fan of torture," Walt went on, as though discussing his preference in fishing lures. "Ain't productive, as a rule. But I've seen it produce results. Tom and I were medics during the Korean War. We saw a lot of pain. You know what I'm talking about. You saw what the Japanese did on the islands."

Sonny made a sour face. "I'm not scared of you, you Texas shit-kicker."

Walt sighed and glanced back at Tom. Then he patted one of the Roadtrek's seats. "Sonny, I've got a toolbox under here. And Tom's got his black bag with him. I feel pretty confident that between us, we can make whatever you and Snake Knox did to them colored boys back in sixty-eight look like a Girl Scout picnic."

Sonny glowered at them in silence.

Walt chuckled patiently. "Yeah, a dull pocketknife dragged over one tooth for ten minutes will turn a bad outlaw into jelly. An old Ranger showed me that trick. When the blade cuts down into the dentin, the pain kicks in something fierce. Most men start talking right then. But if you go all the way down to the nerve . . . hell, you can't shut 'em up after that, not even if you try. You gotta knock 'em out with a two-by-four just to stop the screamin'."

"I've got some local anesthetic," Tom said, playing the good cop as instructed. "Once you tell us what we need to know, I'll make the pain stop."

Sonny's eyes tracked from Tom to Walt, then back again. "All this goddamn gummin'," he muttered. "You haven't said what it is you want."

"Who killed Viola?" Tom asked.

Thornfield looked blank. "*You* did. Didn't you?"

Walt straightened up and kicked him in the gut. Sonny doubled over, gasping for air. After half a minute, he croaked, "That's what everybody says, ain't it?"

"You were there that night," Tom said. "At her sister's house. I saw the pickup truck with the Darlington Academy sticker on the back windshield, parked a quarter mile up the road. Not long before dawn."

Darlington had been founded by the White Citizens' Council in 1969, the year of forced integration in Natchez. "Nobody in that part of town ever went to Darlington Academy."

Sonny was obviously working something out in his head. "Unless you got a picture, nobody's gonna believe you about that."

Walt lifted the seat that concealed his toolbox, then brought out a green metal case and set it in the narrow walkway between the RV's toilet and cooktop counter. Thornfield's eyes locked on to the box. Walt opened it and brought out a small propane torch and a friction striker. With two quick compressions of his forefinger, he lit the torch, which filled the van with a chilling hiss as he adjusted the flame to a blue needle with a white-hot core.

"Hey, hey," Thornfield said, breathing fast while his eyes tracked the blue-white flame. "Wait a minute. Doc . . . I don't feel right. Something's wrong."

"Was Snake with you that night at Viola's?" Tom asked.

Sonny nodded, looking nauseated.

"I'm not kidding," Sonny said, his breaths coming shallow. "Something's wrong."

"You bet your ass something's wrong," Walt said. "But in about thirty seconds, it ain't gonna matter. Your whole brain's gonna feel like it's on fire."

"What the hell do you guys want? Jesus, man!"

Walt cut his eyes at Tom and nodded. Tom took one of his Ziploc bags from a nearby drawer and pulled on a pair of latex gloves. Then he removed two adrenaline vials and a large syringe like the one that had been used to inject Viola.

"*Hey!*" Sonny cried. "What's that? You're not gonna kill me, are you? Doc!"

"That depends," Tom said. "On how cooperative you are in the next thirty seconds. Give me your hand, Sonny."

He reached for Thornfield's hand, but the old Klansman jerked it back. Walt held the blowtorch near his leg and clucked his tongue. The prospect of actually torturing a man sickened Tom, but if Thornfield refused to cooperate, he might have to let Walt proceed. A gun to the head was no good unless you were prepared to use it, and that would defeat the purpose of the whole exercise.

Tom held out his open hand, and this time Sonny lowered his fingers to within reach. With the deft motions that had sutured thousands of wounds, Tom rolled Sonny's thumb and finger over the adrenaline vials several times. With the syringe he took care to place Sonny's prints right where they would have gone had Thornfield injected Viola with adrenaline. As he dropped the vials and syringe back into the Ziploc bag, Sonny stared at him like a puzzled dog.

"Like I told you earlier," Tom said, "I have a proposition for you. I want to talk to you about turning state's evidence."

Sonny's eyes bugged. "You aren't cops. You can't offer me any deal."

"Nevertheless," Walt said, "there's a deal to be had. And it's the only one you're going to get. We've got enough evidence right now to throw you to the wolves on Viola's murder."

"All we've got to do," Walt said, "is put a bullet in your ear, and dump you back at your camp house with that syringe and those vials."

"Then why don't you do it? Why'd you even take the trouble to drive out here?"

"There's a more elegant solution," Tom said. "One more likely to satisfy all parties concerned."

Thornfield shook his head violently. "You're crazy, Doc. You don't know who you're dealing with. I wouldn't live twenty-four hours if I tried something like that." Thornfield was panting for air. "Besides, Snake could just turn around and say I killed her! It'd be my word against his."

Walt grabbed Thornfield's chin and jerked his head straight.

"You've got the wrong idea," Tom said. "Have you ever heard the expression 'Lay the sins of the living at the feet of the dead'?"

Sonny blinked in confusion. Tom was about to explain further when Thornfield doubled over and vomited. "Doc, my chest feels like it's locking up. My heart's skipping something terrible."

"Your heart's smarter than you are," Walt said.

Thornfield hugged himself and sought out Tom's eyes, speaking like a fawning sycophant. "Come on, Doc. Ain't no jury round here gonna convict you. Every nigger round here thinks you walk on water. Just tell 'em you put the old lady out of her misery!"

Tom lowered his head, trying to think of a way to break through Thornfield's fear and stupidity. "Sonny, I'm trying to give you a way out of this that keeps us all out of jail. Will you listen to what I'm saying?"

"He's not listening," Walt said. "He's putting on a show. I say put one in his head and let him take the fall. That's the quickest solution, and I want you clear of this mess before anybody figures out you've jumped bail."

Tom shook his head, wondering if Walt was just trying to scare Thornfield, or if he really meant what he'd said.

Thornfield leaned against a cabinet and moaned in what sounded like real pain. Tom had a wealth of experience with malingering, and this didn't look like it. "Walt—"

"Quiet," Garrity said with sudden urgency.

The old Ranger had gone so still that both Tom and Sonny stared at him in alarm. Walt shut off the torch and scrambled to the front window of the van, which he'd earlier blocked with a sun shield.

"State police!" he hissed, peering out through a crack.

Tom felt his heart lurch, and then the cold sweat of imminent combat covered his skin.

Thornfield started laughing, a hysterical undercurrent in his voice. "I never thought I'd be glad to see the goddamn cops!"

"Shut him up!" Walt snapped. "I'll deal with this, but he can't make a sound."

"How do I do that?" Tom asked.

"Either drug him senseless, or I'll sap him."

A lead-weighted sap could easily kill the old Eagle. As Tom grabbed for the drugs in his bag, he heard an engine outside the van. Then came the slow screech of brake pads. A car had stopped outside. With shaking hands, Tom filled a syringe with Valium.

"Hold his arm, Walt!"

As Walt darted back up the aisle, Sonny tried to rise, but Walt punched him in the solar plexus. Two seconds later, Walt had exposed the antecubital vein.

Tom jabbed in the needle and injected 5 mg of the sedative.

"ATTENTION IN THE VAN!" said a metallic voice.

"PA speaker," Walt said, still holding Sonny. "I've got to go out there."

When Walt let go of Sonny's arm, the old man fell back onto the cushions of the bed and lay still.

"I'd better come with you," Tom said.

"Hide your gun and the drugs first."

Tom nodded, though he couldn't see what good that would do if he couldn't hide Thornfield as well.

"Throw a blanket over him like he's sleeping," Walt ordered. Then he opened the side door of the van and climbed down the step.

"*STOP WHERE YOU ARE!*" ordered the PA voice.

Tom's heart began to thump against his sternum. He wanted to slide the gun into his rear waistband, but he fought the urge and did as Walt had instructed, concealing his black bag and the pistol in a drawer beneath the RV's bed. Red lights began flashing outside, sending sizzling arcs of scarlet light through the van's interior.

A car door slammed outside.

Tom took a deep breath, then went out through the same door Walt had used. A Louisiana state trooper wearing a flat-brim cowboy hat stood beside a white patrol car with its driver's door standing open. The flashing red light bar backlit him like an actor walking into the climactic scene of a film. Tom could hear radio chatter inside the car. Even as he hoped that the trooper hadn't called in Walt's license plate, he realized that the way the van was parked—nose out from the borrow pits—meant the trooper couldn't have seen the plate number yet. Walt had probably parked that way on purpose, just in case.

"What's the problem, Sar'nt?" Walt asked as Tom closed the door.

The trooper walked toward the van, his hand on the butt of his pistol. "What's your name, sir?"

"Captain Walt Garrity, Texas Rangers."

"Texas Rangers?"

"That's right. Retired. But I still work as an investigator for the DA in Houston."

"Where's your ID?"

"In my wallet. Can I take it out?"

"Not just yet. What about you?" asked the trooper, gesturing at Tom.

Tom silently cursed his stupidity. "It's in the van."

"I see. Captain, we've had reports of a van like this one being used to move crystal methamphetamine around the state."

Walt laughed. "You think a couple of old farts like us are pushing meth?"

"You'd be surprised. Why don't we get your friend there to open up the van, so I can take a look inside?"

"Happy to. Our buddy's sleeping inside, though. Hate to wake him. He drank a little too much during Happy Hour tonight."

"He drinks too much *every* damn night," Tom said in a griping tone, flashing back to Korea, where he and Walt had occasionally lied to MPs in similar fashion.

"I'll try not to disturb him," said the cop. "But I need to see both your driver's licenses. Proof of insurance, as well."

Tom guessed the trooper was about forty. He had dark hair and eyes set too close together beneath the brim of his hat.

"Open the van door, sir," he ordered Tom. "Then step away from the vehicle."

Walt nodded that Tom should comply.

I guess we're going to brazen this out, Tom thought. As he walked to the Roadtrek's side door, he prayed that the intravenous Valium would keep Sonny sedated for the duration of their bluff.

"Captain Garrity," said the trooper, "while he's opening that door, I want you to turn around and place your hands behind your head."

"Happy to," Walt said, folding his hands behind his neck. "You're pretty far off the beaten path for patrol, aren't you?"

"I work on loan to the Criminal Investigations Bureau sometimes."

"That right?" Tom saw Walt's right hand flex and unflex behind his head.

Tom's hand was on the Roadtrek's door handle. He sensed more than saw the trooper coming closer, preparing to scan the interior once the door opened. As Tom pressed the button in the door handle, he heard a thud from inside the van.

"Ol' Jimmy must be waking up." Walt laughed. "He'll be wanting some hair of the dog."

The trooper drew his pistol. *"Inside the van!"* he yelled. *"Open the door and come out with your hands out in front of you!"*

Sonny Thornfield shouted something unintelligible from within.

The trooper whirled to make sure Walt's hands were still on his head.

Tom's throat sealed shut with fear.

"How many of you are in there?" called the trooper.

This time there was no response. Tom's back began to ache between his shoulder blades. He prayed it wasn't heart pain.

"Open that damned door!" the trooper yelled at Tom. *"Do it now, then back away!"*

"Hey, take it easy, brother. We got nothing to hide."

The trooper waved his gun at Tom. "You get that goddamn door open." He glared at Walt. "And *you* stay right where you are!"

It is heart pain, Tom realized, rotating one shoulder to try to relieve the ache. *I need a nitro. I guess the sooner this is over, the sooner I'll get one.* He popped the door handle and pulled it open.

"Back away!" shouted the trooper.

Tom took four steps back from the van.

As the trooper edged up to the opening, Tom heard a guttural moan. The cop leaned forward, stood motionless for a few moments, then turned back to Tom with a look that froze his blood. His face was smug, his eyes filled with triumph. When he raised his pistol, Tom reeled backward in terror.

The crack of the gunshot stunned him, but even as he fell, Tom saw the trooper jerk in a way he remembered all too well from Korea. A black circle had appeared on the man's left cheek, just below the eye. Then came another bang, and a second hole appeared beneath the trooper's nose. He wobbled on his feet, then collapsed behind the van and didn't move.

The sound of Walt's running feet startled Tom back into himself.

"You shot him," Tom mumbled, getting unsteadily to his feet. "You *shot* him?"

"He meant to kill you," Walt said, kicking the semiautomatic pistol from the fallen cop's hand. The leather string that always held Walt's derringer around his neck hung from his right hand. While Tom stared at the dead trooper, Walt hung the derringer back around his neck.

When Tom reached toward his friend, a searing pain shot down his left arm. *Oh, no,* he thought, wavering on his feet. *Another heart attack.* "I need a nitro, Walt. Fast."

"Whoa, buddy," Walt said, his eyes showing too much white. "You need more than a nitro. That bastard winged you. Left arm."

Tom looked down and saw blood on his left shoulder. The unexpected sight made him sway on his feet. Walt lunged forward and caught him.

Once Tom had regained his balance, Walt unbuttoned his shirt and checked the wound. "Christ, I thought my combat medic days were over. Straight through. Thank the Lord he was using ball ammo."

"It doesn't feel like he hit an artery."

"No, I think we're good. But it was damned close. Bullet might have nicked the humeral circumflex. I'd feel better if a real doctor checked it out."

Tom swallowed hard and looked at the dead man on the ground. "You just shot a cop, Walt. We need to get out of here."

"You ain't ever lied, brother. We're truly fucked now. Both of us. Let's get you into the van, and I'll clean this scene up double quick."

Tom allowed himself to be led into the van, where Walt retrieved his medical bag from its hiding place. After swallowing one nitro pill and a Lorcet Plus, Tom stuck another nitro tablet and a Valium under his tongue for good measure.

"You'd better come back out with me," Walt said. "I need to be able to see you if you pass out."

Half in a trance, Tom followed his friend back outside. As he leaned against the van, Walt walked over to the state police car, switched off its light bar, took the keys from the ignition, and opened the trunk.

"What are you doing?" Tom called.

Walking back to the driver's door, Walt leaned through it, then straightened up with a shotgun in his hands.

"What the hell are you doing with that?"

Without a word, Walt walked back to the trunk and fired four deafening shots into it. The cruiser rocked on its oversized shocks as it absorbed the impact of the rounds. Walt ducked into the trunk and began fiddling with something. After about thirty seconds, he stood up, triumphantly holding a paper bag in his hand. He carried the bag to Tom and opened it, revealing fragments of metal and plastic.

"What's all that?" Tom asked.

"What's left of a hard drive. The camera in that cruiser filmed everything that just happened. We're taking this with us so no genius from the NSA can put the drive back together."

Tom felt as though he might collapse. "Walt, this is bad. We can't run from this."

The Ranger grabbed his good shoulder and squeezed hard. "Forget the badge, Tom. From the moment he saw Sonny, that guy meant to kill us. Don't ask me how I knew, I just did. Fifty years of experience told me. State cops don't patrol dirt roads in the back of beyond at night. He came here to find *us*. You and me."

"But how could he? We switched off our phones, like you said."

Knowledge dawned in Walt's eyes. "It wasn't *our* phones. I left Sonny's cell phone on so I could monitor his texts and hear his voice mails. Stupid! That trooper was looking for Thornfield, not us. He must have been on the Eagles' payroll."

"A state cop?"

Walt shrugged. "I don't understand it, but now's not the time to figure it out." He looked back at the dead trooper. "I won't lie to you, buddy. Even if he was dirty, it won't make a bit of difference to any cop in this state if they figure out who killed him."

Stinging sweat dripped into Tom's eyes. "I shouldn't have dragged you into this."

Walt's smile had an ironic curve. "A little late for apologies."

A loud cry of pain came from the van.

Walt ran to the Roadtrek, motioning for Tom to follow him into the van. Inside, they found Thornfield lying faceup in the aisle, clenching his left arm, his skin deathly gray.

"He's having a heart attack," Tom said, kneeling.

"Let him," Walt said, trying to pull Tom up without hurting him. "There's nothing we can do."

Tom shook himself from Walt's grasp and checked Thornfield's pulse at the neck. It was thready, and the skin above the artery felt cool. "We need to get him to a hospital."

"A *hospital*?" Walt gawked at Tom. "We can't even take *you* to a hospital. You think we're gonna take this piece of shit, after what we just did?"

Tom had already taken a vial of epinephrine from his bag and loaded a syringe. "He's not going to tell anybody about that. Snake would kill Sonny if he knew we'd questioned him. Come on, Walt. Get us back to Ferriday!"

Walt didn't move as Tom injected the epinephrine into Thornfield's vein. "You realize he may have seen everything. Outside."

Tom thought about it. "I don't think he did."

"But you can't be sure. Even seeing the body would be enough to put us in the death house at Angola."

Walt was right, and this knowledge chilled Tom. "What do you want to do?"

"Leave him here," Walt said flatly. "I can stage this thing where it looks like they shot each other, and the cops'll find the syringe and vials besides. We'll be clear of this thing, and you'll be clear of Viola. It's the only answer, Tom."

Sonny groaned and clenched his left arm with his right fist.

Tom turned and looked up into Walt's hardened eyes. "You're talking about shooting him."

"He's dying anyway."

Walt was still carrying the trooper's shotgun, and it lent him a frighteningly lethal aspect. "We can't," Tom said. "I can't."

"This is no time to get religion, partner. Think of your family."

Tom did. And he understood why Walt was so ready to sacrifice Sonny Thornfield. Along with his fellow Double Eagles, this man had hurt and killed more innocent people than they knew. If Sonny died here (his death staged by Walt's expert hands), and Tom left the syringe and vials behind, they could remove the threat of prosecution for Viola's murder and probably get off the hook for the dead trooper's death as well. With so much pain hanging in the balance for his family (and for Walt, who wouldn't even be in this mess if he hadn't driven hundreds of miles to help Tom), how much of a crime would that be? Was the life of a rapist and killer too high a price to pay for life and freedom? For a chance to make amends to those people he had failed so miserably?

Tom had given up on religion decades ago, but looking down at Thornfield's cyanotic fingernails, he felt his soul in peril. How different was this from finding Frank Knox dying on the floor of his surgery at Viola's feet? Maybe not much. But something deep within him rebelled at the prospect of letting Thornfield die. Maybe he had been carrying so much guilt for so long that he couldn't stand adding another death to his account. Not even the death of a killer.

Tom looked anxiously up at Walt, who was not a man to be easily swayed. "No matter how you stage this, they're going to know someone else was involved. The second you destroyed that hard drive, you proved it."

The Ranger's eyes narrowed as he considered this. "Not if I leave the fragments behind. We'll just have to chance them piecing it back together. They'll never do it without FBI help. Besides, being on Eagle business, he probably found a way to switch off the camera."

"What about our footprints? All that forensic crap?"

Walt set his jaw in frustration. "Goddamn it, Tom. Quit searching for excuses. There's nothing pretty about this, but if we don't do it, we won't get out alive. Guys who kill state cops wind up cornered in barns somewhere. And when the meat wagon finally gets there, they have about thirty holes apiece in them. It's time to buy ourselves some insurance."

Tom slowly straightened up to his full height. He had three inches on Walt, and the new perspective reinforced his sense of moral advantage. "I know you just saved my life. But we can't kill this man. This isn't like the ambulance. This is cold-blooded murder."

Walt looked down at the gray man on the floor. As the barrel of the shotgun drifted toward Sonny's face, Sonny twisted up off the carpet and vomited on himself.

"For God's sake!" Tom pressed. "Let's move!"

With a wild grimace, Garrity carried the shotgun to the front of the van and settled into the driver's seat. For a few seconds he sat in silence, still fighting his instincts. But to Tom's relief, he finally started the Roadtrek and revved the motor in preparation for climbing back up the levee.

"_Shut off his goddamn cell phone!_" Walt shouted. "We don't want his whole outfit coming down on us!"

As Tom moved to obey, the pain of his shoulder wound stabbed him, stealing his breath. He found the cell phone in Thornfield's pocket, its LCD screen glowing blue. As he shut it off, he wondered if more state cops were already homing in on its periodic pings for a tower.

With a lurch, the van began to roll.

"Help me, Doc," Sonny gasped, gripping his arm and imploring him with glassy eyes. "_I'll do anything you say._"

"Don't talk."

"Don't let him kill me. I got a family."

Cursing silently, Tom stepped over Thornfield and moved carefully to the end of the aisle, as though walking in a speedboat. Through one of the van's rear windows, he saw the dead trooper growing smaller in the fading red glow of their taillights. But that vanishing figure was an illusion.

They would never leave that corpse behind them.

CHAPTER 52

IN MY HOUSE on Washington Street, Mom is helping Annie pack a bag upstairs while I sit in our front room, jotting down the most likely explanations for my father jumping bail. It's remarkable how easy this is, now that my faith in his honesty has been stripped away.

If Dad is innocent of Viola's murder, then four explanations seem possible: one, he's trying to solve the murder himself, which would involve proving someone else killed her; two, he's avoiding a DNA paternity test; three, he's trying to avenge Viola's death; or four, he's trying to stop all further investigation by making himself look guilty by flight. This last possibility seems doubtful, since Shad and Sheriff Byrd have already settled on Dad as the killer and are unlikely to pursue any other suspects.

If my father *did* kill Viola, then the possible explanations become simpler—yet far more difficult to believe. One, he might be fleeing the country, which would mean setting up a new life somewhere for himself, and presumably for my mother as well. This seems patently absurd, since Dad would consider being separated from Annie for the rest of his life a fate worse than death. On the other hand, he might prefer that to having Annie watch him be sent to prison. I suppose he might rather vanish than have certain secrets revealed, but if so, those secrets must be truly horrific. I can't imagine that being the father of Lincoln Turner would be sufficient to drive him away from his family.

The sound of an engine on Washington Street draws my attention long enough for me to wait for it to pass. But it doesn't. Someone has parked outside my house, their engine idling.

Taking my .357 Magnum from the table beside me, I go to the window and look out. A white pickup truck is parked across the road. The same white pickup that Lincoln Turner was driving last night. Rather than frightening me, the sight of him stalking our house suddenly pushes me past my limit.

Running to the door, I jerk it open and race down the steps, but before I can reach the truck, Turner guns his motor and screeches away from the curb, headed toward the river. Like last night, I want to follow him, but tonight I can't risk leaving Annie and Mom alone.

Taking out my cell phone, I call Chief Logan and ask why the hell his patrolmen haven't managed to locate Turner yet, when he's obviously stalking my family. Logan apologizes and promises to find Lincoln within the next few hours.

Only slightly mollified, I hang up and trudge back toward the steps of my house. Before I reach them, I hear another engine coming from the direction opposite where Lincoln fled. Crouching behind my car, I watch until I recognize the vehicle, which turns out to be a Concordia Parish sheriff's cruiser. It pulls into the space Lincoln just vacated, and its engine dies. Walker Dennis climbs out and looks up at my front door.

I start to rise from my hiding place, but then I remember John Kaiser asking if Sheriff Dennis might have set up the hit on Henry Sexton—or at least made it possible by pulling his guard patrols. It's certainly possible, but as I watch the new sheriff studying my door, all my instincts tell me he's no threat, but rather a man trying to decide whether I can be trusted.

When I rise from behind the Audi, my pistol in my hand, Dennis stares at me in amazement. "You gonna use that pistol, or whistle Dixie?" he asks, a strange smile on his face. "What the hell are you doing, Mayor?"

"Lincoln Turner was just here. He's stalking me."

Dennis shakes his head, meaning to convey sympathy.

"What are *you* doing here?" I ask.

"I've been thinking about what you asked me this morning. About busting the Knoxes' meth operations."

"I thought you said you couldn't prove they were involved in any of that."

The sheriff waves his hand dismissively. "I didn't want to go into any of that with Henry Sexton around. But I've got a history with Forrest Knox."

An electric chill of presentiment races along my arms. "Tell me."

"Two years back, I lost a cousin who worked undercover in our

department. I was just a deputy then. Mikey ran our K-9 unit. Long
story short, he got shot making an undercover buy with another cop.
Earlier that day, he told me what was supposed to go down. He and this
state-cop-slash-informant were supposed to buy some bulk meth chemicals. When Mikey was killed, the state CIB told us he'd died alone.
They claimed their guy had been working two hundred miles away
with the Gulf Coast High Density Drug Traffic Unit. I tried to follow
up that story, but every door got slammed in my face. So one day I took
Mikey's drug dog to where the bastard was. The dog nearly went crazy.
I pushed for an investigation based on that, but it got quashed. By Lieutenant Colonel Forrest Knox, in case you're wondering."

"I'm sorry, Walker. I had no idea."

"Bottom line, I guess I've been waiting for somebody to come along
who's willing to go to war with the Knox family. My DA sure isn't
hungry to take them on. Most people from Natchez don't care what
happens on my side of the river at all. But after what you did back in
October with that dogfighting ring, I figure you might be the guy."

I nod, weighing the possible outcomes of my earlier plan. "Putting
legal pressure on the Knoxes sounds like a good idea to me. Especially
since they'd be facing mandatory drug sentences. How soon could you
do it?"

"And keep the element of surprise? Twenty-four hours. Maybe
thirty-six. It depends on a lot of variables."

Given that Dad has jumped bail, this doesn't seem fast enough. As
I look into Sheriff Dennis's earnest eyes, another thought strikes me—
something that's been simmering in my mind ever since I visited Pithy
Nolan, and she reminded me of Judge Leo Marston. Back in 1968, J. Edgar
Hoover refused a request by one of his agents to tap Judge Marston's
phone, even though he was a murder suspect. As a result, Special Agent
Dwight Stone broke into Marston's home and planted bugs in every part
of it, including an outdoor gazebo. Then Stone did something he called
"shaking the tree," which, roughly translated, means scaring the hell
out of the suspect. Within hours, Stone got a recording of Judge Marston
discussing the murder with Ray Presley—under the gazebo.

"Walker, do you know a judge who will give you a warrant to tap
Brody Royal's cell phone?"

The sheriff whistles long and low.

"Plus his son-in-law, Randall Regan."

"Jesus, man. I don't know. The requirements to start a tap are pretty stringent. And Brody's a heavy hitter in this state."

"Any chance?"

"Well . . . I know one judge who's no fan of his."

My mother's voice calls from my front door. "Penn? What are you doing?"

"Talking to the Concordia sheriff! Go back inside."

Walker looks over and sees Annie standing beside my mother, a suitcase in her hand.

"You guys going on a trip?" he asks.

I give him a look stripped of all affect. "I'm not going to lose my daughter the way you lost your cousin."

The sheriff's face closes like a curtain. "Will I be able to reach you tomorrow morning?"

"Call my cell."

"Okay. You take care of your family. I'll proceed on all fronts."

"Thanks, Walker. Thanks for taking a stand. Henry was working on his own for too long, and we all share the blame for that."

He shakes his head. "Don't thank me. If I'd manned up this morning, Henry might not have gotten stabbed. Brody Royal and the Knoxes have had their way in my parish for too damn long. It's time to shut 'em down."

After a grim salute, he climbs into his cruiser and pulls away, following the invisible tracks of Lincoln Turner. The memory of that white truck sends a rush of anxiety through me. Where did the man who believes himself my half brother run to? Where is my father at this moment? How long have the two of them known about each other? Have they spoken before? Have they embraced? If so, who brought them together? Who could have, other than Viola Turner? With an exhausted sigh, I turn and walk toward my front steps, praying I can get my mother and daughter to safety without being seen.

CHAPTER 53

TOM HAD BEEN watching the fluorescent glow of the Sidney A. Murray Jr. Hydroelectric Station from a great distance as the Roadtrek hummed over the empty croplands of the Louisiana Delta. Over Walt's protests, he'd deposited Sonny Thornfield in the ambulance bay of Mercy Hospital, and once Walt had got them safely out of town, Tom had come forward and sat in the passenger seat. There was zero risk of a cop pulling them over. They were following the levee road that paralleled the river southward, and it felt like they were driving on the dark side of the moon. No streetlamps, no service stations, not even billboards broke the black monotony that enveloped them. Only the occasional glimmer of moonlight on the borrow pits at the foot of the levee reassured Tom that they were still on Earth.

Walt was so angry that he'd hardly spoken since they left the dead trooper behind. Tom understood, and didn't try to force conversation. He knew his decision might have doomed them both. He also knew he had no right to put Walt into further jeopardy. Yet he didn't regret what he'd done. No matter what Walt believed, another murder wasn't going to save them.

Tom's shoulder still throbbed relentlessly, but he'd endured worse in Korea, and with adequate treatment the bullet wound wouldn't kill him. His angina, however, still lingered high between his shoulder blades like a harbinger of death. He didn't want to take any more nitro until more time had passed, but as soon as they found a safe phone, he would call Drew Elliott and arrange for some clandestine trauma treatment.

Tom had hopes for the hydroelectric station, which was a major installation. Sited at the Old River Control Structure, it harnessed the power of the Mississippi by diverting part of the river through a dammed offshoot channel and converting that inexorable momentum into electricity. The station had a public reception area, and that seemed as good a place as any to find a pay phone.

"We can't risk the power station," Walt said, as though reading Tom's mind.

Tom's shoulder throbbed in reply. "Why not? We haven't heard a thing on your police radio."

"Don't mean they ain't looking for us. And that station's a level-one terrorist target. There're probably fifty cameras around it, and every one wired to the NSA."

"Why?"

"If somebody blew that that dam at high water, it would change the course of the Mississippi by a hundred miles. In ninety days, New Orleans would be a useless marsh and Baton Rouge would be screwed as a port. The stock market would crash a lot quicker than that."

Tom looked at one of the tall control towers and realized Walt was right. Every time the Mississippi flooded, engineers worried that the river would divert through the Atchafalaya Basin and find the Gulf of Mexico by that much shorter route. Once it did, it would never return to its present course.

"Flip down your visor as we pass," Walt said, "and don't even look in that direction. The NSA has facial recognition software, and the FBI can run checks through their system if they want. Since Nine-Eleven, every agency is connected."

Tom kept his face forward, looking at the fallow fields in the glow of the station's floodlights. "Why would a state trooper be hunting for Sonny Thornfield, Walt? Was Thornfield a fugitive?"

Walt squawked a laugh. "Man, you're thinking ass backwards. I told you, that trooper was working *with* the Double Eagles."

"A state cop?" Tom said skeptically.

"State, federal, local—don't make a spit's worth of difference. There's always been a thin line between the black hats and the white in this state. Do you know of any connections between the Double Eagles and the state police? Think of the Eagles you know about, one by one."

The first thing that came into Tom's mind was Ray Presley, dead seven years now. Ray had been a crooked cop in both New Orleans and Natchez, and he'd had shady dealings with the Double Eagles—with Brody Royal, too. Tom also seemed to remember Ray telling him something about one of the Knoxes' sons and the state police. Frank's son, if he remembered right. Tom only recalled this because the boy had been named after a talented Confederate general.

"I believe Frank Knox's son may have been a state trooper at one time," Tom said. "Ray Presley told me that."

Walt didn't react immediately, but after a few seconds, he turned to Tom and spoke in a taut voice. "What's his name?"

"Nathan Bedford Forrest, believe it or not."

"His *last* name is Forrest? Or Knox?"

"Knox. Nathan Bedford Forrest Knox."

"Forrest Knox?" Walt's jaw hung slack.

"I think so, yeah. What is it?"

"Christ, man! There's a Forrest Knox *way* up in the Louisiana State Police. I think he might even be chief of the CIB now."

"What's the CIB?"

"The Criminal Investigations Bureau. That trooper I shot mentioned that he worked for the CIB sometimes. Remember?" Walt shook his head. "That doesn't make sense, though. I know the head of the whole damned outfit—Colonel Griffith Mackiever. Griff spent fifteen years in the Texas Rangers before he took a job with the LSP. No way would he have a dirty cop that high in his organization."

Tom shrugged. "It sure would explain some things, though."

Walt was silent for a few seconds. "I guess it could. Damn. I should have made that connection before."

"Nathan Bedford Forrest was the founder of the original Ku Klux Klan," Tom thought aloud. "Up in Tennessee. That sure sounds like Frank Knox, naming his son that way."

"I've been in Texas too long," Walt muttered. "That, or I'm getting Alzheimer's."

"Do you know this Mackiever well enough to call him?"

"And say what, genius? Hey, Griff, I just shot one of your troopers, and I'm trying to find out whether he was straight or bent?"

Tom didn't respond. Instead, he fiddled with the satellite radio dial until he got it tuned to the 1940s station: Lena Horne was singing "Stormy Weather."

"We've got to get this van under cover," Walt said. "Not to mention getting your shoulder squared away."

"That trooper couldn't have reported our license plate, could he?"

"No, but he could have called in the make and model. And this van's pretty rare in these parts. Once they find his corpse, they'll do everything but call out the National Guard to find us."

"How are we supposed to get this elephant under cover? What is it, ten feet tall?"

"Right at ten. And the LSP's got six choppers in their Air Support Unit. We need some damned thick woods or a warehouse. Boat garage, maybe. You know of anything like that around here?"

Tom shook his head out of reflex, but a moment later a possible answer came to him. "You know, we might be able to kill two birds with one stone. But I need a safe telephone."

"If a call can get us off the road and under cover, I say we go ahead and use my last burn phone." Walt dug a black mobile phone out of his pocket and jabbed it at Tom. "Get on the horn. If we're not under cover by the time the APB goes out, we're going out like Butch and Sundance in Bolivia."

The old Ranger hadn't a trace of humor in his voice.

CHAPTER 54

CAITLIN SAT ALONE in her office at the Natchez *Examiner,* feverishly studying the notes she'd made over the past hour. Since leaving Penn's house, she'd interviewed Sheriff Walker Dennis; Lou Ann Whittington; Hugh Fraser, the publisher of the *Concordia Beacon;* and Sherry Harden, Henry Sexton's girlfriend. Her anger at Penn for failing to trust her had driven those interviews, and her success had left her in a state of excitement that rivaled sexual arousal.

The most thrilling revelation had come from Lou Ann, who (after giving a modest account of saving Henry's life) had confided that Henry had told her he intended to begin writing for the *Examiner.* Henry had asked Lou Ann to keep this quiet for one day, but Henry's decision *had* been the reason he'd been moving his files out of the *Beacon* building. Hugh Fraser confirmed that Henry had asked his permission to write for her, and that he'd given his blessing. The publisher added that Henry had been planning to write a front-page story for Thursday's edition of the *Beacon,* covering his theories about at least five of the cold cases he'd been investigating for so long.

"Now that story might never be written," the publisher had said in a voice freighted with grief. "If I had his files, I'd try it myself, but what those lowlifes didn't steal is going to take weeks to get organized into some kind of order. I think I'm too old for that now."

Caitlin couldn't help wondering whether there might be a rough draft of Henry's story on his office computer, but she hadn't summoned the nerve to ask Mr. Fraser if he would check it. Maybe tomorrow.

Her interviews had yielded other nuggets, too. According to Lou Ann, as Henry slipped from consciousness, he'd been desperate to make sure that someone got certain "keys." No one had any idea what keys he had been referring to, or even if they were physical keys at all. For all anyone knew, Henry might have been talking about digital keys, codes, or important clues to a particular case. From the moment Caitlin heard about those keys, she'd been hoping Sherry Harden would tell her that Henry kept backups of his stolen files somewhere. But the nurse had refused to tell Caitlin anything. She believed Penn's failure to adequately protect Henry had allowed the attempt on his life, and she had no intention of helping Caitlin. Caitlin had tried to pour oil on the waters, but Sherry was having none of it (which was a shame, because what Caitlin most wanted was to go sit by Henry's bed and wait for him to regain consciousness).

Her office door opened, and Jamie Lewis, her editor, stuck his head inside. Jamie had recently transferred down from their Charleston, South Carolina, paper, and he'd made an almost seamless transition into the small-town atmosphere of Natchez.

"I found a file photo of Lou Ann Whittington," he said, obviously pleased with himself. "She belongs to one of the local Mardi Gras krewes, and we have a shot of her riding a float. You want to run it with the story?"

"Is she in costume or anything?"

"No, it's a decent shot."

"Run it. She's going to be a national hero by nine A.M. tomorrow, and people are going to want to see what she looks like."

Jamie grinned. "Granny to punks: *Make my day!* We should change our name to the *Natchez Enquirer.*"

Caitlin grabbed a pen and threw it at him, but Jamie dodged the missile easily. Then he clucked his tongue three times and left.

Caitlin shoved her chair away from the desk and cursed under her breath. She hated playing catch-up. She was on the cusp of a story with national implications, yet she was almost powerless to move forward. She had no way to replicate Henry's years of dogged investigation of the Double Eagle group. And while she did have Henry working for her, at least in theory, he was beyond her reach and might well die before morning.

She was sure of only one thing: Penn knew a lot more about Henry's work than he'd told her so far. Last night he'd spent at least ninety minutes at the *Beacon* offices. Given Henry's respect for Dr. Cage, the reporter had probably told Penn most of what he knew.

Knowing it wasn't the best move she could make, Caitlin lifted her landline and dialed Penn's cell phone. He was probably asleep by now, but she couldn't restrain herself. If she waited until morning, she'd be even farther behind on the story.

"Caitlin?" he said, sounding surprisingly alert.

"Yeah. Look, I'm sorry I was such a bitch before."

"It's okay. This has been a crazy day."

"Is Annie asleep?"

He hesitated. "Not yet."

"You sound funny. What's the matter?"

"Nothing." Penn swallowed something. Probably water beside his bed.

She let the silence drag for a couple of seconds. "I spoke to Lou Ann Whittington, the receptionist who saved Henry's life. She told me that Henry *had* decided to accept my offer. That's why he was moving his files."

"Good for you. I figured that might be it, but that's not what she told Sheriff Dennis."

"Henry asked her not to tell anyone until he did. Penn, listen . . . I can understand you not wanting to break the promise you made to Henry last night. But the whole landscape has changed since then. Henry had decided to come work for me, but now he might not even survive the night. I want to help him, to carry on his work. But I can't do that unless I know where to start."

"I gave you quite a bit last night, and more today."

"Yes, but Henry must have told you more than that. A lot more. His girlfriend has the idea that you two were working together. And you know what I can do if you give me something to work with. I've got people here just waiting to dive into this story."

"Nothing you can do between now and tomorrow morning is going to affect Henry's chances of survival—or Dad's, for that matter. So why don't you work with what you have? In the morning we'll check on Henry and reassess where we are."

She closed her eyes and forced herself not to argue. "What if he dies tonight?"

"If Henry dies, I'll tell you everything I know."

She knew this was all she could reasonably hope for, yet she couldn't help pushing the limit. "Penn, with the right information, I might even crack Viola's murder by tomorrow. I could go a long way toward the solution, anyway. You know that."

When he answered, she heard a warning note in his voice. "Babe, let's just leave it where we are tonight. Okay?"

She grimaced and started to snap at him, but Penn sounded seriously stressed, so in the end she just said, "All right. I'll make do."

"Get Jamie to follow you home, okay? And make him wait until you get inside."

"Truthfully, I'm probably going to stay here all night."

"Even better. Don't leave the building until daylight, all right?"

"Okay." She started to say good-bye, but instinct told her something important remained unsaid. "Has something happened? *Is* everything okay? I mean, apart from the obvious?"

"Everything's fine. We'll talk face-to-face in the morning. Meanwhile, you don't leave that newspaper building. I'm going to have Chief Logan put a cop outside."

"Penn—"

"We'll talk in the morning," he said sharply. "I love you."

And then he was gone.

Caitlin hung up and stared at the telephone. Something was wrong. Or maybe she'd just pushed Penn too hard. She rubbed her eyes to clear the sleep from them. The problem with loving a great guy was that when you needed to bend the rules, he didn't always have the proper flexibility. Yet Penn *had* stretched his ethics last night, and even more today. She was thinking about driving over to Ferriday to sit in the waiting room on Henry's floor (hopefully out of Sherry's sight) when Jamie thrust her door open again.

"Guess what?" he said, his eyes bright with excitement.

"Tell me. I'm desperate here."

"They just had a fire at the *Concordia Beacon*. We caught it on the police radio."

"What?"

"It started in a file room. A flash fire took out a bunch of storage boxes and stuff, then spread to the rest of the building. But get this: their computers *melted*."

Caitlin blinked in confusion. "So? Isn't that what computers do during a fire?"

"Sometimes." Jamie smiled strangely. "But when the firemen got to the *Beacon* fire, they could still get inside the building. Yet the computers looked like someone had turned a blowtorch on them."

This detail raised the hair on the back of her neck. "Oh, man. This is crazy."

"How do you want to handle it?"

Caitlin looked at the phone on her desk and thought about calling Penn back. Instead, she got up, grabbed her coat off her chair, and waved Jamie out the door.

"What are you doing?" he asked.

"We're going to Ferriday."

"You and me?"

"You're a quick study, aren't you? Get your fucking coat."

CHAPTER 55

"DO YOU HAVE the security code?" Walt asked, as the Roadtrek nosed along the road bordering Lake St. John. The oxbow lake looked black in December, and the mostly bare trees didn't offer any sense of warmth or invitation.

"Written on my hand," Tom replied, scanning the mailboxes that lined the road.

"Which one's your partner's?"

"You were here two months ago. You don't remember?"

"It was dark. Just like now."

Tom's eyes were peeled for the tall storage shed that stood beside Drew Elliott's lake house. The former owner hadn't built a boathouse, preferring to keep his ski boat (with its wakeboarding tower) in a prefab storage shed. Drew had complained about the shed when he acquired the property, but he hadn't yet got rid of it. Tom was sure the Roadtrek would fit inside the tall building, so long as they could clear enough floor space.

"This whole damned lake is lined with houses," Walt grumbled. "How are we going to sneak this thing into a garage?"

"The houses on either side of Drew's are empty in the winter. And nobody's moving around this late."

Walt grunted.

Tom had hated to ask Drew to put himself at risk by offering help, but he'd had no alternative. To his credit, Tom's young partner had not only offered his lake house as a sanctuary but also insisted on driving over immediately to treat Tom's wound.

"There!" Tom cried, wincing as he raised his hand to point at a giant shed a couple of hundred yards up the road on the right-hand side.

"I see it."

Walt eased the Roadtrek back to forty miles per hour, then thirty.

The turn was forty yards ahead now. He braked steadily, then swung out to the left so that he could fit the van between the mailbox and a post on the other side of the asphalt drive.

Thirty yards ahead, a gravel offshoot led to the tall storage shed. Walt drove straight up to the overhead door and stopped with a squeal. Tom read the code off his hand, and Walt climbed out and entered it in the keypad on the wall.

The overhead door began to rise, and white light flooded the ground.

Walt scrambled back into the driver's seat, then pulled into the garage as soon as he had sufficient clearance. Then he jumped out and hit a button on the interior wall. Thirty seconds later, the door rattled down to the ground and they were enveloped in darkness.

"Not bad," Walt said in a grudging tone. "About the best we could have hoped for. How's your shoulder?"

"Bad enough. I could use another Lorcet."

"Should you take it, with your ticker weak as it is?"

"No. But if Drew has some Maker's Mark in there, I'll sure drink it."

"Let's find out."

Tom felt dizzy as he sought the van's running board with his foot.

HALF AN HOUR LATER Walt leaned over Tom's bloody shoulder and studied Drew Elliott's handiwork by the light of the reading lamp Drew had used to see while suturing the wound.

"You sewed a drain into it," Walt observed, "just like we used to do in Korea."

Drew stripped off his gloves as Melba Price sponged the skin around the rubber hose protruding from Tom's shoulder. "I wouldn't have used a drain if we were in a hospital. But if Tom insists on staying out here, I want it in there."

Drew had brought Melba along because Tom's nurse had demanded that if he heard anything from Tom—especially about needing help—he should call her. Knowing that he couldn't stay there all night, Drew had done so. Two minutes after crossing the westbound bridge over the Mississippi River—driving in tandem—Melba had noticed a Louisiana State Police cruiser thirty yards behind him, so she'd texted a warning. To test for surveillance, Drew had gone to the Mercy Hospital first to check on Henry Sexton. After that visit, they'd seen no sign of the patrol car, and so had proceeded to the lake house.

"Thanks, Drew," Tom said, forcing a smile. "It feels a lot better already."

"That's just the local, you know that. Once the lidocaine wears off, it's going to hurt like a son of a bitch. And I don't want you hitting that Lorcet too hard."

"Don't worry about that," said Walt. "I took his bottle."

Drew smiled. "Good. Tom's bad about self-prescribing." He leaned over his senior partner. "You know, with your heart the way it is, you really should be in the ICU at St. Catherine's."

Tom shook his head. "They'd put me in the county jail."

"Not if they don't know you've skipped," Walt said.

"And not with your pericardium filling with fluid," Drew added.

"We're talking about Shad Johnson and Billy Byrd," Tom said. "Shad's going to get my bail revoked as soon as he can."

Drew looked troubled. "I think Penn is more than enough lawyer to arrange for you to be held in the ICU while he sorts this mess out."

When Tom shook his head and protested that he'd brought plenty of diuretics with him, Drew raised his hands in surrender. "All right. But if you develop serious complications over here—or God forbid, have a fatal MI—Penn and Peggy will never forgive me. I didn't save your life two months ago to have you die in my lake house."

"You didn't save my life." Tom winked at his nurse. "Melba did. You just plugged up that defib unit and shocked me back into rhythm. It was Melba barging into my bathroom and finding me on the floor that saved me."

Drew laughed, and Melba's eyes shone with pride.

"I don't guess you want to tell me why you skipped bail," Drew said with sudden seriousness.

"You're better off not knowing."

"I don't believe you murdered anybody, Tom. So I'm not worried about getting in trouble for helping you."

"Don't be naïve."

"Hell, I'm already aiding and abetting now, right?"

Walt nodded, and Melba looked worried.

"I wish I could tell you more," Tom said.

"*More?* You haven't told me anything yet."

Tom tried to think of a way to make Drew understand the stakes. "Do you remember when you had your back against the wall a few years ago?" Tom asked. "Shad Johnson had locked *your* ass up, and nobody believed a word you said."

At last his words had penetrated Drew's good humor. The smile had vanished as though it never existed. "I'll never forget it."

"Did you tell anybody *everything*? Even Penn?"

Drew sighed heavily. "No. But I should have. And even though I held back on him, he's the one who got me out of trouble."

"Penn can't get me out of this. You have to trust me on that."

"I guess I have to. It's your life, after all."

"Doc?" Melba said gently. "Are you feeling all right? You look clammy."

Tom forced a smile. "I don't think Drew's going to have a hissy fit if you call me Tom, Melba."

The nurse gave a self-conscious smile. "Old habits die hard, I guess."

"Do you two want me and Captain Garrity to give you some privacy?" Drew asked, carrying his bloody instruments to the sink.

"I'll wash those, Dr. Elliott," Melba said, quickly moving after him.

"No, you won't. You keep our patient comfortable."

Melba came back to Tom's side.

Drew ran water into the sink and waited for it to get hot. "Did you tell him about Mrs. Nolan?"

"Pithy?" asked Tom, suddenly worried. "Has something happened to her?"

"No," said Melba. "Penn asked me to go by her house and give her a steroid shot. I got Dr. Elliott to prescribe it."

Tom knitted his brow. "How the hell did Penn know I missed that house call?"

"He went by there to talk to Pithy," Melba explained.

"About what?"

The nurse shrugged. "He didn't tell me. And Miss Pithy didn't, either. She's sure worried about you, though."

Walt looked down at Tom and shook his head. "That's a big club."

"I appreciate you coming tonight, Mel," Tom said. "But you need to get on back to Natchez."

"I'm not going anywhere. Dr. Elliott, leave those things in the sink and go home. Your family needs you."

Drew nodded, drying his hands. "Will you be at the office tomorrow?"

"I don't know. Let's wait and see how our patient does."

Drew picked up his black bag in preparation for leaving, then looked at Walt. "If you guys absolutely have to drive somewhere, don't drag Melba into it. You can 'steal' the old truck parked down by my pier. The keys are on top of the bathroom medicine cabinet."

Tom saluted his partner with gratitude. Drew chuckled, started to leave, then walked back to the sofa and looked down at Tom with sadness in his eyes.

"Call Penn, Tom. Nobody in the world will work harder to get you out of whatever trouble you're in. Your son is your best hope. You know that."

"He may be, Drew. But I can't call him. Not this time."

The young doctor's face remained hard. "You could die. Right here in my lake house. What do I tell Peggy, if you do? What do I tell Penn?"

Tom looked over at Walt, then back up at Drew, his eyes suddenly wet. "If that happens . . . tell them I was protecting our family. They may not understand it right away. Penn might never understand. But that's what you tell him. One day I think he'll figure it out. Now . . . get going, before the cops show up and arrest you."

Drew stared down at his mentor for a few moments longer; then he snapped his head up, walked to the door, and left his house without looking back.

Tom looked up at Walt, his eyes blurred with tears. "I'm tired, buddy. And I'm so sorry I got you into this."

Walt sat beside Tom, then laid a hand on his forehead with the gentleness he'd always displayed as a combat medic.

"Get some rest, soldier. Tomorrow's another day."

CHAPTER 56

SIX BLOCKS FROM my house on Washington Street, ten blocks from the *Natchez Examiner,* and two hundred feet above the Mississippi River, I kiss my daughter's sleeping face, then roll carefully out of the bed and move to the central staircase. This house, this unexpected sanctuary, is called Edelweiss. I bought the place two months ago as a surprise wedding present for Caitlin, and I've had contractors working practically around the clock to get it ready by the date of our wedding. Three stories high and covered with gingerbread, this authentic German chalet was built on the edge of the Natchez bluff in 1883. You can see fourteen miles of river from its wraparound gallery, and more from its third-floor windows. Rumors have swirled for weeks about the possible new owner: some wags say it's a Hollywood actor who wants to remain anonymous; others claim the owner of one of the casino boats beneath the bluff bought it as a weekend retreat from Las Vegas. Had Viola not been murdered two days ago, the truth would have been revealed two Saturdays hence, when the horse and carriage leaving the gazebo on the bluff carried Caitlin and me only a hundred yards to the steps of our new home. Now it's become a safe house in the middle of a town where almost every citizen knows my face.

At the bottom of the stairs, I turn and go into the kitchen, where my mother waits, her face haggard with exhaustion and guilt. Peggy Cage is remarkably beautiful for a woman of seventy-one, but the past two days have taken a toll, and for once she looks her age. Sitting on the stool beside her, I lay my right hand over hers.

"Annie's finally asleep. Mom, you've got to tell me what's happening."

She nods, but her expression doesn't inspire much hope.

"I simply can't believe Dad would leave you without some way of reaching him."

"But he did, Penn." Her eyes look sincere, but I've had so little experience of deception in my mother, how would I recognize it? "I don't think Tom wanted me to be in a position where I would have to lie to the police."

I give her a few seconds' grace. "Still. I don't believe he'd leave you to face all this alone."

She turns her hand over and squeezes mine. "But I'm not alone. *You're* here. Tom knew that he could count on you to take care of me."

"The last time you saw him was midday today?"

"Yes. An hour after I drove him home from the hearing, he drove himself to the office. I tried to stop him, but he wouldn't listen."

"Did he say anything when he left?"

"No more than usual. But there was something in his face that told me he wasn't coming back. Not for a while, anyway."

"And you didn't try to stop him?"

She gives me a look that says, *Are you serious?* "You know your father."

I nod. "I thought I did. After these past two days, I'm not so sure."

"Oh, hush. This is going to come out all right. You'll see."

Is she really that naïve? "Mom . . . I don't want you to panic, but you have to know how things stand. Now that Dad has jumped bail on a murder charge, any cop can shoot him down with impunity and say he resisted arrest. I suspect that Sheriff Byrd and some Louisiana State Police officials will quietly give orders to do just that, once they know he's gone."

At last I see fear in her eyes.

"If Dad contacts you in any way, you've got to do everything in your power to persuade him to come home."

"I realize that."

As her voice finally cracks, I voice one of my deepest fears. "Dad's not running for real, is he? I mean, leaving the country."

She looks up at the ceiling and blinks back tears. "You know better than that. Tom's never run from anything in his life. Judge Noyes said as much from the bench yesterday."

"So *what the hell is he doing*?"

"Keep your voice down. Remember Annie."

"You'd tell me if he was setting up house for you guys in Brazil or something, right?"

"Oh, for God's sake." She flips her free hand as she might at any absurdity. "We're not leaving our home because some ambitious DA has got it into his head to put Tom in jail. I can't pretend I understand all this. I just have to have faith that what Tom's doing is necessary."

"Mom, don't you think the time for blind faith has passed? Dad's not only risking his own life. Good people are getting hurt. Henry Sexton may die. You and Annie are scared to death. I think we're safe here for the time being, but I honestly don't know. And Dad's leaving us hanging out here without one word of explanation!"

She wipes her cheeks, then takes both my hands in hers. "I've been married to your father for fifty-three years," she says in a voice edged with iron. "Tom has always done right by this family, and I'm not going to start second-guessing him now."

Has he? I ask silently. *Has he always done right by us?* But I won't force my mother to the edge of her faith, where a black maw of disillusionment must surely await. Not at this hour. I may have the strength to choose the truth over my father, but after fifty-three years, perhaps my mother *must* choose her husband over the truth. At least tonight.

"Where should I sleep?" she asks.

"There's a twin bed in the room that connects to the master suite upstairs, where Annie is. You take that."

"Where will you be?"

"Down here. I've got a lot to think about before tomorrow."

My mother slips off the stool, gives me a long hug, then pads into the hall. Soon I hear the stairs creaking.

Alone in the kitchen, I open a Corona Extra and sit at the counter, wondering what in God's name my father thinks he's playing at. If Billy Byrd or Forrest Knox finds out that he's jumped bail, he might not live until John Kaiser and the FBI reach Natchez tomorrow. Even if he does, I can't be sure Kaiser will agree to protect him. By making himself a fugitive, Dad has placed himself outside the pale of the law.

Forcing this insanity from my mind, I remind myself that all I can do in the short run is prove that someone else killed Viola Turner. Putting pressure on Brody Royal and the Double Eagles seems the best way to do that, since they almost certainly planned and executed that crime. And if Walker Dennis can get a warrant to tap Royal's telephones, then all I need to do is find a way to "shake the tree" of Brody Royal.

Last night, Henry Sexton gave me a lot of detail about 1960s-vintage

Double Eagle murders and plots, but I don't think those would worry Royal much. Too many witnesses have died in the decades since. But the nightmare Glenn Morehouse recounted about the murder of the two female whistle-blowers from Royal Insurance is another matter. Royal's son-in-law, Randall Regan, is obviously as sadistic a killer as any Double Eagle from the Jim Crow era. And an investigation that threatens not only the existence of one of Royal's companies, but also Brody himself, would be something Royal simply couldn't ignore. With the horrific details Morehouse gave Henry, I ought to be able to scare the living hell out of Randall Regan, and by extension, Brody himself. I'll just have to make sure that when I do, neither man is in a position to make me suffer for it.

CHAPTER 57

BRODY ROYAL HAD not been spoken to in anger by another man in more than twenty years. Claude Devereux had felt something close to panic as Forrest Knox lambasted the old man for authorizing Randall Regan's abortive attempt to kill Henry Sexton. Claude had watched this confrontation from a club chair in the rear corner of Royal's study, while Forrest stood before Brody's desk, speaking with the cold fury of a field officer reprimanding a deskbound general who'd been insulated from battle for too long. Brody weathered the storm like a craggy rock face on a mountainside, making no excuses, saying nothing at all. Randall Regan and Alphonse Ozan stood behind their principals like seconds at a duel, and Claude had the feeling that each was itching to step in and settle the disagreement with knives or worse.

Claude had always known that Frank Knox's son was tough—Forrest had more than proved himself in Vietnam—but he hadn't known that the boy possessed his father's temper. Seeing the state trooper challenge the silver-haired old multimillionaire had shaken Claude deeply. At bottom, he was watching a young wolf whose power was waxing try to establish his supremacy over an older one whose power, while still considerable, was on the wane. But if Forrest Knox believed Brody Royal would be easily dislodged from his alpha position, he wasn't as astute as Claude believed he was.

Ensconced behind his heavy desk, Brody continued to display a forbearance that Claude had never known he possessed. But with each passing second, Devereux became more certain that this was like the quiet before a hurricane. Brody always kept at least one pistol in his desk drawer, and Claude worried that his old friend might simply shoot Knox out of hand, without even deigning to argue with him. Royal had been raised in a world where that kind of thing was still possible. The Redbone behind Forrest looked like he expected something of the sort; he reminded Claude of a guard dog waiting for an attack command.

"Your *real* problem," Forrest went on, "is that you're acting out of fear. That's a reflex, Brody, and a stupid one."

Royal's eyes narrowed, and for the first time he spoke in answer. "You're not your daddy, boy," he said with venom. "Be careful."

Forrest drew himself to his full height, then gave himself a few seconds before replying. "You're right, I'm not. You and Pop were lions in your day. Everybody knows it. But we're not living in the jungle anymore. You got scared of payback for something you did forty years ago, and you decided the best response was to kill somebody. Worse, you gave the job to *this* guy"—Forrest pointed at Randall Regan, who instantly went red—"and he fucked it up beyond belief."

"Nobody knew that fat secretary had a gun," Regan snapped. "And I want to know where those boys are now. One of 'em was my nephew."

Forrest gave him a contemptuous look. "Then you shouldn't have told him to make his own way when he called you for help."

Before Regan could respond, Forrest stabbed a forefinger at Royal. "Do you sell all your stock when the market starts crashing? No. You buy. This is the same situation. The FBI has had forty years to prove these murders, and they couldn't do it. They won't prove 'em this year, either. So, what are you scared of?"

"Guilt," said Brody, his gray eyes steady in the hawklike face. "Some born-again fool's conscience. I wanted Sexton questioned properly, not killed in the street. I wanted to know the identity of every Eagle he's talked to, everything he told Penn Cage last night, and whatever Viola Turner told him before she died. *Then* I wanted him to disappear. I still do."

"Guilty consciences are a legitimate worry with old men," Forrest conceded. "But let me worry about that from now on. You don't see me trying to run a bank or an agribusiness, do you? Well, shutting people up is one of my specialties. When it has to be done, nobody does it better."

Ozan chuckled ominously behind his master.

"That doesn't reassure me," Brody said. "You've let Henry Sexton write whatever he pleased for years now."

"And what's come of it? Nothing but talk. Not one prosecution. Not even an arrest."

"That could change overnight, son."

Forrest Knox smiled, probably at the idea of being seen as young. Devereux figured he was about fifty-five.

"And you think burning the goddamn *Beacon* is going to help your cause?" Forrest asked. "That fire was like a Jumbotron screaming, *This reporter's on the right track!* Brody, before that fire I had a direct digital line into Sexton's computers. I saw everything that fool was going to publish, days before it appeared. You've destroyed all that. Worse, Randall's rookie crew failed to finish Henry off. Now we have no way of knowing what he's telling the FBI."

Royal lifted the glass of single malt whisky Claude had poured him earlier and drank it off neat. Then he spoke with an unnerving precision that silenced even Forrest Knox, his eyes never leaving Knox's face.

"You don't know as much as you think you do, Lieutenant. For instance, are you aware that Sexton interviewed my daughter, Katy, at her home only one week ago?"

Forrest blinked but said nothing.

"He arranged the interview under false pretenses, then questioned her about that young nigger Wilson, and Albert Norris."

Forrest looked intrigued. "What did he ask her, exactly?"

"Enough to upset her greatly. My daughter is fragile, Lieutenant. I'm not sure what she remembers about that period, but I do know that further questioning of that kind could dredge up information that none of us wants exposed."

Forrest nodded slowly. "I see. Well, I can pay you back for that tidbit. A week ago, some nigger showed up at the deathbed of Pooky Wilson's mother. He knows all about what you and Daddy did back in sixty-four. In fact, he *saw* you and Daddy jump from Norris's store window, and he saw Randall drive you away."

Claude felt his stomach tighten. This was the first he'd heard of such a potentially devastating witness.

"Sexton's been looking all over for him," Forrest went on, "only he doesn't know the man's name. The mama died before he could get it out of her. But now that you've cut off my line into the *Beacon*, we won't even know if Henry finds him."

"All the more reason to deal with the problem at its source!" Royal leaned over his desk, his face darkening with passion. "Do you remember being three years old, boy?"

Forrest looked perplexed by this question.

"I do," Brody said. "It was 1927, and my mama was standing on tiptoe, holding me over her head while the floodwater rose up to her mouth, then her nose. My daddy was diving down to try to find an axe to hack through the roof. If he hadn't found it, we'd all have died that day."

Claude Devereux knew this story well, but few others did. Claude also knew the full extent of his richest client's ambitions. He wondered whether Brody was finally going to reveal his plans to Forrest Knox.

"My daddy owned two stores," Brody went on, speaking softly. "He sold bootleg whisky on the side, and he used the profits to buy land. We lived in St. Bernard Parish. In 1927, as the floodwater came downriver, the bankers who controlled New Orleans started to panic. In the end, they hijacked the government in Baton Rouge and extorted permission to dynamite the levee that protected our parish." Brody nodded, his eyes focused on some faraway scene and time. "They dynamited for three straight days. Everything we had went underwater. When the water finally went down, months later, we'd been wiped out. The stores were gone, and three feet of mud covered the land."

Brody blinked once, which emphasized the stillness of his aquiline features. "Those bankers had promised full reparations before the dynamiting, but they lied. They left us in the mud to rot. Our total compensation, according to those bastards, was twelve dollars and fifty cents. Twelve-fifty for everything we owned. That's when Daddy started bootlegging full-time. He got in with Carlos Marcello, and he never looked back. Along with Huey Long's people, they put slot machines into every parish in this state. In the end, my daddy made back all his money and more. Far more. So did I. But every goddamned day, I thought about the bastards who'd done that to us. And ever *since* that day, I've worked to destroy them."

Forrest nodded but did not speak, obviously sensing that he would gain nothing by interrupting Brody. Claude also figured Knox knew that information was power, and knowing Brody's deepest motives might well come in handy someday.

"One of the highest and mightiest of those New Orleans bankers was originally from Natchez," Brody said. "Twenty years after the flood, I married his daughter. She got me what money couldn't: social position. Fifteen years after that, she climbed into the bathtub drunk, and I held her head under the water until she stopped breathing."

Claude nearly swallowed his tongue when he heard this admission. Forrest and Randall Regan kept poker faces, but Alphonse Ozan actually smiled. Brody pushed on like he didn't give a damn who heard him. "By that time I was managing a lot of her daddy's money. With the stroke of a pen, I cut him out of more than half of it the next day, and he couldn't do a thing about it. He wanted his daughter buried in New Orleans. I didn't care where they put her, but I told him I wanted to take care of the funeral expenses." Brody took another sip of scotch. "I sent him a check for twelve dollars and fifty cents."

No one in the room made a sound.

"I'm a gambler," Brody told Forrest. "But as a general rule, I only bet on sure things. I'm going to tell you about the biggest bet I ever made."

"What's that?" asked Forrest.

"Everybody's always known that if a hurricane ever hit New Orleans head-on, the city would be wiped out. The whole damn town is nothing but a big bowl sitting below sea level—a bowl of filth waiting for a purging flood. Even the people who lived there knew it. But they just kept the party going, and pretended it would never happen. They formed levee boards, and the politicians swept the money under the table as fast as it came in. Everybody got their cut, even me. But I was laughing the whole time. Because I knew their luck couldn't hold. I bought low-lying land and insured the hell out of whatever was on it. St. Bernard Parish, the Lower Ninth Ward, Lakeview, Navarre, Gentilly, even Gert Town. The city dodged Betsy, then Camille, and four or five other near misses over the years. But I kept buying. Tulane/Gravier, New Orleans East . . . because their luck *had* to run out someday. It was simple probability. The only question was, would I live to see it?" Brody smiled for the first time tonight, and his triumph was terrible to see. "Well, I have. At first I thought Katrina was going to be another close call. But then the corruption and the bad engineering and the laissez-faire bullshit tipped the balance. The levees broke, and God swept that city clean like Sodom and Gomorrah."

Brody laughed with deep satisfaction. "I can't tell you how I felt watching that water rise on television. Every extra foot put millions more into my pocket. Three months ago I started getting my settlement checks, and it's more money than you'll ever see in your life. But that's just lagniappe. The real payoff hasn't even started yet! Because the old city's gone now. The municipal whorehouse that all those decadent old Catholic hypocrites loved to call 'the city that care forgot' is dead, and rotting as we speak. A new city will rise in its place, and it's going to be *different*."

Brody took another pull of scotch, his eyes glinting. "You know what killed New Orleans? Not the housing projects or the welfare niggers or even the flood. Those rich bankers did it, with their exclusive clubs and krewes and secret societies. Every time a major corporation moved in there, those arrogant bastards refused to let the officers into the circle. They thought their Gilded Age was going to go on forever. *They* strangled that city. They married among themselves and shut everybody else out, until all the money and business in the South went to Atlanta and Houston and Birmingham and Nashville. And now their idiot descendants sit down there, eating étouffée in their seersucker suits while their trust funds dribble down to nothing. Katrina was just the final shock. The purge. The future belongs to *me*."

To Claude Devereux's surprise, Brody got to his feet and pointed at Forrest Knox with a steady hand. "I've been waiting fifty years for this day, boy. And if you think I'm going to let some bleeding-heart *reporter* screw it up, you need brain surgery. The sooner Henry Sexton and his files cease to exist, the better off we'll all be. I make no apologies for my actions or Randall's. I'll do as I see fit, and you won't say a word. Your job is to *clean up the mess*. Is that clear?"

Forrest stiffened and started to speak, but before he could, Royal added, "I know how bad you want to take over the state police. And *you* know I can blackball you from that post with one phone call."

Forrest paled, but he held his tongue.

"Now," said Brody, taking his seat again, "I believe we're finished."

Behind him, Randall Regan gestured toward the door.

Instead of leaving, Forrest stepped forward and lifted a letter opener from the old man's desk, then held it up in the light. The little knife had a dark leather handle and an ivory-colored blade, and Claude shuddered when he recognized it.

"My daddy made this for you," Forrest said. "He tanned the skin, just like he did the skins of those Japs on the islands back in forty-five. He carved this bone handle, too. He told me it came from that Wilson boy's arm. The skin came from his cock."

Royal nodded, his expression curious but unafraid.

Forrest dropped the letter opener on the green felt, then laid both hands on the desk and leaned so far over it that Royal must have felt his breath. "That nigger still fucked your daughter, Brody. What you did *afterwards* don't mean nothing. You hear me? *You weren't paying attention when it mattered.* Sitting behind a desk for forty years opening letters with a dickskin isn't the proper training for dealing with me. I may not be quite as mean as my daddy was, but I'm smarter. That can be good or bad for you. Take your pick. But if you cross me again—if I have to come back here like this again—it'll be the last time."

The old man's head quivered with rage, but it was his son-in-law who stepped forward, reaching for the desk drawer that held Brody's pistol.

"And *you*," Forrest said, pointing at Regan, who stopped cold. "If you don't leave the operations side to the professionals, I'll have Alphonse come back and make a trophy out of *your* dick—if there's enough down there to work with."

Randall Regan's face went scarlet, then white. He lunged for the gun drawer, but Forrest only turned on his heel and walked past his Redbone bodyguard, who had already drawn a pistol from his ankle holster.

"Open casket or closed?" Ozan said, a smug grin on his lips. "You got a preference?"

CHAPTER 58

LESS THAN FIVE miles from Brody Royal's lake house, Caitlin Masters stood outside the smoking ruin of the *Concordia Beacon* and watched a fire inspector work his way through the building with a high-powered flashlight. Jamie Lewis was sitting in his car, talking on the phone to one of their reporters back at the *Examiner*. She and Jamie had already interviewed every cop and fireman on the scene, and everyone agreed it was arson. Several firemen had reported the smell of tar, which none recalled having encountered in a long time, except at buildings with tarred roofs, which the *Beacon* had not had.

While waiting for the fire crew to leave (so that she could search the building), Caitlin had been discreetly searching the area outside, particularly the ground near where Henry had been attacked. Now that Jamie was occupied in the car, she bent over the soot-covered parking lot and switched on her Palm Treo, using it as a flashlight. The glow of the screen was dim, but she didn't want to risk using the penlight in her purse.

After two or three minutes of searching, she was ready to give up. But just then, something glinted in the soot. Sweeping her gaze in a semicircle, and seeing no one nearby, she reached down and pulled up what appeared to be a small notebook. She brushed off the soot and saw that it was a Moleskine. The cover looked slightly charred, but inside it, between the cover and the first notebook page, she found two photographs. One showed four men in the stern of a fishing boat. The other showed Henry Sexton's face. It had obviously been shot from a distance with a telephoto lens. Caitlin blinked and turned the photo toward the taillights of a nearby truck that had been left idling. Then she froze.

Someone had superimposed a rifle scope over Henry's face.

Sliding that photo aside, she peered at the men in the fishing boat. After a few seconds, her pulse began to race. One of the men in the boat was Tom Cage. Another looked a lot like . . . *Ray Presley*. Had Caitlin not spent all day researching the names Penn gave her last night, she wouldn't have recognized the other two men. But now she placed them as easily as she might have a schoolmate from years ago. The man who appeared to be talking in the photograph was a local attorney, Claude Devereux. The man who looked like Charlton Heston was Brody Royal.

"Jamie!" she called, hurrying to the car and dropping into the passenger seat. "Get this thing in gear!"

"I thought you wanted to search the place."

"I just did," she said, slamming her door. "Get us back to the paper."

WEDNESDAY

CHAPTER 59

CAITLIN ROLLED OVER and shut off her phone alarm, then sat up on the side of the bed. The back of her head pounded dully, probably from too much or too little caffeine. Her body clock had been scrambled over the past two nights. The first edition of today's *Examiner* lay on her bedside table, where she'd dropped it three hours ago, after driving home from the office to grab some sleep in her own bed. Atop the paper lay Henry Sexton's charred Moleskine notebook, and beside that the shocking snapshots she'd discovered inside it. She still couldn't believe the fishing boat photo. The idea that her future father-in-law had been a friend of Brody Royal during the 1960s seemed impossible. She hoped Henry had improved enough overnight for her to question him about the photos (if she could somehow circumvent his girlfriend). But where Henry's notebook was concerned, the photos had been only been the tip of the iceberg.

After skimming through the Moleskine on her way back to the *Examiner*, Caitlin had sequestered herself in her office and read deep into the night, growing more excited—and angrier—with every page she turned. The salvaged notebook contained Henry's notes from his past four weeks' work, including the interviews with Pooky Wilson's mother and Glenn Morehouse, as well as a brief summary of his "war room" conversation with Penn. By the time she read the final entry, Caitlin had a much better idea of how much Penn had kept from her— not only Monday night, but all of last night as well—even after the attack on Henry, and finding out that the reporter had intended to come to work for her.

Monday night, Penn had hinted at unspeakable crimes by telling her about the gang rape of Viola Turner. But Henry's notebook revealed that

Viola's rape—like the murder of her brother—had merely been part of a larger scheme to lure Robert Kennedy to Natchez for a planned assassination. Glenn Morehouse's description of the perverse murder of two female whistle-blowers from Royal Insurance had nauseated Caitlin, and left her shivering with anger. That was exactly the kind of story she lived for, and Penn knew it. The police and FBI had clearly failed in their duty to unravel the Royal Insurance scam and punish the killers. Why, then, hadn't Penn given her the chance to start on that case last night? Granted, his promise to Henry had precluded him from telling her *everything,* at least on Monday night. But as soon as Lou Ann Whittington confirmed that Henry had meant to come work for Caitlin, Penn had lost any justification for keeping Henry's work product from her.

Reaching down to the floor, she fished a bottle of Advil from her purse and dry-swallowed two pills, then bit a NoDoz in half and tried to swallow one jagged, bitter fragment. It refused to go down. Grimacing, she grabbed what remained of last night's Mountain Dew and washed down the pill. After the liquid settled in her stomach, she pushed herself up off the bed and padded into the bathroom, where she froze on the oval rug.

A Clearblue Easy box sat like a silent reprimand on the counter beside the commode. She'd bought the test at Walgreens a week ago, and she'd been riding around with the thing in her car ever since. This morning, as she pulled into her driveway, the box had fallen out of its bag, so she'd carried it inside with the intention of removing that bit of stress from her life before beginning what was bound to be an epic couple of weeks.

With only mild apprehension, she peeled the cellophane wrapper off the testing stick, held the stick between her thighs, and forced herself to relax. After three seconds, she pulled the stick from her urine stream, set it on the counter, and turned the hot water knob in the shower. As she waited for the blessed heat to come down the pipe, she turned to the mirror, took in a deep breath, and raised her arms above her head for a forward fold. After holding that position for sixty seconds, she stepped back into plank position. When she reached the down dog position, she held that until she was sure three minutes had passed, then got to her feet and looked down at the testing stick on the counter. An unexpected tightness in her chest surprised her, but she shook it off, then picked up the stick and squinted at it. The word PREGNANT shone up at her in baby blue, like a mocking Hallmark card.

"Of course," she said. "A week before my wedding. *Fuck.*"

It wasn't that she didn't want to get pregnant—she did. But yesterday she'd postponed her wedding, which would make the timing of this pregnancy a lot more obvious to the curious busybodies that abounded in her adopted hometown. But there was more to it than this, if Caitlin was honest with herself.

At thirty-five, she didn't have a lot of time to burn before getting pregnant. Yet she wanted two or three years of married life before taking on the burden of caring for an infant. After all, she already had Annie in the picture. More disturbing still, the arrival of a child would mark the true end of her all-in approach to journalism. Last night she'd slept only three hours, and she might well be awake for another twenty-four, given what today might bring. A baby could cause the same kind of sleep deprivation, but any positive results of that would accrue to her child, not to her. Selfish thoughts, perhaps, but Caitlin saw no point in pretending she had more maternal instinct than she did. Given her druthers, she'd be overjoyed to deliver a four-year-old child who could be dealt with like an adult.

Too frustrated to shower, she wrapped the testing stick in toilet tissue, dropped it into the trash can, then turned off the water and went back into the bedroom, where she called Jamie at the *Examiner* and began giving orders for the morning. While she was talking, a new call broke in—an unfamiliar number—and she clicked over to it.

"Caitlin Masters."

"Ms. Masters, this is Sherry Harden. Henry's girlfriend."

This announcement did more to wake her than the NoDoz had. "How's he doing?" she asked anxiously. "Better, I hope?"

"A little better. I called because he's been asking for you."

Oh my God, Caitlin thought. A rush of adrenaline started her pacing the bedroom. "What can I do to help? Should I come over?"

"If you have time, I think it would calm him down a little."

"I'm on my way, Sherry. Fifteen minutes, max."

"Thank you."

Caitlin pulled on the jeans she'd been wearing last night, grabbed a fresh blouse from her closet, then put on her tennis shoes. Hair and makeup would have to wait until she got to the *Examiner*. Stuffing Henry's Moleskine and the photos into her purse, she grabbed her keys and her pepper spray off the night table and ran for the front door. The policeman outside looked startled, but she shouted that everything was okay and sprinted to her car.

CHAPTER 60

A DISTANT BELL is ringing in the fog, but no matter how hard I peer into the veil of white, I can't locate the source of the sound. Is it a buoy, or another ship? Suddenly panicked, I jerk upright and realize I'm lying in an unfamiliar bed, my cell phone ringing on the floor beside it. After draining two beers and a shot of vodka in quick succession last night, I slept like the dead, despite the shocks I'd endured during the day. God only knows how many times my phone must have rung to bring me out of my alcohol-induced coma.

Leaning off the edge of the bed, I dig my phone out of my pants pocket and look at the LCD. The caller is Sheriff Walker Dennis.

"Tell me you have good news," I say groggily.

"Not exactly. The judge wouldn't go for it. I couldn't get the wiretap warrant on Brody Royal."

"Goddamn it," I curse, pressing my fist against my forehead. Without a wiretap, shaking Brody's tree won't accomplish a damned thing. "I thought this judge hated Royal."

"He does. But he also wants to get reelected for another term."

"Shit."

"The news isn't all bad, though. He's writing up the warrants for me to go after the meth cookers and mules, even though he knows that means going to war with the Knoxes."

"What about tapping Royal's lines on your own? Do you have the capability?"

"Come on, Penn. If I try that, I might as well write a formal request to be fired and then sued."

I sit up on the edge of the bed. "I know. I was out of line to ask you."

"Look, man, I'm ready to go all-out on these drug busts, if you're still with me. We can put some serious heat on the Knoxes, maybe enough to rattle Brody."

"I doubt it. He probably keeps well clear of the drug stuff."

"Well, what do you want to do? This ain't something to take on lightly. Ask my cousin's widow."

"I hear you. How long would it take you to set up the busts?"

"Twenty-four hours to set it up right—by which I mean keep it quiet."

Though my mind is still on Brody Royal (and my father, always on my father), I give the drug plan ten seconds of hard analysis. "All right, do it."

"Okay. I'm sorry about the phone taps. I know you had your heart set on that."

"Can't be helped. I'll try to think of another way."

"Hey, I went by Henry Sexton's hospital room this morning. He's a little more coherent. He's been asking for your girlfriend, but he also asked me about you. He wants to talk to you."

"I'd like to talk to him. Any leads yet on who attacked him?"

"Nothing. But I'll tell you one thing: the FBI moved into the parish this morning like the damned Third Army. They're out at the Jericho Hole with all kinds of equipment. If you go see Henry, you ought to drive out there and take a look. You won't believe it."

"Thanks, Walker. Stay in touch today."

After he hangs up, I call Caitlin, who sounds breathless when she answers.

"What's going on?" I ask. "You sound like you're running."

"No. I'm on my way to Ferriday. Henry's been asking for me."

"How far have you gotten? Walker Dennis says Henry wants to see me, too."

She doesn't answer.

"Caitlin? Are you there?"

"Yeah," she says awkwardly. "I'm already over the bridge. Why don't you meet me there? I'm sure we're going to be on very different paths today."

Her voice sounds unnaturally cold, but I know I won't get an explanation from her on the phone. Getting to my feet, I head for the bathroom. I want to be present when she sees Henry. I don't want her badgering him if it turns out he's decided not to work for her after all.

"All right," I say, trying not to show my irritation. "I'll see you there."

She hangs up without a word.

CHAPTER 61

FORREST KNOX WAS eating brunch in a temporary shelter erected on the front lawn of the recently destroyed Southern Yacht Club when his secure cell phone buzzed in his pocket. With the lieutenant governor sitting at the end of his table, he figured he'd better ignore it for as long as he could.

Situated on the southern shore of Lake Pontchartrain, the Southern Yacht Club was the second oldest in the United States—older than even Newport—the kind of place to which Forrest's father would only have been admitted to repair something. Tall cotton for a country boy. Forrest had been invited by three men who stood to make millions of dollars out of the reconstruction of the Crescent City.

One of those men sat to Forrest's immediate right. To Forrest's left, two seats away, sat Brody Royal. Royal had become a member only twelve years ago, when his steadily expanding fortune and political power made it impossible for the old-line members to keep him out, despite his plebeian origins. Today's event was part of the campaign to rebuild the clubhouse, which had burned in the hours after the storm, its flames towering above priceless racing vessels that Katrina's surge had tossed into chaotic piles like bathtub toys thrown by a two-year-old.

The lieutenant governor wasn't here for show. While the governor's office might not fully understand the goals of Forrest's benefactors—or agree with their tactics—the politicians in Baton Rouge had to concede that New Orleans was taking a terrible public relations beating, thanks to the media-created impression of a city that might not deserve billions of taxpayer dollars for rebuilding. New Orleans's notorious history of crime and corruption weighed heavily on its national reputation, and something had to be done to address that problem going forward. Since Colonel Mackiever had argued against state police intervention in his official report, Forrest had been asked here today to give his "informal" opinion on the matter.

A black waiter in a white coat set a bowl of garlic cheese grits before him. Forrest's mouth watered at the sight of the pale orange mixture. He was about to tuck into it when his secure cell vibrated again. Down the table, Brody Royal gave him a subtle glare. Forrest reached into his back pocket, took out the phone, and checked its LCD below the level of the table.

PAN-PAN, it read.

He jammed the phone back in his pocket. "Pan-Pan" was a radio code signifying a state of urgency one level below "Mayday," which signaled imminent danger to life or a vessel, requiring all potential rescuers within hearing to cease all activities and begin a rescue attempt. In Forrest's secret world, the "Pan-Pan" code signified a breach of security that could reach all the way up the chain of command.

He glanced to his left, at the main door of the dining room. Alphonse Ozan stood there in uniform, his face tight with concern. A slight inclination of the head told Forrest he needed to leave the dining room immediately.

"Is everything all right, Colonel Knox?" asked the lieutenant governor.

Forrest smiled at the politician, then gave him the old standby cover. "I'm afraid not, sir. We've got a serious situation with the High Density Narcotics Trafficking Unit. I'm afraid I'm going to have to excuse myself early."

One of Forrest's patrons kicked him under the table, but he ignored the blow. Brody tried to catch his eye as he rose, but Forrest pointedly ignored him. No one in his organization had ever transmitted the "Pan-Pan" code, and he wasn't about to waste time finding out what the problem was.

Forrest gave the lieutenant governor a deferential nod, then quickly made his way to the exit. The other diners gawked at his uniform as he passed. It wasn't just the uniform, he knew. The scarred nub of his ear always drew stares in places like this, where he couldn't wear his hat. Those who knew it was a battle wound considered it a badge of honor, but the average asshole usually gave him the freak treatment. He felt a wild compulsion to draw his gun and blast a few of the crystal champagne flutes off the tables.

Ozan didn't begin talking until they'd reached the boardwalk outside, where the fetid smell of Lake Pontchartrain's shore permeated the air.

"We got a major problem, boss. A while ago, Deke Dunn's wife called in to say he hadn't come in from his night shift. I wouldn't have thought much of it, but then I remembered you'd sent him out to tell Snake and Sonny to head for Toledo Bend this morning."

"Go on."

"Deke stopped by Snake's place, then headed toward Sonny's fishing camp on Old River. Nobody heard anything from him after that. But because of your order, nobody worried about it."

"Where is he, Alphonse?"

The Redbone shrugged his big shoulders. "I'm not sure yet. A few minutes ago, Sonny came stumbling up to Snake's house looking like death warmed over. Last night, Dr. Cage and some crazy old Texas Ranger snatched him from his camp at gunpoint."

"*What?*"

"They took him down by the borrow pits, held a gun to his head, and rolled his fingerprints onto some vials and a syringe. Trying to frame him for that old nigger woman's murder!"

Forrest's pulse began to race. "And?"

"Sonny had a goddamn heart attack, right there. He hardly knew a thing after that, but he's pretty sure he heard gunshots. The next thing he remembers is waking up on the concrete outside the Mercy Hospital ER, nurses lifting him onto a gurney. He walked out this morning without the doctor releasing him."

"And Deke?"

Ozan waited for a man in a blue blazer with brass anchor buttons to walk past. "On a hunch, I called Technical Services, and sure enough, somebody using our 'Harlan Black' alias requested a location on Sonny Thornfield's cell number about the time Sonny says all this happened. That had to be Deke. When he saw Sonny was gone from his camp but his truck still there, Deke got his cell phone triangulated and went after him. He must have walked up on Dr. Cage and that Ranger questioning Sonny and shot it out with 'em. The problem is, Deke's phone is dead now. And nobody's seen him, Dr. Cage, or the Ranger since."

"You have the trace coordinates on Deke's phone?"

"Damn straight. I already called Air Support and requested a chopper in your name. It's picking us up at Lakefront Airport in fifteen minutes."

Lakefront Airport was only five miles away. "Let's move."

Forrest's secure phone buzzed again. He looked down at the LCD and cursed. "It's Brody."

Ozan shook his head. "Should we tell the old man what's going on?"

Forrest stuck up his middle finger. "Screw him. From now on, he gets the mushroom treatment. Get the car, Alphonse. I got a bad feeling."

CHAPTER 62

A HALF MILE down the shore of Lake Concordia from Brody Royal's palatial home, his daughter, Katy, sat gazing blankly into her Hollywood-style vanity mirror, which was surrounded by lightbulbs. Her husband stood in the shower a few feet away. Staring into the mirror, Katy saw nothing but fear. In the days since her interview with Henry Sexton, her entire being had been taken over by a steadily encroaching terror, a force that was slowly devouring her, like a lethal infection. She was helpless against this attack, for there was precious little of her left to fight anything external. Katy had lived with fear for as long as she could remember, though she'd never understood its source. Trying to recall her childhood was like dipping her bucket into a well and coming up with India ink. Whenever she'd summoned the courage to dip her hands into that bucket, she'd felt slimy, shapeless things under the surface, things she couldn't catch hold of long enough to lift into the light and identify. At the frayed end of depression, she'd learned, the mind began to lose its grasp on even the most familiar things. Of course, she hadn't done her brain any favors over the years, what with the booze and the drugs. But without those anesthetics, she'd have killed herself long before now.

She picked up a jar of Estée Lauder foundation and unscrewed the lid, then let it sit open. A copy of the *Natchez Examiner* lay on the marble counter, its bottom half faceup. A photograph showed a middle-aged black man standing with his arms folded in front of a music store, several young black men standing proudly beside him. Beside this image, another photo showed the same piece of ground a week later. All that remained were two partially burned pianos standing in a mass of charred wreckage.

Katy heard her husband turn off the water. In her peripheral vision, Randall Regan grabbed a towel from a peg, then stepped out and began drying his hair. With his vision obscured, she stole a glance at the monster who had guarded her since she was a girl. Even at fifty-eight, Randall remained a dense mass of muscle and sinew and anger, stronger than most men twenty years his junior. And when angered, he could be cruel beyond all imagining.

"The fuck you lookin' at?" he asked, noticing her attention. He dropped the towel from his waist. "I *know* you don't want any of this."

Katy whipped her face forward.

"What the hell's wrong with you this week?" He bent to dry his hairy legs. "You walk around like you're in a fog, which ain't far from normal, but this week it's like a damned Alzheimer's ward. You don't even *wash* yourself. You stink. Why don't you take a bath?"

How could she answer that? If she told the truth, Randall or her father would have her committed again—or worse. Neither man had any qualms about killing, and as depressed as Katy was, she didn't want to die yet. She glanced over at the *Examiner.* The side that lay facedown displayed two portraits of Henry Sexton. One showed the reporter as a college intern, questioning an elderly black preacher in Gilbert, Louisiana. The other showed paramedics loading Sexton into an ambulance in front of the *Concordia Beacon,* which had been gutted by fire last night.

Ever since Henry visited this house last week, sparks had been firing through the blank spaces in Katy's brain. Images flashed out of nowhere, like the visions she'd had after alcoholic blackouts, pictures she wasn't sure had ever been real. Henry had asked her about a colored boy, one he'd claimed she once loved. *Pooky Wilson.* The name had scarcely moved her when he'd first said it, like a stone dropped into a deep lake that sank endlessly into darkness. But later that night, as she drifted into uneasy sleep, that stone had finally hit bottom. And when it hit, it jarred something loose.

Over the next few days, painful memories began bubbling to the surface, and each bubble contained its own discrete nightmare. In one of the first, she saw herself as a young girl, peering into her mother's bathroom. Her father sat on the edge of the bathtub, talking to his wife. All Katy could see was her father's broad back. He had never sat in there like that—in fact, Brody Royal hardly spoke to his wife at all. But on *that* day, he'd spoken steadily, and in such a low, cruel voice that Katy had quickly retreated. An hour later, her father called an ambulance and told them his drunken wife had drowned in the bathtub. Ever since remembering this, Katy been unable to get into the bathtub.

"You want to kill me," she said to her husband, voicing her terror for the first time. "Don't you?"

Randall stopped drying himself and looked at her mirror, his actor's mask almost making him appear human. But he must have sensed her state of mind, because suddenly his mask fell away. Forty years of unalloyed hatred blazed out of his eyes like deadly radiation.

"Go on," she goaded, knowing she would pay for her defiance. "Admit it. You want to kill me."

"I ought to," he said. "I've been chained to your pathetic ass for forty years, and you've been trying to kill yourself the whole time. You nearly drank yourself to death in the seventies. You all but blew your heart out with coke in the eighties, and you've been eating tranqs and happy pills ever since. You were hardly alive that whole time. What was the point?"

"You tell me," Katy said quietly. "Why didn't you just put me out of my misery?" *Like Daddy did Mama,* she thought.

Randall shook his head with exasperation, but he didn't answer.

"I know you've wanted to," Katy went on, trying to push him to— to what? "I can see it in your eyes. Right now. You'd like to choke the life out of me, watch my face turn blue. You almost did it a couple of times. That night at Gulf Shores. And the time in Las Vegas, after the dog show."

Randall's face darkened. "Don't even mention your little rat dogs. Brody should have left you in the nuthouse over in Texas."

She shuddered, a physical echo of her year locked inside the Borgen Institute.

"Tell me, Randall," she said in a voice she barely recognized. "Please. Why *am* I still here?"

He stepped closer, staring down like a hunter about to finish a wounded animal. Her brain told her to run, but she remained on her stool. If he killed her . . . what did it matter?

"You really want to know?" he asked, and she shivered at the coldness in his voice. "I'll tell you. You know that river land you own?"

"What about it?"

Randall smiled. "Eleven miles of pristine riverfront farmland.

Eleven *miles*. That came down to you from your mother's family, and it's legally encumbered so that it can never leave her blood family. Well . . . since you can't have kids, that means once you die, it goes to your cousin up in Savannah."

Katy shook her head, lost in confusion. "I don't understand. If you can't get that land, or sell it, what good is it to you?"

Her husband laughed with such harshness that she felt sick. "It ain't me, honey. It's your daddy. Brody might never be able to get *hold* of that land, but as long as you're alive, he can lease it to farmers, cut timber off it, and suck the oil out from under it. And that's what he's been doing since the day I married you." Randall tapped the side of his head and laughed. "You get it now? You're worth more to him alive than you are dead. It's really that simple. Jesus. I thought for sure you'd have figured that out by now. I guess your brain is more scrambled than I thought."

He turned to his closet and pulled a shirt over his still-wet back. "So here I stand, your babysitter. Highest paid babysitter in the world, probably. But it still ain't enough."

She sat in stunned silence, staring at her shattered reflection, finally understanding the riddle of her existence. In her mind, she watched a blurry movie of herself signing various papers in an alcoholic haze.

"I've got a busy day," Randall said. "Brody's in New Orleans, but he'll be back this afternoon. Go play with your dogs, or whatever you're going to do. But do me one favor, please. Take a fucking bath."

He walked out of the room.

Katy sat motionless until she heard the carport door slam. Then she picked up the newspaper, walked to the bathtub, and turned the hot tap wide open. Opening a drawer beside her husband's lavatory, she took out a pair of sharp scissors, which she laid in the edge of the tub. *You get it now?* Randall had said, as though talking to a moron. *You're worth more to him alive than you are dead.* Katy's leg muscles quivered as though barely able to support her weight. How was that possible, since she felt as though she might float away from the earth's surface at any moment? While she waited for the tub to fill, she looked down at the newspaper and read the name beneath the top story.

Caitlin Masters.

CHAPTER 63

DESPITE BREAKING THE speed limit most of the way to Mercy Hospital, I find Caitlin already talking to Drew Elliott in the north wing. She hardly glances over as I approach, since she's giving her full attention to Drew, who looks up and waves at me but keeps talking. At forty-two, Drew remains the television ideal of a doctor: handsome, athletic, super-competent. But like all mortals, he's had his share of personal troubles, and I've done my part to help him out of them.

"We probably should have flown him to Baton Rouge," Drew says, nodding down the hall to where a parish deputy sits glumly on guard in a high school desk. "But between the orthopedist, the surgeon, and myself, we managed to patch Henry back together. Reduced the fractures, took care of the abdomen. Besides, he didn't want to leave. He insisted that we keep him in this hospital. Something to do with Albert Norris being treated here, apparently."

A single-story structure on Highway 15, Mercy Hospital serves the citizens of three surrounding parishes, but it's no level-one trauma center.

"I appreciate you driving back over to check on him," I say. "Has Henry gotten clearheaded enough to say anything more about his attackers?"

Drew nods. "Last night he dreamed that one of his assailants was the son of a guy he played church softball with about ten years ago. Casey Whelan was the kid's name. I don't know how seriously Sheriff Dennis will take that, but Henry sounded sure."

"The FBI will take it seriously. They're in town now." I cut my eyes at Caitlin. "Special Agent Kaiser is supervising an FBI team down at the Jericho Hole. My guess is they're planning to dive on the car Kirk Boisseau found yesterday."

"Has Henry really been asking for me this morning?" Caitlin asks Drew.

"He's spoken both your names, but I think it's you he really wants to see."

"I'd better get in there then. How lucid is he?"

"In and out. He looks bad, but I'm confident his head injury's not life-threatening."

"So he's out of danger?" I ask.

"I'm not sure that's a medical question." Drew nods down the hall at the armed deputy.

I shake Drew's hand. After he gives Caitlin a farewell hug and departs, she and I walk toward the deputy's desk. "Are you going to tell me what's wrong?" I ask her.

"I'm fine."

Sure you are.

We identify ourselves to the deputy, but he asks to see our driver's licenses anyway, which gives me some measure of confidence in Sheriff Dennis's precautions.

As soon as we pass through the door, I see a woman who must be Henry's girlfriend sitting near the foot of his hospital bed in one of those ugly chairs that fold out into a torturous bed. *She's a nurse,* I remember now. *Sherry something.* Sherry wears pink scrubs and looks to be a few years older than Henry. Dark bags hang beneath her bloodshot eyes. She doesn't get up when she sees us, nor does she offer any welcome.

As I pass the corner of Henry's bathroom, I see him at last, and the sight takes my breath away. His neck and face are a swollen collection of contusions, ecchymosis, and hematomas, with only the occasional patch of undamaged flesh showing. A plaster cast encases his left forearm, and his right wrist is purplish-black. Henry's eyes are only half open, yet he acknowledges our arrival by slightly lifting his right hand from the coverlet.

"Sherry?" I venture.

The woman on the chair nods as though against her will.

"Is it all right if we come in?"

"Come on. He been waiting for you long enough."

Her eyes stay mostly on Caitlin, giving an examination worthy of a romantic rival. This might be irrational, but I see it all the time during initial meetings between women.

When I'm far enough into the room, I see a catheter bag and another bag for fluids strapped to Henry's bed. There's probably a drain tube sewn into the stab wound in his belly. A wave of nausea goes through me.

"How's he feeling?" I ask.

Sherry rolls her eyes at the absurdity of this question. "How do you think? You know, I knew this would happen. Sooner or later, it had to, with all those stories he was writing."

Caitlin starts to speak, then wisely thinks better of it.

"I've tried to get him to tone them down," Sherry goes on. "The articles. Things have changed around here, but not that much. Most people have moved on, and the races get along pretty good. But some folks can't let go of the past. And that's who put him in here."

"I'm afraid you're right." I move closer to Henry and touch his foot under the covers. "Hey, buddy. It's Penn. Can you hear me?"

Henry's eyes blink open and stare at the ceiling, then track slowly over to me. When he tries to speak, what emerges is a sort of guttural ululation, and I wonder if pain meds are contributing to his difficulty.

"What have they got him on, Sherry?"

"Zosyn for infection. Dilaudid for the pain."

"*Wiss I could nalk benner,*" Henry groans suddenly. "*Lossa ell you. But . . . I not gon be able work . . . on stery foh while.*" A strained laugh comes through his clenched teeth.

"Is his jaw wired shut?" I whisper to Sherry.

"No. But he bit his tongue during the beating, and some teeth are smashed. They had to stitch the tongue up."

"Christ."

Henry moves his eyes until they settle on Caitlin, who has moved up beside me. "*You gon haf pick up where I lef off.*"

This statement probably sent a blast of endorphins through Caitlin's body, but she hides her excitement well. Demurring with a shake of her head, she says, "Henry, I'm sure you'll be able to dictate stories from here. I'll put one of my reporters at your disposal."

He closes his eyes, squeezing tears from their inside corners.

"Has anybody read you this morning's *Examiner*?" I ask. "Caitlin did a big story on you. You're a hero, man. The online edition has racked up praise from all over the world. You've got comments from India to South Africa."

Sherry steps up to the bed and wipes Henry's tears with a tissue.

"This is still your story," Caitlin says firmly.

His lips move again, but his jaw barely moves. *"No. Uppa you now. But thass not why I call you here. I got . . . sumpin for you."* He motions weakly to Sherry with his right hand. *"Give it her."*

"Are you sure?" Sherry asks, her resentment clear.

Henry nods with obvious difficulty.

Reaching into the pocket of her scrub pants, Sherry produces two small keys, which she hands to Caitlin. Caitlin looks at Henry and raises her eyebrows.

"They shole my case files," he says. *"Or bun 'em. Everysing. 'Ose my keys . . . safe apposit box . . . woy—urr-ROY-al Cotton Bank."*

Excitement is crackling off Caitlin like static electricity. *These* are the keys Henry mentioned to Lou Ann Whittington while he lay bleeding on the pavement. "What's in the safe-deposit boxes?" Caitlin asks.

"Copies," Henry croaks. *"Sranscrip. FBI files . . . disk. Insern did mos of ih foh me . . . lass summuh. Took mohhr . . . moh suff yes'day."*

"My God," Caitlin breathes. "Henry, are you saying I can use your files?"

The reporter nods again, his forehead covered in sweat. He probably couldn't verbalize the trauma of giving away the fruits of a decade's work, even if he wanted to. *"You haff oo,"* he says at length.

Sherry leans over and wipes his purple skin with a washcloth.

"Be cah-ful," Henry warns. *"Nah lige me. Don bee supid lige me."*

Caitlin walks around the bed, lays her hand lightly on his shoulder, and bends to speak close to his ear. Her words are faint but filled with conviction. "I'm going to do everything in my power to live up to the example you've set. You concentrate on getting better. Any time you want to file a story, have Sherry call my cell, and I'll come myself to take dictation."

Caitlin continues speaking, but I'm distracted by Sherry, who comes to my side and begins whispering with great passion.

"Who said my man had to be the one to bring the whole damn Klan to justice? Huh? He's done more than anybody else already. Hasn't he done enough?"

"More than enough," I assure her.

Sherry shakes her head. "I can't live like this anymore. I want a life, you know? A *normal* life. I'm too old to have more kids, but I can sit on the porch and listen to Henry play the guitar. I can work in my garden, and do a lot of other things that don't make people want to kill you."

Unsure of how to comfort her, I take her arm and whisper, "I think Henry's dangerous work is done. A lot of good people are going to take over from here, including the FBI. But without Henry's work, those Klansmen would almost certainly go free forever."

She laughs bitterly. "Do you think that makes it worth it? Look at him. What if that was your girlfriend lying there?"

Henry looks like somebody dragged from a basement after an aerial bombardment. But then I think of the bones Kirk pulled up from the bottom of the Jericho Hole, bones with rusted barbed wire and a bullet embedded in them. "Only Henry can answer that."

She gazes angrily at the man she loves. "He won't quit. Not even after this. I know him too well."

"Maybe he will," I murmur, but I know it's a lie. No man who's come as far as Henry Sexton would stop his quest now. I want to ask him so many things, first and foremost about Brody Royal. But all that will have to wait. "Let's go, Caitlin. Let's let them get some rest."

Caitlin kisses Henry on the forehead. Then she comes over and touches Sherry's hand, whispers something in her ear, and follows me to the door.

"What did you say to her?" I ask when we're outside.

"Girl stuff."

This tells me I will learn no more.

Our cars are parked side by side in the hospital lot. As we walk down the steps at the exit, Caitlin takes my hand and squeezes it, then lets go. I feel her shaking, but it's only when we reach the car that she turns, and I see tears on her face, and her black mascara running down to make a raccoon mask.

"What is it?" I ask. "Henry?"

She shrugs and wipes her cheeks. "I didn't think things like that happened anymore. Even in my job, I just—I don't know. I mean drug murders, sex crimes, sure. But that in there . . . that's something else. This is America, isn't it? He's a *journalist*."

"Henry was a threat to the Double Eagles, so they tried to eliminate him. They want to stay out of jail. They don't think beyond that."

Caitlin wipes her face on her sleeve, then looks up at me with an almost accusing expression. "Are you so sure it was the Double Eagles? Why not Brody Royal?"

"Is that what you're angry about? Something to do with Brody Royal?"

"Penn, you held back so much about him yesterday. I told you last night that Henry was going to work for me. There was so much you could have told me. I've lost so much time."

"Not so much. And we didn't know—"

She holds up her hand, then stares out at the highway with cold resolve. "I'm going to that bank to get Henry's files."

"Yes, and I'm taking you. We'll pick your car up on the way back. Or maybe send a reporter back over here to get it."

"No, I want my car. You can follow me if you want."

"Caitlin, wait. We really need to ride together. You're right, I have held some things back from you. But the biggest thing of all is that Dad has jumped bail."

She drops her hand from her face. "What?"

"I found out late last night, but I couldn't risk telling you on a phone. His life is on the line now. I've moved Mom and Annie to a safe house, and—"

"Excuse me," says an unfamiliar male voice. "Are you Mayor Cage?"

A muscular man wearing a suit and an earpiece has appeared between two cars, and he walks toward us with one hand near the gap in his sport coat.

"Who are you?" I ask warily, wishing I hadn't left my gun in my car.

"Special Agent Loomis." He reaches into his coat, then flips open a wallet, revealing blue and white FBI credentials. "Special Agent John Kaiser would like you to meet him at the Jericho Hole."

Caitlin touches my arm and shakes her head. "I don't have time for that."

"What does Agent Kaiser want to talk to me about?" I ask, not relishing the idea of being interrogated by an FBI agent on this particular day. "Can't he do it by phone?"

Loomis gives me a tight smile and shakes his head. "We've ID'd the car at the bottom of that hole, sir. That's not for publication, by the way," he adds, with a look at Caitlin.

"Who did it belong to?" she asks.

"Sorry. Agent Kaiser may reveal that when you get to the Jericho Hole, but I can't." Agent Loomis looks at Caitlin again. "Are you Caitlin Masters?"

"Yes."

"Agent Kaiser told me to invite you, too."

"Why would he do that? Especially after the stories in this morning's paper."

Caitlin wasn't kind to the FBI in her main story this morning. And she looks very reluctant to divert from the straightest path to Henry's backup files.

"I never know why he does anything, ma'am," Loomis says, "but he usually has a good reason."

"How many people did Kaiser bring with him?" I ask.

"Four agents, plus some techs. But three more agents just left New Orleans. Oh, and his wife is with him."

The effect of this statement on Caitlin is immediate. She looks like a musician after being told Bob Dylan is at a party she just declined an invitation to.

"Jordan Glass is here?" she asks.

"Yes, ma'am. Five minutes from where we stand. She's taking pictures of everything we uncover."

Even before Caitlin speaks, I know she's decided she can afford a stop at the Jericho Hole. "Twenty minutes," she says. "I don't like playing catch-up."

"You go on ahead," I tell Loomis. "We know the way."

The FBI agent looks uncertain, but after I wave him off, he heads for a parked Ford. As soon as he's out of earshot, Caitlin says, "Penn, what the hell is Tom up to?"

"I have no idea. But if a cop spots him, and he resists arrest, they'll kill him. I'm betting Forrest Knox has already given that order."

Suspicion clouds her eyes. "Are you going to tell me what you know about Forrest?"

"On the way to the Jericho Hole." Pulling her to me, I hug her tight, even though she stiffens at my touch. "You'll have Henry's files on your desk in under an hour."

"A lot less than that," she says into my chest. "I'm going to pick up right where he left off." Drawing back her head, she reveals the wrath of a Fury behind her startlingly green eyes. "And whoever did that to him is going to suffer for it."

CHAPTER 64

THE FASTEST WAY to the Jericho Hole is to ride the gravel road atop the Mississippi River levee—fifteen minutes if you drive seventy, and Caitlin is urging me to do just that. The great hole lies in the wooded margin between the north end of Lake St. John and the newer course of the Mississippi River. The oxbow lake is shaped like a C facing the river, about ten miles north of the Natchez-Vidalia bridge, and the Jericho Hole forms an equilateral triangle at the upper end of the C, each of its sides about a third of a mile long. The levee road should bring us directly between the lake and the hole.

As we speed along the levee top, I give Caitlin a much-expanded summary of the theories Henry related to me Monday night—including the story of Brody Royal killing Albert Norris and ordering the downing of Dr. Robb's plane. Since Henry has decided to pass on his files to her, I see no reason to withhold what she'll soon read for herself. She records every word on her handheld Sony, but she seems less excited than I would have expected, which makes me suspicious. She's obviously angry that I withheld so much, but still, to see her sit in tense silence while I describe the murder of two federal witnesses—both women—stretches credibility. Halfway to the Jericho Hole, she tells me that last night she salvaged Henry's most recent notebook from the *Beacon* fire, and from it learned most of what Henry got from Glenn Morehouse, Pooky's mother, and even what he told me on Monday night. That includes Brody's Carlos Marcello connection, the plot to kill Robert Kennedy, and the murders of the two women from Royal Insurance.

"Given that I have all that," she says, "do you still want me to write a comprehensive story in tomorrow's paper, as Henry was planning to do?"

"Yes. Though I think you'd do well to leave out the Marcello-RFK plot. Until you have more proof, that's only going to be a distraction from the civil rights murders."

"But this story isn't just about civil rights murders!" she explodes. "You can't demand that I jump the gun on parts of the story and hold back the rest."

"Did you really look at Henry back there?" I ask. "I don't want you to end up like that. And the best way to prevent it is to convince Royal and the Double Eagles that the information they most fear is already out there. And that the FBI has it."

Caitlin sighs and looks out the window at the river, which appears slate gray today, rather than reddish brown. "This is one of the most complex stories I've ever worked. I can't possibly do it justice by tomorrow. I'm going to pursue it as hard as I can, but methodically. I'm going to get it right. I won't let redneck psychopaths determine my publishing schedule."

"Caitlin . . . Sherry Harden gave you the keys to Henry's safe-deposit boxes. How quiet do you think she'll stay about all she's heard and seen? If the Double Eagles find out you have Henry's files, you'll be next on their hit list. The *only* way to stay off it is to publish the story Henry planned to publish, or one like it."

Caitlin turns back to me and squeezes my arm, her eyes imploring. "But Henry had *years* to digest this stuff. He had it all in his head. I'm starting from zero! If I had his rough draft of the story, maybe I could pull this off. But that was destroyed in the fire last night."

"I'm sorry. But you have a handpicked staff, most of them way over-qualified. If you push your deadline till two or three A.M., you've got plenty of time to put a great story together. Caitlin . . . all you have to do is make the Eagles believe the FBI already has everything you do, even if they don't. I'll be glad to help you sift through Henry's stuff—but I have to track down Dad first."

"I don't need your help," she says sharply. "And I sure can't wait for you to track Tom down. You don't even know where to start looking."

"I suspect Quentin might know where he is."

"I'd start with your mother, if I were you."

"She already lied to me about Dad once."

"Well, you can't blame her for that. What woman wouldn't lie to protect her husband?"

"To her own son?"

Caitlin squeezes her knees in frustration. "We're getting off subject.

I just don't like the way this thing has gone down. I'm still not sure you're telling me everything."

"Are you telling me everything *you* know?"

She blows out a rush of air, then says something unintelligible under her breath.

"Look!" I cry, pointing over the steering wheel as we come to a hard left turn on the levee. "What is that?"

Two hundred yards north of our car—and twenty feet below it—I see two huge tractor trailers with massive blue and white machines like blocky Transformers mounted behind them. Four black SUVs surround the trucks, and even from this distance, I hear a low, powerful rumble through my window glass. Some sort of workboat lies anchored about thirty yards out in the Jericho Hole.

"What the hell's going on over there?" Caitlin asks.

"I have no idea. I figured we'd find an SUV filled with sonar equipment and a couple of FBI divers."

A deeply rutted dirt road leads from the levee down to the Jericho Hole, and I've taken great care not to bottom out or get high-centered on it. Caitlin's impatience is tangible in the car. The Jericho Hole is surrounded by trees except in a few places, but with the branches bare, you can clearly see the great loess bluff of Mississippi a mile across the river. As we draw nearer the semi trucks, I see Kirk Boisseau's Nissan Titan parked at the water's edge.

"How the hell did they find Kirk?" I wonder aloud.

"Look!" says Caitlin, pointing to her right. "That's Jordan Glass."

Forty yards past the trucks, an athletic-looking woman about my age is crouching on a log, shooting pictures through a long telephoto lens. The fleece jacket tied around her waist tells me she's already learned that December in Natchez isn't discernibly cooler than in New Orleans.

Parking beside Kirk's truck, I notice a knot of men standing on the far side of the semi trucks. They seem to be studying a map.

"Penn!" cries a voice from my left, startling me. "You believe this shit?"

I turn and find Kirk Boisseau watching me with flushed cheeks and an excited smile. He's wearing a wetsuit with a down jacket over it.

"What are you doing here?" I ask.

"I had to show them where I found the bones."

"But *how* did you get here? I mean, how did they find you?"

He shrugs. "I figured you gave them my name."

"I didn't."

Kirk shrugs again. "That Kaiser guy just called me out of the blue, late last night. He said the FBI needed my help, and they wanted to hire me as a diver. He's a marine, too. Vietnam. What was I going to say?"

A tall, brown-haired man has detached himself from the group and is coming toward us. He's carrying a neoprene bag in his hand.

"That's him," Kirk says quickly. "He brought a couple of FBI divers up with him, and they're damned good. We've already brought up most of the bones."

Kaiser has almost reached us.

"And those trucks?" I whisper.

"Pumps. King Kong shit, man."

"Hello, Mayor," says Kaiser, leaning forward and shaking my hand with a firm but not overzealous grip. "I see you and Kirk found each other."

I nod and smile, trying to read him as well as I can before we get to anything that matters. John Kaiser looks younger than I imagined, but he has the wise eyes of a man who has seen much—maybe too much. His hair is longer than that of most FBI agents I know.

"Kirk," he says, "do you mind if the mayor and I take a walk?"

"Nah. You guys do what you need to do. I'm gonna get some heat going in my truck."

Kirk heads for his truck, but before we can move away, Caitlin gets out of the car and plants herself in our path. Even as I introduce her, Kaiser takes out his cell phone and calls his wife. Looking up the shoreline, I see the brunette stand and put a cell phone to her ear, then wave and start walking toward us.

Jordan Glass looks very well put together, but not in the way of models or pinup girls. She looks like the kind of woman who could easily run fifteen miles if her car broke down. As she nears us, I sense Caitlin vibrating like there's a motor inside her.

"Jordan Glass," says the woman, holding out her hand to Caitlin. "You're Caitlin Masters?"

"Yes."

"You're younger than I thought you'd be."

Her familiarity leaves Caitlin uncharacteristically quiet. The photographer looks between forty and forty-five, and though she wears little makeup, she doesn't suffer from the lack. Her eyes are clear and bright, her forehead and cheekbones high, and her mouth only faintly lined at the corners. She has shoulder-length hair, but it's pulled back and bound with a multicolored elastic hairband, which gives her an almost bohemian look among the government agents.

"How many bones have you found so far?" Caitlin asks Kaiser. "And from how many different people? Can you tell?"

Kaiser's lips widen in an understanding smile. "Off the record, Ms. Masters?"

"All right," Caitlin concedes, though I know it must pain her to do so.

"All the bones appear to be from one skeleton."

"Have you identified it yet?"

"Not conclusively, so I don't want to say more than that."

"What's in the bag?" I ask.

Kaiser unzips the neoprene bag, then carefully removes a corroded set of handcuffs.

"From the car?" I ask.

The FBI agent nods. "They may have just used them to chain the body to the car. But from what I know about these murders, I'm betting he was alive when he went into the water."

Caitlin's eyes are locked on to the dripping handcuffs, which look like something raised from the wreck of the *Titanic*. "Is it Revels or Davis?" she almost whispers.

Kaiser hesitates. "Probably one or the other. Let's not go any further than that just yet."

Jordan touches Caitlin on the shoulder. "You want to walk down the shore with me? I think these boys are about to go way off the record."

Caitlin gives me a frustrated glare, but after looking back at Glass, who seems to be treating their imminent exclusion as a juvenile exercise by her husband, she says, "Sure. Why not?"

As soon as they are out of earshot, Kaiser's face loses any trace of humor. "Do you know where your father is?"

The shock of this question almost prompts me to speak frankly, but at the last instant my protective instinct kicks in. "I assume he's at work. Why?"

Kaiser studies my face for several seconds in silence. Then he says, "I'm sure you're right. Let's take a walk."

CHAPTER 65

AS THE FBI agent and I walk down the muddy shore of the Jericho Hole, I wave my arm toward the great machines behind us, hoping to buy myself time to think.

"What's on those trucks? Pumps?"

"Not just pumps," Kaiser says, still looking after the girls. "*Monster* pumps. Each one moves twenty-eight thousand cubic feet per minute. This hole has fifty million gallons of water in it, give or take, and they'll drain it dry in fifteen hours. They've already been running for nearly three."

Looking closer, I see a ring of damp earth several feet wide already surrounding the Jericho Hole, and the small hollows of bream beds in the mud.

"Where's the water going? The river?"

He nods and points to four big-bore hoses running off to the east, away from the levee.

"How did you get this equipment up here so fast?"

"Politics. Which I detest. I've cleared this through the U.S. attorney's office, all the way up to Washington."

"All this effort for a couple of musicians who went missing nearly forty years ago?"

Kaiser raises one eyebrow. "Those musicians were kidnapped and murdered by a domestic terror organization, Mayor Cage. A terror cell that murdered FBI informants and probably executed one of its own members only two days ago. Which means that it's still active."

I detect a hint of sarcasm in his voice, but he sounds deadly serious about his motive.

"Are you saying—"

"I'm saying that the Patriot Act, flawed as it may be, has its uses."

"*That's* how you got Morehouse's body. Right?"

He gives me a conspiratorial smile.

"Agent Kaiser, I have a feeling you're not the standard-issue Quantico robot."

"True, I'm afraid. I usually like to do things quietly, but when those bastards tried to kill Henry Sexton, I decided to take the gloves off."

"Kirk said you've already gotten most of the bones up."

"On their way to the crime lab in Washington, as we speak."

"I'm betting they belong to Luther Davis."

Kaiser nods. "But that's not for your girlfriend."

"I know. You already ID'd the car, right?"

Kaiser smiles again. "Nineteen fifty-nine Pontiac Strato Chief. Two-door, full-size convertible. Split grille, twin tailfins, the only year they made them. This one has a 389-cubic-inch Trophy V-8, three-two barrel carburetors, and Wide Track Tiger wheels. Three hundred forty-five horsepower. If the Double Eagles hadn't had Concordia Parish deputies radioing ahead to help them, they'd have never caught Davis and Revels the night they beat them up for going to that all-white drive-in."

"You got all that while it's still under the water?"

"I knew what I was looking for. That's the same car Luther Davis bought used in 1961, right after he was discharged from the army."

A twinge of excitement ripples through my chest. "You're positive?"

Kaiser reaches into his pocket and takes out a folded photo print. At first it looks like a bad underwater shot of the Loch Ness monster. Then I realize I'm looking at a rectangular metal plate with rounded edges and several faint numbers and letters engraved on it.

"One of my divers shot this forty-five minutes ago."

"The numbers look like they're in groups," I muse, taking the photo from him. "One—five-nine—P—four . . . zero-three-five?"

"The VIN number," he explains. "On that model Pontiac, it's on the left front door hinge pillar. The 'one' represents the model series: Catalina. The second number is the year of manufacture: 1959. The *P* means the car was built at the home plant in Pontiac, Michigan. And this last number is the car's serial number: four-zero-three-five. According to Dwight Stone's case notes, Pontiac Catalina number 4035 was registered with the Adams County Department of Motor Vehicles in 1961 by one Luther Elijah Davis, age twenty, a Negro veteran of the U.S. Army."

"Jesus," I breathe, thinking of Henry. "You did it."

"I called Dwight as soon as I matched the VIN. That old hardass was ready to fly down from Colorado and start digging into the case himself. I couldn't allow that, of course, even if his health was good—which it's not. But Dwight's daughter works at headquarters in Washington, and she's helping me grease the skids for all this support."

"Lucky you. But why keep draining the Hole, since you've already ID'd Luther's car? Why not just pull the car up with a cable?"

Kaiser doesn't answer immediately. "We have a lot of unsolved crimes on our books in this parish. I've heard a lot of stories over the years about bodies being dumped into water. I think it's time the sun shone on the bottom of this little lake."

"Is that the only reason?"

Another enigmatic smile. "Well . . . you might say I'm poking my stick in the rattlesnake hole and waiting to see what crawls out."

I point toward the massive pump trucks. "It won't take long for word of all this to get out."

Kaiser starts walking again, and I follow. "I want every ex-Klansman and Double Eagle in this parish to know the federal government just stomped in here with the biggest boots we've put on the ground since 1964. I want 'em pissing their geriatric diapers by morning."

His audacity leaves me speechless for the moment. Pointing to a fallen cottonwood log, he moves toward it, meaning to sit. Before he can, I grab the back of his shirt, then kick the log to scare off any snakes that might be nesting under it.

"Snakes don't hibernate up here any more than in New Orleans," I tell him.

"Thanks." He sits on the thick log and turns his brown eyes on me, reading more than I usually like to let people see. "Penn, I know your father's jumped bail. He's in real trouble, and you need to get him back before anybody else finds out he's gone."

"What makes you think he's jumped bail?" I ask, hoping my face doesn't betray my guilty knowledge.

"Come on, man. Let's not do this. You already knew he skipped."

Blood is pounding in my ears. "My father didn't kill anybody, Agent Kaiser."

He gives me an appraising look. "From what I've read of his history, I tend to believe you. But if he's innocent, why did he jump bail?"

"I'm not sure yet. But this whole prosecution is motivated by revenge. The local sheriff and DA have wanted payback on my father and me for a long time."

Kaiser nods slowly. "I figured it might be something like that."

"How did you find out he skipped?"

"I've got an agent over at the hospital, covering Henry Sexton. Last night, a former Double Eagle named Sonny Thornfield was dropped off outside the Mercy Hospital ER. He was having a heart attack. I wondered if he could have been faking, trying to get close enough to finish the job on Henry. But the ER doc says the coronary was real, and Thornfield made no attempt to reach Henry's room."

"What's the connection to my father?"

"Around the time Thornfield appeared, a nurse saw your father driving a big silver van in the hospital parking lot."

A chill rockets up my spine. *Walt Garrity's Roadtrek.* I remember the sleek silver van parked in front of my house only two months ago.

"The nurse had gone outside to smoke a cigarette," Kaiser goes on. "The van looked empty, but when the hospital's rent-a-cop pulled alongside to check it out, your father suddenly climbed behind the wheel. He moved the van to a parking space near the front. When the guard came around the building again, the van was gone. Do you know anybody with a big silver conversion van?"

Oh, man . . .

"Obviously you do."

"I didn't say that. Was this nurse sure it was my father?"

"Positive. She'd worked with him for fifteen years at St. Catherine's Hospital in Natchez."

I shake my head as though confused, but all I'm thinking is, *What the hell are Walt and Dad trying to accomplish?* "Have you told anyone else about this?"

"No, but it won't stay secret long. Nurses talk. And don't bother trying your dad's cell phone. He's shut it off. Whoever owns that van is giving him good advice."

Thank you, Walt. A low-grade panic has begun to build in my chest. To distract Kaiser, I say, "You know you're about forty years late, if you're here to solve the murders of Jimmy Revels and Luther Davis."

"Better late than never."

"According to Henry, the Bureau hasn't even classified their disappearances as murders."

Kaiser's eyes look somber. "Henry's been holding back a lot from the Bureau. I don't blame him. We didn't give these victims much respect back in the day. Some shine got burned to death in Armpit, Louisiana? If Bobby Kennedy wasn't calling Hoover about it every day, he didn't want to know."

The mention of Bobby Kennedy makes me think of Brody Royal. "Your agency has had a lot of years to make up for that, and it chose not to."

"I know it." Kaiser reaches into his inside coat pocket and takes out a yellowed piece of paper. It looks like an old typed letter, folded twice to fit into an envelope, then once again to fit into a pocket. He hands it to me, and on its face I find three typed sentences:

> *To Mr. J. Edgar Hover,*
> *It was July 18, 1964 on a hot night about eleven o'clock the KKK burned down Albert Norris store and him with it, as of now we have not hear what happen to the hill. Is it possible these men are going to get away with this act without being exposed, even though the police was apart of the gang that permitted this terrible thing to happen. Your office is our only hope so don't fail us.*
>
> *The Colored People of Concordia Parish*

"That came in to Bureau headquarters in Washington five months after Norris was murdered," Kaiser informs me. "I still haven't found out who wrote it. Did you see the bottom of the page?"

Beneath my thumb, scrawled in blue ink, are the letters: *J. E. Hoover.*

"Hoover read that letter," Kaiser says. "He initialed it himself. But he didn't give those people what they deserved. He poured his resources into Neshoba County, the case that would make the Bureau's reputation against the Klan. But I intend to make up for that failure. I'm going to finish what Dwight Stone started back in sixty-eight. We owe it to the families. Not only the families of the victims, but also of the agents who served down here. A lot of them have died already, but there are some left."

No one could deny the fierce resolve in John Kaiser's eyes. "How do you plan to do that?" I ask, passing the letter back to him.

"By busting every Double Eagle still walking this earth. I don't give a shit how old they are. I want life sentences for every last one of them. And I'm not going to rely on any local juries. I can get them under the conspiracy statutes, and also for domestic terrorism."

"Don't sell local juries short. Even Mississippi juries have been doing the right thing on old civil rights murders lately."

Kaiser takes his cell phone out of his pocket, checks a text message, taps quickly on the keypad, then puts it away. "Almost all of Henry's computers and records were stolen or destroyed last night," he says. "I find it hard to believe that he kept no copies, but that's what he's telling me."

Part of me wants to tell Kaiser that Henry did in fact keep backups, but I'm not about to take that step without consulting Caitlin.

"If Henry *does* have copies," Kaiser goes on, "I need them. And if you know about files or ledgers or anything like that, please don't sit on them in the hope that they'll somehow help your father."

"I don't have anything like that," I tell him, praying that Kaiser hasn't bugged Henry's hospital room.

The FBI agent gives me a long look. "You spent nearly two hours alone with Henry in his newspaper office Monday night. He must have confided quite a bit to you."

"He wanted to help my father, if he could. He told me the Double Eagles had threatened to kill Viola if she ever returned to Natchez. He didn't know why. That's mostly what we covered. Then he played his guitar and we talked about old times."

Kaiser pulls a wry face, but he doesn't press me.

"Let me ask you something," I say, as a wild idea strikes me. "If you're investigating the Double Eagles under the Patriot Act, you must have turned on the Big Ears."

Kaiser looks disingenuous. "What do you mean?"

"I mean you have the NSA monitoring their phones and e-mail. Right?"

The FBI agent sniffs and looks down the shore. "Is there a motive behind that question?"

"Absolutely," I reply in a tone that makes him turn back to me. "What do you know about a man named Brody Royal?"

JORDAN GLASS KNELT IN some dead weeds beside Caitlin and began shooting the workboat with her motor-drive Nikon. She clicked off nine shots, then pointed her lens back the way they had come and framed a shot of Penn talking to her husband.

"Do you know why this is happening?" she asked, framing yet another image. "The draining of this massive hole?"

"Because your husband pushed for it?" Caitlin guessed.

"No. Katrina guilt." Jordan pointed at the semi trucks. "See those pumps over there? They're the biggest mobile pumps in North America. They've been sitting down in New Orleans since the hurricane, when they were used to help drain Orleans Parish after the flood. But take my word for it, nobody could have released them to move up here without very high authority. The FBI couldn't do that."

"Then who?"

"The Bush administration is taking a huge hit for its poor handling of Katrina, especially from the black community. Ergo, they're willing to send these pump trucks up here. Why? To win political points by sparing no expense to solve a decades-old civil rights murder they didn't give a shit about last week."

Caitlin could tell by the passion in Jordan's voice that she was the kind of journalist who got personally involved in the stories she covered. "Well, at least they're here."

"Oh, I agree. I just think it's important to understand the context."

Caitlin could hardly believe she was talking to someone she'd admired since she was thirteen years old. She'd first heard of Jordan Glass when a female reporter at one of her father's papers started waving some pictures around the newsroom where Caitlin was working after school. The photos had been shot in the bush in El Salvador, and the massacre they showed was entirely inappropriate for a thirteen-year-old girl; but just as indelible as the bloody images was the reporter's triumphant tone when she boasted that the photos had been shot by a twenty-three-year-old American woman and former reporter for the *New Orleans Times-Picayune*. Now, twenty-two years later, Caitlin was walking beside that very photographer, only now Glass was forty-five and had a string of prestigious prizes behind her. Glass had been *shot* while doing her work, for God's sake.

"Race politics," Caitlin said. "Even in Natchez, it's the subtext of half the stories my paper covers."

"Sorry if I sound pissy," Jordan said, loudly enough to be heard over the rumbling of the pump trucks. She straightened up. "This isn't how I wanted to spend today and tomorrow."

"No?"

"No. I'm flying to Cuba on Friday to shoot Fidel and Raúl Castro. John and I had planned to spend today and Thursday in our house on Lake Pontchartrain—which we haven't gotten to do since Katrina. That was until your boyfriend—"

"My fiancé," Caitlin corrected, a little defensively.

"Oh. Congratulations. When are you getting married?"

"The wedding was scheduled for next week."

"Was?"

"After this stuff came up with Penn's father, I decided we'd better postpone it. Do you know about the murder charge?"

"John told me."

"We're going to wait until we have a better idea of what's going to happen. Maybe until after the trial. If there is a trial."

Glass stopped walking and looked at Caitlin with disconcerting intensity. "You want some free advice? Don't wait. You never know what's going to happen. How old are you, thirty-two?"

"Thirty-five."

Jordan held Caitlin's eyes for another few seconds, then blinked and looked away. "I'm sorry. It's none of my business."

"It's fine," Caitlin said, starting down the shore of the Jericho Hole again. "I just don't want my wedding tainted by Penn's father being in trouble. Dr. Cage's health is pretty fragile."

A cloud seemed to pass over Glass's face before she started walking again. "Seriously, I'm sorry I was bitching. I just . . . John and I have hardly had any time alone since the storm. I sympathize with Henry, believe me. He's done a lot of work that the Bureau should have done decades ago. But frankly—if you don't mind a little oversharing—I've been trying to get pregnant for the past six months, and this little detour doesn't help."

Caitlin instantly flashed back to her morning pregnancy test.

"I know I'm old," the photographer said, as if to counter silent criticism, "but I was always so—"

"I wasn't thinking that," Caitlin said. "I say go for it. You deserve a family as much as anybody else."

Jordan shrugged. "Yeah, well . . . I'm not home much."

"I know," Caitlin said, too loudly. "I see your credit under pictures from all over the world."

Jordan's eyes revealed a shocking vulnerability. "Oh, I lead the glamorous life. A month ago, Angelina Jolie asked how I'd feel about her playing me in a film. It's surreal." She looked at the ground and shook her head sadly. "Why does a woman who's adopting babies left and right want to play a childless woman?" The photographer grimaced, then looked up at Caitlin. "I'm *so* ready to spend some time around joy and innocence instead of pain and death. I let John hire me as a contract photographer for this expedition so we could be together for these two days, but it sucks. He won't even sleep for the next two days, much less take time for me."

"Why is he so gung ho about this case?"

Glass panned her gaze across the horizon, as if searching for new perspectives. "John's very tight with an old-time FBI agent named Dwight Stone. These cold cases from the Ku Klux Klan days are like a holy quest for them."

"I know Dwight," Caitlin said with a touch of pride. "I met him on—"

"The Del Payton case," Glass finished. "I know about that. And I know about your Pulitzer. Good work, by the way. I read your Payton stories last night in the hotel, on the Internet."

Caitlin felt the way she did after being given a blast of nitrous oxide at her dentist's office. She wanted to say thank you, but she found herself strangely tongue-tied by Glass's praise. She was almost never starstruck, but years of hero worship couldn't be easily hidden.

With a fluid motion Glass raised her camera and shot a photo of a mallard coming in low for a shallow landing on the water. "What's it like being with a politician?"

"*Penn?* He's no politician."

"He's not?"

Caitlin laughed. "He's a crusading lawyer with a savior complex. And a part-time novelist. Deep down, he's just a boy who wants to save his hometown."

Jordan smiled at Caitlin's candor. "Can it be saved?"

Caitlin shrugged. "I didn't think so, once. But now I think maybe it can. I've promised to try to help him."

"Good for you." Jordan let her camera rest against her chest. "But if a crusading lawyer with a savior complex is anything like a crusading FBI agent with one, I don't envy you. At least you can work alongside Penn. That's something I really can't do, except by little charades like this one."

Caitlin tried an encouraging smile but felt as though she'd failed.

"I guess you ought to call me Jordan," said Glass. "After my over-share back there."

Caitlin laughed with relief. "Don't worry about it."

"I spent some time on Nexis last night. I couldn't find any *Examiner* stories about the murders Henry has been covering."

"These old cases have been Henry's private preserve, so to speak," Caitlin said, reddening with embarrassment. "But I actually hired Henry yesterday. He was supposed to start writing for me today. But then . . . last night happened."

"So what are you going to do?"

Usually very close with information, Caitlin felt a powerful urge to confide in her childhood hero. Surely Jordan Glass would have sage advice for her. And yet . . . could she trust Jordan not to reveal the conversation to her husband?

"Do you always tell your husband everything about your work?"

Jordan smiled. "No, ma'am. I do not."

"Does he think you do?"

"He pretends to think that."

It was Caitlin's turn to smile. "Does he tell you everything?"

Glass shook her head. "If John told me everything he knows, he could be charged with treason."

"I see. Penn and I operate by a similar set of rules. We keep our two careers as separate as possible."

"Yet you're both here today."

"More separate than together today, to be honest. And we'll split up as soon as we get back to the hospital."

"Which brings me back to my question. What are you going to do now? Pick up where Henry Sexton left off?"

You bet your ass I am. "Isn't that what you'd do?"

"Hell, yes. And I'll tell you something else. I'd rather help you do that than sit around here taking pictures of these guys waiting for a lake to be pumped dry."

Caitlin wondered if her suspicion showed on her face. After several seconds, she made a silent decision. "Tell you what. If you get too bored, and you're still in town tomorrow morning, come see me at the *Examiner*. I could use a world-class combat photographer."

Glass raised an eyebrow. "Are you expecting a war?"

Caitlin saw no reason to hide the anger that was driving her. "Starting one, if nobody manages to stop me."

"What about this afternoon? I could get free for a couple of hours."

Caitlin wondered for a moment if John Kaiser had encouraged his wife to spy on her. But when Caitlin shook her head, it was with genuine regret. "No, I'm sorry. This afternoon I have to work alone."

Jordan nodded, a knowing look in her eyes. "Good for you."

TO MY SURPRISE, JOHN Kaiser has no knowledge of Brody Royal's involvement with the Double Eagles. He knows Royal is a player in the New Orleans real estate market, and that he had ties with Carlos Marcello long ago. He's also aware that two federal witnesses disappeared before they could testify against Royal and his son-in-law in the state insurance fraud case. But beyond this, he seems to know little.

"Last night you mentioned major 1960s assassinations on the telephone," he says. "I did some digging, but I couldn't find any connection between Royal and extreme politics. There was some talk that he might have contributed to the anti-Castro cause back in the day, but that was it."

"I'm not sure Brody's motive was political. But it's not the assassinations I'm worried about right now. It's Viola Turner. I think Royal was behind her death."

Kaiser's skepticism is plain. "Why on earth would he want that woman dead? Dwight and the other agents who worked this area in the sixties never mentioned Royal to me. What do you have on him?"

"I'd rather not answer that just yet. But if you grant me a favor, you may well find most of your work done without lifting another finger."

Now Kaiser looks suspicious. "This must be some favor you want."

"It is. I want you to extend your digital surveillance to include Royal and his right-hand man, Randall Regan. Regan is married to Royal's daughter."

Kaiser runs his tongue around the inside of his cheek. "And why would I do that?"

"Because if you do, within twenty-four hours, you may have proof that Royal ordered the deaths of Albert Norris, Pooky Wilson, Jimmy Revels, Luther Davis, and Dr. Leland Robb. Eventually, you'll find out he was behind the deaths of those two federal witnesses as well."

Kaiser's eyes have gone wide. "You and I obviously need to have a long talk."

I shake my head. "Not yet. I've got things to do. But if you do this for me, we'll have our talk."

He weighs my proposition in silence. Then he says, "There's no evidence suggesting Brody Royal was ever a Double Eagle. How can I justify including him in the surveillance?"

"You said you're operating under the Patriot Act. Don't I count as a reliable informant? I just told you the son of a bitch was the real power behind the Double Eagles during the sixties. That's probable cause, if you really need it. From what I understand, you guys have been playing pretty fast and loose with National Security Letters."

The FBI agent's face hardens.

"Come on, John. Just put the Big Ears on those two bastards. The end will justify the means, I guarantee it."

Kaiser is a tough sell. "What are you really up to, Mayor? Are you trying to use the FBI to prove your father's innocence?"

"If I'm right, that'll be a by-product of your surveillance. But everything I told you is true. If you really want to bring peace to the families of all those dead boys, then turn the NSA loose on Royal and his attack dog."

Kaiser takes a deep breath, then sighs. "What are you going to do while I do that?"

"Poke a stick in the rattlesnake hole. Just like you."

"Why does that scare me?"

"It shouldn't, if you're being honest about your motives. I've told you mine. If my dad has really jumped bail, he could be killed at any moment by an overzealous cop. I've got to move fast to help him."

Kaiser blows out a rush of air like a man getting ready to make a high dive. "If I found your father first, I could protect him as a federal witness."

A tingle runs down my back.

"If you tell me who owns that silver van," he adds, "I could find him pretty quick."

Walt Garrity's name is pushing its way up my throat, but I force it back down. I can't afford to trust Kaiser until he proves himself. After a moment's hesitation, I shake my head. "I'll see what I can find out. Meanwhile, will you promise me one thing? If your people locate my dad, will you call me before anyone else? Especially the state police?"

Kaiser's sudden squint tells me my last question hit a nerve, but he doesn't offer any explanation. "So long as you warn me before you do anything that might disrupt my investigation. I'm no fan of local politicos who use their power to settle personal scores."

"Thanks, John."

The FBI agent stands and offers me his hand. "Let's go get the girls."

I shake his hand, and we start back toward the FBI vehicles. Before we've taken ten steps, a rush of anticipation floods through me. Thanks to Kaiser's link to the NSA, my plan to shake the tree in the Royal camp is back on.

"How soon can you be monitoring Royal and Regan?" I ask.

"One phone call. I'll make it now, if you like."

"Please."

He takes out his cell phone and speed-dials a number. I need to find Randall Regan, fast. As we trudge through the mud beside the disappearing Jericho Hole, Kaiser begins talking, and the rhythmic pounding of the colossal pumps reverberates through the earth like a great beating heart.

CHAPTER 66

TWENTY MINUTES AFTER Forrest Knox and Alphonse Ozan left the Yacht Club, a Eurocopter AS350 from the state police Air Support Unit set down at Lakefront Airport and took the CIB chief and his adjutant into its belly. Then the chopper lifted off and stormed up the Mississippi River with Forrest sitting in the left seat and Alphonse Ozan behind him. Knox and Ozan were linked by a special interphone circuit that could exclude the pilot at the touch of a button, and Forrest had made liberal use of this convenience on the way up. Ozan had already learned that a "silver RV-style van" had been seen near Sonny Thornfield's fishing camp last night, shortly before Trooper Dunn requested a position trace on Sonny's cell phone.

The Roadtrek van was almost certainly the 2005 Anniversary Edition registered to one Walter Garrity, a retired Texas Ranger and former combat medic who'd served in the same unit as Tom Cage during the Korean War. According to state police records, two months ago Garrity had assisted Penn Cage in his battle to break up a gambling and dogfighting operation in Adams County and Concordia Parish. Garrity's name had appeared in several LSP reports at the time, and Forrest figured Colonel Mackiever—himself a former Ranger—probably knew Garrity, even if they weren't personal friends. While some men in Forrest's position might consider this possible connection a problem, Forrest was elated. If a friend of his boss had helped someone jump bail and killed a state trooper, that was bound to offer some unique opportunities.

"Excuse me, Colonel," said the pilot, breaking into Forrest's circuit. "I think I see the cruiser."

Forrest followed the line of the levee with his eyes until he saw what the pilot did. Two SUVs with light bars were parked fifty yards from the borrow pit, while a white state police car with its trunk open stood much nearer to the water.

"Who the hell told the locals about this?" Forrest snapped.

"Some fisherman probably drove up on the scene," said Ozan. "Hell, it's their parish."

"They'd better keep that crime scene pristine!"

"Set her down between those sheriff's cars and our cruiser," Forrest ordered the pilot.

"Yes, sir. I think I see the body. Between the cruiser and the water."

Sure enough, a man in a blue uniform lay sprawled across some muddy sand near a patch of weeds. From eight hundred feet, he looked like a G.I. Joe doll cast aside by a bored little boy. But he wasn't. He was Deke Dunn.

"Take us in, Sergeant. Double quick."

"Yes, sir. Hold on."

THE FEMALE LOAN OFFICER who escorted Caitlin into the vault of the Royal Cotton Bank was far too curious for her taste. She was only allowing Caitlin access to the boxes because she was a personal friend of Sherry Harden, who was on the access list. The waspish loan officer had treated Caitlin with marked coolness in the lobby, probably because of the generally liberal columns she wrote for the *Examiner*. Caitlin didn't care what the nosy bitch thought about her. It had nauseated her even to enter a building owned by Brody Royal, though she appreciated the irony of Henry keeping his backup files in a bank belonging to the man he meant to destroy with them.

"I hate to be rude," Caitlin said, after the woman had inserted her keys into the large drawers, "but I need some privacy."

The loan officer stepped back as though Caitlin had slapped her. "We have a room for that."

"Look, I'm really in a hurry."

After giving a prim shake of the head, the loan officer angrily left the vault.

Caitlin crouched before the two numbered drawers, her heart accelerating. She'd expected regular bank boxes, but both these drawers were triple size. She turned the nearest key, then with some effort dragged open the stainless steel drawer.

A warm glow spread through her chest. There had to be three or four thousand photocopied pages stuffed into the drawer. As quickly as she could, she unlocked the adjacent drawer and gasped when she saw what was inside: several external hard drives; a Ziploc bag containing thumb drives and SD cards; and perhaps most intriguing, a stack of Moleskine notebooks held together by a thick blue rubber band.

"I think I just had an orgasm," she murmured. There was no way she and her team could wade through all this in time to write any sort of comprehensive story by tomorrow. Simply scanning the documents would take days.

She got to her feet and hurried back to the bank's lobby. Sighting the loan officer across the room, Caitlin beckoned her over with an urgent wave. The woman took her sweet time about coming, but when she finally arrived, Caitlin said, "I'm going to need some boxes and a cart."

"We don't provide boxes."

"How about garbage bags, then? I'll pay you for them. But I know you've got a cart somewhere, and I need it ASAP."

She turned on her heel and went back to the vault without waiting for an answer. Then she knelt beside the first drawer and began stacking files beside her on the floor, her nerves singing with anticipation.

FORREST KNOX TOOK A last look at the bullet holes in Deke Dunn's face, then got to his feet and addressed Ozan.

"Small caliber. Didn't even exit the skull. I'm betting a .22 derringer."

The Redbone nodded. "Dunn fired a single round from his weapon. I wonder if he hit either of them."

"And who shot first?" Forrest worked his lower lip around a plug of Copenhagen. "Not that it matters. I can't figure them leaving Deke's gun here. That's damned odd."

He looked over Ozan's shoulder, past the chopper with its spinning rotors, at the three Concordia Parish deputies he'd ordered away from the body.

Ozan said, "The records in that *Magnolia Queen* case say Penn Cage killed the Irish casino manager with a derringer. The weapon was lost in the river, but it belonged to Garrity. You figure the old man replaced it?"

"Everybody's got a favorite gun. Garrity probably likes his ace in the hole. Get somebody to look back through his Ranger reports. I think Garrity must be making the decisions. Dr. Cage wouldn't know how to blast the hard drive of the cruiser's video recorder."

"True dat, boss. But why didn't Deke call one of us?"

"My Al Qaeda order," Forrest said. "If I'd waited one more hour to issue it, he probably would have called you. But he observed radio silence, like a good soldier. Let's get photos and casts of the tire tracks by the water. Footprints, too."

"Have the locals do it?" Ozan asked. "Or wait on our evidence team?"

"I don't want a parish deputy anywhere near this scene." Forrest spat beside Dunn's corpse. "I'm going to put out an APB for Cage and Garrity: wanted for killing a state trooper."

Ozan whistled. "What evidence you gonna hang it on?"

"Sonny Thornfield. We'll keep his name out of the media, just refer to him as a confidential informant. But I'm going to tell Mackiever the truth. Cage and Garrity kidnapped an old Klansman and tried to frame him for Viola Turner's murder. He can choke on that. We can bolster the APB with the van sighting, and as soon as we confirm the derringer, we'll update the bulletin. Every cop in Louisiana will be shooting to kill."

The Redbone nodded with admiration.

Forrest stepped away from the body and glared at the deputies staring in their direction. "What we need now is some pressure points, in case something unexpected happens. I already know about Cage's family. What about Garrity?"

"He's got a Mexican wife in Navasota." Ozan grinned. "Dry as an old boot, probably, but I imagine she bleeds like any other woman."

"Make some calls. Before we get back in the chopper."

"Will do, boss."

CHAPTER 67

I'M SITTING IN my Audi outside the Kuntry Kafé, an old-time diner not far from the music store where Henry and I met Kirk Boisseau after he discovered the bones in the Jericho Hole. Three minutes ago, Randall Regan walked inside alone to eat lunch. As I got up to follow him, I saw through the window that he'd sat down with an attractive woman thirty years his junior, a woman most definitely not his wife. I know from Caitlin's research that Katy Royal Regan is fifty-nine. The girl laughing with Randall inside is barely thirty. *His mistress? A casual conquest? Or an innocent flirtation?* The diner is nearly full, yet Regan obviously has no qualms about eating with an attractive young lady, even though he's married to Brody Royal's daughter.

For a few seconds I consider waiting for a better opportunity to confront him. But the sooner I rattle the son of a bitch, the sooner he and Brody are liable to say something incriminating on the telephone (or via e-mail or text). After a brief argument with myself, I put my .357 in the glove compartment, lock my car, and walk into the Kuntry Kafé, my entry announced by Christmas bells hanging from the door.

Several people recognize me, and wave, but I walk straight to Regan's table and sit in one of the two empty chairs. Regan gives me a mildly curious look, but the young woman appears shaken. She looks anxiously at Randall, but he seems content to wait and see what I intend to do.

"I know you," she says, peering closer at me. "You're the . . . the mayor of Natchez."

I give her a politician's smile. "That's right. And everybody else in here is figuring out the same thing about now. They're all staring at us, and trying to figure out who you are, and why you're eating with Randall here."

She looks around at the watchful crowd, then back at Regan, who tilts his head toward the door. Blushing red, she grabs her purse and bolts without a word. Randall chuckles, then gives the crowd a hard look, one face at a time, and they go back to their meals.

Pithy Nolan described him as Black Irish, and as usual, she was right. Regan's eyes are dark and fey, his nose an off-center testament to the risks of boxing (or street fighting), and his curly black hair lined with silver. Rangy and rawboned, he looks like he's done enough manual labor to make him harder than most athletes ever get. If a weight lifter challenged him to an arm-wrestling contest, he'd probably snap the man's wrist just for spite.

Since Regan shows no inclination to question my sudden appearance, I simply start talking. After all, my purpose is to rattle the man into panicking, not to have a conversation with him. I speak just below conversational volume, softly enough that the people at the nearest tables can't hear exactly what I'm saying, but not whispering, either. I start out by describing the murder of the two Royal Insurance employees at the hunting camp in South Louisiana, using every vivid detail Glenn Morehouse provided to Henry. Then I give Regan a devastatingly accurate summary of Brody Royal's involvement in the murders of Albert Norris, Pooky Wilson, Jimmy Revels, Luther Davis, and Leland Robb. To my surprise, the man doesn't say a word during my monologue. Nor does he get up and walk away.

I've had conversations like this before, usually during interrogations of hardened criminals. They'd sit and smoke, or pick their noses, or just give me what they thought was a thousand-yard stare. Eventually most of them broke down, once I found the right psychological lever. But Randall Regan is different. He doesn't try to intimidate me like most hardasses would. He tucks into his country-fried steak as though I'm some traveling salesman who happened to sit down in the last available seat, and he's content to endure my patter, like a plowing farmer must endure the rain.

Despite his apparent nonchalance, the one or two times he does meet my gaze, I realize he's got some of the coldest eyes I've ever come across. Recalling Morehouse's tale of this man who forced one woman to kill her coworker, then raped her and ordered her death, I lose track of my words for a second. Into this gap rushes an image of my father and Walt Garrity running for their lives from men like Randall Regan.

Banishing that nightmare, I push on, exercising my practiced prosecutor's gift for detail. When I finally stop talking, Regan wipes his mouth with his napkin, takes out his wallet, leaves a ten-dollar bill on the table, then tosses his head once and walks out the front door.

I've seen that casual toss of the head countless times in my life, usually under friendly circumstances. It generally means "Be seein' you." Today it means the same thing, but the context isn't friendly at all.

As Regan's V-shaped back disappears through the door, the obvious reality finally breaks through the daze that Walker's news knocked me into: *Regan assumed I was wearing a wire. That's why he didn't speak to me.* If I had been wearing one, anyone listening to the recording would have concluded that I'd sat in the diner and talked to myself for ten minutes. Still, I reflect, that doesn't mean my plan didn't work.

"Randy left already?" asks the waitress, startling me.

"Yes."

"Well, dern. He usually orders dessert. I've got it right here."

She lowers a saucer with a slice of chocolate pie on it. "You want it instead?"

"No, thank you."

As she walks away, I go to the restroom to get some privacy. I don't fancy walking out into the parking lot until I know Regan is gone. Once inside, I sit on the edge of the sink and call John Kaiser's cell phone. He answers immediately.

"Get ready," I tell him. "I think the music's about to start."

"What did you do?"

"Poked a stick in the rattlesnake's hole."

Kaiser is quiet for too long. "You haven't heard, have you?"

"Heard what?"

"Penn, there's no good way to tell you this. A few minutes ago the Louisiana State Police sent a flash APB across five states for Thomas Jefferson Cage, M.D., and Walter Roark Garrity, a retired Texas Ranger. They're wanted in connection with the murder of Trooper Darrell Deke Dunn, who was shot and killed last night near the borrow pits in rural Concordia Parish."

As I sit dumbstruck on the sink, my head roars as though I'm standing in the middle of a highway. I feel like someone just told me that a friend of mine ran over a child in the street and fled the scene. Life will never be the same.

"The bulletin says both fugitives are known to be proficient with firearms and should be considered armed and dangerous. Penn? Are you there?"

"Yeah," I manage to grunt. "What else can you tell me?"

"Forrest Knox visited the crime scene in a helicopter a little while ago. He issued the APB himself, and there's not a chance in hell of getting it recalled. I'm sorry. I know this is tough, on top of everything else."

"John, what the hell is going on? There's no way my dad killed a cop."

"What about Garrity?"

The time it takes me to ponder this possibility tells Kaiser all he needs to know.

"John, it doesn't matter if they did it or not. When an alert goes out for a cop killer, it's open season. Every cop within five hundred square miles will be looking to shoot them on sight."

"I know. The only good news is that your father seems to have dropped off the face of the earth, right along with Captain Garrity. My advice is, put on your thinking cap and try to figure where he'd go to ground with his life on the line. Nobody knows him better than you, right?"

I shake my head, not sure of this at all.

"I'll let you know if I hear anything else," Kaiser promises. "And I'll be monitoring Royal's and Regan's communications for you."

I almost laugh at this. "Like it matters at this point? After what you told me, who killed Viola Turner rates about a two on a one-to-ten scale. At this point I'd be happy to have Dad on trial for murder. At least he'd stand a decent chance of surviving."

"You work on finding him, Penn. I'll work on a way to take him into federal custody."

My heart leaps. "Will you really?"

"I don't think Dr. Cage will survive an encounter with Forrest Knox's troops, even if he gives himself up with his hands over his head."

"Thank you, John."

"Keep your head high, man. I know who the good guys are."

As I press END, my eyes well with hot tears, and my throat spasms shut. Never have I felt so angry or impotent or cut off from my family.

Two minutes ago, I was trying to save my father by solving a murder mystery. Now I'll be lucky if I can keep him alive long enough to go to prison.

My bladder, which felt like stone as I talked to Kaiser, suddenly ambushes me with a desperate need to pee. Stepping up to the urinal on the wall, I see a piece of duct tape stretched across it. A handwritten sign reads: BROKEN! USE THE STALL!

Pushing open the stall door, I unzip and stand over the commode, but despite my urgency, nothing comes. My heart is pounding, and sweat has broken out on my face and neck. Did the news of the APB cause this? Or did it begin during my confrontation with Royal's son-in-law? Though Regan didn't say one word throughout, he made it clear that a state of war now exists between us. Just as my urine starts to flow, the restroom door opens.

"It's a one-holer today!" I call. "I'll be out in a second."

"No problem," says an amicable voice.

While I strain to empty my bladder, the stall door crashes against my back, knocking me into the wall and spraying piss all over me. An arm like an iron bar locks around my neck and bends my spine back over what must be a knee, pulling me into an agonizing bow. A blast of air bursts from my diaphragm, but the choke hold traps it in my throat. I can neither speak nor breathe. While I try in vain to free myself, a big hand gropes me from armpits to ankles, not missing any place where I could conceal a weapon or a wire.

My vision's going black. The hold loosens slightly. When the voice speaks again, it's a savage rasp in my right ear, the mouth so close I feel its heat and moisture.

"You think you're smart, don't you? Well, you've got a lot to learn, Mayor. You think you saw some shit over in Houston? Well, you didn't. That's bush league over there, and you're about to find it out."

Steeling my muscles, I try to hurl us both away from the wall, but Regan has such a bind on me that I can't muster sufficient leverage. His knee digs deeper into my spine, which feels on the verge of snapping. Laughing, he lowers his voice to an intimate whisper.

"Everything you said out there," he hisses, *"you got from Glenn Morehouse, and that fat-ass is dead as a hammer. All you did today is guarantee your little girl's gonna grow up an orphan—if she makes it herself. Your old*

man's as good as dead already, and you're next. It won't be quick, either, I promise you that. It'll be more pain than you think a human body can stand. I've had a lot of practice killing slow. You'll beg me to finish you." Again the knee digs into my spine. *"And after I'm done? I'm gonna send your little girl the pictures. How does that sound, Mayor?"*

He wrenches my neck backward, and something pops near the middle of my spine. Then he lets me fall and backs out of the stall.

I clutch the toilet paper dispenser to stay erect, and it's all I can do to keep from collapsing over the commode.

Regan grabs a handful of paper towels and throws them at me, laughing. "You pissed yourself, Mayor. Better clean up before you go out there to your adoring fans."

Gripping the top of one of the stall walls, I manage to pull myself to a standing position. Regan watches me with animal curiosity, his wild eyes showing genuine pleasure. His blitz attack scrambled my higher thought processes, but my lower brain functions are still active. Fight-or-flee chemicals course through me like amphetamines, and Regan has barred the way to flight. As I stand paralyzed, the atavistic core of my being speaks in the voice of my old friend Daniel Kelly.

When it's life or death, forget the eyes, the balls, and all the rest of that crap they teach women. When it counts, there's only one target—

Knowing I must draw Regan closer, I begin to laugh. First a chuckle, then a snigger that grows into a hysterical cackle, like something out of a horror movie.

"What the fuck you laughing at?" he growls, obviously annoyed. *"Freak.* I think your damn egg got shook."

My brittle laughter bounces off the mirror, filling the little room. "You'd better get moving. The FBI's got everything you just said. You should have left while you were ahead."

Regan's eyes narrow. He steps forward as though to give me another blow.

"You missed the wire, Randall. The Bureau's got a whole new bag of tricks since Nine-Eleven. You couldn't find this bug in a week. They call it the 'tick.' "

He lunges forward, meaning to strip-search me, but as his right hand comes up, I drive my fist deep beneath his chin, hard into his Adam's apple. Nothing cracks, but Regan reels backward, both hands flying to his throat. His eyes bulge when he hits the wall, and his mouth gapes while he slides down it. With one blow I've scrambled his cerebral cortex, as he did mine. Desperately clutching his throat, he sits heavily on the floor, looking like nothing so much as an actor trying to panto-mime choking to death.

Strangely, my lawyer's mind tallies up the charges this assault could expose me to, up to and including murder. But I'm not a lawyer now. I'm a father. A father and a son. Randall Regan threatened my family, and he meant what he said. He assaulted me first. For a couple of sec-onds I consider calling 911, but that would trigger too many questions. Besides, if his larynx is just bruised, and he lives, I want him out on the street calling his father-in-law, not stuck in a police station explaining this fight to local cops.

A high-pitched wheeze tells me that at least some oxygen is reach-ing his lungs, and therefore his brain. Otherwise he'd already be blue. Though it costs me blinding back pain, I kneel in front of him and speak close to his ear, as he did in mine.

"Don't make the mistake of thinking you're dealing with a lawyer, Randall. Or a mayor, or a writer. If you ever come near me or my fam-ily, I'll kill you. And if you kill me first, then a friend of mine will square it. He eats assholes like you for breakfast, and he'll square it if it takes ten years. You hear me?"

Regan still can't speak.

Using the sink, I pull myself back to my feet, then walk out of the restroom and make my way through the close-packed tables to the door. Our waitress gives me a puzzled wave, and I wave back. Then I'm out in the cold wind and winter sun.

I doubt Regan is even off the bathroom floor yet, but just in case, I climb straight into my car, back up, and pull onto Carter Street, heading for the Natchez bridge. I was damned lucky back there. Regan thought he'd hurt me too badly to retaliate against him. I only pray that in the next hour or so, he and Brody Royal say enough on their phones to allow Kaiser to arrest them. Because if they don't, he's going to come after me. And the friend I warned him about is seven thousand miles away, in Afghanistan.

CHAPTER 68

"I TOLD YOU we should have killed that son of a bitch last night," Walt Garrity growled. "He was dying anyway. Now every cop in five states is hunting us."

The Ranger sat in a leather chair in the den of Drew Elliott's lake house, pecking irritably on a laptop he'd found on Drew's desk. Tom lay on the nearby sofa, trying not to bitch about Walt's steady typing. The only illumination in the room came from an overhead lamp. They had closed all the curtains to prevent anyone from seeing movement inside the house. Tom wasn't much in the mood to talk. Walt had doled out three Lorcet today, and the hydrocodone had quieted his pain for a while, but now his shoulder throbbed relentlessly.

"We did the right thing about Thornfield," he repeated, recalling the terror in the old Klansman's eyes as he realized he was having a heart attack—a terror Tom had experienced firsthand.

"He might have seen me shoot that trooper," Walt said. "Not that it matters. All he has to do is put us at the scene and tell what we did to him."

Walt looked over at the kitchen counter, where he'd rigged his police scanner to the battery he'd brought in from the van last night. This time the cop chatter was about something besides the APB, for a change.

"I'm sorry, Walt," Tom said for the twentieth time. "I should never have called you to help me with this. I realize that now."

The Ranger gave a sullen grunt. "Who else could you call? We need to get some more burn phones. Maybe Melba will take Dr. Elliott's truck to the Ferriday Walmart and buy us a handful."

Having tended Tom's wound throughout the night, Melba Price was napping in the back bedroom of the lake house.

"Calling Mackiever was a big risk," Walt said, "but I'm glad I did it. If we'd left this house not knowing about that, we'd likely be dead already."

A half hour ago, Walt had used his last TracFone to call the superintendent of the Louisiana State Police. Griffith Mackiever had served in the Texas Rangers early in his career and knew Walt personally. Walt believed there was no way Colonel Mackiever would knowingly tolerate a crook like Forrest Knox as the chief of his Criminal Investigations Bureau, but whatever the truth of that, they had little choice if they hoped to find a way out of the mess they'd created last night. A simple ruse had gotten Walt past Mackiever's receptionist, but as soon as his old comrade in arms learned who the caller was, he'd told Walt about the APB, then given him a different number to call in two hours.

"I can't see a damned thing anymore," Walt complained, squinting at the computer keys.

"What are you trying to find out?" Tom asked, as Walt stabbed angrily at the keyboard.

"I sent a text message to Carmelita over the Internet. Once she gets it, she's supposed to log on to a chat site on a special Hotmail account. That's the only secure way I can talk to her."

Walt's voice told Tom he was worried about his wife. Carmelita Cruz had come along late in Walt's life, and maybe for that reason he treasured her more than the women he'd known as a younger man. Of Mexican descent, Carmelita was twenty years his junior, but Walt claimed she ran the roost back in Navasota, refusing to put up with any of his "bachelor ways." She had adult children of her own in Mexico, but she'd become an American citizen two years ago, after steadfastly refusing to marry Walt to get her green card.

"Here she is!" Walt said with relief. "Wait—oh, no."

Tom's heart thumped at the fear in Walt's voice. "What is it?"

"Something happened a little while ago. Hang on."

"Tell me, Walt."

Walt began typing with desperate intensity. "Somebody slipped a manila folder under our door. Photographs of a family that had been murdered. Their heads had been cut off. Goddamn it. That's Mexican cartel bullshit."

"This happened because of us? You think the Double Eagles got someone to Navasota that fast?"

"Distance doesn't mean anything these days. Forrest Knox probably has contacts all over the South. Convicts, cops, Border Patrol guys."

Tom rose painfully into a sitting position, his shoulder screaming. "Take Drew's pickup and go to her, Walt. Right now. Didn't he say the keys are in the bathroom? Top of the medicine cabinet."

Walt stopped typing and turned to him. "She's too far away to help that way. Seven hours, at least. They could take her and do whatever they want before I even got to Monroe. Besides, the whole reason they did this was to separate me from you."

"Well, they used the right tactic. There's no way you're sticking with me while Carmelita's in danger. I won't let you. I'll be fine on my own, and I've got Melba to tend my wound."

Walt's furrowed face was set with anger. "How long do you think the two of you could last here? They'd find you sooner or later. The police or Knox's men, don't matter which."

"What else can you do but go to her?"

Walt worked his mouth around as though he were chewing tobacco. "When you Rangered as long as I did, you get pretty tight with the boys you work with. I think that's something Mr. Knox ain't countin' on."

"Do you know anybody close enough to get to Carmelita fast?"

After one brief nod, Walt went back to typing. "I've got a Ranger buddy who lives four miles outside of town. Still fish with him now and then. Got two more within fifty miles. Carmelita already called 911 and reported a prowler. And she's got her own gun in the house, of course. Plus my collection."

"Are all these friends retired Rangers?"

"Yep. And they've forgotten more about gunplay than most men will ever know."

Tom tried to gauge whether Walt was as optimistic as he sounded, or whether he was just trying to keep his wounded friend calm. Tom couldn't help but recall the motto Walt had always quoted with mild sarcasm.

"One riot, one Ranger?" he said.

Walt's lips barely cracked in acknowledgment. "I've told you that's practically an inside joke. But three Rangers can sling a lot of lead, and they generally hit what they aim at." He stopped typing and looked over at Tom. "How does that shoulder feel now?"

Tom blinked in surprise. "I don't even feel it."

A fierce grin split Walt's leathery cheeks. "Ain't that always the way?"

CHAPTER 69

SONNY THORNFIELD HAD never been as afraid as when he walked around the side of Snake Knox's house after returning from the hospital. He hadn't been sure whether to lie or to tell the truth, but in the end he decided his best chance of survival was to come clean with his old friend. He'd known Snake for too long to successfully deceive him, and the prospect of lying to Forrest Knox made his bowels squirm. Things seemed to have gone all right, so far. Snake had used some emergency communication system to pass Sonny's story up the chain of command, and the fact that he was still alive was encouraging. But until he knew for sure how Forrest had reacted to the news, Sonny wouldn't take an easy breath. That's what he and Snake were waiting for now.

Snake sat in a green metal lawn chair, chewing Red Man and watching a ring-tailed raccoon stare back at him from a rectangular wire cage. The cage was a live trap, meant to capture varmints so that they could be released into the wild or exterminated at close range. You baited the trap with fish heads, then waited for the greedy coon to walk in and trip the screen, jailing himself. The coon in Snake's trap was a big female, maybe twenty pounds. Sonny could see her quivering with fear and rage. The slightest provocation would send her into a frenzy. Snake picked up an old golf club and tapped the top of the trap with it. The coon flew at the club, claws and teeth bared, screaming and hissing like a demon.

"You little bitch," Snake said, chuckling. "I was gonna pop you with a .22 short and let my neighbor's feist come get you. But you've got a date with destiny. We're going to put on a little show tonight, and you're the star."

Sonny didn't know what Snake was talking about, but he didn't feel confident enough to ask.

"How's your chest feeling?" Snake asked.

"It aches something fierce," Sonny said truthfully, remembering the crazy Texas Ranger who'd threatened him with the blowtorch in the back of the RV.

Snake leaned his rifle against the lawn chair and laughed. "You salty son of a bitch. Walking right out of the hospital!"

Sonny forced himself to laugh despite the pain. "It sounds like something's on for tonight, huh?"

Snake grinned. "Yeah. A nice little op. Billy's left for Toledo Bend already."

A vague answer, at best, but Sonny didn't ask for clarification. Billy Knox owned a luxurious home on Toledo Bend, the vast man-made reservoir that lay on the Louisiana-Texas border. He called it his "fishing camp," but it was nicer than the homes in the most affluent subdivisions of Natchez.

Snake reached into an Igloo and handed Sonny an ice-cold Schaefer. "Yeah, him and Joelle Brennan pulled out before six this morning." Joelle was Billy's latest squeeze; she ran a local health club and was built like a brick shithouse. "You and me can leave as soon as you're feeling steady."

"Are we flying over?"

Snake shook his head. "Drivin'. Flying back, though. Alibi city."

Sonny couldn't begin to fathom this strange arrangement. He looked at the beer, then handed the can back to Snake. "I'd better pass after all the drugs they give me."

Snake downed the Schaefer in five gulps.

"You gonna fly drunk?" Sonny asked.

"Shit. I'm twice the pilot drunk that most men are sober."

Sonny was only making conversation to divert his friend; Snake had walked away from a half-dozen crashes that would have killed less hardy men.

"What gun is that?" Sonny asked, pointing to the rifle leaning against the chair. "That ain't your regular .22, is it?"

Snake gave Sonny an odd leer, then picked up the rifle and ran his fingers down its long barrel and checkered stock. "Something special. For tonight." He held the rifle out to Sonny. "Check it out."

Sonny groaned as he reached for the gun. One of the bruises on his chest was shaped like the heel of a Red Wing boot.

"Never mind," Snake said, noticing his grimace.

"You gonna shoot that damn coon or just torment it some more?"

Snake laughed and looked down at the cage. "I was, but this little lady has a job to do tonight." He touched the trap with the rifle barrel, and the coon went batshit. A blood-chilling scream came from the needle-toothed mouth and pointed snout.

A shiver of foreboding went down Sonny's spine. "Granny always said, if a coon was big as a bear, it'd be the baddest thing on God's earth."

"She was right!" Snake kicked the cage, then whooped when the coon went for his boot. "*Look* at that bitch go. She'd rip my throat out if she could!"

"Run right up your leg," Sonny agreed.

Snake stopped smiling. "Why do you think Dr. Cage and that Ranger didn't kill you last night? That was a hell of a risk, dropping you off at the hospital like that."

A swarm of yellow jackets rose up in Sonny's chest. "The Ranger wanted to. It was Dr. Cage who saved me. He said he couldn't kill a man in cold blood."

Snake shook his head in wonder. "I wish we *could* fly over to Toledo Bend. You oughta rack out in the backseat of the truck while I drive."

Not a chance, Sonny thought, despite his exhaustion. If Forrest decided that last night's events made him a liability, he would never reach Toledo Bend alive. It was even possible that this decision had already been made. Billy Knox was a businessman; sentiment didn't figure into things. And Forrest was like an admiral on a battleship, moving plastic figures around on maps with a stick. To him every soldier under his command was expendable.

Sonny turned at what he thought was the sound of footsteps, and a tall, rangy man in black pants and a high-collared shirt walked around the corner of the house. Sonny was so jumpy that he leaped to his feet, but Snake raised his rifle in greeting. The newcomer was Randall Regan, Brody Royal's right-hand man.

"What are you doing here?" Snake asked.

"Delivering a message," Regan rasped, like a man with laryngitis. "Last night Forrest said no phones, period. And I think ours are being tapped."

"What's wrong with your voice?" Snake asked. "You swallow a wasp or something?"

Regan scowled, then unbuttoned his collar, revealing a nasty reddish-purple bruise that covered his throat.

"What the hell did that?" Snake asked.

"Penn Cage. He braced me in a public restaurant about the Royal Insurance bitches you dumped out in the swamp. He knew every detail. I didn't say a word. But later, he sucker-punched me in the bathroom."

This answer worried Sonny, but Snake started laughing so hard that Regan buttoned his collar again, all the while looking like he wanted to strangle Snake Knox.

Once Snake stopped laughing, he said, "What's your message?"

Regan's reply sounded like the wheeze of a diphtheria patient. "Brody doesn't want you to wait until tonight. He wants it done right now. Or as soon as it can be done. He wants you to get word to Forrest."

"Tell Brody not to worry. Forrest knows what has to be done."

Regan pointed at the cage on the ground. "What the hell are you doing with that thing?"

"You'll find out." Snake chuckled and kicked the trap again. The raccoon went crazy, biting the steel wire in a futile effort to reach her tormentor.

I know how you feel, Sonny thought, touching his chest where the Texas Ranger's boot had driven into his sternum. *Jesus God.*

CHAPTER 70

IN ALL HER life, Caitlin had never felt the kind of journalistic responsibility she did today, nor such frustration. Last night she'd been stunned by the horrific details contained in the single Moleskine notebook she'd found near the burned hulk of the *Concordia Beacon*. But today Henry Sexton had given her the fruits of decades of painstaking investigation into one of the darkest chapters in American history. Whatever it cost in time and money, she meant to vindicate the full measure of Henry's faith. Yet Penn had made that impossible, by insisting that her story must run in tomorrow's newspaper, as Henry had originally intended. Penn's intentions were good—he meant for the story to render physical violence against Caitlin and his family pointless—but the result, she was sure, could only be a journalistic embarrassment.

The sheer volume of Henry's files astounded her. The multiple murder cases were unimaginably complex; the historical context alone would consume all the column inches usually devoted to news stories. Pursuing Penn's plan would be like trying to tackle the Watergate story in a single night. She and her staff might be able to produce a sketch of the Double Eagle group's crimes over the years, but they couldn't possibly explore the larger implications, or the FBI's failure to achieve justice for the victims and their families. Henry Sexton's solitary struggle on behalf of the victims deserved a book in itself. And yet, Caitlin reminded herself, Henry *had* planned to publish one comprehensive story tomorrow, in the interest of his loved ones' safety. Henry's publisher had verified this plan by telephone.

If only Henry's first draft hadn't been destroyed with his computer, she thought.

Never one to shrink from a challenge, Caitlin had brought the full resources of her staff to bear on the problem. They'd begun with brute-force analysis. For the past two hours, five *Examiner* employees had been scanning every scrap of Henry's files into their computer system using high-speed imaging machines. Their goal was to create a searchable database of Henry's archive. From this epic record they would distill the macro story into discrete parts that could be handled by specific reporters. Caitlin would act as editor in chief, and write a master story that functioned as a hub for the others. Some stories would only be published in the *Examiner*'s online edition, and for the first time, stories in the actual paper would carry footnotes directing readers to the website for further detail. Caitlin had another groundbreaking idea, but executing it would require the permission of her father, and he had yet to call her back with an answer.

She took a sip of green tea and went back to her computer display. In studying Henry's files so far, she'd learned three things: Sexton was a gifted investigator, a solid writer, but a twentieth-century organizer. To address the organizational challenge, a Columbia-educated reporter named Donald Pinter had begun creating data maps and spreadsheets containing breakdowns of every major and minor personality related to the 1960s-era murders. Victims were highlighted in blue, Double Eagles and Klansmen in red, and police and FBI informants in orange, which denoted uncertain allegiance. Any local police officer of that era had to be considered potentially corrupt or ideologically loyal to the Ku Klux Klan, while FBI agents could have been motivated more by fear of or loyalty to J. Edgar Hoover than by a sense of justice.

Pinter was also building a master timeline that began with the birth of Albert Norris in 1908 and ran to the present day. Contained within that master line were markers that kicked viewers to "sub-lines" with more detail. The most important of these gave a month-by-month chronology from January 1963 to December 1968. The watershed assassinations bookended this timeline in flaming red—Medgar Evers and John Kennedy at the beginning, Reverend King and Bobby Kennedy at the end—while local race murders were highlighted in dark blue. The simple beatings and "rabbit hunts," as the Klan had called nonlethal attacks, were marked in yellow and dotted the line like a chain of daisies. Pinter had created a digital masterpiece of organization, yet still Caitlin felt overwhelmed by the data. Her personal story notes had already run to fifteen pages, and even her *outline* was already three pages long. In truth, she hadn't been planning a news story, but a comprehensive investigation that would take weeks to accomplish, at the least.

Despite the importance of the historical murders, Caitlin's mind gravitated to Henry's most recent discoveries, detailed in the Moleskine notebook she'd found at the fire. Last night, descriptions of savage beatings, flayings, and a possible crucifixion had still retained the power to shock her. But the sheer weight of the horrors Henry had uncovered had begun to deaden her sensibilities. The same thing could easily happen to the *Examiner*'s readers, so she had to choose her focus carefully. The dozen-odd murders committed by the Double Eagles comprised a diffuse mass of data spanning a decade and involving unknown witnesses who could take years to locate, if they weren't dead already. Nailing a few wrinkled old Klansmen who'd been peddling crystal meth to pay their rent might sell a few newspapers, but it wouldn't win her any prizes. Glenn Morehouse's sickening account of the murder of the whistle-blowers from Royal Insurance was the kind of story that grabbed modern readers by the throat. Further, Brody Royal was about the juiciest target imaginable in terms of a marketable story. If she brought down one of the richest men in the state by tying him to Carlos Marcello and the attempted assassination of Robert Kennedy, the story would break worldwide in a matter of hours.

Caitlin set down her teacup, her heart racing. The last thing she needed now was more caffeine. To nail Brody Royal for murder, she needed one of two things: a witness who could tie him to one of the murders, or a line into his secret life that could yield damning evidence. The only witness she knew about was the one Henry had dubbed "Huggy Bear" in his notebooks—an unidentified black man who had mysteriously appeared at the bedside of Pooky Wilson's dying mother. Yet Henry had committed many hours to finding this man, and he'd failed, even with the advantage of having known many of the boys who'd worked at Albert Norris's store. As for finding a door into Royal's secret life, Caitlin's possible lines of infiltration were few. One was Brody's daughter, Katy Royal Regan, who'd been Pooky Wilson's lover forty years ago. Another was Royal's homicidal son-in-law, who was as likely to rape and kill her as talk to her. And then there was Claude Devereux, Royal's wily old attorney. Caitlin didn't hold out much hope of tricking a lawyer into admitting anything damaging about a client, much less his richest one. The daughter, on the other hand, might make a vulnerable interview subject. Henry had interviewed Katy Royal and come up dry, but then . . . Henry was a man.

Caitlin felt sure she could do better.

The only problem was that after leaving the Jericho Hole, she'd promised Penn not to publish anything about Brody Royal until midnight tonight. She regretted that promise now, but Penn had told her that he and John Kaiser were working together to obtain proof of Royal's involvement in Viola Turner's death. She couldn't very well argue against a strategy that might gain Tom his freedom.

As her mind shifted to thoughts of Tom on the run, someone cleared their throat in her doorway. She looked up and saw Jenna Cross, her personal assistant, looking harried.

"What is it, Jen?"

"Your father's on line two, returning your call."

Caitlin nodded and lifted the landline next to her computer. She often called her father to authorize extra funds for specific stories, and their pattern of negotiation was invariable. John Masters would complain for a while, but in the end he would give his daughter what she wanted. But this time Caitlin's request had been unusual. She'd asked her father to publish tomorrow's Double Eagle stories not only in the *Natchez Examiner,* but in all twenty-six other papers of his chain. Since most Masters papers were based in the Southeast, the public reaction would come like a storm. But Penn's goal of making the story so big that attacking Caitlin or Annie or Peggy would seem pointless would be well and truly accomplished.

"Hello, Daddy. What did you decide?"

Her father's deep chuckle filled the earpiece. "I'll run your story in ten papers."

Caitlin started to argue out of reflex, then reconsidered. "Which ten?"

"The urban markets. Charleston, Wilmington, Savannah, Birmingham, et cetera, down the line."

She closed her eyes and suppressed the impulse to ask for more. Agreeing to run her story in ten papers was an unprecedented concession from her father, whose strategy of expansion had always been based on giving small cities what they wanted: good news rather than strong medicine.

"Thank you, Daddy."

"How much space are these stories going to take up?"

"Pretty much the whole edition here, excepting the sports page."

"You know I can't give you that in the other papers."

"What can you give me? This story's going to go international sixty seconds after we go out with it."

"Three related stories, a total of . . . three thousand words."

This was like a gift from the gods, but still she clenched her jaw and said, "Four."

"Thirty-five hundred, Cait, and that's pushing it."

Caitlin wanted to press him, but she stifled herself. She'd have to be content with adding links to the full suite of stories on the *Examiner*'s Web edition. "Done," she said.

"When will you be finished with these stories?"

She was going to have to lie now and beg forgiveness later. "What's the absolute latest I can get them out?"

"Midnight, if you want them in the other papers. That's nonnegotiable. I can't pay the staffs of ten papers overtime because you're late getting a story in. If you need more time, we can run it day after tomorrow."

"I'd like nothing better. But Penn says no."

"Is Penn making your publishing decisions now?"

She quickly explained her fiancé's theory of achieving security for the family by running the story as soon as possible.

"I agree with Penn," her father said. "You have those stories done by eleven—no ifs, ands, or buts. If you don't, I'll call Penn and have him dictate a story. I'm not suffering through one more night like I did two months ago."

Caitlin closed her eyes and tried to remain in the present. "I'll make the deadline. And you'd better get ready. We're going to have every TV network in the country calling us tomorrow."

"I'll let the other editors know."

Caitlin thanked him again, then hung up and looked at her watch.

It was 4:42 P.M. She had approximately seven hours to produce the stories that would run in the chain's flagship papers tomorrow. Maybe a couple of extra hours to write additional material that would run only in the *Examiner*. That meant she had a decision to make. Would she write those stories based on Henry's work alone? Or would she use part of her time to try to accomplish what Henry Sexton had not?

Seven hours. Fourteen if I'm willing to break a story in the online edition alone. Could brazenness, daring, and insight allow her to crack the most explosive mystery of this complex epic in a single night? An image of Katy Royal Regan rose into her mind—her most promising target of opportunity. But to take that shot, she would have to break her promise to Penn, and possibly damage Tom's chances of a quick dismissal of his case. With a resentful sigh, she got up and closed her door, then picked up Henry Sexton's charred Moleskine and began to reread his most recent entries, hoping to find something she'd missed before.

A hard knocking at her door startled her, and before she could call "Come in," the door opened.

Jamie Lewis came into her office and shut the door behind him. A professional cynic, he rarely delivered news without a smartass remark. But Caitlin could tell by his manner that he had bad news.

"Tell me," she said.

"An APB has gone out for Tom Cage and his friend Walt Garrity. The Louisiana State Police issued it."

Caitlin's palms went cold. "What's it for? Jumping bail?"

"No. Killing a cop. A state trooper."

The blood drained from her face. She waved Jamie out, then grabbed the telephone, all her anger at Penn forgotten.

CHAPTER 71

"THAT'S ALL I can say on the phone," I tell Caitlin, driving down Washington Street toward Edelweiss. "Just keep working on your story, and I'll come to you as soon as I can."

"But Tom—"

"I'm doing the only thing that I think might possibly get Dad to safety. That's really all I can say. I'm checking on Mom and Annie now. Don't leave your office if you can avoid it. Okay?"

"All right. But please come down here as soon as you can."

"I will."

Taking a sharp turn, I pull into the backyard of Edelweiss, which is only accessible by a small opening in the overgrown fence on the Washington Street side. I park behind a small brick outbuilding, trot to the back door of the ground floor, let myself in, then climb the stairs to the main floor.

From the sound, Mom and Annie must be watching TV in the third-floor master suite. When I call up the long staircase, Annie comes to the head of the stairs. I smile and wave to her, but then I hold up my hand and ask her to send her grandmother down. Annie is clearly worried, but I don't want her to see me too closely. A reddish-blue bruise is already spreading around my neck where Randall Regan choked me.

As soon as Mom reaches the bottom of the steep stairs, I walk her into the kitchen. She can tell that something has happened, and suddenly her gaze settles on my neck. Raising my hand to stop her question, I speak in a low voice.

"Mom, you need to brace yourself."

Her right hand flicks out and seizes mine, her eyes wild. "Tom's not dead!"

"No, no. But a Louisiana state trooper was found shot to death this morning, by one of the borrow pits across the river. The state police

have already put out an APB for Dad and Walt Garrity. Every cop in
three states is hunting them now."

My mother's face looks as though it's turned to wax. "But . . . why
would they think Tom would kill a state trooper?"

"You knew Dad was with Walt, didn't you?"

"No! But I'm glad he is. What else do you know?"

"A lot. I just talked to Sheriff Dennis. Basically, all the physical
evidence looks bad for Dad, and the state police have a witness who'll
place both him and Walt at the murder scene. A man named Sonny
Thornfield."

Mom is shaking her head in denial or disbelief.

"Do you have *any* idea what Dad's plan was when he jumped bail?
If you do, tell me now. If I can reach him by phone, I can try to arrange
a surrender to the FBI. One of their agents is willing to protect Dad as a
federal witness. Or to try, anyway."

She stares back at me with a look I recognize from my experience
with the wives and mothers of criminal defendants: uncertainty about
what to say to support the unknown alibi of a loved one.

"Mom, listen to me. There's an officer high up in the LSP who
wants Dad to go down for Viola's murder. He's the son of Frank Knox,
the founder of the Double Eagle group. And the best way he can get the
result he wants is to have Dad shot as a fugitive while resisting arrest."

"Annie's going to come down in a minute," Mom says, looking
bewildered. "She's terrified, Penn."

"I know she must be. Mom, I need you to focus."

She grabs my wrists with surprising strength. "You don't really
think Tom or Walt could have killed a police officer?"

I've been pondering this question from the moment John Kaiser
told me about it. "I'd like to say no, but even an honest cop might have
drawn down on Dad if he saw him as a bail jumper. And if they were
dealing with a dirty cop . . . I can see Walt shooting to protect Dad in
either case."

She sags against the kitchen counter. "Oh, God. This can't be."

I hug her tight against me. "Where would he go, Mom? Who would
he trust with his life on the line?"

"Oh, Lord," she says into my chest. "Tom must have treated ten
thousand people since we moved here. Three-quarters of them would

probably help him if he asked, and ten percent would probably risk their lives for him."

She's right. "That's a thousand places to search, right there."

Her wet face nods against me. "Maybe he wasn't so crazy to run. Maybe he's sure they can't find him."

"But they will, sooner or later. They have too much technology, and the Knox family knows this area like their own backyard."

Her arms clench me with the strength of near panic, and she shudders against my chest. After half a minute, I kiss the top of her head and draw back.

"Mom, I don't want Annie to see me this way. I need to look for Dad, even if the chance is slim. Please reassure her all you can. And whatever you do, *don't leave this house.* Don't even stand by the windows. I've called all the contractors, so no one should be showing up. If I decide to send someone to protect you, I'll call you first."

She nods with grim determination. "I've got my pistol in my purse."

"I'll come back as soon as I can. Tell Annie I'll be back by dark. And call my cell if you think of any way I might be able to reach Dad."

Mom nods helplessly as I disappear through the back door, but she bolts it shut as soon as I'm outside.

My cell phone rings when I take out my keys—a number I don't recognize. Clicking the talk button, I say, "Hang on!" then climb into the Audi and start the engine. "Who is this?"

"John Kaiser."

"Thank God. Have you got anywhere on being able to help my father come in?"

"I'm working on it. The best we can hope for is a surrender to us on federal charges. But with a dead state trooper, the politicos down here are going to light up the phones in Washington if I try to take him away from them. I'm pressing for it, but my SAC has been fighting turf battles with the locals every day since Katrina."

I grit my teeth in frustration. "Please do what you can. I haven't had any luck finding him yet, but I will."

"Watch your tail while you look. I checked up on Randall Regan. He's a bad son of a bitch."

"I learned the hard way, as usual. Hey, have you got anything on the Big Ears yet?"

"Uh, yeah. I've got Regan telling Brody Royal that you assaulted him in the restroom of a restaurant. He's thinking of pressing charges."

"Is that all they said? No mention of what I said to Regan in the diner?"

"Nope. He told Royal you sat down at his table and harassed a coworker he was with. Then he went into the restroom to take a leak and you attacked him. Two waitresses have already confirmed that story, by the way. If you go by what they said on the phone, Regan and Royal are as clean as a nun's drawers."

"Damn it, John. They must have figured out my game. Regan didn't say a word in the restaurant, like he expected me to be wearing a wire."

The FBI agent sighs. "You know the odds of getting quick results are low, especially pushing as hard as you are. You're so keyed up Regan probably read you like a book. Setups always take time. Just promise me you're not going to make the same kind of approach to Brody Royal."

Not unless I have no other option. "You can rest easy on that score."

"Good. Stay in touch."

Hanging up, I back my Audi onto Washington Street, then pull onto Broadway and drive along the bluff to State Street, wondering where to go next. Where *would* Dad run with his life on the line? Even if a thousand people would risk their lives for him, there can't be more than a handful whom he would place in the line of fire. I quickly discard my first few ideas, but then a chill raises the hair on my arms and neck.

Could Dad be hiding at Quentin's house? When the old lawyer's not working in Washington, D.C., he lives on seventy acres in Jefferson County, Mississippi, and I can hardly think of a more isolated sanctuary for Walt and my father to hide in. Whether Quentin would risk his law license to hide a client fleeing a murder warrant is another question. But of course my father is more than a client to Quentin. This half-crazy idea gives me the first hope I've felt since I learned Dad jumped bail, but the only way I can safely confirm it is to drive the thirty-five miles to Quentin's place.

Turning right on Franklin Street, I cruise past the turn to City Hall and continue north, half convinced I should make the drive right away. There's not much else I can accomplish in the next couple of hours. Since my altercation with Randall Regan didn't trigger any incriminating phone chatter, he and Brody are obviously smarter than I'd hoped.

The only other thing that might push them to incriminate themselves is Sheriff Dennis hitting the Knoxes' drug operations, which won't happen for another eighteen hours, at the earliest. *Why am I even thinking about that? Now that Dad and Walt have been painted as cop killers, everything else is academic—*

When my phone rings, I assume it's Kaiser calling back, but it turns out to be Chief Logan of the Natchez police.

"Don? What's happening?"

"I found what you were looking for. Are you still interested?"

"Can you be more specific?" I ask, confused.

"L.T."

Lincoln Turner. My heartbeat picks up immediately. "Where?"

"His white pickup is parked at a juke joint out by Anna's Bottom. It's called CC's Rhythm Club. Looks like your basic dump to me."

Having been thwarted on all fronts today, the idea of confronting the man who started this nightmare—and who's been stalking my family—appeals to me. Moreover, Anna's Bottom lies in roughly the same direction as Quentin Avery's place. You could almost say it's on the way.

"Keep him there, Don. I'm on my way."

"Keep him there? He's outside the city limits, Penn. I've got no grounds to detain the guy if he tries to leave."

"He's in a jook house, right? If he tries to leave, give him a field sobriety test. I'll be there in fifteen minutes."

"I don't even have jurisdiction out here! This is the county. Billy Byrd's territory. Penn, wait. You don't sound like yourself. I heard about that APB, too. What exactly you are planning to do?"

"Just keep the subject where he is, Don. I'm on my way."

Hanging up, I whip my Audi left onto Martin Luther King Street and head out into the county, toward a bend in the Mississippi River. Before I cover a mile, a new thought strikes me with chilling power. Last night, when I was jotting down reasons that Dad might have jumped bail, I omitted one potential answer—probably because it was so primal and obvious. Of course, at that point I didn't know Walt was with Dad.

What if Henry was right the first night we talked? What if the Double Eagles have threatened violence against our family unless Dad takes the fall for Viola's murder? If they have, I can easily imagine Dad and Walt going on the offensive, rather than letting Dad die in jail. He and Walt could have gone to the borrow pits in search of the men who threatened us. That dead trooper could have been one of them, a soldier in the secret army of Forrest Knox. If I'm right, then I made a terrible mistake by having the FBI eavesdrop on Brody Royal and his son-in-law. I may well have set up the technology that will record my father and Walt Garrity wiping out the men who framed Dad for Viola's murder. With fear filling my mind, I press my foot to the floor and lean into the curves that lead into the thickly wooded hills above Anna's Bottom.

CHAPTER 72

ANNA'S BOTTOM IS a vast, fertile floodplain that swells like a pregnant belly into the old course of the Mississippi River north of Natchez. For 250 years cotton has been cultivated in that plain, and black men and women have toiled there without cease. Though their equipment has changed, little else has, and it's on the high rim of those fields that Lincoln Turner has chosen to while away his hours this afternoon.

The road to Anna's Bottom winds through densely forested hills between Highway 61 and the river, and my Audi easily hugs the bulging curves at eighty. All this land was once part of plantations, and many of the big houses still stand amid cattle ponds and old slave quarters. Quite a few people make this drive purely for the exhilaration. The hills rise steadily above the river, the road narrows, and then at three hundred feet above sea level the blacktop plunges down the most precipitous slope in ten counties, snaking back and forth as it falls toward the bottomland. Your mind reels from the sudden change in perspective; the forest drops away, and your gaze flies out over the flatlands of Louisiana toward Texas, while far beneath you a couple of oil wells pump with lazy persistence, all that remain of the fifty that once sucked thirty million barrels of black gold out of these cotton fields..

Today I will not make that plunge, for the "jook joint" that Chief Logan directed me to squats in the trees on the ledge overlooking that wild drop. It's a juke, all right, just like the ones that used to dot Highway 61 all the way through the Delta. The Crayola purple cinder-block building has eight or ten vehicles parked out front, and a tin-roofed appendage spews smoke into the sky from a rusted vent pipe, spreading the mouthwatering smell of cooking pork for miles. The building's black-painted windows have been covered with airbrushed paintings of martini glasses, Colt .45 Malt Liquor cans, and bubbling champagne bottles. Above this hodgepodge of images someone has splashed the words "CC's Rhythm Club" in bold graffiti script. Most juke owners would have chosen CC's Blues Club, which make me wonder whether the eponymous C.C. named his (or her) establishment after the infamous Rhythm Club in Natchez, where 209 African-Americans burned to death in 1940. This whole building could easily fit inside Pithy Nolan's parlor at Corinth, but more human drama unfolds within these walls over a Labor Day weekend than has in Pithy's mansion over the past twenty years.

Lincoln Turner's white pickup is parked on the right end of the line of vehicles—I confirm it by the Illinois plates—so I park my Audi on the left end. Given that Lincoln has no idea I'm coming, keeping a reasonably clear line of retreat seems prudent. I see no police car as I walk to the front door, and I don't know whether to feel better or worse about that. Since CC's stands outside Chief Logan's jurisdiction, it'll be one of Sheriff Billy Byrd's deputies who responds to any 911 call made from here. Of course, most of CC's customers don't think of the police in terms of aid, so emergency calls are rare.

When I walk through the door, the club's patrons don't turn to me and freeze, nor does the jukebox screech to a halt, as it does in schlock movies. About half the patrons glance in my direction, but most quickly go back to their business. Only the bartender stares, waiting to see what my intentions might be.

I scan the room, searching for the man I've only seen up close in a pickup truck window, and for a brief time in the Justice Court. The interior of the juke isn't as dim as I expected, but it smells like every other one I've entered in my life. The first wave of odors confuses the olfactory senses—a strange brew of delicious aromas and suspicious funk. Frying chicken, sizzling lard, baking biscuits, fresh corn bread, and onions battle dead fish, stale beer, old garbage, disinfectant, sugary wine, and cigarette smoke that's permeated even the cinder-block walls. Eight tables with red-checkered cloths have been squeezed between the bar and the corner stage, and four more stand along the far wall beneath narrow windows that actually allow some daylight through. A painting of a naked and bejeweled black girl floating above a smoldering volcano serves as a backdrop for the stage, where a glittering red drum set awaits the next show. The flashing jukebox in the corner sends Bobby "Blue" Bland throughout the club with bone-shaking bass. I can guess the other artists in that machine without looking: Little Walter, B. B. King, Big Mama Thornton, Wilson Pickett, Muddy Waters, Irma Thomas, Robert Johnson, Beverly "Guitar" Watkins, Ray Charles, and probably a couple of tracks by Merle Haggard or Hank Williams to round out the list.

No one in CC's is younger than forty, except a tall, skinny busboy moving between the tables with a mop and bucket. It's too dark to see faces clearly, so I try to differentiate Lincoln by his size. As I search the tables, a woman wearing jeans and a red bandanna tied around her head walks up and gives me a skeptical look. "What you lookin' for? Your car break down or somethin'?"

"No, ma'am. I'm Mayor Penn Cage, from Natchez. I'm looking for a man from Chicago. His name is Lincoln Turner."

She looks at me like I just announced I'm selling burial insurance. "Don't know him."

"His truck's parked outside."

"Well, you can look around, if you buy a beer."

"Budweiser."

She spins and heads for the bar.

The scents of cooking food are emanating from the ramshackle kitchen beneath the vent pipe I saw outside. Only a greasy curtain separates it from the main room, and it's near this curtain that I spy Lincoln Turner, sitting alone at a half-size table. *Did he consciously choose the table with the shortest path to the back door?* Maybe not. He's sitting hunched over a Colt .45 tallboy, facing away from me, and he seems oblivious to my entrance.

When the waitress places a sweating beer can in my hand, I move cautiously toward Lincoln's table. He's actually bent over a plate, not his beer, eating as though he hasn't had anything for days.

"Mind if I sit down?" I ask from four feet away.

Lincoln doesn't turn at first, and when he does, he turns slowly, as though already certain of what he'll see.

"Take a seat, Mayor," he says, not smiling. "I can't say I was expecting you."

As I slide into the chair opposite him, he says, "How'd you find me? Put your local Gestapo on the case?"

I don't answer, and it's several seconds before I realize why. I'm searching his broad face for similarities to my father's—or my own. I see no obvious resemblance, but it's strange to search for your own features in a face of a different color. Lincoln is an imposing man, if not conventionally handsome. He has an oval face, as I do, but not the prominent jaw that my father and I share. His eyes are brown, like mine, but almost disturbingly dark. I don't recognize his nose or cheekbones, and his hair is as nappy as that of any black man I ever knew. Only Lincoln's high forehead strikes a resonant note and, if I'm honest, reminds me of my father. The lack of overall similarity comforts me, and yet . . . something bothers me that I can't put my finger on.

"I'm surprised you had the nerve to walk in here," he says. "White boy like you in a black jook? Out on the edge of nowhere? Most white boys would be nervous as a whore in church."

"I'd be a lot more nervous in a shitkicking honky-tonk. People come here for the food and the music."

Turner chuckles. "You're right. When rednecks drink, they want to fuck or fight, and not necessarily in that order."

I want to ask him what he was doing outside my house earlier this afternoon, but that might force our conversation to an abrupt conclusion. Better to learn what I can before confronting him. "I didn't even know this place existed."

He looks around as though appraising the value of the place. "When I was a boy in Chicago, there were jooks like this on the South Side. No name, usually, just an address. Mississippi folks who moved up there re-created what they'd known back home. My stepfather did a lot of his business in corner jook joints. He'd sit there eating pork sausage and cat-head biscuits, running half a dozen scams from the pay phone while he ate. I guess I got to like it. The *funk* of it, you know?"

My stepfather. I try to recall what Dad told me about the man Viola married in Chicago. The phrase "charming rogue" comes back to me.

"I know why you're here," Lincoln says, his dark eyes suddenly serious. "I see you studyin' my face."

"Why don't you enlighten me?"

"No. I'll let you tell your lie before I tell the truth. Why do you *think* you're here?"

"I came to find out why you're trying to railroad my father for murder."

He shakes his head with confidence. "That's no mystery. What son wouldn't want vengeance on the man who killed his mama? That's logic, plain and simple. No, Mr. Mayor . . . you're here to answer a deeper question. And you're scared."

"What were you doing parked outside my house an hour ago?"

Lincoln shrugs. "It's a free country, ain't it?"

"Oh, cut the shit. What 'deeper question' am I here to answer?"

He seems to weigh the issue for a bit. "You ever hear that expression, 'brothers from a different mother'?"

My stomach does a slow flip. "I've heard it."

"That's what we are." He grins, showing his big teeth. "You and me. Literally. We got the same father." His eyebrows arch expectantly. "Ain't that some shit, Mayor?"

"I don't believe you." I'm speaking truthfully, despite my doubts about my father's honesty.

"Yes, you do. The truth is already there, down deep in you. All I did was pick off the scab. Take a minute to adjust, if you need it. Nobody's going to ask for our table."

"What year were you born?" I ask.

"Nineteen sixty-eight, in December. Nine months after my mama left Natchez."

I'm reluctant to raise Henry Sexton's explanation of this juxtaposition of events, but what choice do I have? Lincoln has forced my hand.

"A lot of terrible things happened to your mother and her family in 1968," I say in a neutral tone. "Her brother was kidnapped and murdered, for one thing. Viola had several good reasons to leave this town."

"None measure up to being pregnant by her white, married boss. A man she loved, but who would never leave his wife."

This simple, vivid description stops me for a few moments, but I press on. "Something else happened in 1968, Mr. Turner. Something a lot worse than what you just described."

"What's that, Mayor?"

"Your mother was raped by the Ku Klux Klan. Or several former members of it, anyway."

The dark eyes smolder with anger. "You think I don't know that?"

"I don't know what you know."

Lincoln stabs a thick forefinger at me. "You think I was sired by one of them cracker assholes?"

"I don't know. It seems possible."

Lincoln's chest rumbles with contemptuous laughter. "You wish I was, don't you? You and your daddy. That would make your lives a whole lot easier. Keep that fairy tale you was raised in intact. But I told you that first night who I am. I'm the chicken come home to roost. It's taken damn near forty years, but I'm here now. Here to stay. And I know what I know. I had to break through a lot of lies to find out, but now I know."

"Are you saying you have proof of your paternity?"

"I'm saying I *know*, brother."

"We're both lawyers, Mr. Turner. There's a world of difference between 'knowing' something and proving it. With all respect, I can't help raising what seems a pretty obvious objection to your assertion. You've got a very dark skin tone, considerably darker than your mother's. So how do you figure that my father, who's got the pale skin of Scots-English descent, is your father?"

Lincoln grins again. "Your lack of education's showing, Counselor. It's obvious you're a lawyer and not a doctor. You ever read a genetics textbook?"

"No."

"Well, I have. And that idea you've got of what mixed-race people look like belongs on the trash pile with phrenology and all the other hokum from that era. Did you know you can get a black mouse from two white ones? Luck of the draw, in genetic terms. I've seen the face of a white man when the high-yellow woman he married popped out a black baby. I'm talking 'bout a woman who'd been passing for *white*. There's no expression like it, my man. No, indeed. *Sur-priiise*."

I'm not sure how to respond to this. I know a lot of black people, and in my mind those on the lighter end of the spectrum—those with "yellow" or "bright" skin tones—represent the mixed-race types that my ancestors called mulattos, quadroons, or octoroons, those classifications based on the percentage of African blood. We all develop preconceptions about such matters based on folk wisdom rather than science, and until I learn more, there's no point in debating the issue.

Lincoln leans closer to me. "The man you called Daddy your whole life is my daddy, too. Only I never saw him in person till yesterday. That's no mystery, either. What white man ever wanted the world to know he had a nigger baby? Huh? Because that's what it comes down to, *brother*. Simple as that."

"Are you suggesting that my father has known all this time that he had a son by Viola, and did nothing to help support her?"

Lincoln shakes his head almost sadly. "I'm not saying he did nothing. A rich man can always spread a little money around to ease his conscience. But as far as acknowledging my existence, he did nothing. He wanted Mama to stay up in Chicago, same as the Klan did. They wanted it for different reasons, I guess. Though when you strip away all the bullshit, the reasons weren't so different after all."

Turner is filled with the accreted anger of thirty-seven years. And by the circular logic of every bastard son in history, he's transformed supposition into "facts" to prove he's the son of a great man. Arguing this point with him would be like arguing with a convert about religion. I should get out of here as quickly and quietly as possible.

While I try to think of a graceful excuse to leave, he takes a bite of pulled pork and speaks as he chews. "Now that you understand the situation, the idea of murder doesn't seem so far-fetched, does it?"

"That's ridiculous. Killing Viola wouldn't keep your existence secret, if that's what you're implying. Dad would have to kill everyone else who knew, as well."

"Almost nobody did." Lincoln finishes chewing, then swallows and watches me for a few seconds, seeming to enjoy my discomfiture. "But by the other night, he knew that *I* knew."

"So, killing your mother wouldn't keep the alleged secret."

"It would, if he killed me, too."

I draw back from him in shock. "You're not seriously suggesting . . . ?"

Lincoln shrugs. "When was the last time you talked to him?"

I try to keep my face immobile.

"Uh-huh. What do you think I'm doing out in this dump? I can afford to eat at the Castle if I want to. But I can't show my face in Natchez until Tom Cage is in jail. Even then, I can't be sure I'm safe. He's got plenty of redneck patients who'd be happy to do him a favor by making me disappear."

I shove my chair back from the table. "You're crazy. What do you really hope to get out of this?"

"Justice. Plain and simple."

I have a practiced eye at reading deception, and there's something more than sincerity in Lincoln Turner's eyes. He radiates the cool certainty of a con artist rather than the sincerity of a wronged child. For an instant I feel I'm on the verge of a revelation, but the insight fades. Instead of trying to recapture it, I voice a question that's been nagging me since Shad called Monday morning with the news of Viola's death.

"Why were you thirty minutes north of Natchez on the morning your mother died? Why haven't you been here for the past month, while she was dying? You're about to be disbarred in Illinois. And you just told me you have enough money to stay at a nice hotel. Why weren't you down here easing her last weeks on earth? Why were you sitting up in Chicago while your mother suffered at death's door?"

He has no ready answer for this, and the anger in his eyes deepens appreciably.

"I think I know why you want to punish my father," I say softly. "Viola knew she couldn't rely on you for the hard duties of being a son. That's why she came back here to die. My father had the guts and the patience and the love to sit with her while she wasted away, but you couldn't. And you want him to pay for that. You want to blame somebody for your own shortcomings, and your mother's lack of faith in you."

Lincoln's dark face darkens still more with blood. Then he speaks with unsettling conviction. "When a child finds out his parents have been lying to him for his whole life—not about some little thing, but about who he is, and who *they* are—it doesn't exactly predispose him toward feelings of charity. Do you feel me, bro?" Lincoln tilts his head toward mine. "Yeah, you do. The next time you look dear old Daddy in the eye, you're gonna feel like puking. 'Cause there's nothing worse than a self-serving lie to a child."

"Is that what you believe? That your mother lied to you out of self-interest?"

"No. Her motive was worse than that. She didn't lie to protect herself. That would have made sense, at least. No, she lied to protect *him*." Unalloyed rage enters Lincoln's voice. "My mother thought more of Tom Cage's happiness than she did her own. Or mine. Isn't that pathetic? She and I paid the price for your family's shiny little life."

I feel my hands shaking as my heart rebels against this twisted view of my personal history, but Lincoln goes on relentlessly.

"You ever read that story, 'The Secret Sharer'? Well, I'm your dark twin, Mayor. The shadow you never knew you had, leading you to your destiny. We're like two parallel lines that finally converge, against all odds. We were conceived in the same town, from the same pair of balls, the same pool of protoplasm, the same strands of DNA. But we were born and lived our lives seven hundred miles apart."

My face has grown hot with blood. "If that's true . . . will you agree to take a DNA test?"

Lincoln smiles. "Any time, so long as it's not in Natchez, Mississippi. You won't hear Tom Cage make that promise."

Nothing could have stunned me more than this offer to subject his claim to scientific testing. Clearly, Lincoln believes what he's saying.

He drains his beer glass, and the waitress moves toward the table, but I wave her away.

"She's out of pain now," Lincoln says. "There's nothing left to worry me now but earthly justice. Before long, Tom Cage is gonna be standing in the dock in handcuffs, just like any old nigger brought there by the sheriff. He'll stand there while all his lies are stripped away and his soul is laid bare before the town he's been worshipped in so long. It's taken a lot of years, but the truth he tried so long to bury has finally found its way up to the light."

The specter Lincoln has conjured sends a shiver down to my bones. To see Dad publicly shamed as a liar might be worse than hearing he's been shot by a cop somewhere. I know *he* would rather die than be seen to have betrayed the code he tried to live by all his life.

"What you thinking?" Lincoln asks, a strange gleam in his eyes. "You thinking life would be a lot simpler if my truck ran off the road halfway back to town?"

"No."

He laughs softly. "You sure, Mayor? Aren't I just like some girl you fucked and hoped never to see again, come back to tell you I'm pregnant? You want me to disappear. That hope is smoldering deep in that overheated brain of yours, even if you don't know it yet. And the fact that it's there ought to prove something to you."

I lay my hands on the table and push my chair back. "I think we're done here, Mr. Turner."

"Sure. Go home to your little girl and pull the covers over your head. You won't forget one word of what I've said. This is exactly what you hunted me down to hear."

I reach for my wallet, but Lincoln waves his hand to stop me. "My treat, brother."

This time when he laughs, it comes from deep within his chest, like the laugh of the voodoo master in *Live and Let Die*.

"What the hell's goin' on here?" drawls a redneck voice. "Family reunion?"

Somehow Sheriff Billy Byrd has materialized beside our table, his potbelly straining against his starred brown shirt, and his red-tinged cheeks shadowed by the brim of his Stetson hat. His high-pitched cackle merges with and then drowns out the resonant laugh of Lincoln Turner, but it's the pistol jutting from his gun belt that holds my attention.

Lincoln is staring at the sheriff, but I can't tell whether he's been expecting Byrd or not.

"Mayor Cage," Billy says, "we don't like people threatening witnesses in this county. And this looks to me like harassment of a witness. This man here's gonna help put your father in jail for murder, which means you need to steer clear of him till the trial."

"I haven't threatened anybody. This man was parked outside my house an hour ago, and when I pulled up, he took off like he was leaving the scene of a crime."

Byrd grunts skeptically, then looks down at Lincoln. "That right, Mr. Turner?"

"The mayor's mistaken, Sheriff. I was just sitting here having an early supper. He walked in, sat down, and started asking me where his father was. To tell the truth, I think he's confused."

"I imagine he is," Billy says. "Now that his daddy's jumped bail. I call that damned peculiar behavior for a model citizen. Hell, the Louisiana State Police say Dr. Cage killed a trooper over there. I don't figure he's got long before somebody puts a bullet in him."

Lincoln's mouth drops open. This is clearly new information to him.

"Yeah," Billy goes on, "at this rate, your mama's case might not even get to trial. Dr. Cage is liable to be bagged and tagged by sundown. But that's no reason to let the mayor abuse his position."

Sheriff Byrd looks toward the end of the bar, where my waitress stands whispering to the big bartender. "Hey, hon! Fix me a coupla them cat-head biscuits to go. Put some gravy in there with 'em."

If Lincoln or the club management didn't summon Sheriff Byrd here, then Billy himself—or one of his minions—was already nearby when I arrived, keeping an eye on Lincoln. The sheriff might have several reasons for doing that, but at this moment, in my mind, one overrides the rest.

"I just realized what you're doing here, Billy. You think Dad might try to contact Lincoln, or even hurt him. Lincoln is nothing but a goat tied to a tree. You want to put a bullet in my father before some Louisiana state trooper beats you to it. And all because Dad knows what a rotten son of a bitch you really are."

Billy's hand drops to the pistol at his side.

"You're quick to reach for that gun, aren't you? That temper's going to get you in trouble someday. Soon, maybe."

"Aren't you late for a meeting?" Byrd asks, his eyes burning. "That Joint Governance Committee you started gets going in ten minutes, and you're twenty miles from the courthouse."

He's right, I realize, looking at my watch. "I do have a meeting," I tell Lincoln, getting to my feet.

Byrd looks down at Turner. "Did you know the mayor wants to rebuild the old slave market for tourists to gawk at? 'Cultural tourism,' he calls it. What you think about that? As an Afro-American? Would you pay money to come look at the block they sold your ancestors on?"

Lincoln wipes his mouth with a napkin and gets up from the table. He towers six inches above Billy Byrd, and he doesn't make any effort to give the sheriff the space he's accustomed to.

"You in the wrong jook, Sheriff," he says. "We settle our own business up in here. Ain't no place for the law."

Byrd seems stunned by "his" witness's behavior. Leaving his hand on his pistol grip, he takes a step back and says, "I'm the high sheriff of this county, boy. I go any damn place I please."

"Then go," Lincoln says. "Before somebody decides to disabuse you of your notions."

Sheriff Byrd glances over his shoulder. The big bartender stares back at him, both hands invisible behind the bar. The waitress and cook are watching from the kitchen curtain, and there's a cleaver in the cook's hand.

"All right, now!" Billy says loudly, backing away from our table. "Nobody do nothin' stupid!"

"That sounds like good advice," Lincoln says.

Billy finally looks to me for help—the only other white man in the room. But I simply turn up my palms.

"Where's my damn biscuits?" he calls, trying to assert the old hierarchy.

The bandanna-clad waitress slides between two tables with a small brown sack in her hand. As Billy reaches out with his free hand, she drops the sack on the floor at his feet.

"Sorry 'bout that," she says, making no effort to pick it up.

"You people need a little reeducation," Billy mutters. "Oh, yeah."

The sheriff looks like he's going to say something else, but instead he shakes his head and marches out to the parking lot, leaving his biscuits on the floor.

"I thought you were working with him," I say to Lincoln.

"I'm not working with anybody, Mayor. I'm here for justice. I'll use a cracker like Byrd if I have no choice, but I don't have to like it."

"What about Shad Johnson?"

Lincoln shrugs. "Same for that Oreo. But he's the man in the DA's office."

"What *were* you doing outside my house this afternoon?"

"Looking at the life I might have lived, if things had been different." He gazes down into my eyes with emotion that I can't begin to read. "Think about what I've told you today. Think about what the Bible says: 'I the Lord your God am a jealous God, visiting the iniquity of the father on the sons unto the third and fourth generation.'"

As he quotes the Bible, I sense a malevolent urge within him, something darker and more primitive than anything he's voiced today.

"Lincoln . . . you wish history was something less terrible than it was for your mother. I wish the same thing. But you shouldn't try to punish my father for pain inflicted by someone else. My father loved your mother. He proved that in the last month of her life. Why can't you leave it at that?"

Lincoln lays a twenty-dollar bill on the table and prepares to go.

"You talk about sin like you've never committed any yourself," I observe.

His eyes blaze with sudden passion. "Whatever evil I've done goes on Tom Cage's account. You hear me? I *am* his sin, alive in the world."

Lincoln's ominously resonant voice makes my skin prickle. "If that's true, then what am I?"

He looks back at me for several silent seconds. "You're what he could have been."

Lincoln turns toward the door and walks out without looking back.

Before I follow, the bartender calls: "Don't come back here no more, Mayor. I don't want that sheriff up in here again."

I acknowledge his order with a wave, then walk out of the juke in the footsteps of a man who just might be my brother.

CHAPTER 73

A MILE DOWN the road from CC's Rhythm Club, something breaks in my mind, like a steel restraining pin giving way inside some complex machine. For the past two and a half days, my father's behavior has stumped me. Nothing about it has made sense from the moment Shad Johnson called to tell me that Viola was dead and Lincoln wanted my father charged with murder.

But if I simply accept Lincoln Turner's assertion to be true—*that my father is also his father*—then logic leads me to a sequence of deductions that can't be refuted. One: If Lincoln *is* my father's son, then he's family in my father's eyes. Two: If Lincoln is family, then he deserves my father's protection as much as I or my sister would. My heart clenches as the next question forms in my mind: In what circumstance would my father risk his life to protect Lincoln Turner?

Lincoln's life must be at risk.

How could Lincoln's life be at risk?

He's either been threatened, or he's guilty of a serious crime.

Who might have threatened him?

No way to know.

Of what crime could Lincoln be guilty?

"Killing his mother," I say aloud. *Killing his mother . . .*

My heart flexes like a straining biceps, but still my mind races down the interrogatory chain. "How could Lincoln kill his mother if he was thirty miles outside Natchez?"

He couldn't.

The next question flares in my mind like a bottle rocket in a black sky: *What if Lincoln was in Natchez when Viola died?*

In some process infinitely faster than conscious thought, a new relationship between the principals in this deadly drama forms in my mind. If Lincoln *was* in Natchez when Viola died, then he would surely have agreed to help her end her life—especially if my father had already refused. If my mother were dying of a terminal illness, wracked with pain and with no hope of recovery, I'd do whatever she asked without question. Would the man I just spoke to in CC's Rhythm Club do less? *No.* But if Lincoln euthanized his mother in the wee hours of Monday morning . . . then my father did not.

Unless they did it together, whispers a voice in my head.

"No," I say softly, my mind racing. "No way."

Yet once I accept the possibility that both Lincoln and Dad could have been in that house at the same time—or even within minutes of each other—a dozen new scenarios become possible.

Lincoln could have botched the morphine injection, causing Dad to try desperately to revive Viola. (Only Dad wouldn't have given an adrenaline overdose under those circumstances.) Lincoln could have botched the morphine injection, panicked, *then tried to revive Viola himself.* A son overcome by guilt might easily do that. If something like that did happen—after Dad had left the house with Viola alive—then Dad may have deduced that Lincoln probably killed his mother. He might even know that for a fact. Cora Revels might have told him. Or he might have returned to the scene and found Lincoln grieving over Viola's body. I saw dozens of crazier death scenes as a prosecutor.

If any of these scenarios occurred, then Dad knows he's innocent of Viola's murder. But knowing him as I do, that awareness—in those circumstances—would probably cause him to behave *just as he has* since he learned of his potential prosecution for murder. For if Dad really believes that Lincoln is his son, then his guilt over failing that son for four decades would make him all too willing to take the fall for Lincoln, regardless of the cost to himself.

But . . .

There would be no fall to take, had not Lincoln pushed Shad Johnson to press murder charges. And if Lincoln actually killed his mother, why would he risk pressing the DA to punish my father?

"Oh, no," I whisper, certain I've found the truth at last. "Because he'll risk almost anything to punish *his* father."

I can't imagine a purer, more righteous anger than that of a son who helped his mother to die after a life ruined by a man who'd refused to marry her or acknowledge him. The situation must have been tempting for a lawyer. If Lincoln knew Dad had been in Cora's house before him, he would have instantly seen how easily Dad could be framed for his mother's death. The necessary props for the deception were ready to hand: the syringe with Dad's fingerprints, the vial of morphine prescribed by the man Lincoln longed to punish. And Cora Revels probably told Lincoln about the euthanasia pact between Dad and Viola. If fate handed Lincoln a chance like that—a chance to make "his father" pay for a lifetime of neglect—would he refuse? I doubt it.

This scenario easily explains Lincoln's behavior. But does it explain Dad's? His refusal to say what happened in Cora's house that night? Holding his silence in the face of deputies handcuffing him and leading him to court? Silence in the face of indictment for murder? *Yes, yes, and yes.* In the mind of a guilt-ridden father, all these acts must have seemed noble efforts to protect the son he'd failed throughout his life.

But jumping bail?

This takes me a little longer, but at last the answer comes. So long as Dad remained silent while awaiting trial—and so long as I and others protested his innocence—people might continue to investigate Viola's death. Friends like Jewel Washington might have gone back over the crime scene, or probed more deeply into Lincoln's whereabouts on the night of her death. They might have asked, as I did, why Lincoln hadn't been in Natchez for the past month while his mother slipped inexorably toward death. But by jumping bail, Dad swept all those possibilities off the table. From the moment his flight became public, every cop, lawyer, and average citizen would view him as a killer trying to escape punishment.

I can't begin to guess what Dad was doing with Sonny Thornfield last night at the Ferriday hospital. Maybe he wasn't there with Thornfield at all. Maybe he had coronary symptoms himself, and stopped to get a nurse or doc he knew to provide him some meds or do an EKG. Hell, maybe he was meeting Drew there. Whatever his reason, it doesn't matter now. What matters is that every cop in Mississippi and Louisiana is chasing the wrong man. And now I know who the right man is. There's just one little problem—

Proof.

Could anyone other than my father prove that Lincoln euthanized his mother? Lincoln has a perfectly defensible reason for his fingerprints to be all over Cora Revels's house. Even if they're on the medicine vials and the syringe, that only proves he handled those items at some point—after the fact, he would argue. Worst of all, the case is being handled by a hostile DA and sheriff who'll ignore any evidence I present them, short of a videotape showing someone other than Dad killing Viola.

With that thought, I recall the missing tape from the camcorder Henry left in Viola's sickroom. The hard drive attached to Henry's camera showed only Viola's death throes, not what precipitated them. But according to Henry, what triggered that hard drive to start recording was the mini-DV tape in the camera running out. And that tape was supposedly missing when the deputies arrived at the scene. *Who took it?* When I questioned Dad in his office on Monday evening, I got the feeling he might have taken it. But what if *Lincoln* removed that tape before the deputies arrived? Could that tape show Viola's actual murder? And if so, does it still exist?

Before I can second-guess myself, I speed-dial Quentin Avery's house in Jefferson County, thirty miles north of here. I'm not going to ask Quentin if Dad and Walt are hiding out there—as badly as I'd like to. No one answers my call, just as they haven't for the past two days. But this time, when the beep of the answering machine sounds, I leave a message.

"Quentin, it's Penn. I just spoke to Lincoln Turner, and my world-view changed radically. I think you probably know what I'm talking about. If you don't, you need to catch up in a hurry. If you don't call me back in ten minutes, I'm going to drive up there and tell the police I'm worried you've had a heart attack. That'll—"

"Hold on, Penn," says a female voice. "This is Doris. Quentin's right here."

"Thanks. I'm sorry to make threats, but things are pretty serious down here."

"They're serious up here, too, but here he is."

After several clicks and grunts, Quentin says, "Telling me you'd call the police was a veiled threat against my weed stash, boy. Don't think I don't know that."

"Lincoln Turner just told me Dad is his father."

Quentin is silent for several seconds. "And that surprised you?"

"Are you telling me it's true?"

"I don't know whether it's true or not. But it doesn't surprise me that he said it. Hell, a blind mule could see that boy's game from twelve rows away."

"Quentin, what are you talking about?"

"Why wouldn't Viola tell that boy Tom was his father? Beats the hell out of telling him he was fathered by some booger-eating Ku Klux Klansman."

"You're deflecting, Quentin. I'm asking you what's *true*. Has Dad ever told you he had an illegitimate son?"

"That's privileged information, as you well know. But I'll tell you anyway. Hell, no."

"Lincoln offered to take a DNA test."

"Well, it may come to that. But that's not the primary issue right now."

"What is?"

"I would have said the trial, until I heard about the dead state trooper and the APB."

At this, I fall silent. Quentin doesn't sound like a lawyer hiding his client from the police, but he's a subtle character. "And . . . ?"

"I wish Tom had come to me rather than go running off with Walt Garrity. But I don't control the man."

If Dad and Walt are hiding out at Quentin's isolated compound, then Quentin is a consummate actor. *He is,* says a voice in my mind. *There's no one better.*

"How about we get back to Lincoln for a minute?" I quickly summarize my deductions since leaving the CC's Rhythm Club, culminating with my theory that Dad is protecting Lincoln, who probably killed his mother. Quentin listens in surprising silence. "Well, what do you think?" I ask.

"That all makes sense, I'm sorry to say. Covering for Lincoln sounds exactly like Tom. Sacrificing himself out of guilt, I mean. He'd probably do that on Viola's word alone, without even checking to make sure the boy was his."

"But he hasn't said anything to you along these lines?"

"No. But I can imagine what you're thinking now. You figure that if you can prove Lincoln killed Viola, your father's home free."

"*If* I can get him into protective custody before some gung ho cop shoots him."

"You're wrong, Penn. Think about it. So long as Tom is willing to get up on a witness stand and say that he killed Viola, you've got no play. If your father wants to go to jail for someone, he's going to jail."

This stark truth silences me like news of a death. After several stunned seconds, I say, "He'll be lucky to make jail, Quentin."

"Well . . . if Walt Garrity's with him, he just might be okay. And don't assume you're right about Lincoln. Those damned Double Eagles may well have killed Viola. Don't give up on that angle yet."

"If they did, how do you explain Dad's behavior?"

"I can't. But your father's no fool. Keep using that brain of yours, and maybe you'll get to the bottom of this. I've got to go. Doris has got to give me my medicine."

As the old lawyer hangs up, I hear him say, "What the *hell* is Tom thinking?"

When the connection dies, a smothering solitude closes around me. In five minutes I'll be sitting in a room watching six yellow-dog Democrats and six Fox News–addicted Republicans argue about the prospect of rebuilding the second-largest slave market in America. This notion is almost unbearable, yet I must bear it, for I set the process in motion. The best thing I can do now is make use of my last minutes of freedom.

While I can't prove or disprove Lincoln's paternity on my own, I can try to find out whether he was in Natchez at the time of his mother's death. Chief Logan has access to all kinds of digital records, and what he can't find out, John Kaiser can. As my Audi skids onto Highway 61, I call up Chief Logan on my cell phone.

"How'd it go at CC's?" he asks by way of greeting. "You're still breathing, obviously. Is Turner?"

"You sound nervous, Don."

"You could say that."

"Billy Byrd paid us a visit, and he almost got stomped for his trouble. Everything's cool now, but I need another favor."

"Your wish is my command," he says sourly.

CHAPTER 74

CAITLIN PUT DOWN her office telephone and sat motionless, save for her finger rubbing her upper lip. Penn had just called her with a new theory of Viola Turner's murder, this one generated by a face-to-face meeting with Lincoln Turner. She'd been so shocked to learn that Penn had met with Lincoln that she'd had difficulty concentrating on what he was saying. But after a couple of minutes, she got it. While the logic of the theory made sense, she disagreed with the assumption upon which the whole concept rested: that Tom was Lincoln Turner's father. She'd begun offering objections, but Penn hadn't wanted to hear them. He was late for a joint meeting that he claimed he couldn't afford to miss. Caitlin had hung up with a sour taste in her mouth and resentment in her heart.

Turning away from the phone, she picked up one of Henry Sexton's old Moleskines and thought over all she had read in the past hour. Getting these notebooks was like being given the key to a hidden library, one in which the secret histories of Natchez and Concordia Parish had been recorded by a monk working in fanatical solitude. They weren't merely a record of Henry's work, but quasi-journalistic diaries containing sketches, theories, meditations on life, guitar tablature, even snatches of poetry and song lyrics. And out of all the tales Henry had so meticulously documented, one shone like a beacon: the reporter's personal stake in the solution of the crimes he sought to solve.

Caitlin's heart skipped when four black-and-white photographs dropped out of the back of the journal in her hand. The first showed an African-American girl of extraordinary beauty sitting on a piano bench, her back to a Baldwin piano. She couldn't have been more than seventeen, but her eyes held the self-possession of a woman ten years older. There was an ethereal quality about her, yet Caitlin could see from the shape of her neck and collarbones that she was no delicate flower. Turning over the photo, Caitlin read: *Swan, 1964,* written lightly in pencil.

The second photo showed the same girl standing next to a skinny white boy with a nervous grin on his pimpled face, hands locked in front of him as though he were afraid of what he might do with them if they got loose. *Henry,* Caitlin thought with a pang of guilt. *Henry at fourteen. My God. And now he's lying over in that hospital, stabbed and beaten half to death.*

A heartbreaking passage in one notebook had described a Saturday afternoon when Henry had walked into Albert's store and found Swan and Jimmy Revels making love in the back room. Though Henry desperately loved Swan, she had loved the heroic and gifted young leader whom Henry himself had looked up to as a kind of demigod. On that terrible day, Henry had sprinted all the way home, his youth pouring out of him in the tears he shed along the way.

Still thinking about Penn's call, Caitlin picked up the third photo from her desk. It showed Albert Norris leaning against a pickup truck with a piano loaded in its bed. He was a strong, dignified-looking man with a smile of greeting on his face, though Caitlin thought his eyes seemed slightly veiled, like those of a sage accustomed to concealing his wisdom.

"You poor man," she murmured, recalling that Norris had served as a cook in the navy during World War II. "Why didn't you go north after the war?"

The man in the snapshot didn't answer. History remained unalterable: Albert Norris had stayed in the South and done about as well as a black man could in the town where he was born—until the night he was burned alive. Caitlin's black hair fell across the photograph. She brushed it back, then slid the photo aside.

The last picture showed four teenage boys playing instruments in what must have been the interior of Norris's Music Emporium. Two guitarists stood up front: one white, the other black. The pimply white boy was Henry Sexton, staring in awe at the left hand of the black guitarist, who was more pretty than handsome. With his head thrown back and his eyes closed, he looked like a young Jimi Hendrix effortlessly channeling the muses through his fingertips. Jimmy Revels, Caitlin guessed. Behind and between the two guitarists, a shirtless, muscular black man with brilliant white teeth pounded blue-glitter drums. *Luther Davis.* And to the drummer's left, almost out of the frame, stood a skinny black boy with a huge Fender bass hanging from one lopsided shoulder.

"Pooky Wilson," she said aloud. "My God."

To look at the pure joy captured in this image, and then be forced to associate it with words like *flayed* and *crucified*, made her skin clammy with revulsion. This world of music and friendship—an oasis in a desert of hatred and mistrust—had been utterly obliterated by the rage of one man, Brody Royal. Not only had all three black boys in this picture been tortured, murdered, and mutilated, but the building itself had been burned to the ground, and its owner immolated. Why was anyone surprised that Henry Sexton had spent decades in his quest to gain justice for these people?

Reaching into her bottom drawer, she took out the snapshot of Tom Cage in the back of the fishing boat with Brody Royal, Claude Devereux, and Ray Presley. *What in God's name are you doing with these assholes?* she wondered. Strangely energized, she snatched up a pen and scrawled a list of leads on her notepad:

- *The Jericho Hole (Kaiser has monopoly)*
- *The Bone Tree (Start tomorrow?)*
- *Pooky's "Huggy Bear" (No clue to ID. Publish plea to come forward?)*
- *Albert's ledgers (No clue to location)*
- *Brody Royal (Too dangerous to approach)*
- *Claude Devereux (Too smart/attorney)*
- *Randall Regan (Brutal rapist, killer)*
- *Katy Royal Regan (Penn would freak. Henry, too.)*

One scan of this list made the truth painfully obvious: Only one avenue of investigation was practical in her existing time frame. Katy Royal. But following that avenue could be dangerous, if Randall Regan discovered she'd made contact with his wife. Interviewing Katy today would surely damage Caitlin's relationship with Penn, and possibly with Henry as well. Could she justify doing that? *That's not the question,* she thought. *Penn didn't even lift the phone to tell me he was meeting Lincoln Turner at a juke club out in the boonies. The question is, can I bear to publish this story tomorrow without adding one iota of original information to it? Can I be merely a mouthpiece for Henry Sexton, however noble that might be?*

"*That's* not even the question," she said aloud. "The question is, can I get to Katy Royal in the next hour without her husband finding out about it?"

Going back over her conversations with Penn, Caitlin realized that she'd only promised to hold off *publishing* anything about Brody Royal until midnight tonight. Technically, she wouldn't be breaking her word by simply investigating him. She knew what Penn would say about this Clintonian parsing of language, but right now, his only interest was saving his father from being shot by police. Caitlin wanted the same thing, of course, but she didn't want *only* that. It wasn't even within her power to help Tom get to safety. And now that the terrifying scope of Brody Royal's and the Double Eagles' crimes had been revealed, she couldn't simply turn away. This was the kind of story she'd originally moved south to cover. Never mind that the old Savage South of her mother's imagination no longer existed; the Double Eagles were still alive—as was Brody Royal—and they'd already proved they would kill to remain free. A bloody wake of violence trailed back through history behind those old men, and the families they had wounded suffered to this day. If Caitlin had a chance to bring peace and justice to those families by succeeding where Henry had failed, how could Penn expect her to turn away? *Besides,* she thought with a bracing thrill, *Penn will be stuck in that meeting for at least two hours.*

As a sop to Penn, she dialed Mercy Hospital and asked for Henry Sexton's room. A few moments later, Sherry Harden came on the line.

"Sherry, this is Caitlin Masters. Is Henry doing any better?"

"Nobody knows," Sherry said curtly. "He's sleeping. He's been out for most of the day."

"I'm sorry. I was hoping to verify something about the story he wants me to publish tomorrow. I need to know if he tried to reinterview someone who refused to tell him anything the first time."

"Are you serious? I can't wake him up for that. You'll just have to do the best you can. And please don't call back. The phone disturbs him."

Sherry hung up.

Thank you very much, Caitlin thought with perverse satisfaction. Now Penn couldn't argue that she'd tried to circumvent Henry.

She saved her open computer files in an encrypted format, then logged into a White Pages website and typed *Katy Royal Regan* in the search field. The search engine instantly kicked back *Randall and Katy Regan, 18 Royal Road, Lake Concordia, Louisiana*. She memorized the address and scrawled the phone number on a Post-it, then typed in *Royal Insurance Company, Vidalia, Louisiana*. Adding this phone number to the Post-it, she made a quick plan.

Lake Concordia was ten miles from the *Examiner* offices. She could call Royal Insurance on her way to Louisiana, and with any luck verify Randall Regan's presence at his office. If he wasn't there, she'd have to find a way to make sure he wasn't home with his wife. But given what she'd learned about that relationship, Caitlin felt confident that home was the last place Randall Regan would be. With adrenaline pumping through her like fuel, she stuck the Post-it to her Treo, dropped a Sony tape recorder into her purse (next to her pistol), and headed for the front door.

CHAPTER 75

CAITLIN KNEW SHE was risking her life to interview Katy Royal Regan. To minimize that risk, while driving over the bridge to Louisiana, she'd called Royal Insurance and asked for Randall Regan. When the receptionist asked for her name, Caitlin answered that she was Special Agent Glass of the FBI. When Regan came on the line, speaking like he had a bad case of laryngitis, she informed him that an FBI search team would arrive at Royal Insurance in thirty minutes with a warrant, and that he should be prepared to produce all files pertaining to the state insurance fraud case of 2003. If Regan had any trouble remembering which case that was, she said, it was the one in which two female employees who had given evidence to federal agents had disappeared. Before Regan could do anything but curse, she'd hung up.

As for Katy Regan, Caitlin had reluctantly decided on an ambush interview. According to Henry's notes, the woman hadn't been upset by his questions about Pooky Wilson during his interview, and she'd been gracious to Henry throughout. But when he'd called back two days ago, she'd angrily rebuffed him. Caitlin wasn't going to risk spooking her quarry before getting inside her house.

Dusk was falling by the time Caitlin reached Lake Concordia, and the first thing she saw was a line of houses decorated with Christmas lights. None could compete with the Regan home for gaudy splendor. Every surface of the house had been lined with colored bulbs, and the yard boasted at least six inflatable displays, one depicting Santa landing in a helicopter. Caitlin called the house immediately, identified herself, then told Mrs. Regan that the *Examiner* was doing a lifestyle story on Christmas displays. Could she possibly stop by for ten minutes to discuss Mrs. Regan's decorative sense? When Katy agreed, Caitlin hung up before the woman could change her mind. Five minutes later, she presented herself at the front door, which had been covered with red foil wrap.

The interior of the Regan home looked like a photo spread out of *Southern Living* magazine—French country fireplaces, contemporary furniture, and three antlered deer staring down from the living room walls. Katy herself looked like a Stepford wife of indeterminate age. Caitlin knew from research that Brody Royal's daughter was fifty-nine, but Katy already had the scared-cat face of the plastic surgery addict. When she answered the door, her eyes had a glaze that Caitlin read as the result of a couple of gin-and-tonics. Her polite drawl had the beginnings of a slur, as well. Caitlin hoped the alcohol might loosen the woman's tongue.

The Regans' living room looked out over the narrow oxbow of Lake Concordia, which reflected a thousand colored lights. Caitlin accepted the offer of a glass of sherry, though she detested the stuff, and watched her hostess walk to her kitchen to pour it. While Katy was out of sight, Caitlin switched on the miniature tape recorder in her purse.

Soon her glassy-eyed hostess handed her the sherry, then went to the chair opposite Caitlin and sat with her legs crossed so perfectly that she must have learned the art at some finishing school for southern belles. Caitlin found it difficult to reconcile this poise with her knowledge that Katy Regan had been forcibly committed to a mental institution where she'd been subjected to primitive electroshock therapy for nearly a year.

"You look very chic," Mrs. Regan said, nodding at Caitlin's black silk T-shirt and jeans. "I could never carry off that look."

"Of course you could," Caitlin said, smiling.

"Oh, no. But thank you. Aren't you and the mayor getting married soon?"

Caitlin forced her mind to shift gears. "Ah . . . yes, we are. I mean, we were getting married this weekend, but some family issues came up. We'll probably have the ceremony this spring."

Katy Regan's smile broadened. "Will it be a *big* wedding? Dunleith and the carriage? All that? I *love* big weddings."

Caitlin forced herself to sip the sherry, then set down her glass. "Mrs. Regan, I'm sort of under a deadline."

"Of course, dear. What would you like to know?"

She took a deep breath, then spoke in the most sympathetic voice she could muster. "I'm going to be honest with you. I didn't really come here to talk about Christmas lights."

The surgically augmented lips flattened into a tense smile. "I never thought you did. I've read your stories, Ms. Masters. You've never written anything but hard news."

Caitlin was startled to hear such frank clarity from this seemingly airheaded woman. "The truth is, I've been working with Henry Sexton, and—"

"Oh, *Lord*," Mrs. Regan cut in, her face a caricature of shock. "Wasn't that terrible what happened to him?"

"Yes," Caitlin said, sensing a chance for cooperation. "That's why I'm working on this story now. And Mrs. Regan, I must tell you—"

"Please call me Katy, dear."

"Katy," Caitlin said thankfully. "Both Henry and I believe—we fervently hope—that you can shed some light on one particularly heinous crime."

Mrs. Regan blinked like a young ingénue auditioning for a lead role. "What crime is that?"

"The murder of a boy named Justus Wilson. His friends called him 'Pooky.'"

Katy Royal kept looking back at Caitlin as though she hadn't spoken a word. Then, after an interminable silence, she blinked once, like a patient bird. "Who, dear?"

Caitlin leaned forward and gave Katy the full intensity of her gaze. She knew that her bright green eyes sometimes unnerved people, and she hoped they would have that effect now. "Pooky—Wilson," she enunciated. "He was a young black man who worked for Albert Norris, the music store owner, back in 1964. He disappeared on July nineteenth, the day after his boss was murdered. He was never seen again."

If anything, Katy's eyes had grown glassier still.

Purely on instinct, Caitlin took the photo of Pooky and his band from her purse, then crossed to Katy's chair and held the picture before her.

"That's Pooky on the right," she said, "playing the bass guitar. He was murdered in 1964, and I finally know why."

"Why?" Katy asked, her eyes glued to the photograph, her voice as distant as the echo in a canyon.

"Because he loved a white girl. A beautiful eighteen-year-old girl."

"No."

"Yes," Caitlin said softly. "A girl named Katy."

"No." Mrs. Regan shook her head. "He didn't love her."

This was the last thing Caitlin had expected to hear. "He didn't?"

The stretched-taut face began to twist with emotion. "No, no, no. He just wanted to touch her. *Use* her. Do dirty things to her."

Caitlin couldn't quite read what lay behind the troubled face, but the voice sounded angry. "Who are you talking about, Katy?"

Mrs. Regan shook her head like someone trying to wake herself from a trance. Then she looked at Caitlin with unsettling directness. "You're taping this, aren't you?"

Caitlin swallowed. "No."

"*Liar, liar, pants on fire,*" Katy chanted in a childlike voice. "I'm not *blind*, you know."

Caitlin felt as though she'd awakened in a 1950s horror movie.

"If you want me to keep talking," Katy said, "turn off your tape machine."

Caitlin thought about it for a few seconds. Then she went back to her chair and replaced the photograph in her purse. Lifting the Sony so that Katy could see its red light, she switched off the recorder.

The woman smiled with childish satisfaction. "Now. Where were we?"

"Pooky Wilson." Caitlin dropped the recorder back into her purse. "I was confused, because you were speaking in the third person. You said, 'He didn't love her. He just wanted to do dirty things to her.' But I assume you were talking about yourself."

"Yourself, myself, himself . . . no-self. What's the difference?"

Caitlin took a stab in the dark. "Were you talking about Katy Royal?"

"*Katy Ann Royal!*" Mrs. Regan barked. "*You get those shoes off and get ready for dinner!*" Then she answered in a child's plaintive voice, as though acting two roles in a play. "Yes, ma'am, I will." Then a third voice, oddly detached, began to chant: "*Katy Ann, tall and tan. She was a good girl, but she's gone again. All gone. Nobody left now . . . nobody but me. Daddy and Dr. Borgen made sure of that.*"

"Dr. Borgen?" Caitlin said, wishing the Sony were still on.

Katy gave her an eerie, knowing look. "Mm-hm. You'd know him if you saw him. His eyes sparkle, and his hair is made of blue fire."

Caitlin jumped as her Treo vibrated in her purse, but she didn't dare reach for it. Mrs. Regan's eyes tracked the sound like the buzzing of a rattlesnake. "Are you still taping me, Miss Priss?"

"No! I promise. That was my cell phone. I'm going to set it to silent so we won't be interrupted."

Katy looked uncertain, then nodded her assent.

As Caitlin reached for the vibrating phone, an idea struck her. As casually as she could, she opened her Treo's voice note program and hit the record button. Then she switched off the vibrate setting and laid the phone atop the pistol in her purse.

"Katy . . . you were talking about your time in the Borgen Institute?"

The woman raised up her hands and hugged herself as though she'd been airdropped into the middle of an ice storm. "*Shhhh.* That's not its real name. That's what they call it on the *outside*. But when you go there, when they *lock you in,* you learn its real name. The secret name."

"What was its secret name?"

Katy Regan lifted her chin and spoke in an exaggerated whisper. "*Hay-des.* The main building was built over a humongous hole. Down under the basement there's a hole that goes all the way to the center of the earth. It has an electric door that crackles and burns. Dr. Borgen has the switch that works the door."

Caitlin wasn't sure how to respond to this.

"They have a furnace, too. A furnace where they burn people they don't want anymore."

Caitlin shivered at the conviction in the woman's voice. "Katy . . . are you all right? Can I get you something?"

Mrs. Regan giggled, then let her arms fall and said: "No drinky-poo for Katy-boo! She's had too much already."

Caitlin found herself at a loss. Obviously Katy Regan was mentally unbalanced, but was that sufficient reason to stop trying to find out what she knew about Pooky Wilson's murder? Katy had already implied that Pooky had done things to her against her will. Was it possible that Henry had got the story wrong? Had Pooky's "Huggy Bear" ever known the truth about Pooky and Katy? Had Justus "Pooky" Wilson forced himself on a rich white girl and then paid a medieval price for his transgression? *No,* Caitlin thought. *That's the classic stereotype. Why would a well-liked black boy risk being castrated or killed for a few minutes with a white girl who didn't want him?*

"Katy?" Caitlin said gently. "What can you tell me about the day Pooky disappeared? Were you happy or sad?"

Mrs. Regan scrunched up her face like a child, then shook her head.

"Did you love Pooky?"

"I don't remember."

"Are you sure?"

Katy squeezed her eyes shut like a little kid. "Don't! Dirty! *Dirty bird!*"

"Katy?"

"That dirty bird put it in me! He had to be punished!"

Caitlin suddenly realized that Mrs. Regan was sweating profusely. "Who are you talking about, Katy? Are you talking about Pooky?"

The woman nodded, but again the gesture seemed to have been against her will. Then she cried, "Dr. Borgen did it! *He* put it in me. When the nurses were gone. Every day Katy had to play, or else stay longer in the hole."

A shudder ran through Caitlin. She wanted to ask for details of what she gathered was sexual abuse by a psychiatrist, but she didn't know how long Katy would stay coherent. More than this, her first priority remained unshaken: *Brody Royal.*

"Tell me about your father, Katy."

Mrs. Regan's eyes went wide, as though she'd mistakenly opened a door into a theater showing a slasher film. Yet once again the voice that came from her mouth was soft and childlike. "Daddy took care of me. Always. He takes care of us all. When I had the blue devils, Daddy chased them away. When I was alone, he found me a husband. Did you know that?"

"What do you mean?"

"Daddy owns the company Randall works for. He owns Randall, too. Bought him a long time ago, right after I got back from *Hay*—" Katy winked—"from the *institute.*"

Without Caitlin realizing it, Katy had uncrossed her legs and sunk deep into her chair. If she sank any farther, she would probably slide right out of it. As Caitlin began to despair of learning anything useful,

Katy said, "Pooky was so sweet. He sang pretty, too, all the time. Can you keep a secret?"

Caitlin nodded with what she hoped was girlish enthusiasm.

"Pooky wanted to marry me. With the carriage and everything. But all he had was a bicycle and his daddy's old mule. The night I got married for real"—Katy's voice dropped to a whisper—"I thought about Pooky the whole time. Poor Poo. I knew he was gone, though."

"Where did he go?"

Katy shook her head. "It's too terrible," she whispered.

"I need to know, Katy. For Pooky's sake."

Mrs. Regan looked around the room, paying special attention to the windows and the door, as though she expected to find white-coated attendants peering in at her. "There's another place like . . . like the place I was. Another hole in the world. It's for the dark people. A tree grows over it. A big twisted tree with branches that reach almost to the sky. And it's filled with bones. The dark people who break the law are taken there."

"Why are they taken there?"

Katy looked into her lap and spoke in the voice of a two-year-old. "To get punished."

"Do they ever come back?"

Now Katy's face held the sober concentration of a child given its first glimpse of human cruelty. "Never."

Caitlin sensed she was on the verge of a revelation. All she could think about was a place described in Henry's journals as the Bone Tree—a place where Indians and black men had been murdered for years, and dead bodies dumped to prevent their being found. "Who took Pooky to that tree?"

"I was always going to tell," she said softly. "But I have to wait until Daddy *passes*. Then he can't hurt me."

"Katy—"

"Shh! He might hear us. Daddy can hear from miles away sometimes. You know . . . before Henry came and talked to me, all this was blank. Everything had fallen down Dr. Borgen's hole. But then it started to come back. First the bathtub . . . Daddy killed Mama in the bath. Did you know that? I thought he was just talking to her—and he was. But later I figured it out. He was holding her head under the water while he talked."

Every hair on Caitlin's body was standing erect. She swallowed hard. She couldn't find her voice.

"Then, when you called a few minutes ago," Katy said, "I knew."

"Knew what?"

The woman shook her head again. "It doesn't matter. It's too late."

"What do you mean? Too late for what?"

Brody Royal's daughter listed to the left in her chair. "For *me*. For Katy-Poo."

"*Katy*," Caitlin said firmly. "Whatever you were waiting to tell, you can tell me. Now. No one will hurt you anymore. I'll make sure of that."

The woman's eyes rose and met Caitlin's with conspiratorial slyness. "Will you promise not to tell?"

"Yes. I promise."

A manicured fingernail rose to the red lips, its scarlet nail gleaming. "Cross your heart and hope to die?"

"Stick a needle in my eye."

Katy looked right, then left, then finally spoke with the certitude of a courier who had carried a message through miles of bloody trenches. *"Daddy did it."*

Caitlin's heart thumped against her sternum. "Did what? What did Daddy do, Katy?"

The heavy lidded eyes fluttered. "Like Jesus," she whispered.

Like Jesus? Caitlin shivered again, though she didn't know why. "Did your father kill Pooky, Katy?"

The woman nodded once more. "And Dr. Leland. He killed Mr. Henry," she said softly. "And that colored nurse, too."

At this, Caitlin's voice deserted her again.

Katy was listing to the other side now; she looked as though she might fall out of the chair at any moment.

"*Katy?*" Caitlin said, coming to her feet.

Mrs. Regan opened her mouth, but no sound passed her lips. Then she went as limp as a rag doll and slid to the floor. Her head hit the carpet with a wooden thump.

Caitlin stared, momentarily paralyzed. Then she jumped down and felt for a carotid pulse. It was there, but very weak.

"Katy!" Caitlin shouted. *"Katy Regan! Can you hear me?"*

The woman gave no sign of having heard.

"How long have you been drinking? Did you take something?"

Katy groaned but formed no coherent words.

Crawling to her purse for her Treo, Caitlin heard a bang from the side of the house. Then heavy footsteps clunked up the hallway. She looked at her watch, and a bolt of fear shot through her. *Randall Regan?*

She got to her feet, instinctively looking for a place to hide. As she glanced toward the hall door, she saw a large brown pill bottle sitting on the fireplace hearth. She hadn't noticed it before, but now it seemed the largest object in the room. The bottle had no lid, and it was empty.

"Who are you?" shouted a male voice. "What the hell's happening here?"

Caitlin turned to see a tall, dark-haired man in his fifties kneeling beside Katy. In one glance Caitlin knew this was the man who had raped and murdered two former employees of Royal Insurance. God only knew what he'd done to Katy behind the locked doors of this house—or what he would do to Caitlin if he caught her.

"I think she took some pills," Caitlin said, casting about for a lie that would buy the time she needed to escape. "See there?" She pointed to the empty bottle by the fireplace. "I was about to call 911."

Regan's eyes didn't leave her for a second. "Who *are* you?"

He stood and took a step toward her.

Caitlin grabbed her purse off the floor, spilling out half its contents. Regan was still closing the space between them when she got her pistol out and held it in front of her.

The sight of the .38 stopped him, but she wasn't sure it would hold Regan long. He had the eyes of an enraged animal.

"Call 911!" she shouted. "And let me out of here! Just *let me go!*"

"You're that Masters bitch," he said in a low, cracked voice. "Penn Cage's whore. You're not gonna shoot me."

Caitlin felt her arm shaking. Regan was calling her bluff. What would happen if she shot a man in his own home, after having gained entry under false pretenses? Did it even matter? *Not if I don't get out of here alive.*

"Let me out, I said! I'll shoot!"

Regan laughed and started forward.

Caitlin fired into the floor at his feet. He stopped, and the smell of gunpowder filled the room. Caitlin moved quickly around him, keeping the gun pointed at him all the time. Regan turned to track her movements, but the door wasn't far away now. Then a horrifying thought struck her.

"You'd *better* call 911," she said. "Because I'm calling it as soon as I leave. You can't let her die on the floor."

"You're dead," Regan rasped, his eyes burning. "You and your boyfriend both. *Dead*."

Caitlin whirled and ran for her car.

CHAPTER 76

I'M SITTING ON the second floor of the old City Jail, now refurbished as a meeting hall for the Board of Selectmen but still known as the "old jail." Tonight the jail is being used for the Joint Governance Meeting, which brings the city and county governments together, an event as rare as a U.S.-Chinese summit. For nearly two hours I've listened in excruciating agony while black and white politicians with only one thing in common—a profound ignorance of history—debate the merits of creating a unique but racially sensitive historical park and memorial. As a result, I've developed a detailed fantasy of dropping several of my colleagues through the long-disused hangman's trapdoor upstairs.

Four days ago, the two projects we've met to discuss were the chief goals of my administration (after reforming the public school system). Now they seem like obscure public works projects I read about in the back pages of *Newsweek*. This is the kind of meeting where I wish the only two people on my side would get off of it. One ally is black, the other white, and neither seems to realize that his impassioned rant will only hurt our chances of securing the votes and funding required to get this park built.

Not that I give a damn at this moment.

For the first hour, all I could think about was what Lincoln Turner told me in the juke near Anna's Bottom, and the deductions I made afterward. Then Sheriff Dennis called my cell. When I stepped out of the meeting, Dennis told me that, not long before, someone identifying himself only as "Mr. Brown" had called his office and insisted on speaking to the sheriff. When Walker got on the line, "Mr. Brown" told him that on the previous night, he'd witnessed a pickup truck bearing the Royal Oil Company logo smash the front door of the *Concordia Beacon* with its right front fender. Then he'd seen two men get out, one of whom appeared to be carrying a large backpack. They entered the newspaper, and moments later, an intense glow became visible through the smashed door. About a minute later, the arsonists had emerged and fled the scene in the truck.

"Did you ask this 'Mr. Brown' if he recognized them?" I asked.

"He said he did," Walker answered in the tone of a man telling a good joke. "He said one was Randall Regan, and the other was Brody Royal himself. Those were his exact words. *Himself.*"

This news actually lifted me out of my trance. "He told you Brody Royal torched the *Concordia Beacon*?"

"Yep. What do you think I ought to do about that tip?"

"Have you told anybody else about it?"

"Not yet."

"Not even your deputies?"

"No."

"Then don't. Don't say anything about it to anybody. I'll get back to you about this later. Okay?"

"If you say so."

I remembered then that Walker had no idea about the existence of Henry's "Huggy Bear." "I do, Walker. This could be important."

After hanging up with Sheriff Dennis, I returned to my Kafkaesque civic meeting. At this moment, a white Republican is trying to reassure his colleagues that a rebuilt slave market is really "just a king-size diorama, like the ones they have at Civil War battlefield parks," while a black Democrat makes sweeping statements about forcing white elites to acknowledge the greatest crime in American history. My fantasy about the old hangman's trapdoor upstairs gives way to a compulsion to offer dueling pistols to each side and let them shoot it out. Or better yet . . . the silver-handled straight razor Pithy Nolan gave me yesterday is still in my inside coat pocket. I never took it out last night, and the thing is so slim that I forgot it was there until now. *What would these blowhards do if I pulled out the "Lady's Best Friend" and sliced off their ties just below their half-Windsors?*

As I try to banish this thought, one of the saner supervisors suggests that we should suspend discussion of the slave market and move on to the intentional flooding of St. Catherine's Creek, which flows through the middle of Natchez, but she's instantly shouted down. Apparently even the problems of eminent domain pale next to those involving race.

When my cell phone vibrates on the table yet again, two selectmen glare at me, almost daring me to check the LCD. Leaning forward, I see Caitlin's name.

"Just tell me this!" snaps a supervisor. "If this is such an all-fired great idea, why hasn't somebody on the South Carolina coast started rebuilding slave ships? Huh? Tell me that!"

Caitlin's text message reads:

Call me NOW. Urgent!

Lifting my left hand in apology, I say, "Excuse me again, ladies and gentlemen. Family emergency." With a screech of chair legs, I get to my feet and decamp to the anteroom, where I speed-dial Caitlin.

"Are you alone?" she asks, her voice quavering.

"What's the matter?"

"I think I just killed somebody."

My chest goes so tight that my next breath takes conscious effort. "What do you mean? With your car?"

"No. I just interviewed Brody Royal's daughter, Katy Regan."

"*What?*"

"I know, I know, I'm sorry. I just felt that I couldn't write the story without at least trying to talk to her."

My intimate knowledge of Caitlin's ambition fills me with foreboding. "What did you do?"

"I ambushed her. I know it was wrong, but it was the only way. Henry had interviewed her about Pooky before, and it hadn't upset her, so I figured it was okay. She let me into her house quite happily—"

"Jesus. You know Randall Regan is a killer."

"I know. Please just listen. She seemed fine with it, seriously. Even when I told her why I was really there. I figured she might be ready open up to another woman, you know?"

Cold dread closes around my heart. "What happened, Caitlin?"

"It went fine for a while, and then she passed out right in front of me. She'd taken an overdose of pills before I got there."

"Is she alive?"

"She's in a coma at St. Catherine's Hospital."

I blow out a rush of air and force myself to start breathing again. "Caitlin, you—"

"I *know*," she says again. "I should have told you."

"No, you should have *waited*. Christ, this is a disaster."

"Not totally."

"What do you mean?"

"I'd rather not say anything on the phone. I'm almost outside the Selectmen's Building. Can you come out and talk for a second?"

I feel like screaming at her, but that's not going to solve anything. And if she knows anything that can mitigate this tragedy, I need to hear it. "How close are you?"

"I'll be out front in twenty seconds."

"I'm on my way down."

THE INTERIOR OF CAITLIN'S car is twenty degrees warmer than the outside air, but the voice of the disturbed woman coming from Caitlin's Treo chills me more deeply than any wind. Katy Royal Regan's voice as she accuses her psychiatrist of using her for sex sounds like that of a little girl shaken awake in the midst of a nightmare.

"Let me skip ahead," Caitlin says, fiddling with the phone's controls. "Right here. She's talking about the Bone Tree that Henry wrote about in his journals. That's a killing ground that dates back to Indian and slave times, but the Klan also used it, and they dumped bodies there. Just listen to this shit."

Caitlin presses PLAY.

"*Who took Pooky to that tree?*"

"*I was always going to tell,*" says the childlike voice. "*But I have to wait until Daddy passes. Then he can't hurt me.*"

"*Katy—*"

"*Shh! He might hear us. Daddy can hear from miles away sometimes. You know . . . before Henry came and talked to me, all this was blank. Everything had fallen down Dr. Borgen's hole. But then it started to come back. First the bathtub . . . Daddy killed Mama in the bath. Did you know that? I thought he was just talking to her—and he was. But later I figured it out. He was holding her head under the water while he talked.*" There was a pause. "*Then, when you called a few minutes ago, I knew.*"

"*Knew what?*"

"*It doesn't matter. It's too late.*"

"*What do you mean? Too late for what?*"

"*For me. For Katy-Poo.*"

"Jesus," I mutter. "This woman belongs in a hospital."

"Oh, yeah. Just listen."

"*Katy. Whatever you were waiting to tell, you can tell me. Now. No one will hurt you anymore. I'll make sure of that.*"

"*Will you promise not to tell?*"

"*Yes. I promise.*"

"*Cross your heart and hope to die?*"

"*Stick a needle in my eye.*"

"*Daddy did it.*"

I clench the door handle so hard my arm shakes.

"*Did what?*" Caitlin presses. "*What did Daddy do, Katy?*"

"*Like Jesus.*"

"Whoa," I breathe, shuddering at the implication of these words. She must be talking about the crucifixion that Henry has always heard rumors about.

"*Did your father kill Pooky, Katy?*"

"She nodded right here," Caitlin says in a taut voice.

"*And Dr. Leland. He killed Mr. Henry . . . and that colored nurse, too.*"

"Oh my God. Does she say Viola's name?"

"No. She slides out of her chair right about here. Totally unconscious."

"*Katy?*" Caitlin cries on the recording.

The sound of a blunt impact follows.

"*Katy! Katy Regan! Can you hear me?*" Silence. "*How long have you been drinking? Did you take something?*"

I hear a groan but no coherent words. Then there's a bang, and heavy footsteps on hardwood.

"Right here I saw the empty bottle of pills by the fireplace."

"*Who are you?*" yells a male voice, one I recognize from earlier today. Caitlin stops the recording. "That's Randall Regan. He came at me, Penn. He would have killed me if he could. I had to fire a shot into the floor to stop him. He got my tape recorder. It fell out of my purse. But at least we have *this*." She holds up her phone in triumph. "So, what do you think? As a lawyer?"

I shake my head in disbelief. "As your future husband, I think you're crazy. As a lawyer . . . it's the closest anyone's gotten to real evidence in the Albert Norris case."

"The *Norris* case! Penn, Katy Royal just said her father killed at least seven people, if you count the plane crash—*including Viola Turner.*"

"I know," I murmur, troubled by something I can't quite pin down. "Five minutes ago, I was sure Lincoln Turner had euthanized his mother. Or screwed up trying to revive her."

"Based on pure conjecture. That's a theory, and a damned complicated one." She shakes the phone in my face. "This is *Royal's daughter* saying he killed Viola. On *tape*. Or in digital memory, whatever."

"She didn't use Viola's name."

Caitlin's mouth forms an O of disbelief. "What other 'colored nurse' could she be talking about?"

"But my scenario explained Dad's behavior. His willingness to take the fall."

"Because he believes Lincoln is his son?"

"Right."

She gives an exasperated sigh. "Maybe Tom does believe that. Maybe Lincoln believes it, too. That explains his willingness to take a DNA test. But *I* don't. No way is Tom the father of that man."

"Why not?"

"Logic, for one thing. You told me Lincoln is blacker than Viola was, right? Tom's ancestors were Scots-English. He's as light as I am, and that's saying something."

"Lincoln says that's possible. He's checked the genetics of it."

"He's a disbarred lawyer with zero objectivity! I'd prefer the opinion of an actual geneticist on that." Her voice gains certainty as she goes on. "Lincoln claims your father has known about him for years, right? Again—no way. Tom wouldn't have kept that secret for forty years. He would have owned up to it."

"I'm not sure. Dad has his secrets. He's never told me what happened to him in Korea."

"A lot of veterans are like that. If you'd been drafted to go fight somewhere, he'd have told you about Korea. Did Lincoln say or imply that your mother knows anything about him?"

"No."

She gives me a pointed look. "Do you plan on asking Peggy about Lincoln?"

"Hell, no! Not if I can avoid it."

"Let me give you the female perspective. Viola was terminally ill.

She'd had a hard life, and Lincoln's probably wasn't much better. At some point, somebody probably told him he was someone else's kid. Maybe the stepfather. Lincoln would have confronted Viola, asked who his real father was. What's she going to say? Your father was a Klan rapist from Mississippi? The math is the same as a pregnancy by your father, you know. And a black woman impregnated by a Klansman has a lot better reason to keep a boy's paternity secret than one pregnant by a white physician she loved." Caitlin shakes her head with conviction. "No, she lied. She blamed a one-night stand, a long-gone boyfriend from Chicago, something. Because if she'd told Lincoln his father was a rich white doctor, Tom would have heard from the boy long before now. But he *didn't.*"

Before I can interject anything, she says, "But *later*—after she got cancer—she was overwhelmed by guilt. She's facing an early death and failure as a mother. Her son's a disbarred lawyer, no prospects. She wants to leave him some security, give him the best life she can."

"So she tells him Dad is his father?"

"Yep. But it's not what she told Lincoln that's important. It's what she told *Tom* that matters."

The heat of recognition flushes my skin.

"You know your father. Atticus Finch with a stethoscope. If Viola told him they'd had a son that she'd kept secret for forty years to protect your family—what would he do?"

"Whatever Viola asked him to."

"Exactly! Tom probably called an attorney the next day to start setting up a trust fund for Lincoln."

I have the feeling Caitlin's scenario may be close to the truth. "None of that weakens my theory about Lincoln killing his mother. Both he and Dad would be acting in the belief that they were father and son."

"I don't pretend to know exactly how Viola died," she says. Then she holds up her Treo. "But my money's on the Double Eagles, under orders from Brody Royal."

Caitlin seizes my wrist and looks hard into my eyes. "Penn, you've got to forget all this Gothic crap. We've got a recording of Brody's daughter saying he committed murder, and Viola's included in that. The only question is, what are we going to do with it?"

I do my best to suppress my personal issues and analyze the evidence. "The recording is problematic. If Katy doesn't come out of that coma, she can't be cross-examined, and she's clearly got mental issues, as evidenced on the tape. Plus she's under the influence of a potentially suicidal dose of narcotics. The recording would be a lot more effective with her alive on the stand to verify and elaborate on it.

"*If* she would verify it. She's clearly been terrified of her father for years. Her husband, too. If she doesn't wake up from the coma, could this stand as a dying utterance?"

Caitlin's ambition is like a third person in the car.

"I doubt it. But if you could get it admitted, the circumstances might lend weight to her statements. Except . . ."

"What?"

"She said her father killed Henry. Didn't she?"

"Yeah. 'Mr. Henry,' she said. Like a little girl."

"Henry Sexton's not dead."

Caitlin shrugs as though this is inconsequential. "I'm sure she meant that Brody *ordered* the hit on Henry. They did try to kill him, right?"

"Yes, but that's a big problem, as far as using this recording as trial evidence. It calls everything else she said into question. God, I wish she'd spoken Viola's name."

Caitlin turns and stares out at the darkened courthouse. "Are you saying I shouldn't use it?"

"No. But what are you thinking of doing with it?"

"If this were any other case . . . I'd go straight over to St. Catherine's Hospital and interview Brody Royal right now—if he's even there. That's what Henry would do, if he could."

I strive to keep my voice level. "But this *isn't* any other case. And given Royal's past, and what you just did to his daughter—and her husband—that could be suicidal."

Caitlin whirls on me. "I'm sorry the woman tried to kill herself, okay? But she's been mentally unstable for years. And I see no reason not to use this recording as the linchpin of tomorrow's stories."

I draw back in surprise. "You want to publish the contents of this recording? Tomorrow?"

"Maybe," she says defiantly.

As I try to think of a way to prevent this, a revolutionary idea comes to me. "You know something? From an evidentiary point of view, that recording has serious problems. But as an existential reality . . . it's one hell of a weapon."

She looks suspicious. "What exactly do you mean?"

"I know you're focused on tomorrow's story. But tomorrow is a world away right now. At this moment, Dad and Walt are being hunted as cop killers. Their lives are measured in hours, maybe minutes. The *only* way to save them is to get that APB revoked. And the only way I can see to do that is to go to the very men who want Dad dead and blamed for Viola's murder."

Caitlin's eyes narrow still further. "Brody? And . . . ?"

"Forrest Knox. Knox issued the APB. They're the only ones with the stroke to change the public narrative and stop that manhunt."

"Bullshit! *I* can change the public narrative. With this recording, and with Henry's files."

"Not fast enough to save Dad."

When Caitlin covers her eyes with her hands, I know it's all she can do not to hit me in the face.

"There's more," I go on. "Earlier today, I got into a fight with Randall Regan myself. I didn't tell you because I didn't want you to worry. But it was brutal. Now you've driven Brody's daughter to suicide, and fired a gun at Regan in his own house. Do you really think they're going to sit around and wait for you to destroy them in tomorrow's *Examiner?* We really shouldn't even be sitting out here on the street."

As though realizing the danger for the first time, she scans the dark street around us.

"To save Dad, we've got to go straight at them," I tell her, squeezing her arm. "Right now. They won't expect that, and it'll give us the initiative."

"But why would they agree to help Tom?"

"Because I'm going to show them a greater threat than Dad. Between what you've got on that phone, what I know from Henry, and some exaggerations about witnesses, I can make them see that killing Dad isn't worth what it will cost them in the end."

"What witnesses are you talking about?"

"Huggy Bear. Walker Dennis got a call today from a guy who claims he saw Brody and Regan burn the *Beacon* last night. He didn't give his real name, but I think it's the same guy who saw Brody burn Norris's store forty years ago—only he's a man now."

Caitlin's eyes flash with interest, but then she settles back into her seat, her jaw muscles flexing. "I don't like this. It sounds more like *bribery* than intimidation. Those bastards aren't going to give you anything without getting something in return. You know that."

"Who cares! The point is getting Dad safely into federal custody. After that, you can throw Brody to the wolves. You just might have to wait a day to do it. That's all. For them to call off the dogs, and for me to get Dad safely in."

Her cheeks go red. "Now you want me to hold off publishing for a day? This afternoon you were demanding that I publish everything immediately!"

"Don't postpone the story. Just leave Brody and the tape out of it for a day. Those old murders have waited nearly forty years to be solved. They can wait another twenty-four hours."

There's a war going on inside Caitlin, her code of honor and blazing ambition on one side, love for my father on the other.

"Penn . . . Brody Royal is like a cobra in tall grass. Regan, too. You're saying you want to walk into the grass with them and make some kind of deal—then go back on it and nail them. *I* say the only way to get them is to slash and burn their cover, expose them for everyone to see. That's the only way to stop monsters like that. If you try your way . . . I'm afraid you'll wind up like Henry, or worse."

Reaching into my coat, I take out the straight razor I carried up to the selectmen's meeting and open my palm. "I went to see Pithy Nolan yesterday. She gave me a little present. Be careful with it."

Caitlin takes the gleaming object from my hand, runs a fingernail down the groove between the handle and blade.

"Brody Royal gave Pithy that just after World War Two. For her protection, he said. He was hoping to marry her, but she saw him for the gangster he was."

Caitlin sucks in her breath as she flips the ugly blade from its silver handle. "Jesus."

"Pithy gave that to me as a reminder of who I was dealing with, if I chose to go up against Brody."

Caitlin squints at the handle in the dim light. "What does this inscription say?"

"'A Lady's Best Friend.' Can you imagine? Brody gave that to a Natchez belle."

Caitlin clucks her tongue softly. "After reading Henry's journals . . . I believe it."

Taking back the razor, I carefully fold it closed. "I haven't forgotten what Brody did to those black boys, or those women who tried to go to the feds about the insurance fraud. I don't have any illusions, and I won't confront him or Regan alone."

Caitlin sighs and lets her head fall on my chest. "Who would you take with you? John Kaiser?"

Wanting to embrace her, I slip the razor into my back pocket. "Kaiser wouldn't let me try something like this. His goal is to put the Double Eagles in prison, and maybe Forrest Knox. He's going to go by the book, more or less. He has no choice."

"Who, then?"

"I think Kirk Boisseau will go with me."

She blows out a rush of air. "Where would you confront them?"

"The hospital, if that's where Brody is. If he's not with his daughter, then some other public place."

Her right forefinger rises to her philtrum, then runs down the sculpted curve. "Does Kirk understand the risks?"

"I'll make sure he does."

Her eyes find mine again. "What if you play Brody Royal that tape, and he decides to unplug his daughter's ventilator because of it?"

I've never considered this. "I don't think he will. Royal thinks he's invincible. All his life experience up to now has confirmed that belief. He'll think he can deal his way out of this, and I'll confirm that instinct."

She grunts skeptically. "I think when he's threatened, he lashes out."

I take her hand and squeeze it hard. "You may be right. But I know one thing for sure: if we do this by the book, Dad's never coming home again."

Her eyes focus somewhere above me. She looks like she's performing a complicated equation in her head. After a long silence, she says, "We can make a copy of the recording at the paper."

A flood of relief goes through me. "Thank you."

"Are you going back up to the selectmen's meeting?"

"Only to adjourn it. I'll be back down in two minutes."

She leans over the console and hugs me, then draws back, her eyes wet. "Do you want me to wait, or should I go on over?"

"Do you still have your gun?"

She reaches down to the floor and pulls up the black .38 Special my father gave her seven years ago. "Only fired once in anger."

"Take off the second I step out of the car."

She nods. "I'll have the copy made by the time you get there."

CHAPTER 77

WALKING DOWN THE hall toward Henry Sexton's hospital room, Caitlin saw the deputy guarding the door watching her approach. He was sitting in the same high school desk, his cell phone glowing on the desktop like he'd been playing a game on it. His eyes followed her as surely as any high school boy's would have, and his mouth hung just as slack. She smiled as she signed her name in his notebook, but her mind was otherwise engaged. She'd gotten her press operator to drive her to Ferriday in his car, hoping to evade anyone watching the *Examiner* building. Penn would scream to high heaven if he knew she'd left the building, but she meant to get all she could from Henry before tomorrow.

She'd hoped to find him alone, but her luck wasn't running that way. Sherry Harden was still here, guarding her man with bleary eyes. Henry's hospital room looked messier than it had during the morning, though with a lot more flowers. Henry's eyes were half open but dull, and his bruises darker than before. When he saw Caitlin, he moved his hand on the coverlet and gave a guttural moan that resembled speech, but Caitlin couldn't distinguish the words. As she moved closer to listen, Sherry raised herself higher in her chair like someone startled out of a nap.

"His pain is worse," she said, recognizing Caitlin. "They've got him on Dilaudid. But the swelling in his mouth has gone down some. He can talk a lot better, when he's not too drugged up."

Henry tried to speak again, and this time Caitlin translated the sounds as "Learn anything new today?"

She wasn't about to show Henry what she'd come to ask about with Sherry in the room, so she stalled as best she could. "Not much. Background, mostly. Catching up on your magnum opus."

"Are you printing a story tomorrow?"

"Probably. Penn thinks that printing the story will reduce the danger to all of us."

Henry inclined his head a quarter of an inch. "He's right."

"I suppose. But he wants me to hold back some of my best information." Caitlin tried desperately to think of a way to get Henry's girlfriend out of the room. Almost anything she might say about confidentiality was bound to offend Sherry. "Anyway, that's why I'm here. I was hoping to verify some things before publication. Do you feel well enough?"

"Feel like . . . what the cat drug up and the dog wouldn't eat."

"You're speaking more clearly, though."

Henry grunted. "How do I look? Sherry won't show me a mirror."

Caitlin glanced back at Sherry, whose face tensed. Caitlin considered lying, then gently laid her hand on Henry's arm and said, "You look like crap, dude."

Henry closed his eyes, but a faint smile touched his swollen lips. "Honest woman."

"He was about to take a nap when you came in," Sherry said. "Dr. Elliott isn't as worried about the head injury now, so he upped the limit on the pain pump. He'll probably feel better tomorrow, if you want to come back."

Caitlin wasn't about to leave without speaking to Henry alone. "I'd like to stay, if you don't mind. I can wait until he wakes up if I have to. I can work on my stories in the waiting room. I really need to be sure of my facts. I won't bother him until he's ready, I promise." Caitlin could see she was making no headway with Sherry, so she threw out some bait for Henry. "I could even read him some of my story, if he wants to hear it. I'd love to get your input, Henry."

Before Sherry could argue, Henry said, "Yeah . . . sit with me awhile. I want to hear."

"Have it your way," Sherry said. She closed her eyes for a couple of seconds, and when she opened them, Caitlin saw not anger, but something else. *Cabin fever,* she realized.

"Actually," Sherry said, "if you can sit with him awhile, I could run home and pick up some things. I haven't had a shower or seen my son since yesterday. He's sixteen, but he still needs me."

Trying to conceal her elation, Caitlin gave what she hoped was an accommodating smile. "Of course he does. I'm happy to stay. Take a couple of hours if you need it."

Sherry took the pain pump controller from Henry's hand and pressed its button once. "Hit that every twelve minutes if he falls asleep," she said. "He can't OD from it. The maximum dose is preset. But you don't want to get behind the pain curve."

"Every twelve minutes," Caitlin promised.

Sherry hiked her purse strap over her shoulder, then walked to the window ledge and picked up a vase of bloodred roses. As she passed Caitlin, she took the plastic card holder from among the flowers and held it up for her to see. The card read: *To the World Champion Nigger-Lover. Die soon, okay?*

"I didn't show him this one," she whispered.

"We need to give that card to the FBI. Do you mind?"

Sherry shrugged.

Caitlin took the plastic rod with its three-pronged pitchfork end and stood it upright inside her purse.

"What are you girls talking about?" Henry asked in a jealous tone.

"None of your beeswax," Sherry said. "I'll be back soon. Don't you hit on this pretty girl while I'm gone."

Something like a laugh came from Henry's puffy lips.

Then Sherry was gone.

Caitlin opened her computer case, took out two photographs, then moved quickly to the right side of the bed and leaned over Henry. She figured she only had a couple of minutes before the Dilaudid knocked him out. "I needed to see you alone. Don't speak any more than you need to. Just lift your hand to show you understand or if you mean yes. For no, move your hand sideways. Okay?"

Henry lifted his bandaged hand slightly.

"Good. I've been through almost everything from your safe-deposit boxes."

Worry flickered in Henry's eyes.

"Sherry doesn't know about Swan Norris, does she?"

"No."

"I'll make sure she never does, if that's how you want it."

He nodded.

"But I did something big today, Henry. I want you to be the first to know. I have proof that Brody Royal killed Albert Norris. Pooky, too."

The reporter's eyes went so wide that it frightened her.

She touched his wrist. "Take it easy. I went back and saw Katy Royal, and she opened up about her father. She told me she'd been sexually abused in that sanatorium in Texas. Then she implicated her father in Albert's and Pooky's murders. Dr. Robb's, too. She even said that Brody killed her mother. Drowned her in the bathtub. And that's how she died, all right. I checked. But the main thing is, I recorded almost every word of it."

A high color had come into Henry's cheeks. "My God . . . after all this time. On tape, you said?"

"Well, on my phone. And that's not all. Katy also blamed her father for the attack on you, and for Viola's death."

Henry looked more confused than incredulous, and Caitlin realized from the rapid ping of his monitors that his heart rate had increased. "Henry, *please* try to calm down. You're in a vulnerable state, and we don't want the nurses coming in here, do we?"

"I'm all right," he croaked. "Just . . . I've waited so long for this. To get that . . . *monster*. And you did it in one day."

"Well. My news isn't all good, I'm afraid."

"Whassa matter?"

Caitlin almost couldn't bring herself to say the words. But having come this far, she had to tell the rest. "Katy took some pills, Henry. A lot of pills. She attempted suicide. She's over in St. Catherine's Hospital—alive, but in a coma."

He closed his eyes and swallowed hard. "I knew she was . . . fragile. But I can't blame you. I tried to go back to her myself."

"I know. I was just trying to do what I thought you'd do."

Henry's eyes remained closed. The corner of his left eye expressed what looked like a tear, but she couldn't be sure. "Henry?"

"Nnhh?" he groaned sleepily.

The Dilaudid was kicking in. "I brought some things to show you. I found some old photos in one of your notebooks." She didn't want to mention the fire, in case no one had told him about it. "Would you look at them for just one second?"

The reporter opened his eyes with difficulty. Caitlin held the first snapshot up and tilted it so the overhead light shone on the paper.

"This is Tom Cage with Brody Royal," she said. "In a fishing boat. Can you see it?"

"Don't need to."

"Why was Tom with Royal?"

"Don't know. That picture always worried me. . . ." Henry blinked and opened his mouth, but no sound came out.

"Henry?" She fought the urge to shake him. "Can you hear me?"

"Doc . . . never let me . . . interview him. I . . . gave Penn copy."

Caitlin's mouth fell open as Henry groaned. *One more thing Penn had withheld from her.*

"Doc told Penn . . . wasn't nothing. One-time . . . thing." Henry jerked as though at a sharp pain. Her stomach clenched in sympathetic reaction.

"There's some writing on the back of the picture," she said in his ear. "It says 'BT,' and then 'T. Rambin.' *Henry,*" she said sharply, feeling him slipping away. "Henry! Can you hear me?"

"*Unnhh,*" he moaned. "Bad now . . . push the pump."

Caitlin sighed and pressed the pain pump three times in quick succession.

Henry murmured something, but she couldn't make out the words Then his eyes slowly closed, and he began to snore. The Dilaudid had overcome both pain and consciousness.

Caitlin prayed he would awaken before Sherry returned.

TOM AND WALT LOOKED at each other over empty Chinet plates that smelled of fried fish and ketchup. Melba walked over to them with the flat paper bag she'd used to blot the grease from the bream fillets and french fries.

"Still got some left," she said. "Any takers?"

Walt groaned and rubbed his belly. "If I eat another bite, I'll pop. You did a fine job, Melba."

The nurse smiled and laid a hand on Tom's good shoulder. "How bad's that pain, Doc?"

"Nothing two more Lorcet wouldn't fix."

Melba humphed like chiding nurses around the world. "Two more

Lorcet and you're liable to quit breathing when you doze off on that couch."

Tom winked at Walt, who smiled briefly, then wiped his hands on a paper towel, stood, and flattened his trousers. "I hate leaving you two, but until I meet Colonel Mackiever, we're not going to have a prayer of leaving this place."

"You're sure it's not a trap?" Tom asked.

"Mac and I Rangered together. That's the best answer I can give you. Anyway, he's the only man in this state who can cancel that APB."

"But you think he wants some kind of quid pro quo in exchange for helping us?"

Walt nodded. "Sounded to me like Mac's got a Knox problem. Which is exactly what we've got. So maybe things'll fit together just right for all of us."

"How long will you be gone?" Melba asked.

Walt looked at his watch. "I figure six hours. Ninety minutes each way, plus whatever it takes to deal with Mac. I can't risk getting pulled over by a Louisiana highway patrolman. He might just put a bullet in my ear. I could be back in five hours, if nothing unexpected happens."

"What if it does?" Tom asked.

"Put it this way: I'll be back by dawn no matter what happens. Will you two be all right? Or should we try to get some kind of guard help over here?"

"We'll be fine," Tom said, hoping it was true. "The fewer people who know we're here, the safer we'll be."

Walt nodded. "I think you're right."

"I hate for Melba to be here. There's not only the legal risk for her, but the physical one, as well. I think you should drop her in Natchez on your way through."

Melba put her hands on her generous hips and glared at Tom. "And what do you plan to do after you have a heart attack and pass out? You going to call the ambulance with ESP?"

"She's got you," Walt said. "And be glad for it. I couldn't leave you here alone."

In the awkward silence that followed, Walt looked uncomfortable.

He wasn't the type for small talk or long good-byes. "I'd better get moving. You two kids don't get up to nothin' while I'm gone, tempting as it might be."

While Melba shook her head, Walt picked up the small bag he'd packed for the ride, then went to the door. "Back before you know it," he said.

As he walked out of the lake house, Tom felt the way an old bomber pilot he'd known had described feeling when the P-47s reached the limit of their range and peeled away, headed back for England, leaving the bombers alone for their final push into Germany.

"I guess it's just you and me now, Mel. Let me give you a hand with those dishes."

"Stay where you are," she replied. "I'm used to doing dishes. We're gonna be just fine, Doc."

"I know we are," he said, smiling. "Just like always."

When Melba turned to the sink, Tom's smile died, leaving dread and regret in its place. Something told him they were never going to see Walt Garrity alive again.

EIGHTY-FIVE MINUTES AFTER HE passed out, Henry Sexton began to stir in his bed. Caitlin's heart began to race, and she rushed to finish the text she had been writing to Tom. She'd slept fitfully for much of the past hour, despite her intention to work on her master story. A steady flow of nurses and aides had cycled through the room, checking tubes, taking readings, and monitoring the catheter and drain bags. One had even gotten Henry awake enough to check his vital signs, but he'd fallen right back to sleep. Caitlin had hit the pain pump at least three times while he slept—probably not as often as Sherry would have done, but as cruel as it might seem, she hadn't wanted to miss her chance to speak further with him alone.

She doubted Tom would even see her text message, since he'd probably switched his phone off, but she wanted to do what she could to prevent some cop from shooting him as a fugitive. Though no one else knew it, Caitlin had unique leverage over her future father-in-law, and she meant to use it. Her text read:

Tom. Whatever happened the night Viola died, you don't have the

right to sacrifice yourself, because I'm pregnant. Penn doesn't know.
I'm telling you because my child needs you in his life. It's time for you
to come home. This family can get through ANYTHING together.
Caitlin Masters Cage (☺ your future daughter-in-law).

Henry started awake and called out for Albert Norris. Caitlin
pressed SEND, then leaped out of her chair and took his hand, reassuring
him that he wasn't alone.

"Did you see him?" Henry asked through his teeth.

"Albert?" Caitlin asked hesitantly.

"No . . . no. The other guy."

"What other guy?"

"The black guy."

Caitlin looked around the room as though she might actually find
an unexpected visitor. "Who was he?"

"He wouldn't say." Henry's eyes looked dreamy with narcotics.
"Just one of Albert's boys, he said."

"One of Albert's boys?" Caitlin had read that phrase in Henry's journals. "Like Pooky and Jimmy?"

"Yeah."

"How old was he?" she asked, figuring Henry had hallucinated a
teenager from his youth in Albert's store.

"'Bout sixty."

Caitlin blinked in puzzlement. "Was he here just now?"

"I don't know," Henry said groggily. "Maybe it was earlier. Maybe
when Sherry stepped out."

"What did he look like?"

"Just a black guy, you know. Had on a black baseball cap. An old
one with a white *D* on it. For Detroit maybe? Yeah. The Detroit Tigers."

"What did he want here?"

"He thanked me for all the good work I've done. That's all. He said
it didn't matter who he was. It made sense to me."

I'll bet, with all the Dilaudid in your system. Caitlin made a mental
note to check the deputy's book for visitors.

"Hey," Henry said. "Do you think he could have been the one who
went to see Pooky's mama before she died? 'Huggy Bear'?"

Caitlin recalled Penn telling her about the anonymous caller who'd

contacted Sheriff Dennis about the burning of the *Beacon* building. But
the whole idea of that man sneaking in here with a guard outside seemed
far-fetched.

"Maybe it was," she said, deciding not to get Henry too excited with
that story. "Henry, do you remember the photograph I showed you
before you fell asleep?"

"What?"

"The one of Tom and Brody Royal in the boat. It has writing on the
back. It reads 'BT,' and then 'T. Rambin.' It looks like your writing to me."

At first Henry said nothing. Then in a reluctant tone, he said, "It is."

His eyes looked wary, almost hunted. Caitlin said, "I was wondering if 'BT' might stand for 'Bone Tree'?"

The reporter avoided her gaze.

"You see, I read all about the Bone Tree in your journals, and the
more I read, the more I started thinking Pooky's bones might be out
there. Maybe Jimmy Revels's, too. The FBI only brought Luther's up out
of the Jericho Hole."

"Could be," Henry said vaguely. "But I looked for that tree . . . and I
never found it. So did the FBI."

Katy Royal talked about a tree like this, too, Caitlin wanted to say, but
she stifled herself. "Who's T. Rambin, Henry?"

Still the reporter refused to meet her eye.

Caitlin laid her hand softly against Henry's hair and stroked it. "I
know this is hard, to be trapped in this room while other people go out
and try to finish what you started. It's not fair, and I won't pretend it is.
But whatever I find, Henry, your name will be there with mine. I promise you that. Not for the glory—because I know that's not what you care
about—but for the closure. So the families will know it was you who
brought them justice." She lowered her voice to a whisper. "And for
Swan. She'll see it, too."

Henry finally turned to her, his eyes more alert than she'd seen
them since the attack. "If you try to find the Bone Tree, you could end
up just like me. Or worse."

"I know that. But it's worth it to me."

After some moments, he nodded slowly. He tried to roll to his left,
but failed. "My cell phone," he groaned. "In my pants. In that bag, there.
Get it."

Caitlin quickly found a soiled pair of trousers in a shopping bag beside the chair she'd been sitting in. In their right front pocket was a Nokia cell phone.

"Look in my contacts," he said. "Toby Rambin."

Caitlin flicked through the buttons with manic dexterity. "Who is he? I looked for a phone number and couldn't find one."

"A poacher. Rambin hunts the swamp down in Lusahatcha County. I only found him a few days ago. Didn't tell anybody. Not Penn . . . nobody. All he has is a cell phone. Talked to him Monday night. Rambin says he knows where the Bone Tree is. I was setting up a meeting, but . . . this happened."

Caitlin's heart thumped as her eyes zeroed in on the name in tiny text. "Got it." Quickly, she memorized Rambin's name and number, then entered the characters in her Treo. "Do you think this guy is for real?"

"Maybe. He sounded scared enough. He wants money, though."

With a twinge of guilt, she edited Henry's "Toby Rambin" contact so that the surname "Rambin" became "Smith." Then she altered the area code of Rambin's phone number to that of South Carolina. Unwilling to go so far as to delete the information altogether, she saved the changes, then slipped the phone back into Henry's pants.

When she looked up, Henry was holding out his bandaged hand. Caitlin hurried to his bedside and took it in hers. "You be careful," he said. "They play rough down in Lusahatcha County. The Knoxes own land down there."

"I will. Let me ask you one more thing. I found a telephoto shot of you with a rifle scope over your face. What's the story on that?"

Henry took a couple of shallow breaths, and his eyes clouded with anxiety. "I was . . . checking into Brody Royal's land deals . . . with Carlos Marcello. Got that picture in the mail. Showed the FBI. . . . They never traced it. I backed off. Too chicken, I guess. That time, anyway."

Caitlin leaned over and kissed the reporter's forehead. "Screw that. You're a hero, Henry. I mean it. This is Captain America stuff you've been doing."

Henry's skin reddened between his bruises. He was blushing.

"We're going to get them all in the end," she promised. "Royal, his son-in-law, the Knoxes . . . every last one. And when we do, it'll be because of you."

Henry began coughing, hard. "Hope so," he finally croaked. "Won't bring Albert back, though. Or Jimmy . . . or Pooky."

Caitlin glanced back at the door, toward the little hall that led to the door. She felt as though Sherry were standing just out of sight, listening intently.

"Can you tell me anything else about Brody?" she whispered. "Is there anything else you didn't put in your notebooks?"

Henry's breaths were coming shallow. He flinched suddenly, then raised his hand. *"Ohhh.* Belly hurts again . . . bad."

Caitlin picked up the pain med controller and started pumping. "I'd better let you rest some more."

"Pump it," he said, his face sweating. "Pump. . ."

She pressed the button four times.

"Muhhfckrs," Henry mumbled.

Caitlin looked up. "Did you say 'motherfuckers'?"

"Yeah. Listen . . . if you go see Toby Rambin . . . don't go alone."

"I won't."

Henry's eyes widened. *"Promise me."*

"I promise!"

"Talk to Dr. Cage, too. He knows more than anybody."

"I will, as soon as I find him."

"Oh, Jesus . . . pump some more."

Caitlin pressed the button four more times. "It's coming, Henry. I'm pressing. I think you're at the limit, though."

Henry lay silent but for his stertorous breathing. Then his eyes popped open and flickered like lantern flames. "I've tried to forgive them," he said. "But I can't. Jimmy talked to me about forgiveness once. He wasn't but twenty-five . . . but he was *wise*. He said forgiving somebody doesn't mean . . . they shouldn't . . . pay a price for what they'd done. But that's God's business, he said. Hating somebody just poisons you . . . not them."

Caitlin felt a sudden urge to unburden herself, a desire to know what Henry would do in her predicament. "Penn wants me to hold back the recording of Katy," she said. "He wants to use it against Brody, to try to save his father."

The reporter blinked several times, his head moving side to side on the pillow. Then he looked at her as though trying to make her out from a great distance. "Dr. Cage is a good man. But . . . can't let Brody go free. Not even for . . ."

The reporter's eyelids fell and did not rise again.

Hearing the door creak, Caitlin stepped back from the bed, afraid it would be Sherry rather than another nurse. Henry's girlfriend wouldn't like seeing her leaning so close over him.

The first thing Caitlin saw was a huge, flower-print weekend tote. Then came a grease-stained McDonald's bag, followed by Sherry herself, dressed in a flannel shirt and jeans.

"*Look what Sherry's got,*" Caitlin sang, hoping to break the spell of intimacy in the room.

"Is he awake?" Sherry asked, looking for floor space to set down her bag.

Henry's lips moved, but as Sherry dropped her tote against the exterior wall, his head jerked to the right and his eyelids fluttered, then froze in the open position.

"Did you say something, hon?" Sherry asked, straightening up with a weary sigh.

In the silence that followed this question, a shard of glass fell out of the window. It tinkled against the air-conditioning unit, then shattered on the floor with a flat crack like a broken Christmas ornament. Caitlin stared at the shard in confusion, then looked up at Henry.

A single runnel of bright red blood trailed from his temple down to the white pillow. His head jerked again, but his eyes remained open. Caitlin's gaze went to the window again and finally took in the state of the mini-blinds.

When were those opened? she wondered. *They were supposed to be closed at all times—*

"Henry?" Sherry said, puzzled but still not worried.

"Shut the blinds!" Caitlin screamed. "*Sherry, shut the blinds!*"

Flooded with adrenaline, she grabbed the foot of the hospital bed and pulled it away from the wall. Various cords and tubes resisted her, but she yanked hard and the bed came away on its wheels.

Sherry stared at Caitlin as if she were about to start pulling the bed back toward the wall.

"Shut the fucking blinds!" Caitlin yelled again. *"Someone's shooting!"*

Another piece of glass popped out of the window, and Caitlin sensed more than felt something ricochet through the room. At last Sherry grasped what was happening. Without any thought for herself, she lunged for the plastic rod that controlled the blinds.

Caitlin manhandled the head of Henry's bed past the bathroom door and slammed it against the main door of the hospital room. Then she kick-locked the bed's wheels to stop anyone getting in from the hall.

Someone was pounding on the door—the deputy, probably—but Caitlin wasn't about to let anybody inside. She shouted that he should call the FBI and lock down the hospital, but he just kept yelling for her to open the door. Scanning the room for her purse (meaning to get her pistol), she saw Sherry spin away from the window, both hands clutching her throat. The woman hung in the air for a surreal second, blood pouring from her left eye socket, then fell so heavily that Caitlin knew she was dead before she hit the floor.

Terrified that the gunman outside would rush the shattered window, Caitlin snatched up her pistol from her purse, then backed into the narrow crack between Henry's bed and the wall. The deputy was still shouting, but he didn't have the weight to overcome the resistance of both Caitlin and the locked wheels under the bed.

"Lock down the hospital!" she shouted. "There's been a murder!"

With shaking hands, she took out her phone and speed-dialed John Kaiser. The FBI agent answered after two rings. Caitlin spat out what facts she could. Her words sounded garbled to her own ears, but Kaiser seemed to understand them perfectly. He was parking his car behind the hospital, having returned to question Henry, and said he would be outside Henry's door in forty seconds. Then he said something that chilled Caitlin to the marrow: *"If anyone tries to enter that room before you hear my voice, pull the trigger and keep pulling it until your gun is empty. Door or window, you take them down."*

The deputy had stopped pounding on the door. Caitlin glanced fearfully at the shattered window, then looked down at Henry, whose eyes still had life in them—or seemed to. She wanted to cradle his head, but she worried she might kill him by doing that. Very lightly, she pressed one fingertip beneath his jaw and felt for a carotid pulse. *There!* He was alive.

Caitlin aimed her pistol at the window and tried not to look at Sherry's body lying motionless on the floor. Even a child could have seen she was beyond help. *"Please hurry,"* she whispered, picturing John Kaiser's confident eyes and military bearing. *"Please, please, please . . ."*

At last a Klaxon alarm began to ring.

CHAPTER 78

TO SPARE KIRK BOISSEAU conflict with his girlfriend, who had complained bitterly about him diving the Jericho Hole yesterday, I e-mailed him from the *Examiner* and asked him to meet me at a corner house, two down from his, as soon as he could manage it. Kirk spends most of his off hours on the Web, networking with other kayakers and ex-marines, so I felt sure that he'd see my mail quickly. In the end, I had to sit outside his place for forty-five minutes before he texted me that he'd be out soon. Another ten passed before he actually appeared in my passenger window.

"Back already?" he asks with a grin, dropping into the seat beside me. "I must have done good yesterday."

"You got your name in the paper. Did you mind that?"

"Not me, man. Nancy wasn't too happy about it, but hey. My life, right?"

"I guess so."

"Sorry I took so long. Domestic issues." He taps my dashboard with irrepressible energy. "So, what's up now? More bones to salvage?"

I shake my head and let him see that tonight's errand is far more serious. "I need to question somebody, Kirk. And he's not going to like it."

He nods slowly. "Like a field interrogation?"

"You could call it that."

"Tough guy?"

"Not exactly. He's probably over eighty."

"*What?*"

"But he might have some people with him that I wouldn't want to have to handle on my own."

"I get you. Do I know him?"

"Brody Royal."

Kirk whistles long and low. "Whoa, brah. Hey, we just heard his daughter was in the hospital."

"That's right."

The marine's eyes widen. "Don't tell me you had something to do with that."

"No comment."

He makes a sound I cannot decipher. "Well . . . I'll help you, but there's one little problem."

"What's that?"

"Royal owns the Royal Cotton Bank, and I've got an outstanding note there on my dozer. He sees me working as muscle for you, he's liable to call my note tomorrow."

"How much is left on the note?"

"About twenty grand."

Less than I figured. "Tell you what. If Royal calls the note, I'll pay the balance, and you can pay me if and when you get the money."

The silence lasts a few seconds. "This is some serious shit, huh."

"Yep. That's the second part of this conversation. Brody's son-in-law is a real bastard. A killer, Kirk. He attacked me in a restaurant at lunch, and Caitlin had to shoot at him earlier tonight to keep him off her."

"And you need me to keep him in line?"

"Discreet backup, let's say. But things could get violent fast."

He shrugs, then rolls his enormous shoulders with fluid grace. "Sounds better than watching *Sex and the freakin' City* with Nancy."

"This isn't diving the Jericho Hole. Brody Royal's tied in with the Double Eagles and some corrupt state cops in Louisiana. There's drugs involved, and God knows what. They've killed a lot of people."

"You're shitting me. I thought Royal was like a model citizen."

"As far from that as you can imagine. That guy whose bones you brought up yesterday? Him and his buddy Jimmy Revels were both in the service. One army, the other navy. Before Brody's thugs killed them, they sliced off their service tattoos and tanned them as trophies."

Kirk's left fist flexes and unflexes on the console of my Audi. "Brody Royal was behind that?"

"Yep. I'll tell you something else. Most of the Double Eagles were bastards, but at least they served their country. Brody Royal had mob connections who fixed it so he could stay home during the war and rake in black market money while everybody else risked their ass overseas."

"I'm starting to look forward to this." Boisseau sniffs and gives me a nonchalant look. "Where's this friendly conversation likely to take place?"

"Probably St. Catherine's Hospital. But if not, then some other semi-public place. I don't think we should go to Royal's place on Lake Concordia."

"Does it have to be tonight?"

"Yes."

Kirk rubs his chin. "Does this have to do with your dad's trouble?"

"Yes. These guys want Dad shot as a fugitive. I've got to convince them to cancel an APB."

"I got you. Only one question, Bwana. Will they be armed or not?"

"Probably so."

"Okay."

"I just want you with me as a stabilizing presence. Ideally, nobody will lose his cool. But like I said, Randall Regan could get crazy and go for us."

Kirk shrugs. "I got no problem with self-defense. If fact, I'm kind of—"

The ring of my cell phone stops him in midsentence. I start to ignore it, but then I check the LCD and see it's Caitlin. I hit the button to answer.

"Hey. Can I call you back?"

"Penn, Henry's been shot."

The blood drains from my head so fast that I feel dizzy, even though I'm sitting. "Shot dead?"

Kirk tenses beside me.

"No. The bullet grazed his head, and then I yanked his bed clear."

"You were *there*? I thought you were at the paper!"

"I needed to check something with Henry. Penn, Sherry Harden's dead." Caitlin sounds near to hyperventilating. "They shot her through the window. I still can't believe it."

"Are you safe now?"

"Yeah. Kaiser has FBI agents here, and Sheriff Dennis is on the way. Penn . . . what about the recording? Katy must have known her father was going to try to kill Henry. Do I tell Kaiser about it?"

My stomach knots. "Ahhh . . . not yet. Stay close to Sheriff Dennis and away from the windows. I'm on my way."

"What happened?" Kirk asks as I hit END.

"A sniper just shot Henry Sexton through his hospital window. They only grazed him, but they killed his girlfriend."

Kirk holds up his hands like weapons at the ready. "This is wild, man. Tell me what to do. Is our thing still on?"

"Yes. I want you to track down Royal for me. As soon as I can get loose from this murder scene, I'll come to you."

Kirk grips my hand with startling strength, then springs out of the Audi, closes the door, and leans back through the window. "Do what you gotta do, man. I'll stay on these guys till you're ready to brace them. And if it turns out they shot Henry Sexton . . . I might just take it out of their asses myself."

CHAPTER 79

SONNY THORNFIELD THOUGHT he'd been afraid during the afternoon, but that had been nothing compared to now. This was like the war all over again. The plan that put a bullet into Henry Sexton's brain had been pure genius; nobody would argue that. It was the aftermath that had Sonny worried. He and Snake were flying five thousand feet over the Atchafalaya Swamp in a darkened Cessna Caravan with two half-drunk boys in the backseats: Jake Whitten and Charley Wise, the two surviving punks who'd bungled Brody Royal's first hit on Sexton. Sonny had been told that his job was to help Snake kill the boys and dump them in the swamp, but he feared that the real purpose of this mission was to leave him in the same dark hole.

Until he'd heard about this flight, Sonny had felt pretty sure that Forrest still trusted him, despite his being kidnapped by Tom Cage and that Ranger bastard. But then—on Forrest's orders—Snake had carried him to Claude Devereux's office to videotape a statement about what happened, which was then notarized and duplicated on the spot. With that video statement in Devereux's safe, Forrest could still order Sonny's death whenever he liked. Sonny looked out at the stars and thought about the successful hit on Sexton. Surely Forrest would give him partial credit for that?

Forty minutes ago, he and Snake had dropped out of the clouds over an empty Concordia Parish cotton field, then descended toward a line of chemical glow sticks. Snake had set the floatplane down on a narrow stretch of water owned by a friend of Billy Knox, then taxied to a stop near the shore, where a Chevrolet parked at water's edge switched on its headlights. Charley and Jake had brought this car to meet the plane, with Snake's raccoon trap in the trunk.

Snake took the trap out of the trunk, shot the terrified coon, then climbed into the Chevy and headed for Mercy Hospital. Twenty minutes later, he dumped the dead coon beneath Henry's window, then set up his rifle on a spot he'd marked that morning with a tent stake, just thirty yards from the window. Using a modified photographic tripod as a bench rest (just as he had when practicing the shot through the windows of an abandoned house near Jonesville), he executed Henry Sexton with a perfect head shot, then took out his girlfriend, just in case she'd seen something.

Sixty seconds after killing the reporter, Snake was back in the Chevy and headed for the Cessna, where Sonny and the boys waited. Slick as snot on a doorknob. No flight plan, no airport, not even a dirt strip. Just an airplane floating on a patch of water in some empty fields. Charley and Jake had no idea they were going to take the return flight to Toledo Bend, but they didn't argue much, especially after Snake pulled his pistol. They left their keys in the Chevy as instructed, then handed over their cell phones to Snake and climbed into the rear of the plane.

Sixty seconds after the Cessna lifted off, a four-wheeled ATV carrying two former Double Eagles emerged from the trees. It stopped beside the Chevy long enough for one man to dismount and get behind the wheel. After driving out to the highway, he wouldn't stop until he reached Memphis, Tennessee, where he'd dump the Chevy in an abandoned salvage yard, then ride the bus back to Natchez. After the four-wheeler disappeared, it was as though none of the vehicles had ever been there.

But they had, Sonny reflected. *And now Henry Sexton is dead.*

Snake had ordered him to keep the boys calm while he flew them toward their deaths. That was easier said than done. You could smell the fear coming through the boys' skins, a sour sweat that permeated the Caravan's cabin. But they'd tried to put on brave faces and pretend this was all part of some grand plan to protect them, rather than the opposite. Sonny knew exactly how they felt.

Twenty minutes into the flight, he'd given each of them a bottle of Budweiser laced with Versed, a short-acting benzodiazepine often given to children to sedate them for medical procedures. Sonny and Snake were drinking Schaefer (supposedly to be sure they got the non-doctored beers, but Sonny kept thinking his tasted funny, and tried to drink as little as possible). Long before the plane reached the black glassy sheet of the Atchafalaya Swamp, the two boys fell unconscious. The longer Sonny remained conscious, the better he began to feel.

He tensed again when Snake checked his GPS unit, then began descending rapidly toward the swamp. There was a big stretch of open water about twenty-five miles east of Lafayette, Louisiana. A mile north of Des Glaise, it ran north-to-south and was not accessible by road. True Cajun country. Snake had a lot of years under his belt flying as a crop duster, skimming beneath power lines and dodging trees. But it took all the guts and skill he had to set the Caravan down in that swamp without lights.

When the plane finally settled heavily into the water, Sonny climbed down onto a rocking pontoon and shone a spotlight in front of the plane while Snake taxied toward a wall of cypresses in the distance. It took them four minutes to reach the trees. Once there, Snake steered the plane into a long channel and taxied for another minute. Then he cut the engine.

Sonny's heart banged like an antique pump in his chest. There was so much adrenaline flushing through him that he felt like he'd been doing coke for two hours. He quickly realized that he couldn't manhandle the boys out of the plane on his own. After bitching for most of a minute, Snake got out of his seat and helped Sonny muscle the boys through the door and down into the water. Neither boy stirred when they were dropped in, though the water had to be freezing.

When Sonny turned to get back into the plane, Snake told him they couldn't chance either kid waking up in time to swim to shore or climb into a cypress and save himself. He told Sonny to hold each kid's head under the water for at least three minutes. It wasn't drowning the boys that freaked Sonny out—though he'd never cared for killing—it was turning his back on Snake to do it. But in the end he didn't have a choice. Snake had the only gun.

One by one, Sonny held the boys' heads under the water for the allotted time. Jake Whitten twitched after about a minute under the surface, but then he stopped, and Sonny tried not to think about his freezing hands or Snake's pistol as he waited for Snake to call time. The colder he got, the easier it was to imagine Snake saying, "Sorry, Sonny boy, Forrest's orders."

But Snake never said that.

After catching his breath on the pontoon, Sonny climbed back into the Cessna and collapsed into his seat while Snake taxied back to open water. Forty seconds later, they were airborne again, climbing for the clouds. Snake remarked that two missions had just been accomplished with a minimum of conversation, and that mostly curses. That was how vets worked in combat zones, he said with nostalgia, and Sonny grunted in agreement. But inside, Sonny was still a wreck.

"Forrest may be slow to pull the trigger," Snake said, "but once he makes up his mind, he don't take chances or prisoners. Ask them jelly-legs we left back there in the swamp." Snake's harsh laughter bounced off the windscreen and hurt Sonny's ears. "Ask Henry Sexton," he added.

Shivering in his seat, Sonny gave the obligatory laugh.

I've gotta calm down, he thought. *Snake's gonna see I've got the yips. And if he does, he'll start to worry. And if Snake starts worrying, Forrest will, too. And I won't live to see my grandson again.*

"A perfect head shot, you said?" Sonny asked with feigned awe.

"Punched right through his skull. Got his girlfriend in the eye. Wish you coulda seen it, Son. She dropped like a sack of meal."

"Damn," Sonny said, trying to hold down the contents of his stomach. "I wish I could have, boy."

CHAPTER 80

BY THE TIME I penetrated Sheriff Dennis's outer perimeter and started looking for Caitlin, John Kaiser and a couple of his agents were on the scene and working to restore calm at the hospital. Nevertheless, I found weeping nurses, a panicked administrator, and rattled deputies milling through the halls. Just as I saw Caitlin down a corridor, Walker Dennis appeared beside me, grabbed my arm, and pulled me into an empty hospital room.

"You and I need to talk," he said in an urgent tone, "before we see anybody else."

"What is it, Walker?"

"A little while ago you asked me to keep that 'Mr. Brown' call about Brody Royal to myself. Is that still how you want to play it? With the FBI, I mean? Because in light of what's happened, I'm thinking anything could be important, no matter how crazy it might sound."

All I can think about is the copied audio recording of Katy Royal in my back pocket—something I don't want John Kaiser to know about until my father has reached some safe place. "Walker, this may not make much sense to you, but I'd still prefer to keep that call between the two of us."

His eyes narrow. "Are you onto something about Brody? Even without the wiretaps?"

I nod. "Please don't ask me what it is now. I'll tell you as soon as I can. I'm trying to save my father's life, or I wouldn't ask this of you. Can you live with that?"

Sheriff Dennis looks into my eyes for several seconds, then sighs. "I guess I can. But if you think Brody ordered Henry shot tonight, I wish you'd tell me now."

"I don't know, Walker. If I had to lay money on it, I'd say the Knoxes are behind this. That's who Henry was stirring up the most. You don't happen to know where Brody is now, do you?"

"I just checked on that, as a matter of fact. He and his family are over at St. Catherine's Hospital. His daughter's in a coma in their ICU."

"Thanks, buddy."

Walker's eyes radiate suspicion from beneath his hat brim. "You don't happen to know how she got that way, do you?"

"I'll tell you that story later, too."

The sheriff shakes his head like he's not looking forward to hearing the answer. "All right. We'd better go see if Kaiser's turned up anything. He used to be a big dog in the Investigative Support Unit, you know. And I'm not going to pretend I don't need the help."

When Sheriff Dennis and I reach the end of the corridor, we find John Kaiser questioning Caitlin and the deputy who was guarding the door during the shooting. Jordan Glass stands a discreet distance away. Caitlin looks like she's barely holding herself together. Unlike Kaiser's wife, she hasn't had much direct exposure to violence. When Kaiser asks the deputy a question, I hug Caitlin tight, then whisper into the shell of her ear: "Don't say anything about Katy's tape. Okay?"

She nods once into my chest.

Only after I draw back do I realize we're standing outside the room where Henry was shot. Henry himself has been moved to a window-less office in the administration area and placed under FBI guard. Using mobile equipment, the staff converted the office into a makeshift hospital room.

Two more FBI agents arrive in short order, one of them the evidence specialist who processed the bones that came out of the Jericho Hole. With silent proficiency, they begin working the scene as a Concordia Parish sheriff's detective observes. It quickly becomes obvious that John Kaiser knows more about homicide investigations than anybody else on the scene, but he takes pains to make sure Sheriff Dennis doesn't feel the Bureau is running roughshod over his turf.

This détente lasts until Kaiser resumes questioning the deputy who was guarding the door to Henry's room. The man had been instructed to keep a careful log of everyone entering or leaving, but no nurse or aide on his list has admitted to opening the window blinds—which made the head shot possible. Kaiser obviously believes the deputy was lax in his logging, and as he presses the man, Sheriff Dennis boils toward the limit of his forbearance.

"White uniforms all start to look the same after a while, don't they?" Kaiser asks with apparent empathy. "They become sort of an official pass in a hospital environment."

"Nobody went in without me logging them," the deputy says doggedly, but I sense that he isn't sure.

"Could you have dozed a little bit? Even for a minute? Standing post in an empty hallway is pretty boring, I know from experience. And you had the desk."

The deputy's lips lock shut in a thin white line. Then he says, "I wasn't sleeping, damn it. I told you that."

"Ease up, Agent Kaiser," Sheriff Dennis says in a tense voice. "Tommy's had a rough night."

Kaiser turns to Walker and speaks with grim purpose. "A material witness in several major murder cases nearly died because somebody reached up and turned a plastic rod on a window blind. The person who opened those blinds was almost certainly working with the shooter."

"How do you know that?" asks the deputy, who then points at Caitlin. "*She* was in there for two hours."

Caitlin looks up in shock from beside Jordan Glass.

The harassed deputy sticks his chin out angrily. "How do we know she didn't just reach up and open them blinds without even thinking about it?"

"I *didn't*," Caitlin insists.

"Agent Kaiser," I cut in, "didn't you tell me you were going to make sure Henry was covered? Were there any FBI agents in the hospital?"

Kaiser sighs with frustration. "We were shorthanded at the Jericho Hole. I thought Sheriff Dennis had two more men over here."

Walker's face is turning redder by the second.

"I'm not accusing anyone of negligence," Kaiser goes on. "We're here to find out what happened, not whose fault it was. But whoever opened those blinds almost certainly knows who the shooter is. It could have been a hospital employee, or it could have been a walk-in."

He turns back to the deputy. "Your list shows five names in the past three hours, aside from the people with us here. One nurse is positive the blinds were closed shortly before Sherry left to go home. Caitlin says she didn't open them, nor does she remember seeing anyone open them. But she was working on her computer while Henry slept, and she dozed some herself, so we have to assume that's when the blinds were opened. We need to bring everybody on your list back down here, so you and Caitlin can verify who you remember, and see if you recall anyone else not in that group. Okay?"

The deputy nods sullenly.

Kaiser waves at one of his men, who takes the log and heads down to the central area of the one-floor hospital. Sheriff Dennis whispers to his deputy, who nods and walks down the hall toward the restroom.

Hiking up his gun belt, Walker leans close to Kaiser. "We screwed up, okay? But I went to school with Henry Sexton. I played peewee football with his little brother. And I just got off the phone with his mama, whose scream I won't forget for the rest of my life. I appreciate your help on this case, but I'm telling you—in the nicest way possible—to *ease the fuck up* on my deputy. You hear?"

"I understand, Sheriff. I'll go as easy as I can." Kaiser turns and focuses on Caitlin. "Tell me about the shots. How many did you hear?"

"None. The first thing I heard was glass falling out of the window. That's when I saw the blood. The same thing with the shots that killed Sherry. Just glass getting punched out of the window."

"Silencer?" Sheriff Dennis says to Kaiser.

Kaiser nods absently. He appears to be pondering some complex question. "Shooting through glass is no simple thing. That difficulty is the only thing that saved Henry's life. SWAT teams have a special technique for that kind of shot. They use two shooters. The first shoots out the glass, and the second takes out the target. They make the shots so fast that the target doesn't have time to react to the first shot. Which means the primary shooter—the one making the kill shot—fires even before the hole he will fire through actually exists. To an untrained ear, it might sound like a single shot."

"Never heard of *that*," says a deputy on the periphery of our group.

"But unless we have a pair of police- or military-trained snipers roaming this parish," I point out, "that's not what happened."

"The glass in there looked pretty thin," Jordan observes.

"When was this hospital built?" asks Kaiser.

"Nineteen sixty-one," says the hospital administrator.

"No polymers back then," says Kaiser. "Thin glass to start with, and it would be brittle after all this time. If the shooter fired at a right angle to the glass, the bullet's deflection would be minimal, even with a small caliber."

"How small?" asks Sheriff Dennis. "Not a .22, huh?"

"Twenty-two Magnum." Kaiser takes a plastic pill bottle from his pocket and holds it up. "We dug this round out of the wall a few minutes ago. This is the one that grazed Henry's skull. The glass probably affected the rotation of the bullet just enough to save his life."

The FBI agent looks up the hallway. Four of the five people listed in the deputy's log have arrived for the mini-lineup. (One male aide apparently went off-duty but is on his way back to the hospital.) Caitlin and the deputy quickly agree that these four nurses and aides did in fact enter Henry's room. What they can't remember is whether anyone else did.

"Wait a second," Caitlin says. "When Henry woke up, he told me he'd gotten a visit from somebody. I thought he was hallucinating. He said the guy thanked him for his good work, and then left."

"Did he mention a name?" Kaiser asks.

"No. He said it was a black guy . . . about sixty years old. Henry said the man said he was 'just one of Albert's boys.' That's why I thought he was hallucinating. Oh, and he was supposedly wearing a Detroit Tigers baseball cap."

"Detroit Tigers?" Kaiser echoes. "Henry was talking like the guy had just been there?"

"Yes, but he wasn't sure. He said it might have been when Sherry stepped out for something."

"There was a guy like that stopped by a good while back," offers the deputy. "When I first came on duty, before lunch."

"And you didn't think he was suspicious?" Walker asks in a challenging tone.

The deputy shrugs. "Well . . . he was black, you know? I figured he was a friend of Henry's. He sure wasn't no Double Eagle. But I got his name, boss. It oughta be there on the list."

Kaiser grabs the list and scans it. At first he says nothing, but then he starts shaking his head, and his mouth shows the hint of a smile.

"What is it?" asks the sheriff.

"Gates Brown," says Kaiser. "Ever hear that name?"

"Sounds familiar," says Dennis, cutting his eyes at me. "Who is he?"

Kaiser laughs outright. "Gates Brown was a pinch hitter for the Detroit Tigers in the late sixties and seventies. Batted left-handed but threw right-handed. He won a World Series with the Tigers in 1968. Batted four-fifty."

"How do you know all that?" asks the deputy, marveling at the FBI agent's encyclopedic memory.

"I had a radioman from Detroit in my platoon in Vietnam. Black kid. He never stopped talking about Gates Brown. He liked him because Brown had been discovered while playing for a reform school team."

"Well, what the hell does this mean?" asks Sheriff Dennis, glancing at me every few seconds.

Kaiser looks hard at the frazzled deputy. "Did you ask to see Mr. Brown's ID, or did you just ask him to sign the book?"

"I looked at his driver's license."

"Did the name on the license match the signature?"

The deputy goes red again.

"Goddamn it," Walker curses.

Kaiser holds up his hand to calm the sheriff. "So—Henry had a visitor who used an assumed name. A man who may have worked for Albert Norris when he was a boy. We'll have to try to find out what we can about 'Mr. Brown.'"

Sheriff Dennis gives me yet another sidelong glance, but I look away. As I do, I see Caitlin watching me carefully. She's come to the same conclusion I have: "Gates Brown" must be "Huggy Bear"—the childhood friend of Pooky Wilson, who visited his mother on her deathbed. Henry's mystery witness is still in town—or at least he was this morning.

"Agent Kaiser?" says a new FBI agent from the edge of the group.

"Yes?"

"We've been grid-searching the grounds on the highway side of the building. We just found a dead raccoon out there. Still warm."

"So?"

"It was right under the victim's window."

"Show me." Kaiser slips through the knot of bodies and heads toward the exit.

As the FBI men move away, Walker grabs my arm and leans close to my ear. "That's got to be that same 'Mr. Brown' who told me he saw Brody Royal burning the *Beacon,* right?"

"I imagine so."

"What the hell is going on, Penn?"

"I don't know, Walker. Let's go see the raccoon."

CHAPTER 81

HENRY SEXTON LAY half-conscious in a windowless room that only an hour ago had been an administrative office. Two doctors, four FBI agents, and a squad of nurses had hastily converted the office into a protective cocoon for the reporter-turned-assassination-target. Only one nurse had been with Henry since the ER doctor had patched the grazing wound to his skull, and at least one plainclothes FBI agent was standing guard outside his door. The nurse had been ordered not to speak to anyone about Henry's condition, or even to confirm that he was alive.

To Henry's dismay, neither Sherry nor Caitlin nor Penn Cage had been in to check on him. The FBI agents he'd questioned had been brusque, but as the dazing effect of his head wound began to wear off, Henry recognized his nurse as an old grade school classmate—Irma McKay. When he told Irma he recognized her, she lingered to talk to him, and he'd taken advantage of the opportunity to ask about the shooting. Nurse McKay tried to obey her orders not to reveal Sherry's death, but Henry quickly read the truth in her eyes. Seconds later she broke down and admitted that Sherry was dead.

Although Henry had feared this from the start, something broke inside him when the nurse told him the truth. Not since the murder of Albert Norris had a death hit him like Sherry's did. Her loss proved the cliché: you never knew what you had until it was gone. For years he had taken her for granted—the thousand things she did to make his life easier and, more important, the rock-solid support she'd given him when no one else gave a damn about his work. Sherry had always begged him to pursue a different type of story, but she'd finally accepted his need to see his quest through. She'd even helped him when she could. But now she had paid for his stubbornness with her life, while he had survived.

Try as he might, Henry simply couldn't process the shock. As he lay on his back in a drug-induced haze, a conviction grew in him that soon became an obsession. He had to get out of the hospital. Before an hour passed, his obsession had become a compulsion, irresistible and beyond all logic. The goal of his escape seemed almost secondary. As though in self-defense, his mind had focused on logistical considerations rather than philosophical ones.

The problem was, escape seemed impossible—at least at first. He'd considered and rejected a host of wacky ideas. A diversion was a common component of prison escapes, he knew, but with the FBI on high alert, the slightest disturbance would only tighten the protective cordon around him. Floating in an opium-derived cloud, Henry's mind began to search for a more original solution. As the medical machines clicked and beeped around him, he recalled an older boy telling his underaged self how to sneak into adult bars. *You walk in like you own the damn place, man. Show no fear. No doubt whatsoever.* Henry had used this tactic many times as a journalist, and often gained exclusive access to restricted areas and crime scenes.

Might not that same tactic serve him now?

The next time Irma McKay returned to check his vitals, Henry gave her the saddest smile he could muster.

"How are you holding up, Henry?" she asked. "I'm so sorry about Sherry. I should never have told you. That wasn't my place."

"Yes, it was. Better to hear it from an old friend than from some grouchy government agent. It's all right, Irma. I won't tell anybody that you told me."

"Really?" she said hopefully, making notations on his chart.

"Not if you'll you do me one little favor."

She looked up quickly, anxiety in her eyes. "I can't get you no cigarettes, Henry."

He laughed at the absurdity of her misjudgment.

"No, that's not it. The FBI guys never brought me my cell phone. Maybe it's evidence now or something. But I really need to talk to my mama. She's got to be frantic by now."

"I don't know, Henry. The FBI doesn't want anybody knowing anything about your status."

"I know. But you know how this town is. The news is bound to be all over the place by now. Mama could hear it any minute. She might even hear I'm dead." He shook his head, then regretted it as his skull pounded in response. "Sherry and Mama weren't best friends or any-thing, but when word gets out . . . Lord, I hate to think what Mama might do."

Irma patted his upper arm. "I know, Henry. You're right." The nurse reached into her scrubs pocket. "If you promise not to tell, you can use my phone. Will that help?"

"You're a blessing, Irma." He gratefully accepted the phone. "Um . . . is there any way you could give me a little privacy? I don't want to—get emotional in front of you."

"Oh, Henry. We see men cry all the time in this place."

He closed his eyes and gently shook his head.

"All right. I'll go in the boss's private bathroom while you call."

Henry thanked her, then waited for Irma to fulfill her promise. As soon as she pulled the bathroom door shut, he looked down at the phone and carefully dialed his mother's number.

CHAPTER 82

"COON'S RIGHT THERE," says an FBI agent, pointing to a dark hump in the grass beneath the shattered window of Henry's hospital room.

John Kaiser takes a small but powerful flashlight from his pocket and shines its beam on the gray animal, which appears to have been shot more than once. Then he pushes through the bushes beneath the window. I look right, then left, surprised to see how many volunteer trees and shrubs have obscured the windows that line the hospital wall.

"Hold my light, Penn?" Kaiser says, handing me the black metal tube. "Shine it on this tree trunk."

I do.

With a penknife, Kaiser digs into a small hole in the bark of a sapling by Henry's window.

"You got another slug in there?" asks Sheriff Dennis.

"Yep." Kaiser turns and nudges me out of the bushes. When he steps into the open, his hand held in front of him, I shine the light beam into it. Lying in his palm is a small, deformed slug.

"Twenty-two Magnum?" Sheriff Dennis asks.

"Just like the ones inside."

A deputy behind me whistles. "I'll be damned."

"Is that a sniper rifle?" Caitlin asks.

Kaiser shakes his head. "It's a varmint gun, basically. People like them because they're not as loud as a .308, but they have more killing power than a .22 long rifle. You can kill a coyote at seventy yards with a head shot."

"You can also shoot coons and armadillos without waking up the neighbors," Sheriff Dennis observes.

Everybody falls silent. Speculation about the bullet's caliber temporarily blinded everyone to what is right before us. We have a dead raccoon and a dead woman within a few yards of each other.

"You see any other holes in that tree?" Sheriff Dennis asks Kaiser. "Maybe the wall?"

I shine the light at the window, and Kaiser points to the right of it. "Looks like one embedded in the wall there."

"Shit," says Dennis. "You think some kid could have been popping off rounds at that coon and accidentally shot through the window?"

"No way in hell," says Kaiser.

Walker doesn't look so sure. "Every kid in this parish owns a .22. They get BB guns for Christmas when they're four years old. If you stand outside around here on any given night, you're gonna hear shots. What if some kid was chasin' that coon and run him up that tree you dug the slug out of? That's just what a coon does. One miss would put a bullet right through Henry's window."

"Why would a kid fire with a lighted window right there?" Kaiser asks. "And why multiple shots? No. You're reaching, Sheriff."

"*Buck fever,*" says a new voice from behind us—a voice that sounds almost as amused as it does certain. "There's prob'ly a ten-year-old kid crappin' his pants somewhere right now, wondering if he shot a hole in somebody's bedpan."

As Kaiser turns to argue, the deputies part for the newcomer. I shine Kaiser's flashlight on a man with a hard, angular, copper-hued face, gold bars on his shoulders, and a gold badge in the shape of the Pelican State gleaming on the breast of his blue uniform shirt.

"Who are you?" asks Kaiser.

"Captain Alphonse Ozan, state police. Who are you?"

Kaiser hesitates before answering, his perceptive eyes taking in the new man. "Special Agent John Kaiser, FBI."

Captain Ozan grins as though at a private joke. "Oh, yeah. I've heard of you." He points at me. "Get that light out of my eyes."

I lower the light but leave it high enough to keep his face illuminated.

"What are you doing here?" Kaiser asks.

"I was in the area working a drug case, and my CO asked me to stop by and make sure this murder was being handled properly."

"It is," Sheriff Dennis says in a defensive tone.

"Who's your CO?" asks Kaiser.

"Lieutenant Colonel Forrest Knox, Criminal Investigations Bureau."

A brittle silence descends on the group.

"Ain't that some shit," Sheriff Dennis says under his breath.

"What was that?" Ozan asks.

"We were talking about the bullets," says Walker, looking back at the building. "And this coon. Mighty queer situation, I've got to say."

Captain Ozan steps forward and prods the dead raccoon with his boot. "We see this kind of tragedy all the time in rural areas. You know what they say about sport shooting these days? Every bullet you fire comes with a lawyer attached."

"It's a tragedy, all right," Kaiser remarks. "But I can think of a dozen men who'll be celebrating tonight."

"Who you talking about?" Captain Ozan asks.

"The Double Eagle group." Kaiser's gaze is like a laser locked on Ozan's face. "And the Knox family."

Ozan returns the stare without a word, but he radiates the same energy as a wild animal in captivity—seemingly docile, but capable of lashing out with lethal speed and effect at any moment.

"That raccoon is the killer's idea of a joke," Kaiser says. "The Double Eagles are laughing their asses off right now."

A strange smile stretches Ozan's lips. "How do you figure that?"

Kaiser smiles back, but the expression contains no goodwill. "When the FBI came to Natchez in the mid-1960s, the Klan wrangled up a mess of rattlesnakes and snuck them into the agents' hotel rooms. The agents killed all the rattlers and barbecued them in front of their hotel. The Klan guys drove by laughing and whistling. It was all a big game to them. This is the same kind of crap. I'll bet they're watching us *right now*." Kaiser points across the highway. "I wish I had a thermal scope to scan that tree line."

Everybody turns and peers into the dark field opposite the hospital.

"I want a time of death on that raccoon," Kaiser says.

Ozan laughs out loud.

"Is he kidding?" asks a deputy from the surrounding darkness.

Kaiser's eyes almost blaze in the dark. "Do I sound like I'm kidding?"

"How the hell are we gonna get that?"

"Shove a thermometer up its ass! Somebody in the Smithsonian will know the cooling curve on a dead raccoon. I want to know how long ago that goddamn ringtail was shot."

"We'll get it," Walker says, hoping to keep the peace.

"High-tech law enforcement, boys," Ozan says in a mocking tone. "The FBI wants to send a dead raccoon to the Smithsonian Institute."

Muffled laughter comes out of the dark.

Kaiser ignores the disrespect and speaks with military precision. "Has anyone found shell casings out here yet?"

"Not yet," answers a Yankee-accented voice.

"You need metal detectors and floodlights out here. Anything that comes out of this field other than grass or dirt, I want it. Bag it and tag it, no matter how trivial it may seem. Find out where the shooter fired from. I'm guessing inside thirty yards, at a perfect right angle to the window glass. That's how—"

"Hold up there, fellas," Captain Ozan calls. "This is now a state police crime scene, and you'll be taking your orders from me. FBI assistance has not been requested and won't be required."

Kaiser can't hide his shock, and Ozan doesn't give him time to argue. "If you have any questions, Agent Kaiser, have your SAC in New Orleans call the governor. That's who we take our orders from down here. Washington's about as much use to us as tits on a boar hog, which Katrina just proved for all time. You can go back to your sump pumps and your forty-year-old bones. We'll handle this crime scene."

Kaiser stares at Ozan in furious silence. Though neither man speaks, the air between them seems on the verge of ionizing in a blue flash. The rest of us have become an audience to a confrontation we don't quite understand. I'm not sure it will end without a blow being struck until Caitlin steps up and speaks to Ozan in a strong voice.

"Actually, you're wrong, Captain. This is a hate crime. One of the victims received a card calling him a 'nigger-lover' and telling him to 'die soon.' That's a quote. I have the card in my purse. Doesn't the FBI have jurisdiction over hate crimes?"

I'm about to pull her away from Ozan when a piercing beep sounds, and Kaiser takes his cell phone from his pocket.

"Yes? . . . Understood. Where? . . . Good, that's good. I'm on my way."

He pockets his phone, then cocks his head slightly as though sizing up Ozan one last time. The state cop looks braced for an argument, but Kaiser only turns to Walker Dennis and says, "Sheriff, feel free to call if you need us."

Walker nods but says nothing in reply.

As Kaiser starts back toward the hospital entrance, he takes his flashlight from my hand and whispers, "Meet me in the parking lot. Bring Caitlin."

Captain Ozan's eyes follow Kaiser as he walks away. In the shadows, it's hard to see much of the captain's face, but I'm left with the impression that he has Indian blood.

"Are you Mayor Cage?" he asks, turning to me after Kaiser disappears into the dark.

"That's right."

"I understand your fiancée was standing a couple of feet from the victim when he was hit."

"I was," Caitlin says defiantly.

Jordan Glass steps up protectively beside her.

"You're a lucky girl," Ozan goes on. "To walk out of that room alive. Mighty lucky, I'd say. It's a lucky thing I was in town, too." He looks over at Sheriff Dennis. "This parish has been going to hell for a long time, and you don't seem to be able to handle it."

Walker looks like he's about to have a stroke, but he doesn't argue.

After holding my ground long enough to prove that Ozan's scrutiny doesn't rattle me, I take Caitlin's hand and lead her back toward the main hospital doors. Jordan takes up station at Caitlin's other shoulder as we walk.

"This is nuts," Caitlin says shakily. "Who was that guy?"

"A killer," Jordan says in a cool voice. "I've shot enough of them to know."

CHAPTER 83

JORDAN, KAISER, CAITLIN, and I stand by my car like two couples after a mugging. We stare at each other in dazed incomprehension, the hospital's sodium vapor lamps rendering everything around us in an eerie, dichromatic world of yellow and gray.

"What just happened?" Caitlin asks.

"One of the killers just showed up to investigate the murder," Kaiser answers. "Or one of his flunkies, anyway. This state is something. It's like it's still 1964."

"Are you saying the state police were involved in killing Henry Sexton?" Caitlin asks.

"Off the record?"

Caitlin glances at Jordan, who looks embarrassed by Kaiser's insistence on secrecy among the four of us. "Off the record," she says grudgingly.

"That's what I'm saying. And I appreciate you standing up for federal jurisdiction back there. That took guts. But next time leave the turf battles to me, okay?"

Caitlin doesn't know whether to be flattered or angry.

"Do you really have that card you mentioned?"

She takes a card from her purse and hands it to Kaiser, who reads it, then slips it into his pocket.

"Are you really just going to give up the crime scene?" I ask, stepping up to Kaiser. "Caitlin's right about the hate crime angle, and Walker already invited you to consult on the case."

Kaiser looks like a man trying to wrap his mind around something. "They shot Henry *knowing* that my team could respond in a matter of minutes. That's balls, you know?"

"But maybe not brains. Although Ozan could be destroying critical evidence as we speak."

The FBI agent shakes his head. "Don't kid yourself. This murder won't be solved unless the shooter confesses or a co-conspirator fingers him. They've been planning this hit since they missed Henry the first time."

"What was that phone call you got at the end?"

Kaiser cuts his eyes at Caitlin as though deciding whether he should speak candidly. "My people found something in the trunk of Luther Davis's car." He points to a Suburban parked twenty yards away, its engine running. "It's in the back of that SUV over there."

"What is it?" she asks, glancing at the vehicle.

Kaiser steps closer to her. "Before I answer that, let's talk about Henry Sexton's backup files. I know you have them, and I need access to them."

As Caitlin looks to me for help, I realize that what I feared this morning must have happened during the afternoon: Sherry Harden told Kaiser about Henry's safe-deposit box keys.

"If Henry wanted you to have any of his case materials," Caitlin says, "he would have given them to you before now."

Kaiser's face looks as serious as I've ever seen it. "Henry didn't realize how much danger he was in. With all due respect, Ms. Masters, I think you have the same problem. Those files are a bullet magnet. Or worse. The Double Eagles are big fans of explosives, and old hands at using them. The *Beacon* building has already been burned. The *Natchez Examiner* isn't exactly a fortress. Do you want to wait until Penn is picking out a casket before you face what you're caught up in?"

Caitlin takes an aggressive step toward Kaiser. "Whoever shot Henry could have blown me away two seconds later. But he didn't. I think I'm relatively safe, for the time being anyway."

Kaiser shakes his head. "Maybe the triggerman didn't know you were going to be there. Maybe he didn't want to risk a cell call to get the go-order."

"If things are really that dangerous, what are we doing standing out here? A sniper could shoot us from across the highway, couldn't he?"

"Not at this moment. I've had a sniper on the hospital roof sweeping that field with a thermal imaging scope for the past four minutes."

This silences us all.

"The Double Eagles probably don't know you have those files yet," Kaiser goes on. "But they will. Henry's girlfriend was no fan of yours. She's bound to have talked to somebody."

"You think you're going to scare me into cooperating with you?" Caitlin challenges.

"No. But I don't understand your reluctance. Are you hoping to solve these murders yourself? Henry tried that, and look at the result."

"At least he didn't sit on his ass for forty years, like the FBI."

I step between them, silently warning the Bureau man to back off.

"Look," says Kaiser, trying to stay calm, "we all have different pieces of this puzzle, and we all want the same result. Don't we?"

"Do we?" asks Caitlin.

"You can't blame her, John," I interject. "The Bureau has got a pretty bad record in the sharing department. Henry wasn't the Bureau's biggest fan, either."

"I'm not the Bureau," he says angrily. "Not on this case. I'm Dwight Stone. Dwight and every other agent who bucked Hoover and the system to try to do the right thing, all the way back to 1963, when Medgar Evers was shot. This won't be a one-way flow of information. I'm not keeping things from you guys."

He turns on his heel, walks to the Suburban, and knocks on the driver's window. The glass slides down and someone hands him a bag. When he returns, he takes his flashlight from his pocket, unzips the bag, and removes a large clear Ziploc containing a badly rusted hunk of metal with a strangely familiar shape. That shape hurls me back to every World War II movie I've ever seen.

"That looks like a Luger," I comment.

"Doesn't it?" says Kaiser. "This was rusted to the inner wall of Luther Davis's trunk. The agent who found it said he thought about *The Rat Patrol* the second he saw it."

"*Is* it a Luger?"

"No." Kaiser opens the Ziploc and takes out the heavily oxidized but still graceful weapon and examines it from several angles in the beam of the flashlight.

"What is it?" asks Caitlin.

"A Nambu."

"A what?"

"N-A-M-B-U. It's a Japanese pistol widely used by their officers during both world wars. It was designed by General Kijiro Nambu, the Japanese John Browning. Takes an eight-millimeter cartridge. It looks like a Luger, but the works are completely different. Quite a few Pacific vets brought them home as trophies."

"Like Frank Knox?" I guess.

Kaiser's eyes glint with triumph. "Yes, sir. Frank Knox was known to possess a Nambu. Picked it up on Tarawa. Best of all? Nobody's seen that gun in forty years."

"Oh, man. You knew this all along?"

"Let's just say I had a feeling this gun might have gone into the ground wherever Jimmy Revels and Luther Davis were buried. I wasn't far wrong, by God."

"Why would they dump the gun with the body?" I ask. "They should have thrown it in the river."

"Frank Knox would have," Kaiser says. "But Frank was dead by the time Jimmy and Luther were killed. Whoever shot Luther obviously had access to Frank's pistol, though."

"His little brother?" I guess. "Snake?"

Kaiser nods. "Snake Knox is an arrogant man. Crazier than his big brother, and not nearly so careful. Snake took over the Eagles the day Frank died, and Jimmy and Luther were never seen again."

"Any chance of getting a serial number off this gun?" Caitlin asks.

"No, but that's irrelevant. This weapon was a battle trophy, never registered." Kaiser turns to his wife, who's standing just behind me. "We need a good set of photos of this pistol. A set of high-res print-outs, too."

"No problem," Jordan says.

"Make sure Ms. Masters gets a good one for the *Examiner.*"

Caitlin goes still, her eyes wide.

Kaiser looks her full in the face. "You have my permission to report this find in your paper. Same with the handcuffs and Luther's ID. That'll make a hell of a headline. After what happened tonight, we're about to be enveloped in a media storm, but you'll have the exclusive story."

"But only if I turn over Henry's files to you?"

"Fair's fair," says Kaiser, looking to me for support. "Right now I need to know who the mysterious 'Gates Brown' is. I'm guessing that information is somewhere in Henry's files." He looks back at Caitlin, his eyebrows arched. "Or maybe you already know?"

"No." She debates silently with herself. "I'm sorry. I'm not ready to make that trade. Not without more thought. Too much has happened tonight."

"I need to see those files, Ms. Masters. And your withholding them comes very close to obstruction of justice."

"Whoa, John," I cut in. "If you're going to talk like that, you'd better talk to her lawyer. And tonight that's me."

Kaiser starts to speak, but Caitlin holds up her hand and says, "I feel sick. Seriously. I need to get to the ladies' room."

Kaiser looks more suspicious than sympathetic. "You'd better go with her," he says to Jordan. "With Ozan's people coming and going, the hospital's no longer secure."

"I'll go with her," I say, but Kaiser grabs my upper arm and holds me in place. "I still need to talk to you. Please." He gives Caitlin a look of apology. "We'll be here in the car when you guys come back."

I'm tempted to jerk my arm from Kaiser's hand, but Caitlin shakes her head at me, then nods assent to Jordan and starts toward the hospital entrance.

As Jordan follows her, Kaiser bags the Nambu and beckons me toward a black Crown Victoria two spaces away. He puts the evidence bag in the backseat, then starts the car and turns on the heater. By the time I close the passenger door, the front windshield is completely fogged.

"You were a little rough on her back there," I tell him.

He turns to me with startling urgency. "I need those files, Penn. The Double Eagles came within an inch of assassinating Henry Sexton while he was under police protection. I don't have time for your fiancée to play Lois Lane, or whoever the current role model is."

"I think Caitlin's hero is your wife."

Exasperated, Kaiser leans forward and wipes the windshield so that he can observe the hospital entrance.

"Why didn't you tell Ozan to get the hell away from here?" I ask. "You've got the authority, especially being here on a terrorism case."

"I honestly wasn't expecting such a brazen move. I was hoping to put out the word that Henry had died, but that's not going to fly now. As for Ozan, I'm giving him rope and hoping that he and his boss will hang themselves with it."

"Forrest Knox?"

"That's right. My man Forrest just unzipped his fly. I've been playing a long game with that bastard, but his time is coming."

Kaiser may be playing a long game, but I don't have time for such luxuries. My game will be won or lost in the next eight hours or so, and I don't want to sit here long enough for Kaiser to start questioning me. To forestall any interrogation, I ask whether his digital surveillance has picked up anything further between Brody Royal and his son-in-law.

He rolls his eyes and says, "They know what we're up to. That's the only explanation. So, do you want to tell me what you have on Royal?"

While I try to think of a credible answer, I realize that Randall Regan must not have said anything on the phone about Caitlin firing a gun in his house. If he had, Kaiser would certainly have said something to Caitlin about it.

Kaiser is clearly getting impatient, but before he can press me, an FBI agent taps on his window, then tells him that Henry Sexton is demanding that his mother be let in to visit him when she arrives. Preoccupied with me, Kaiser grants permission, so long as Mrs. Sexton presents valid ID and matches the picture on it. As he concludes this conversation, Caitlin appears in front of the car and signals for me to get out.

"I need to speak to her," I tell Kaiser, and quickly make my escape.

"Are you okay?" I ask Caitlin.

She nods but says nothing. Then I see Jordan standing a few feet behind her.

"Delayed shock," Jordan says. "I've seen it plenty of times in war zones. She'll be all right. She's plenty tough."

"Maybe I should drive you back," I suggest.

Caitlin shakes her head, her eyes fraught with conflicting emotions. "Thanks, but my press operator drove me over, and he's still here. Jamie texted me while we were inside. The deadline's crashing down on us. They need me back at the paper now. I'm going to go say good-bye to Henry, then get back to work."

This seems like an overly thorough explanation, but something tells me not to question her. Kaiser looks a little suspicious as well, but his buzzing cell phone distracts him. He checks a text message, then says, "I've got to get back inside. Apparently Captain Ozan has been questioning hospital employees about Henry's status. I need to call my SAC."

I shake Kaiser's hand, thank Jordan, then take Caitlin's hand and pull her toward my car. She follows without resistance. Once there, I lean in and start the engine, but we stand outside, our breath fogging in the cold.

She raises her eyebrows in silent reproach. "Did you tell him anything about Henry's files?"

"No."

"The recording of Katy Royal?"

"Hell, no."

Caitlin relaxes a little, then rubs her hands together. "Can you believe he tried to extort me like that?"

"Kaiser's serious about nailing the Double Eagles. And he's got a point. Without Henry's files, he's got one hand tied behind his back."

Caitlin's eyes flash. "I could say the same about the recording of Katy Royal, but you're not giving him that."

"You're right."

She looks around cautiously, then reaches into her pocket and pulls out a small photograph. When she turns up her palm, I see Henry Sexton with a rifle scope superimposed over his face.

"Where did you get that?"

"Someone sent it to Henry a few months ago. He was in New Orleans, looking into old real estate deals between Brody Royal and Carlos Marcello. He showed it to the FBI at the time, but they didn't come up with anything. It's one more thing to keep in mind when you confront Brody."

"Thanks."

"Have you talked to Kirk?"

"He's waiting for me now."

She gives me a long look. "Promise me you won't give Royal anything that matters. You can't trust him, Penn."

"I know that."

"Stop by the newspaper when you're done. I can't make any final decisions about tomorrow's editions until I know where you stand with him."

"I will."

"All right, then." Slipping the photo back into her coat, she stands on tiptoe and kisses me.

As she starts toward the hospital entrance, Jordan Glass gets out of a car to my right and follows her to the doors. Maybe Kaiser told his wife to keep an eye on Caitlin, or maybe she's just concerned.

Shaking off my worry, I climb into my Audi, throw it into gear, back out of the space, and race out of the parking lot. As soon as I hit Highway 15, something in my chest comes loose. It's not empathy for Henry, or grief over the woman he loved. The reckless attack on Henry—with Caitlin standing only feet away—has penetrated the most primitive fibers of my brain. I feel myself gearing down into survival mode, a state without sentiment, hesitation, or moral constraint. Instead of apprehension, I feel an almost surreal sense of calm.

The ambient glow of Vidalia fills the sky ahead, and the lights of Natchez flicker like stars high on the bluff across the river. Taking out my cell phone, I call Kirk's number.

"I'm on him," he says. "Still at St. Catherine's. Whole family's outside the ICU."

"Randall Regan, too?"

"Oh, yeah."

"Are you still up for this?"

"*Oo-rah,* brah. Let the games begin."

CHAPTER 84

AS SOON AS the guard passed Caitlin through the front entrance of the hospital, Jordan Glass called out her name, then beckoned her toward some chairs in the corner of the darkened lobby. The seats had cracked covers, but they were comfortable enough. The coffee table was strewn with well-thumbed magazines. Jordan sat beneath a poster warning about heart disease in women, then waited while Caitlin took a chair to her right. Caitlin's skin felt cold, and her ears were ringing. She wondered if she was finally going into shock.

"You saved Henry," Jordan said, as though they had been discussing the issue for the past twenty minutes.

Henry's frozen face kept floating behind Caitlin's eyes, the trickle of blood running down to the pillow, then Sherry whirling from the window, her hands flying to her throat as one eye socket poured blood. Caitlin didn't want to say anything about it, for fear of sounding like a baby in front of a woman who'd spent years in war zones. *Who opened those damned window blinds?* she asked herself for the hundredth time.

"And Sherry died doing what she could to save the man she loved," Jordan added.

"She died doing what I told her to do," Caitlin corrected.

"If you hadn't told her to do that, Henry might be dead instead of her. Or both of them. Or *you.*"

Caitlin stared at a tattered issue of *Self* on the table.

"In 1992," Jordan said, "a man I loved got blown apart while standing in line to fill a canteen with water for me. I was hiding twenty yards away. A mortar round took off the top of his head and killed four other people, two of them children. I didn't even get a bruise. I can't tell you how many 'if onlys' I suffered through over that. He died because of me, no question. But he was also there for himself, just like Henry Sexton. And I almost got myself killed a week later because I was still dwelling on it. I don't want you to end up like Sherry tomorrow because you're not paying attention."

Caitlin said nothing. The story seemed like a magazine article she'd read long ago. Still, the accuracy of Glass's intuition was unnerving.

"Did Henry tell you anything important before he was shot?" Jordan asked.

Caitlin's thoughts leaped to Toby Rambin, the poacher Henry had told her about—the man who supposedly knew the location of the Bone Tree. With a stab of guilt she recalled entering Rambin's name and number into her phone, then altering it in Henry's so that no one else could discover it there. She hoped the FBI had no way to detect recent editing on a SIM card.

"You don't trust me," Jordan said.

A simple statement of fact.

"It's not that," Caitlin lied. "This morning you told me that you don't always share everything with your husband. But I'm sure you share a lot. Where's the line?"

The photographer smiled with an inward sadness. "That's not always clear. But I wouldn't betray anything you're working on to John."

"Are you asking me to tell you everything Henry's confided in me?"

"No. But I figured you wouldn't have been in that room tonight unless you hoped to learn something more from him."

Caitlin's head snapped up, angry words on the tip of her tongue.

"Hey, hey," Jordan said gently. "No offense, okay? But if there's one thing I know, it's reporters."

"I'm the publisher of my paper, not a reporter."

Glass gave her a knowing smile. "I've read your stories. You're a reporter."

Caitlin resented the confidence with which Glass had pigeonholed her, but a little part of her glowed, as well.

Jordan hooked her hands around one knee and leaned back in her chair, her perceptive eyes on Caitlin. "I'm about to tell you something I shouldn't."

"What?" Caitlin asked, intrigued by the tone of Glass's voice.

"Tomorrow John is going to subpoena the files you got from Henry Sexton. He's going to take them from you legally."

A jolt of alarm made Caitlin sit upright. "He can't do that! That's crazy."

"John wouldn't do it if he didn't think he'd get the files."

"But Henry *gave* me those files. Those are a journalist's records. He was my employee at the time! I can prove that. He still is. His publisher will swear to that."

Jordan held up her hands to stop Caitlin. "Remember what I told you at the Jericho Hole? How John got things moving so quickly on this case? He's operating under provisions of the Patriot Act."

Caitlin felt a cold sweat inside her shirt.

"When a federal judge considers Henry's files in that light—and his attempted assassination—he'll probably decide they're critical evidence in the hunt for an out-of-control domestic terror cell. So—here's my free advice. Go back to your office and make copies of everything Henry gave you, if you haven't already. Then give John either the copies or the originals. Because he's going to get them anyway. Things will go a lot smoother if you do it voluntarily, and I think after you get a little sleep, you're going to realize what it will mean to have John giving you exclusive information."

A dozen different emotions swirled through Caitlin's exhausted brain. "Did your husband tell you to talk me out of those files?"

Jordan smiled sadly, then shook her head. "I'm on your side. I loved it when you got in that trooper's face out there. I look at you and see my younger self. I want you to *own* this story. But John's right: tomorrow an army of print and TV journalists is going to descend on this area. Your window of exclusivity is going to slam shut fast. Hiding those files may feel instinctively right, but it's not. People are dying. John and his team are the best hope of stopping this violence. He won't let any other journalist see those files. And if you give him access, he'll pay you back ten times over. I know him."

Caitlin's heart told her to believe Glass, but skepticism had been drilled into her from infancy.

"If you need to hold something back," Jordan said, "then do it. Something special that Henry gave you, maybe. But the rest of it . . . let it go. That's the safest thing for your family, too."

Caitlin thought about the Moleskine notebook she'd discovered outside the burned *Beacon* building, the Toby Rambin lead, the recording of Katy Royal. "Are you going to tell John you told me that?"

Jordan laughed without humor. "If I ever do manage to get pregnant, I'd prefer to be married, not divorced. So, no, I'm not going to tell him."

Caitlin rubbed her eyes so hard she saw spots. Then she set her elbows on her knees and gave Glass an unguarded gaze. "When I was thirteen, I worked at one of my father's newspapers. I saw some photographs there that had just been shot in El Salvador. A massacre by a death squad. A lady who worked at our paper was so proud that a young American woman had shot those pictures. Do you remember who shot them?"

Jordan tapped the coffee table as though bored or frustrated. "Me."

"Those pictures went a long way toward leading me to where I am now."

Glass's smile looked forced. She'd obviously heard this kind of thing a thousand times before. Her eyes focused somewhere in the darkness across the lobby. "I'm not the same person I was then. I'm tired. I'm ready to stop—for a while anyway." She put her face in her hands and massaged her temples as though to relieve a headache. "I'm not that girl who sneaked into a village and shot those pictures anymore." She looked up at Caitlin. "But *you are.* That's why I gave you that advice. You're not thinking straight right now, because of what happened. But tomorrow you will be again."

Caitlin had never felt so validated as she did in that moment.

"John's not exactly himself right now, either," Jordan said. "You should know that. When you criticized the Bureau out there, it really hurt him."

Caitlin shrugged, but she didn't apologize.

"John knows the Bureau failed all those years ago. It failed the murder victims, the families, even its own agents. He wants to make that right. When he tells you he's on your side, he means it."

"He's gotten a lot done in a short time, I'll give him that."

"Thanks to Henry and Penn. And you."

Caitlin was suddenly nervous. "I haven't done anything yet. But I'm going to."

Jordan's eyebrows rose. "Something you probably shouldn't be doing?"

"That depends on your point of view."

"What's your plan? Just between us and the coffee table? No shit."

What the hell? Caitlin thought, suddenly realizing that she trusted

Jordan Glass more than many people she'd known for years. "I want to find Pooky Wilson's bones. I think Pooky and Jimmy may have been killed or dumped at the same place."

"And you know where that is?"

"Maybe. I've got a good lead. One nobody else has. Maybe that's what I'll keep for myself."

"Does Penn know what you know?"

"No."

Jordan smiled in the shadows. "A girl after my own heart. So where are these mysterious bones?"

As badly as Caitlin wanted to confide in her idol, something held her back. While she wondered how to tactfully evade the question, her Treo pinged with a text message. She took it out and entered her privacy code, then saw a message from Jamie Lewis, her editor.

> In 1970, Dr. Wilhelm Borgen was indicted for multiple counts of
> sexual abuse of psychiatric patients at his Texas institute. Crimes
> date from 1956–1968. Testimony of nurses indicated he used
> electroshock to erase the memories of his victims. Aborted fetuses of
> impregnated patients under his care. This story getting sicker by the
> minute. HURRY BACK!

Caitlin's heart fluttered. She thought of trying to hide her excitement, but Jordan was far too sensitive to be deceived.

"Everything okay?" Jordan asked in a leading tone.

"Yes." Caitlin typed a quick response to Jamie, then texted her press operator that he should pick her up out front. "But I think I've got to skip saying good-bye to Henry."

Glass gave her a sisterly smile. "Do what you need to do."

Caitlin stood and slung her purse over her shoulder. "If you find yourself at loose ends tomorrow morning, come by the _Examiner_. I might have some work for you."

"I might do that." Jordan stood and offered Caitlin her hand.

Instead of shaking it, Caitlin hugged the older woman tight, then stepped back blushing. "Thank you. I mean it."

"I know. Get going."

Caitlin hurried to the exit, gave the guard a familiar wave, then darted through the door and ran for her ride.

CHAPTER 85

WHEN THE HOSPITAL security guard recognizes me as the mayor—and Dr. Cage's son—he not only allows Kirk and me to pass unchallenged into the main building, but also answers my questions about "poor Mr. Royal and his family." I'm actually a little surprised to find Brody Royal at the hospital after 11 P.M., but given that the administrator has cleared three patient rooms near the ICU for the use of his family (Brody is on the hospital board), the old man is exempt from the usual discomforts of late-night visitors.

I've known the way to the ICU ever since I accompanied my father on emergency calls as a kid. Walking up the deserted corridor, I remind Kirk that I want him to stay cool and quiet, and only intervene if any of Royal's people try to get physical. If they do, he should use the minimum force required to restrain them. I've brought Pithy Nolan's straight razor in my back pocket, but only as a prop to intimidate the old man into thinking I know everything there is to know about him.

Brody's oldest son, Andy, sees me first, glancing to his left as he passes between the big ICU double doors and a regular room. Andy looks away, then turns angrily back as he makes the connection between Caitlin and me.

"What the hell are you doing here?" he challenges.

"I'm here to speak to your father."

President of his father's bank, Andy Royal is a big man of thirty-five with more gut than muscle. He takes a couple of steps toward me, his face turning scarlet. "You've got some damn nerve, Cage."

"You don't understand the situation. Where's your dad?"

Andy Royal grinds his jaws with fury. "My sister's lying in there in a *coma,* thanks to your goddamn girlfriend. And you—"

"I'm sorry about your sister, Andy. More than you know. But your dad is going to want to talk to me. If he doesn't, he's not going to like what he reads in tomorrow's paper."

His eyes bulge. "*What?* Man, we've already talked to our lawyers about what happened this afternoon, and they think we've got a hell of a case against your girlfriend *and* her father's media group."

"Then you didn't tell your lawyers the whole story. But of course you don't know it. So how about you take me to the man who does?"

Andy points at Kirk, who decided to wear a sock cap in the hope of concealing his identity. "Who's this guy?"

"A Good Samaritan. Come on, Andy."

"Dad's in 119," he says, still eyeing Kirk, whose powerful physique is a little too obvious to ignore.

Three doors down from the ICU, the patriarch of the Royal clan is holding court from a padded chair beside a buffet of sandwiches, dough-nuts, fruit, and cheese. A half-empty fifth of Maker's Mark stands on a table beside him. Compared to his son, who looks like a high school tackle who never matured into a man, Brody Royal looks like a weather-beaten falcon. His slim face and aquiline nose contribute to this impression, but it's the deep-set, predatory eyes beneath sleek gray brows that first mark me in the doorway. They flit to Kirk for a second, then lock back on me as though gauging the distance for a killing dive. My peripheral vision registers five other people in the room, three of them women. I glance away from Brody long enough to recognize two red-faced Royal nephews in their fifties—both employees of Royal Oil.

"Everybody out," Brody says with the casual authority of a monarch.

Nobody questions his order. They don't even hesitate. Brody glares at Andy, who has lingered in the doorway, and says, "Shut the door."

Andy steps inside to obey, but his father says, "From the other side."

After an awkward silence, his son yields. "Holler if you need me," Andy says, backing out of the room.

After the door closes, Brody beckons me nearer. As I move toward him, I realize that age has not robbed him of his virility. He projects a restrained power, more like the aged Burt Lancaster than Charlton Heston, to whom Henry Sexton compared him. Royal has an acrobat's proportions, which are accented by his tailored shirt.

"To what do I owe this honor, Mr. Mayor?" he asks without a trace of irony.

This opening takes me aback. I'd expected to confront a querulous old caricature of Theodore G. Bilbo, the red-faced, overweight arche-type of Big Daddy, Boss Hogg, and all the other southern shouters.

Finding myself facing a trim and courteous businessman is more than a little disconcerting.

"I need to tell you some rather unpleasant things, Mr. Royal. And then I need to ask you a favor—a couple of them, actually."

The cool gray eyes don't blink. "I'm a captive audience. Fire away."

"Somebody shot Henry Sexton tonight. He survived, in case you didn't know."

Royal shrugs as if nothing could interest him less. "Can't say I'm surprised. That boy's been pushing certain people for a long time. Stands to reason they'd push back eventually."

"And you know nothing about it?"

The eyes remain steady. "What would I know?"

I can't help but smile in appreciation of Royal's poker face—and at my knowledge of what is about to happen. This consummate power broker hasn't had his will challenged for years.

"I've got good news and bad news for you, sir. The bad news is, I've got enough evidence to buy you a guaranteed seat on death row at Angola. That's in the long run. In the short run, I've got enough information to destroy your reputation and the value of most of your companies by noon tomorrow."

Royal's face alters less than the surface of a rock when the wind passes over it. "What's the good news?"

"I'm not that interested in forty-year-old murders today. I'm interested in one that happened this past Monday at five thirty in the morning. A woman named Viola Turner."

Royal studies me like a gambler watching his opponent deal cards. "You haven't said what you want, Mayor. You want to know who killed that old colored woman? Your daddy's old squeeze? Is that what you came for?"

"No."

"What then?"

"I want you to listen for a minute. I want you to think about what I've told you. Then decide whether or not you're going to do what I need you to do."

"Well, get started. You're boring the hell out of me so far."

It suddenly strikes me that Brody Royal hasn't said one word about his comatose daughter. Squatting before him, I look into the opaque gray eyes and begin my pitch.

"In July of 1964, you ordered the deaths of Pooky Wilson and Albert Norris. You threatened Norris in his shop the afternoon of the night he died, and you went back later that night to help kill him with a flame-thrower. I know that because there was a witness. A witness who's still alive, healthy, and willing to testify against you."

Royal shows no reaction to this.

"The day after Norris's store was burned, the Brookhaven klavern of the Ku Klux Klan kidnapped Pooky Wilson from a train station and delivered him to the Double Eagles for punishment. One of those men is ready to testify as to how and where Pooky died, and about your involvement in it."

"Bullshit," he says calmly.

Royal is right. That last part was a lie, but he can't know for sure. And part of my purpose is to sow seeds of paranoia in the enemy camp. The predatory eyes narrow, the mind behind them judging odds based on variables unknown to me.

"You ordered the deaths of Dr. Leland Robb and everyone else on his plane. You told Snake Knox to sabotage it, and after Robb was dead, you married his wife. Killed two birds with one stone there. Nice trick. Only before Dr. Robb died, he told my father what Albert Norris had told him. And my father will testify to that in court."

"You're a book writer, aren't you?" Royal says in a conversational tone. "I can see you'd be good at it. Because every bit of this sounds like hearsay to me."

Reaching into my back pocket, I take out Caitlin's tape recorder. "Let's see if this sounds like hearsay. You might want to take a shot of that whiskey before I press play."

The falcon's eyes settle on the tiny Sony. "What's that you got there?"

"You'll understand soon enough. Listen up."

Before Kirk and I entered the hospital, I cued the recorder to the point where Katy begins to implicate her father. As her slurred voice repeats the damning words, the old man's face goes gray, then white.

By the way Brody is staring at the recorder, I'm betting that Randall Regan already told him about the tape recorder Caitlin left behind—which contained no incriminating information. Brody probably doesn't know enough about cell phones to know they can also record memos.

"Speaking as a former prosecutor," I tell him, "that doesn't sound like hearsay to me. It sounds like your daughter is accusing you of murdering her mother, among other people. And if she dies, I'd say that what you just heard becomes a dying declaration given prior to suicide. Claude Devereux could challenge the recording in court, of course, along with your daughter's mental status, but by that time your reputation will long since have been destroyed. So . . . if you don't do exactly as I ask—tonight—what you just heard will be published tomorrow morning in every newspaper owned by the Masters Media Group. That's six or seven million readers, at least. By noon you'll have CNN setting up cameras in the lobby of your bank. There's nothing like a Klan story to give the liberal media a taste for blood. Think about Trent Lott. He had ten times the connections you've got, and he quietly exited stage left when only a hint of this kind of scandal touched him."

"You print that," Brody says calmly, "and I'll own John Masters's media group."

"No you won't. You'll be watching a jury listen to how you forcibly committed your teenage daughter to an institution where she was given electroshock therapy against her will—and sexually abused—all because she fell in love with a black boy. Crucifixion, flaying . . . the murder of those women from Royal Insurance. Christ, man. The DA will have a hell of a time even seating a jury who doesn't want to string you up on the courthouse lawn. But you might actually prefer that to spending your last years in Angola with large, angry African-American gentlemen who are well informed about your past."

Royal's eyes are still on the tape recorder.

"Don't waste time wondering how I got this. It's only a copy. One of many, and soon to be number one, unless you do what I ask—tonight."

Royal raises a hand and rakes the gray stubble on his chin. I sense anxiety mounting in him, charging him with energy, like the armature of an electric motor. Despite all his wealth and power, in this moment Brody Royal is nothing more than a cornered animal searching for escape. I half expect him to come out of the chair and throttle me. Instead, he rolls his shoulders to loosen them, then gets to his feet, takes a pull of Maker's Mark, and gives me a knowing smile.

"Why don't you tell me about this favor you need?"

I glance back at Kirk Boisseau, who's staring at us in amazement.

"You want a sandwich?" Brody asks Kirk. "That chicken salad's pretty good."

"No thanks."

A fraction of a second before I speak, inspiration strikes me. *If I have Brody Royal by the balls, I'm a fool not to ask for everything I can get. After all, the APB is inextricably tied to the dead trooper.* "I need two things from you," I say, and then another possibility hits me. "Three, actually."

"I'm all ears, son."

"First, there's a Louisiana State Police APB out for my father and a man named Walt Garrity, accusing them of killing a state trooper. I want that rescinded tonight."

"I see. What else?"

"The death of that trooper will have to be written off somehow. Blamed on drug dealers or whatever else you can make work. I'm almost certain he was a dirty cop, but one way or another, you kill that case."

"And the third favor?"

"I want Viola Turner's case closed. To get the Natchez DA to do that, you'll probably have to sacrifice a Double Eagle. I don't care which, but you'd better pick one fast."

Brody takes a deep breath, then nods amicably. "Is that it?"

"That's it."

The multimillionaire gives me an expansive smile, then chooses a chicken salad sandwich from the tray, takes a bite, and washes it down with Maker's Mark.

"Mayor, I can see you're upset. All I can say to you is, I wish you'd come to me sooner. Because you've come to the right place, if you want a situation handled in Louisiana. My daddy worked hand-in-glove with Huey Long, and I worked with Earl K. and Russell myself. When the public officials couldn't quite make the mare go, I worked with the Little Man and his family in New Orleans. Hell, I've worked with every senator and governor all the way down to Edwin Edwards and his successors. I even dealt with the colored congressmen, these past few years. You've got to have an open mind to thrive in my state."

Royal is actually bragging about working with Carlos Marcello, one of the most powerful Mafia chiefs in America during the twentieth century.

"Listen," he goes on, "getting that APB canceled shouldn't be more than a matter of making the right telephone call."

Having come in ready for a pitched battle, I blink in surprise. "Even on the murder of a cop?"

Royal makes a clicking sound with his mouth. "That complicates matters a little. But Mayor, your father has treated me and members of my family many times during emergencies over the years. I can personally vouch for his integrity in the highest quarters. Why, I can't understand how a decorated veteran and pillar of the community like Tom Cage could be caught up in such a sordid business."

"How fast can you make that APB go away?"

Brody scoops some ice into a glass and pours himself a Diet Coke. "With a little luck, maybe two hours. More likely by nine or ten tomorrow morning."

"And the Viola Turner case?"

Brody holds up his glass, watches the ice cubes as he swirls it around, then adds some whiskey to it. "On that matter, I'm going to have to confer with some people I'd prefer not to mention. They can be unreasonable at times, but one is a pragmatist. I feel certain that he can offer a solution—and maybe even a candidate, warm or cold—to fill the role of Nurse Turner's killer by close of business tomorrow. You might say this kind of thing is his stock-in-trade."

Royal's got to be talking about Forrest Knox. But it's the *way* he's talking that leaves me speechless. His daughter lies comatose only a few feet away, yet he seems completely unconcerned about her. He's discussing the commission of felonies as casually as he might a real estate deal. Despite having seen some abominable exercises of influence in Houston, I thought the time had passed when men could dispose of murder cases with telephone calls. But in Brody Royal's world, all things remain possible. Apparently, laws are but inconveniences to fearless men who live by their appetites.

"Obviously," Royal adds in a less casual voice, "I need to know what I'm getting in return. Every bargain has two sides, after all."

I glance back at Kirk, who has picked up a banana from another tray and stands chewing it while he watches the door, now seemingly oblivious to our conversation.

"You obviously can't grant me legal immunity," Brody observes, "since you're no longer a prosecutor. So what are you selling, exactly? I'll need that tape, naturally, plus any and all copies."

"You'll get it. Also, a series of stories about Henry Sexton's death and the old civil rights murders will break in the Masters papers tomorrow. If you deliver, neither your name nor your daughter's will appear in those stories."

"Or elsewhere in the papers," Royal adds.

"Naturally."

"What else? You mentioned several other potential problems."

"My father's lived a long time without telling what he knows about that plane crash. You play ball, he can stay quiet for a few more years."

Royal smiles. "And the witness? The one who was there at the fire? I assume he was a friend of the Wilson boy?"

It's perfectly legal for police detectives and prosecutors to lie to suspects to prompt a confession, and in this situation, I'm not bound by any rules at all. "I'll give you the kid's name," I lie. "He's not a kid anymore, of course. I'll leave it to you to make sure he doesn't tell his story to anybody. I'm assuming you'll pay for his silence, but that's your decision."

Royal's eyes glint with interest in my apparent pragmatism. "Who has he talked to, so far?"

"Only Sexton, who's conveniently unconscious and almost sure to die by morning."

Royal ponders these points for a few seconds. "How could I ever know I had all the copies of that tape?"

"You won't. But you don't need to lose sleep over that. The tape alone wouldn't put you in the pen, especially if you can get your daughter to recant."

He nods thoughtfully. "When do I get the witness's name?"

"After my father's safe in federal custody. That's nonnegotiable. The same man saw you burn the *Beacon* last night, by the way."

Royal finishes off his sandwich, sips his drink, then sets his glass on the credenza. "I don't like it. But I guess I can live with it. There's just one thing I don't understand."

"What's that?"

"You." The cool gray eyes gleam with curiosity. "I know about you, Cage. You're a goddamn crusader. A bleeding heart. Why on earth would you do this deal?"

"In a word? Family. My father's safety means more to me than some black guys who died thirty years ago. Nothing's going to bring those men back. But this deal can keep my father alive."

I almost believed this when I said it, to the point that it worries me. How far *would* I go to protect my father?

Royal considers my words, then chuckles with recognition. "Ain't it something? When it comes down to family, a man's basically got no choices. Everything else goes by the board. Blood trumps all."

"We're agreed, then?"

He cocks his head to one side, and again I see the raptor in him. "How do I know that once I give you what you want, your girlfriend won't throw me to the dogs?"

"All I can give you is my word. But Caitlin loves my father, too. Even more than her career, and that's saying something. She knows I'm here, and why I came. I can't promise you that the FBI won't eventually pick up on something and come after you, but you and Forrest ought to be able to blame those old murders on the older Double Eagles. Maybe even dead ones. Hell, blame Norris and Pooky Wilson on Frank Knox."

After a long last look, Royal holds out his hand to shake, but I can't bring myself to go that far. "I'll give you my cell number," I tell him.

The old man gives me a haughty look and withdraws his arm. "Don't worry about it. I can find you anytime I need you."

"I hope so. The clock's ticking."

As I turn to make my exit, the door flies open and slams against the wall. Randall Regan fills the doorway, a large purple bruise covering his throat. He looks like he rear-ended someone and slammed into the steering wheel.

"What the fuck are *you* doing here?" he demands, starting toward me.

For the first time I remember the straight razor in my back pocket.

"Easy, Randall!" Brody barks, raising his hand to stop the charge. "Mayor, I believe you know Randall Regan, my son-in-law."

"We've met."

"Screw this," Regan hisses. "I'm done playing with this guy, Brody."

Regan takes another step toward me and reaches for my throat, but just then a soft yet commanding voice says, "Hold it, ace. Listen up a sec."

Regan's hand stops within inches of my throat, and he turns his head enough to locate the speaker. "Who the fuck are you?" he asks Kirk.

"Just an interested bystander." Kirk faces Regan from an angle, as though prepared to throw him across the room if necessary. "But I'm not going to let you hurt anybody. Strictly for informational purposes, if you touch the mayor, you're going to wake up in the ICU next to your wife."

Regan's eyes rake up and down Kirk Boisseau's frame, estimating his speed and power.

"Randall?" Brody says, "I appreciate you coming to check on me, but you ought to get back with Katy. The mayor and I have come to an understanding."

Regan straightens his jacket, his jaw working as he tries to ratchet down his fury. He's had a hell of a day, and the idea of beating me senseless must be tempting. But Kirk looks a little too much like a spoiler to risk that. Regan holds his ground for a few face-saving seconds, his left cheek twitching, but at last he turns and stalks out, leaving the door wide open.

Brody is looking intently at Kirk. "I know you," he says at length. "You're Marguerite Boisseau's boy."

"That's right."

Royal laughs softly. "You owe me for a bulldozer, don't you?"

Kirk rolls his eyes with resignation.

"Don't worry about it, son. Seeing that little standoff was worth the balance of your loan. Now, you boys get out of here and let me tend to my daughter." He points his forefinger at my chest. "I'll call *you* later. Don't let your girlfriend do anything stupid before you hear from me. I'm not the forgiving type."

OUTSIDE THE HOSPITAL, KIRK and I stop between our vehicles, each digging for our keys. I'm glad I decided not to show Pithy Nolan's straight razor to Brody after all. The last thing that old woman needs is that bastard angry at her.

"I feel like I need a shower after that," Kirk says. "I knew a son of a bitch like Royal in the corps. A colonel. He covered up a blatant rape by a buddy of his. Buried the whole mess, and the girl was really messed up, too. But they never even thought twice about it."

"The world's full of bastards like him," I mutter, just wanting to get away from this place. "Hopefully they're dying off. Can you follow me to the newspaper office?"

"No problem."

My ride across town is quick and uneventful, but about halfway to the *Examiner,* I remember that I never stopped by Edelweiss to see Mom and Annie as I promised. I told Mom to tell Annie I'd be back by dark, and I've gone many hours past that deadline. For a moment I consider stopping by, but Caitlin is waiting to hear the result of my meeting with Royal, and the longer I take to bring her the news, the angrier she's going to get. I'll wake Annie when I'm done arguing with Caitlin.

After I park in the rear lot of the *Examiner,* Kirk pulls in behind me, then gets out to shake hands. I'm glad to see a cop guarding the back lot, and I make a mental note to thank Chief Logan for this courtesy. Kirk greets the policeman, then peers into my eyes with a measuring gaze. Kirk is too good a friend to question my character outright, but his doubts are plain enough.

"I heard a lot of what you said up there," he says. "You didn't sound much like the guy I remember."

"I know. I didn't much like doing that. But I'd deal with the devil to save my father. I guess I just proved that."

Kirk nods philosophically. "Do you think Royal can do what he claimed?"

"If he can't, neither of us is likely to see my dad again."

Kirk stares into my soul a little longer, then squeezes my left shoulder. "Call me if you need me, bud. I'm here for you. You and your father."

"Thank you."

The ex-marine climbs back in his truck and gives me a crisp salute. "*Oo-rah,* brother."

"Oo-rah," I echo dispiritedly, already dreading my conversation with Caitlin.

CHAPTER 86

WALT GARRITY PULLED Drew Elliott's nondescript pickup truck off Highway 61 and drove west into downtown Baton Rouge, where the state capitol towered above the Mississippi River. Colonel Mackiever had chosen the city's riverfront casino hotel as their meeting place. Walt wasn't excited by this; any casino-related business was bound to have security cameras. With the APB out, he worried that his face might be picked up by the NSA's facial recognition software, which could lead to a lightning-quick arrest. Surely Mackiever understood that risk, yet Walt gauged the probability that his old friend was setting a trap for him at less than 1 percent. Still . . . that didn't mean Forrest Knox wasn't watching his boss's movements. Walt decided not to stay in the hotel any longer than he had to, and to keep his derringer cocked in his pocket both going in and coming out.

The seven stories of the Sheraton hotel squatted behind the downtown levee, linked by a skywalk to the riverside casino, the Belle of Baton Rouge. Walt pulled his hat low over his face, gave Drew's pickup keys to a valet, told him to park it close, then walked into a large, glass-ceilinged lobby that looked like a bastard child of the Crystal Palace, which had burned down in London when Walt was a boy. When he asked the desk clerk to connect him to "Mr. Griffith's" room, the clerk asked him to wait. Walt kept his head down to avoid being recorded by the elevated cameras behind the desk, and he didn't raise it when the clerk took an envelope from a slot behind him and handed it across the counter. Walt walked a couple of steps away from the desk, opened the envelope with one hand, and read the faxed handwritten message inside:

> *Ranger Captain,*
> *I had to take an unexpected trip to New Orleans regarding our*
> *mutual problem. Tough times, partner. They're coming after me,*

too. I hope to be back tonight, ASAP. Please check into a room under the name Bill McDonald and wait as long as you can. It won't be time wasted, and you'll be safe here. No bushwhackers on this ride.

Captain M.

Walt didn't like the idea of waiting, but he didn't have any doubt that this message was from Griffith Mackiever. For one thing, he'd signed his old Texas Ranger rank, when in fact he was a colonel of the Louisiana State Police. For another, Mackiever had instructed Walt to check in under the name of one of the most respected Rangers ever to wear the badge. It was Captain Bill McDonald who'd said, "No man in the wrong can stand up against a fellow that's in the right and keeps on a-comin'." In later years, Walt had heard more educated men hold forth on the "moral advantage," but no one had ever put the idea quite as succinctly as Cap'n Bill.

Checking into a hotel and waiting like a lazy duck on a glassy pond didn't strike Walt as the smartest of options, and Mackiever's mention of being assailed himself was worrisome. If Forrest Knox knew Mackiever was onto him, he might decide that a good offense was the best defense and strike preemptively. Given how quickly Trooper Dunn had gone for Tom by the river last night, Knox might already have gone over to the offensive.

With an ache of presentiment in his chest, Walt followed his friend's instructions about the room, then walked to the elevator and waited for the door to close. He thought of Tom and Melba, waiting for him ninety miles upriver. He hoped they hadn't let the isolation of the lake house lull them into a false sense of security. He hoped they were being as careful as he was. Not one moment while he was in the lobby had Walt taken his finger off the trigger of his derringer.

CHAPTER 87

TOM AND MELBA sat on bar stools at Drew's counter, finishing some eggs Melba had scrambled. They'd watched television for a while, but nothing held their interest, and Drew's satellite offered no local news. Melba's eyes betrayed exhaustion, but she'd brewed some coffee to stay awake.

"Don't just sit there brooding," she said. "You might as well talk about it. The time will pass faster."

Tom wasn't so sure. But after a while, he said, "I've got two sons, Mel. One is trying to save me, the other to destroy me. There must be a deep truth in there somewhere."

His nurse kept her eyes on her plate. "Don't be too sure. This world is hard. Always has been, always will be, till Judgment comes."

Tom marveled at the certainty of her faith. Melba never proselytized, but she had an adamantine faith in God, and in the teachings of Jesus.

"*Judgment*," he said. "That's an ominous word."

She looked up, her deep eyes holding his. "Not just for you. I've got my own stains on the inside, that no one but God knows about. We do the best we can, Doc. That's all we can do. Though it don't hurt to kneel in prayer now and then. You could have done a little more of that over the years. Wouldn't have hurt you none."

"I suppose not," Tom said, though he disagreed. If you didn't believe in a God who heard or answered prayers, then wasn't prayer a kind of secular heresy? A failure of character—or at least of nerve? "Melba, I want you to go home after you finish that coffee."

She looked up sharply. "Have you lost your mind? Captain Garrity left me here to watch over you, and I mean to do it. There's no way I'm going to stand beside your casket and tell Mrs. Peggy I left you here alone to die."

"What exactly will you do if I have a coronary? The nearest ambulance is thirty minutes away. All you'd be doing by calling 911 is open-ing yourself to criminal charges for aiding and abetting a fugitive."

Melba looked indignant. "I'm a nurse, aren't I? I can do compres-sions till the paramedics get here. And you've got adrenaline in your overnight bag. I checked it when you were in the bathroom."

Tom smiled and laid his hand on her wrist. "And if a bunch of old klukkers find us?"

Melba drew back her hand and folded her arms across her chest. "I reckon I can shoot a pistol as well as most men. And it wouldn't trouble me much to shoot a Klansman, I can tell you."

Tom laughed. "I believe you. But it's not worth your life, Mel. You've got grandchildren, and they need you."

"So do you, old man!"

"Yes. But I made the choices that put me here. You didn't."

Melba's eyes glistened. "I'm here by choice, too."

"You're here because you're a good woman, and a good friend. But you can't give your life for me. I won't let you. You're going to finish that coffee and drive home. Walt will be back well before dawn."

This time, Tom could see he'd gotten through to her. The nurse shook her head, then wiped her tired eyes. "Dr. Cage, please tell me you know what you're doing. All the years I've been with you, I've never doubted you. But this time . . . maybe you're not thinking straight. People do crazy things when they feel guilty about something. Tell me you're not planning to do something crazy."

When he realized what she feared, he felt ashamed. "I'm not going to kill myself, if that's what you mean."

Melba lowered her chin and looked up at Tom like the experienced nurse she was. "Maybe not with your own hands. But if you put yourself beyond medical help, or where harm is likely to come to you, that's just as much of a sin."

Tom didn't know how to answer this.

She leaned forward and touched the center of his chest. "Your patients *need* you. Where could they go if you passed? These young docs don't care about folks the way you do. Especially old folks. You owe it to them to keep going as long as you can."

Tom didn't verbalize the obvious, which was that he had to die someday, and it would likely be sooner rather than later, no matter what happened tonight. Melba was right that his patients would suffer, especially those with chronic illnesses, but what could be done?

"There's nobody here but us," he said gently. "Won't you call me Tom now?"

She shook her head almost involuntarily, and Tom wondered what troubled her so about crossing that formal boundary. "What if I called you Nurse Price out here? How would that make you feel?"

Blood rose into Melba's dark cheeks. After some thought, she said, "If I call you Tom, will you let me stay until Captain Garrity comes back?"

"No. I can't make you leave, but I'm asking you to. My heart will beat a lot easier if you go."

Melba picked up her fork and tapped it on the china plate. "I can't believe it's come to this. All those good works you've done, and it's come to running like a common criminal."

"We never outrun our sins, Melba. None of us."

"And you tell me you don't believe in God! How can you believe in sin, if you don't believe in God?"

"I don't know what I mean, exactly. I just use the words I know."

A tear rolled down the nurse's cheek. "I still have hopes for you . . . Tom. You've always done God's work, whether you know it or not."

His throat tightened so much that for a moment he couldn't breathe, much less speak. "Thank you, Melba. Now, you give me a good, long hug, and then walk out to your car and drive home. Walt will be back soon, and we'll resolve this mess."

"Do you really believe that? Don't lie to me."

"I do. That old dog still has a trick or two left."

Melba looked grateful for the lie. After a moment, she rose from the stool, and once he'd followed suit, she took him into her arms and hugged him, taking care not to put pressure on his wounded shoulder. At first the embrace felt awkward and stiff, but then Tom felt something let go in the nurse's frame, and it was as though they'd been married for thirty years. In a way, he supposed, they had—just as he and Esther Ford had, and of course Viola, though their relationship had crossed into something far more intimate.

"Don't you sit here studyin' 'bout Viola and that boy of hers," Melba said in his ear. "You don't know for sure he's yours. And even if he is, you never knew about him. Viola made that choice. And if that boy hates you now, well . . . if you let him know you, he'll come around."

"He's not a boy anymore."

Melba drew far enough back to look into his eyes. "Yes, he is. Down deep, he is. And a black boy is a hard thing to be, especially without a daddy. Take it from me."

"I believe you, Mel."

The nurse hugged him tight again. "I feel like I'm never going to see you again."

"You will. I promise."

She shook her head stubbornly. "I feel it. And I want to say something to you."

"What?"

She finally released him and stepped back, but she kept hold of his arthritic hands. "Don't give up. Please. Don't let them take you without a fight. Nobody's perfect. Not even you. You deserve all the time you've got left."

Tom felt his eyes getting wet. "Thank you, Mel. You go now."

"I will. But I'm only going because I know you're not alone here."

As his nurse turned and walked to the door, Tom felt the familiar and terrible weight he had borne all his life, the faith of simple people who had believed too much in him.

CHAPTER 88

AS SOON AS Caitlin got back to the *Examiner* building, she'd found herself in the eye of a hurricane. Not only was her full staff working frantically to finish the stories they planned to run on various threads of Henry Sexton's murder investigations, but the editors of her father's satellite papers were screaming for the stories they'd been promised by a deadline that had passed an hour ago. After passing a taped copy of her phone recording to Penn, Caitlin had deflected her staff by issuing a quick barrage of orders, then told Jamie to call his counterparts at the satellites and tell them thirty minutes of overtime had been authorized. It was a lie, but one she was banking no one would test by waking her father in Charlotte. As everyone left to implement her instructions, she'd retreated to her private office and locked the door.

She was confident that the six stories on Henry's murder investigations had been well written; she trusted Jamie to make sure of that. But without her master story to provide historical context, readers would have no way to place the dramatic events that her reporters had dealt with elsewhere. And her master story had one major problem. If Brody Royal agreed to Penn's demand, and Penn asked her to leave Royal out of her story—even for one day—the resulting gaps would be like antitank trenches dug in the highway of her narrative. She didn't know if she could bear to butcher her story that way. Reality was fast overtaking Penn's concerns anyway. The rumor mill had already spread the news of Katy Royal's attempted suicide to every corner of Adams County and Concordia Parish. Speculation about her motive was rampant, and right now Caitlin was the only journalist in the world who knew the truth. Better still, she understood how that motive fit into the forty-year-old matrix of rape and murder that had divided the community and triggered two assassination attempts on one of the South's best journalists.

Bottom line: the Katy Royal tape had changed everything.

The revelation that a man of Brody Royal's wealth and position had ordered (and possibly taken part in) the murders of Albert Norris, Pooky Wilson, Dr. Leland Robb, Jimmy Revels, Luther Davis, Viola Turner, and other collateral victims dwarfed Caitlin's 1998 story of the murder of black Korean war vet Delano Payton, and *that* story had won her a Pulitzer. If she wrote tonight's story as she wanted to—as it demanded to be written—a second Pulitzer was a lock, a prize she would happily share with Henry Sexton.

To write that story, though, she might have to break faith with Penn. With him still closeted somewhere with Royal, she saw no way to finish her story before the other Masters papers closed out their editions— not if she waited to find out Royal's answer about the APB. Caitlin had never felt so strangled by conflicting loyalties. She loved Tom as she loved her own father. But how could she abandon her duty to Henry Sexton, Katy Royal, and all the families of the victims of the Double Eagle group to save a man who had refused to try to save himself?

Taking a Mountain Dew from the mini-fridge in the corner, she poured several ounces into her mouth and swished it around so that the caffeine would be absorbed more quickly. Then she called up iTunes, selected David Gray's "Please Forgive Me," and opened a clean page in her word processor. The text of the toolbar swam before her eyes for several seconds, then resolved into black letters on a field of taupe, her preferred color scheme. Thus prepared, in a single sustained burst of clarity she wrote a nine-hundred-word lead story titled LOCAL JOURNALIST SURVIVES SNIPER ATTACK.

She led off with a firsthand account of the attack on Henry Sexton and Sherry Harden, and concluded with the contents of the Katy Royal interview. She spared Brody Royal nothing. The only person she treated with kid gloves was Tom Cage. As she corrected the last typo, she knew in her gut that this was the story to print tomorrow. Penn might hate her for it, but he would be judging her by inverted priorities. He was so deep inside the nightmare that he could no longer tell right from wrong. She was preparing to send the story to Jamie for a read-through when someone knocked at her door.

"*Working!*" she shouted.

"It's Penn," said a male voice, muffled by the wood.

Was that a male staffer telling her Penn was out front? she wondered. Or was Penn actually at the door?

"Caitlin!" Penn shouted. *"Open up!"*

A ripple of irrational fear crossed her skin. She sat frozen for three
seconds, then got up and opened the door. Penn stood there, looking as
tired as she'd ever seen him.

"You talked to Royal?" she asked.

He nodded.

She took his hand and pulled him into her office, then closed the
door. "And?"

Penn's other hand held a leather holster with his .357 inside. He laid
the pistol on the credenza to his right. Caitlin stared at it for a couple of
seconds, realizing how seriously he was taking the danger. "So? What
did he say?"

"He's going to do it. He's going to get the APB canceled. He didn't
have any choice, really. He's going to fix everything."

"Fix everything?" she echoed, unable to conceal her disappointment. "What does that mean?"

"The APB, the dead trooper, even Viola's murder case."

"And you believed him?"

"I did. I do. The whole conversation was anticlimactic. More surreal
than confrontational, like a weird business deal. I think Royal has dealt
with this kind of crap his whole life, though not with quite so much at
stake. He realizes that his freedom and wealth are in danger, so he'll do
whatever's necessary to preserve them."

Caitlin shook her head in disbelief. *"How* can he do those things?
Magic?"

Penn ran his hands through his hair, then collapsed into the chair
opposite her desk. "By calling the right people, apparently. It's not what
you know, right? It's who."

She knew her disgust showed on her face. "There's got to be more
to it than that. How can he muzzle Shad Johnson? And Sheriff Byrd?"

Penn laughed with bitter amusement. "I don't think Shad or Billy
would even *flirt* with the idea of crossing Brody Royal."

A sudden wave of nausea nearly made Caitlin double over. Grabbing her lukewarm Mountain Dew, she drank what was left to try to
settle her stomach. "I don't understand. This is exactly the kind of back-
room deal you've despised all your life."

"You're right. But I had no choice. Why are you so upset? I told you what I was going to do."

"You told me you were going to try to get the APB revoked, and Tom into federal custody. But from what you described, Brody's giving your father a world-class get-out-of-jail-free card. A free pass on everything."

"Well, I figured as long as I had him over a barrel, I'd push for everything I could."

Caitlin felt her bottom lip shaking. She was usually good at hiding her emotions, but now it was impossible. "Royal's obviously not going to move heaven and earth for free. What did you promise him in return?" A sickening thought struck her. "Did you tell him you'd give him the tape I made of his daughter?"

"Of course I did."

Stunned by his casual tone, she walked around her desk and sat down, then fixed him with a level stare. "Did you promise that I would keep his name out of the *Examiner*?"

Penn didn't answer immediately. Then he looked off to the side and said, "I had to, babe."

She closed her eyes, and a sensation of falling in slow motion enveloped her. "You had no right to do that," she said softly. Then she opened her eyes, her voice rising. "You can't make a promise for me. You can't make a deal with the devil in my name. You can't *sell my soul* for me. Only I can do that!"

"Sell your soul? You're blowing this out of proportion. This is my father's life we're talking about."

Galvanized by righteous anger, Caitlin leaned forward and snapped, "Brody Royal's a fucking murderer. Do you really think your father would want a man who's killed innocent people to go free to protect him?"

"I don't know," Penn replied in a maddeningly mild voice. "I think Dad's known some pretty bad things about Brody Royal for thirty-five years, and he kept them quiet to protect our family."

Caitlin felt paralyzed; she wished Tom were here to argue for her. "For all you know, Royal is just stalling you. He could be packing his bags for Brazil right now."

"Brazil isn't a nonextradition country."

"Oh, stop talking like a fucking *lawyer*."

Penn rubbed the back of his neck, looking more haggard by the minute. "What do you think I'm trying to do here? Sabotage your career?"

"What *are* you doing? In the past, your motto was 'Let justice be done though the heavens fall.' And I loved you for it. But now that your father's in trouble, suddenly Albert and Pooky and the others are just regrettable deaths. What about Henry and Sherry, for God's sake?"

Penn took his time answering. "Caitlin, throughout my career, I had to compromise. Every single case eventually came down to that. Perfect justice does not exist in this world."

"*Perfect* justice? This is the *opposite* of justice! It's a black hole sucking in everything good that comes near it. It's a singularity of shit!"

Penn's nostrils flared, and she almost welcomed the prospect that he'd stand up and fight—but he didn't. She sensed that he was seeing himself in a new light, and not enjoying what he saw. When he spoke again, it was in a tone of infinite regret. "If justice for those victims and families was truly your goal, you wouldn't be trying to keep Henry's files from the FBI. You'd have given Kaiser copies as soon as you got them."

She stiffened, feeling her face go red. "I am giving them to him. Jordan and I talked about it tonight. I'm giving Kaiser copies of everything tomorrow morning."

Penn was staring at her as though at a stranger. "Everything?"

God, how well he knows me. "That's right."

He didn't bother to challenge this. "Maybe I'm not being clear. I'm not asking you to live up to this deal with Royal. I'm asking you to hold off on the man for one or two days."

"One day in my business is like a month in yours. You know that. If we're not first with a story, we're irrelevant."

Penn turned up his palms. "If Royal doesn't do what he promised by tomorrow afternoon, you're welcome to tear him to pieces. You can start posting in your online edition right after lunch."

"But what if he *does* cooperate? You want me to bury the story forever? I can't do that. I *won't*. And what if he just strings you along some more? You'll be back in here pleading with me to protect him."

"No, I won't. But this is Royal's only way out, other than running. And if he runs, you can rip him to shreds. But for God's sake—for *Dad's* sake—let Royal pull these strings and remove the immediate threat."

"You can't trust a man like Royal, Penn. Some way or other, he's going to screw you. You *and* Tom. Remember what he did to his wife? To his own daughter?"

Penn let her words hang in the air. Then he said, "You know something? You're right. My father's life means more to me than Albert Norris's. Or Pooky Wilson's, or even Henry's. *After* Dad is safe, I'll do everything in my power to send their killers to prison. But *until then,* I can't worry about them. My father, my mother, Annie, you—all of you mean more to me than anyone else on this planet. There's nothing I wouldn't do to protect you, and I'm not ashamed of that."

A smothering wave of emotion swept through her, for she knew that he meant every word. "I understand," she said. "But I don't want to mean that much to somebody. I don't want a travesty of justice committed in my name. We can't compound this evil. We have to fight it."

"By publishing everything about Brody tomorrow morning?"

She nodded, her breaths coming shallow. "I've already written the story. I would have called and told you, but I assumed you were with Royal."

"And you couldn't wait a few extra minutes to see how that went?"

She felt her cheeks heat up again. "Not and make my deadline. But truthfully . . . maybe I was afraid I knew how it would go."

He leaned back in his chair. "I see. And I suppose it's just a coincidence that this decision gives you the biggest scoop of your career? On the same morning that a flock of vultures will land here to cover the same story?"

Her temper finally flared beyond her control. "I'm not going to apologize for doing my job! You think some other media outlet might not get to Katy Royal in the hospital? What if she tells *them* about her father's crime?"

"She's in a coma! Please tell me this isn't about hanging another Pulitzer on your wall."

His words stung like a swarm of hornets, because they were partly true. He got up and flattened his hands on her desk, his lips pale with emotion. "Are you seriously willing to keep my father's life at risk so that you can beat everyone else into print with this story?"

Penn's unfiltered anger was hard to withstand, but she found strength in her conviction that only the truth could gain justice for the victims who had suffered so long. "I think your father has always had it in his power to resolve this situation. If Tom is going to be saved, it won't be by us. He's going to have to do it himself. All we can do is what we think is best, each by our own lights. That's why I have to write this story."

"How can you face Annie and my mother if you do that?"

She turned up her palms. "I think we'll both have a lot to explain, if it comes to that."

He sagged against her desk. "Maybe it's a blood thing. Maybe if it was *your* father running for his life, you'd feel like I do."

She was too exhausted to think anymore. "I don't know. I honestly don't."

Caitlin glanced at her watch. The absolute deadline was coming at her like a train out of a dark tunnel. "I really have no more time. None. Not if we're going to get this mess out tomorrow."

Penn regarded her with disconcerting intensity. "It's your decision. You know how I feel. Do what you think is right, and we'll go on from there . . . if we can."

She felt dizzy. "Are you serious?"

He reached out and took her left hand. His skin felt cold. "We've been together for most of the past seven years," he said. "That's a long time to be involved without getting married. And if we really look at what's kept us from taking that last step . . . it was your career. We met during the biggest murder case this town ever saw. You won your Pulitzer for your coverage. But deep down, you've always felt constrained here. Every couple of years, you've had to break out and hitch your wagon to some shooting star of a story to keep from going crazy. And that's okay. But I also think it says something about what's most important to you."

Caitlin was trembling. She knew he could feel it through her hand. "That's really going around the world for an insult. I think I've made my case tonight. And I think a lot of people would say my motives are purer than yours."

"Now who's talking like a lawyer?" he asked gently. "You're right about one thing: this story is huge. But what matters in it are the people involved, not the articles written about it. You know me, Caitlin. I won't let Brody Royal escape punishment for the things he did."

"You promised him that you would."

"I'm not bound by a promise to a murderer. In the end, justice will be done, no matter who prints the story. I'll make sure of that. Kaiser will, too."

"What's written about it matters," Caitlin insisted, her voice quavering. "The story matters."

Penn nodded, but she could see that he didn't agree. Not really. And if she were brutally honest with herself, she didn't only want the story told; *she wanted to be the one to tell it.*

"Tell me one thing," she said. "Did you mention 'Huggy Bear' to Royal? Or 'Gates Brown'? Did you tell Royal there was a witness who could put him inside Albert Norris's store on the day of that murder?"

"Yes. I had to frighten him into a corner."

Her cheeks felt cold. "Did you promise to give Royal that man's name?"

"I don't even know his name!"

She shook her head slowly. "Brody might not need the name. You know? Just the Detroit Tigers baseball cap, or the Detroit connection. That might be all a man like him needs to find and kill that man, whoever he is."

"I didn't give him that stuff!"

"It won't be hard for him to find out. That's why I haven't published a plea for 'Huggy Bear' to come forward, or to call my cell. I knew the risk was too great." Caitlin suddenly knew what she had to do. "I'm standing by my story," she said in a flat voice. "I'm printing it all in tomorrow's edition. I'll show it to you now, if you want to read it."

Penn dropped her hand and stared at her in disbelief.

"I protected your father. But I didn't spare Brody Royal anything."

She stepped behind her chair and laid her quivering hands on its back, as though it were a shield. "I've got editors standing by at nine papers, and every one's on overtime. I'm seriously pissing my father off to make all this happen. Please let me get on with it."

Penn walked to the credenza, picked up his pistol, and went to the door. With his hand on the knob he let out a long sigh, then turned back to her. "Are you coming home tonight?"

"I can't—not with all this going on. As soon as the story goes up online, we're going to have people calling from around the country. Around the world, probably."

Penn only nodded, but his eyes said, *Which is exactly the way you want it. You and your paper at the center of a media storm.*

"Please don't leave this building by yourself," he said. "If you do decide to come home, get one of the guys to drive you."

"I will." She stood in the awkward silence, searching for words that could magically separate them without pain. "I hope Forrest Knox cancels that APB, anyway."

Penn started to speak, then apparently thought better of it and went out, quietly closing the door behind him.

For the first time in what seemed a very great while, Caitlin felt tears running down her cheeks. As she tried to catch her breath, Jamie Lewis flung open her door and walked in, a sheaf of paper in his hand.

"Shit!" he cursed. "I thought you guys would never finish. Where are you on the hub story?"

Caitlin shook her head, then looked up and tried to blink away the tears.

"Jesus," Jamie said. "Are you *crying*?"

CAITLIN LEFT HER EDITOR standing openmouthed in her office and raced for the back door, hoping to catch Penn before he left the employee parking lot. She didn't really expect to overtake him, but when she threw open the door, she saw him standing about ten feet away, as though waiting for her. Blessed relief surged through her, until she saw two men standing beside Penn with pistols in their hands. There was blood over Penn's left eye, and a cop lying prostrate on the ground behind him. She felt herself backing up even before she knew what she was doing.

"If you go back inside," said one of the gunmen, "we'll shoot him right here."

"Go, Caitlin," Penn said firmly. "Right now. Lock the door and call 911."

The older man raised his pistol and pressed the barrel against Penn's right temple. The gunman's face was pale and bland beneath his long hair, and appeared to be without mercy or even concern.

Go, Penn mouthed silently. *I love you.*

"What is it you want?" Caitlin asked.

"Mr. Royal wants to talk to you," said the younger gunman, who had a crew cut and looked slightly less ruthless than his partner. "Both of you."

Brody Royal. Caitlin saw a van parked beyond the men, smoke puffing from its tailpipe. Penn stared into her eyes with chilling urgency. Then he shook his head.

"I'll go with you," he said, "but she stays here. If we don't go soon, one of Chief Logan's squad cars is going to circle through this lot."

"He's right," said the younger man.

"Just a second," said Longhair. He was looking at a cell phone while he covered Penn with the gun in his other hand. "This is going to be good. Watch."

"Go, Caitlin," Penn said again. *"Right now."*

She wanted to obey, but deep within her brain, a bundle of nerve fibers told her that if she tried to flee, the tall man would kill Penn while his partner went after her. Penn's eyes fairly blazed out an order to run, but before she could make a decision, someone flung her purse through the door behind her, then pulled it shut. She heard the bolt slide home.

What the hell? she thought, unable to believe that one of her employees would participate in her kidnapping. Then a thought flashed through her—

My .38's in that purse! Her heart began to pound. *Should I grab for it, or just act like I'm casually picking it up?*

The younger gunman made the decision for her. Aiming his automatic at her head, he lunged forward and snatched up the purse.

"Get in the fucking van!" he shouted.

With a last desolate look at Caitlin, Penn turned and walked to the van's side door as though in complete surrender. As Longhair slid the door open, Penn hurled himself backward and shouted, *"Run, Caitlin! Run for the street!"*

She broke to her left, then hesitated as Longhair hammered his pistol against Penn's neck, knocking him to the concrete. Her hesitation doomed her. The younger man was two steps faster than she, and fifteen yards down the wall he rode her into the cement. When she struggled to her knees, he punched the side of her head, and she felt her jaw rattle. Blinking away tears, she tried to clear her head, then toppled over like an animal darted with a tranquilizer.

The hands that grabbed her armpits felt made of stone, and they lifted her without effort. The last thing she remembered was the sound of duct tape being ripped from a roll.

CHAPTER 89

WHEN HENRY'S MOTHER finally reached his secret treatment room, she took off her 1950s-vintage hat and began sobbing as though he were dead. He tried to reassure her, but any embrace was prevented by the hastily assembled equipment that surrounded his hospital bed.

"Do you know what the FBI agent outside told me?" his mother asked, after they'd both regained their composure.

"What?"

"Not to tell you Sherry had passed away." His mother suppressed another sob, wiped her eyes. "As if I would lie to my own son."

Henry nodded. The FBI still seemed intent on keeping him in the dark about Sherry's fate. They probably meant well, but he resented it nonetheless. "I guess they think I'm a basket case," he said. "And maybe they're right."

"This doesn't make any sense," she said, her jaw setting with anger. "They're the ones who let you get shot!"

"You're right." They fell into a tense but companionable silence. After what seemed to Henry a couple of minutes, he said, "Did you bring the things I asked for?"

She nodded, worry etched in her face.

"Good. We may not have much time. Can you help me with these IVs?"

A retired nurse, Mrs. Sexton had no problem removing the IV lines from his hands, then placing bandages over the infusion sites. "Compress that left one," she said. "The problem is your cardiac leads. As soon as we disconnect them, somebody's gonna come running."

Henry had already solved this problem. "Uh-uh. You're going to put them on in my place. You know exactly where they go, don't you?"

His mother sighed, then nodded in resignation. "I hope you know what you're doing. You know I don't believe in violence. Not without grave provocation, anyway. Old Testament provocation."

Henry met her gaze and uncloaked a small fraction of his anguish. His mother shut her eyes, then turned away.

"But you brought what I asked for?" he repeated. "Everything?"

"Yes."

Lifting a shopping bag from the floor, she removed three items Henry had requested and laid them gently on the bed. Then she unbuttoned her blouse and unsnapped her brassiere. When both she and Henry were ready, she rapidly transferred the cardiac sensors to her own body. An alarm tripped for a few seconds, then returned to normal.

"You'd better go now," she advised.

On his first try to rise from the bed, Henry got so dizzy that he fell back on the mattress. His mother told him to forget it, but he only redoubled his efforts. The second time, with her help, he managed to get to his feet. The pain took his breath away—worse in his head than in his belly, where the knife had gone in. *Probably from the bullet,* he realized.

While waiting for his mother, Henry had shaved his mustache, his goatee, his lower legs, and the backs of his hands, thanks to a cup of water and a toiletry kit begged from Irma McKay. From his mother's handbag he took her extra wig and fitted it over his head. She made a few small adjustments, then lay back on the bed. Finally he donned an old raincoat of his father's that resembled the coat she'd worn into the hospital. He hated wearing anything that reminded him of that man, but tonight he was willing to bear it. The coat pockets held a pair of sturdy sandals, which he carefully donned by dropping them to the floor and sliding his feet into them.

"You're not on IV pain meds anymore," his mother said. "I had some OxyContin left at home from my last surgery, so you'll have to make do with that. But it's not the same as Dilaudid or fentanyl."

"I'll be all right," he assured her, his head feeling like a water-filled balloon. "Just as long as I make it past the guard at the side door."

His mother rose up far enough to put an arm around his waist and gently hug him. "I wish I could help you more. But I know God is watching over you. If he wasn't, you would have died tonight."

With great effort, Henry bent and kissed the top of her head. Then he put on her hat, picked up her purse, walked slowly to the door, and gave her their prearranged signal: the "okay" sign.

"You take care of yourself, honey!" his mother called loudly. "I'll be back first thing in the morning. Don't you bother these nurses too much, all right? They need some rest, too."

"I won't," Henry said in a dull voice.

Then he opened the door and, with his chin touching his chest, walked right past the FBI guard stationed outside, who sat in a folding chair, typing a text message. Henry made his way down the hall to the right, aping his mother's painful stoop with an ache that he didn't have to fake. With his mother's purse hanging on his arm, he brushed back the hair of the wig with what he fancied an authentically feminine gesture and padded slowly toward the hospital's side exit. The pain wasn't as bad as he'd expected, thanks to the Dilaudid still coursing through his system, no doubt. But soon that cushion would vanish. All the way down the hall, he waited for the cry of "Halt!" like a POW trying to escape from some prison camp. But the FBI agent never called out. Nobody did.

When Henry reached the side entrance, the man standing post outside scarcely even registered one more woman walking out after the night shift—especially one who ignored him like she owned the place.

It took Henry quite some time to make his way around to the front parking lot, where his mother had left her old Impala. With a prayer of thanks on his lips, he unlocked the door, then very carefully slid behind the wheel and waited for his heart to stop pounding. Once it did, he opened the pill bottle she'd given him and crunched an OxyContin between his back teeth. The bitterness surprised him, but he swallowed the fragments gratefully.

Two men who looked like FBI agents stood talking in the light of the hospital's porte cochere entrance. Henry shut his eyes for a few seconds, wondering if they were real. When he opened them, the men were gone.

Wiping tears of confusion from his eyes, he craned his neck over the front seat and looked down at the floor. His mother's 12-gauge Winchester pump shotgun lay there, just as he'd requested. His father had bought the gun in 1957, the last year they'd made that model, and it was one of the few of his possessions that Henry's mother hadn't given to the Goodwill or burned in the backyard. Encouraged to have come so far, Henry slid her key into the ignition, started the Impala, then put it in gear and drove slowly out the of hospital lot. Barring unforeseen complications, he would arrive at his destination before the pain became too intense to bear. After that . . .

What would be, would be.

CHAPTER 90

CONSCIOUSNESS RETURNED AS a hammer pounding the base of my skull and lights flashing in the stinking dark. I'm lying on the metal floor of a van, Caitlin beside me, still unconscious. Duct tape binds our hands and ankles, and Chief Logan's cop lies senseless at our feet, near the van's rear doors. Two minutes ago I pried off one shoe with the other and searched for his carotid pulse with my toe, but I felt nothing.

I didn't recognize either of the men waiting for me outside the *Examiner* building—didn't even see them until one clubbed me with the butt of his pistol. They were trying to force me to ask Caitlin via text to come outside when she obligingly ran out on her own. I half wish she'd gone back inside when I told her to—but if she had, I'd be dead.

I can't see our abductors clearly; a dense wire partition divides the cab of the van from its cargo area. I remember two thugs: one older with long hair, one younger with a crew cut. Flexing my wrists and ankles as hard as I can, I quickly learn this duct tape doesn't give. As silver steel girders continue flashing through the long horizontal windows above me, I realize we're crossing the Mississippi River Bridge, heading into Louisiana. For a few moments I consider waking Caitlin, but Royal's men will do that soon enough, and the prospect of being delivered to the psychos who forced one female employee to kill another is something I'd like to spare her for as long as possible.

Brody Royal. How smoothly that old man played me. The consummate deal maker, he told me exactly what I wanted to hear, buying just enough time to arrange a permanent solution to the threat picture I'd painted for him. I briefly wonder whether Royal might have some subtler plan than killing us in mind, but the pragmatist in me knows the truth. If Brody has his way, after tonight, no one will ever see Penn Cage or Caitlin Masters again—alive or dead. We'll disappear into the same void that Pooky Wilson and Jimmy Revels did.

Despite my intent to leave her unconscious, after a couple of miles, Caitlin's eyelids flutter, then pop open. As full comprehension dawns, she glances at me, then closes them tight again, expressing tears from their corners.

Very softly, I lean close and whisper, "Do you have your phone?"

She opens her eyes and shakes her head, then mouths, *You?*

"They took it."

"Gun?"

"Same."

I watch her absorb what this means for our chances of survival. Looking toward her feet, she whispers, "Is that the cop who was guarding the parking lot?"

I nod.

"Is he dead?"

"I think so. I kicked off one shoe and touched his throat. I couldn't feel a pulse. And I felt something wet."

She looks back at me, her face bereft.

"I'm sorry, Cait. I should never have pushed Royal that hard."

She looks at the dark roof of the van. "I'm the one who went after Katy and made the tape."

We stare into each other's eyes, painfully, yet thankfully, aware that we share responsibility for our fate. As I try to think of some way to comfort her, her lips part, and her face brightens with hope.

"They can't kill us, right? I mean—you're the mayor, for God's sake. I'm the publisher of the newspaper. Royal can't imagine he could get away with that. The outcry would be *huge*. The investigation would never stop."

This is the logic of a woman raised with privilege. If they've killed a cop to get us, and they know we know that, how can they possibly let us go? But I see no profit in pointing this out to Caitlin, who's desperately searching for any hope of life.

"Royal's a businessman," she says, biting her bottom lip. "You said that back in my office. He's doing this to make sure you hold up your end of the deal. He knows if he doesn't, we could destroy him as soon as your father is safe. That's only logical, right?"

"Yes," I say.

"If he believes we'll protect him, why take the risk of killing us?"

"He wants that witness dead. Pooky's friend. 'Huggy Bear.' That's what Brody wants from us. His real name."

Her eyes narrow. "We don't have it."

"That's right. And if he figures that out . . . we're dead."

Her eyes widen, then close. "We screwed ourselves," she whispers. "By keeping what we knew about Royal secret, we made this happen."

"We have one chance. Walker Dennis knows Royal is dirty, and it bothered him to keep what he knew from Kaiser. After what happened to Henry, he may tell Kaiser about it tonight. Just pray these bastards didn't switch off our cell phones. Kaiser can track the pings."

Caitlin puts on a brave face, but we both know the likelihood of this sort of luck is almost nil. With a glance up at the wire mesh, she says, "Tell me you left the Katy Royal tape in your car, at least?"

I shake my head. "It was in my coat pocket. They got it."

With this, we fall silent. Further conversation seems pointless. Even the argument we had in her office, while shattering at the time, now seems trivial. If we could embrace, the essential redundancy of all words would be manifest. But we can't. All we can do is look into each other's eyes like condemned prisoners riding a cart to the guillotine.

"Will you kiss me?" she asks. "Before we get where we're going?"

Glancing up at the wire screen, I scoot carefully across the metal floor, trying to bring our bodies into contact. As I do, something jabs my behind. I try to raise my butt over it, but the hard object keeps jabbing me. Lowering myself again, I rock softly from side to side, trying to tell what's beneath me. When I finally understand, my heart begins to pound.

"What is it?" Caitlin hisses. "What's the matter?"

"Pithy's straight razor is in my back pocket. They missed it when they patted me down. It's lying along the bottom seam of my jeans."

Her eyes widen. "Can you get it out?"

"Not with my hands taped in front. But you can."

She nods quickly.

As quietly as possible, I flex my body until I've turned my back to her. Twenty seconds later, I feel her fingers fishing in my pocket. Almost before I'm aware of it, the razor is gone.

Her lips touch the shell of my ear. "I think I should try to cut the tape on your wrists. You've got the best chance of fighting them. You can free mine after you cut your feet loose."

"Get some while you can, bro!" shouts one of the men up front, laughing wildly. "We're almost there!"

Tilting back my head, I see a dark oval staring down through the mesh screen. It's Crew Cut. "If you get turned right," he says, "maybe she can unzip you. I'd give it a go, man, considering the circumstances."

"Why don't you blow your partner while he drives?" Caitlin snaps. "We could use some privacy."

I guess she figured sarcasm might make him lose interest, but instead of facing forward again, Crew Cut starts telling her what she can expect when we get where we're going. The gist is that a quick bullet would be infinitely better than what awaits us, but we won't be lucky enough to get one.

"You're pretty damn hot, girl," says the shadow face. "But you're about to get a *whole lot hotter,* where you're going."

As he sniggers, the invisible driver busts out laughing. Crew Cut is still talking when his partner hits the brakes, makes a right turn, then cruises slowly for a couple of hundred yards. "Showtime, boys and girls," he says, cackling softly through the mesh.

When the engine dies, I press my forehead against Caitlin's. "Listen to me. That razor—"

"Turn over!" she hisses. *"Hurry! Let me cut your hands loose!"*

"There's no time. Listen, Caitlin, that razor is useless against guns."

"What?" Her eyes are frantic. "You want me to leave it here?"

"No. Hide it if you can."

The sound of slamming doors reverberates through a closed space.

"Hide it for what? When do I use it?"

I don't want to answer, but her mind has not yet allowed her to face the final extremity. "It's for you now," I tell her. "Not them. Do you understand?"

In some terrible fraction of time, confusion becomes comprehension, and her head begins shaking as though from a nerve tremor.

"No," she whispers, but it's only a token denial. At last she has glimpsed what the end might be, what she might have to do to find a humane death.

Before I can speak again, our guards jerk open the doors and heave the dead cop out of the van. Then they slash the tape binding our ankles, drag us out by the feet—past the prone policeman—and stand us up beside a brick wall.

We seem to be in a closed residential garage. A blue Range Rover is parked beside the van. Prodding us with pistols, they force us through a door and into a spacious pantry, which leads to a kitchen gleaming with stainless steel and granite. Caitlin and I share quick glances, but I can tell she's never been to this house, either. Just past the kitchen is a door that opens onto a staircase.

"What's down there?" I ask, stopping at the head of the stairs with a pistol jammed into my back.

"A basement," says the older guard behind me. "What's it to you?"

As an assistant DA in Houston, I visited dozens of murder scenes and saw hundreds more on police videotape. The majority involved journeys like this one: a walk into a basement, an industrial freezer, or a rented storeroom where screams could not be heard, smells would not be noticed, and cleanup could be carried out in peace. This terrible knowledge compels me to repeatedly warn both Caitlin and my daughter: *If a man ever tries to get you into a vehicle, run, even if he has a gun. The odds are, he won't hit you. Even if he does, he probably won't hit a vital organ. But if he ever gets control of you . . . if he ever takes you to some isolated place . . . you're dead. Or worse—*

"Don't even think about it," says the man behind me, sensing rebellion. "I'll shoot you in the spine. Start walking. You first, then her."

We descend the stairs single file, me leading the way. The steps end at yet another door.

"Open it," says the man behind me.

Few homes in this part of the country have basements. I have no idea what I might find beyond this door. When I open it, I see an oak-floored room furnished like a British gentlemen's club. Glass-fronted display cases line three walls, within which hang an astonishing assortment of military weapons. At the center of the room, Brody Royal and Randall Regan sit on a leather sofa, watching us expectantly.

"Well, well," Brody says with a sly smile. "We have company."

CHAPTER 91

BRODY ROYAL IS still wearing the suit pants he had on at the hospital, but he's stripped down to his shirtsleeves. Randall Regan has a notebook computer on his lap and a cigarette in his mouth. The bruise marking his throat looks even darker, and he stares at me with barely contained rage.

Turning to one of the guards, Brody says, "Give Randall their phones, then wait upstairs. Let me know immediately if you hear from Chalmers."

"Yes, sir." Crew Cut hands Regan a paper sack. Then the pair move back to the staircase. As the door slams, I look past Royal and Regan. Unlike the other walls, which are lined with glass-fronted gun cabinets, the far wall has six recesses like library carrels set in it. Suddenly, I realize what I'm looking at: an indoor firing range—a wealthy sportsman's toy. I've seen less lavish versions in several homes. Five of the "doors" are actually shooting stations. Only the portal on the far right is a true door. Beyond those shooting stations will be long lanes with human silhouette targets hanging from automated tracks.

Looking back at the luxurious seating area, I catch Brody appraising Caitlin's lithe body while Regan extracts the SIM card from my cell phone and slips it into a USB device connected to his computer. With the smoldering cigarette dangling from his lower lip, he taps the keys with surprising speed and dexterity. I've always thought of Randall Regan as a killer, but I suppose he learned some other skills during decades of running an insurance company.

"I apologize for the circumstances of your transport, Ms. Masters," Brody says in a congenial voice. "I hope you can forgive the—*abruptness* of the journey. Randall, cut her wrists loose."

Regan obviously doesn't agree with this gesture, but he sets aside his laptop long enough to get up and cut the duct tape binding Caitlin's wrists. From the expression on her face, I sense that Caitlin is thinking about the dead cop. I only pray she doesn't say anything. If Brody wants to pretend he's civilized, I'm perfectly willing to let him do it all night.

"You're here, my dear," he goes on, "because your fiancé and I made a business arrangement earlier this evening. And before I fulfill my half of the bargain, I need to be sure he's going to do the same."

"I can understand that," Caitlin says carefully, glancing at me to check my reaction.

"Excellent." Brody gives her an expansive smile. "Well, it so happens, you're part of that arrangement. The mayor here has promised that my name will never appear in your newspaper—or any of your father's papers—in connection with any crimes. Are you aware of those terms?"

Again I feel the sting of her gaze. "I am."

"And do you intend to abide by them?"

She hesitates, then nods. "I do."

"Why?" Brody asks, taking her off guard. "Why would you do that?"

She takes some time with this question. "Because Tom Cage means more to me than any newspaper story."

"Does he indeed?" Royal picks up two sheets of printer paper off the sofa. "Then perhaps you can explain something to me. I have here a story titled 'Local Journalist Survives Sniper Attack.'"

Caitlin blanches, her eyes wide.

"The smaller headline," Brody goes on, tilting his head back to better focus on the page, "reads, 'Vidalia Nurse Perishes.' I figure quite prominently in this story, Ms. Masters. And not in a flattering light."

Caitlin cannot hide her astonishment, and Brody savors it like a wolf licking blood. "I wrote that before I knew about the deal," she says.

Brody nods slowly. "I've calculated the timing, and I have to admit that's possible. But you can imagine this doesn't do much for my confidence in our arrangement holding very long."

"I'll delete the story."

Another smile, this one a little cooler. "It's already been deleted. Your editor in chief never even saw it."

While Caitlin tries to fathom whether this could be true, he says, "I bought myself a source at the *Examiner*. Took a page from Forrest Knox's book. Remarkable how cheaply you can buy a journalist. I should have remembered. Carlos always kept a few scribblers on the payroll in New Orleans."

In my mind, I see Caitlin's purse being flung outside the building and the door being yanked shut behind her. She's doing a workmanlike job of hiding her fear, but I sense how deeply Royal's seeming omnipotence has shocked her.

Royal starts to go on, but his cell phone rings. He presses a button and holds it to his ear. "Yes? . . . How many? . . . Bring them here immediately, and deal with the car afterward. . . . Right."

He pockets the phone and studies Caitlin's face for several seconds.

"Let me be frank, Ms. Masters. I have both copies of the recording of my daughter. Henry Sexton will likely be dead by morning. If he's not, the Knoxes will surely finish him off. I'm confident that Dr. Cage won't try to attack me, if I secure his freedom. He's done me a similar service for the past forty years, so why change now? But what I *don't* have—and what I absolutely require before I will order Colonel Knox to cancel that APB and arrest warrant—is the name of the witness who can place me at Albert Norris's store the night he died. Without that, I'm afraid we have no deal. And without a deal . . . the mayor here will never see his father alive again."

Just as in the hospital, Brody presents himself as a pragmatic negotiator rather than a ruthless predator. Could this show of civility mean Caitlin is right? Might he actually consider making a deal? Maybe killing us *would* cause too much of an uproar. Maybe he only wanted to scare us sufficiently before making his demands. But then I remember . . . his men just killed a cop.

"I asked for more than the APB to be canceled," I remind him. "What about the dead state trooper?"

Brody shrugs as if this is of no consequence. "Trooper Dunn was murdered by a Mexican drug gang operating out of South Louisiana. Two witnesses will testify to that, and Sonny Thornfield will repudiate his earlier accusations about Dr. Cage. They were the result of hallucinations brought on by a reaction to prescription drugs. In actuality, Dr. Cage saved Thornfield's life."

Caitlin shakes her head in wonder. "Black is white, and white is black."

A glint of pride shines in the cold gray eyes. "In the right hands, my dear, that's true."

"And Viola's death?" I ask.

"Viola Turner was murdered by either Glenn Morehouse or Sonny

Thornfield. Frankly, I'm not sure that's been decided yet. Perhaps both. But does it really matter?"

"Thornfield would confess?" I ask.

Royal smiles. "I'm not sure he'll be able to. I think last night's heart attack may prove fatal after all."

"My God," Caitlin breathes. "Why would they kill their own man?"

Brody steeples his fingers and speaks with disinterested precision. "After Sonny's meeting with Dr. Cage and Ranger Garrity, I'm not sure Forrest is fully convinced of Thornfield's—reliability."

"I'm not seeing anything like what we want," Randall Regan interjects, still scanning his computer screen. "I've checked his SIM card and phone. I just killed the backup power source on Cage's phone—the Bureau can track that, even with the main battery removed. Moving on to hers now."

Brody waves his hand as though dealing with a manservant. "Clearly a lot of people are going to great lengths to accommodate you, Mayor. And to spare Dr. Cage a trial, or even his life. So . . . I'll have the name of the witness now."

I glance at Caitlin, who's giving a good impression of calm self-possession. "One question, Brody, before we give you that name. For my own knowledge. Who *really* killed Viola Turner? You? Did you order it?"

The sleek head tilts, and once again I see the eyes of a falcon sighting down on prey a thousand feet below it. "Are you stalling, Mayor? It's really not worth it. The cavalry's not coming. You already received a text from Sheriff Dennis, during the drive over. Read it, Randall."

Regan taps some keys, then says: "'Good luck with whatever your play is, brother. I'm praying for your daddy. Get some rest tonight, and I'll get the other thing going.'"

"I wonder what the 'other thing' is," Brody says, almost whimsically, as my last hope dies. "Care to tell me?"

"I don't know."

"Pity."

Regan holds up Caitlin's silver Treo. "And her editor thinks she and the mayor got into a fight and left to argue it out. Good thing we moved your Audi. I texted him back that she's fine."

Caitlin groans softly.

With surprising flexibility, Brody Royal crosses his legs on the sofa. "Well, then. As you see, for you two, there's only one way out of here alive. The witness's name. Colonel Knox is waiting for my call, and every minute your father stays on the run is a minute he could be shot as a cop killer."

Cornered at last, I run through possible names that might buy us an hour. If I make up a name out of whole cloth, they'll soon discover my ruse, but at least that will eat a little time. A real name would buy us more but would also put someone's life at risk. The best course might be to tell Brody that I won't give him the name until he cancels the APB, but given the circumstances of our abduction, I'm unlikely to get far with that.

"There *is* no witness," Caitlin says, as though tired of keeping up a charade.

Brody's eyes narrow. "What?"

"Nobody ever saw you at Albert Norris's store that night. Nobody but Albert himself. Penn made up another witness to try to force you to help Tom. That's all we want—Tom back safe. We don't care about the cases anymore."

The boldness of her gambit takes me aback, but there's genius in it. *We don't know the witness's name because there isn't one. No threat exists, at least from that quarter,* ergo *you don't need to kill us.*

Brody draws back his head, looking smug. "Nice try, Princess. But I already saw a reference to that witness in your personal computer file. I believe Henry Sexton calls him 'Huggy Bear'? Randall tells me that was the name of a colored pimp on an old cop show."

My heart thumps against my breastbone. Royal is two steps ahead of us, and maybe more. "I think Huggy ran a bar," I say uselessly.

"Huggy was a nigger *pimp*," Regan declares, looking up from his computer. "A jive-talking pimp who dressed like Superfly."

Brody sighs, for the first time showing his irritation. "I think we're drifting from the main point. I've tried to be reasonable, but clearly neither of you is acting in good faith. Your plan was to push me to get Dr. Cage to some safe place, then throw me to the dogs. Obviously, I can't let that happen."

"Here's a name," Regan says, lifting his fingers from the keyboard. "It's a Lusahatcha County number, nothing but a name with it. Toby Rambin. That sounds familiar to me."

I cut my eyes at Caitlin, who's lost a shade of color. "You can read my personal computer files?" she asks Royal.

"We're inside your intranet," Regan brags.

"Is Rambin the witness?" Royal asks evenly.

Caitlin shakes her head. "No. He's lived in Mississippi his whole life."

Brody watches her in silence for an uncomfortable period, then gives an enigmatic smile. *How this man loves his games.* I can't see much point in maintaining a pretense of a negotiation. "You're not going to let us out of here no matter what we tell you," I say. "Your men already killed a cop right in front of me."

Royal looks genuinely surprised. "That man's not dead. They Tased him when he wasn't looking, then injected him with a sedative. I'm a businessman, Cage. Killing Natchez cops wouldn't be good for business. In five hours, he'll wake up behind the Duck's Nest bar with no idea how he got there."

Could this be true? "I felt his neck with my foot. No pulse."

"Why don't you leave the medicine to your father?" Rising from the sofa, Brody looks deeper into Caitlin's eyes. "Before things deteriorate any further, let me say this: For thirty seconds, my offer remains open. I'll stand by the deal I made at the hospital. But you *must* give me the witness's real name. Otherwise, I'm going to have you both taken into the next room." He nods toward the door to the firing range. "Take my word for it . . . you don't want to go in there."

Randall Regan's dark eyes move from Caitlin's face to mine, then back again. "They don't *know* the name," he says, utter certainty in his voice. "Cage doesn't, anyway. Maybe the girl does. But I don't think so."

Clearly Regan has more gifts than I've given him credit for.

"Is Randall correct?" Brody asks us both.

"I know the name," I lie, trying to pull him away from Caitlin. "But we're not giving it to you until you take care of the APB. Have Forrest Knox put a press release out to the wire services. I can check it on Regan's computer."

Royal is already shaking his head. "We're past that point, I'm afraid. You're going to have to prove your good faith, Mayor."

"Why are we wasting time with this?" Regan asks irritably. "Let's take them into the range. Introduce her to the Flammenwerfer. If she knows the witness's name, we'll have it in thirty seconds."

Brody gives his son-in-law a chiding look. "Patience, Randall. We've got a few minutes before the packages arrive. The problem is that Ms. Masters doesn't really understand the stakes. And I know why." He walks very close to Caitlin, then circles slowly around her, missing nothing. "You have my congratulations, Cage. I'd plow this filly all day long just to watch her walk."

His crude words are all the more startling for the civility that preceded them. "What do you think, Randall?"

Regan looks up from his screen and tilts his head to one side. "A little skinny, but still prime."

Caitlin's face goes red, and she looks away from both men.

"You can't fake that haughtiness," Royal says with an appreciative smile. "Raised with a silver spoon, this one. Thinks the world has *rules*, and that her job is to make people abide by them. Except herself, of course. And what she most wants . . . is to be a star. But she wouldn't even have the chance, if Daddy didn't own the company."

"And you?" she flashes back. "You're richer than my father ever was."

Brody barks a laugh. "You really don't know anything, do you? I met your father once. At the Kentucky Derby. The second I heard him speak, I knew he came from money. And you're his pride and joy, aren't you."

"I hope so." Pink blotches have come up on her throat.

The old man glances at his watch, then looks at her with startling intensity. "My story's a little different, princess. My mother died when I was just a tot. We were living on the levee after the Great Flood. The only dry land for fifty miles around. My father was out in a boat, helping rescue trapper families from the marshes. Everybody on the levee was starving, black and white both. One morning, a huge hog swam by. It was eating a bloated old nigra woman. I'll never forget that sight, so long as I live. Most of the bodies floating past were nigras. They never learned to swim, see? Lots of them still don't. Anyway, a National Guardsman shot the hog, and two men jumped into the water to get it. They shoved the woman's corpse away with a pole and dragged the hog back. They gutted it right quick, then strung it up and built a fire under it. But the people were so hungry . . . they couldn't wait."

Royal lowers his voice, and his eyes grow remote. "We were ripping meat off that hog long before it was cooked. I wasn't much more than a baby, so I was grabbing from down low, where I could reach. The meat I got was cooked, I guess. But Mama pulled hers from higher up, where it was almost raw. I got sick, but I lived. Mama died in agony, five weeks later. Worms in her brain."

Brody shakes his head, looking lost for a moment. "Rich folks don't die like that, do they, Ms. Masters? I'll bet all your people died on clean white sheets, surrounded by nurses."

I'm stunned to see sympathy in Caitlin's face. Reflexive guilt over her privileged background? *How can she possibly feel guilt when facing a monster?*

"But I don't think *you're* going to die that way," Brody says, his voice suddenly brittle. "Not unless you start talking *right now*. No clean white sheets for you. No painless passing. Just everlasting fire, like Albert Norris got."

"I know you're upset," Caitlin says carefully. "I'm sure you blame me for what your daughter did. I can understand that. But she needs you now. When I talked to her . . ." Caitlin trails off when she sees the glacial coldness in Royal's eyes.

"Tell her, Randall."

"Katy's dead, you stupid bitch."

Caitlin whips her head back toward Royal.

"She died twenty minutes after your fiancé left the hospital," says the old man.

Even as Caitlin says, "I'm sorry," the timing of Royal's daughter's demise strikes me as highly improbable.

"You killed her," I say softly, my eyes boring into his.

"You left me no choice. It was a mercy, in a way. Especially for Randall."

Regan looks at me like a man who has had a crippling burden lifted from his shoulders. Undoubtedly he did the deed himself.

Brody looks hard at Caitlin, who appears horrified by the ultimate consequences of her interview with Katy Royal. "I don't need your apologies, Ms. Masters. All I need from you is a name."

Caitlin's eyes flick back and forth like those of a trapped animal. She's where I was a few minutes ago. *Make up a name and pay the price for lying? Or give Royal a real name and possibly trigger someone's death? Is there even any point to stalling? John Kaiser seems our only possible deliverance, but without Walker Dennis leading him to Royal . . . why would he show up?*

"Randall, I think it's time you show Ms. Masters that we're not playing games here."

"About time," Regan says, setting his computer aside and getting to his feet with his cigarette clamped between his teeth.

I start toward Caitlin to protect her, but instead of moving toward her, Regan walks straight to me, spreads his hands wide, and claps them over my ears with stunning force. Though I see the blow coming, my taped hands give me no chance to block it. The simultaneous concussions stun me like nails driven through my eardrums, scrambling all thought.

I hit the floor even before I realize I'm falling.

As I lie on my back, heaving for breath, Regan drops a crushing knee onto my chest and leans over me, the orange eye of his cigarette burning white as he sucks air through it. Grabbing the butt from his mouth, he jams the burning tobacco into my left cheek.

Searing agony whites out his laughing face. For a wild rush of heartbeats there's only fire in my skin and a hammer pounding in my skull. The next thing to register is a high-pitched scream. Turning my head toward the sound, I see Caitlin's mouth wide, her eyes red and pouring tears. Royal gives an order that registers faintly in my brain, and then Regan gets off my chest and pulls me to my feet.

Brody walks up and squints into my eyes like a neurologist. "Can you hear me, Cage?"

I nod once, my head ringing like a struck anvil, my cheek radiating arcs of fire.

Brody signals Regan to bring Caitlin closer. The tall Irishman grabs her arm and drags her to within five feet of me. Her jet-black hair hangs lank over her eyes, but while her jaw hangs slack in shock, her emerald eyes still burn with intelligence.

"The *name*," Brody urges.

Even in my dazed state, I sense Caitlin's mind working at blinding speed, simultaneously racing down a dozen pathways, desperately searching for some ingenious blocking move. But there isn't one. I've known that since we were in the van.

"They're here," Regan says from my left.

Royal nods, preoccupied. "I tell you what, dear," he says with sudden gentleness. "Walk with me while you think about it. You, too, Mayor. Let me show you the pride of my collection."

Putting his arm around Caitlin, Brody walks us down the line of display cases. Regan prods me from behind, and the object poking me feels more like a gun barrel than a finger. Glancing backward, I see a Glock semiautomatic in his hand. As my eyes rise to his face, I read sadistic hunger in his eyes. Worse, we're already halfway to the firing range door.

Inside the display cases are MP40 and Mauser machine pistols, a Walther P38, the Fallschirmjägergewehr 42, a Sturmgewehr 44, even a Panzerfaust antitank weapon—each labeled with a brass plaque and a descriptive caption. Between a British Sten and a Mosin-Nagant sniper rifle, I see a Thompson submachine gun, one of the few pieces I would have recognized without the tag.

"Did you serve in combat?" I ask Brody.

"I was exempted from the draft," he answers over his shoulder. "War-critical work."

"Bootlegging?" Caitlin says with scathing contempt.

A hitch in Royal's stride tell me this barb hit home. "A little advice, Princess. Don't insult the alligator until you've crossed the river."

A few steps more, then Brody pauses before a cabinet at the end of the row, one wider than the rest. Despite its size, this case holds only two weapons: civilian hunting rifles, by the look of them. Below the rifles sits a large empty shelf with a plaque that reads: FLAMMENWERFER 41. ST. VITH. DECEMBER 1944.

"Do you know what you're looking at?" Brody asks, his voice oddly hushed.

Leaning forward to read the plaques beneath the rifles, I freeze, barely breathing. The first reads, *November 22, 1963*. The second: *April 4, 1968*. Juxtaposed in this setting, those two dates blow what coherence I've regained to smithereens. Yet out of the resulting chaos bounces Henry's tale of Snake Knox claiming to have killed Martin Luther King, and my father's story of being trapped on the fishing boat with Brody Royal and the drunk CIA man who kept cursing about the botched job in Dallas. Caitlin's gaze presses on my right cheek, silently asking if these weapons could be authentic. Unwilling to give Brody the satisfaction of seeing my distress, I straighten and turn to him as I would to a fool who'd paid top dollar for lead bricks painted gold.

"How much did you give the Knoxes for these fakes?" I ask. "Not much, I hope."

The steady certainty in Royal's eyes rattles me, and he knows it. In his mind, at least, these rifles are the genuine article.

As Caitlin straightens up, I try to catch her eyes, but she's whipped her head toward the staircase by which we entered. Two strangers have entered the room. They're better dressed than our van crew, and walk with distinctly military bearing. Each carries what looks to be a heavy banker's box. The sight hardly affects me, but Caitlin looks as though someone just gut-punched her. Behind us, Brody Royal chuckles softly.

"You obviously recognize those boxes. Take those into the firing range, Chalmers. Then deal with the mayor's car and our Natchez PD officer as quickly as possible."

Both men walk quickly to the door on the far right, then disappear through it. "What's in the boxes?" I ask.

"Henry Sexton's backup files and notebooks." Brody smiles with triumph. "Another excellent return on my investment at the *Examiner*. Now, no matter what the paper might print, no one will be able to substantiate the stories. And the FBI will never see them."

Behind me, Regan says, "The *Examiner's* scanned copies of those files are being systematically erased as we speak."

Caitlin's face now has the blankness of a condemned prisoner. She looks like she could scarcely string two thoughts together; I can hardly credit that she made the crack about Royal's bootlegging past only seconds ago.

Brody nods to Regan, who presses his pistol against my spine. Then Brody lays a hand on Caitlin's shoulder. "We're going to step through this door over here, darling. Last one on the right. Nothing to worry about."

How have we come to this point? Death stands behind us, and death waits before. In this situation, many people simply allow themselves to be led forward, grasping whatever extra seconds of life they can, until they get the bullet in the neck, or the gas, or whatever end has been devised.

I will not die that way. Better to fight here and force them to kill us both than to endure some depraved game like the one Brody forced on the two women from his insurance company.

I'm tensing my legs to hurl myself back against Regan when Caitlin says softly: "All right—I'll tell you."

Brody stops in mid-stride and turns to her. "What?"

"The witness. I'll give you his name."

Royal glances back at Regan, who shrugs.

The firing range door opens, and the two guards walk quickly to the staircase at the opposite end of the room. After they've gone, Brody looks at Caitlin and says, "I'm listening."

Caitlin looks so shamefully resigned that a terrifying notion comes to me. *Has she known the real name all along? Has she forced us to endure this in an effort to protect Henry's witness? The "friend" who held his silence for forty-one years?* With a rush of clarity I understand how she could justify such a thing. If she believed we were going to die no matter what, better to die saving the one man who might someday send Royal to death row for his crimes. Only now that we truly stand at the threshold of the abyss, she can't resist the hope that giving Royal what he wants might spare us terrible pain, if not our lives.

Brody leans toward her like a Hollywood vampire, his cold eyes burning into hers, searching for deception. "Don't lie to me, child. You'll *burn* if you lie."

Her chin is quivering, and when she speaks, two wheezing syllables emerge, but I can't make them out. Neither can Royal, because he leans still closer and says, "Once more, dear."

As the last syllable leaves Brody's lips, Caitlin catches his shoulder and spins him against her with feline quickness. The bright steel of Pithy's razor flashes beneath his chin as she lays the blade against his throat.

Regan knocks me aside and tries to get close enough for a shot, but Brody throws up a hand to stop him. *As would I.* Gone from her eyes is the dull glaze of a moment ago. Now they glow with green fire, and she holds the straight razor against his pulsing throat with the sure hand of an executioner.

"Get *back*," she warns, her voice like a second blade. Her eyes drill into Regan's. "Give Penn your cell phone. If you don't, I'm going to lay open his windpipe and sever his carotid."

Regan looks to Brody for guidance.

"I'll paint this fucking floor with his blood," Caitlin promises.

When Royal starts to speak, Caitlin slices his neck above the jugular. A dark rivulet of blood rolls down to his shirt collar. "The *phone*, moron," she says, tucking her head behind Royal's for protection. "Do you recognize this blade, Brody? The handle says 'A Lady's Best Friend.' Sound familiar?"

The old man looks almost hypnotized by her words.

"Nobody's giving you a phone," Brody rasps, his eyes regaining focus and confidence. "Randall, put your gun to the mayor's head."

Regan presses the barrel of his Glock against my right temple.

"Count to ten, then blow his brains out."

Caitlin's jaw is set tight with purpose, but I see doubt in her eyes. Even if Regan can't see the same, I sense that she's already lost the initiative. At least she tried—

"I'm counting to *five*," Caitlin snaps, before Regan even starts counting. "Then it's hog-killing time. ONE—"

"*What do I do?*" Regan cries, his Glock scraping against my temple.

For the first time I see fear in Brody's eyes. He knows there's nothing more dangerous than a cornered animal.

"Give him your phone!" Caitlin screams. "And your gun. TWO!"

Blood rolls steadily down Royal's neck.

Turning my head slightly to the right, I say, "Give me the gun, man."

Regan's eyes are filled with indecision. He jumps at the sound of a closing door.

Caitlin whips her head around Brody's, her eyes wild with suspicion. To my right, the van crew has slipped back into the basement. *Probably drawn from upstairs by the screaming.* Caitlin curses and drags Brody backward, into the corner shooting station. Crew Cut heads for the firing range door, while the older man takes a pistol from his belt and moves cautiously closer to Caitlin, angling for a shot.

"Watch that guy!" I tell her, pointing at the man making for the door.

"THREE!" Caitlin cries, her eyes jittery. "FOUR—"

"*Stop!*" Brody screams. "Put down your guns! Give Cage the phone. Stay out of there, Dwayne!"

The Glock's barrel falls away from my temple.

Caitlin's eyes flick back and forth, trying to read every intention. As Regan digs in his pocket for his cell phone, Brody sags with relief, then cracks his elbow into Caitlin's ribs and tries to wrench himself away. With a cry she rips the razor upward, spraying blood—and then they are two, not one.

Brody's shirt is a fountain of scarlet, and blood pours through his hands, which are at his throat. I leap forward to shield Caitlin, afraid

Regan will shoot her outright, but he appears stunned by the sight of Royal frantically probing the wound in his neck. Caitlin still has the razor in her hand, but it's useless now, except as a tool for suicide. Crew Cut and his partner have now trained their guns on us. They walk forward, bodies turned at an angle, lining up their shots. When I turn and find Caitlin's eyes, I see something I'd rather have died than witness: despair.

"Take them into the range!" Brody bellows, still probing his lacerated neck.

"Are you all right?" Randall asks, incredulous.

"I will be. Get me some goddamn superglue!"

Energized, Regan yells, "Put the mayor on the chain! The bitch gets the pole!"

This is the end. As Crew Cut reaches me, I grab his gun and twist hard enough to tear ligaments from bone. He shrieks, and my left hand closes firmly around cold steel. I sense more than see Caitlin flailing the razor to my left, but then something crashes into my neck, stunning me nearly senseless. I try once more to twist the gun free, but a second blow batters my skull, blotting out the light.

CHAPTER 92

HENRY SEXTON FORCED himself to keep the Impala's speedometer on forty as he drove up the lane toward Brody Royal's lake house. The IV narcotics were fading; he knew because his abdominal pain was climbing quickly up the scale. He'd taken a second OxyContin to compensate for the missing pump, and a couple of minutes ago, he'd realized he was only driving ten miles per hour.

He was breathing pretty well, in spite of his swollen tongue, and the pounding in his head had settled down to a tolerable backbeat. The cast on his left arm gave him no difficulty driving, but he worried about what might come later. As he neared the lake house, he tried to keep his mind engaged with reality. He couldn't allow the combination of white-hot anger and potent painkillers to handicap him.

He braked as he spied a pickup truck parked on the street beneath some trees at the border of Brody Royal's property. There was a man sitting behind the wheel. For a moment Henry was paralyzed. If he stopped and tried to turn around now, he'd look suspicious as hell. But if he went on . . .

He must be a guard of some sort, Henry decided, *posted to stop people like me.* Henry lifted his foot off the brake, thanking God he hadn't removed his mother's wig from his head. *My brights are on,* he thought. *I should just drive past like I'm headed home after a late night.*

As he came within a few feet of the pickup, Henry realized that the man sitting outside Brody's house was black.

That made no sense.

Twenty yards past the truck, Henry braked again. *A black security guard? Here?* He shook his head. Emboldened by the drugs, he put the Impala in reverse and backed up until he was even with the truck. Then he pulled off his wig and rolled down his window.

The man in the cab of the pickup turned his head casually toward Henry, peering through his window with open curiosity. Something about him seemed familiar. He was about Henry's age, for one thing. *Maybe I know him*, Henry thought. *But . . . no*. He couldn't place the man.

"Are you Henry Sexton?" asked the black man, sounding far from certain.

Henry nodded slowly.

"You shaved off your goatee?"

Henry laughed painfully. He'd been through a hell of a lot more changes than that in the past two days.

"Well, I guess you found me," said the man. "What you doin' out here? I thought you were in the hospital."

"I sneaked out." Henry cocked his head. "Who *are* you?"

"Sleepy Johnston. I'm from Wisner, originally. I been living in Detroit for the past forty-one years."

This revelation arced like lightning through Henry's narcotic fog. *One of Albert's boys*, he thought. With considerable effort, he opened the door and got out of the Impala, a movement that quickly punctured his OxyContin cushion.

Sleepy Johnston got out and carefully shook his hand, each man assessing the other. With gray hair and whiskers showing under his Detroit Tigers cap, Sleepy looked close to seventy, but his body appeared strong and healthy.

"Did you work for Albert Norris?" Henry asked. "I don't remember you."

After he puzzled out Henry's mumbled words, Johnston smiled. "Not officially. But I hung around the store whenever I could. By the time you came along, I was on the road, playing with bands. I only came back this way for family reunion gigs, things like that. That's how I met Pooky. He sat in with my band a couple times. But I knew Jimmy and Luther real good."

Henry shook his head, still dazed by the sudden appearance of a man he had hunted so hard.

"So," Sleepy went on, "why'd you sneak out of the hospital?"

A knot of foreboding formed in Henry's stomach. He pointed at the darkened Royal house. "I've come to see the man who lives in there. He killed my girlfriend tonight. And he damn near killed me."

It took Johnston a while to make out the words, but as he absorbed their meaning, his eyes widened. "Have you come to kill Old Man Royal?"

Henry thought about this. "I don't know. I just had to come. When a man kills the woman you love, you're supposed to do something about it. Aren't you?"

"I reckon so. But there's a lot of distance between 's'posed to' and actually doing. I can tell you all about that."

"Have you seen Brody here tonight?" Henry asked. "Is he in there?"

Sleepy licked his lips and nodded. "He's in there, all right. Just before you got here, two of Brody's thugs drove up in a van. They took a man and woman into the basement, all tied up."

Henry felt adrenaline rush into his bloodstream, mixing with the heady cocktail of drugs that were keeping him upright. "Black or white?"

"White, both of them."

"What did they look like?"

Sleepy ran a hand across his mouth, thinking. "Tall man, dressed pretty good. The woman had dark hair, classy looking. I was prowling back near the garage, and I saw the bastards drag them out of the van."

Penn Cage and Caitlin Masters. Henry knew it as surely as he knew that he had to abandon his confrontation plan and call for help.

"What you doing?" called Sleepy as Henry turned and opened his passenger door.

"I'm—" Henry slapped his forehead. In his haste at the hospital, he'd forgotten to ask his mother for her cell phone. The drugs were having more of an effect than he'd realized. He turned around. "We need to call for help. Not the local police. We can't trust them. We need the FBI. Or . . . wait." Henry fought through the cobwebs in his head. "Maybe we should call Royal's house. Let him know we know they have the mayor and his girlfriend in there."

"The *mayor*? Hold on," said Sleepy. "I don't know any of those numbers."

"Well, we could call Information—"

"*Hands up!*" ordered a sharp voice from behind Sleepy.

A middle-aged white man in a dark jacket held a pistol to the back of Sleepy's head.

There's the guard, thought Henry numbly. *The real one this time.*

Sleepy put up his hands, and Henry slowly followed his example. He thought of the shotgun in the backseat of his mother's car, but he couldn't make a move toward it without endangering Sleepy. Especially in his current condition.

The guard searched Sleepy's windbreaker pockets and pulled out his cell phone. Taking a step back, he dropped it on the asphalt and crushed it with his boot heel. Then he walked forward and patted down Henry.

"You got a gun in that truck?" he asked Sleepy, straightening up. Without waiting for an answer, he opened the driver's door of the truck. "Move back," he ordered. Then he searched the truck, quickly coming up with what appeared to be a small-caliber revolver.

"Head to the house," he barked. "Both of you. Walk in front of me. Double time."

In a daze, Henry began trudging ahead of Sleepy toward Brody Royal's lake house, which lay some eighty yards away.

"Hurry up," said the guard. "You old fucks." He prodded Henry with the pistol. "What's wrong with you, anyway? You bust out of an asylum or something?"

Henry stopped and turned, which forced Sleepy and the guard to stop as well. "I'm going as fast as I can," he said. "They've got me on strong medicine."

Sleepy, hands jammed in his coat pockets, turned to face the guard. "Can't you see the man's hurt? What's your problem?"

"You're my problem, asshole."

As the guard reached out to prod Henry forward, Sleepy's right hand rose from his pocket in a fluid motion, and a bright blade flicked in the moonlight. Before the guard could jerk back, Sleepy had buried his knife in the man's neck with one hand and swatted his gun away with the other.

The guard staggered, both hands gripping the wound in his throat. Henry watched black blood pump through the man's hands. As the guard fell backward, Sleepy quickly closed the distance between them and pressed a boot onto his chest.

Henry tried to recover his composure, but something kept causing breaks in his train of thought. "See if he has a phone!"

The guard had stopped moving. His eyes were open, but they looked sightless to Henry. Sleepy knelt over him, rummaged through his clothes, then stood. "Nothing but a walkie-talkie and some keys."

Henry tried to think clearly. "Do you think we should call inside? Tell Brody we know who he's got in there? Tell him the FBI is coming?"

Sleepy considered this suggestion, then shook his head. "We can either drive back to town and call the cops, or go in there and do what we can. But we *ain't* calling and letting them know we're out here. Mr. Royal don't react like other men would. You radio that we're out here, he'll kill your friends and us, too."

Henry nodded slowly. "If the guard has a house key . . . we could call 911 from inside the house as soon as we get in."

Sleepy nodded. "I guess we could. Especially if they're still in the basement."

The guard suddenly groaned in pain, startling Henry so badly that he almost fell over.

"Wait here," Henry said. "Let me get my gun."

He turned and trudged back to his mother's Impala. The altercation with the guard had apparently spurred his metabolism. Or maybe it was just the exercise, loosening unused muscles. He was moving much faster than before.

Back at the car, he paused, his mind a frazzle of conflicting impulses. Sleepy Johnston represented the Holy Grail he'd sought for years: a witness who could put Brody Royal on death row. Taking Sleepy into Royal's house was like finding the grail and then carrying it into Hell. Yet something had driven Sleepy to this place, as surely as it had Henry. What was it? A private quest for justice? Foolish, perhaps, but maybe that compulsion had put them both in a position to save Penn and Caitlin. To *prevent* more murders like Albert's, and Sherry's, instead of avenging them. Gritting his teeth against imminent pain, Henry opened the back door of the car, bent at the waist, and lifted the shotgun from the backseat floor. Then he staggered back to where Sleepy awaited him.

"Glad to see that scattergun," Johnston said. "You're not in much of a state for target shooting."

"That's why I brought this. What you want to do?"

"Our buddy on the ground said the mayor and his lady are in the basement. There are two more guards in the house." Sleepy held up the walkie-talkie. "Been listening to this. From what I can tell, I think he told the truth."

Henry looked at the man on the ground. "I thought he was dead."

"He is now. Let's go."

Henry took two deep breaths and shifted his weight from foot to foot, trying to be sure of his balance.

Sleepy reached out and gripped his left arm. "You sure you're ready for this, Henry? You're hurt pretty bad already."

"I'm going. You can stay out here if you want, or go for help. But if I don't come back . . . swear to me you'll tell the FBI what happened to Albert that night. And who did it."

Sleepy shook his head. "Take it easy, brother. I was just askin' for your sake. I got Albert on my mind, myself. Pooky, too. Have had for too many years now."

Henry saw his own grief reflected in the black man's face. "Yeah. It's Swan I see, though. That bastard in there killed Swan's daddy."

Sleepy's teeth flashed in the moonlight. "Swan Norris," he said, as though hearing a song he'd forgotten years ago. "Lord, that man in there owes for a lot of people. For a long time, too. He's got a big account to pay."

"Maybe it's time we collected."

Sleepy nodded, then turned and started toward the great dark house beside the lake.

Holding his shotgun like a balancing pole, Henry followed in his wake. When they neared the front porch, Henry covered the approaches to the house while Johnston opened the front door with the guard's key. Holding a finger to his lips, Sleepy stepped over the threshold, into a dark foyer. Henry followed, trying not to stumble.

No alarm sounded.

There was a lighted keypad on the wall, but the LED read DISARMED. Henry saw no other light, except the flicker of a television far down a hallway to their right. Gripping his shotgun like a lifeline, he started forward, but Sleepy caught his arm and held him back. The black man reached down to a credenza in the foyer and lifted an envelope from a pile of mail. Then he took a cigarette lighter out of his pocket and set the envelope alight.

Henry watched in bewilderment. Was Sleepy Johnston crazy, or was it that Henry's addled brain couldn't keep up? Johnston scanned the ceiling, then walked over to a smoke alarm and held the burning envelope directly beneath it. At last Henry understood. Even with the security system disarmed, the fire alarm should sound and summon the fire department.

He waited for an earsplitting Klaxon, but again none came. Sleepy stretched up higher, until the flame actually touched the smoke alarm.

Still nothing.

Henry went back to the keypad on the wall and punched the fire alarm and police buttons. When nothing happened, he pressed several buttons, trying to arm the system, but the readout didn't change.

"Don't make sense," Sleepy whispered. "Something ain't right."

Why would Brody Royal disable his own alarm system? Henry wondered. *Especially when he's holding people prisoner downstairs?* He shuffled quietly into the first darkened room off the hall, watching the light of the television flicker at the end of the long corridor.

A guest room. *There.* A telephone sat on the bedside table. A landline. Laying his shotgun on the bed, Henry dialed 911 with shaking hands, then lifted the receiver to his ear and waited. He heard neither a ring nor an answer.

"Hello?" he said, wondering if the drugs were playing tricks on him.

"Hey, Lee!" called a male voice from the direction of the TV's glow. "What the hell you doing inside? Mr. Royal said not to leave your post unless we relieved you."

Still confused by the silent telephone, Henry set down the receiver and considered trying to fake a response. Before he could try, Sleepy raised his finger to his lips, then pointed at the shotgun. Tensing for the shock of pain, Henry bent at the waist and picked up his father's old Winchester.

CHAPTER 93

I COME AWAKE with my head pounding like a kettledrum, but a baritone counterpoint of voices penetrates the pain. My captors must be close. Keeping my eyes closed, I try to glean what I can of my surroundings. I'm lying on my side, on a cold concrete floor. The voices belong to Brody Royal and Randall Regan, and they're coming from beyond my head, not my feet. Before I can make sense of their words, Caitlin's higher-pitched voice asks a question. As the old man answers, a stunning realization hits me: *my hands have been freed.* The sticky residue of duct tape remains on my wrists, but the tape itself is gone. After a moment, I carefully open one eye and realize why. My left leg has been manacled to a ring bolt set in a cinder-block wall.

My chain appears to have about five feet of play in it. The slightest leg movement will make it rattle. As slowly as I can, I arch my neck back, searching for Caitlin. *There.* Fifteen feet away, she stands trussed to a steel pole like a witch condemned to burn at the stake. Her right cheek looks pink and swollen, as from a blow, and her eyes are bereft of hope.

Beyond my line of sight, Brody says something to Randall Regan in a low voice, but I hear nothing of the men from the van. With any luck, they're gone. Hoping to further assess our situation before Royal or Regan realizes I'm awake, I tilt my head a little farther back, taking great care to keep my eyes barely open.

Brody Royal's firing range appears to be a long tunnel cut deep into the earth. Five shooting lanes wide and forty yards long, it's lined with cinder-block walls, floored with cement, and fitted with ceiling-mounted sprinkler heads every few yards. Steel support poles rise from the concrete floor to the basement ceiling, and it's one of these to which Caitlin has been tied. Harsh fluorescent light floods the vast space, giving it the look of a chamber Reinhard Heydrich designed to torture Czech resistance fighters.

As I expected, long metal tracks line the ceiling, receding into the distance, where targets with human figures printed on them hang against a wall of bullet-pocked railroad ties. Three targets show Muslim terrorists with red crescents painted on their checked keffiyehs. Two more show the famous "running nigger" from the 1960s: a cartoon-ish silhouette of a black man with an Afro haircut, running in profile, with red target dots printed on his kneecaps, his buttocks, his chest, his mouth, and his temple.

Halfway to the far wall sit the two boxes brought by the professional guards, as though awaiting disposal. A few feet away from me sits an odd collection of equipment, so carefully laid out that it must have been brought here for us: a large chrome fire extinguisher; a thick roll of Visqueen; a red plastic bucket; and, strangest of all, what looks like some sort of man-portable welding system, with two gas cylinders on a frame, connected to a woven hose and a pipe. Beside this antique-looking apparatus I see the legs of Royal and Regan, who seem to be staring at Caitlin.

As I try to divine the purpose of the equipment, Regan takes a couple of steps toward me and kicks me savagely in the ribs. Air explodes from my throat as something cracks in my side.

"He's awake now."

"Then let's find out where we stand and get this done," Brody says. "Suit up, Randall."

Regan hands Brody his pistol, then walks to the eerily familiar contraption on the floor. Slipping his arm through one khaki strap, he shoulders the horizontal cylinders like a backpack, then settles the thing squarely on his frame. It actually looks like some sort of antique scuba rig, but instinct tells me its purpose is to end life, not to preserve it.

"Recognize that?" Royal asks, as I finally guess what Regan is wearing. "It's a Flammenwerfer 41. Kraut flamethrower. Excellent unit, like most German-engineered gear. Shoots a mixture of oil and tar. The combination comes out a lot like napalm."

To my amazement, Brody seems to have patched his neck wound with duct tape, though I remember him saying something about super-glue. "As a point of interest," he goes on, "this is the very weapon we used on Albert Norris. It's a bit heavy for me now, so I'm going to let Randall do the preliminary work."

Henry Sexton's description of Norris's awful death comes back to me in a rush, triggering a cold sweat from head to toe. Caitlin's eyes beseech mine, searching for a sign of hope, but I can't summon any.

Royal turns a valve on the back of the unit, then taps one of the cylinders twice and says, "Light up the jet pipe, Randall."

When Regan pulls a trigger on a striker unit, the basement fills with a sound that starts my bowels roiling. It's a hiss blended with a soft roar, the sound of liquid fire waiting to be unleashed. At the end of the firing pipe in Regan's hand, a deep blue jet with an orange core glows like the key to hell.

"Hydrogen pilot flame," says Royal, taking a pack of Camel cigarettes from his pocket and shaking one loose. As if replaying an old routine, Regan holds up the jet pipe and Brody leans down over the hissing flame with the Camel in his mouth. He draws on the cigarette once, puffing blue smoke, then straightens up and takes a long drag.

"Best damned cigarette lighter in the world. Ask any Wehrmacht veteran. Singe off your eyebrows, though, if you're not careful."

"Let's do it," Regan says.

"Wait," says Brody, picking up the paper bag from in the gun room and dumping our cell phones into the red bucket. Then he removes the microcassette from the recorder we used to make my copy. "A little demonstration." After dropping the crumpled bag into the bucket, he carries it downrange and sets it atop the two banker's boxes.

An involuntary whimper comes from Caitlin's throat.

Regan laughs.

"Aim low," Brody tells him, taking care to stay near the wall as he walks back to us. "I switched off the fire alarms. You don't want to burn the goddamn house down."

Bracing the pipe against his hip, Regan pulls the trigger.

A blast of flame reaches downrange like the hand of Lucifer. In less than three seconds, the ravenous fire devours the bucket and its contents like a campfire eating a paper cup, and the smell of burnt plastic joins that of gasoline and tar. When the flame vanishes, what remains is a red puddle on the burning boxes. Half the oxygen seems to have been sucked from the tunnel.

"So much for your evidence," Brody says.

Acrid black petroleum smoke is gathering beneath the ceiling like a fog, but he appears unconcerned. "Don't worry, this place has OSHA-grade air handlers and a world-class sprinkler system."

"There are two more copies of that tape," I tell him, wondering why I didn't go this route before. "They're with lawyer friends of mine, and they'll be given to the FBI upon my death."

Royal probes me with his gambler's eyes. "The tapes don't actually worry me much, Mayor. My daughter was delusional all her life. Katy was a known alcoholic and drug addict, and she had a suicidal dose of narcotics in her system when that recording was made. It's the witness I care about. He's the only reason you're still alive."

Holding the cigarette at shoulder height—the height of Caitlin's face—Brody steps closer to her. While her eyes track the glowing orange flame, Royal takes Pithy's straight razor from his back pocket and turns it in the air until it catches the light.

"I do remember this," he murmurs. "Quite well, actually. I bought it off a madam who'd worked in Storyville as a girl. It's a terror weapon, really, made for teaching whores lessons, not for killing. The blade is too fragile." He cocks his head at Caitlin. "You actually remind me of Pithy Nolan in some ways. She thought she knew it all, too. How strange that this gift circled all the way back to me after all this time . . . and nearly killed me. I believe I'll pay Pithy a visit next week. Get reacquainted."

As I try to hide my fear for Pithy, he says, "Ladies' choice, Ms. Masters. The flame or the knife?"

She gazes back at him without fear. "What are you hoping to find out? I don't know the name."

Royal touches the duct tape ringing his neck. "I'm sorry I can't take your word for that."

After another contemplative drag off the Camel, he reaches out and cups his left hand behind Caitlin's head. Then he draws the blade of the straight razor from the corner of her eye to the crease at the edge of her mouth.

I scream, but when he pulls away the blade, I see no blood. *He was just teasing her. . . .*

As Caitlin and I sag with relief, Royal stabs the tip of the cigarette into her left cheek, pressing it deep into the skin. The pole clangs as she yanks her head away, banging her skull against the steel.

An angry red welt like a bullet wound has risen in the center of her once-perfect cheek. I kick my manacled leg away from the pillar, hoping to break a weak link, but it's pointless. Caitlin is moaning now. Tears pour from her eyes. Stooping, I seize the chain with both hands and yank it as hard as I can. In seconds, my palms are lacerated and bleeding.

"All is vanity," murmurs Royal, stepping behind her. "Amazing what the prospect of a permanent scar will do to motivate a woman."

Now Caitlin's trembling from head to toe. The old man draws on the cigarette, and its tip glows bright again. My chain clinks and rattles as I try to break free from the wall, but it's no use.

Royal beckons his son-in-law forward, and Regan obeys, brandishing the flamethrower. "Do you know what German infantrymen nicknamed the Flammenwerfer?" Brody muses. *"Skinstealer."*

This nickname has its intended effect. Brody may not see it, but the threat of imminent agony and disfigurement has unsettled the deepest part of Caitlin's being. Outwardly, though, she somehow remains composed.

"Now . . . about that witness."

Caitlin closes her eyes and turns her head away from her tormentor.

"The tip of that cigarette was about a thousand degrees Fahrenheit," Brody says. "The Flammenwerfer burns at twenty-five hundred. The pain you feel now is like a paper cut compared to it." He pulls a strand of black hair from her eyes. "Can you imagine? I honestly can't."

As I struggle maniacally to free myself, Brody stares at me as he might a troublesome dog. "Save yourself the pain, Cage. That chain is tempered steel."

Still I struggle, shredding my palms on the chain. Only one thing is going to stop this torture—a name. But whose? I don't even have enough raw data to make up a credible candidate for "Huggy Bear." What was the name from her phone? Rambin . . . ?

"I don't know the witness's name," Caitlin says in an exhausted voice, "but he's out there. And he *will* tell his story. It will probably be our deaths that finally push him to go to the FBI. He'll tell them what he knows"—Caitlin looks Royal full in the face—"and that will be the end of *you.*"

He peers into her eyes as though intrigued. "How subtle are you, I wonder?" Then he walks behind her again, and her whole body shudders. When Brody circles back in front of her, she practically folds her shoulder blades around the pole to get away from him. On the third circuit, he takes out the razor and severs the rope binding her wrists. Then he backs away to give his son-in-law a clear field of fire.

"Pay attention, Princess. I want you to hold your arm as far away from your body as you can. It's for your own good, believe me. If you can keep it far enough away, you might lose no more than your hand and forearm."

I realize I'm clenching and unclenching my own hands. Why else would they have freed my hands except to use them in the same way?

Whatever self-control Caitlin still possesses is fast draining away. Her face is so pale that even the cigarette burn has lost its redness.

"*We don't know the name!*" I scream at Brody. "Torturing us won't change that!"

"*You* don't know it," he says with calm assurance. "But I'll tell you what I think. I think she winkled the name out of Sexton but kept it from you. She knew she couldn't trust you not to use it as currency to buy your father back."

Could he be right?

"Your arm," Brody says patiently, trying to penetrate Caitlin's now-infantile terror. "Hold it *way* out to the side, like this." The old man extends his left arm, then tilts his head far in the opposite direction and covers his eyes with his other hand. "You don't want your face spoiled any worse than it already is, do you?"

As Randall Regan tests the trigger, a three-foot jet of fire spurts from the pipe in his hand, roaring like an overfilled propane barbecue grill erupting into flame. Royal motions him farther back.

Regan backs up until he's twenty yards away from Caitlin, then squares the cylinders on his shoulders, preparing to fire. "I'm going to walk it up from the floor."

"Try to keep it off her legs. I want her able to talk, at least, after the first blast."

My field of vision tunnels down to Caitlin's face: the fresh burn scar on her cheek, the abject terror in her eyes. I half expect her to faint, but after five or six seconds, she slowly lifts her right hand and holds it away from her body. As the pilot jet roars softly, I say a silent prayer: *For God's sake, give him a name, any name at all—*

Regan's finger crooks into the trigger guard.

"*Gates Brown!*" Caitlin screams. "His name is Gates Brown!"

After so much tension, these two simple words silence the room as surely as the arrival of a stranger.

To my surprise, Brody holds up his hand to stop Regan from firing.

Caitlin is sobbing softly, like a broken woman. "Gates Brown" seems to have triggered some association in Royal's mind, one he can't quite place. I only pray that he's not as big a baseball fan as John Kaiser's radio-man in Vietnam. Of course, his son-in-law might be—

"She's lying," Regan says. "Look at her. Let me do her, Brody. It's the only way to know for sure."

"Quiet," Royal snaps, watching Caitlin with suspicion. "I remember that name, Randall. *Gates Brown . . .*"

Sweat glistens on Regan's face. "She's lying, I tell you!"

When Brody ignores him, Regan fires another blast downrange, filling the tunnel with a hellish flare. The burning oil flies thirty yards in the air, then hits the concrete floor and slides along it like a fiery flood until it meets the wall of rail ties.

"*Goddamn* it!" Brody shouts. "I said *wait!*"

Regan refuses to meet Brody's eyes. "She's not gonna tell you without the fire."

Picking up the fire extinguisher, Brody hurries down to the wall and sprays the base of the blaze that Regan unleashed, but the foam does little to smother the napalm-like mixture. After a few more attempts, he sets down the silver canister and walks back up to Caitlin.

"Are you playing me, girl?"

"No. Gates Brown visited Henry Sexton in the hospital, and he signed the deputy's book. The man had to show his driver's license. I'll bet Forrest Knox can have somebody check that."

As Brody reaches into his pocket for his cell phone, a staccato series of bangs reverberates through the house above us. The ceiling muffles the explosions, but they're clearly gunfire.

"Son of a bitch," Regan curses, trying to shrug the straps of the flamethrower off his shoulders. "Time to bolt. We'll take them with us. The Rover's in the garage."

"Stay where you are," Brody says, watching the ceiling like an astronomer trying to decipher unexpected celestial movements. "It's too late to run anyway."

"But—"

"Shut up, damn you! *Listen.*"

CHAPTER 94

HENRY SEXTON FELT like he was trapped in a childhood nightmare, so slowly did his body obey his brain. The gunfight had started in the hall, as soon as Sleepy Johnston tried and failed to respond to a question called by one of the guards to "Lee"—who now lay dead out by the road. Sleepy had already fired half a clip, crossing the hall to another bedroom as he did, trying to get a clean shot at the men at the end of the dark corridor. A man had screamed down there, and Henry hoped he'd been hit, but he couldn't be sure.

"*Henry!*" Johnston screamed from across the hall. "Need some help here!"

When Henry finally reached the bedroom door, three shots blasted from the end of the hall, and splinters of Sheetrock stung his eyes. Sleepy let off two quick shots in return, and something fell heavily down the hall.

"*Don't fire!*" Sleepy shouted, and then he rushed into the hall, firing as he ran. As Henry peeked out, four shots exploded from the direction of the TV room. Something punched his left shoulder, and wetness ran down the left side of his rib cage. He looked down. Dark blood covered the white plaster of his cast.

Not again, he thought dully.

Henry backed into the bedroom, wobbling as he went, then fell on his ass. From the noise in the hall, Sleepy seemed to be holding his own, but then everything went quiet. That silence filled Henry with dread. If Sleepy was dead, he'd never make it out, either.

He heard footsteps creeping up the hallway.

"*I'm empty!*" Sleepy shouted, his voice desperate. "*Now or never, Henry!*"

Swearing to himself, Henry scrabbled to his knees, then knee-walked to the open door, twisted to his right, and fired blindly at a figure only ten feet away.

The shotgun roared, then roared again, lighting the hall with fire. The dark figure hurtled backward and fell heavily to the floor. A forearm rose like a flag of surrender, but then Henry saw a pistol in its hand. He shut his eyes and fired twice more, then began crawling forward.

"Sleepy?" he called. "Where are you?"

Johnston stepped out of a door to Henry's left, his dark face covered with white dust. "Jesus, man, you sure took your time." He carefully pulled Henry to his feet. "They got your shoulder, looks like. Hurt bad?"

Henry shook his head. "I can't really feel it yet. I've got a lot of drugs in me."

Sleepy looked down at the gunman lying nearest them. Henry followed his gaze. At least one of Henry's shots had taken the man dead center. *Dead*, he thought, thankful that his emotions were dulled by chemicals.

"We'd better move," Sleepy said. "Shouldn't be anybody left but Mr. Royal and his son-in-law, if that guy outside told the truth. But if we don't find that basement quick, they'll be gone and your friends dead."

A searing pain arced through Henry's abdomen, and the OxyContin didn't blunt it at all. Either his knife wound had reopened, or something else was going on. As he tried to gather himself, the hand that held his mother's shotgun began to shake.

"Let's go," he gasped, after he got his breath. "You're right. I don't think we have much time."

CHAPTER 95

WHILE THE GUNS thundered upstairs, Royal told his son-in-law that if the FBI had come, there was no point trying to break out. Better to wait for an arrest and try to find a way to flee the country. But as he listened to the pounding of feet, the quick pops of pistols, and the muffled roar of a shotgun, he said, "I don't think that's the FBI. They'd have hit both floors at once. And we wouldn't be hearing their rounds."

"Sheriff Dennis?" Regan suggests, his body taut with the effort of holding his ground while his instincts tell him to run.

Royal shakes his head, one hand held high like a sensitive antenna. No guns have fired for several seconds. "Get over by a shooting station and cover them. Then sit tight and see what comes through that door."

In the subsequent silence, Caitlin and I look steadily at each other, more feeling passing between us than ever has through the medium of language. A few moments ago, death seemed certain; now our hearts thunder with hope that someone has come for us.

Regan backs into one of the shooting-station partitions, his flamethrower trained on Caitlin and me, but we ignore him. Brody moves quietly across the floor to the firing range door. Flattening himself to one side, he waits with his pistol drawn and ready.

In the adjoining gun room, a door crashes open with a muted impact. Twenty seconds of silence follow.

"Mayor Cage!" shouts an unfamiliar voice. "Are you in there?"

My heart leaps. Whoever has come for us seems to have won the gun battle upstairs. *But who are they?* SWAT officers led by either John Kaiser or Walker Dennis? The leader's voice sounds older, though. *Walt Garrity, maybe? Or Chief Logan, from Natchez?* Sometimes the local departments practice mobilizing a multi-force SWAT team.

I want to shout a warning, but Regan's face tells me he'll fire the flamethrower if I do. Yet waiting will guarantee casualties among our rescuers. No amount of body armor will protect a man from burning gasoline.

Brody tenses at the sound of further movement in the gun room, but there's no fear in his face or posture. Still glaring at me, Regan aims the flamethrower at Caitlin to ensure my silence.

"Royal!" yells the voice from the gun room, now sounding strangely familiar. "We know you have Mayor Cage and Caitlin Masters down here! Send them out!"

I know that voice, but the speech seems impaired . . . yet even that sounds familiar. "Oh, no," I say under my breath. *Henry? Impossible—*

"The FBI's on their way!" yells the voice.

Hope dies within me. In Caitlin, too, I can tell. If John Kaiser were coming for us, Henry Sexton would still be back in his hospital bed.

Brody looks back at Regan with a smile, then gives him a thumbs-up. Ever the astute gambler, he's already guessed the truth: a SWAT assault would have unfolded very differently from this. I'm almost ready to shout a warning regardless of the consequences, but Caitlin beats me to it.

"Stay back, Henry! It's an ambush!"

Before her last word fades, someone kicks open the firing-range door.

No one comes through.

As we stare at the empty doorway, a black object skitters through it and slides across the floor. Royal and Regan throw up their arms, expecting a grenade, but it's only a walkie-talkie.

A tinny version of Henry Sexton's voice emerges from the black radio. "You're surrounded, Royal. Send out your hostages."

While Royal and Regan stare at the walkie-talkie, a black man darts through the door, a pistol held in front of him as he scans the room for targets.

Brody takes one step and lays his gun against the back of the man's head. "Drop it," he says. "Drop it now, or I pull the trigger."

Left with no choice, the man drops his gun.

He's obviously no SWAT operator. Dressed in work boots, jeans, and a dark jacket, he looks like a stranger to me. A sixty-five-year-old stranger. Then I see the gothic *D* on his black baseball cap, and a sadness unlike anything I've ever known suffuses me. Henry has done the *one thing* that could worsen our situation—and make our defeat more complete. He's brought "Gates Brown" straight into the arms of Brody Royal.

As I turn toward Caitlin, Henry steps through the basement door in a raincoat, a shotgun held before him, its barrel aimed at Royal's head. Henry's head is bandaged, and a huge bloodstain soaks his shoulder and sleeve, but he looks ready and willing to pull the trigger.

"*Wait!*" Brody cries, total submission embodied in the word.

Henry shakes his head and answers in a mournful voice: "I'm tired of waiting." And then he fires.

The deadest click in the world echoes through the tunnel.

Brody reels backward as though hit, then rebounds and cracks his pistol across Henry's face. The black man starts to go for Brody, but spies Regan covering him with the flamethrower from his left. Henry wobbles on his feet, then falls to the concrete like dead weight and doesn't move. I jump to the end of my chain, but it's pointless. Brody and the stranger are at least fifteen yards away from me, and Regan is even farther.

Brody kicks the black man's gun across the floor to Regan, who aims the jet pipe at the stranger and barks, "Who the fuck are you?"

"You heard the man," says Brody, covering the newcomer with his pistol.

"Nobody," says the stranger. "I ain't nobody."

Brody knocks the baseball cap off the man's head, exposing nappy white hair. "Henry?" Brody says with obvious curiosity. "Who's your pet nigger?"

Henry doesn't stir. Brody steps hard on the reporter's shoulder wound, but a muffled groan is the only response.

"Give me your wallet, boy," Brody says, jerking his pistol.

The stranger stares sullenly into Brody's eyes, but he obeys.

Royal snatches the outstretched wallet, extracts a driver's license, and reads aloud from it: "Marshall Johnston, Junior. Detroit, Michigan. *Michigan?*"

Randall Regan shrugs.

Brody pulls out his cell phone and dials a number. "Claude Devereux knows every family in this parish, black or white."

One minute later, Royal's lawyer fulfills his client's faith. Marshall Johnston Jr. belongs to a black family from Wisner, a one-horse cotton town about fifteen miles away. According to Claude Devereux, folks called the son "Sleepy."

"Well, well," Brody says to Johnston. "You're the friend of that Wilson boy, aren't you? The one who raped my daughter."

"Pooky never raped nobody," says Sleepy Johnston. "Your little girl chased him first. That's what got them together in the first place."

A strange tremor goes through Brody. He walks slowly around Johnston. "You know what's pathetic, boy? You ran away from Louisiana after your friend died. You did whatever you did up north all these years—some factory job, I imagine—but you never really got away. All that time you were circling right back home, like a rabbit to the hunter."

Brody stares at Johnston for several seconds, then motions for Regan to cover him as he walks back to the gun room. I hear a drawer open and close. When Brody returns, he's holding something in his hand. All the humanity has drained out of his face, leaving only stony hatred.

"Your daughter loved Pooky Wilson," Caitlin says suddenly. "I could see it this afternoon, when I spoke to her."

"That's a *lie*," Brody growls. "That boy defiled my flesh and blood. He broke the law."

"What law?"

"The *first* law."

"Miscegenation?" I offer.

Brody nods. "Trust a lawyer to know his history. But that's not what I'm talking about. I meant the *unwritten* law. I never had any real problem with nigras. But you don't mix blood through the white female. Albert Norris knew that rule, and he flouted it. The Wilson boy did, too. Even his friends warned him away from my daughter, but he wouldn't listen. *That* nigger had to have his way, like a mutt wanting to mount a pure-blooded bitch. And the result?"

Brody holds up the item in his hand. About eight inches long, it looks like an ivory file with a leather handle. "I've been opening letters with that boy's cock for forty-one years."

Caitlin gasps.

Johnston stares in horror at the obscene artifact.

"Handsome, isn't it?" Brody turns it in the light, which reflects dully off the osseous material. "Frank Knox carved the blade out of that boy's arm bone, and Snake tanned the skin of his cock for the handle. They made me a razor strop, too. White man's skin on one side, black on the other. The black side is used for coarse sharpening, the white for finishing. I'll use that on Pithy's razor before I go see her." He touches the duct tape on his neck. "I think it's gone a little dull over the years."

"How did Pooky die?" Johnston asks through clenched teeth, eyeing the gun that Brody still wields with his other hand. "You crucify him, like I've heard?"

"Not exactly. When I first heard he'd spilled his seed in my little girl, I told Frank I wanted that boy skinned alive. Well, they caught him quick enough. And they took him out to that tree in Lusahatcha County. The Bone Tree. But flaying a man's a tricky business. To do it right, you need a knife called a dermatome. Snake didn't have one. He tried his best with a Buck knife, but it turned into such a mess they couldn't hold that boy still no matter what they used."

Hearing the old man describe this atrocity with such clinical detachment short-circuits some part of my being, leaving me nearly paralyzed.

"You were *there*," Caitlin intones.

The light in Brody's eyes tells me that he was. "In the end, they just nailed him up to the tree. Frank said it had been done there before, back during the War Between the States."

With a sound like the voice of retribution, Johnston says, "I know why you done what you did. Why you tore that poor boy up so bad. Your little girl not only loved Pooky. She was carrying his child."

Brody jerks back as though the words had struck him physically. Then he smacks Johnston across the face with his gun.

Johnston staggers but holds his feet, his eyes filled with irrefutable truth. "You didn't just kill Pooky. I know that child was never born. You killed your *own flesh and blood*. You might as well have killed your daughter, too. You killed her soul right then. And you damned your own."

Mouth agape, Brody is clearly stunned that any black man would speak to him this way. He presses the gun barrel to Sleepy Johnston's sternum. "You got anything else to say?"

When Johnston speaks again, his voice is filled with emotion I can't quite read. Then I recognize it—pity. "You ain't nothing, Mister," he says softly. "All your money and land don't make you worth the mud on Albert Norris's shoes. And what's more . . . *you know it*."

Brody fires.

Sleepy's body jerks, then drops to the floor. His blank eyes stare sightless at the low ceiling.

Brody wipes a sheen of sweat from his face, then turns to face Caitlin and me. The man I spoke to only a minute ago seems to have fled the body before me. Caitlin appears frozen, as am I. We might have been in shock before, but the cold-blooded execution has taken our desperation to a new level.

Henry, who seemed only half-conscious before, rolls onto his side and stares at Johnston's body on the floor.

Brody points his smoking pistol at Henry. Caitlin screams, and I shrink from the imminent shot. Instead of shooting, though, Brody crouches so that Henry can see his eyes. "You spent thirty years trying to get me, boy, and in the end you delivered the *only* thing that could have destroyed me. Like *room service*. I do believe you're the saddest white man I ever saw."

Henry gazes up at Brody but says nothing. He looks more like a stroke victim than an active participant in a conversation.

"See that fire downrange?" Brody asks, pointing at the burning bucket and banker's boxes. "Thirty years of notes and diaries? Nobody's ever going to see it. Shit, son . . . don't you realize we could drive back to Ferriday right now and start asking people on the street who Pooky Wilson was, or Joe Louis Lewis, and not three in ten would know? Not one in a hundred, if we asked people under thirty. And Ferriday's ninety percent black! Thirty miles from here, nobody's even heard those names. Nobody gives a shit, black or white. The nigras living in Ferriday now aren't thinking about anything but how to fill their crack pipes tomorrow."

Brody looks down at Henry as though waiting for agreement. "You know I'm right, son. You wrote all those stories, and what thanks did you get? Did anybody hand you the key to the city? Nobody cares but a few New York Jews and liberal, guilt-ridden princesses like Ms. Masters over there."

With a last shake of his head, Brody straightens up and turns slowly back to me, his face haggard and finally looking its age. "Well, Mayor . . . nothing left now but the final act. But never fear. Nobody's gonna leave the theater bored."

"For God's sake, Brody. You've got all the fucking money in the world. Just take it and go. Surely you've got some nonextradition haven somewhere? You can't kill everybody who knows about you. You're going to be found out. It's inevitable. If you kill us, John Kaiser will never stop trying to nail you. Never. Go *now*."

Royal looks at me like I'm mad. "*Go?* Why would I leave?" He kicks Sleepy Johnston's corpse. "With this fool dead, I'm washed clean. 'Washed in the blood,' as they say. Henry's dying, and his files are ashes. Katy's gone, and those tapes, too." He takes one step toward me, then another. "About the only thing in this world I have left to worry about is *you*. You and Princess there."

"If you kill us, you'll trigger the biggest manhunt in the history of this state."

One eyebrow goes up. "You think so?"

Regan moves out of the shooting station and approaches us with the flamethrower.

"I think it's human nature to overestimate our own importance," Brody says. "Here's the ending, son. You and your girlfriend are going to disappear down the drain of this room, just like Henry and Mr. Johnston there. Randall's going to melt you into barbecue drippings, then feed your bones to the pigs on my daughter's farm, miles from here. Your father will be dead by morning." Royal comes still closer, so close that I smell his breath, a mix of whiskey and dirty dentures. "Last of all, your mother and your little girl."

For one shattering moment, I fear that he's located Mom and Annie at Edelweiss. But I see in his eyes that he hasn't—and then I understand the final act that remains to be played.

"It's only fitting," he says, "when you think about what happened to my Katy. So—"

"You're insane. You think you can get away with killing my whole family?"

"I do. When morning comes, there won't be anything left but three empty houses. There'll be some hullabaloo, of course. The FBI will run all over town like ants in a stepped-on pile. But meanwhile, Forrest will quietly spread the word that your family went into witness protection somewhere. And you know what? *Folks will believe it.* They'll figure they were right all along—Doc Cage couldn't have really killed anybody! Yeah, they'll figure that whole story of him being a fugitive was some kind of cover story."

"What kind of cover story? That's ridiculous."

Royal purses his lips like a storyteller asked to make up a good one on the spot. "I'm thinking Sonny Thornfield might disappear tonight as well. Maybe Snake Knox with him. Those two have had their runs. And Agent Kaiser *has* declared the Double Eagles a domestic terror group. And then there are those rumors that Snake's been claiming he killed Martin Luther King. Yes . . . I think that story's got legs, Mayor. And I think the more loudly the Bureau denies it, the more people will believe it."

He's right. . . .

Brody stares at me as he might at a wayward nephew. "You still don't understand, do you? I built what I have from nothing. From that godforsaken levee where my mother ate raw pig. Hundreds of people depend on me now. *Thousands.* And you want to tear all that down because a couple of niggers forgot their place forty years ago? It defies understanding. Hell, Cage, not even the FBI was working those cases until Henry started embarrassing them in the newspaper every week!"

He turns away, rubbing his chin in silence.

"Now?" Regan asks eagerly.

Royal holds up one hand, then turns slowly around the firing range and focuses on me again. "You know the tragic irony of all this? It's only happening because of your father. All of it. All these deaths go back to him."

I blink in confusion. "What?"

"Back in the gun room you asked me if I killed Viola. Well, I didn't, as a matter of fact. I *would* have, thirty-seven years ago." Brody steps to within inches of my face, his eyes gleaming like those of an old lecher. "I'll tell you this: she was a sweet piece, boy. I had my taste out at a machine shop in the woods. Snake and his boys had her tied to a work-table, taking turns. I wore a hood while I took mine, just to be safe, but I could sure see her. My God . . . like a brown-skinned angel she was. But Snake had said too much in front of her, and she needed to die."

Caitlin is watching Brody with visceral hatred.

"That's ancient history," I say in a shaky voice. "*Who killed* her?"

He shakes his head in amazement. "Don't you see it yet? Viola would have died forty years ago if it was up to me. Or Snake. We *all* wanted her silenced. It was your daddy who kept her alive. St. Thomas Cage, M.D."

"I know that. But *how* did he save her?"

Royal shrugs as if the answer is self-evident. "The same way I was going to get that APB canceled, or blame Morehouse for her murder. *Power.* The crazy irony of this whole goat rope is that, after giving up so much to keep that colored nurse alive back *then,* Doc killed her himself forty years later."

My blood pressure plummets so fast that I feel I might faint. But Royal only mutters, "It defies understanding, I tell you."

I don't want to believe a word he's saying, but I see only truth in the old man's eyes.

"Tom thinks that damn son of hers is his," Brody goes on. "And I suppose he could be. But like as not, he's mine—or Snake's, or Frank's, or God-knows-who-else's." Royal pokes me in the chest. "*That's* why you're down in this hole, son. That's why you and yours are going to die. You're paying for the sins of the father, just like the Bible says." He shrugs philosophically. "It'll kill your daddy to hear you died this way, but he's got no one to blame but himself."

Royal takes a long last look at me, then turns away as though I'm already dead and says, "All right, Randall."

"You won't get my mother and daughter," I promise his back. "My father, either. You don't know where they are."

Royal nods, then smiles sadly. "I'll know in about thirty seconds, when your fiancée is screaming like a heretic at the stake."

Caitlin closes her eyes.

"I don't know myself," I tell him.

"Yes, you do. You hid your mother and daughter. Had to have. And as for your father . . . you may not know where he is, but you know how to reach him. As soon as I had Forrest cancel that APB, you were going to call him and Garrity and tell them it was okay to come in."

I'll never be able to convince Royal otherwise.

Regan braces the firing pipe on his hip and aims it at Caitlin's helpless body.

"Oh," Brody says, as though he's just remembered something. He takes a small derringer from his pocket, breaks it open, and removes one of its two rounds, which he slips into his pocket. "I've always been a student of human behavior, and I'm curious about something."

He bends over and slides the pistol across the concrete to me.

"You've got one bullet," he says. "What will you do with it? Once Ms. Masters is on fire, will you put her out of her misery? Or will you try to kill me?"

Like a suspicious primate taunted by a cruel zoo worker, I hesitate to reach for the derringer. But in the end, I snatch it up. Maybe I can inflict some degree of harm on Brody before I die. Breaking open the weapon, I check the remaining round—a .22 long rifle bullet. It seems to be live, but it's practically useless from this range. To reliably kill from this gun, this bullet should be fired from a foot or less.

"There's a third choice, Brody," Randall says. "He might save the bullet for himself. To spare himself the pain."

Royal laughs. "Are you that blind, Randall? Not Mayor Cage. He's a white-knight type. He's *Ivanhoe,* son. Chivalry and honor. He's his daddy all over again. Nope . . . he'll shoot the girl. I'd stake my fortune on it."

"Look at his eyes," Regan says, watching me warily. "I'd take a step back, if I were you."

"Oh, he'd love to kill me," Brody concedes, like a sportsman arguing about a casual bet. "But he'll save the bullet for her. That's true love, Randall. Pay close attention. It's something you never felt in your whole life."

While Caitlin silently reaches out to me with her eyes, I force myself to ignore her, quickly calculating the relevant distances, not only from where I stand, but from where my gun hand could reach if I leaped toward Brody. With the full length of the chain, my body, and my gun arm, a dive forward might buy me an additional six or seven feet. But I'd have to time the shot perfectly to kill him, and still Regan would remain free to burn Caitlin and me to death. No . . . the only way to prevent that outcome is somehow to kill Brody *and* take his pistol—then shoot Regan before the man incinerates us.

Impossible—

"You want me to light her up now?" Regan asks, his eyes on Caitlin.

Brody peers into Caitlin's bloodshot eyes as though he could subsist on her tears alone. "No," he says softly. "Give me that unit, Randall."

"What?"

"I said, give me the damn thing. Take my pistol."

Regan looks like a wolf cheated of a tasty meal by his alpha male.

"Help me put it on," Brody orders.

Regan unhooks the khaki straps, then helps settle the pack onto Royal's shoulders. The old man scarcely bends under the weapon's weight. "Heavier than I remember," he says, adjusting the straps on each shoulder and closing his hands around the hissing jet pipe.

"Can you handle it?"

"Long enough to cook this piece of chicken." He turns the jet pipe on Caitlin and curls two fingers into the trigger mechanism. The hiss of the pilot flame sounds like an angry viper in the room, and oily fire drips from its opening.

Regan practically licks Caitlin with his eyes. "Scorched on the outside, pink on the inside."

As Brody moves farther away from her to avoid any backsplash from the pressurized fuel, a bolt of instinct flashes through my brain: *Shoot the gas tank!* But which one? One of the two cylinders probably contains inert propellant, the other the gasoline and tar mixture. The upper tank looks smaller than the lower one. *Which one holds the fuel? Top or bottom?*

"Hey, Brody!" cries Regan, astonished by something. "Look at this gimp motherfucker."

He's pointing at Henry Sexton, who has begun crawling slowly toward Caitlin, his bloody cast leaving a scarlet trail across the floor. "You want me to shoot him?"

Brody stares, fascinated, as the reporter reaches a bare support pole, grips it with both hands, and begins to pull himself erect.

"Unbelievable."

Regan aims his semiautomatic at Henry's head.

"Put down your gun," Brody commands, like a boy watching a mortally wounded animal. "Let's see what he does."

Once Henry regains his balance, he staggers across to Caitlin, leans against her for a few seconds, then turns and faces Brody as a human shield.

"I'll be damned," Royal says with obvious admiration.

"You will," I promise, shamed by the bravery of Henry's hopeless act.

Sobbing softly, Caitlin says something to Henry that I can't make out, nor can I tell whether Henry understood her. To my surprise, she seems to be praying.

There are no atheists in foxholes, my father always said. *Trust me, I've been there.*

But I'm not praying. I'm wondering if a .22 slug in the proper tank could turn Brody Royal into the Human Torch. As the old man braces the pipe against his hip and aims at Henry and Caitlin, the hiss of the gas pilot brings every hair on my body erect.

"Do it," Regan urges, pumping his fist in the air. "Cook her!"

I step to the limit of my chain, then extend the derringer, sighting along its two-inch barrel toward the larger of the two cylinders. With Brody standing in profile, I can only see the heads of the cylinders in cross-section—a vanishingly small target, considering my weapon. But I have no choice.

"Drop it, Cage!" Regan shouts, turning his pistol on me. "I'll blow your shit away, I swear to God!"

As I start to depress the trigger, Henry says, "No," in a clear and distinct voice. "No more." Then he starts walking toward Brody.

The reporter's eyes shine with the ecstasy of a martyr walking into the flames. His first step is tentative, as though he might fall, but his next is stronger, and then suddenly he's closing the distance between himself and the hissing jet pipe with the flame rising from its mouth. Startled, Brody retreats a couple of feet and tries to brace the firing pipe again. Clearly, he fears the weapon in his hands more than he does Henry Sexton.

"Burn him!" Regan shouts, shifting his pistol toward Henry. *"Now!"*

"Regan!" I yell, whipping my aim from the flamethrower to his head. Now he knows he can't fire on Henry without taking a shot from me.

But it's Henry we're all watching: he's much too close now for Brody to fire the flamethrower without risking self-immolation.

Their collision is anticlimactic: so weakened is Henry by his wounds that the older man easily absorbs the shock without falling. Even encumbered by the Flammenwerfer's cylinders, Royal is clearly the stronger of the two on this night. Any second he will knock Henry to the floor, where he can be easily dispatched by Regan. *Yet he doesn't.* Henry clings to Brody with fierce tenacity, and for the first time I see panic in Royal's eyes. As they tear at each other, Brody's face tightens like that of a desperate fighter who feels his strength ebbing. Henry's face shows strain but not fear, and conviction blazes in his eyes.

At last Regan turns fully away from me, trying to find a safe shot at Henry. *Should I fire into Regan's back and hope to hit his heart? The .22 wouldn't likely pierce his back muscles—*

"Don't!" Regan shouts in a high-pitched voice. *"Brody, look out!"*

Henry's left hand has disappeared between the two wrestling bodies.

"Henry, don't!" I scream. *"HENRY!"*

The instant he finds the flamethrower's trigger, Henry pulls it, and a white-orange sphere of burning tar and gasoline engulfs the two men. A screech of agony splits the air, then dies as the windpipe that produced it melts shut. The blast of ignition throws off a broiling wall of heat, driving Regan backward with his gun arm raised as a shield against the blast.

I fire the derringer between his shoulder blades a half second before his back crashes into my chest, knocking me to the floor and driving the breath from my lungs. With his full weight crushing me, I can't get a breath. For a couple of seconds he seems dead, but then he jerks as though coming awake and roars in pain. Desperately aware of the pistol in his right hand, I drop the derringer and push my arm between his arm and body, grasping for his wrist. If I hadn't shot him before he landed on me, he would already have blown my brains out. But there's no guarantee that the little .22 slug will do more than stun him. I've got to kill Regan before he can recover his senses.

As my right hand closes around his thick wrist, I clamp my left forearm around his throat and try to cut off his oxygen. This triggers a thrashing movement, as though I'm trying to throttle an alligator and not a man. Regan's muscles strain with frightening power as he tries to bring his pistol up to my head. I squeeze his neck as hard as I can, but trapped beneath him as I am, it's hard to get enough leverage to completely cut off his air with only one arm. With a whiplike motion he raises his head, then slams it back into my face—once, then again. White stars explode in my field of vision. I feel his pistol rising to my head, but I can't stop it. He's simply stronger than I am.

A deafening blast of flame and thunder scorches my face, and Regan tries to twist from my grasp. If my strength fails now—if he moves the gun another inch upward—I will die. There's no way I can strangle him before he brings that pistol to bear. Purely out of instinct, I release my forearm lock from his neck, then chop the inner edge of my hand back down on his injured throat with all my strength. His body jerks, and the power in his gun arm wavers. Before he can recover, I drive my hand down three more times, each blow harder than the last. Cartilage crunches beneath my final strike, and then both Regan's hands fly to his throat, the gun forgotten.

With a single heave I roll him off me, then grab his gun and scramble to my knees. Smoke is billowing through the basement tunnel. Regan's mouth gapes as he gasps for oxygen, his eyes wide with terror. As I aim the pistol at his chest, he claws the air like a drowning man grasping at a rescuer. Then he slowly drops his arms and goes still.

Sprinklers in the ceiling have begun spraying water like rain. Fans must be churning somewhere, but I feel like I'm choking on soot. The heat and smoke will soon overwhelm me. Laying the muzzle of Regan's pistol against my leg chain, I fire. The first bullet fractures one link; the second severs the chain.

Getting to my feet in the smoke, I make my way to Caitlin's pole. Freeing her proves more difficult, but a third and fourth bullet snap the ropes, and she stumbles away from the pole.

"We've got to get out!" I shout. "Now!"

"Make sure Johnston's dead!" she cries, lifting the fire extinguisher and stumbling downrange to where the bank boxes still burn.

I turn and find my way to Sleepy's body, then drop to the floor and press two fingers into his neck, searching for a carotid pulse. I feel nothing at first, but as I dig for any pressure, he says, "I can't move, man. I think my back's broke."

"He's alive!" I shout, scarcely able to believe it.

I whip my head back and forth, trying to find Caitlin again. Then the smoke parts, and I see her charging toward me with a charred box in her arms. Beyond her, orange flame still rages in the smoke. At the center of a burning sphere, two black figures appear locked in eternal combat, like soot-shadows seared onto a Hiroshima wall.

"Is Mr. Royal dead?" Sleepy Johnston rasps from beneath me.

"Yes," I assure him, squeezing his hand.

The black man settles into a deeper stillness.

The charred banker's box drops heavily to the ground beside me, then Caitlin falls to her knees. "We've got to get him out," she says.

"We can't move him. His spine's hit."

"He'll burn alive!"

She's right, of course. I must be in shock. We're *all* about to burn.

"I'll take his arms!" she says, scrambling to her feet and the suffocating smoke. "You get his legs. I'll do what I can."

"What about Henry's files?"

She looks down at the charred box, then shakes her head. "Screw it. This man saved our lives."

"Get back," I tell her, recalling a moment much like this one seven years ago, when I carried my maid from our burning house. "Take your box and go."

"Penn, you can't—"

"Go, goddamn it! Don't wait for me!"

Stunned by my anger, Caitlin bends and shoves her hands beneath the heavy box, then heaves it up to her waist. With an inchoate fury impossible to contain, I set my knees against the floor, shove my right arm under Sleepy's back, then strain to heave him bodily over my shoulder. Fear and adrenaline surge through me, and my muscles bulge with blood.

"You're going to fall!" Caitlin yells.

"Get out!"

Straining every fiber of muscle, I get one foot under me, then balance the load across my right shoulder and lunge upward, whipping my left foot under me as I rise. Once both feet are beneath me, it's only a matter of steadying myself before I can start across the floor toward the far door.

Caitlin leads the way, and I follow the white flag of her blouse through the smoke. She pauses at the stairs, meaning to help, but I bull forward and she scrambles out of the way.

There are only a few steps to climb. This stairwell leads out to the yard and not up to the next floor. As I reach the top, pure cold air flows into my lungs like the breath of God, and the load on my shoulders vanishes to nothing.

CHAPTER 96

TOM STOOD AT the edge of the lake, shivering in a raincoat he'd found in Drew's closet. His wounded shoulder throbbed relentlessly, but he fought the urge to take another pain pill. The dose of narcotics required to dull that pain could easily depress his respiratory function to a lethal level. On the other hand, going without relief might raise his stress level to the point that it triggered another heart attack. The bullet wound was relatively minor, as missile injuries went. A battlefield medic would have popped him with a syrette of morphine, patched the holes, and moved on to the next foxhole. But at seventy-three, alone in the night, he felt the pain of that wound beginning to work on him.

Most M.D.s understood pain about as well as most lawyers understood prison. Doctors *believed* they understood pain, since they'd experienced the mild or moderate forms at some point in their lives. But two years in Korea—and twenty years of living with psoriatic arthritis and diabetes and coronary artery disease—had taught Tom the true nature of pain, from the slicing, electric burn of a nerve to the bluntest fist crushing the chest. Melba hadn't been gone long, but already her words of faith seemed distant and ephemeral. In all his life, he had never felt so alone as he did now.

Just after his nurse left, he'd sat on the sofa and immediately fallen asleep. Jerking awake a few minutes later, he was gripped by the certainty that if he sank into deep sleep he would never wake again. Many of his patients had experienced this premonition over the years, and often enough reality had borne it out. In the end, he'd chewed up half a Lorcet with a nitro chaser, then walked down to the water's edge, where the cold would keep him awake.

He sensed that his mind had come partly unmoored from the present. That might be a result of the wound, or the drugs, but it might simply be sleep deprivation, or the cumulative shocks he'd sustained over the past three days. His emotions swirled and eddied like a dark body of water in his skull, and his thoughts bobbed and slipped over the surface, only tenuously tied to reality.

Snatches of his last conversation with Melba sounded in his mind, like something overheard on a train. The word *sin* resonated again and again. Tom had committed the usual sins during his life, but there were other, more profound transgressions that he seldom acknowledged, even to himself. He'd done terrible things during the war. He knew the common guilt of the combat survivor, and the special guilt of the combat medic. He carried the deadened grief sense of the civilian physician, who lost so many battles with death in lonely sickrooms, his only weapon at the end his ability to ease pain, and sometimes not even that. As for the more universal sins: the familiar guilt of the adulterer had been dwarfed by that of the absentee father, who brought life into the world and then left it to struggle like a seed abandoned on the ground. A dozen rationalizations came to him, of course, the first being that he hadn't known of the boy's existence. But at his core, that brought no comfort.

Ever since Viola had told him about her son, Tom had been reflecting on Thomas Jefferson. Tom been named after the third president, but that was only an accidental irony. At some level, though, he had always strived to follow in Jefferson's footsteps. How could you not love a man whose library had contained six thousand books in an era when public libraries held only half as many volumes? A man who called himself a Christian but spent six years painstakingly cobbling together a customized Bible that contained no miracles, prophecies, angels, or resurrections?

Six days hence, historians would celebrate the nation's acquisition of the very land beneath Tom's feet, one of Jefferson's greatest accomplishments. And yet, this mental giant whom he'd studied in school like a demigod now shared with him a unique sin. Upon his death, Jefferson had left behind an enslaved black mistress and mixed-race children. He had freed some of his Negro descendants before his death, but others, along with most of his remaining slaves—more than a hundred human beings—had been sold at auction to pay his debts, a monumental hypocrisy and surely a sin by any measure. *How,* historians asked, *could the man who authored the Declaration of Independence have done this?*

Tom knew the answer. Moving with the same passive blindness, he had fathered a child by a black employee in her twenties. And though

Viola had loved him as surely as Sally Hemings must have loved Jefferson, Tom had to wonder how much choice either woman had really had in their circumstances. He hated to think of himself as a man who during difficult times had offered a troubled woman only temporary comfort and not real help. He was no Thomas Jefferson in intellectual terms, but that probably meant only that Jefferson had found some more facile way to justify actions that went against the grain of all he had championed during his life.

Rubbing his hands together against the cold, Tom recalled a quote from Peggy's distant cousin, Robert Penn Warren: *"And what we students of history always learn is that the human being is a very complicated contraption and that they are not good or bad but are good and bad and the good comes out of the bad and the bad out of the good, and the devil take the hindmost."*

An image of Penn rose in Tom's mind, but he pushed it away. *What of my other son?* he thought in desolation. *I don't even know him, much less love him. My Sally Hemings is dead, and my own dark descendant wants only to see me die behind bars. Would Jefferson's bastards have wanted the same, if they'd had the power to bring about that result? Would they have punished the man who gave them life but not his name?* Tom knew one thing: he would not compound his sin by following Jefferson's example of neglect. If he lived through this nightmare, he would take steps to ensure that his illegitimate child would never suffer in the same way, no matter how much he might hate his father.

Tom felt his keenest guilt over his firstborn son, and all those loved ones who he knew would risk everything to save him. Walt Garrity was risking his life now, though he had a wife waiting for him at home. Melba would have stayed all night, knowing full well that she might die because of it. Tom couldn't bear to think of what Penn and Peggy would give up to save him, and he had no intention of letting them do so. To that end, he had struck out on his own, separated himself from the lawful community of men, because he believed he had one chance to keep his family intact. The death of the state trooper had complicated matters, but one chance remained. The attempt might cost him his life, but Tom had risked his life before, and only for his country, not his family. This time, if he died, he would do so knowing he hadn't died in vain.

But the price of freedom would be high. In order to keep his family together, he would have to make a deal with the devil, or that incarnation which had prospered in this country for the past fifty years. Tom was intimately acquainted with evil in its many forms, and in a way that Penn was not. Penn had seen some of the horrific things that humans did to one another, but almost always from the safe perspective of the government prosecutor. As young men, Tom and Walt had entered that transformative zone where the border between "moral" and "amoral" blurred into something not distinguishable by the human mind. In that existential arena, the soul could be seared and scarred or lifted into radiant ecstasy, but none who entered it emerged unchanged.

Most of the Knox family had spent decades in that zone. After leaving sanctioned combat, they hadn't weaned themselves from the extreme emotions experienced there, but instead found ways to continue living in that realm where violence held ultimate sway. Inevitably, this involved crime, for only in life-and-death struggle could the most primitive and intense emotions be experienced. Normal men brushed up against those feelings by hunting animals or participating in dangerous sports, but men who had known combat—and thrived in it—achieved no rush from substitutes. And such men, Tom knew, were capable of any act. Even normal men and women would kill to protect their families or themselves. What, then, would monsters like the Knoxes do to preserve their freedom?

Tom had never forgotten something Leland Robb told him back in 1965, four years before he died in that plane crash. Lee had been home eating supper with his family when an FBI agent called with a medical question. The agent wanted to know whether it was possible for a human being to survive being skinned alive. He hadn't given the reason for his inquiry, but Dr. Robb had known that it must concern the fate of one of the young black men who had recently disappeared. Strange to think that the FBI had so little forensic knowledge at that time, since now they were considered the experts. Dr. Robb had been unable to answer the agent's question. But Tom, as an amateur historian, would have referred the agent to any detailed history of the medieval period, when flayings were quite commonplace. To think of such things in academic terms was one thing; to contemplate dealing with men who had actually performed such horrors was another. Yet Tom now found himself in exactly this position.

As if summoned by Tom's thought, the low hum of an engine

rolled down the slope to the shore of the lake. He wondered if his ears were playing tricks on him. Maybe a night fisherman had taken to the lake, and his motor was reverberating along the shore. But the sound steadied and continued, long enough for Tom to realize that a vehicle had parked in the driveway of Drew's lake house. Logic said Walt had returned from Baton Rouge. And yet . . . something deeper told Tom not to walk up the hill just yet. The engine of Drew's old pickup hadn't sounded nearly so smooth as Walt had chugged way from the house.

As suddenly as it had appeared, the engine noise died.

Some part of Tom hoped that Drew or Melba had broken their promises and told Penn where to find him; another hoped that Lincoln had somehow run him to earth. At least then he could pose the questions he longed to ask the boy, with no one around to witness his pain upon hearing the answers. And yet, without any evidence, Tom knew that none of those people was at the top of the slope.

The men in that vehicle had come to kill him.

Tom was armed, but even as he felt the pistol in his pocket, cold against his skin, he knew he didn't have the will to murder a stranger in order to remain free for a few more hours. What was the point? At bottom, he believed that Walt was already dead. Killed on a fool's errand, trying to save a friend who had doomed himself.

Sure that he was living his last moments on earth, Tom did what Walt had warned him countless times not to do. He took out his cell phone and switched it on. If it connected with a tower fast enough, he might be able to call Penn and tell him he was sorry. Peggy, too, if he had time. Turning his back to the house on the hill, he cupped the glowing screen inside his coat to block the light, then watched the device strain to link with a transmission tower.

There! Two bars . . .

Tom was about to dial Penn's number when a string of text messages appeared on his screen. Seventeen of them. He started to ignore them, but the most recent had been sent by Caitlin, and for some reason, he tapped on it. The message expanded to fill the tiny screen:

Tom. Whatever happened the night Viola died, you don't have the right to sacrifice yourself, because I'm pregnant. Penn doesn't know. I'm telling you because my child needs you in his life. It's time for you

to come home. This family can get through ANYTHING together.
Caitlin Masters Cage (☺ your future daughter-in-law).

As Tom stared in dazed comprehension, he heard a wet compression behind him. Then another. *Footsteps. On damp grass.* He turned. Two shadowy figures were moving swiftly down the hill, toward the water.

With his heart pounding dangerously, Tom slipped the phone into his coat and shoved both hands into his trouser pockets.

Ten seconds later, they stood only a few feet away: two strangers in their thirties, their pale faces lighted by the moon. One pointed a pistol at Tom's belly. As it glinted ominously in the moonlight, a nauseating flash of déjà vu went through him: two Chinese soldiers had confronted him exactly this way in Korea. Only it had been snowing then, and Walt had shot them both.

"Don't shoot," he said in a level voice. "I need to talk to your boss."

"Just who do you think we work for?" asked the man on the left, the shorter of the two.

Tom's life now depended on a fifty-fifty gamble. Was the answer Brody Royal? Or had Frank Knox's son eclipsed the older man in power? After a moment's hesitation, he said, "Forrest Knox."

The two men looked at each other. Then the one on the right said, "You've got a syringe and some vials with Sonny Thornfield's fingerprints on them. Where are they?"

"I'll discuss that with Forrest when I see him."

The man with the pistol shook his head. "You ain't goin' nowhere, Doc. This is the end of the road for you."

Tom was sickened by the fear that surged through him. Only minutes ago he had resigned himself to death. But Caitlin's message had resurrected the hope of something he'd given up expecting to live to see. Another grandchild. Maybe a grandson, this time. The realization that these two men meant to take that from him—to kill him on this lonely black shore—summoned a blast of adrenaline from his aging glands. Pain stabbed him beneath the left shoulder blade. He needed a nitro tablet, fast. But if he reached for one, the man holding the pistol would fire.

"That stuff isn't here," Tom said in a strained voice, closing his right hand around the pistol in his pocket. "Walt's got it."

"That Texas Ranger?"

"He's lying," said the taller man. "I'll bet that junk's right up there in the house."

The shorter man was working up the nerve to pull the trigger—Tom could see it. The abstract thoughts that occupied his mind earlier had flown from his head like dandelion seeds. He was back in Korea, facing two captors who couldn't understand a word he said. What he'd learned all those years ago was that speed didn't matter that much in a gunfight. It was deliberation that counted. Deliberation and steady nerves.

Tom had already turned the gun in his pocket. For once he was grateful for the "geezer" slacks that did nothing to flatter their wearer. His vision telescoped down into a few square feet of the world: the shorter man's eyes jumping from Tom's face to his comrade's, his gun trembling from the weight of the pistol and the knowledge of what he meant to do with it—

Tom fired as the taller man gave the order to execute him. The gunman staggered back and looked down at his belly, where a grapefruit-sized bloodstain was rapidly growing. As the short man tried to figure out where the bullet had come from, his partner grabbed for an ankle holster. Tom slowly pulled his pistol and aimed it at the man's head.

"Be still, or I'll kill you."

When the man hesitated, Tom laid the barrel against the crown of his head. "Draw it slowly, with two fingers, then toss it into the water and stand up straight."

After a couple of seconds' hesitation, the man obeyed. After the splash, he rose slowly and gaped at Tom, clearly stunned by the sudden reversal of circumstances.

"Pick up your buddy and carry him up the hill," Tom said, tensed against the pain in his shoulder and back.

"You're not gonna shoot me?"

"I am if you don't carry him up that hill."

The tall man bent over and tried clumsily to lift his dead companion. While he did, Tom stuck a nitro tablet under his tongue.

"I can't get him up," the man almost whined. "I sure as hell can't carry him all the way up to the truck. How 'bout I drag him?"

"Goddamn it!" Tom snapped, furious that he'd had to kill the man.

"I once carried a wounded marine six hundred yards through barbed wire and shell holes. Grab him under the arms! That's right . . . now get him up on his feet, like you're hugging him from behind. Once he's up, turn him around and heave him over your shoulders."

Following Tom's instructions, the thug heaved and grunted and cursed until he got the corpse over his shoulder in a fireman's carry. Then he started trudging up the slope. Behind him, Tom powered down his cell phone and put it back in his pocket. After his heartbeat steadied, he slowly followed his would-be assassins up the hill. The pain in his shoulder burned like white phosphorous, but it reassured him of one thing as nothing else could.

He was alive.

CHAPTER 97

WITH CAITLIN'S HELP, I lay Sleepy Johnston down in the grass. Only now do I see the glitter of lights reflecting on water thirty yards away. *That's Lake Concordia*, I think. *This is Brody's lake house.*

"He's alive," Caitlin says. "We need a cell phone."

"Don't call no ambulance," says Johnston. "We're too far from the hospital. I ain't gon' make it. Just let me breathe this sweet air."

Despite his request, Caitlin digs in the man's pocket but finds only a walkie-talkie. She presses the transmission button and starts to speak, but I gently pull the radio from her hand. She stares at me with what seems like anger, but slowly her face softens into resignation. Below us, the ashy face and bloodshot eyes look up at the stars, seeing something I can't begin to guess at.

"Don't you want to live?" Caitlin whispers. "You can tell the world the truth about what happened all those years ago."

Sleepy Johnston shakes his head. "That's your job now. At least that old bastard's gone. That's enough for me."

"You saved our lives, Mr. Johnston. You're a hero."

"No. I was Pooky's friend . . . that's all. Just one of Albert's boys. That's all I ever wanted to be."

Caitlin shakes her head, then wipes her eyes and begins to sob.

"Why did you call yourself Gates Brown?" I ask, leaning over him.

The gray mouth splits into a smile. "Gates was my man when I got to Detroit . . . that brother won the Series in sixty-eight. Tigers recruited him right out of reform school . . . helped him make good, just like Albert had done." Two long, rasping breaths stop his speech. "You tell this story, miss," he whispers, his eyes on Caitlin. "Just like Henry would have. Tell people what that Royal done . . . what people *let* him do."

"I will," she promises.

"He ain't the last, you know."

"We know," I tell him. "Take it easy, man."

"I'm sorry," he croaks. "It took me so long . . . to find the guts to come back."

He lifts his hand as though searching for a familiar grasp. Caitlin takes hold of it and presses the hand to her breast.

"Thank you for what you did. We'll never forget you." Squeezing her eyes shut, she shakes her head helplessly.

Johnston, too, has closed his eyes. Caitlin leans over him, her ear against his mouth. I lay my hand on her back and rub softly.

When she rises, tears streak her face, and her mascara has bled into a bandit mask. "Jesus," she says. "All of this out of some black kid liking a white girl?"

"That's right. Just like Dad and Viola. We're tribes, just like we were ten thousand years ago."

She shakes her head as though to negate reality. "Nothing's changed?"

"Sure it has. In the law. In people's hearts? Maybe. In the blood . . . ? No."

Caitlin gets to her feet and staggers away, obviously distraught.

I get up and follow. After leaving her in peace for a few yards, I come alongside her.

"Did you see Henry?" she asks, her voice slightly hysterical. "He was like a monk immolating himself in the street. He did that to save me."

"He did. And to stop Brody. He did it for everyone he couldn't save before tonight."

She shakes her head with violent intensity. "I feel *sick*. I don't know how to process that."

"That's who Henry was. He probably would have been useless in a combat platoon, until someone threw a hand grenade into a foxhole. Henry was the guy who'd jump on a grenade to save his buddies."

Caitlin stops and turns back toward the lake house. Flames have reached the first floor, and smoke is gathering under the eaves. "What happened tonight? What am I supposed to write tomorrow? Everybody's *dead*. I mean . . . what was the point?"

For a long moment I remain silent. "I don't know, but I think maybe I finally understand why my father couldn't tell me about the war."

Caitlin gingerly touches the puckered burn on her face. "I wanted this story so bad. Now I'm *in* it. We *are* the story. And I have no idea what to say about it."

"The things Brody and the Knoxes did . . . that pain echoes through a lot of years. Generations. That's what kept Henry going, and what brought Sleepy Johnston back here. This is the end of Brody's thread, that's all. Albert's and Pooky's, too. It's justice of a kind, I guess."

"No one will understand this. I don't, and I was here."

"Because it's not over. Forrest and the Double Eagles are still out there. And Henry's work is truly yours now. Just write the story up to this point. That's all you can do. The meaning comes later, if at all."

The sound of sirens grows to a wail, and a convoy of spinning red lights comes flying up the lake road.

"How much do we tell?" she asks. "To the police, I mean."

Brody Royal's last accusation against my father echoes in my mind. "Is it worth lying at this point?"

She turns to me, her survivor's will burning through the shock and exhaustion in her eyes. "I hate to say it, but we may have to. We'd better decide fast."

Dreading contact with the larger world, we walk back to wait beside the body of Sleepy Johnston. A low thump makes the ground shudder, and then a tower of flame rises from the burning lake house.

"The flamethrower?" Caitlin asks.

"Probably."

As the orange and blue geyser rises into the night sky, I realize I'm witnessing the cremation of a man who three days ago meant little more to me than a byline under a newspaper article. But without him, Caitlin and I would now be charred flesh and ligaments over scorched bone. In this moment, it comes to me that my father is somewhere out in this same darkness, lost in a maze of his own making. Yet he's never seemed farther from me in my life. The question of who really killed Viola Turner seems like some mystery from another age, like the death of Amelia Earhart.

What happened tonight? Caitlin asked me.

For my part, only this: to save my father, I tried to make a deal with the devil, and I almost lost everything because of it. My father is going to have to save himself.

And the rest of it? What was the point? For most of his life, Henry Sexton fought to gain justice for nameless victims and for families who had no voice. Did he accomplish that? Will anyone care? I don't know. But Henry did something that police detectives, FBI agents, and attorneys with a lot more training and resources than he possessed had failed to do for forty years.

Henry got his man.

AFTERWORD

WHILE THIS NOVEL is entirely fictional, many of the background cases were inspired by unsolved race murders that occurred in Concordia Parish, Louisiana, and southwest Mississippi during the 1960s. To date, only one conviction has resulted from these horrific crimes. Stanley Nelson of the *Concordia Sentinel* has been working to solve those cases for many years, and he's made remarkable progress. This is an often thankless job that angers many, but with limited resources Stanley has persisted in the face of both apathy and obstruction. In some cases he has solved murders, but the killers were already dead. In others, the outcome has yet to be decided.

Despite the FBI's cold cases initiative, which began in 2007, the behavior of the FBI and the Justice Department regarding these cases is puzzling and sometimes inexplicable. Where official progress has been made, it has been due to the commitment of dedicated family members, reporters, and individual prosecutors or U.S. attorneys, rather than the sustained efforts of the FBI and the Justice Department. Today's FBI agents are as dedicated as those of the 1960s, but they have been given neither the time nor the resources required to mount an effort comparable to that of their fellow agents from the earlier era.

The solutions to my fictional cases are different from what I believe happened in the actual cases that inspired them, but the emotional realities are true. In creating the characters of some of my fictional victims, I used theories and rumors that circulated during the early phases of the investigations. Many of those I no longer believe to be founded in reality. The primary example is Frank Morris, the shoe repairman, who I believe was guilty of nothing more than serving both white and black patrons and refusing to mend a corrupt white deputy's boots for free. Morris was a fine man, and not involved in bootlegging or prostitution, as was suggested by rumor and by evidence likely planted at the site of his burned-out shop. The same holds true for the terrible plane crash at Concordia Airport in 1970. That was almost surely an accident, though had justice been done in an earlier murder case, one pilot would have been incarcerated, and the subsequent collision could not have happened. Life is often more prosaic (and tragic) than the stuff of good fiction.

If you would like to learn more about the actual crimes that form the backdrop of *Natchez Burning,* please visit the Web page of the *Concordia Sentinel* and read Stanley Nelson's articles. You will also find a link on my website. Stanley expects to have his own book published soon, so watch for that as well.

I cannot possibly thank everyone who assisted me with this novel. However, I must include the following:

Dr. Jerry Iles, gone but never forgotten.

Betty Iles, for everything.

Uncle Joe Iles, for standing in for his big brother when it mattered most.

Madeline Iles, Mark Iles, Geoff Iles, and Colin Kemp.

Caroline Hungerford, for too many reasons to count.

Dan Conaway and Simon Lipskar, for vision.

David Highfill, Liate Stehlik, and the whole team at William Morrow/HarperCollins, for putting their full faith into this epic endeavor.

Courtney Aldridge and Rod Givens, M.D.: wise friends; Jim Easterling and James Schuchs, southern philosophers; Billy Ray Farmer, who's got the instincts.

Stanley Nelson, the journalist/detective; Rusty Fortenberry, for great stories about law in Mississippi; Mimi Miller, the memory of Natchez (and still young!).

Ed Stackler, for riding shotgun ever since I put Rudolf Hess back into the cockpit of his Messerschmitt.

Jerry Mitchell of the *Clarion-Ledger;* John M. Barry, author of *Rising Tide;* Kevin Cooper and Ben Hillyer of the *Natchez Democrat.*

Tony Byrne; Charles Evers; Sheriff Chuck Mayfield; Darryl
    Grennell; D. P. Lyle, M.D.; Nancy Hungerford; Kevin
    Colbert; Keith Benoist; John White, M.D.; Brent Bourland;
    Mark Brockway; Mark Coffey; Grayson Lewis; and Brooke
    Moore.

Judge George Ward (John, Win, Stan, and Ann, too!).

Jane Hargrove, who worked faithfully beside me through many
    novels.

Bruce Kuehnle and Alan J. Kaufman, lawyers who helped when
    it counted.

My deepest thanks to all the doctors, nurses, and paramedics (and
chopper crew) who helped to save my life: those at the University of
Mississippi Medical Center, Natchez Regional Medical Center, Method-
ist Rehab, and Prime Care Nursing. I particularly want to thank: Dr.
Matt Graves (ortho trauma guru); Dr. Peter Arnold (plastic surgeon/
fighter pilot); Dr. Fred Rushton (thanks for patching my aorta, yo!); Dr.
Gregory Timberlake and Dr. Wesley Vanderlan (critical care); Dr. Joe
Files; and Kim Hoover, dean of nursing, UMMC. I also want to thank
Richard Boleware, Rick Psonak, and Blake Carr at UMMC Orthot-
ics and Prosthetics. Special thanks to Claudia, Felecia, and Renee, my
supernurses. Thanks also to Karl Edwards of Natchez, for many great
conversations during rehab.

Finally, thanks to the Rock Bottom Remainders, for forcing me to
have fun regardless of what life throws at us.

As usual, all mistakes are mine.